LOVE AND LYRICS

The Complete Series

USA TODAY BESTSELLING AUTHOR
NIKKI ASH

Gage

Braxton

Declan

Camden

Controlled Chaos

A LOVE & LYRICS NOVEL

It should be me, kissing you, touching you, inside you
But instead, it's him, getting you, every fuckin' piece
of you
Those pieces should be mine

– Camden Blackwood, Raging Chaos

One

CAMDEN

THE PRESENT:
HIGH SCHOOL PRE-GRADUATION PARTY

"SO YOU'RE REALLY GOING TO LET IT HAPPEN, HUH?" DECLAN ASKS, TAKING A SIP OF HIS BEER. "YOU'RE going to let her go off to college with that asshole without telling her how you feel?"

I flip the hood of my jacket up and tug on the strings, tightening it to cover my head. "She's in love," I say dryly, then take a swig of my beer, chugging it down in the hopes of getting drunk enough to believe the words I'm spewing.

"I missed my chance, and I'm not about to be *that* guy." Draining the last of my beer, I drop the empty bottle onto the table and stand so I can grab another one.

"I'd bet my ass if she knew how you felt, she wouldn't be with him," Declan points out as we push through the crowded room of our classmates celebrating our impending graduation in various ways—some legal, some not so much—to the kitchen.

"She knows how I feel." I scoff, grabbing a Solo cup and a bottle of vodka so I can mix myself a stronger drink. Beer isn't going to cut it tonight. Not if I want to forget.

Declan barks out an obnoxious laugh. "Sure, she knows you care about her...as a *friend*, but you've never actually told her you're in love with her."

"And when the hell was I supposed to do that?" I huff, forgetting the cup and guzzling straight from the bottle. I welcome the burn as the liquid slides down my throat and into my belly, warming my insides.

"I don't know, but if you don't tell her soon, it really will be too late."

"What if she turns me down?" I ask, sounding like a damn pussy.

"I can't imagine it," Declan says, taking a sip of his drink. "For the past three years, every time that girl looks at you, it's as if you both are the only two people in the room."

I love my best friend, but the guy is such a fucking hopeless romantic, which is ironic since his parents are the least loving people I've ever met in my life. "Then why is she with him?"

"Maybe because she doesn't know you're an option."

Like a moth to a flame, my eyes find her as she makes her way through the living room alone. I'm shocked her boyfriend isn't with her. The guy never leaves her side, especially if he knows I'll be there. She's dressed in a sexy as hell red minidress that shows off all of her curves, with her chestnut hair down in long waves. Our gazes lock, and like it always does when I see her, my heart thumps against my rib cage. It's been like this every time I've seen her since we met.

"It's what my mom says I do when I'm upset." She looks out at the road in front of us. "I just want to sit here and wallow."

"Here." I pull one earbud out and hand it to her. "I have the perfect wallowing music."

I scroll through my selection of songs on my phone until I find one that she might be able to connect with and click play.

We sit together, listening to "Here Without You" by 3 Doors Down, while Layla cries. I'm not sure what to do, so I do the only thing I can think of and put my arm around her, pulling her closer to me so I can try to comfort this sad girl who's now my next-door neighbor. I'm shocked when she not only comes willingly but lays her head on my shoulder.

When the song ends, I find another one—"Home" by Machine Gun Kelly—and after that, in hope of lightening the mood, I click on "I Can See Clearly Now" by Johnny Nash. When the lyrics start, I feel Layla's shoulders shake with laughter. She glances up at me and grants me a full ear-to-ear smile. And holy shit, she is pretty. She's got two dimples, one on each cheek, and when she isn't crying, her brown eyes brighten up to the color of caramel. Lyrics flood my head, and I have to shake them out to focus on what she's saying.

"You have quite the playlist," she points out, her smile remaining.

"I love music." I shrug. "All of it."

"Even country?"

"Country, pop, rap, rock...If the lyrics say something worth hearing, I'll listen."

"Camden," a voice calls out. I look over and find my mom standing on the doorstep. "Everything okay?"

"Yeah." I stand, and Layla joins me. When I look at her, my earlier suspicions are confirmed. I'm five-ten, and she only comes up to the top of my chest, putting her a good half a foot shorter than me. "This is Layla, our new neighbor."

Mom meets us halfway. "Nice to meet you. I'm Sophia Blackwood."

"It's nice to meet you," Layla says softly.

"Will you be attending Brooklyn High?" Mom asks.

"Yeah, my mom got me registered, so I can start tomorrow."

"You'll love it," Mom says before turning her attention to me. "It's late, and you have school in the morning as well. Come in soon, please." She looks back at Layla. "It was nice to meet you. I'll have to stop by tomorrow to introduce myself to...your parents?"

"Yeah, my mom and dad."

"Good luck on your first day tomorrow. If you need anything, I'm sure Camden can help you." With a smile and a wink, Mom excuses herself.

"Here, put your number in," I say, handing her my phone. She raises a single brow. "So if you're lost or anything tomorrow, you can text me," I add. "Don't worry, I heard the part about you having a boyfriend."

Her face falls at the mention of the guy she had to leave behind. She inputs her number, and once she hands me back my phone, I pull it up and hit call. Her phone rings in her pocket, and I click end. "Now you have my number, in case you need anything."

"CAN WE PLEASE STOP BY STARBUCKS ON THE WAY TO SCHOOL?" BAILEY GROANS AS WE WALK TO THE car. Oscar, our driver, opens the door, and I'm about to get in when I see Layla stepping outside with a frown marring her features. She's dressed in the girls' version of our school uniform—a blue, yellow, and white plaid skirt, a white button-down shirt with a matching plaid tie, and black flats—with her backpack situated on her shoulders and her camera around her neck.

When she sees me watching her, a small smile appears.

"Who's that?" my younger sister asks.

"Our new neighbor." I wave Layla over. "You on your way to school?"

"Yeah. I have my GPS pulled up…"

"Get in," I tell her. "It'll take a good thirty minutes to walk and even longer on the train since it's the morning rush."

She eyes the vehicle, Oscar, then my sister.

"This is Oscar, our driver." Oscar tips his hat—yes, he actually has a hat like the drivers you see in movies and speaks in a British accent. He's been our driver for years and is awesome about not telling on us for the shit he sees us do.

"And this is my little sister, Bailey. She's a freshman."

"His much *cooler* sister," Bailey adds with a side-eye.

After Layla introduces herself, we pile in, and Oscar stops by Starbucks so we can run in and grab coffee and breakfast on our way to school. Layla asks if she can roll down the window during our drive, and she snaps pictures of everything in sight.

When she says she's never even so much as visited the city before moving here, I offer to show her around this weekend.

"That would be amazing," she gushes in excitement. "This place is like a photographer's playground."

When we arrive, Bailey takes off toward her friends, and Layla stands in place with a coffee in her hand, checking everything out. It must be daunting coming from a small town to the city. Brooklyn isn't huge compared to Manhattan, but our high school is three stories and houses almost three thousand students. Even though my dad is a famous musician, and my family is hella rich, we've gone to a public school our entire lives. My parents want us to stay humble, and that's fine by me. Had I been forced to attend private school, I never would've met my boys.

"You're not going to take any pictures?" I ask, nodding toward the camera still around her neck.

She glances down as if just remembering it's still there and pulls it over her head, pushing it into her backpack. When I give her a questioning look, she simply shrugs and says, "Don't want to be the weird new girl with a camera around her neck."

I nudge her hip lightly. "There's nothing weird about you, Shutterbug."

She smiles at the nickname. It's not original by any means, but it fits her.

"You ready?" I ask, taking her hand in mine.

She glances down at our joined hands, swallows thickly, and briefly closes her eyes. "Not even close." But then, she opens her lids and, with renewed strength, nods once and saunters forward.

While she's speaking to the lady in the front office to get her schedule, Braxton texts me in our group chat asking where I am, and I tell him I'll see him at lunch.

We find out Layla has three classes with me, including first period, so after she finishes in the office, I walk her to class. When we get inside, the bell is just ringing, and everyone is piling in. I always sit in the back with Declan, who also has English first period.

When he walks in, he notices Layla right away, giving me a raised brow, clearly appreciating what he sees. Feeling an odd sense of protectiveness over Layla, I shake my head, making it clear she's off-limits. Sure, she has a boyfriend, but he isn't here—and let's be honest, at fifteen and living hundreds of miles apart, they aren't going to last. Her simply having a boyfriend won't stop the guys from swooping in like vultures and trying to pick apart the fresh meat.

As I'm introducing Layla to Declan, Kaylee and Tori walk in. They're cool chicks, so I nod for them to come over and introduce them to Layla. The girls hit it off right away and spend the next few minutes getting to know each other while we wait for the teacher to start class.

"WHAT'S WITH YOU AND THE NEW GIRL?" BRAXTON ASKS LATER AT LUNCH. WORD HAS ALREADY GOTTEN out around school that there's a new girl, and since I walked her to our first three classes, she's obviously been linked to me.

I'm scribbling words into my notebook, hoping eventually some of them will get turned into lyrics, so I don't look up when I say, "Nothing. She's my new next-door neighbor."

"She's hot as hell," Gage says, sitting next to me and dropping his tray of shitty food on the table.

"Fuck yeah, she is," Declan agrees, sitting next to Braxton and across from me. "But not as hot as your sister."

I look up and glare at him. "Don't talk about my sister." I point my finger at him. Fucking dick has been obsessed with my older sister, Kendall, since he met her. She's seven years older than us and doesn't even know he exists. "And she's off-limits."

"No shit. She's dating that actor…"

"Not her…though she's definitely off-limits as well, even if she wasn't dating that dumbass. I'm talking about Layla. She's off-limits."

Braxton's brows hit his forehead. "You laying claim on her?"

"She has a boyfriend back in Michigan. But even if she didn't, it's not happening." There's no way I'm letting my asshole friends anywhere near her. They would use her up and spit her out just like they do the rest of the girls at this school.

Declan scoffs. "It's sounding a whole lot like her boyfriend is sitting at this table."

"We're friends," I say dryly, going back to working on some lyrics.

"Whatcha got there?" a feminine voice asks a few minutes later.

Looking up, I find Layla sitting next to me, her raspberry-vanilla scent invading my nostrils, and her eyes on my notebook.

"That's his journal," Braxton says, answering for me. "It's where he writes all his secrets."

"Aw, that's cute," Layla coos. "I have one too. I keep it under my bed…" She scrunches her face up in an adorable way, making her twin dimples pop out. "But I probably shouldn't have said that out loud, huh?"

"Good to know," Braxton says, "in case I'm ever in your room." He shoots her a wink, and I kick him in the shin, making him groan in pain.

"This isn't a journal like that. It's where I jot down my ideas for songs."

"You write songs?" Her voice perks up, and she moves closer to sneak a peek.

I close my book. Nobody's allowed to see what I write—hence Braxton talking shit. "I do," I tell her. "We're in a band." I nod to the other guys.

"Really? You didn't tell me that last night." She playfully jabs my side. "You any good?"

"Damn good," Kaylee says. "They'll be playing Friday night at the party Ricky's throwing. You should totally come."

"I'm there." Layla's eyes meet mine. "I can't wait to see you guys play."

After school, since Layla and I don't have our last class together, I text her, telling her to meet me in the student pickup so she can ride home with the guys and me. Bailey texts that she's going home with a friend.

When we get home, Layla says she'll see us tomorrow and then heads over to her house. Before she gets to her door, I call out her name. "We'll be practicing all afternoon if you want to come over and hang out."

A huge grin spreads across her face. "Let me just say hi to my mom, and then I'll come over."

The afternoon is spent practicing while Layla videos and takes pictures. I'm not sure what she's doing, but she's so into the music and us, I don't question it. At some point, Dad comes home, and I introduce him to Layla.

"Did you make that today?" he asks her from behind her laptop. I'm on the other side so I can't see what he's talking about.

"Yeah, I'm just messing around. My dad bought me this new program."

"Can you play it back for me from the beginning?" he asks.

Curious, the guys and I walk around behind her to check it out. It's a rough cut of us practicing, homing in on each of us from different angles—still shots, video clips—showcasing each of our best attributes. I've seen my sister and dad play, have watched their live performances and music videos, but this is the first time I've seen myself and the guys as an outsider. We've been playing for years, but at this moment as I watch ourselves from Layla's perspective, I feel like we're actually a fucking band.

"This is really good," Dad says, making Layla blush with his compliment. "You considering videography as a career?"

She nods. "I'm not sure what I want to do with it, but yeah."

"From that video, it's clear you have a keen eye for detail. The way you captured their passion and love for the music. You could make a very good living working in the music industry. If you ever want to intern at Blackwood, just say the word."

Her eyes light up, and I can't help the way my insides tighten. "Really?" she says. "That would be amazing."

Three

CAMDEN

JUNIOR YEAR

Layla: SOS My house.

"SHIT, I GOTTA GO." WITHOUT WAITING FOR ANY OF THE GUYS TO SAY ANYTHING, I HAUL ASS UPSTAIRS AND head straight for the front door. Layla only texts me SOS when it's an emergency—it's our thing. When one of us needs the other to bail us out, or when we're having a bad day and need to talk, we text SOS. Layla was supposed to be in Michigan, staying with her aunt so she could visit her friends and boyfriend for two weeks before school starts back up. She's been looking forward to this all summer. She's only been gone for a few days, so for her to be back already means something went wrong.

Without knocking, since I know her dad's at work and her mom treats me like I'm her own son, I swing the door open and go in search of Layla.

"She's in her room," her mom says with a sad smile from the kitchen where she's stirring something on the stove.

"Thanks."

I sprint up the stairs to the fourth floor, where her room is, and with a small knock, walk right in, stopping in my place for a moment when I see her lying in her bed, curled up like a shrimp, with tears streaming down her cheeks.

"Ah, hell, Shutterbug, what happened?"

Lifting her into my arms, I sit against the headboard and hold her tight while she sobs against my chest. I have a feeling I know what, or I should say *who*, has caused her to cry: Taylor, her dumbass boyfriend. And while I hate to see her cry, if he's the cause of her tears, that probably means one thing—they broke up—and selfishly, that makes me happy because Layla deserves better than that guy.

When she's finally calmed down enough to talk, she sniffles a few times and glances up at me with her red-rimmed eyes that have me wanting to kill the fucker who would dare to break her heart.

"He's been cheating on me for the past several months," she chokes out, "with Mariah." A fresh sob wracks her body, and she nestles her face back into my chest. I lean over and kiss the top of her head, inhaling the raspberry scent of her hair and the vanilla from her lotion. "I showed up as a surprise, and instead, I was the one surprised."

Over winter and spring break, she offered to visit Taylor, but he gave her excuses that he was too busy with school and sports and work and wouldn't be able to spend quality time with her. I wanted to call bullshit, tell her to dump that asshole and find someone who would make her the center of his world, but I kept my mouth shut, knowing she needed to get through this her way. I knew he would eventually fuck up, and once he did, I'd be here for her. When summer came around, he mentioned he had football camp in the beginning, so she called his mom to ask when it was over to plan a visit and surprise him.

I had a bad feeling something like this was going to happen. I could see the signs that he'd been pulling back, not calling and texting her like he used to when she first moved here, but for Layla's sake, I was hoping I was wrong. Because, with the way she wears her heart on her sleeve, I knew she'd be devastated the day he broke her heart. I've learned over the past year from getting to know Layla that when she gives you her heart, she's all in. She's loyal to a fault and probably the most forgiving person I've ever met. She's also the best person I know.

"I'm such an idiot."

"You are *not* an idiot," I tell her, tipping her chin up to look at me. "He doesn't deserve you." Nobody does...but if she would ever give me a chance, I'd do everything in my power to be worthy of her love.

"It hurts," she croaks, fresh tears filling her lids.

"I know, but you'll get through this." I kiss her forehead and hold her tighter while she continues to cry in my arms. When her eyes eventually shut, I spend the next couple of hours watching her, wondering how long it will take for her to get over this guy. I know that sounds bad, but the truth is, at some point in the past year, I fell in love with Layla. I've waited for the day I can finally tell her and hopefully make her mine.

Eventually, her eyes flutter open, and she stretches her limbs, glancing up at me with a soft smile. "Sorry, I guess I fell asleep."

"It's all good."

As if she suddenly remembers something, her eyes light up slightly. "I have something for you." She reaches across the bed and grabs a small box off the nightstand. "When I first flew into Michigan, my aunt took me to this cute little shop she opened up a few months ago. She makes all types of jewelry and house stuff. Anyway, when I was looking around, I saw this necklace." She opens the box and pulls it out. "My aunt said it's a friendship necklace." She opens the clasp and puts it around my neck. "I know you're a guy, but lots of guys wear jewelry, and it's manly."

I glance down at it and smile. I've never been one to wear jewelry, but as far as jewelry goes, it's not half bad. The beads are all black, with pieces of metal between them.

"Thanks."

Layla sniffles softly and encircles her arms around me. "Thank you for being my friend. I don't know what I would do without you in my life."

"Well, it's a good thing you'll never have to find out." And once she gets past her dumbass ex-boyfriend hurting her, hopefully, we can work on our friendship becoming something more.

"I'M READY!" LAYLA SAYS, JOGGING DOWN THE STAIRS TO THE STUDIO A COUPLE OF DAYS LATER. AFTER I held her all night, we spent the next day watching chick flicks while eating a shitload of junk food that her mom swore would heal her broken heart. That night, I reluctantly left to go home since my mom was giving me crap about being gone for so long, but sometime in the middle of the night, Layla texted me she needed me, and I ended up back at her house, in her bed, holding her for the rest of the night. Yesterday, Kaylee and Tori came over and dragged her out for a girls' day, where they got their nails and hair done. Once she was home, she snuck over after her parents fell asleep and slept in my arms, leaving some time before I woke up.

"What are you ready for?" I ask, flipping my hood onto my head and tugging on the strings as I take in her appearance. Unlike the past couple of days, when she's been dressing in sweats and oversized hoodies, today, she's wearing a tiny jean skirt, a light-pink tank top that shows off her belly ring, and flip-flops. She's wearing more makeup than usual, and her usually wavy hair is straight.

"Life," she says with a wide grin, making those damn dimples pop out. My heart pounds against my chest at how beautiful and happy she looks. "I'm ready to finally live my life."

I set my notebook on the table and walk toward her, wondering how long I have to wait to tell her how I feel. Then she speaks her next words, halting me in place.

"More specifically, the single life." Her hands land on her hips, and she nods once quickly for emphasis. "I've spent the past two years locked down by a boy who didn't deserve me. I spent too many hours giving him my time when I should've been focusing on me. So this year is all about me. And to start it off, guess what I'm doing?"

Her eyes light up in excitement while my heart deflates.

When I don't answer quick enough, Braxton does for me. "What're you doing?"

"I'm trying out for cheerleading!"

Kaylee and Tori cheer—since they're both on the squad and have been begging Layla to join—at the same time the guys snort out a laugh.

"This is going to be so much fun!" Kaylee squeals, running over to Layla and hugging her. "Guys are overrated. I say we make this year about girl power!"

"I'm in!" Tori agrees.

So much for telling her how I feel.

Four

CAMDEN

SENIOR YEAR

"CAMDEN, I SERIOUSLY CAN'T THANK YOU ENOUGH." MY SISTER, KENDALL, WRAPS HER ARMS AROUND ME and kisses my cheek. "I know you would've rather been hanging with your friends all summer." She isn't wrong. I was definitely looking forward to hanging out with my friends and relaxing all summer, but when Kendall broke up with her boyfriend—who's opening up for her while on tour—and begged me to join her, I couldn't say no to my sister. She's several years older than me, but we've always been close.

"It's all good. I had fun on the road with you, and I learned a shit ton about touring."

She grins. "Never know...I could be visiting you while you're on tour in a few years."

"Oh, it's happening," I tell her, stepping off Blackwood Records's private jet. "Mark my words, within a year of us graduating, we'll be touring."

Her shoulders shake with laughter. "How is it that we grew up listening to nothing but pop and country, and you ended up being a metalhead?"

"Hey!" I feign offense. "I am *not* a metalhead. Would you call Aerosmith a metalhead? How about Matchbox Twenty or OneRepublic? No, you wouldn't, and I'm not either." Not that there's anything wrong with someone being one. I grew up listening to Led Zeppelin and Black Sabbath. They're just a couple of the reasons I fell in love with rock instead of the pop shit my dad and sister sing.

But when Braxton and I sat down in the sixth grade and decided to start a band, I knew I wanted my lyrics to be less heavy and a bit more soulful. Braxton agreed. And when we met Declan—who is a hopeless romantic—and a year later, Gage—who didn't give a fuck what we sang as long as he could beat the shit out of the drums—they were both on board with the vibe we wanted to create.

"Whatever." Kendall rolls her eyes playfully. "It all sounds the same to me."

"And so does your bubblegum pop crap."

She laughs as we get into the Town Car taking us home. Technically, Kendall lives in California, but after a tour, she always spends time at home so our parents can spoil the shit out of her before she goes back to LA to record her next album. She could easily record her album in New York, but she swears the California beach speaks to her, and she has no desire to live anywhere else.

Dad has already said if he signs us after graduation—yeah, *if*, because he refuses to agree to anything until after the four of us have our diplomas—we'll have to move to LA, at least for a while since that's where Earl James is located—one of the best producers in our genre.

When we get to the house, our mom fawns over us, crying about how much she's missed us, while Dad asks us how the tour went, even though he knows everything that goes on with Blackwood.

"Breakfast is ready," Maria says, popping her head in and shooting a wink my way, silently telling me she's made my favorite. Maria is officially our nanny/housekeeper, but unofficially, she's our nanna—at least that's what we've been calling her since I was born. She was hired to help when Mom was pregnant with me and eventually moved in.

While our parents have always been there, they're still busy with Blackwood since Dad is the president, and Mom is Blackwood's attorney and VP. When Dad's parents retired several years ago, they stepped down. Dad retired from making music and instead focuses on running the family business. The first musician he signed was none other than Kendall.

"Cream cheese French toast," Mom says, sitting at the table. "You haven't made these since—"

"Since my birthday," I say, stabbing a piece with my fork. "Because they're my favorite. Thanks, Nanna."

She smiles brightly, sitting at the table with her own plate of food. She's in her late seventies now, and Mom insisted years ago that she stop doing anything around the house and relax. She's hired someone else to do the cleaning and cooking, but Maria swears she gets bored if she's not taking care of our family. I'm not going to argue since she always makes my favorites and cleans my dirty clothes even though we do our own laundry. And before you get on me, I've never asked her to do it. She's like the laundry fairy. My clothes go from the hamper to my drawers, and I've never even seen her do it, but I know it's her. Nanna's been spoiling me since I was born, and everyone knows I'm her favorite.

"Anything for you, my boy," Nanna says with a wink that has everyone at the table, besides me, groaning. "It's been quiet around here all summer without you and those boys making a ruckus downstairs." Her eyes meet mine, and they're a bit glassy. "Sure gonna miss you when you're in LA."

"Oh, Maria!" Mom wraps her arms around her. "No crying. Besides, we still have a year before they leave." She glances at my sister, then back at Maria. "And they always come back."

"But if you're worried about missing me, you're more than welcome to tag along. You can live with me, enjoy the beach and the sun, and make me French toast every morning."

Dad kicks me under the table, Mom glares, and my youngest sister, Phoebe, who's eleven, scoffs. "She's not going anywhere. She still has to take care of me. Right, Nanna?"

Nanna laughs. "I'm not going anywhere, dear. If your brother wants my famous French toast, he'll have to come back here."

"You couldn't keep me away," I tell her as I stuff a bite of delicious food into my mouth.

After breakfast is over, I head up to my room to shower. While I'm waiting for the water to heat, I scroll through my social media, checking out Layla's photos. She hasn't posted a lot this summer, but the few pictures from her time at the beach have all been saved to my phone. And one in particular, where she's lying on a towel and laughing at the camera, has become my background. We've texted almost every day, up until a couple of weeks ago, when the tour went overseas. Between the time difference and my phone rarely having reliable service, we've only spoken a few times.

Before I get into the shower, I pull up her name and shoot her a quick text: **I'm home. Where are you? I need to talk to you.**

This past year, I've given her the space she wanted and remained her friend while she stuck to her ridiculous no-boy pact. At first, I didn't believe she would last all year. I figured she was just heartbroken and needed time, but she stuck to that shit like glue. She joined the cheer squad like she wanted to, and she, Tori, and Kaylee spent the year boyfriend-less. Luckily, staying away from guys doesn't include me, so nothing between us has changed. She still spent plenty of afternoons and weekends hanging out in the studio and going to the parties we performed at. Layla also started a YouTube channel, documenting our shows and practices, and it's blown up like crazy.

I'm excited as hell to be back. I've written several songs while on tour with my sister, and I can't wait to get back to practicing and performing and hanging out with my girl. This year is going to be my year. I can feel it. Braxton mentioned he and Kaylee started dating this summer, and so did Gage and Tori. I was shocked as shit my friends actually got girlfriends, but I'm happy for them. I'm also happy because that means the no-boyfriend pact is over, and I can finally tell Layla how I feel.

Since Layla hasn't texted back yet, I take a quick shower, then get dressed, ready to go find her ass. I shoot a text to the group chat with the guys, letting them know I'm home and asking where they are, figuring since they're dating Layla's best friends, they're probably all together.

Within seconds Braxton texts me back: **At Serendipities. It's hot AF today, and the girls wanted ice cream. <insert rolling eyes emoji>**

I chuckle at my pussy-whipped friend.

Me: Layla with you guys?

Braxton: Yeah

Me: See if everyone wants to come over and chill in the studio.

Before he can respond, Layla responds to my text: **Hey you! Welcome home. Brax said we're going to your house. See you soon! <insert kissing emoji>**

About thirty minutes later, everyone piles into my studio. Declan is the first to enter, and he's alone, followed by Braxton, who has his arm around Kaylee, Gage, who's holding hands with Tori, and Layla, who's…What in the actual fuck? She's holding hands with some asshole I've never seen before.

I'm about to ask what the hell is going on when Layla locks eyes with me, her twin dimples I've missed the hell out of popping out. "Camden!" she squeals, running into my arms. "I've missed you so much!"

Her arms wrap around my neck, and I inhale her signature raspberry-vanilla scent. Fuck, I've missed this girl. My gaze goes over her shoulder to the guy she was holding hands with, and he's glaring daggers my way. I tell myself this can't be right. There's no way I left for two months, and she found a boyfriend, but when we separate, and she walks over to stand next to him, my heart sinks, knowing that's exactly what happened.

"Camden, I want you to meet David Kessler…my boyfriend."

My eyes dart from him over to my friends, who are all standing silent, waiting to see how I'm going to handle this. They know I'm in love with Layla and have been waiting for her to be ready. And based on the way they're avoiding looking my way, they've known about Layla and this guy for however long this has been going on and didn't fucking tell me.

"David," Layla continues. "This is the guy I've been telling you about. Camden, my best friend."

And just like that, I've been friend-zoned.

Just. Fucking. Great.

Five

CAMDEN

PRESENT DAY
HIGH SCHOOL PRE-GRADUATION PARTY

"YOU KNOW WHAT? YOU'RE RIGHT," I SAY, MY GAZE LOCKED ON LAYLA AS SHE ATTEMPTS TO MAKE HER WAY over here only to get stopped by several people. "I'm going to tell her how I feel."

While Layla and I have remained close, it hasn't been easy. David is a possessive asshole—not that I can blame him since Layla is the entire package, and he's worried she'll leave him for someone else. But if Layla and I were together, I wouldn't treat her the way he does—trying to keep her from her friends and hog all her time. I wouldn't fear she'd leave me because I'd treat her so good she wouldn't want to be with anyone else.

We still ride to school together every day, but once we're there, David makes it a point to drag her away, wanting alone time with her. She still hangs out in the studio, but it doesn't take long before he's texting her, wanting to hang out. She still goes to parties, but he's always all over her, not giving her any space. Kaylee once said he only acts like that around me, that when I'm not around, he's normal and doesn't get all possessive, which tells me he's scared of losing her to me.

The funny thing is, up until now, I'd never go after another man's woman, so he had nothing to be worried about. But now, despite knowing it's wrong, I need to finally be honest with her. I'm not going to ask her to break up with David, but I need for her to at least know how I feel before she takes off to college with him—because once she said where she wanted to go, suddenly, he wanted to go there as well. The fact is, I've been holding on to these feelings for three years, and I need to get them out, so at least she knows.

I steal one of the shots Declan poured for himself and throw it back, needing a bit of liquid courage. "Fuck it. At this point, what do I have to lose?"

"That's what I'm talking about." Declan clasps his hand on my shoulder.

As I'm pushing off the counter, ready to lay it all out to her, a couple of our fellow students speaking next to me stops me in my place.

"…that picture…Braxton is going to kill him."

"Kill who?"

The two girls look up, their eyes going wide. "Umm…"

"Who the fuck is Braxton going to kill?" I snatch the phone from the girl's hand so I can see what she's looking at. The last thing we need is Braxton getting into any fights the night before we all walk across that damn stage and get our diplomas. Sure, technically, we're graduates, but who knows what the school would do if he got arrested for fighting, and Braxton is notorious for his no-shits-given attitude.

When I see the photo on the screen of his girlfriend half-naked in bed with another guy, I fling the phone back at the girl. "Where is this?"

"I don't know." She shrugs. "Probably here since I saw Kaylee earlier." She turns back to her friend. "I always knew she was a skank. Always trying to act like she's so perfect. Guess the homecoming queen has been dethroned."

"What happened?" Declan asks.

"We need to find Brax. Now."

I sprint out of the kitchen, already dialing Braxton's number, but before it goes through, Gage's name appears on my screen.

"Hey, man, have you seen Brax?" There's silence over the line. "Gage, you there? This is important. Gage…"

"She…She's gone."

I halt on the sidewalk, a shiver racing up my spine. Gage's girlfriend, Tori, has been going through some shit lately, but there's no way he could mean…

"Gage, what the hell are you talking about? Where is she?"

"Tori's dead. I'm at the hospital. She's gone, man." A choked sob comes through the phone, sending goose bumps up my arms.

"Stay right there," I tell him. "I'm on my way. Don't fucking move!"

The line goes dead, and I glance over at Declan. "Something happened to Tori. I need to go to Gage. I need you to find Braxton. There's a picture going around of Kaylee and another guy. Find Braxton and don't let him kill anyone."

Declan nods, and we take off in opposite directions. I call my parents on the way and ask them to meet me at the hospital.

We arrive at the same time, finding Gage sitting in a chair at the hospital, his head in his hands, his entire body shaking uncontrollably.

"Gage." His face pops up, his bloodshot eyes meeting mine. "What happened?"

He shakes his head, and I drop onto the ground next to him. "She texted she wouldn't be able to make it to the party. I knew she'd been down lately, and I didn't want her to miss our last night." A sob escapes his lips. "I showed up at her house…" He swallows thickly. "I was too late…Fuck!" He roars. "I was too fucking late. She's gone." Tears slide down his face, and I pull him into my arms, holding him tight. "She's gone," he repeats over and over again while we sit here, me holding him while he cries into my chest.

At some point, he gets himself together and stands. "Where are you going?"

"I don't know," he says, looking around. "I…I don't fucking know. Her parents wouldn't even let me see her. I just wanted to see her."

"You're coming home with us," my mom insists. "We'll deal with this together as a family."

I give her a sad smile, thankful as hell to have the parents I have. A few months ago, Gage aged out of the system, and the people giving him a place to live said he needed to go. Without hesitation, Mom told him he'd be staying with us.

My phone buzzes in my pocket, and remembering everything that's going on, I pull it out so I can get everyone caught up to speed.

Declan: Not good. Kaylee cheated on Brax, and I can't find him.

I check to make sure Declan didn't text me in the group chat and then reply: **Gage found Tori dead. Find Brax and get to my house ASAP. He needs us.**

Declan: Fuck…There's something you need to know. It's bad timing, but I don't want you finding out from someone else.

Me: Worse than Kaylee cheating and Tori dying?

A link comes through, and I click on it, waiting for it to open so I can see what the next blow tonight will be.

When it loads, I find a picture of Layla and David with smiling faces, but that's not what has my attention. Because also in the picture is her hand, with a diamond ring on her left finger. The caption reads: **He asked, and I said yes!**

And just like that, my entire world is blown apart.

 Six

LAYLA

FIVE YEARS LATER

"MOM, CHECK OUT THIS MOVE," FELIX SAYS, SHAKING HIS BUTT TO JUSTIN BIEBER'S "BABY." HE TURNS IN a circle, mimicking what Justin is doing on the television. Justin drops into some cool dance move I couldn't replicate to save my life, but somehow, my four-year-old does it perfectly, making it look like he's part of the concert, only in our living room.

"Good job," I tell him. "After this song, I need you to stop and clean up before—"

My sentence is cut off by the opening and slamming of the front door. Felix's eyes go wide, and he runs to turn off the TV, but he's not fast enough. Before he can cut it off, David steps into the living room with a scowl on his face.

"What did I say about letting our son spend his time dancing?" he barks. "Dancing is for girls. If he's bored, enroll him in a damn sport."

I mentally roll my eyes at his sexist remark, not bothering to comment on it. We've had this argument too many times lately. With my passion for videography, Felix has grown up watching various music videos, and along the way, he found his love of dance—and for his age, he's actually really freaking good. When I mentioned him taking dance lessons, David nearly flipped his shit and refused to allow it. Since then, I've made it a point not to have Felix dance when David is around. That way, he can't make Felix feel bad about it.

"Well, aren't you in a lovely mood," I say dryly, then glance over at Felix. "Why don't you go clean your room? I'll let you know when dinner is ready."

Felix nods and runs out of the room, thankful for the out.

"I take it you didn't get the promotion you were hoping for?" I say to David once we're alone. David lives and breathes his job. If he didn't get this promotion he's been working hard for, he's going to be a pain in the ass to live with. Our marriage is already rocky as it is. I'm not sure we'll be able to weather an unplanned storm.

I sigh, wondering how we got here. Things between us weren't always this bad. At least I don't think they were. It's hard, now, to remember a time when we actually got along, but I'm sure we did. Otherwise, we wouldn't have gotten engaged and left for Boston together. But somewhere along the way, between college and my accidental pregnancy and life, things between us shifted—and not for the better. I keep hoping the rift between us can be fixed, but at some point, I'm going to have to face the facts—that rift is split open so wide, there's no repairing it.

David glares at me. "Actually, I did get the promotion. Thanks for your vote of confidence...but it comes with a stipulation I wasn't aware of: relocation."

"Relocation? Like we have to move?" We've been living in Boston since we moved here for college. I had hoped to move back to New York after college, but when David graduated, he got the job of his dreams, which meant staying—regardless of what I wanted.

"Yeah," he says with a bite in his tone. "Actually, this should make you happy. We're moving back to New York."

"Really?" I gasp because he's right. This does make me happy. I should be totally peeved that he's made the decision without me, but since it means moving back to the place I consider home, I'm not going to bother arguing. Especially since it will mean being closer to my mom.

Last year, we lost my dad, and since then, she's been having a hard time. I know getting to see Felix more often will help. And since David is practically married to his job, it will mean getting to spend lots of quality time with my mom as well.

"Yeah," he says, his nostrils flaring. "We're moving back. But I'm telling you right now, if you think that means you'll be spending all your time with those loser metalheads, you're wrong. I don't want my son around them."

"They're not metalheads," I argue. "And in case you forgot, they don't even live in New York." I'll never understand why David has such an issue with the guys. They've never done anything wrong to him. But if they come on the radio or get mentioned, he damn near loses his shit, like them simply being alive and existing personally offends him.

"His parents do." *His* meaning Camden, who I haven't talked to in several years. But that doesn't stop David from making crazy accusations anyway. "All I'm saying is when we move back there, you need to remember who you're married to."

"I'm well aware of who I'm married to. So when do we move?"

"Soon. With the promotion comes a relocation bonus. I found a place not too far from my parents and signed a six-month lease." Of course, he only mentions his parents because he and my mom don't exactly get along. When she was visiting us after Felix was born, he was rude to me in front of her, and she made a comment about it. Ever since then, he acts like she's trying to break up our marriage when, the truth is, he's doing a fine job of it himself. I already have one foot out the door. And now we're moving home. He might've found a place near his parents, but my mom lives near them.

"When it's up, I'll figure out what I want to do," he continues. "They're opening up a new office and want me to oversee it. I'm hoping once it's up and running, they'll move us somewhere else."

"I don't want to keep moving," I tell him. "Felix is about to start school. I want stability for him. You know how much I hated moving when I was younger. Moving to New York means being close to our families. I want to stay there."

"Well, you don't really have a say," he snaps. "My job pays the bills, so I decide where we live, and New York is not where I want to live."

And here we go again...

"And I'd gladly work, but you keep giving me shit about it."

"Because you belong at home taking care of our son. How about being a little more appreciative that you're able to be home? My mom's been home since I was born, and she appreciates it. Stop acting spoiled."

"I am appreciative of it," I grind out. "I love being home with him, but once he starts school, I'd like to get a job. That doesn't make me spoiled. I want to follow my passions and contribute just like you're doing."

"Your passions?" He scoffs. "Taking pictures is a hobby, not a job. Focus on our son, and I'll focus on taking care of us." He loosens his tie. "I need to get everything in order. We're leaving next Friday."

"FELIX! COME AND EAT, PLEASE," I YELL OVER THE SOUND OF JUSTIN BIEBER. I CAN'T SEE HIM SINCE HE'S upstairs, but I can imagine him dancing his little butt off to the new music video that just came out. When he doesn't respond, I add, "I made chocolate chip pancakes."

"Coming!" he yells. The music comes to a halt, and then the distinct sound of his feet padding against the wood floor is heard. He flies down the stairs and plops into his chair, diving right into his breakfast.

"Are you excited about school?" I ask, my stomach in knots at the thought of my little boy starting preschool.

"I'm a little scared," he admits. "Ms. Derby seems nice, but I don't know anyone, and I miss my friends."

"I get that, but the good thing is we're close to Grandma and Nona and Papa. And you'll make new friends, I promise." School started a couple of days ago, but it's still early enough that he won't feel too much like the new kid.

I hate that Felix will miss the friends he's made in Boston, but the truth is, I won't miss the place at all. Everyone and everything I love is in New York, and had I not gotten pregnant our freshman year, I doubt I would've stayed in Boston as long as I did. Actually, I know I wouldn't have.

Felix nods slowly, not completely convinced, and continues to eat his food. A few minutes later, he's done, and after cleaning him up, we're off to his new school, which is only a few blocks from where we live. It's September in New York, and still nice out, in the low seventies. Unfortunately, that won't last long, and snow will soon be blanketing the ground.

After snapping several photos of Felix next to his desk and then introducing himself to a couple of kids and being reassured by Mrs. Derby that he'll have a great day and she'll see me later when I pick him up, I head back home to get my chores done. David likes a neat house and tends to bitch and moan when things are amiss, so I straighten up, run the vacuum, wash the dishes from breakfast, and throw a load of laundry into the washer.

When I glance at the time and see it's only been an hour, I send a text to my mom to see what she's up to.

Mom: Walking into yoga. Dinner tonight?

Me: Have fun! And sure. I'll come over after Felix gets out of school.

Then I text Kaylee to see if she's free for coffee.

Kaylee: I wish. Classes all day. Boo.

Kaylee had a rough go of it after her breakup with Braxton. Despite my best efforts to help her get through her first year of college, she failed out and moved back home. She took the rest of the year off and started over again the following year. She buckled down the second time around and will graduate in December. She already has a job lined up that she's excited about.

Bored, I pull up my social media and scroll through everyone's Monday morning posts, a mixture of inspirational and hating Monday memes.

I stop on one post in particular and hover my finger over it, deciding whether to like and comment. It's from Raging Chaos's official page. The picture was taken at a recent award show—Gage, Declan, and Braxton are standing around the man in the middle, who's holding the award in his hand with a huge grin spread across his face: Camden Blackwood. My best friend. Well, my ex-best friend. We haven't spoken in years, not since *that* night when everything changed. When Tori took her life, Kaylee cheated on Braxton, and David asked me to marry him.

Braxton and Kaylee broke up.

We buried Tori.

And then the guys left for LA, never looking back.

None of us even bothered to walk across the stage—our diplomas were mailed to us.

I tried to call Camden, but he said they needed time. Needed some space. So I did what he asked. A few months later, while I was in my dorm room listening to music while studying, their first song hit the radio. "Raging Chaos." It was the name of the song and their band—their introduction to the world.

A couple of months into college, David and I were going through a rough patch—being in college was different than being in high school. I was close to calling off the engagement and ending things between us, but then fate intervened, and despite being on birth control, I found out I was pregnant. David insisted on us getting married before Felix was born, so, in December, we were married. It was a small wedding, just close family and friends. I sent the guys and Camden an invite to our wedding, but they RSVP'd they couldn't make it. The day of the wedding, a gift arrived from Camden congratulating us—it was the newest camera out at the time with a note that read: *So you can capture all the memories.*

In June, I gave birth to Felix, and once again, a box was waiting for me when I got home. It was a baby book to print the pictures I took and create a scrapbook. There was a note inside as well that read: *You're going to make a wonderful mom.*

My heart hurt that he could easily throw our friendship away, reducing it to gifts for the occasions, but I didn't know what to do or how to fix it, so I followed his pages and watched him and the other guys climb up the ladder of fame. I always knew they'd be successful. Between Camden's soothing voice and the raw talent of Gage, Declan, and Braxton backing him up, it was a given. But what I don't think anyone expected was how quickly they would blow up.

Every song has topped the charts for weeks, every album has won awards, and every tour has sold out. I'm so proud of them. And I miss Camden so damn much.

I click on the picture and comment congratulations even though I'm sure they probably have people handling their social media for them, and none of the guys will even see it.

Closing the app, I pull up Google. Without thinking about it, I find myself searching for videography jobs. With Felix in school and David busy at work, there's no way I'm just going to sit around here doing nothing. I got my videography degree for a reason, and it's time I actually put it to use.

As I'm searching for possible job leads, my phone rings. It's Bailey.

"Hey, long time no hear," I say when I answer.

"Hey, you. I just saw your mom at yoga, and she said you're back! When were you planning to let us know?"

"Umm...soon..."

"That doesn't sound convincing."

The truth is, since Camden stopped talking to me, I kind of shied away from the rest of his family. I always comment and like their posts, but I haven't seen any of them since I moved to Boston, and since David despises New York, my mom always visited us.

"We just got back a few days ago and are still settling in. We actually rented a place not too far from my mom."

"That's awesome. I know how much your mom misses you. Every time Mom and I have lunch with her, she's always talking nonstop about you and Felix."

My heart swells at her words. Even though I was gone, I'm glad she has Sophia. Since we moved in eight years ago, they clicked and have been the best of friends ever since.

"Thank you for keeping her company. I've missed her like crazy." *I've missed everyone like crazy.*

"We should totally catch up. Hey! Friday night, I have to attend a charity concert. It's for a good cause, and I have an extra ticket. You should come."

"I don't know." It's been so long since I've been out. David always works late on Friday nights, and I hate to ask my mom to watch Felix when we've just moved back.

"Come on, please. It's been forever since we hung out," she begs.

"Let me see if my mom minds watching Felix, and I'll let you know."

Seven

LAYLA

"A charity concert in the park."

"Who will be there?"

"Bailey, for sure, and I'm assuming her friends."

"Will *they* be there?"

"Who?" I ask incredulously, confused as to why the hell my husband all of a sudden cares where I'm going and who I'm going with. For the past five years, he's never asked me a single question. He's always been too busy with school and work and doing his own thing.

"Don't play stupid with me, Layla. Raging Chaos." His face twists together like just the name of the band is enough to make him sick.

"You know, you used to be friends with them," I point out. When we first met at the beach, he hit it off with Declan, Gage, and Braxton. We spent two weeks, all of us hanging out. It wasn't until Camden got home that David decided he was above hanging out with a bunch of rockers.

"I put up with them to hang out with you," he corrects. "And once we were together, I didn't have to do that."

What the hell? Not liking his attitude, I throw it back at him. "Well, Camden used to be my best friend, and now that we're home, I wouldn't doubt that we'll see more of them, so you better play nice. You know our families are close."

"I don't give a shit how close your families are. You're married to me, and he isn't welcome anywhere near *my* family."

"Whatever. I'm going tonight. Does you coming home early mean you're keeping Felix?"

"I have a meeting I need to get to. I thought your mom was taking him."

"She is," I snap. "I need to get ready. Keep an eye on Felix, please." After stomping upstairs, I put on an olive-green maxi dress with a halter top and pair it with a cute dark-wash denim jacket. After I finish curling my hair into beach waves, since it's too humid to straighten it, and throw on a pair of strappy sandals, I head back downstairs.

David is in the living room typing away on his computer, and when he sees me enter the room, he does a double take before setting his computer aside and walking toward me.

"You look beautiful," he says, placing his hands on my hips. "We should go out tonight, just the two of us." His tone is gentle, sweet, and very unlike him. It reminds me of when we were in high school, and for a second, my heart softens at it.

"I thought you had to work."

"I can reschedule the meeting. We can drop Felix off at your mom's and go to dinner. What do you say?" He places a tender kiss on the corner of my mouth. "Cancel with Bailey and go out with me."

His last statement has me rearing back. "Or you can go with us?"

His eyes turn into thin slits. "I'm not going to that shit." And there he is... The *real* David Kessler.

"It's for a good cause," I repeat what Bailey had said. "We can get dinner and go to the concert. It will be nice—"

"I have work to do," he says, stepping back. "I grew up years ago. You should try it."

His harsh words hit me like a slap to the face even though they shouldn't surprise me anymore. "Music isn't just for teenagers. You might think of it as a hobby, but many people view it as a career. One I plan to pursue."

He glares like he always does when the subject of me working gets brought up. "If you're bored, you can always reconsider getting pregnant..."

Ugh, not this again. "I already told you that I'm not ready to have another baby." The truth is, I always imagined my kids being close in age, but there's no way I'm bringing another child into our already rocky marriage.

"Fine," he barks. "Then you should do something productive like volunteer at Felix's school. My mom did that when I was little."

"You're such an asshole," I hiss, completely fed up with his shit. "You've known what I've wanted to do for years, and you used to be supportive. What happened?"

"I assumed you would grow out of it."

"Grow out of it? It's my passion, my livelihood. My dream is to make music videos, film documentaries, and photograph musicians. That's never going to change."

During the years I was friends with Camden, I would record them, edit the footage, and post it on YouTube. It was then I realized I wanted to do that on a larger scale one day. The summer before our junior and senior year, Easton, Camden's dad, even let me hang around the studio and learn from one of their videographers. He told me after I finished school, I would always be welcome if I wanted to intern with them. Maybe I should talk to Easton. It would piss off David, but at this point, I don't even care.

"I need to get going," David says, snapping me from my thoughts.

"Of course you do." I roll my eyes.

He ignores my annoyance, gathering his stuff and heading to the front door. Before he walks out, he turns back to me, eyeing me one last time. "Do you think that dress is appropriate for a mom to wear?"

My jaw drops—literally drops. "You just said I looked beautiful."

"And you do. When you're at home or with your husband. I'm just not sure about the kind of message it will send if you're wearing it to a concert, surrounded by drunken men."

"It's a *charity event,* and I don't care if I show up naked. Nothing I wear should send any message to any man, drunk or not. Have a great night at work," I sneer, turning my back on him, done with this asinine conversation.

"ARE YOU *SURE* YOU DON'T MIND WATCHING HIM?" I ASK AS MY MOM PUSHES ME OUT THE DOOR, EVEN though she told me several times she has absolutely no problem with watching her grandson. In fact, she insisted on keeping him for the night to make up for all the time they've missed out on while we were living apart and told me not to pick him up until at least after breakfast tomorrow.

"Layla Isabella, if you ask me that one more time…"

"Okay, okay." I throw my hands up, waving the white flag. "I'm going."

"Have fun, Mommy!" Felix yells from the living room, not even bothering to come over and properly say goodbye since he's too busy checking out all the toys my mom bought for him once she found out she'd be watching him tonight.

"Bye, love you."

I close the door behind me and walk down the steps and over to the Blackwoods, where Bailey told me to meet her. When her mom found out we were going out tonight, she insisted I stop by to see her before we went out.

"Oh my God, Layla!" Sophia wraps me up in a motherly hug. "Seeing pictures of you online is not the same thing. I swear, when you left here, you were still a little girl, but now"—she backs up and drags her gaze up and down, taking me in—"you're a beautiful woman." She hugs me again. "We missed you so much."

"Okay, Mom, we get it," Bailey says, sauntering into the room, dressed in a pair of dark-wash skinny jeans and a black wraparound halter top, complete with tall lace-up stiletto boots. "Now give her some breathing room before you scare her away."

Sophia rolls her eyes lovingly at her daughter and kisses her cheek. "Have a good time tonight and give my boys some lovin' from me. Tell them I expect to see them before they take off back to the other side of the country."

Her words have me freezing in my place. "The guys are going to be there?"

Bailey and Sophia both eye me curiously, and I make it a point to school my features, not wanting them to know just how much I've missed Camden. Hell, how much I've missed them all.

"They're playing at the event," Bailey says, a cautious smile on her face. "I assumed you knew. I'm technically working tonight. I'm sorry. I should've mentioned that. If you don't want to go—"

"What? No! It's all good." I cringe when I hear the false cheer in my voice. "It's just been forever since I've seen them play live," I add, trying to play it off.

Sophia and Bailey both frown, but thankfully, neither one comments on how awkward I sound, like I'm talking about a band and not my once best friend.

"You sure?" Bailey asks.

"Yeah, I can't wait to see them play in person." I should've known the event wasn't just for pleasure. Bailey works for Blackwood, so it only makes sense.

The ride to the concert is long in the city traffic, but Bailey and I use the time to catch up. I learn she's dating someone new—her name is Cynthia, and she works in marketing at Blackwood. She's the first woman Bailey's dated who she can see a future with, so they're taking it slow. Bailey graduated last year and is using her marketing degree to run Blackwood's media department, and when she asks me if I'm still planning to do something in videography, I tell her I've been researching possible internships and jobs.

"You know my dad would be offended if you don't intern with us."

"I wasn't really sure if that was still on the table." I shrug, not wanting Easton to think I've disappeared and then expect him to take me in.

"Layla," she says, placing her hand on my thigh. "I know you and Camden don't…" She flinches, not finishing the sentence, but we both know what she was saying: *we don't talk anymore*. "But that doesn't change the fact that you're like family."

"I appreciate that. I think, for now, I'll keep looking. I don't want to stir the pot."

I can tell she wants to argue, but instead, she says, "Okay, but if you change your mind…"

"I know. Thank you."

When we get to the venue, we're taken backstage. With Bailey's hand in mine, we walk through the throng of people running around and getting ready for the show to start. It's complete madness and makes me smile. I always dreamed of working with musicians, and although I've only been to a handful of concerts, those I've been to, I was lucky enough to be with Camden and get to experience it all from behind the scenes. Every show he took me to solidified what I wanted to do for a living. Being back here amid the chaos reminds me of my dreams. And if David thinks he's going to stop me from achieving them, he's got another thing coming.

"I just need to check in with Cade real quick," she says. "Actually, you'll love to meet him." She grins back at me. "He's our videographer. I'm doing a promotional YouTube series leading up to the next tour for Raging Chaos, and he's getting footage for it."

She searches for him in several areas he should be in, and when she can't find him, she stops and calls him. After the second attempt, he answers. "Hey, Cade, where are you?"

I can't hear what's being said but based on the frown now marring her features, it can't be good. "Is everything okay?" Her frown deepens. "I understand...No, it's okay. You need to focus on her. If you need anything, please let me know."

"What happened?" I ask when she hangs up.

"Cade's girlfriend has been put on bed rest. She's only eighteen weeks pregnant. He's been so distraught that he forgot to call me. He's in LA with her right now."

"Is she okay?"

"Yeah, but he's worried about leaving her. I really wanted to get some footage of the show tonight, but there'll be other shows."

"I could do it," I blurt out. "If you have the camera equipment and lighting, I could record the footage. It's not that hard." Her eyes go wide, and I immediately backtrack. "I mean, I haven't done anything like that in a while, but while I was in college, I videoed a few shows and made some music videos. No, actually, I can't do it. I don't know what I was thinking. Just ignore me. I'm an idiot. I have no idea what I'm even talking about." When a smile spreads across Bailey's face, I stop my rambling. "What?"

"Nothing, I was just listening to you have an entire conversation with yourself. Do you do that often?"

I snort out a laugh. "It's one of the side effects of being a stay-at-home mom."

She laughs. "Sounds like you need some adult interaction."

"David works a lot," I mumble, immediately regretting it when Bailey looks at me curiously. "I mean, he's working his way up the corporate ladder, and with the promotions, he has to be at the office a lot, so it's usually just Felix and me." I sigh, willing myself to shut up.

"So you can do it?" she asks, changing gears.

"Do what?" I ask dumbly.

She rolls her eyes. "Record the show. It would just be during the guys' set, which is only two songs."

"I don't know."

"You would be doing me a huge favor, and let's be real…" She steps closer and leans in like she's about to tell me a secret. "We both know you want to. I bet you're itching to get behind a camera again."

She's right. I totally do, and I totally am. My fingers are literally tingling at the thought of getting my hands on the professional equipment. It's been too long since I've gotten to do anything like this and never at an event this big.

"Yeah, I do," I admit.

She grins. "Then let's do it."

Eight

LAYLA

SINCE THE GUYS DON'T GO ON UNTIL LAST, AFTER BAILEY SHOWS ME WHERE ALL THE EQUIPMENT IS AND I get situated, we go to the VIP seats and watch several performances. Some of my favorite bands are playing, and I get lost in the music. It's been way too long since I've been able to let loose and enjoy myself. We dance and laugh and sing and even have a couple of drinks. I'm so wrapped up in the show that I'm momentarily confused when Bailey says it's time to head backstage. Until I remember I'm recording Raging Chaos. Then my heart goes into overdrive because what the hell was I thinking? I haven't seen these guys in person in five years.

Thankfully, since they're on stage and I'm recording from the side, they won't even know I'm there. My plan is to get in and get out.

As I'm setting up, the crowd goes crazy, and a second later, Camden's voice echoes across the speakers. My gaze lands on him, and my heart leaps in my chest. Time has been good to him. He's older looking, more mature. His brown hair is messy, and his skin is sun-kissed from the California sun, making him look more like a surfer than a rock star. I briefly wonder if he lives near the water. If he goes to the beach on his days off.

Camden thanks everyone for being here, and once the crowd has calmed a bit, he explains that them being here is helping a cause close to their heart. My chest tightens at his words as he speaks about it, though he doesn't specifically say Tori's name. It's been years since I've allowed myself to think about her. What happened was so tragic, and it was hard to deal with as a teenager. The night she died, everything changed for all of us. We were young and heartbroken, and we just didn't know how to handle adult shit. Hell, five years later, I might be older, but I still don't think I would be able to handle the seriousness of what went down.

Gage starts the song by counting off on his drums, and I press record, focusing on him. His face is stoic, but I know him well enough to know he was affected by Camden's speech and is hiding his emotions. He looks darker and edgier than he did the last time I saw him five years ago. He's never been carefree, not with everything he's been through in his life, but before, he still had a lightness to him. Now, it's as if it's been snuffed out.

Declan joins in with the bass a few seconds later, smirking playfully at the crowd. Like Camden and Gage, he's now less boy and more man. Braxton adds his guitar, his eyes meeting Declan's for a moment before he gives the crowd his attention. He smirks as well, but it's more devilish. While the band has been good at keeping themselves away from any negative publicity, Braxton's been caught quite a few times in compromising positions with various women, alongside Gage. The media chalks it up to them being manwhores, but since I'm personally familiar with their history, I know it's more about burying their broken hearts than the need to sleep around.

Declan and Braxton move closer, and I zoom in on their instruments and then on their faces as they bob their heads in time with the music. And then Camden belts out the beginning lyrics of the song "Hate to Love You" from their last album. Their sound is fluid. They've been playing together for so many years, they could probably do it in their sleep. One song blends into two and then three.

Camden's shirt comes off at some point, and sweat glistens on his skin. He chucks it to the side, making fans freak out over who's going to snag it. I've seen plenty of pictures of him shirtless, but none of them compare to seeing him in person. He's all man, rippled and hard everywhere, yet still so damn beautiful.

When the lyrics come to an end, Camden grins while Braxton riles the crowd up with his solo just before the lights flicker off, officially ending the song.

Everyone cheers when the lights come back on, and Camden is sitting on a stool with a mic in his hand. He holds his hand up, and like magic, the place goes silent.

"I thought tonight, here with you, would be the perfect time to play something new. It's a bit slower. What do you think?" The fans scream and shriek, and Camden chuckles under his breath. "All right, since you asked so nicely." More screams.

Gage starts in on the drums, and then the other guys join in. I'm videoing just fine, focusing on what I'm doing...and then Camden opens his mouth. His raspy voice is filled with raw emotion, and I find myself locked on him, forgetting what I'm supposed to be doing. From the moment the first words leave his mouth, I can tell that this song is different from his norm.

> *Lately, I've been sitting in the dark*
> *Drinking whiskey*
> *Wondering how the hell I let her get ahold of my heart*
> *It wasn't hers to take*

It sure as fuck wasn't hers to break

I quickly realize he's singing about a woman who has broken his heart, and I wonder who it could be. As far as I know, he's never been in a serious relationship. Sure, he's been seen out with various women but never more than a few times. Maybe he kept it quiet, under wraps, not wanting his business to be out there.

> *Looking back, I have to wonder if I was ever even in the game*
> *Guess it doesn't fuckin' matter*
> *'Cause the outcome was always meant to be the same*
>
> *Sharp, jagged pieces all over the floor*
> *That's all that was left when she walked out the door*
>
> *Camera in her hands*
> *All I wanted was to see the world through her lens*
> *Would it be beautiful, magical, or would it all be a blur?*
> *Would I ever know what she's thinking?*
> *Or would I always wonder why I was never enough for her?*
>
> *Sharp, jagged pieces all over the floor*
> *That's all that was left when she walked out the door*

At his words, my body stills, chills racing up my spine. My eyes stay locked on Camden as he sings about a woman with a camera. He couldn't be talking about me. There's no way. Mentally, I shake my head for even coming up with such an outlandish notion. It has to be a coincidence. It wouldn't even make any sense because we've never dated, so how could I have possibly broken his heart. No, I'm clearly overthinking things. I chalk my crazy thinking up to the shit David was giving me earlier about Camden, mixed with the couple of drinks Bailey convinced me to get...until he sings the next few lines.

> *Nobody warned me how hard it would be*
> *To watch that gorgeous woman walk away from me*
> *Thousands of miles apart*
> *Should've been easier than this to piece back together my heart*

I suck in a sharp breath, tears filling my lids. This can't be a coincidence. I'm the girl with the camera. I left for Boston and didn't return until now. He moved thousands of miles away. Too many pieces fit together, but none of them make any sense.

Like the perfect lens has been shattered
I'm trying to see past her, but she's all that mattered
Life has turned into one blurry mess
I need to refocus, finally put her to rest

Sharp, jagged pieces of my broken heart all over the floor
That's all that was left when she walked out the door

The crowd cheers when the song ends, clearly loving it. The guys make their way off the stage, but I can't move. My feet are stuck, and my head is numb. My heart is racing beneath my rib cage, causing my body to vibrate. Thoughts of all the times David was pissed about Camden, accusing him of wanting to get in my pants, saying we can't be friends because guys and girls can't just be friends hit me hard. I chalked it up to him being jealous over nothing. But was he right? Was I blind? Did Camden want more with me, and I had no idea?

And then, just before they disappear, Camden stops and glances my way. His eyes land on mine, and I swear, my heart stops. Like literally stops. His eyes widen slightly, his nostrils flaring. I wait with bated breath to see what he'll do. Will he come over? Walk away?

My questions are answered when he steps toward me, not stopping until we're mere inches apart. He's still shirtless, dripping with sweat. It's hard to breathe, and my head is spinning. I open my mouth—to say what, I'm not sure—but before any words can come out, Camden leans in. I think he's going to say something, but his lips softly land on my cheek. Unconsciously, I inhale, and the scent of him damn near knocks me on my ass. He still smells like the same cologne—warm with a spicy undertone. It's the same cologne he's been wearing for years. It's not until his scent hits me that I realize how much I've missed that smell...missed *him*. It's like sitting by the fire on a cold night. I could wrap myself up in his scent and feel content.

He pulls back slightly, and his green eyes bore into mine for a long moment before he finally speaks. "You look good, Shutterbug. Really damn good." Then without another word, he turns his back on me and disappears, leaving me wondering what the hell just happened.

"Layla," a feminine voice says, clearing some of the fog in my head. "Are you okay?"

I look at Bailey, who's biting her lip in worry. "Was that...?" I drag in a breath, then release it harshly. "Was that song...about...?" I can't even finish my question, a lump of emotion clogging my voice. I already know the answer, but I need someone else to say it, to confirm it.

"About you?" she finishes. "Yeah."

"Did you know?"

She shakes her head. "I mean, I knew he wrote it. I'm back and forth between here and LA, and I hear the songs they're recording. But I didn't know he was going to sing it tonight. I swear."

"I don't understand," I breathe. "He said I broke his heart, but it doesn't make any sense. He's the one who left without so much as a goodbye. He's the one who said he needed space."

Bailey eyes me for a moment before she sighs. "Why don't we get out of here and go get a drink?"

We end up at Mitchell's, a hole-in-the-wall dive bar that Bailey frequents when she's in town, and Kaylee, who apparently was watching the performance online, meets us there since she lives in the city and attends NYU.

"It's been too damn long." Kaylee wraps her arms around me for a hug. "I can't believe the warden actually let you out."

"K," I groan, not wanting to hear, *again*, how much she can't stand my husband. Once upon a time, they got along. Until we moved to Boston and shit hit the fan. He wanted to focus on school while Kaylee wanted to drown her sorrows in the bottom of a bottle, and I was stuck in the middle. It led to a lot of fights and me staying home with David and studying instead of partying. She'd constantly tell me he was too controlling and would ruin my college experience. It didn't matter, though, because shortly after the start of our freshman year, I got pregnant, and after that, my life revolved around Felix, school, and David.

After three double shots of Johnny, and an hour of playing catch-up, I bring up the elephant in the room. "So that song...Care to explain it?"

Both women laugh. "I'm pretty sure it was self-explanatory," Bailey says. "That was my brother's poetic attempt to get over you."

"When the hell was he ever into me?" I ask, throwing my hands up in frustration.

"He's been in love with you since you moved here," Kaylee says.

"What?" I gasp in shock. "No..."

"Yes," they both say in unison.

"You're the only one who didn't notice," Kaylee says. "We all saw it, but since you never reciprocated, everyone assumed you didn't feel the same way. And then you got together with David."

"I...I didn't know." I rack my brain, trying to think of any indication Camden would've given that he had feelings for me, but I can't think of anything. "We were just friends."

"Yeah, because you were either dating someone or on a man-break," Kaylee points out. "The guy was head over heels in love with you, and you totally friend-zoned his ass."

"What? No, he wasn't!" This doesn't make any sense. "He never said anything!"

"Because he's not the kind of guy to fuck with a girl while she's in a relationship," Bailey points out.

"Didn't you ever wonder why David hated Camden so much?" Kaylee adds.

"I thought he was just acting crazy." The bartender serves us another round of shots, and I down mine, then ask for another.

"Slow down," Kaylee warns. "When's the last time you drank?"

"Don't worry about me. I can handle it."

Nine

LAYLA

I OPEN MY EYES, AND THE BRIGHT LIGHTS PEERING THROUGH THE SLATS OF THE BLINDS HAVE ME QUICKLY shutting my lids. The room feels like it's spinning, and my head is pounding to the beat of an off-tune drum.

"I think...I drank too much," I groan to myself.

"No shit," Kaylee says, making me jump up and screech.

I push up onto my elbows and glance around, noting that I'm lying in bed with Kaylee, and it's not my bed. "Where am I?"

"My place." She quirks a brow. "Don't you remember?"

I drop back down and grab a pillow to cover my face, willing the throbbing in my head to go away while I try to recall last night. I remember the charity concert, Camden singing the love, *er*, heartbreak song about me, getting drunk at the bar, going to a tattoo shop...

"Oh, shit!" I pop back up, and the room swirls around me. It takes a second for everything to become clear, and once it does, I jump out of bed and run into the en suite bathroom, tugging the sleeve of my shirt down as I go to expose my collarbone.

"I got a tattoo?" I gasp. "Oh, my God! I got a freaking tattoo."

"Were you really that drunk?" Kaylee asks, sitting on the toilet to go pee.

"No...Yes...Ugh, I don't know. I remember getting it. I just can't believe I did that." I stare at the black, gray, and white shaded camera with the cracked lens. There's one word written in script across the front of it: Shattered. The name of the song Camden sang last night. Shards of glass dance up the front of my shoulder and across the top. It's beautiful and sad and...

"What the hell was I thinking?" I murmur, pulling my shirt back up to cover the ink and wondering how the fuck I'm going to hide this from David. He's going to flip his shit when he sees this. Just the idea of me talking to Camden sends him damn near over the edge. When he finds out I got a tattoo...a freaking tattoo with the title of his song on it, he's going to kill me.

Kaylee flushes the toilet and washes her hands, then follows me out of the bathroom. "Only you can answer that, but if I were to guess..." She locks eyes with me. "I think hearing that song stirred something deep inside you."

"Like what?"

"Like feelings for the lead singer of Raging Chaos."

"I'm married," I argue, refusing to acknowledge that what she's saying might be true. Not that it matters because the fact is, *I am married,* and while Camden and I used to be best friends, we're not even acquaintances anymore. "I love my husband."

But as I say those words, a sadness creeps into my chest. Because while it's true, I do love David—he's the father of my son, and I've given him every part of me for the past six years—if I'm honest with myself, I don't think I've been *in love* with him for quite some time. I keep holding out hope that he's going to change, that we're going to fix the broken in our marriage so we don't have to tear our family apart, but the truth is, I'm not sure if that's possible.

"That doesn't mean you can't have feelings for another man." I'm not sure if she's right or wrong, but I've been cheated on, and it sucks. Having feelings for another man while I'm married might not actually be cheating, but it still doesn't sit right with me.

"I don't want to talk about this anymore," I say, needing to shut down the conversation and get dressed so I can pick up Felix from my mom's. It's already well after breakfast.

When I text her I'm on my way, she replies that she's taken him to the children's museum and to meet her at the house for dinner.

I pull up the thread of texts with David, scrolling through them. He apologized for his attitude and asked what time I'd be home, and apparently, in my drunken state, I told him never. *Yikes.* He proceeded to tell me he's sorry and that he loves me, and I told him I'd be spending the night at Kaylee's. Of course the mention of her pissed him off, and the conversation ended with him telling me not to let her slut rub off on me.

As soon as I get home, I shower, careful with the new tattoo, and then get dressed, putting on a bit more makeup than usual to cover my hangover. David isn't home, which means he's probably working all weekend again. I make sure the shirt I'm wearing fully covers my ink and then head to his office to surprise him for lunch, stopping at his favorite Italian restaurant to get us food. *Yeah, I know. You can smell the guilt I'm bathed in from a mile away.*

When I arrive, the office is locked, and I have to text him that I'm here, so he can let me up. When he comes down, the lack of emotion on his face has my stomach churning. *Something is wrong.*

"I brought a peace offering," I tell him, holding up the bag of food. "Rossi's, your favorite."

David nods, and I swallow thickly as I walk past him and over to the elevator. He's silent the entire ride up to his office floor and doesn't say a word once we're in his office. The silence has my head spinning in worry. Is it possible he heard the song? Does he know it's about me?

The moment we're in his office, he slams the door, making me jump, and is on me, pushing me against the desk. Out of shock, I drop the bag of food and drinks onto the floor as his mouth descends on mine in a punishing kiss. At first, I think he's turned on and wants me, but when he bites my lip hard, making me yelp out in pain, goose bumps prickle my flesh. He's pissed, and I highly doubt it's over our half-assed argument last night. We've had a million of those over the years.

"Ow!" I hiss. "That hurts."

"That hurts?" he barks. "You know what fucking hurts? Learning that my wife was out last night with another man!"

"What the hell are you talking about?" I ask in confusion. "I wasn't with anyone but Bailey and Kaylee last night."

"You're going to lie and say you didn't go to that concert to see Camden fucking Blackwood?" He grips my chin to force me to look at him. "Is that why you didn't want me to go?"

"Are you insane?" I scoff, tugging my face out of his grip. "I asked you to join us. *You* had to work." I might've seen him last night, but I sure as hell didn't go there with the intent to.

"So while I'm busting my ass to provide a cushy life for you and our family, you go out with *him*?" He steps back slightly and runs his fingers through his hair.

"You knew there was a chance he would be playing there. You bitched about it before I left."

"Yeah, but I didn't know you would be all fucking over him!" he booms.

"What? I don't—"

Before I can finish my sentence, he pulls his phone out and turns it around, and taking up his entire screen is a picture of me...and Camden. It was taken when he approached me after his performance. Somebody must've been recording them walking off stage, and when he stopped to talk to me, they got a picture.

"I...I can explain," I say, staring at the image of Camden leaning so close into me, it looks like he's about to kiss me on the lips instead of on the cheek where he actually kissed me. "It's not what it looks like."

"I knew this move was a bad idea." David glares, throwing his phone onto his desk. "I'm talking to Paul on Monday. They haven't filled my old position yet. I'm telling him I want it back. Moving here was a mistake. I knew this shit would happen."

His eyes are manic, and they scare the shit out of me. I get it. Camden apparently had feelings for me years ago, but the fact is, I never knew that, and I never once cheated on David. I've given him all of me. Even though he hasn't done the same.

"You're acting ridiculous," I tell him, sliding out from between him and the desk. "You might not like Camden, but you have no reason to act like this toward me. Unlike you, I've always been faithful."

"Really? You're going to throw that shit in my face again?" David barks, stalking toward me. "It was one fuckup, and I've apologized a million damn times."

"And I forgave you. I'm just pointing out there's no reason for you to act crazy with jealousy when I haven't done anything wrong. I haven't even seen him in five years. Aside from sending us a wedding and baby gift, he hasn't once tried to speak to me. He saw me standing on the side of the stage and quickly said hello. That's it."

"Why the fuck were you on the side of the stage anyway?"

"Because Raging Chaos's videographer had an emergency, and Bailey asked me to record their performance."

David's eyes bore into mine. "Don't even fucking think about it."

"Think about what?"

"Getting a job at that fucking record label."

"Blackwood is a huge label. I doubt they'd even hire someone like me... someone with zero experience." I step toward him, putting my hands on his biceps, hoping to calm him down. We can't keep doing this. Going rounds every damn day. It's exhausting, and it's eventually going to affect Felix.

"Please stop acting like this. I didn't know he was performing last night, and when Bailey asked me to fill in, I couldn't say no. You know how much I love videography. It was nothing more than me doing a favor for an old friend. You have nothing to worry about. Camden isn't even part of the equation. I'm married to you."

"Damn right you are, and since I'm the one who pays the bills, I make the decisions, and we're moving back to Boston."

"No, we're not," I say defiantly. "I didn't like it there. It never felt like home. Here, we're close to our families."

"And Camden."

"Would you stop with him already? He lives in California. I'm done with this stupid conversation," I say, walking toward the door.

"Where are you going?"

"To my mom's. I told her I'd have dinner with her when I picked up Felix. You obviously need time to cool off and figure your shit out. I'll see you at home." I glance at the bag of food on the floor we never ate. "Enjoy your food."

Before David can argue, I'm out the door and speed-walking to the elevator. I should probably feel bad that I blew off his accusations, but the truth is, I have nothing to feel guilty about. Well...except for the fact that I got a tattoo in response to a song that Camden sang about me with the title etched across the top. But in my defense, I was drunk, and it's not like I got his name tattooed on me. It's of a camera, something that has meaning for me.

Jesus, if David is pissed about me simply going to a concert where Camden was performing and talking to him for a quick second, I can't imagine how he's going to react when that song hits the radio, and he hears it. Hopefully, he won't listen to it since he hates everything about Raging Chaos. Because if he does, I have no idea how the hell I'm going to explain this tattoo. And there's no way I'm moving back to Boston. He can scratch that crazy idea right out of his head.

By the time I get to my mom's, I'm so worked up over everything, I'm not paying attention when I walk inside...and come face-to-face with Camden Blackwood.

"What are you doing here?"

"Well, hello to you too, Shutterbug." He smirks.

Hearing my nickname on his lips sends liquid heat through my veins. I haven't heard it in five years, and now he's said it twice in twelve hours. It shouldn't affect me like this. *He* shouldn't affect me like this...but it does. *He* does. Fuck, this isn't good.

"Why are you here?"

"Umm...because I live here?" he says with a chuckle.

"No, you live in LA, and I thought you were on tour." *Please don't say you've moved back. My marriage will never survive it.*

"Keeping tabs on me? That's sweet. We are on tour, but in case you forgot, we performed here last night. And since we have a few days before our next show, I'm staying with my parents to get some family time in."

I sigh in relief. Okay, that's okay. It's temporary. Soon, he'll be on his way out of here, and then everything can go back to normal.

We're both silent for a second, and then it hits me...

"Why are you here?"

Camden's brows furrow. "Didn't we just go over this? I'm spending time with—"

"I mean, here, in my house."

He glances around and then laughs. "I'm pretty sure it's your mom's house, and I'm here for dinner. My entire family is."

Oh, shit. This cannot be happening.

Before I can respond, Felix comes barreling down the hall. "Mommy, you're back!" he squeals, throwing himself into my arms. I lift him up, prying my gaze off Camden to give my son my full attention. "I went to the museum with Grandma, and she got me an ice cream. And we made cool art, and I made you something, but it's a secret."

"A secret, huh? What kind of secret?"

Felix's eyes go wide, realizing he let something he wasn't supposed to tell me slip. "I can't tell you! It's a secret."

"Maybe...I'll...tickle it out of you." I tickle his sides playfully, and he squirms.

"No, Mommy! It's a secret."

"Fine." I sigh and stop tickling him. "Were you good for Grandma?"

"Duh." He rolls his eyes, and Camden laughs, reminding me that he's still here.

Our eyes lock, and the softness in his eyes reminds me that he wrote a song about me.

"Mommy, put me down," Felix whines, wiggling his body to get down. "Nanna is letting me mix the potatoes."

"Nanna's here?" I ask, putting him down. I haven't seen her since I moved. Because I spent so much time at Camden's house in high school, she became like a grandma to me, doting on me as much as she did Camden.

Without answering me, Felix runs out of the room and back into the kitchen.

"Nanna's here?" I ask Camden, since he's still standing in the foyer with me.

"Yeah. She and my mom came over earlier to help your mom cook."

"Well, then you know the food is going to be delicious." I rub my belly. "I can't remember the last time I had a home-cooked meal. I can't cook for shit."

Camden laughs. "That doesn't surprise me in the least. I can still recall putting out quite a few fires when you would try back in the day."

"Oh, hush." I shove him playfully, but before I can move my hand, he grabs it and tugs me toward him, so we're close...too close.

"It's been a long time, Layles." With the hand he's not holding mine with, he tucks a wayward strand of hair behind my ear, causing me to shiver when his flesh brushes against mine.

He notices, and a knowing smirk quirks up on one side of his mouth. "How are you?"

"I'm good," I say, internally cringing at how breathless those two words come out.

"I heard you're back for good. Is that true?"

"Yeah, *we're* back for good." I emphasize the *we're* to remind him—and me—that I'm married.

Camden nods. "That's good. *You* were definitely missed."

I know I'm playing with fire when I say my next words, but I blame it on that damn song because I can't stop thinking about the words and what they mean. Everything about Camden's and my relationship now feels like a lie. I'm overanalyzing every word, every touch, wondering if what everyone said is true. If he really had feelings for me. The song said he had to put me to rest. Does that mean he's over me? Or is he trying to get over me? Could he still have feelings for me?

"Who missed me?"

His eyes dance with what looks like mirth, and when he leans in like he's about to tell me a secret, I hold my breath, waiting for what he's going to say.

"Your mom, of course." He steps back slightly, keeping my hand in his, and looks into my eyes. "I didn't know you'd be at the concert last night. What did you think?"

"About what?" I swallow thickly, completely overwhelmed by this conversation. I imagined seeing Camden again one day, but I never thought our reunion would go like this. Like he didn't just up and leave, and we didn't spend five years apart without saying a single word to each other. Like he didn't become a huge rock star, and I didn't go to college, get pregnant, and then get married.

"The band," he says, knocking me from my chaotic thoughts. "Our performance. Bailey said you videoed it for Cade. Did you enjoy it?"

"You guys were amazing," I say truthfully. "Better than you were in high school."

Camden nods. "And what about the last song?" He squeezes the hand he's holding against his chest, and my heartbeat picks up speed. "What'd you think about it?"

Holy shit. Did he seriously just straight out ask me about that song?

"I think…" I inhale deeply, the scent of him making me feel slightly dizzy, then release a harsh breath, unsure what to say. Thankfully, before I can finish my thought, my mom calls my name, breaking the moment.

"I think I better go see what my mom wants." I pull my hand away from his and turn my back on him, trying to get away quickly without making it look like I'm running.

I'm almost to the kitchen when Camden's strong hand lands on my shoulder, halting me in place. His front presses against my back, and his lips brush against the shell of my ear. I stand here, frozen in my spot, waiting to see what he's going to do, when he leans in and murmurs, "For the record, your mom isn't the only one who missed you, Shutterbug. I've missed you too."

And with those words, he steps around me and saunters into the kitchen, looking unaffected by our interaction as he asks the women if dinner's ready. While I wonder if maybe David was right and moving here was a bad idea. Because the butterflies in my belly that are swarming around…they're not for my husband.

And that's a problem—a big problem.

Ten

LAYLA

"I DON'T WANNA GO HOME," FELIX WHINES, RUBBING HIS FISTS AGAINST HIS EYES IN EXHAUSTION. "I wanna play with Camden."

"You've played enough," I tell him, lifting him into my arms while Camden takes the controller from him.

"But Mom…" he says in a voice that tells me he's about to have a meltdown. He's spent the past few hours playing *Sonic the Hedgehog* with Camden after he found an old Sega Genesis my dad had in the cabinet from many years ago because he loved the classic games—and after asking what it was, Camden set it up so they could play. It's late now, and David texted asking when we would be home. Not wanting to fight anymore, I told him soon.

"Hey, bud," Camden says. "How about you head home with your mom, and if it's okay with her, the next time you come to see your grandma, I'll come over and play with you?"

Felix sighs, not liking it, but then he gives in and nods. "Fine."

I don't bother to mention by then Camden should be back on tour and far away from here. If it means getting Felix to leave without a fight, I'll go along with it and hope he doesn't remember this conversation later.

We make our rounds, saying goodbye to everyone, and then Camden shocks me when he walks us out, holding the door for me while I carry Felix to my car. We don't live far, but I drove, knowing we would be here until after dark.

He opens the passenger door for me, and I slip Felix into his booster seat. He says bye to Camden, his eyes already fluttering closed, and I shut the door, leaving Camden and me alone.

He steps toward me, and I take a step back, not wanting to fall under his trance again.

"Look," I say, putting my hand out so he can't come any closer. "I don't know what happened in there earlier, during our conversation, but…" I swallow down the lump of emotion in my throat, knowing what I say next will most likely send us back to square one—and not the square in high school when we first met, but the one where he left and didn't speak to me for years. "I'm married."

"I know," he says, his mouth curving into a slight frown, which is so unlike the cocky guy I've been in the presence of all night.

"It's inappropriate to flirt with a married woman."

His gaze meets mine. "Who said anything about flirting? I'm just catching up with my best friend." He shrugs innocently.

"Your best friend?" I scoff. "No. You lost that title five years ago when you moved to the West Coast without so much as a goodbye. We *were* best friends. Now..." I look at the older version of the boy I used to know, realizing I know nothing about him anymore. "Now, we're strangers."

His mouth pops open, but before he can say anything, I open my door and slide into my car. "Have a good rest of your tour," I say, closing my door and ending the conversation.

When Felix and I get home, since he's passed out, I take him up to his room and tuck him into bed, not bothering to change him into his pajamas. If he wakes up, he'll be up for hours.

Afterward, I go in search of David, hoping we can talk. I find him in his office, sitting at his desk and drinking whiskey.

"Hey," I say, making my presence known. "Felix is in bed."

The second his dark eyes lock with mine, I know something is wrong. "Come in here and close the door."

I hesitate for a moment, but not wanting to wake Felix with whatever argument we're about to have, I do as he says.

When I turn around, he's standing close to me. He backs me up against his desk until my back hits the hard edge of the wood. "Have you seen social media?"

I shake my head.

"Everyone is linking you to that fucking song. The one where Blackwood admits to being fucking obsessed with you for years. They're wondering who the woman is that Blackwood poured his broken heart out to. I was in a meeting today, and Vanessa asked how you knew Camden Blackwood because that photo is every-fucking-where!" he barks.

Vanessa is his assistant from Boston who moved here to New York. She's always been civil with me, but I could sense a bit of hostility beneath her placating smile, like maybe she has a crush on my husband or doesn't like me for whatever reason. Of course she would be the one to throw me under the bus.

"David, I—"

"Not a fucking word," he booms, reaching down and unbuttoning my shorts. "Do you know how fucked up it is to find out from my assistant that another man wrote and sang a fucking love song about my wife?" He pushes my shorts down, confusing me.

"I didn't know—"

"I said, not a word!" He forcefully cups my jaw, making me jump. "We haven't even been back for a week, and you're already making a fool out of yourself and me. The song, the photo of you all over him. And don't get me started on the fact that you spent the night with him."

My eyes go wide, and he chuckles humorlessly. "Yeah, your mom loves to post her entire life on social media since you showed her how to use it. Tonight, she posted about her daughter and grandson being home. And in the background, I saw you two." He squeezes my face harder, and the pain in my mouth from his tight grip has me pulling my head back.

"David, I understand it all looks bad, but if you'd let me explain."

"This is mine." He grabs my breast and squeezes. "*You* are mine." His hands fist the two sides of my shirt, and before I can stop him, he yanks it apart. Buttons fly everywhere, leaving me in only my bra and underwear.

I'm so focused on the fact that he just ripped my shirt, I'm not thinking about what he's just exposed. Until his wild eyes land on my collarbone.

"Are you fucking serious right now? This is what you were doing last night after you were all over that fucking loser?"

"It...It doesn't mean anything," I lie because I've never seen David this mad before, and at this moment, I have no idea what he's capable of.

"Don't fucking lie to me!" He whips his hand around, landing on my cheek. The feel of his palm connecting with my face stings like hell, and instinctually, I reach up to rub the area.

It takes me a second to comprehend what just happened, but once I do, I push against his chest as hard as I can. "Get the hell away from me!" I demand, refusing to let him put his hands on me in a violent manner.

David doesn't listen, though, grabbing my wrists and twisting my arms behind my back. My back hits the edge of the desk again, this time harder, and I flinch at the bite of pain.

"What the fuck were you thinking, getting branded with the title of that fucking declaration of his obsession with you?" He shocks me when he pulls his head back and then spits in my face. "Less than a week here and you're turning into a slut!" Who the hell is this man? Because this is not the guy I married. I shake my head, trying to get the spittle out of my eyes.

"You need to get that shit removed immediately." He locks both my wrists with one hand and grips my face with his other, squeezing my cheeks and chin painfully.

"Fuck you!" I hiss. "I'm not removing shit." I shouldn't provoke him, but I've had enough.

"Yes, the fuck you are," he says lowly. "We both know you've been in love with him for years, and I will *not* fuck my wife while she's marred by another man's words. Understand?"

Without waiting for an answer, he releases my wrists. I assume he's going to let me go, but then he fists my mane and yanks me to my knees.

My knees hit the tiled floor, and I cry out in pain. "David, stop!" I beg as he tugs on my hair, causing my scalp to burn painfully.

He pulls harder, forcing my chin up. "I'm not sticking my dick in you until you're rid of that shit, but since you want to act like a little slut, you can suck my dick like one." He unzips his fly and pulls his soft dick out. "Wrap your perfect dick-sucking lips around me, so you can remember who the fuck your husband is."

"I'm not touching you!" I yell. "Let go of me!"

He grabs his dick and strokes it a few times and then pulls my face toward it. I try to shake my head and keep my mouth closed, but he stuffs it into my mouth. I'm in shock, filled with disgust. I never imagined the man I've spent the past six years with could be this cruel. I knew he had a temper, but I didn't think he was capable of this. My body trembles in fear, and I know there's a chance I'm going to regret my next move, but I refuse to be a victim, to sit here while he forces himself on me.

When his dick is all the way in my mouth, I open wide and then bite down on it so hard I taste blood.

"You fucking bitch!" he shouts, yanking on my hair until he brings me to the ground. He slaps me across the face, then straddles my torso. "You want to act like a whore, then I guess I'll have to treat you like one."

He lets go of my hair and flips me onto my stomach, trapping my wrists in his hand and pulling my arms painfully behind my back. At the same time, he rips my underwear to the side. I fight to break free, yelling and cursing at him to stop, but he ignores me as he roughly enters me from behind, tearing me apart. We've never had sex this way, and it burns so badly, tears sting my eyes. The hand not holding my wrists together fists my hair, pulling on it so hard it feels as if my hair is being ripped from my scalp.

The entire time my husband rapes me, I never once give up trying to stop him, but he's stronger, and I can't get away. The more I fight, the harder he pulls my hair, the tighter he locks my wrists together, the deeper he thrusts into me. Finally, when he's found his release, he pushes off me and gets up, leaving me lying on the ground, in pain, shaking and crying and wishing he were dead.

"Get the fuck out of my office," he says, his voice filled with anger and disgust like he isn't the one who just forced himself on his wife. "And don't come anywhere near me until that tattoo is off your body."

I scramble up, grabbing my clothes and putting them on. I want to yell and tell him to go fuck himself, make it clear if I have it my way, he'll never see me again after what he's just done, but I keep my mouth shut, not wanting to give him a reason to hurt me any further. My goal: to get as far away from him as possible. And then, once I do, I can figure out what the hell just happened, so I can ensure it never happens again.

"HE RAPED YOU?" KAYLEE SCREECHES. "ARE YOU FUCKING SERIOUS RIGHT NOW?"

After David stalked out of his office, declaring he'd be at the office working the rest of the night and then left, I showered, trying to rid myself of what he'd done to me. And then I called Kaylee to come over, needing my best friend.

"He...he did it...in my butt," I admit shakily, recalling the bleeding he caused. "It hurt so bad." Fresh tears fill my eyes, and Kaylee pulls me into her arms, hugging me tightly.

"He's dead," she says softly. "I'm going to kill him."

"You can't do that, then you'll be sent to jail, and I need you with me."

She nods in understanding. "What are you going to do?"

"I'm going to file for divorce."

Her eyes go wide, obviously shocked.

"You don't think I should?"

"No, I do," she says. "I absolutely think you should. I also think you should file a restraining order against him. I'm just shocked. I thought you'd say you were going to talk to him, and I would have to convince you to leave him."

"He put his hands on me, spat at me, he *raped* me." The pain, the visual, burns in my brain, like the worst reel on repeat. "I get he's upset over Camden and my drunken tattoo, but that doesn't give him the right to do what he did. There's no coming back from that. *Ever.* I thought about filing a restraining order, but I don't want it to get ugly, and trying to prove my husband raped me will get messy. While I was waiting for you to come over, I was reading about it online and found so many women who tried to prove their husbands were raping them and couldn't. But I am filing for divorce as soon as possible."

"Good. My stepdad will know someone. I'll call him first thing in the morning, and we'll get the ball rolling. But if he so much as lays a finger on you again, you need to file a restraining order so you know you're safe." She takes my hand in hers and squeezes it. "I'm proud of you."

"For what?"

"A lot of women would've made excuses, tried to fix it, or blamed themselves. For years, that's what my mom did with my dad after his accident.

He became addicted to drugs and would drink to numb the pain. She felt bad for him and kept hoping he would get better. It took her nearly getting beat to death before she finally left him. I'm proud of you for knowing what he did was wrong and unacceptable and not giving him the chance to do it again." She wraps her arms around me. "We'll get through this. He'll never fucking touch you again."

The next morning, I drop Felix off at my mom's, and Kaylee and I go to the divorce attorney her stepdad recommended. It's Sunday, but he apparently owes her stepdad a favor so he meets with us. After spending the night thinking about what David did to me, I decide to mention the rape, asking his opinion on what I should do.

He tells me what I feared—proving my husband raped me will get messy, and since there are no marks on me from where he slapped me, it would be my word versus his. He tells me he can take it on, but he can't be sure we'll win. It would be a battle that I would most likely lose because our judicial system is far from perfect. Knowing David will get away with it pisses me off and makes me feel sick to my stomach, but I can't drag my son through a messy court battle. Maybe that makes me weak or a horrible person, but I just can't do it.

After agreeing the best course of action is to simply file for divorce, we go over all the details, and when we're done, he says he'll have the papers filed first thing in the morning, and David will be served by the end of the day. When I explain I'm not sure how I'll be able to pay for this since I'm currently jobless, Kaylee insists she'll cover it, and I can pay her back. I want to argue, but I also want this over with as soon as possible, so I agree and thank her.

Not wanting to be home when David gets the papers, I head over to my mom's so I can tell her everything that's happened. She cries when I give her a less descriptive version and offers to have Felix and me move in with her.

David never calls or texts all day Sunday, so I know he never came home, but we spend the night at my mom's anyway. I don't want to take the chance of being there when he does go home. Monday morning, instead of dropping Felix off at school, I keep him home, unsure of how David will react when he gets the papers. I never thought he was capable of violence, but I was clearly wrong, and I'm not going to risk something happening to my son or me. He'll need time to cool down, and it's best if we stay away until he can do that.

I know when David gets served because my phone starts blowing up with phone calls and texts from him. The texts start off with him upset, asking to talk, but then quickly morph into anger.

"He's going to come here," I tell my mom when I read the text from him that says he was just at the house and we're not there.

Mom nods. "Why don't we have Felix go over to the Blackwood's to play so he's not here?"

"I hate involving them."

"They're like family, Layla. And it's to protect your son."

I agree, and after Mom calls Sophia, I take Felix over there with the Sega Genesis he's become obsessed with. Thankfully, it's only Nanna, Sophia, and Easton at home, so I don't have to see Camden. I thank them for watching Felix and ask that if by some chance David shows up, to please not open the door. Easton promises he'll keep my son safe.

After kissing Felix and telling him I love him and I'll be back soon, I head back over to my mom's. I'm almost to her house when David pulls up. I try to rush inside, but he's faster and catches me before I can make it.

"Were you just at the Blackwood's?" he hisses, pushing me against the front door. "Were you over there fucking him? Is that why you're divorcing me? Because you're fucking that loser?"

"I'm not fucking anyone," I hiss, the vision of him forcing himself on me hitting me hard. It feels like every time I close my eyes, I can see him, feel him, hurting me. "I'm divorcing you because you turned into someone I don't know. You hit and raped me."

"I didn't mean to," he says, his tone softening into the man I used to know. "I was just so upset. The guy's had a hard-on for you for years, and then we move back here, and not even a week later, you're in pictures with him and getting tattoos of his songs on your body."

"It doesn't matter if I got a tattoo of his name on my body. You don't have the right to ever put your hands on me violently. You raped me, David. You hurt me."

"You're my wife! I had sex with my wife. I didn't rape you."

"I begged you to stop. You hurt me. You made me bleed."

"You're overreacting," he scoffs. "Please, Layla." He raises his hand, and I flinch, afraid of what he's going to do. "Don't be afraid of me. I messed up. I was upset, but I love you. You know I love you, right?"

"I know that you hurt me, and I can't let that ever happen again. I want a divorce, and I'm going to live with my mom until everything is final."

He looks at me in pain, reminding me of the man I married, and my heart cracks. We created a life together, a family, and in one day, it all got blown to bits. "I told you moving here was a bad idea," he mutters, scrubbing his hand over his face.

"You can't blame the move or anyone or anything for what happened. *You* did this."

He nods solemnly. "I don't want you to uproot Felix. You can stay in the house. It's your home. I work a lot anyway. I can stay in the office until it all gets sorted."

I release a sigh, grateful that he's calmed down and is acting maturely.

"Thank you."

"Maybe you just need some time," he says. "We can go to therapy."

"I don't think so. After what happened, I can't be with you." I don't apologize because I'm not sorry. I didn't do anything wrong, nothing that would ever make it okay for my husband to hurt me the way he did.

He nods and leans in, kissing my cheek. "I'm not giving up yet, but I'll go with the flow for now. I know I fucked up, and you need some time. But I love you, and I'm not giving up on us."

With those final words, he walks back to his vehicle and drives away, leaving me wondering how my life got so messed up so quickly.

Eleven

CAMDEN

TWO MONTHS LATER

"OH, MY GOD, YES! JUST LIKE THAT. FUCK ME HARDER!" AN ALL TOO FAMILIAR VOICE SCREAMS OUT AS Declan and I walk into the penthouse suite we're sharing with Gage and Braxton. Sometimes, we get our own rooms, but at this hotel, in order for security to stay tight, they had to book the only penthouse available, which meant the four of us sharing.

"Yes, yes. Harder!" she yells, moaning loudly.

"Oh, shit," Declan says with a laugh. "I'd recognize that voice anywhere."

Of course he would because we spent the past several months listening to it every damn day. Sure enough, when we step into the living room, we find Everly, our publicist, sandwiched between Braxton and Gage, getting fucked in both her holes. Gage looks like he's barely involved, aside from his dick being part of the equation, and Braxton is angry-fucking her ass with his eyes closed as he pulls on her long brown hair.

"Seriously?" I bark. Both guys glance over at me at the same time, and Everly squeals in embarrassment. "Again?" This isn't the first damn time one of these assholes has fucked a member of our team. And it always ends the same way—her becoming attached and getting her heart broken or us having to fire her because she turns crazy.

"It's the last day of the tour," Braxton says, continuing to fuck her. "She wasn't even all that good at her job. It's not like we're going to hire her back."

Everly gasps in outrage, and I groan, knowing what's coming next.

Pushing Braxton back, she climbs off Gage, who's so high that he doesn't even bother moving. Gage simply lets his head drop back, and his eyes close, leaving his condom-covered dick out in the open for everyone to see.

"Fuck you, Braxton!" she hisses. "I'm good at my job."

"Of course you are," he purrs. "You're awesome at your job. I was just kidding. Now get back on my dick so I can finish, please."

Everly glares, gathering up her clothes and putting them back on in haste.

"You can finish your damn self," she says, grabbing her heels and stomping out the door.

"Great," Braxton says dryly. "This"—he points at his now soft dick—"is all your fault. Which one of you is going to suck me off so I don't get blue balls?"

Declan snorts out a laugh, and I roll my eyes. "Thank fuck this tour is over. I need a few months without walking in on you fucking your way across the globe." I shove Gage awake. "And you need to lay off the drugs."

Gage grunts in response, pulling the condom off and dropping it onto the floor as he gets up and stumbles toward his room. "Will do, *Dad*."

"I'm worried about him," Declan says once we can hear his snoring from the other room.

"Yeah, I am too," I agree. "But we'll be back home in a few days, and we'll keep an eye on him. I spoke to my dad, and aside from a few shows we've already committed to, we're going to take the next six months off to write and record our next album."

"Sounds good," Braxton says, grabbing his pants and pulling them on. "I'm going to take a shower."

"Want a drink?" Declan asks, raising a bottle of Jack.

"Sure."

We take our drinks out onto the balcony, and I pull out my phone to text our tour manager to let her know what happened and to find out what time we're flying out tomorrow. But when my screen lights up, I find several missed calls from damn near everyone in my family.

My stomach drops. Something is wrong.

Since my mom was the last one to call, I hit her name and wait as the phone rings. "Camden, we've been trying to reach you," she says, her voice filled with emotion.

"My phone was on silent, sorry. Everything okay?"

There's a moment of silence on the other end before she says, "No, it's not. Maria is in the hospital, and the doctors aren't sure how long she'll be able to hold on for."

I shoot up in my seat, knocking my drink to the ground. The glass shatters everywhere, but I ignore it, too focused on what my mom just said. "What are you talking about?" I just saw her a couple of months ago when we were in town for the charity concert. She was fine. She even made me my favorite French toast.

"She's been tired a lot lately. I asked her if she was okay, but she blew me off. Today, she had a dizzy spell while she was in her room and hit her head," she chokes out. "She was rushed to the hospital, and the doctors said she has stage four cancer. She never told us. Didn't want to worry us because it was too late."

"Fuck!" My heart squeezes in pain. "There has to be something we can do. A doctor we can call."

"We've spoken to the oncologist, and there's nothing that can be done. They gave her roughly six months to live. It's been three, but her body is shutting down. They said it can be days or weeks, but she doesn't have long. Right now, she's coherent, and she's asking for you."

"I'm on my way. I'll get a flight out as soon as I can. Tell Nanna I'm coming."

"OH, THERE'S MY BOY," NANNA MURMURS WHEN I WALK INTO THE ROOM SEVERAL HOURS LATER. SHE'S lying in a hospital bed in a private room, looking so small and fragile. Like simply touching her will break her.

"Nanna," I breathe, tears welling in my eyes.

"Come give me a hug, sweetheart."

I do as she says, hugging her gently and kissing her cheek before I drag a chair over and sit next to her. My parents and Bailey excuse themselves to give us some time alone, but I don't pay them any attention, focusing on the woman in front of me. "Why didn't you tell anyone?" I ask her. "We could've called someone."

"No, you couldn't have," she says softly. "I always hated going to the doctor. Kept putting it off. By the time I went, it was too late."

"You still should've told us."

"So you'd spend my last few months worrying about me?" Her wrinkled hand pats mine gently. "I didn't want anyone fussing over me. You and your sister were both on tour. Bailey is so busy with her internet, and I didn't want to upset Phoebe."

"I would've come home sooner."

"I know you would've. That's why I didn't tell you."

I squeeze her hand. "What did—"

"Oh, I'm so sorry," a feminine voice says. My eyes dart over to Layla standing in the doorway, dressed in ripped jeans, an off-the-shoulder cream sweater, and brown leather boots since it's cold as hell in New York. "I didn't know you were here with her. I'll come back later." Before I can get a word in, she backs out and closes the door behind her.

"Such a sweet girl," Nanna says. "Shame everything she's going through."

"What do you mean?"

"The divorce," she says like it's obvious. "I always knew that man she married wasn't any good for her. I never met him, but from the way he kept her from everyone all these years, a woman my age gets a feeling. At least he agreed to give her primary custody of that sweet little boy. She's been looking for a job but is having trouble finding one."

"Wait, what?" I say, my head spinning with all of this information. "Layla got a divorce?"

"Yes. I've spent some time with Felix while Patricia has watched him so she can look for a job. Such a good boy. Reminds me of you when you were little. Polite and funny. And he loves my French toast." She winks playfully, and I can't help but smile.

"I always thought it would be you two that ended up together. Then she met him…" She scrunches up her nose in disgust. "But he's gone now. Who knows? This could be your second chance."

"Maybe…"

"I heard the song." She smiles. "'Shattered.' Your mom always plays them for me on her phone. I'm so proud of you. Of whom you've become. But that song…it made me sad for you. I remember when your parents got together. Your mom found out she was pregnant with you, and she was so scared but strong. She had a wall built thirty feet high, but your dad busted it down piece by piece. And once he did…well, their love was a beautiful sight to behold."

She takes her hand in mine and gently squeezes. "That boy…David…he hurt her, and I imagine her wall will be really high, but I have no doubt you'll be able to knock it down." She winks playfully. "And once you do, I bet your love will be just as beautiful."

I nod, unsure what to say in response. I came in here expecting to see her in bad shape, but instead, she's giving me relationship advice.

With a yawn, she removes her hand from mine and pats the top of it. "Thank you for coming. You'll be staying, right?"

"I'm not going anywhere, Nanna. Not until you're better."

She frowns. "Didn't you just hear me? You have a wall to take down, and you can't do that from across the country." Another yawn. "I'm feeling a little tired. It's been a helluva day. I think I'm going to rest my eyes for a few minutes." She closes her eyes. "I'll see you when I wake up, and we can come up with a plan of attack to tear down that wall and woo the hell out of your woman."

"I'll be here," I say with a laugh. Growing up, my grandpa and my dad always talked about how men have to woo the women they love. I always laughed at them, but now that I'm older, I get it.

I watch Nanna sleep for several minutes, trying to wrap my head around everything I've learned about her—about Layla. Once I know she's in a deep sleep, I head outside to see where my family is.

I find them in the waiting room with the guys…and Layla. Declan has his arm around her, and she's smiling up at him. He must say something funny because she throws her head back in a laugh, exposing her slim neck.

Declan lets go of her, and then Gage pulls her into his side, kissing her temple. It's been five and a half years since we've left, since they've spent any real time with her, so it should be awkward, but they're acting like no time has passed...and that's because despite her saying we're strangers, we're not. We never could be because those three years together—through good times and bad—cemented our friendships. Those guys care about her almost as much as I do. She became a part of us, and even though we had to walk away, we never stopped thinking about her. We just couldn't be with her. We had to let her go. And fuck if it wasn't the hardest thing we'd ever done.

Layla is the first to notice me. She dips out from under Gage's arm and walks over to me. "How is she?"

"She's sleeping. Thank you for coming. I'm sorry you didn't get to see her. Tomorrow—"

"Oh, no. I saw her. I've been here all morning. Felix insisted we make her a card. They won't let him visit because he's not family, and kids have tons of germs, so I brought it to her."

We stare at each other for several beats. There's so much I want to ask her, but then Declan comes over. "How's she doing?"

"She's okay. Aside from looking fatigued, you wouldn't know her body is giving up on her." I look at my dad. "There's nothing we can do?"

"I'm sorry, son." He puts his arm around me. "Her organs are shutting down. The doctors are shocked she's doing as well as she is and talking as much as she is. They said to prepare ourselves because it won't be like that for long."

"This fucking sucks."

"Yeah, it does," Mom agrees. "Why don't you go home and get situated? I know it was a long flight."

"I'm not going anywhere. I promised Nanna I'd be here when she woke up. I just wanted to come out here and properly say hello." I give her a hug and a kiss on her cheek, then turn to the guys. "If you want to check in to a hotel..."

"Nonsense," Mom says. "You guys can stay with us."

"We appreciate that, Sophia," Declan says. "But you haven't lived with these assholes in a few years, and trust me, you don't want them stinking up your place."

In other words, the guys need their space to fuck, smoke, and do their own thing.

"I'm not sure how long I'll be here," I tell them. "If you want to head back..."

"Fuck that," Gage says, looking somewhat sober. "If you're here, we're here. Besides, I need to say hi to Nanna."

"I'll let you know when she wakes—"

"Excuse me," a female doctor cuts in. "Are you the family of Maria Garcia?"

"We are," Mom says, speaking for all of us.

"Maria went into cardiac arrest. Because she signed a DNR, we weren't able to resuscitate her. I'm sorry, but she didn't make it."

And just like that, my heart implodes inside my chest.

"THIS SUCKS."

I glance over and find Layla sitting next to me. The funeral has ended, and Maria's casket has been lowered into the ground.

"Are you going to your parents'?" she asks when I don't say anything. There's a repast taking place at my parents' house, but I can't find it in me to move.

When I stay quiet, she reaches over and threads our fingers together. I look down at our joined hands, noticing her left hand is missing her wedding ring. In its place is a pale strip where the ring once was.

"The last time I was home, she made me French toast. I told her not to, said she should be relaxing, but she insisted. She said she would make them every time I came home as long as I keep returning." My voice chokes up on the last word, tears filling my eyes.

"She made them for Felix a couple of weeks ago. He said they were his favorite, so I tried to make them for him the other morning." She laughs softly. "He said they were good, but they weren't as special as the ones she made him." I laugh at that, knowing exactly what he means. Nothing compares to her French toast.

"Going home will make it real," I say, answering her earlier question. "And I'm just not ready for it to feel real yet. She won't be there to offer to make me food or do my laundry when I'm not home. She won't leave me a snack when I sneak in after curfew or gripe about the guys leaving a mess even though she insists they come over...because she's gone, and she'll never be back."

Layla squeezes my hand. "She is. I can't say I completely understand because my dad and I were never that close. He worked far too much and wasn't around enough. But it still hurt when he died. Every morning on his way into the office, he would call me to say hi. The first day he didn't call, it was hard. My heart hurt, and I cried. The next day, though, I was ready for the heartbreak. Each day got easier, my heart healing more and more. It still hurts, and I miss him, but it's bearable now."

She looks at me, her brown eyes shining. "It won't be today or tomorrow or the next day, but eventually, your heart will heal."

When she squeezes my hand again, I look down at our hands, remembering the last conversation Nanna and I had. I've never been the type of person to believe in fate. But right now, while I would give anything to have Nanna back, I'm wondering if maybe, as her last gift to me, she brought Layla and me together. Because had she not passed away, I'd still be across the country instead of sitting right here holding hands with the only woman I've ever loved.

"I think you're right," I tell Layla. "I think my heart will eventually heal."

Twelve

CAMDEN

Declan looks up from the paper where he's scribbling lyrics, Braxton stops strumming his bass, and Gage removes the joint from his lips.

"What's up?" Declan asks, reaching over and taking the joint from Gage so he can take a hit.

"We've done everything together from day one," I begin, nervous at what I need to speak to them about. "Every decision, every show, when we decided to move to LA—"

"Just get to the damn point," Braxton cuts in, snatching the joint from Declan. "You want to stay in New York, and you need us to agree."

I open my mouth, shocked as shit that he hit the nail on the head. "How did you know?"

"It doesn't take a brain surgeon," Declan says. "We saw you walk in with her after the funeral, holding hands."

"It's not like that," I start.

"Of course it's not," Declan replies. "Because it's too soon. She's only just gotten a divorce. She needs time to get over whatever that fucker did."

"But this time, how about you *not* wait until she's moved on and found someone else, yeah?" Braxton hands me the joint, and I take a hit. "I hate this fucking city, so if I'm going to be stuck here for the foreseeable future, you better fucking man up and do something this time."

"Do what?" Bailey asks, strolling into the studio. Her nose scrunches up in disgust at the smell of weed, and she steals the joint from me, dropping it into my can of soda.

"Get the girl," Declan says with a smirk.

"What girl?" she asks, confused.

"Layla...duh." Declan rolls his eyes. "Is there any other girl for your brother?"

"Does this mean you're staying?" she asks, her voice rising several octaves in excitement.

"Yeah," Braxton tells her.

"But you guys hate New York," she points out.

"Camden doesn't," Gage says, speaking for the first time. "Camden never had his shot. When shit went down"—he swallows thickly—"he got on that plane for us. Now, regardless of how much we hate this city, it's our turn to stay for him."

Fuck, these guys.

Gage glances at me, taking another joint from behind his ear and lighting it, despite knowing Bailey will grab it and snuff it out. "This time, get the fucking girl. Don't make us being here a waste."

Bailey does just as I thought and snatches the joint, dropping it into Gage's beer. "Have you told Dad? You're supposed to be working on your next album. We're going to have to make adjustments." I can see her brain shifting into work mode as she pulls out her phone and starts typing. "Shit, Cade has to stay in LA. Now, I'm going to have to find someone else to film the web series."

"Hire Layla," I say.

Her head pops up. "What?"

"Hire Layla to film the series. We'll also have music videos we have to do. She can do those as well."

"She's never worked in the music industry," Bailey says.

"I don't care." I shrug, propping my feet up on the table. "She has natural talent. I want her. Cade can work with someone else in LA, and we can record our album here."

"THANK YOU FOR MEETING WITH US," BAILEY SAYS TWO DAYS LATER IN THE CONFERENCE ROOM IN Blackwood Records's office.

"I'm not sure what I'm doing here," Layla says, glancing around at everyone sitting at the table. Because everything is done through Blackwood, my dad—our manager—and my mom—Blackwood's attorney—are here, along with me, Bailey, since she's in charge of all media, and the guys, who I brought in as reinforcements because she likes them and has always had trouble telling them no.

"Raging Chaos has decided to relocate to New York for the foreseeable future," Bailey says.

Layla's eyes dart over to me in shock. "You're...You're moving back here?"

"Figured it was time I came home. Missed my family."

The guys chuckle but keep their mouths closed as Layla nods slowly. "Okay, what does that have to do with me being here? I actually have an interview at Picture Perfect soon." She glances at her phone to look at the time. "I told Bailey, but she said she just needed to speak to me for a moment."

"We want to hire you," I say, cutting to the chase. "Cade, the videographer you covered for at the charity concert, has to stay in LA, so we need someone to document us. Since we have a few shows to attend, there will be some travel, but mostly it will be here, at the place we're renting, at the studio. We're doing a web series for the fans to get a behind-the-scenes look at what goes down when we're recording an album, from us writing the songs to recording them. We're also going to need to do a couple of music videos. One of them will be fan-based, the footage from over the years...from the beginning, spanning over various tours, meet and greets, etcetera."

Layla slow blinks several times before she finally speaks. "Why me?"

I knew she would ask that, especially since she hasn't done shit in the music industry, so I'm prepared to answer her. "Because you're talented. We're picky about who we let into our world, and we're extremely private. Cade has been with us for years, but he can't be here. So we talked, and we want you."

"I don't know what I'm doing."

"Yes, you do," Declan says, joining in as backup. "You did it for us before we became who we are. The hits on those YouTube videos are why we blew up so quickly. They're still huge. You're real and raw, and you know us. The real us. We don't want to bring some fake person in who has no idea who we are."

"I...I can't," Layla says softly. "I appreciate the offer, even though I'm ninety-nine percent sure this is out of pity since Bailey knows I'm jobless. I have Felix, and David—" Her phone rings, cutting her off. She glances down at it, her lips turning down into a frown. "I need to get this." She answers the call and steps away from us. "Yes, this is Felix's mom...Is he okay? No, absolutely. I'll be right there. Okay, thank you."

She hangs up, pockets her phone, and darts her eyes around at each of us. "That was Felix's school. He's not feeling well and has a slight fever. I need to go pick him up."

"Oh, no," Mom says. "We can continue this another day."

"That's okay," Layla rasps. "There's nothing to continue. One day, I would love to work with musicians. I would love to make documentaries and music videos, but that can't be right now. Being a newly single mom means having to put my son first. Like now...going to pick him up from school because he's sick.

"My life, my priorities, doesn't meld with that of a rock star's." She looks at me, and I feel the double meaning in her words: our lives, even though she knows I'm here for her, knows I'm in love with her, would never work because we're two different people. She's a mom, and I'm a musician. Well, fuck that.

"My mom was a single mom when she met my dad. She was putting herself through college when she got pregnant with me. She got through law school with the help of my dad and my aunt Naomi. She didn't allow being a mom to stop her from doing what she wanted. She and my dad worked it out. She traveled when she could, stayed home when she had to. They handled it. Everyone in this room is your support system. You don't want to work at Picture Perfect, taking family portraits all day. That's not who you are. You're interviewing there because you think that's what you're supposed to do. That's the safe route."

"I'm doing what's best for my family," she says. "I'm sorry. I have to go." And with a small, sad smile, she walks out the door.

"Well, that didn't go as planned," Bailey says. "I honestly thought she would go for it. She had a blast videoing you guys at the concert. I thought we would offer her the job, she would say okay, and we'd sign the papers."

Dad laughs. "Nothing with women is ever that easy." He puts his arm around my mom and kisses her temple. "I had to work hard to get this woman to be with me." He glances at me. "But the best women are usually the hardest to rein in."

"This isn't over," I tell them. "Not by a long shot. I'm only just getting started."

KNOCK. KNOCK. KNOCK.

I stand at Layla's front door, waiting for her to answer. Bailey said to give her time, but I can't do it. Every time I give her time, she slips through my fingers. I can't let that happen again.

"Who is it?" a tiny voice says on the other side of the door—her son.

"Camden."

"Who?"

I chuckle. "Camden Blackwood. We played *Sonic* together at your grandma's."

A second later, the lock clicks, and the door opens, exposing Felix in his pajamas, his brown hair wet like he just took a bath. "Hey, Cam! Are you here to play with me?"

"Felix!" Layla gasps, running down the stairs...in nothing but a damn towel. "Did you just open the door?"

"It's Cam, Mom. He's here to play with me."

"You know better than to open the door for anyone," she says, kneeling in front of her son. "Only adults can answer the door."

"But..." He frowns.

"No buts. It's different here than in Boston. Anybody can knock on the door. You can't open it unless I say you can."

"What if it's Dad?" he asks.

"You don't open it for anybody," she says again. "Now, please go lie down."

"But I'm not sick anymore. I feel good."

Layla rolls her eyes. "That's because you just threw up everywhere, so your belly doesn't hurt right now. But you're still sick. Go lie down. You can watch a show."

"Fine." He sighs, then glances at me. "Can we play when I'm not sick?"

"Sure, bud," I tell him. "Feel better."

"I already do," he grumbles, dragging his feet over to the couch.

"What are you doing here?" Layla asks. When I glance back at her, I'm able to get a good look at her up close. Her hair is up in a loose bun, and her towel is wrapped around her body, being held together with a tight knot that's nestled in the middle of her breasts. The towel covers all the important parts but stops short, showing off her tanned, creamy thighs.

"Camden!" she hisses, making my eyes rise. On my way up to her face, I catch sight of something I've never seen before.

"I brought Felix some chicken soup," I say, lifting the brown bag up and setting it on the table. "Is that...?" I step closer, taking in the black ink etched into her skin between her collarbone and shoulder. It's a camera, similar to the one she used to carry with her everywhere she went. Only instead of it being put together, the lens is broken, and pieces of it ascend up and over her shoulder. "Holy shit," I breathe when I see the single word that's scribbled across the front of the camera, where the brand name should go. "You got a tattoo of the song I wrote about you."

Her eyes go wide, and then she drops her gaze to her towel-covered chest. Her hands fly across her body as if just realizing she's been standing here this entire time in nothing but a towel.

"Oh my God!" she gasps. She's about to run away, but before she can, I reach out and grab her arm, pulling her into the kitchen, where Felix can't see us, but we're close enough to hear him.

"Let me see it," I insist, once I've backed her against the edge of the counter.

"No! Let go of me," she hisses. "I need to get dressed."

"Not until I see it." I place my hands over hers on either side of her body and get a good look at the tattoo, shocked as shit that she actually inked herself permanently with the title of my song.

"When did you do this?" I ask, looking up and meeting her eyes, our faces only a few inches apart.

"The night of the concert. I had too much to drink. It was a drunken—"

"No." I press my fingers to her lips to silence her. "Don't you dare blame drinking on this. You never do shit without thinking it through. You're the most levelheaded person I know."

"I—" she breathes, but I cut her off.

"We'll talk about your tattoo later...when we're alone. What I want to discuss right now is the job offer."

Her eyes go wide, confused as to why I'm changing the subject. What she doesn't understand is that I plan to have my chance with her, but it won't be until she's ready—and based on that tattoo, it's clear she has some kind of feelings for me—but her lame excuse of being drunk tells me she's not ready to pursue those feelings yet. So I'll wait until she's ready. Because I'm a patient guy.

"The job pays six figures and requires light travel. It would start as a ninety-day trial period, and once the ninety days are up, if both sides are happy, we'll sign a one-year contract."

"Six figures?" she chokes out. "But I have Felix..."

"We know you have a son and that he'll always come first. You don't think my parents know a thing or two about raising kids while working in the music industry? You've got this, Shutterbug, and we all have your back."

Thirteen

LAYLA

"MOMMY! LOOK WHAT I MADE FOR DADDY'S BIRTHDAY." FELIX THRUSTS A CARD AND A DRAWING AT ME. "IT says Happy Birthday, Daddy. I love you, and I hope you have yummy cake and share it with me."

I look at the random letters that most definitely do *not* spell any of those words and then smile down at Felix. "This is beautiful. Your dad is going to love it. And I bet he'll share his cake with you."

Felix beams. "I wanna give it to him now."

"Oh, umm," I say, unsure what to do. David hasn't taken Felix overnight with the excuse that he's getting everything together. We've met a few times at the park and a couple of times for dinner, but every time, it ends with him begging me to work things out and him getting mad when I tell him it's not happening. I'm starting to wonder if maybe he's hoping if he prolongs getting his own place long enough, I'll give in and take him back, even though I've made it clear that's not going to happen. Simply looking at him disgusts me, and if I could have it my way, he would drop off the face of the planet and leave Felix and me alone, but that's not how real life works. David is Felix's dad, and by law, he gets to see him every other weekend and every Wednesday until he's eighteen.

"Please." Felix looks up at me with puppy dog eyes that I have a hard time saying no to.

"Okay, sure. We can go by his office."

"And bring him cake?"

Oh, Lord. "Sure, we can pick one up on the way."

"Yay!" He jumps up and down in excitement.

We take the train downtown and then stop by the bakery across from the building David works in. When we arrive at his office, no one is at the receptionist's desk, so we walk past it and head straight to David's office.

In Felix's excitement, he runs ahead and, without stopping to knock, crashes right into his father's office. "Happy Birthday, Daddy!" he yells.

There's a screech and then a hiss. When I catch up, entering the office,

I find David's assistant pulling her skirt down while David blocks her the best he can. It's obvious from the bulge in David's pants that they were in a compromising position.

"Layla, get him out of here," David barks when neither of us moves.

"Felix, c'mon, sweetie. Daddy's busy."

"But I made him a birthday card!" Felix whines, confused.

"You can give it to him another time," I tell him.

"But...But..." Tears fill his eyes. "I got him a cake."

When he refuses to move, I drop the cake onto the table and pick him up. "I know, but we have to go."

"Wait, please," David calls out as I stalk out of the room. "Shit, Layla, wait!"

"Nope, not going there," I tell him.

"Stop!" He grabs my shoulder and whirls me around. Memories of him forcing himself on me resurface, and I jump back as if I've been burned.

"Don't you dare touch me," I hiss. "We're divorced. You're free to do as you want. But maybe you can stop begging me to take you—" I stop myself, remembering Felix is in my arms. He deserves better than this. Better than to listen to his parents go at it in front of him.

"Begging you?" the woman screeches. "He hasn't been with you in over a year."

"Not now, Vanessa," David barks.

I snort out a laugh. "We've only been divorced for a couple of weeks." We haven't been living together for two months, but it took six weeks to finalize the divorce.

"You said you haven't been together in over a year," she continues. "Are you telling me you were with me while you were with her?" Her eyes turn into thin slits.

"We moved here together," I point out because c'mon, she can't be that stupid.

"He said you moved here so he could see his son, but that you guys weren't together." She stalks toward him as he yells at her to shut up, and I use that as my cue to get my son and me out of here.

I don't put Felix down until we're on the train heading home. He's quiet for the entire ride, and while I doubt he knows all that happened, kids can sense moods, and I'm sure he knows something is wrong.

Afraid that David will try to show up, I text my mom, asking if she's up for company. When she doesn't respond, I assume she left her phone somewhere and head to her house. But when we get there, she's not home.

"Looking for your mom?" a masculine voice says.

I glance over and see Camden standing on the front porch steps of his parents' house.

"I want cake, but Mommy left it with Daddy." Felix huffs in frustration, his only concern the abandoned cake. Thankfully, he isn't aware of what he walked in on, nor does he understand what we argued about.

"What kind is your favorite?" Camden asks, walking over.

"Vanilla. Mommy loves chocolate, so she buys cakes with both, and I give her my chocolate, and she gives me her vanilla."

"That sounds like the perfect way to eat a cake," Camden says, smiling at Felix before he looks at me. "Our moms are at their book club."

"Oh, shoot." I knew that. It just slipped my mind in all the craziness. Every month, the ladies meet and discuss a new book they read while they get drunk on wine and gossip.

"Juniors has some delicious cake," Camden says with a knowing smirk.

Damn him. He knows Juniors is my favorite restaurant. At his words, Felix perks up. "I wanna go! I love delicious cake! Can we go, Mom?"

"Fine, but you have to eat first." I give him a playful side-eye. "Then we can have cake." I glance back at Camden. "Have a good night."

"Damn, so I bring up the restaurant, and I'm not even invited." He pouts, his lips curving down and making him look hella sexy. Ever since I heard that song and learned how he felt about me, I can't stop thinking about him. I was always attracted to Camden, but the truth is, I never knew he felt that way about me. He and the other guys always had girls surrounding them. It comes with the territory of making beautiful music. I always assumed he just saw me as the girl with a camera attached to her face, tagging along.

But now that I know he wanted more, I can't help but wonder how different things could've been had he told me...until I think about the fact that I wouldn't have Felix. Then I have to tell myself that everything happens for a reason. While the teenage Camden was sweet and sexy, albeit a little cocky, the older version of Camden is gorgeous, slightly harder, and a hell of a lot more confident. He left for LA trying to find his place in this chaotic world and found it in his music.

"I didn't think you'd want to spend your Friday night eating chicken fingers and cake," I say with a laugh. "Surely, a famous rock star like yourself has other, more interesting plans."

"I thought I heard you out here," my mom says, stepping outside.

"I thought you were at your book club." I glance at Camden.

"We were. Sophia held it here this week." She envelops Felix in a hug. "This is such a pleasant surprise. Sophia made brownies. Would you like one?"

"Yes!" Felix lights up.

"Oh, actually, we were going to go to Juniors," I tell her.

"Nonsense. We have tons of sweets here," she says as the other women in the book club file out, saying goodbye to all of us. "I feel like I haven't seen my grandbaby all week. Have you been hiding?" she asks Felix playfully.

"I made Daddy a card for his birthday, and Mommy got him a cake, but he yelled at Mommy and made us leave."

Mom's eyes fling over to me as my heart sinks. Guess he understood a bit more than I thought.

"Daddy's just having a bad day," I explain, the defense of David's disgusting actions tasting like sour lemons on my tongue.

"There he is!" Gage booms, stepping out of a Town Car, followed by Declan and Braxton. "We've been blowing your phone up. Lush. Tonight."

"Did you say Lush?" Bailey asks, rushing out the door. "I've been dying to check out that club. It's hard as hell to get into, but of course you got an invite. I'm in."

Declan snorts. "Who said you're invited?" He pulls Bailey into a side hug and ruffles her hair.

"Me," Bailey sasses. "What time are we leaving?" She glances at me. "Layla and I need time to get ready, and I need to let Cynthia know. She's been dying to check out that club."

"Wait...what?" I say, confused at the turn of events.

"Not sure," Declan says. "Camden, what time do you want to head out?"

"Eh..." He shrugs. "I think I'm going to sit this one out."

The guys, all at once, start giving him shit.

"You should go," Mom says to me. "You haven't been out in a while. I can spend the evening with Felix."

"We were supposed to go to Juniors," I say again.

"I wanna stay with Grandma. Please." Felix hits me with his damn puppy eyes. "I'll go with you to Juniors tomorrow. C'mon, Grandma, let's go eat brownies. Bye, Mom!" he yells, dragging my mom inside the Blackwoods'.

"You in?" Declan asks me.

"Sure, why not."

"Nice. Now, what time are we leaving, Pretty Boy?" Declan asks, calling Camden by his nickname the guys dubbed him years ago because he doesn't look like your typical rocker. He's, well, pretty. With gorgeous emerald eyes, soft, wavy hair, a natural tan that women would kill for, and a face that looks way too innocent and sweet to be singing the crude words he sings on a nightly basis, Camden is the face of Raging Chaos. He's also, without a doubt, the *prettiest* of the four guys, who are in contrast rough and dark and exactly what you'd imagine a bad boy rock star to look like—covered in tattoos with piercings in various places. Camden, on the other hand, has no tattoos or piercings...as far as I know.

"I thought you said you weren't going," I say to Camden, whose eyes are locked on me.

"I am now." He glances at the guys. "Let's leave around nine."

"Oh, should I be filming this?" I ask, switching into work mode.

"No," Camden says. "You should focus on having a good time."

IT'S MY FIRST TIME AT A NIGHTCLUB, AND I'M HAVING A BLAST. THE LIQUOR IS FLOWING, THE MUSIC IS thumping, and Bailey, Cynthia, and I are dancing our hearts out on the dance floor. Cynthia is sweet and totally has googly eyes for Bailey. They're so cute together, and I hope it works out between them.

When I stepped out of Bailey's room, dressed in one of her strapless mini dresses, I could feel Camden's heated stare. My tattoo was on full display, and if the way his eyes seared into me was anything to go by, he was thinking about when he saw it peeking out from under my towel the other day—when I lied and told him it was a drunken mistake.

Because it's November in New York and cold as hell outside, I covered up with a thick coat, hiding it away. But the second I removed it at the club, he was back to staring at it. If the other guys noticed it, they didn't comment.

We were escorted straight to VIP with the guys' security, where we've spent the night drinking and dancing. Camden hasn't said much, but the way his eyes haven't left me almost all night feels like he has a lot to say—only I'm too chicken to find out what.

"Oh, check out that guy eyeing you," Bailey says, her words coming out a bit slurred. I don't even bother to look.

"He totally is," Cynthia agrees, waggling her brows.

"Nope, not happening." I shake my head to emphasize my point. "I'm on a hiatus from men."

"Oh, fuck," Gage says. "Again?"

"What's that supposed to mean?"

"It means you did that shit our junior year, right before you chose to go out with David the Dick."

"Huh...I did, didn't I?" I shrug. "Well, at least I didn't get cheated on during that year."

"David cheated?" Bailey gasps.

"Yep," I say, choosing not to elaborate. "I've only seriously dated two guys in my life, and both cheated on me." My eyes drop to the shots of liquor. I grab one, down it, and slam the empty glass on the table. "What does that say about me?"

"It says absolutely nothing about you and everything about them." Camden twirls me around so we're facing each other, our chests almost touching. "You're perfect, Layla. You're smart and sweet, and those assholes cheating on you is their issue, not yours."

"Maybe." I shrug, suddenly feeling kind of sorry for myself.

"No, not maybe." His large hand covers mine, and he pulls me over to a more secluded area, pushing me gently against the wall. "Do you have any idea how fucking beautiful you are?" He drags his knuckles down the side of my cheek and neck, landing on the spot where my tattoo is. "And this tattoo? It's the sexiest thing I've ever seen."

His touch causes chills to race up my spine, and my entire body visibly shivers.

"Tell me the truth, Shutterbug." He leans in and whispers into my ear. "Why did you get this tattoo? And don't you dare say it was a drunken mistake."

"I...I never knew you felt that way," I admit, not quite answering his question but also kind of answering it. "I was shocked, confused...Bailey and Kaylee knew. Hell, even David knew, but I didn't. I drank...a lot, and then I got the tattoo. But...no," I murmur. "It wasn't a mistake."

He leans back slightly, his face only inches from mine.

"Nanna saw it," I continue. "It peeked out of my top one night when I was picking up Felix from my mom's. She loved it. Said she always knew you had feelings for me, and it was about time you admitted it." I laugh softly, shaking my head.

"When we spoke in the hospital, she mentioned you got divorced," he admits. "We were supposed to come up with a plan of attack."

"For what?"

"To break down your wall and get you to fall in love with me."

Holy shit...He's not holding back at all.

"Why didn't you ever tell me how you felt?"

"Isn't that the million-dollar question...?" He rests one hand against the wall next to my head, and the other goes back to my face, dusting several strands of sweaty hair out of my eyes. "It never felt like the right time. You were either taken or on an anti-boyfriend kick." He playfully rolls his eyes, making me laugh. "And then, before you were about to leave for college, I was going to. I was gonna throw it all on the table...And then all that shit went down at the party, and you posted that David proposed, and I...*fuck*, I just felt like maybe it wasn't meant to be. Gage and Brax needed me, so I left."

"Without even saying goodbye."

"It was too damn hard. You needed to focus on your future, and I needed to be with my band."

"And now that I'm divorced, you're back?" I tilt my head up slightly, and our mouths are so close. If Camden just moved a little closer, they would touch.

"This is my second chance," he says, shocking me. "I let you go once, but I can't do it again without telling you how I feel. I'm in love with you. I probably have been since the day I saw you crying on your front steps. I know you need time to get over David, and I'm going to give you that time."

"Cam," I gasp. "I don't know—"

"You don't need to know anything right now except that I'll be waiting for you to be ready, and once you are, I want my chance with you."

"I can't jump into something again. I have Felix now, and...I barely know you. Yeah, I knew you years ago, but we've both changed, and this time, I need to be careful. It's not just my heart that's at stake but also my little boy's too. We haven't hung out or talked in five years. I might not even be the same girl you once loved. I meant what I said before...we're practically strangers."

"I get it," he says, smiling softly. "And the fact that you're protecting your heart and your son's only makes me love you that much more."

"So then what do we do? Where does that leave us?"

"We get to know each other all over again," Camden says, rubbing his thumb across my bottom lip before he steps back, breaking all contact. "Starting right now." He extends his hand. "I'm Camden Rocco Blackwood, lead singer of Raging Chaos. It's nice to meet you."

I snort out a laugh at his introduction and accept his hand. "I'm Layla Isabella Kessler. Can I have your autograph?" I flip my hair playfully, making him laugh.

"Oh, Shutterbug, you can have way more than that."

"Oh, yeah?" I play along. "Like what?"

"Me," he says, using my hand to tug me toward him. "You can have me."

Fourteen

LAYLA

"I'M THANKFUL FOR MY MOMMY BECAUSE SHE LETS ME STAY UP PAST MY BEDTIME SOMETIMES AND because she signed me up for dance classes, and Grandma because she lets me have another cupcake when Mommy says no…" Felix looks around the table and stops on Camden. "My friend Cam for buying me the new *Sonic* game."

Everyone laughs under their breath as he continues to thank everyone he can think of for doing something for him or letting him do something he shouldn't do. It's Thanksgiving, and we're all at the Blackwoods for lunch. We've finished eating dessert, and Sophia insisted we continue Nanna's tradition of everyone going around and saying what they're thankful for. Normally, we would eat later, but with my custody agreement, David gets Felix at two o'clock, so everyone agreed to eat earlier so Felix and I could join.

It's going to be the first time Felix spends the night with David, and I'm not looking forward to it. After the craziness at his office, he showed up at my house the next day, begging to talk, but I refused. I think he's finally gotten the message because he texted me to let me know he rented a condo near his work and would like to take Felix for the weekend starting on Thanksgiving. It'll probably be the most time they've spent together since he was born, since David always works. He assured me he would spend the weekend with him and not pawn him off onto his parents—although that might not be a bad thing since his parents are actually good grandparents—or drag him into the office, so hopefully he's telling the truth because I officially start my job for Raging Chaos this weekend.

I've signed the contract and am going away with them early tomorrow morning for the weekend to LA for Escape, a music festival that takes place all weekend. The guys will be performing on Saturday night, but they will also attend meet and greets and panels, where they'll be asked questions about their music and band. Since David is taking Felix for the weekend, I'm able to go. It will be my first weekend away from Felix, so at least I'll be busy instead of wallowing by myself.

And then there's the fact that I haven't seen or heard from Camden since our conversation at Lush, where I allowed the alcohol flowing through me to speak honestly and even flirt with him. After he made it crystal clear that he wanted me, we spent the rest of the night dancing, and then we headed back home when the club closed. They had the car drop me off first, and after Camden made sure I was in safely, he kissed me on my forehead and wished me a good night, leaving me to spend the rest of the night thinking about everything he said.

"Camden, it's your turn," Sophia says, snapping me out of my thoughts. "What are you thankful for?"

Everyone turns their attention to Camden.

"Hmm…" he says as if thinking about what he wants to say. "Despite losing one of my favorite people, I have a lot to be thankful for this year. It's the first time in a few years that we've been able to be home." His gaze skates over to Declan, Braxton, and Gage. "I'm thankful for another year of success with Raging Chaos. It's been a wild ride thus far, and I can't imagine being on it with anyone but you guys." The guys raise their glasses and tip their chins up, silently agreeing.

"I'm thankful for the home-cooked meal," he continues, glancing at my mom and then his. "It's been a tough few weeks without Nanna. I miss her daily phone calls and her reminders to do my laundry." He looks at his sisters and chuckles under his breath. "I'm thankful my sisters have stepped up to call me every day. Now, if they could just do my laundry, I'd be set." He shrugs, and everyone laughs. "And…" His eyes meet mine. "I'm thankful for opportunities I never thought possible."

Everyone goes quiet, waiting for him to elaborate, but instead, he takes his glass and raises it, his eyes never leaving mine. "Happy Thanksgiving, everyone."

As everyone raises their glasses, I notice my mom is smirking, her gaze darting back and forth between Camden and me. Dammit. She totally knows.

"SO I HEARD YOU'RE TAKING DANCE LESSONS?" CAMDEN ASKS FELIX, COMING OVER AND SITTING NEXT TO him. Lunch is over, and everyone is relaxing before dessert since we all just pigged out on way too much food.

Felix looks up from his iPad, where he's probably bulldozing some crops or building a house out of blocks. "Yeah," he says softly. "Mommy signed me up."

"That's cool. I took dance lessons when I was younger too."

Felix's eyes light up. "You did? Daddy said it's only for girls, but Mommy and I went there, and the lady said there will be other boys too."

Camden's jaw ticks in anger, and I hold my breath, waiting for him to say something rude about David. Instead, he says, "Well, I'm a boy, and I can dance better than a lot of girls. As a matter of fact, I was in a music video once."

Felix gasps. "Really? Was it Justin Bieber's?"

Camden laughs. "No, it was my sister Kendall's, but she's big like Justin. Want to see the video?"

"Yeah!" Felix yells, practically bouncing in his seat.

Camden hooks his phone up to the television, and a minute later, an older music video of Kendall's pops up. I smile as we watch it, and Camden points out where he is, remembering this music video like it was yesterday. Camden was a fill-in for a dancer who got food poisoning, and they wanted a certain number of dancers. Since he had taken dance lessons growing up, he had no problem filling in. I spent the day watching the production and fell even more in love with the music industry, cementing that I wanted to do that one day.

"That's so cool!" Felix says, jumping up at the part when they break into a hip-hop type of dance. "Can you show me how to do that?"

"Sure," Camden says, standing. He does the move, and Felix watches, his eyes wide with excitement. "Need me to show you again?" Camden asks when he's done.

"Nope. I got it!" Felix busts into the same moves Camden just did, mimicking move for move. Granted, they're not as fluid since he's only four, but he gets every one right. When he finishes, he looks at Camden nervously, waiting for him to tell him how he did.

"Holy shit, little man," Braxton says from the couch. "You can bust some moves."

"Yeah, you can," Camden adds, raising his hand for a high five.

With the biggest grin on his face, Felix slaps his hand, soaking up the praise.

"Maybe one day you'll be dancing in a music video," Camden says.

"Yeah," Felix says. "And my mommy is going to make it."

Camden smiles at me. "I have no doubt, bud. And I bet it will be one awesome video."

"WHAT'S WITH THE FROWN?" MOM ASKS, COMING UP BEHIND ME. I WAS IN THE KITCHEN HELPING WITH THE dessert dishes, but when my phone went off with a text from David, letting me know he's running late, I excused myself outside to call him. Of course, he didn't answer. Instead, he texted me that he had to run into the office for an emergency.

"David won't be picking up Felix until later." I glance up and force a smile. "I think we're going to head home. I'm pretty sure more cake ended up on Felix's clothes than in his mouth."

Mom nods. "I know this is hard on you, but you're handling it all very well. I'm proud of you."

"Yeah?" I laugh humorlessly. "Because it feels like my entire life has completely spun out of control."

"Oh, Layla…" Mom sits next to me and pats my thigh. "It's just a bad moment. It will pass."

"A bad moment?" I scoff. "It feels like a bad life." I lay my head on her shoulder, and she wraps her arms around me.

"Not all bad," she says. "I saw the way Camden has been looking at you all day. That boy always had a crush on you."

"Of course you knew," I mutter. "Because apparently everyone knew but me."

Mom chuckles. "Any chance of something happening between you two?"

"I don't know. He wants there to be, but…" I close my eyes and release a harsh breath. "I feel broken. I know I shouldn't. I know what David did to me wasn't my fault, and it's on him. He allowed his anger and jealousy to steer his decisions. I know…I know I didn't do anything wrong…at least not that warranted to be raped."

"But?" she prompts.

"But setting the rape aside, he's been cheating on me with his assistant for God knows how long." She knew about David raping me, but I haven't told her about him cheating. "And it wasn't the first time. I don't even care that he cheated. We're over, and after what he did, I lost every ounce of love and respect I had for him. It's just…I can't help but wonder if it's me. I keep thinking, why wasn't I enough? Am I not pretty enough? Sexy enough? Am I not good enough in bed?" I choke out, a ball of emotion clogging my throat.

"And then I think about Camden and how he wants me to give him a chance. The other night when I mentioned that I was cheated on by the only two guys I've been with, he said it's them, not me, but how can it be them and not me, when both of them cheated on me? And if I couldn't keep them satisfied and only wanting me, how the hell would I ever keep a man like Camden satisfied? He's a rock star, for God's sake. He has beautiful women throwing themselves at him every damn day. What do I possibly have to offer him that he can't get from all those other women?"

I glance up at my mom, needing her motherly wisdom, but my eyes lock on Camden, who is standing just behind us.

"Felix was looking for you," he says. "I thought I saw you come out here. I wasn't trying to eavesdrop." He swallows thickly, his Adam's apple bobbing.

"I only heard the end of what you were saying."

"Great," I mutter, dropping my head into my hands.

My mom's arm leaves me just as a strong hand grips my hand and gently tugs it. I'm forced to look at Camden, who's now crouching in front of me. I look for my mom to save me, but she's already disappeared inside. Damn traitor.

"But I'm glad I did," he says, palming the side of my face. "I don't know all that went on in your marriage, but what I do know is that I'd give anything to be able to come home to you every day. Your boyfriend from high school cheated on you because you moved away, and he was young and not thinking about forever, and your husband...he cheated on you because he's a damn fool. But neither of those circumstances were because of you."

I start to argue, but he presses two fingers against my lips. "Sex is sex, Layles. Guys can get off with anyone. Give them a warm hole to sink into, and they're good to go. But what a guy *can't* get just anywhere is a good woman. Someone who supports and loves him. Who is there, day in and day out, making sure their family is taken care of. And all of those things are found *in the home*, not outside of it. David made the same mistake many men make. He was too busy looking outside to pay attention to what was inside."

"What if...?" I sniffle, hating that I'm crying in front of Camden. "What if what's outside is better than what's inside?" I ask, tears filling my eyes and falling without my permission.

"If *you're* inside, that's impossible."

"David didn't think so," I murmur.

"And we've already concluded that he's a fool. David didn't deserve you. He didn't appreciate you. Because if he did, he would've been too busy looking inside to notice anything beyond those walls. He had everything. The beautiful wife, the adorable kid. A loving home. And he lost it all because he chose to look outside instead of cherishing and appreciating what he had on the inside. But that's on him, not you, and it's sure as hell not fair to throw his dumbass choices on me."

His emerald eyes sear into me. "If I had you, I know I'd never look outside. Them fucking blinds would stay closed." He smirks, and I find myself laughing. "You're beautiful and smart and sexy as fuck, and if I'm ever lucky enough to get you inside my four walls, I will prove to you every damn day that you're all I see...all I want. That there's nothing worth looking outside for.

"I hate that he hurt you. I hate that he ruined your family, and Felix will be affected. But selfishly, I'm so fucking thankful he showed his true colors, and because of his stupidity, I was able to tell you how I feel. I missed my chance all those years ago, but I'll be damned if I let you slip through my fingers again."

"I need a little bit of time," I tell him, needing to be honest. "I heard everything you said, but the truth is, I never knew you felt that way. Right now, I'm trying to wade through my mess of a life, and I don't think I'm in a place where I can be what you need. I know you said you'd never cheat on me, but I don't want to enter into a relationship feeling insecure. And I know that's not fair to you because you haven't done anything wrong, but I can't help how I feel."

Camden nods, his lips turning into a sad smile. "I get it. I heard you. When I shook your hand at the club, it was us starting over...as friends. I'm here, as your friend, and hopefully, one day when you're ready, I can be more. But just know that I'm here, no matter what. I fucked up when I walked away five years ago. I did what I had to at the time for Gage and Brax, and even myself, but I still fucked up. And to be given a second chance...I won't fuck it up again. Even if it's only as your friend."

I sigh in relief and wrap my arms around Camden, needing to hug him. "Thank you," I tell him, breathing in his warm, comforting scent. "I don't know what the future holds, but I can tell you that right now, I can definitely use a friend."

"THIS IS ALL THE INFORMATION YOU NEED IN CASE OF AN EMERGENCY." I HAND DAVID A FOLDER THAT contains copies of Felix's insurance card, birth certificate, social security card, his pediatrician's number and address, the local hospital's information, my phone number (I know, I know, I'm acting crazy), my mom's information, and a bunch of other numbers he might need.

"Poison control?" he asks, glancing up at me and raising a brow. "Do you really think all of this is necessary? I'm his dad. I can handle things. I don't need a file on my own kid."

"Please take it, just in case," I insist, my heart pounding against my rib cage at the thought of my little boy leaving for the weekend. Of him possibly needing me and me not being there. This is why so many women stay in bad relationships—for their kids, so they can be there for their kids. Because the worst part of being divorced is having to let your child walk out the door without you over and over again. What if he gets hurt? What if he has a nightmare and calls out to me in the middle of the night? What if...? What if...? What if...?

"If there's an issue, which I doubt there will be, I can just call you." He closes the folder and drops it onto the table.

"Yeah...I know," I say, picking it back up and handing it to him again. "But just in case. Please." I debated whether to tell him that I'll be in California this weekend but decided against it. For one, he'll give me tons of shit for it, which will sour Felix's first weekend at his dad's. He's already been acting off since we moved here and got divorced. I don't need to add to his craziness right before I leave our son in his care for seventy-two hours. And also, I don't want to deal with him. He'll eventually find out, but for now, I'm okay with him not knowing. It's not even his business, but I'm sure when he finds out, he'll try to make it so, as well as try to make my life a living hell.

The problem is, by not telling him, he thinks I'm going to be here in New York, so he doesn't understand my need to make sure Felix is taken care of. It will be my first time without my little boy for longer than one night, and on top of it, I'm going to be across the damn country, where I can't just jump into an Uber and get to him in minutes.

"Whatever," he grumbles, shoving it into the front pocket of the suitcase Felix packed. David and I explained to him that he'll be getting his own room, but he's only four and doesn't get it, so he insisted on packing his favorite stuff to take with him.

"I'm ready!" Felix yells, running down the stairs. When he stops in front of us, he glances at me. "Mommy, you have to put on your shoes so we can go to our new house."

Oh, jeez...Because I didn't already feel like the worst mother in the world for ripping my son's family apart—even though it needed to happen and is for the best.

I get down on my knees, so Felix and I are at eye level. "The new house is only for you and Daddy," I explain. "This house is still mine and yours. You have two houses and two rooms. Sometimes, like right now, you'll go with your dad, and I'll stay here by myself until you come back here."

Felix's brows knit together. "But...I wanna stay with you. I don't want you to be lonely."

Be still my heart.

"I love you so much," I tell him, pulling him into a hug. "And I'm going to miss you, but you're going to have fun with your dad. I won't be lonely, I promise."

"Hey, Felix," David says. "I was thinking we could go to the park this weekend. Maybe we can convince your mom to join us."

"David," I hiss, knowing exactly what he's up to. The guy switches between hot and cold like a drunken Mother Nature. He's either pissed at me or apologizing to me. He either tells me I'm a shitty person for ending our marriage or begs me to take him back. And just when I think he's finally accepting where we stand, he pulls this shit.

"The park sounds like so much fun," I tell Felix in an upbeat voice so he doesn't catch on to the stifling tension between his parents. David might disgust me on a deep level, and I might've lost all love and respect for him, but he's still Felix's dad, which means I have to deal with him for the rest of our damn lives. His *only* saving grace is that his son absolutely adores his father, and I can't simply take Felix away from his dad because of what went down between us. But one wrong move on David's part, and I won't hesitate to strike against him.

"Can you go?" Felix asks before I can finish my sentence.

"I can't," I tell him, hating the heartbroken look on his face. "This weekend is all about you and your daddy. I want you to have tons of fun and call me every night before bed to tell me how your day went, okay?"

"Okay," he says, nodding.

"I love you, and I'll miss you." I pull him into a hug and inhale the scent of his shampoo.

"Love you, Mommy."

The moment David and Felix take off, I break down sobbing and call my best friend, needing her.

"Did they leave?" she asks, already knowing what was going down tonight.

"Yeah. I know this is what I wanted, but…"

"No," she says in a stern voice. "This is not what you wanted. You wanted a husband who would love and cherish you, who would treat you with respect and honor the vows he made. Unfortunately, David turned out to be a rapist asshole. Now, you're doing what you have to do, not what you *wanted* to do, and if it means you cry, then fucking cry, and I'll sit on the phone with you while you do."

And that's exactly what I do. I cry over the phone and to Kaylee until the tears dry up, and I fall asleep with the phone to my ear, wishing I could fix my broken life.

Fifteen

CAMDEN

dressed in a pair of dark wash skinny jeans, a thick coat since it's cold as shit, and boots that almost reach her knees. Her brown hair is up in a loose ponytail, and her makeup is a bit on the heavier side—almost like she's trying to cover something up. It doesn't look bad. It's just not how I've seen her wear it since we've reconnected.

"Is that your way of telling me I look like shit?" she grumbles. "Thanks."

Declan snorts from inside the SUV. "Sounds like operation *Get Layla* is going smoothly."

I reach in and punch him in the arm, then round the vehicle so I can open the door for Layla. She hands our driver her suitcase, and he throws it into the trunk. As she's getting in, her eyes land on the other vehicle.

"What's that?"

"Our security team. We don't really need them much in New York since the people here are too busy to give a shit about us. But LA is another story. We have a team of four, and they have to go everywhere we go when we're in LA. Two of them were actually with us at Lush, but they make it a point to blend in unless we need them."

She nods and gets in, scooting to the other side, so I can sit next to her. Declan's already moved to the second row to sit next to Braxton, and Gage is sleeping in the front seat. Since the vehicle is warm inside, she unzips her coat and shrugs out of it, exposing a tight long-sleeved shirt that shows off the swells of her perfect round breasts.

"What's wrong?" I ask her when the vehicle lurches forward to head to the airport.

"I couldn't sleep. Felix is with David for the weekend. It's our first time away from each other for this long." Tears well in her eyes, and my heart shatters at her voice's broken tone.

Without thinking, I pull her into my arms and kiss her temple. "I'm so sorry you're going through this." I can understand on a certain level because of my parents being in the music industry. They had to travel a lot, and oftentimes, we couldn't go. But I've never been on the other side of it. When I have kids one day, I'll be where she is, only it won't always be for just a weekend but for weeks at a time. It's the downside of the business we're in. Touring is where we make the majority of our money. It's why so many artists go on tour every year. Why we've been going on tour every year. My dad's advice was to hit the iron while it's hot, so later, when we're ready to settle down, we can travel less like he did.

"I'll get through it," she says. I expect her to pull away since she's so hell-bent on taking shit slow, so I'm a bit surprised when she snuggles against me and sighs into my chest. A few minutes later, the soft sound of her snoring tells me she's fallen asleep. She stays like this for the entire ride. I use my available hand to go through my phone, double-checking the agenda Jill sent us. While my dad is our band manager, we also have a tour manager—Jill—who handles everything we do on the road, whether it's a tour or a festival like the one we're attending this weekend.

Since we're not performing until tomorrow, she left today open for us to do what we want. The guys already know I've made plans for Layla and me for the day. My goal is to reconnect with her and remind her of the friendship we once had while wooing the hell out of her. I only get one day alone with her, so I'm determined to make the most out of it.

A few minutes into the drive, my phone goes off with a text from Kendall. When I click on it, I see she actually texted Gage, Braxton, Declan, and me.

Kendall: Hey! Mom said you guys are flying in. Let's meet up. I miss you!

One of the nice things about living in LA for the past five years is that, even though the majority of my family lives in New York, Kendall owns a home just up the street from us in Calabasas. With us both touring like crazy, we don't see each other often. But during the rare occasion we're both in LA at the same time, we hang out. Kendall loves her house and loves to throw pool parties, which leaves me to man the grill.

Me: You're back?

Kendall: About to land. I was thinking I could fly home with you guys on Sunday since I couldn't make it home yesterday for Thanksgiving. I'm going to surprise Mom and Dad and chill in New York for a while. I'm exhausted.

In other words, she and her latest boyfriend broke up, and she's going to New York to hide out. My sister is what you'd call a serial dater. No matter who she's with, she finds something wrong with him. And when they break up, she writes a shit ton of songs about him. Ever heard what people say about Taylor Swift's exes? They've been *Swifted*. Well, my sister's exes...they get *Stiffed*. It's a play off the wood in Blackwood. Lame, I know. But it doesn't change the fact that, like Taylor, my sister has developed quite the reputation for luring men in, making them fall in love, and then kicking them to the curb. I love my sister, she's one of my best friends, but I pity the men she hooks. I honestly don't think she does it to be cruel. I think my sister loves the idea of being in love. She has it in her head what it should look like, feel like, sound like, and when the guy she's with does something she doesn't like, she drops him quicker than a bad habit. Hell, she has yet to bring a single guy home with her to meet our parents.

Me: I can do breakfast. Layla's with us. She's our new videographer. I made plans with her for the rest of the day.

Kendall: I heard...and of course you did. I need to shower and get some shut-eye, so breakfast is a no-go, bro.

Braxton: Sleeping all fucking day. Club LA tonight.

Club LA is our go-to place to chill. It's owned by a good friend of ours, so whenever we go, we get VIP, which allows us to party without all the craziness that comes with being who we are.

Gage responds next—guess he woke up: **Same**

I'm about to put my phone away when another text comes through from Declan: **I'm down for lunch or dinner.**

I mentally roll my eyes. Of course he is. The guy has had a crush on my sister since we first met. Normally, a brother would be worried about his friends hooking up with his sister, but in my case, if Kendall ever gave in to Declan, I'd be more concerned about him. Because Declan is a hopeless romantic. He's the sweet to Braxton's jaded. The light to Gage's dark. And the optimistic to my—until recently—pessimistic ass. He keeps us all grounded. Never allowing the scales to tip too much one way.

Kendall: Sounds good! I'll text you when I wake up.

When we arrive at the airport, we're taken straight to the Blackwood jet that's waiting for us. Layla walks on board with wide eyes, checking it all out. It reminds me of the first time the guys came on board. I was raised in this lifestyle, so for me, it's a normal occurrence. Don't get me wrong, I don't for a second take it for granted or not appreciate what I have, but the wow factor just isn't there.

We take off, and the guys find a place to crash, leaving Layla and me on the couch. "Any plans for today?" she asks, constantly glancing at her phone. "I didn't see anything on the agenda." When I made the plans for us today, it was to reconnect, but now I'm hoping they'll take her mind off the fact that she's away from her son all weekend. Because of her divorce, she'd be in the same position she's in now, but I'm sure it's harder knowing she's hours away from him.

"Actually, yeah. I was hoping we could spend the day together."

Her gaze pops up. "Like all of us or just the two of us?"

"Just the two of us...if that's okay with you. I thought it could be a good way to get things back to a starting point with us. See if the adult us still connects like the teenage us used to."

She sucks in her bottom lip, then slowly releases it, and I wonder how she tastes, and if one day I'll get a chance to find out. I have no doubt the adult me still wants the adult her, but I know that since she hasn't shared the same feelings I have all these years, I need to show her how good things can be between us.

"Yeah, that's okay with me." She slides a bit closer. "Things have been crazy since I returned to New York. Between the move, the divorce, and finding out that after all this time, you wanted more, and I had no idea, I think spending some alone time together is a good idea."

I pull her into my side and kiss the top of her head. "I'm going to woo the hell out of you, Layles."

She laughs, shaking her head. She isn't a stranger to that term. My family's used it as long as she's been around.

"I think...I think I'm okay with that," she says softly, shocking the hell out of me. She lays her head back on my chest, and a few minutes later, she's fallen back asleep.

Sixteen

CAMDEN

Declan chuckles. "More like six of your houses. But yeah, this is home."

"We figured sharing a house would be better than living separately," I explain. "Last year, we had a studio built so we don't have to go to the Blackwood studio every time we want to work on our music. Traffic in LA is a bitch. Not as bad as New York, but still pretty bad."

The guys all go their separate ways to their rooms while I give Layla a quick tour, leading her to the guest room. "This is your room. It has an en suite bathroom, and the balcony overlooks the infinity pool, rolling hills, and a bit farther out, the stadium."

"This is perfect. Thank you." She pulls the French doors open, leading to the outside. We picked this house because it's in a gated community but on a good-sized piece of property. It's our very own sanctuary.

"Wow, it's so warm." She laughs. "A weekend here and I might be convinced to move the hell out of frigid New York City."

"If you think the weather will convince you, wait until you see what I have planned."

She twirls around. "What are you up to?"

"You'll see," I say, giving her a playful wink. "I'll give you a few minutes to freshen up if you need to and change into something cooler. Oh, and make sure you're wearing comfortable shoes. We'll be doing a good amount of walking. I'll meet you downstairs."

When she enters the living room about twenty minutes later, she's in the same jeans and shirt, but in place of her boots are sneakers. When I glance up at her, I find her eyes are rimmed red, and her nose and cheeks are splotchy.

"What's wrong?"

She shakes her head, but the second I'm off my seat and over to her, palming her face, she breaks. "David is being a dick. I tried to call to talk to Felix, but he said they're busy. I should've known he would act like this."

"Because you're with me?"

"No, he doesn't know I'm here or that I work for Blackwood. I didn't want to chance him freaking out. I'll have to tell him eventually, but…"

"I get it. But why is he acting like this?" I didn't want to pry. I was hoping she would eventually tell me all that went down, but I can't be there for her if I don't know what's going on.

Layla flinches, and my hackles rise. "Layles," I say gently. "You know you can trust me, right?"

"I know," she says softly. "I really just want to spend the day with you without bringing David into the mix. Can we please just enjoy our day? I promise I'll tell you everything soon. I'm just not ready to right now."

"Okay," I concede, hearing the pleading in her voice. "We can do that. And when you're ready to talk, I'll be here."

"Thank you," she says, sagging in visible relief.

Since we won't require any security where we're going, we take off in my Mercedes C-Series Coup. It's not often I get to actually drive it, and since it's nice out, I ask Layla if she's okay with rolling the windows down. Of course she is.

The ride is made in comfortable silence with Layla sticking her hand out the window and reveling in the cool breeze. I can't help but constantly glance at her. She's so fucking beautiful, and despite everything going on, she actually looks almost content right now.

Twenty minutes later, when we arrive at the heliport, her eyes swing over to me. "We're going in a helicopter?" she squeaks. "Are you freaking serious?"

"It's the quickest way to get around." I shrug, loving that she's obviously excited.

"Oh, shit," she says when she meets me around the front of the car. I take her hand, leading her to the one we're taking.

"What?"

"I knew you were going to woo me, but this…You're pulling out all the stops, aren't you?"

I have to laugh at that. "Damn right." I tug on her hand so she's forced to spin around into my arms. "I'm not taking any chances this time. I've wanted you for eight years. When you got pregnant and then married David, I thought I'd lost my shot. I'm not gonna lie, a part of me kept holding on to hope, which makes me sound like a dick because that means I was banking on you eventually getting a divorce, and I shouldn't have wanted that for you. You deserve to be happy, even if it's not with me. But still, here we are, and as I said before, I'm not taking this second chance lightly. If we don't end up together, it's because you don't want to be with me. And if that's the case, it is what it is. No matter what you decide, unless you walk away, I'll never go another five years without talking to you again."

She smiles softly. "That makes me happy because I really did miss you." She wraps her arms around me and places a chaste kiss on my neck. "I'm sorry I didn't know how you felt."

"It's not your fault. I should've made it clear. But now I am."

While I knew she'd be wowed by the helicopter, I wasn't lying when I said it's the quickest way to get around. Within fifteen minutes after taking off, we're landing on Catalina Island and stepping off the helicopter. A taxi is waiting for us, and a few minutes later, he drops us off at the Avalon Resort.

During the entire trip so far, Layla's been taking picture after picture with her camera hanging around her neck. It reminds me so much of the girl from high school. I'm glad she's back in my life and that I get to spend so much time with her since she's working with us.

"Wow," she breathes when we make our walk out to the beach. "This is amazing. Do you come here a lot?"

"Actually, I've never been here," I admit.

"What?"

"I considered showing you around LA since that's what I'm familiar with, but the thought of being recognized and fans getting crazy...I just wanted some time with you. So I did some research and found this place. I think it's a lot like New York. When you're a tourist, you visit everywhere, but when you live there, you forget to actually enjoy it."

"I get that," she agrees.

Threading our fingers together, I guide her over to the private picnic the resort set up for us inside the cabana I booked ahead of time. There's an assortment of meats and cheeses on a charcuterie board, a pitcher of sangria, and several other plates of food for us to snack on.

I fix us each a plate while she pours us a couple of drinks, and then we take them over to the double lounger, where we can lie down and enjoy the nice weather and view.

Layla's the first to speak. Between bites, she says, "How are Brax and Gage doing? Like really doing. We've kind of kept in touch over the years, but it was mostly commenting and liking each other's pics."

"They're okay." When she glances at me, raising a single knowing brow, I sigh. "Brax's okay. I mean, he's turned into a bit of a slut, but I think he's just trying to move forward."

Layla nods. "Kaylee kind of did the same thing right after. She lashed out, got caught up in some bad stuff, and failed out of Boston."

Damn, I had no idea. Not that I feel too bad for her. She chose to do what she did. But if I'm going to have a shot at being with Layla, I have to be accepting of all the parts of her life, including Kaylee...and David.

"She's graduating in December from NYU," she adds.

"That's good," I say evenly.

"And Gage?" she prompts.

"He's…not so good," I admit truthfully. "My dad has mentioned rehab a few times but hasn't pushed because he's not a danger to himself. He's just always kind of high."

"I just want to hug him and never let go," she says with a sigh.

I look over at her. "I know they've missed you. They don't talk about you much since they knew how I felt…how I *feel*. But I've caught them talking about Felix a few times. Checking out his birthday pictures. Commenting on when you graduated from college. We were so proud of you."

Her eyes fill with liquid. "I did the same thing with all of you. I hated seeing everything as an outsider, but I loved getting glimpses of you guys. You did what you dreamed of, and I'm so happy for you guys." She laughs softly. "Of course, now every time I hear a song, I wonder if you're singing about me."

I chuckle at that, glancing at the tattoo of the camera peeking out of the top of her shirt. "If they were written by me, and they're about love, they're about you."

She shakes her head, an adorable light blush creeping up her neck and cheeks. "I can't believe I had no idea. Everyone knew…"

I have to laugh at that because she isn't lying. Literally, everyone knew but her.

"You had no clue at all?"

"No. I always thought you were good looking, so had I known…" She shrugs. "Ever since I found out, I can't stop thinking about it. Analyzing everything, questioning my feelings." She frowns. "David knew. He hated anyone even mentioning you. But I just thought he was being crazy."

"He is crazy."

"Yeah," she says solemnly. Then she takes a deep breath and releases a harsh sigh. "Sorry, I said no bringing him up, and then I did."

"He's your ex, and he's Felix's dad. I know that in order for us to have a real chance at being in a relationship, I have to be open to hearing about him."

"Thank you." She leans over and kisses my cheek. "That means a lot to me."

We spend the rest of the day exploring the island. We don't bring up David or the guys anymore and instead focus on getting to know each other again. At one point during our hike, she starts a game of twenty questions, which leads to *would you rather*. I don't know if it's being away from the city or everyone, but she opens up, allowing me into her adult thoughts, feelings, goals, and dreams. She's light and playful, laughing and making jokes. I already knew I wanted her, but by the time we're climbing back into the helicopter, I can say with certainty that I'm still in love with her. She might be a few years older and a mom, but she's still the same person I fell in love with on the steps of her family's home all those years ago.

"Too bad we didn't leave a little later," she says once we're situated in our seats and buckled in. "I bet the sunset from up here is beautiful."

"Actually," I say, feeling on top of the world. "I booked a tour for on the way back. We're going to see all of LA from above, along with the sunset."

She shakes her head and smiles, those damn dimples popping out. "Oh, Camden, your wooing game is seriously on point."

We put on our headsets, and the rotors start spinning. A few minutes later, we're on top of California, listening to the pilot tell us about what we're flying over. Layla stares outside the window, mesmerized, while I stare at her.

When she glances over at me with a gorgeous smile splayed across her face, my heart stutters in my chest, and without thinking, I thread my fingers through the back of her hair and pull her to me for a kiss.

Seventeen

LAYLA

TODAY HAS BEEN ONE OF THE BEST DAYS OF MY LIFE. BETWEEN THE HELICOPTER RIDES, EXPLORING THE island, and spending time with Camden, getting to know him all over again, I'm in heaven. The past several years have consisted of me being a student and becoming a mom and a wife. Don't get me wrong, I love my son, but it means my days have been spent watching children's shows and having conversations with someone who thinks it's funny to fart in the tub and make bubbles.

And I hadn't realized until today just how off David and I were. He worked and provided for us, but we never actually spent time together, and because I was so busy going to school and taking care of Felix, I never stopped to question it. We didn't go away or have date nights. He worked, and I took care of our home and Felix. But spending the day with Camden made me see that I want more. I learned more about him today than I think I ever learned about David in our years together.

And if I was worried about picking up where we left off five years later, it was a waste of a worry because Camden made it so easy. Our conversations flowed. We laughed and joked, and for the first time, I felt like more than a caregiver. I felt a lot like me. And sadly, it made me realize that somewhere along the way, I forgot who I was.

We're on the helicopter, on our way back to LA, and when I turn to thank Camden for today, our gazes clash. Before I know what he's doing, he tugs me toward him, our mouths colliding in the sweetest yet most intense kiss I've ever experienced in my life.

Our lips caress, our tongues stroke. He tastes like the beer he was drinking earlier and something uniquely Camden. I sigh into him, wishing we were alone so I could climb into his lap and burrow myself into him. I want to deepen the kiss, to feel him everywhere and get lost in him.

And then his fist tightens in my hair, and without my permission, my brain goes back there...Instantly, I jump back, smacking the back of my head on the glass.

Camden's eyes widen. "Are you okay? I'm sorry...I shouldn't...I should've asked."

"I'm okay," I tell him as traitorous tears fill my lids. "It's okay." I nod emphatically, trying to convince myself.

He doesn't take his eyes off me. "Layles," he begins as if he can see through me. He knows something is wrong, and I'm going to have to explain because before those memories popped up, I was immensely enjoying that kiss. Butterflies were attacking my belly, and sparks were flying behind my lids. And I knew at that moment I wanted Camden. I want to try. I don't care that I've only been divorced for a short time. I've spent the past five years alone while David was cheating on me. He was living two lives while I was barely living, and now it's my turn to live.

"Can we talk when we get back to your place?"

"Of course," he says. I can feel him mentally taking a step back because he thinks I didn't want the kiss, but in a helicopter isn't the place to have this conversation. Hopefully, when we're done talking, he'll know how I feel and what I want.

"YOU GUYS COMING?" BRAXTON ASKS WHEN WE WALK THROUGH THE DOOR. HE'S DRESSED IN A PAIR OF skinny jeans, a shirt taut across his chest that reads: *My other shirt is at your mom's house*, showing off several tattoos up and down his arms, a pair of Vans, and a matching Vans hat. One thing I've noticed about all four of the guys is that while they've spent the past five years playing their heart out, they've also spent a lot of time working out.

"You checking me out, Layla?" Braxton says, lifting a playful brow.

"What? No!" I say with a laugh. "I was...well, kind of." I shrug. "In my defense, you guys are all tattooed and buff now. Except Cam. He's just buff."

Braxton throws his head back with a laugh. "Buff?"

"You know..." I squeeze his forearm. "Hard and muscular."

"Quit touching my boy," Camden says with a mock glare as he pulls me away from Braxton and drops his arm around my waist. "If you want to feel something hard and muscular, you can touch me."

I reach over and make a show of squeezing his bicep. "Damn, Cam, you are hard."

"Oh jeez, please don't stroke his ego anymore," Declan says, entering the room. "The guy already thinks he's God's gift to...well, the entire human race."

"Shut the hell up," Camden says without any conviction in his tone.

"What? It's the truth." Declan shrugs. "And it doesn't help that women fawn all over your pretty boy face." Declan reaches out to stroke Camden's face, but Camden smacks his hand away.

"You leaving soon?" Camden asks.

Declan laughs. "Yes, don't worry, we're getting out of here so you can continue your wooing in a few minutes. We're just waiting on Gage."

"Where are you guys going?" I ask. While Braxton is dressed all wannabe grunge, Declan's wearing nice denim jeans, a button-down collared shirt, and clean white Nikes. He's not wearing a hat, and his long hair is tied neatly in a bun.

"The club," Declan says just as Gage walks out from wherever he was. His bright blue eyes are bloodshot, and when he gets closer, the scent of cannabis fills the air. Like Braxton, he's dressed like he's going to a skate park instead of a club with his shoulder-length curly hair down and still wet from his shower.

"Hey, you," Gage says, pulling me out of Camden's arms and giving me a side hug. "Glad to see you coming around again."

"I'm glad to be back around," I tell him, snaking my arm around his back.

"You guys joining us?" he asks.

I glance at Camden. I was hoping we could talk, but I won't stop him if he wants to go out.

As if he can read my mind, he shakes his head. "Nah, we're gonna stay in, order some grub, and make it a Netflix and chill kind of night," he says, winking at me.

I laugh at the same time Declan snorts. "Yeah, okay. You gonna watch *Friends*?"

"Funny," Camden says dryly. "Speaking of *Friends*...How was lunch with my sister?"

Declan clears his throat, his demeanor going serious. "Good. We went to La Grande. She mentioned meeting us at the club."

"That's good. Well, you guys have fun. Make sure you're ready to go in the morning by nine. We have the panel at eleven and the meet and greet afterward."

"Yes, Dad," Braxton says, mock saluting him.

Gage kisses my temple, then leans in and whispers, "Go easy on our boy, yeah? He's been waiting for you for a long-ass time." Then he releases me and follows Declan and Braxton out, leaving Camden and me alone.

Once the guys are gone, Camden turns his attention on me. "What would you like to order in? We have pretty much anything available."

"Chinese?" I suggest since I know we both love it.

"Sure, I know a good place," he says, pulling out his phone and then handing it to me so I can see the menu. After I tell him what I want, I excuse myself to try to call David again so I can talk to Felix.

"Mommy!" Felix shouts, answering the phone.

My heart swells, and I release a breath of relief at his voice. "Hey, sweetie.

How are you?"

"I'm good."

"Yeah? What are you doing?"

"Talking to you." He giggles, making me laugh as well. "Are you having a good time with Daddy?"

"I'm bored. When can I come home?"

My heart falls. "Did you guys go to the park?"

"No, Daddy had to work. We're at his office. It's borinnnnnggggg. He let me watch videos on his phone."

That must be why he answered it when I called.

"Where is your dad now?"

"He's…" There's shuffling, and then Felix says, "It's Mommy!" He must be talking to David.

"Hello?" David says.

"Are you seriously at the office?"

He sighs. "I know you don't understand this since you've never worked a day in your life, but some of us have responsibilities. Something came up, and I needed to handle it."

"You told Felix you were going to take him to the park."

"And I'm going to…tomorrow. Is this what you called for, to nag the hell out of me? If you're so concerned, how about you stop acting stubborn and let me put our family back together?"

"I'm not having this conversation with you again. Let me talk to Felix so I can say goodbye."

"Mommy!"

"It's me. I love you, sweetie, and I'll see you in two days. Okay?"

"Okay. Love you. Bye."

The call ends, and I sigh in frustration.

"Everything okay?" Camden asks.

"Not really," I say honestly. "There's some stuff I need to talk to you about. The reason I abruptly ended our kiss."

"Then let's talk." He guides us over to the couch and sits down, pulling me with him, so I'm sitting up against him.

"I'm a little nervous," I admit, pulling back slightly. "I know you say you like me, and while you might think I'm still the same person I was five years ago, a lot has changed. I'm a mom now, and with that comes a lot of responsibility."

"Layles, I know you're a mom, and I know you've changed. We both have. But that doesn't hinder my feelings for you. Spending the day with you showed me that we're still as compatible as we were before, and if anything, seeing you be an amazing mom to Felix the few times I've been around you guys only adds to your appeal."

I can't help but smile at his admission. "Thank you. But thinking I'm a good mom is different from being part of our lives. And unfortunately, that also will include David. And after what I tell you, you might want to kill him, but you won't be able to because he's Felix's dad and...yeah."

I exhale a harsh breath and then just say what I need to say. "The reason I ended our kiss, which I was enjoying, is because when you pulled my hair, it brought back horrific memories of when"—I clear my throat—"David raped me."

Camden's eyes bug out, and his jaw ticks. "He did what?"

"It's why we got divorced. He found out that I saw you at the concert. A picture went around of us."

"Yeah, I saw it. When I briefly spoke to you as I was walking off the stage."

"He's always been jealous of you. Even in high school, we would constantly argue about me spending too much time with you. Anyway, between the picture and the tattoo, he flipped his shit. He spat at me and slapped me and then forced himself on me. Today, when we were kissing, you tugged on my hair, and without meaning to, that day flashed in my mind. When he was forcing me to give him head and then raping me, he kept pulling on my hair. I have nightmares sometimes about it, but I didn't realize being sexual with someone would trigger a flashback."

"What in the actual fuck," he says slowly. "Your husband raped you?"

I nod, choking up at the pained expression on his face. "Yeah. He hurt me...bad."

"Why the fuck isn't he in jail?"

"Because I searched *proving your husband raped you,* and it scared the hell out of me because most women said they couldn't prove it. It'd be a messy battle, and I was afraid if I was accused of lying, he could somehow take Felix away from me. I believe in the judicial system, but it's not without flaws, and I couldn't risk it. So instead, I hired an attorney and divorced him."

"I'm going to kill him." Camden's body visibly vibrates in anger. "When Nanna said David hurt you, I thought she meant emotionally. I had no idea she meant literally."

"One, you're not going to kill him because that will end with you in prison, and that would make David all too happy." I palm his cheek. "And while physically he did hurt me, it hurt just as bad emotionally. I felt violated on many levels."

"Fine, I won't kill him," he relents. "But I'm not throwing *destroying him* off the table. He's going to pay," he says in a tone that brooks no argument. I won't let him make good on his threats, but for right now, since he's thousands of miles away, I'll let him make his warnings. Kaylee and my mom did the same thing.

I stroke his cheek, and he seems to calm down somewhat.

"What can I do?" he says, leaning into my touch. He brings his hand up to mine and holds it against his face for a second before he turns slightly and kisses the inside of my palm. "How do I fix this for you?"

My heart warms. "You're doing it. This weekend away, despite missing Felix, is exactly what I needed. I feel like I have a small piece of me back for the first time in a long time. Being with you feels good, feels right. And the truth is, things haven't felt right for a long time."

He grabs my hips and pulls me onto his lap to straddle his thighs. "I feel the same way. Since the day I got on the plane to California, it's felt like a piece of me was missing, and being with you, spending time with you, it's as though the pieces have clicked into place. We can take things slow—"

"I don't want to take things slow or fast. I just want to be with you and see where it leads. We take it at our pace, do whatever feels *right*." I lower my top, exposing the tattoo. "The night I got this tattoo, I think I already knew I had feelings for you. I've never permanently marked my body before, but when I heard that song, I did it without even thinking twice." My eyes descend in shame. "At the time, when David confronted me, I was in denial, but he wasn't wrong in his accusations. I was married and got a tattoo to represent you and the way you feel about me."

"Hey." Camden lifts my chin. "I happen to love that tattoo."

"Yeah, but you wouldn't have if I were with you and got one about another guy."

"That's true, but maybe everything happens for a reason. I wrote that song years ago, but I couldn't find it in me to actually sing it. At the last second, without knowing you'd be there, I decided to, and that song led to you finally hearing my words and in turn getting that tattoo."

"And was the reason for my divorce."

"No," he says. "David forcing himself on you was the reason for your divorce. If my wife came home with a tattoo of a song by another man, I wouldn't be happy, and I'd definitely question our relationship and where we stand, but I sure as fuck wouldn't rape her."

"I know you're right, and it's for the best...the divorce, not the rape. But I think what has me feeling guilty is that I don't feel guilty about getting the tattoo, but I feel like I should. Does that make sense?" I ask with a laugh.

Camden smiles. "I get it, but everything that happened led us to right here, so I say fuck feeling what you think you should feel. It's over and done with, and I love seeing that tattoo on your body."

"I do too. Although, I think you should rewrite the ending...the part about finally moving on."

Camden's mouth quirks into a sexy grin. "How about we leave that song the way it is and instead write our own song?" He tugs on the front of my shirt, pulling me toward him, and my heart swells, knowing he did that so he wouldn't use the back of my head. His lips brush softly against mine, once, twice, then he coaxes my lips open, slipping his tongue into my mouth.

My hands glide over his shoulders, up his neck, and land on the back of his head, my fingers threading through his soft, messy hair. Camden's tongue wraps around my own, and he sucks it into his mouth. I find myself grinding against him, deepening the kiss and needing to be closer to him.

And then a buzzer goes off, breaking the moment.

"That would be the food," he groans, resting his forehead against mine.

Eighteen

CAMDEN

MY HEAD IS ALL OVER THE PLACE, MY THOUGHTS SWIRLING AROUND LIKE A DAMN TORNADO. ON THE ONE hand, I'm ecstatic that Layla is willing to give us a chance and see where things go. She admitted to my feelings not being completely one-sided and the tattoo meaning more than she was willing to admit at the time. On the other hand, it feels like every admission has been blanketed with a dark cloud thanks to David. I always knew he was an asshole, good at hiding who he really was. He had everyone fooled, but not me. I should've pushed harder back then and convinced Layla he wasn't the one for her, but I pussied out and let her walk away, and in the end, he hurt her on so many damn levels.

I tried to be positive, telling her everything happens for a reason, and to an extent, I believe that, but on the other side of the coin, I'll always wonder if what happened could've been prevented had I stepped in years ago. I know... It's pointless to live with what-ifs, but I can't help it.

All I can do at this point is make sure I'm there for Layla and her son and keep a close eye on that rapist fucker. One wrong move, and he's going down.

After bringing the food in, Layla and I spend the next couple of hours chowing down and watching some Horny Housewives in England show. That's not what it's called, but the show is about some British folks who spend their days trying to hook up with each other.

When the main chick's brother pushes his woman against the tree and starts fucking her like a savage, I notice Layla squirm in her seat. She's turned on. And while I want nothing more than to tend to her needs, I also want to let her lead at her own pace. Knowing the last time she had sex was when her ex-husband raped her changes shit.

"Is the show boring you?" Layla asks when she catches me staring at her instead of watching the show.

"What show?" I joke.

She rolls her eyes and swats my chest playfully. "It's still kind of early. If you want to go to the club—"

"Hell no." I pull her into my arms. "The only thing I want to do is hang out with you."

A small smile curls on the edge of her lips as I lean in to press my mouth to hers. I still can't believe that I can finally kiss her whenever the hell I want after all these years. When our lips touch, she sighs into the kiss, tugging on my shirt so I'm forced closer, deepening the kiss.

Layla edges backward until she's on her back, her head resting on the arm of the couch, and then she reaches out for me, but I don't go. Not yet. Because I need a moment to look at her, to appreciate what I finally have in front of me.

"What?" she asks, her voice coming out breathy and impatient.

"You're beautiful."

Her nose scrunches up, and her cheeks turn a gorgeous shade of pink. "Cam…" she whines. "Come here."

I pull my phone out, needing a picture, and her eyes go wide. "You're always the one taking the pictures," I explain. "I want one of you. On my couch, looking relaxed, with a bit of a tan from our day on the island, with your hair fanned out, and a slight blush on your cheeks." I snap a photo of her, and I'm about to put my phone away when she leans forward slightly and removes her top, exposing a sexy as fuck pink lacy bra. It's slightly see-through, and her hard nipples are poking through it.

With her eyes on me, she reaches down and unbuttons and unzips her pants. "Help me take them off."

I do as she says and peel them down her hips and thighs. Underneath is matching lacy underwear. All see-through, showing off her trimmed pussy underneath.

"You always wear matching bras and underwear?" I ask curiously.

The corner of her lips quirks up, knowing exactly where I'm going with this. "Only when I think there's a chance someone might see."

I absorb her words, my insides lighting off fireworks that she came here thinking there'd be a chance I'd see. This was before we talked, which means she was thinking about me.

"Take a picture," she says. "I want to see myself through your eyes."

I do as she says, taking a few pictures. But when I click on them to show her, my attention strays back to her because she's arching her back now, unclipping her bra and taking it all the way off. Her perfect round tits are paler than the rest of her from wearing a bathing suit, and my mouth waters, wanting to take her rose-dusted nipples into my mouth.

As if she can hear my thoughts, she drags her hands down her chest slowly, seductively, landing on her nipples. She tweaks them, making them even harder than what they already were, before she continues downward to her underwear. She hooks her fingers into the sides and drags them down her creamy thighs. She has the perfect triangle of neatly trimmed hair between her legs, and all I can think about is burying my face in her pussy.

"Are you going to take a picture?" she asks softly.

"No, I wouldn't risk it." Too many celebrities have gotten their phones hacked, their private pictures stolen. I shouldn't have even taken the ones I did.

"Here," she says, reaching forward and grabbing her camera. "Use this."

I take it from her and turn it on. I have no idea how the hell to use this thing, but I'm assuming I can just point and click. I do as such and take several pictures of Layla sprawled out on my couch, naked and fucking gorgeous.

I'm taking a picture of her when I notice through the lens that she's spread her legs, exposing her pussy. Pictures forgotten, I drop the camera onto the coffee table and give her my full attention.

"We were supposed to take things slow. If you don't want—"

She presses two fingers against my lips, silencing me the same way I've done to her in the past. "Our pace...not fast or slow. We do what we want, and tonight, I want to be with you. Some would say it's too fast since we've only just decided to give this thing between us a go. And some, our friends and probably you, would say this has been a long time coming." She laughs softly. "So we do what we want because I want this. I want you."

I stare into her eyes for several seconds, looking for any sign that she's not sure, but all I see is a beautiful, confident woman lying on the couch, wanting to be with me. But still, I have to ask.

"This isn't..." I clear my throat, hating to bring that asshole into my home, into this moment. "This isn't to try to rid what happened with *him*, right?"

I don't have to say his name for her to know who and what I'm talking about. "No," she says with conviction in her tone. "I will admit, I'm looking forward to having a new experience to fill my head, but I'm not using you to make what he did go away. Nothing we do will make what he did go away. Also..." She releases a harsh breath. "I don't think..." She flinches, suddenly looking nervous, maybe embarrassed, for the first time.

"What? Tell me."

"He...He did it in my...butt." She whispers the last word, her face flushing in embarrassment. "We'd never had sex like that before, and when he forced me, it was back there. So maybe we don't..."

"I won't touch you there," I promise while mentally counting backward from ten to calm myself. If we were in New York, I'm not sure I'd be able to hold back from going after him. No, that's not true. I *know* I wouldn't be able to because what the fuck is wrong with him to not only rape Layla, but there? Knowing it would hurt her worse. He's going to pay. I don't care what it takes. I will *make* him pay for what he's done to her.

"Maybe one day," she continues, her voice small.

"Layles…" I pull her legs toward me, so I can get closer to her face, and her legs hug my waist. "Everything we do or don't do is up to you. You're leading, baby. I'm just following. Okay? You tell me what you want, and I'll make it happen. You tell me there's something you don't like, and it goes into the no pile."

She nods, a tiny smile appearing. "Well, if that's the case, I would like for you to fuck me now."

A short laugh shoots out of me. "Oh, yeah? Is that what you want?"

"Uh-huh."

"Your wish is my command. But first…" I scoop her up into my arms, making her squeal in shock. "I'm going to make you come several times."

"What are you doing?" she asks as I carry her down the hall.

"Taking you to my room. There's no way I'm risking anyone seeing you like this."

Once we're in my room, I slam the door closed, then walk us over to my bed. I set her down in the middle, loving her here, in my bed, in my home. She's naked and on display and so goddamn beautiful.

"What are you thinking about?" she asks, raising a single brow.

"That I can't believe you're actually here, naked in my bed." I reach down and stroke her soft cheek. "I dreamed of this so many times."

"Well, believe it." She beams up at me, her brown eyes twinkling with happiness. "You know what would make this even better?"

"What?"

"You taking off your clothes." She grips the edge of my shirt and lifts it over my head. When her gaze lands on my naked upper body, her eyes turn molten with lust. "Sometimes, when I would watch your concerts online, I would pause it on the parts after you took your shirt off."

"You used to watch us?" I smirk, loving her admission.

She grabs the necklace, the one she gave me years ago, and tugs on it gently, bringing me close to her. "The first time I saw you wearing this necklace, I thought I was seeing things. I zoomed in and couldn't believe it. Every concert I would watch, I'd check. As soon as your shirt would come off, I'd look for it. And every time you were wearing it."

She shakes her head. "I thought maybe it was a sign not to give up on our friendship. I wanted so badly to call or text you, but I didn't know what to do. So I just kept watching, telling myself the day I saw you without it on would mean you'd moved on from our friendship. But you never took it off."

"Never." I brush my lips against hers. "It was my only connection to you. I never took it off. When we were doing a cover for *Rolling Stone*, they tried to make me, but I refused." I move to her neck, and she tilts her head, giving me better access to trail kisses along her heated flesh. She visibly shivers, and I chuckle softly, loving the way I affect her.

"I love that," she breathes, her fingers dragging through my hair as I kiss my way downward, stopping every couple of inches to suck on her flesh. Layla moans, her legs tightening around me. "I missed you so much. Every day...I hate that—"

"Stop," I tell her, pressing my lips to hers. "What's done is done. All that matters is that we're here, right here, right now, together." I kiss along her jawline, then work my way down to her chest, inhaling the sexy as fuck vanilla scent she slathers all over her damn body. When I get to her nipple, I wrap my lips around it, darting my tongue out and slowly licking the hardened peak until she's squirming under me. Then I switch to her other breast, giving it the same attention. Layla gasps and moans, grinding against me.

"Cam, please," she begs, wanting more.

"Shh." I kiss my way down her torso. "Stop rushing me."

"But—" she whines.

"No," I say firmly, spreading her legs and planting a kiss on the top of her pussy. "I've waited too damn long for this." I glance up and find her looking down at me with hooded eyes. "I'm not going to rush. I'm going to explore every..." I part her lips. "Single..." I run my finger along her seam, finding it dripping wet and ready for me. "Inch of you." I dip down and dart my tongue out, licking up her center and stopping at her clit. One taste and I'm already addicted.

I eat Layla's pussy, listening to her moans of pleasure, learning what she likes and what turns her on. I work her up higher and higher until she screams out my name, coming so hard, her body arches off the mattress, her legs shake, and she leaves a wet spot on my sheets. Goddamn, I'm never washing these fucking sheets.

"Come fuck me," she says, her voice soft and sated. Her eyes are barely open, and she looks like she's flying on a damn cloud. Mentally, I thump my chest with my fist because I did that. I brought her pleasure. And I'm nowhere near done.

Shucking off my pants and briefs, I crawl up her body, kissing her flesh. When I get up to her face, I palm it with one hand, using the other to hold myself up, and look into her eyes.

"I need you inside me," she says, wrapping her legs around me, causing my dick to stroke her pussy lips.

"Soon," I tell her, pressing my lips to hers. "But first, I need to make sure we're on the same page." Her brows furrow, and I drop a kiss to the middle of them. "This isn't a one-time thing or just two friends reconnecting. I want you in every way that matters. I want all of your days and your nights. Your happiness and your sadness. I want your tears and your laughter. I want your body…and your heart."

A small gasp escapes past her lips. "You have me. I don't know how this will all work, but you have me. All of me. I'm all in."

The surety in her words and the way her eyes bore into mine have me pushing inside her. Our mouths collide, our tongues caress. I get lost in her perfect warmth. In the way her pussy tightens around my shaft. She feels so damn good. We fit perfectly together. When I open my eyes, needing to see her, to remind myself that I finally get to have her, I find her eyes already open, looking at me.

"You okay?" I murmur against her lips, fucking her slow and deep.

"Yeah," she breathes, smiling at me. "It feels so good…*this* feels so good."

She finds her release first—moaning so loudly if the guys were here, they'd hear her through the walls. Her perfect pussy chokes the hell out of my dick, coaxing my own release out of me. I nuzzle my face into the crook of her neck, suckling on her hot flesh, and I come harder than I've ever come in my life.

We lay like this for several minutes, our sweaty bodies wrapped around each other. When we've both caught our breath, I pull out of her, noting the way my cum seeps out of her hole.

"We didn't use protection," I voice.

Her eyes go wide. "I'm on the pill."

"I'm clean. I haven't been with anyone in…a while."

She nods. "I got tested after *him*."

Sensing the mood darkening at the mention of her ex-husband, I jump off the bed and pull her into my arms.

"What are you doing?" she asks with a laugh.

"*We're* going to shower." I drop a chaste kiss to her lips. "I'm going to clean you, every part of you, so I can dirty you up all over again."

"Ohhh." She grins. "I like that plan."

Eighteen

BONUS SCENE

LAYLA

CAMDEN CARRIES ME INTO HIS MASSIVE EN SUITE BATHROOM AND SETS ME ON THE COUNTER. HE TURNS the water on in the shower and then returns, spreading my legs and stepping between them. His mouth crashes down on mine, and he thrusts his tongue past my parted lips, devouring me.

"I can't get enough of kissing you," he murmurs against my mouth. His hand glides up my calf and thigh. "Touching you." His fingers skate across my flesh and enter me. "Feeling you."

He thrusts a finger inside and then another. "Knowing that it's my cum inside you turns me the fuck on," he says, pushing his digits in and out of me. His fingers mixed with my wetness make a squelching sound that I would be embarrassed about if it were anyone but Camden.

He drops to his knees, and his face is eye level with my center. "What are you doing?" I ask, leaning over slightly so I can see him.

"Tasting you." He spreads my legs wide and licks up my center, not caring that his cum is dripping out of my hole.

"Fuck, you taste good," he mutters, sticking his tongue into me. He licks and sucks my sensitive flesh, ascending toward my clit. Once his lips wrap around the swollen nub, he shoves his fingers back inside me and pumps them in and out, not stopping until my orgasm rips through me.

I've only barely come down when Camden's mouth is on mine. "You taste that?" he says. "That's you and me."

We continue to kiss as he lifts and carries me over to the shower. He sets me on the bench, then breaks the kiss, proceeding to wash every inch of me, paying special attention to my breasts and sex. When my front is complete, he pulls me to my feet and turns me around to face the wall. I use the tiles to keep my balance, and Camden slowly and carefully washes my back side.

When he's done, he peppers soft kisses along my shoulders and back. Wanting to feel him inside me again, I turn around and lift my leg, setting my foot onto the bench, and reach down, stroking his hard length until it's as hard as granite.

"Fuck me," I murmur.

Hooking my leg over his arm, he slides his hard length into me, stopping when he bottoms out. He grabs my chin with his other hand and captures my mouth with his. His mouth makes love to me as our bodies move together in a slow sensual rhythm. When we both find our release, Camden pulls out and sits on the bench, pulling me into his lap. "I don't think I'll ever get enough of you," he says, kissing me softly.

We sit like this, holding each other until the water starts to cool. Then Camden cleans me all over again. When he's done, I take the loofah from him and return the favor, using the opportunity to explore his body. Once we're both clean, he shuts the water off and grabs a couple of towels, wrapping one around him and the other around me.

As I step out, my stomach rumbles loudly, making both of us laugh.

"It sounds like I need to feed you," he says, encircling his arms around me.

"Well, technically, you did feed me." I smirk, cupping his dick and making it clear I wasn't referring to the Chinese we ate earlier. "But yeah, a little snack would be good."

Nineteen

LAYLA

"Nope." Camden shakes his head, pinching his lips tightly together.

"C'mon...one bite." I playfully push the food toward his mouth.

"No," he insists, the word coming out muffled since he's not chancing opening it and me shoving the snack in.

"I promise, it's delicious." I'm straddling his lap in the living room, the movie we were watching long forgotten. After Camden gave me another orgasm in the bathroom, followed by a round of shower sex, my stomach rumbled in hunger, so we got dressed and went to the kitchen in search of something to eat. He warned me that because they're only in town for the weekend, their stock of food is limited.

He was right. But upon inspection, I found they had bananas, raisin bread, and mayonnaise. And everyone knows banana and mayo sandwiches are the shit. Well, everyone except Camden. When we used to hang out, I'd make them all the time, and he'd refuse to even try them. Damn man is so stubborn.

"If you take one bite, I'll…" I lower my hand and rub it against his groin, then lean in and whisper, "give you the best blowjob of your life."

Camden groans, and I can tell he's about to give in because he's eyeing the banana-and-mayo-covered bread when the alarm chimes, indicating the door has been opened, and a few seconds later, Braxton, Gage, and Declan saunter in with a few scantily clad women. The way they're all talking and laughing loudly, their words slightly slurred, tells me they've had a good amount to drink.

The women are draped over them and giggling like they're five, and when the guys see us, they stop. Gage smirks, and Braxton grins. And that's when I remember I'm on Camden's lap in nothing but his shirt.

"About time," Braxton says, extending his fist to bump it against Camden's. When Camden doesn't react, he drops his fist and shrugs. "Damn, I thought once you finally got laid, you'd loosen up."

Camden continues to glare, so I jump in. "Did you have a good night?"

Braxton's grin grows. "Night's just getting started." He waggles his brows, and I stifle my gag, looking at Gage, who's resting against the wall with one of the women groping him like they're not in front of other people.

His eyes meet mine, and I notice they're bloodshot and sad. Unlike Braxton, who's drunk and happy.

"C'mon, Brax," one of the women says. "Show me your room."

"Specifically your bed," another woman adds with a giggle that has my ears bleeding.

"Gotta go," Braxton says. "And before you go all parental on us..." He looks at Camden. "We're taking them out to the pool house. We would've gone around back, but we forgot our keys."

"Remember we have to leave tomorrow at nine," Camden reminds him.

"Yes, Dad." Braxton mock salutes him, then wraps his arms around two women, yelling out, "Night!" while Gage and the other two women follow.

As they leave, I count how many women there are: two brunettes, a redhead, a blonde...

"That's four women for three guys," I point out. "Someone's going to feel left out."

Declan barks out a laugh. "That's four women for two guys, and trust me, none of them are going to feel left out."

It takes me a second, but once I put together what he's saying, I actually do gag this time. "They're sleeping with two women *each*?"

Declan chuckles, and Camden shakes his head.

"Won't be the first time," Declan says. "I'm off to bed. See ya in the morning."

Once he disappears down the hall, I turn my attention back on Camden. "You better have that pool house bleached." I mock shiver. "I can't even imagine the fluids that are getting swapped in there."

Camden rolls his eyes playfully. "Forget them. What I want to focus on is that blow job you were talking about before we were interrupted."

"Oh yes, in exchange for trying this." I pick up the bread I had placed on the plate and lift it to his mouth. Just as he's opening to take a bite, my phone vibrates, reminding me—for the second time, since I clicked ignore earlier when we were busy in the bedroom—to take my birth control and iron pills.

"Be right back." I drop the bread, kiss him quickly, and run to his bedroom to grab my pills, swallowing them with a mouth full of water.

"Okay, now where were we?" I say when I sit back on the couch. "Oh, right! You're going to take a bite of this delicious sandwich." I'm bringing it to his mouth when an alarm sounds, indicating a door somewhere in the house has been opened.

I give Camden a look, silently asking who's coming in, but he shakes his head and bites down. He chews slowly, making a face similar to the face Felix makes when I force him to eat his vegetables, then audibly swallows.

"Fuck, that was horrible."

"What? It's yummy. Maybe you need one more—"

"Nope!" He snatches the bread from me, drops it onto the plate, and tosses the plate onto the coffee table. "One bite is what I agreed to." He scoops me up into his arms and stands. "Now it's time to pay up."

As he's walking us out of the living room, there's a clatter from the direction of the kitchen, and then a "Fuck!" Braxton pops his head out of the kitchen. "I need condoms and lube. Who the fuck used the last of it in the pool house and didn't restock?"

"You're looking in the kitchen for condoms?" I ask, confused.

"And lube," Braxton adds.

"Why—"

Camden shuts me up by kissing me and continues walking us to his bedroom, ignoring Braxton. Once we're inside and the door is shut, he sets me on the bed and steps between my legs, then goes about kissing my face and neck, but I can't get my question out of my head.

"Why would he be looking for condoms and lube in the kitchen?"

"Because there's usually some in the kitchen drawer," he says, peppering kisses along my neck.

His answer leads to another question. "Do you guys have sex a lot in the kitchen?"

He shrugs, then gently pushes me down so I'm on my back and he's hovering over me. His mouth lands on my ear, and he tugs on the lobe.

I should be focusing on him, but now I'm wondering…"Have you had sex in the kitchen?"

This makes him stop in place. His eyes meet mine. "We're not having this conversation."

"What conversation?"

"The one where you ask me how many women I've slept with, and my number will undoubtedly be higher than yours because you've only been with one guy…well, now two, with me. That'll lead to you asking questions you don't really want the answers to, which will end with you becoming insecure and getting upset."

"Wow, you just had an entire conversation for us both *and* told me my feelings."

Camden sighs and rolls off me, landing on his side. "I just got you. The last thing I want is for you to run scared."

"That bad, huh?" I joke. Camden doesn't laugh, though, and that makes my stomach roil. I know he hasn't been a saint all these years. He's in a rock band. The sex and drugs are expected to go along with the rock and roll. But he's right...Now that I'm thinking about it, I can't help the insecurity from rearing its ugly head. It's one thing to speculate, but it's another to actually see Braxton and Gage walk in with multiple women.

"Have you had sex with multiple women?" I blurt out.

Camden's eyes roll up to the ceiling. "I guess we're going to have this conversation anyway." He sighs and flops onto his back, and I hate that I've just ruined the moment, but I can't help my curiosity.

"Have I had sex? Of course," he says, glancing over at me. "With more than one woman? Yeah. But not as often as you're thinking and not in a long time. When the fame first hit, women flocked to us. I was heartbroken, learning you were getting married and then you got pregnant, and I lost myself in a few women. But it got old real quick. The fake women, the fake emotions. It's not for me."

I nod in understanding, hating that I hurt Camden when I didn't even know I was.

"I can't take back what I've done, but I can tell you, none of the women I was with compare to being with you."

I roll my eyes playfully and he palms the side of my face. "I'm serious, Shutterbug. Being with you...it's incomparable. I told you before, for a guy, sex is usually just sex, but with you, it's so much more. I always knew it would be like this, but I never imagined it would actually happen."

I wrap my arms around his neck, and he pulls me on top of him so he's leaning against the headboard, and I'm straddling his waist. "I get it. I appreciate you explaining it to me, and I won't ask how many or anything like that. Am I a bit self-conscious after seeing those women? Yeah." I shrug. "Those women from earlier were nothing like me. They were dressed in tight, sexy dresses, faces full of makeup, fake breasts, and based on how tiny they were, I doubt they've had any kids."

"They're fake. Fake hair, fake makeup, fake tits. Fake tan. All fake." He squeezes my hips. "You're all real, and no man wants fake over real."

"You said you did. And Brax and Gage obviously do."

"I didn't *want* fake. I went for fake because it was easy. Brax's heart is fucked, and Gage..." He shakes his head. "In their own time, they'll come around. They'll find someone real, like you, and it will be a game changer, just like you are for me, but right now, the fake is what's getting them through each day. Not having to think too hard, not having to feel. The fake is how those who can't have the real survive."

His words burrow into my chest and squeeze my heart. I never thought of it like that, but he's right because looking back, what I had with David wasn't real—it was fake. It was how I got by. Only I didn't know it until Camden came back into my life and showed me the real.

I edge down and lay my head on his chest, wrapping my arms around him. "I hope one day Brax and Gage find the real because the fake really sucks."

Twenty

LAYLA

"WHAT'S UP, LA?" CAMDEN YELLS OUT TO THE CROWD OF THOUSANDS OF PEOPLE. OF COURSE, THEY ALL scream back like he's a damn god. "Hell yeah! We just got done with a hundred and fifty–show tour, but I have to tell you, there's *nothing* like being home."

The crowd erupts in even louder cheers—if that's even possible—and I make sure to record their reaction. The festival has been going on all day, but not a single band has had the same response as Raging Chaos.

Gage starts drumming the beginning instrumentals to their first song, then Braxton and Declan join in. A few seconds later, Camden starts singing, and the crowd goes crazy.

I move my camera from the guys over to the crowd, zooming in on various fans. One woman is holding up a sign that reads: I <3 you Brax. MARRY ME! Several women are flashing the guys their breasts, and a few are even crying. It's insane. The charity concert I attended was tame because it was for a charity. But out here, anything goes. The smell of weed permeates the air, smoke creating a hazy fog across the area.

I shift my focus back to the guys as they get lost in song after song. Knowing how Camden has felt for me all these years gives every song, every lyric, new meaning. I can tell which songs Braxton and Gage wrote because they're all bitter and angry and filled with rage. But Camden's...they're filled with heart and love mixed with evident sadness.

At some point, Declan's hair falls out of its knot and his long hair curtains his face. Gage's shirt has come off, exposing his tattoos and six-pack abs. Braxton's eye-fucking several of the women in the front row, and Camden's hoodie is coated in sweat, sticking to his muscular torso and showing off the outlines of his shoulders and back.

The fans eat up every minute they're on stage, and I don't blame them because I can't take my eyes off them. This is nothing like watching it on the internet. The electricity, the spark. They're a force to be reckoned with when they're on stage like this and in their element. My gaze goes back to Camden, who's now singing about wanting what he can't have.

It should be me, kissing you, touching you, inside you
But instead, it's him, getting you, every fuckin' piece of you
Those pieces should be mine

My heart swells at the words, at the implication behind them. I wonder if he'll write songs about us now that we're together.

When Camden announces the last song, they boo, and when it ends, they beg for more. Of course, Camden messes with them, asking if they deserve an extra song. They scream the place down, so with a panty-melting wink, he gives in, and the guys give them one last song before saying good night and walking off the stage.

Since they're done, I make my way to the back, handing over my equipment to the sound manager and crew. Then I head to the guys' private room for tonight. A few minutes later, I'm checking my phone when the door swings open, and the guys, along with their security and tour manager, enter.

Gage immediately lights up a joint, Braxton rips his shirt off, and Declan pulls his phone out. Camden's eyes find me, and his entire face lights up. He stalks across the room and pulls me into his arms, not giving a shit that he's covered in sweat or that we're not alone. My legs wrap around his waist at the same time as his mouth crashes against my own. The kiss is filled with heat and intensity. My back hits the wall, and his fingers squeeze my ass. As the kiss deepens, my fingers tug the strands of his hair, and I grind my center against him, needing more.

"Get a fucking room," Declan yells through a laugh.

"Or you can all get the hell out of this one," Camden fires back.

His beautiful green eyes, filled with a mixture of mirth and lust, stare into my own. "I loved having you here, standing only a few feet away, knowing I could kiss you, touch you, be inside you afterward." His confession that his words were about me has me wanting to get him alone and make good on every one of his wants.

"Do you have anything you have to do now?"

"Only you." He smirks.

We leave the crew to handle everything and are on our way back to Camden's house when my phone rings: David.

Since Felix is with him and it's late in New York, I immediately answer it. "Hello."

"I need you to come over."

Before I can ask why, I hear the sound of my little boy crying in the background. "What happened?" I ask, my heart bottoming out in my stomach. I know that cry. He's hurt. Something is wrong.

"I don't know," David says, his tone dripping with impatience and frustration. "He was asleep and then woke up crying. He won't stop! I need you to come over here."

"I can't," I tell him, closing my eyes in pain. Felix's crying doesn't stop, and the sound has me wanting to reach through the phone and comfort him, but of course, I'm hours away. "I'm…not in New York. You need to ask him what hurts. If it's his stomach or—"

"Where the fuck are you?" David barks.

"It doesn't matter. Just focus on Felix. Ask him what hurts."

"He won't stop crying!"

"Because he's in pain. Is he holding his belly or maybe pulling on his ear?"

"His ear. He's pulling on his ear. Now, where are you?"

"David!" I snap. "Forget about me. I'm not there, and I can't be there right now. You need to give him Tylenol for kids."

"I don't have any."

Of course he doesn't. And I didn't think to pack any. Dammit. "You'll have to go buy some."

"I can't believe you're not here. What did you do? Go away? Our fucking son needs you, and you're not even here."

I know his accusation is super hypocritical since he's never been there for Felix a day in his damn life, but it still hurts knowing I'm not there.

"Look," I say with a sigh, not wanting to fight. "I'm going to get there as soon as I can." My eyes meet Camden's, who nods in understanding. "But it won't be for a few hours. I need you to get him Tylenol to help with the pain. If you can't do that, you need to take him to the ER, so they can. Ear infections hurt really bad. Hence, his crying. He's in a lot of pain."

"Fine."

"Also, make—" Before I can finish my sentence, I realize the crying has stopped in the background because David's hung up on me. I call him back, but he sends me to voicemail. I try again—same thing.

"I can't believe this." I drop my head into my hands, and Camden tucks me into his side.

"We're heading to the airport," he says.

My head pops up. "Right now?"

"I've already told Jill to schedule a pilot. The jet's been on standby, ready to go tomorrow."

"What about the guys and our stuff?"

"They'll grab it for us, and the jet will come back for them."

"That's such a waste, though," I say, feeling guilty.

"The only important thing right now is getting to your son. I have the means to do it, so it's being done." He kisses my temple, and I sink deeper into his side.

During the entire plane ride home, I try to call David, but he refuses to answer, sending me to voicemail or letting the phone ring every single time. Hours later, we land, and there's a car waiting for us. I try to tell Camden we should take separate vehicles so I can go straight to David's, but he insists on going with me.

When we pull up to the building David lives in, I turn toward him. "I appreciate you getting me here so quickly, and I get why you wanted to come with me because you're worried about what he'll do, but I don't think you should come in with me. It'll only rile him up and—"

"I get it," he assures me. "I'll be right here, waiting for you."

"Thank you." I plant a chaste kiss on his lips.

"I need you to do something for me before you go."

"What?"

He pulls his phone out and dials, and a second later, my phone is ringing. "Answer it."

I do as he says, confused, and his face shows up since it's a video call.

"Keep the phone in your pocket, so I can hear, just in case. I'm going to record the call...just in case."

I nod once in understanding. I hope nothing bad happens, but I love that Camden is looking out for me.

After walking up to David's complex, I press the number of his apartment to be buzzed in. Since he's on the first floor, I find his number quickly and knock. A few seconds later, the door opens, and with a look that could kill, David widens the opening, silently telling me to come in. My stomach drops at his cold demeanor, and I'm glad Camden can hear everything going on.

"Where's Felix?" I ask.

I'm glancing around at David's new place since I've yet to see it, so I'm taken aback when he shoves me against the wall, caging me in.

"Where's Felix? What the fuck do you care?" David hisses, slamming his palm against the wall. "I saw the pictures! You were in fucking LA with him! While your son was here, crying in pain, you were off with him!"

"David, you need to lower your voice and back up," I say slowly, trying to calm him down. "It's not what you think." It kind of is, but I'm not about to say that.

"Then what is it?"

"I got a job working for Blackwood as a videographer."

"You mean you got a job working for *him*! You're such a fucking slut. You've probably been fucking all of them for years. Haven't you?"

I knew him finding out I work for Blackwood would piss him off, which was why I hadn't told him yet. But now I'm wishing I would've because somehow, a picture must've leaked, and he found out anyway.

"I'm not having sex with them. I was given an opportunity," I explain calmly. "Now, please, before you do something you're going to regret, back up."

His eyes turn into thin slits, and a second later, his fingers wrap around my throat. The back of my head hits the wall hard, and I yelp out in pain. "The only opportunity that asshole is giving you is to suck his fucking dick!" He slaps me across the face and then squeezes my throat harder, making it difficult to suck in air. I claw at his arms, trying to get him to let go, but he ignores me.

"I would rather watch you take your last breath than to support you fucking that piece of shit." He tightens his hold on me, and my vision turns blurry. I'm scared he's actually going to kill me, and then the door swings open and in walks Camden.

"Get your hands off her!"

The shock of seeing him has David releasing me. "Fuck you!" he barks. "You always wanted my wife, didn't you?" He stalks over to Camden and punches him in the face. Camden stumbles back slightly but quickly gets himself together, refusing to take the bait. David's about to punch him again when Felix screams, "Mommy!" and runs down the hall and into my arms.

Camden glances at Felix, and David uses the moment to sucker punch him again.

"Stop it!" I yell.

"Get the fuck out of my house!" David barks at Camden.

"Mommy, my ear hurts," Felix cries.

"I know, baby. Did Daddy give you medicine?"

He shakes his head.

"Why didn't you give him medicine?"

"You're raising this kid to be a damn brat. He wouldn't stop crying all fucking night."

"Because he's in pain!" I hiss. "What the hell is wrong with you?"

"It was late. I wasn't running out with him in the middle of the night."

"I'm done with you," I say, knowing this conversation is pointless. I never should've left Felix with David. He's a selfish asshole and has no idea how to parent.

"You're not taking my son with that piece of shit!" David booms, trying to block me from leaving.

"Yes, I am. Now move. I need to get my son some medicine. He's got to be in excruciating pain right now."

"You're not—"

"Yes, she is," a masculine voice says. Camden's huge-ass bodyguard, along with two other guys, just as big, step in and surround David. "Go ahead, Layla. Take your boy home."

"Thank you," I say, scurrying out the door with Camden and Felix.

"Are you okay?" I ask Felix once we're in the car and Camden's driver has taken off. "How does your ear feel?"

"It hurts," he says softly. "Daddy yelled at me and wouldn't fix it. I wasn't trying to be a brat." His eyes turn watery, and he looks down in shame.

I glance at Camden for a moment. His jaw is locked, and his fists are clenched in his lap. I want to thank him for stopping David, for not fighting back, for having his security as backup, which I had no idea about, but right now, I need to focus on Felix.

"You are not a brat," I tell him, pulling him into my lap. "You're in pain, and your dad should've given you medicine. I'm so sorry I wasn't here." I hug him tightly. "I'm going to make you feel better." He nods into my neck and then rests his head on my shoulder.

Since it's Sunday, and his doctor's office isn't open, we go straight to the pediatric wing at the hospital. Thankfully, it's not too busy, and they can get us in quickly. Since he's being checked out, they have Felix change into a hospital gown, and then the nurse comes in to take his blood pressure and temperature.

When she lifts the sleeve, I notice a large purple mark on Felix's arm. "How did you get this?" I ask. I didn't notice it before because he was wearing a long-sleeved shirt.

"Daddy got mad at me."

I hear Camden curse under his breath.

"Are you saying Daddy did this to you?" I confirm.

"I was crying, and he got mad."

While the nurse finishes up, I pull my phone out and text Camden: **Can you find a police officer, please? I want to file charges, and I don't want to wait.**

I'm done. I never should've let David get away with raping me. I tried to take the easy way out, the route that wouldn't make waves and put Felix in the middle of a nasty custody battle. Never in a million years did I imagine he would hurt our son, but he has. And now I'm fucking done. I don't care what it takes. He's never taking Felix again. Not as long as I'm alive.

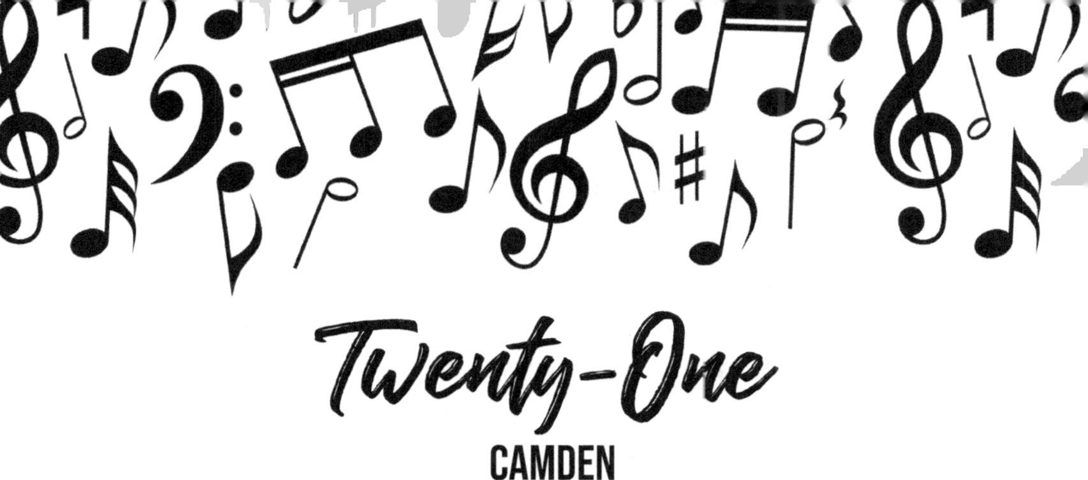

Twenty-One

CAMDEN

Layla: SOS my house

IT'S BEEN YEARS SINCE I'VE GOTTEN AN SOS TEXT FROM LAYLA. I'M SITTING IN MY PARENTS' LIVING ROOM, talking to them about everything that's happened, but the second I see it, I shoot up, telling them I have to go. Since Layla's house is only a couple of blocks away, it doesn't take long to get there. When I do, I find her sitting on her front steps with her head in her hands, her body shaking.

"Hey, what happened?" I ask, sitting next to her. "Where's Felix?"

She looks up, her tear-filled eyes meeting mine. Her face is splotchy, and she has tear stains running down her cheeks. It's only been a few hours since I last saw her, and I already miss the hell out of her.

"He's in bed asleep. The attorney said he can file for emergency custody tomorrow morning, but he doesn't believe I'll get it. He said the judge usually needs more than that to take away a parent's rights. It's going to take time to build a case."

"More than someone leaving bruises on his son's body and his ex-wife's throat?"

"Apparently so," she chokes out. "I don't know what I'm going to do. Something is wrong with him. He's snapped. And I'm so afraid he's going to take it out on Felix. He already has! The bruise on his arm. The way he emotionally fucked with him." She looks over at me with such fear, I want to kill David with my bare hands.

"I can't let him take him," she says softly. "We have joint custody. He gets him every other weekend and every Wednesday. I can't let it happen."

"So what are you going to do?"

"I'm going to run."

"What?" I ask in shock. She can't just leave. Where would she go? What would she do? "You can't do that. You'd be committing a felony, and if he ever found you, he'd get Felix."

"Then I'll make sure he never finds me," she says, conviction stitched into every word. Her phone that's sitting on her lap beeps three times, but she ignores it. "I already fucked up once letting my son go with him. I should've run with him after David raped me. I was scared, and I fucked up, but I won't make that mistake again. I won't leave my son with that man ever again."

"You didn't fuck up. You made the best choice you could in a shitty-ass situation."

Wordlessly, she stands and heads inside her house, and I follow her in, my mind reeling with everything. While she goes about pulling out some luggage from a hall closet, I pull my phone out and text my dad. I don't want to say anything to her because I don't know for sure, but one of his best friends is actually a judge here, and if anyone can help us, it's him. I quickly explain what her attorney said and what she's planning to do since he already knows what happened with Layla and Felix earlier today—I told him when I went over there for dinner, needing to talk to someone about it all.

Dad: Give me a few minutes.

I put my phone away and follow Layla into her bedroom as she pulls clothes out from her drawers. I want to stop her, tell her to think about this, but I don't because I know she feels completely helpless and is in mama bear mode. I've seen my mom in it many times over the years, and there's no arguing with her when she's like that. Based on the determined look in Layla's features, I imagine it's the same for her.

Beep. Beep. Beep.

When her phone sounds again, Layla stops what she's doing and goes to the bathroom. I don't know why I follow her, but I do. It's not like she's going to disappear right this second. She presses a button on a gadget that's sitting on the sink, and a couple of pills drop into her hand.

"What's that?"

"My mom bought it for my birthday," she says. "I have a horrible memory and forget to take my pills, so it's synced with my phone to remind me. It'll keep going off every few minutes until I take them." She fills her cup with water and downs the pills. "It's my birth control and an iron supplement because I'm at risk for anemia."

I press the button, but nothing happens.

"It's not a candy dispenser," she says with a laugh. "It only dispenses when it's supposed to."

"What do you do when you're traveling?"

"You can select the days you're traveling, and it will dispense it ahead of time so you can take them with you. The app will still remind me."

"That's pretty cool. My grandma is always complaining about my grandpa forgetting to take his heart medication. I should buy him one."

My phone vibrates in my pocket, so I pull it out.

Dad: Daniel said to call him. I can't make any promises.

I click on the number he's included and walk out of the room, so Layla won't hear me. After a couple of rings, he answers. "Camden, how are you, son?"

Daniel Maxwell was my family's attorney in LA before he moved to the East Coast and eventually became one of the most powerful judges in New York. I'm not sure how it all works, but from what I've heard over the years, he's really high up there.

"I'm okay. Just...fuck. I'm assuming my dad filled you in?"

"He did. I normally don't do this sort of thing, but I have a soft spot for women in abusive relationships, especially when children are involved. Send me over the police reports filed and all of her information and give me twenty-four hours."

"I CAN'T BELIEVE YOU DID THIS," LAYLA SAYS TO ME, TEARS BRIMMING IN HER EYES. "THANK YOU!" SHE wraps her arms around me and hugs me tightly, and I breathe in her comforting scent. "I don't know how I'll ever repay you."

"There's nothing to repay." I tilt her chin up and kiss her supple lips. "I would do anything for you and Felix."

More tears fill her eyes. "Thank you."

I take her hand in mine, and we walk out of the courthouse. Daniel came through big time. Not only was Layla given emergency temporary custody, but David has to attend six months of anger management and therapy, and the only way he can see Felix is with a social worker for supervised visits, one day a week in a public place. The judge will reassess after the six months are up and he's met with a court-appointed psychologist to be reevaluated. He's also not allowed to go within five hundred feet of Layla. And all of that was done in seventy-two hours before David could pick up Felix for his scheduled night.

"I really hope David gets the help he needs," she says as we step outside and walk over to my waiting car. "We never had the perfect relationship, but he wasn't always like this."

I love and hate that she's defending him. The fact that she sees the best in everyone and, despite the shit he's pulled, wants him to get better shows what a good person she is. But it also makes me feel like a shitty person because I'd rather David be given a death sentence for what he's done to her than a second chance.

"I have to get Felix from school and take him to his first dance class, but do you want to come over for dinner afterward?"

"Sounds good to me." I give her a playful wink that has her lighting up. The past few days, while we waited to see how it would all pan out, were stressful for Layla. She wasn't her usual bubbly, carefree self, so it's good to see her smiling again.

"Actually, you should invite your parents too," she adds. "I really want to thank your dad for calling the judge."

"I'll see what they're up to."

"Oh! And I should invite my mom. She's been so worried."

I laugh. "Layles, you realize you have a four-person table, right?"

She pouts adorably.

"How about we go out to dinner? Invite everyone."

She gnaws on her lip for a second. "Should we be celebrating the fact that Felix won't see his dad but once a week for only two hours?"

God, I love this woman. "I wouldn't look at it like we're celebrating the downfall of David, but more of the fact that you've made it through this shitty, dark part of your life. You deserve to feel safe and not have to worry about what he'll do. This outcome doesn't happen often enough for women in your shoes, so it's okay for you to celebrate that you now feel safe once again."

"I hate that," she says. "That this happens to women and children every day, and they don't get the same outcome. If I were rich, I would pay to help every one of them I could."

Her words give me an idea...but I don't mention it out loud.

"So dinner?"

"Yeah, that sounds good."

After telling Layla I'll pick them up later, I go by my parents' place and tell them the outcome and invite them to dinner. Then I head to the hotel to get changed. The guys are there, hanging out and discussing their plans for the night. When I tell them about Layla, they take it as an invite and agree they want to see for themselves that she and Felix are okay.

"Can we discuss finding a place?" Declan asks. "I'm sick of living out of my suitcase. We're finally off tour, and I feel like we're still on the road."

I roll my eyes at his dramatics. We're currently residing in a hotel room that's bigger than most people's homes in New York, but I also get it.

"You guys are still good with living in New York?" If they're not, I'll figure it out, even if it means flying back and forth.

"I assumed this was a permanent decision," Braxton says. "Is there any chance Layla would be willing to move to LA?"

"Willing? Maybe. But can she? No. David still has rights to Felix. She has to be here for him to see Felix every week."

"Then it looks like we'll need to find a place to live." Braxton shrugs. "You still want to live together, or are you thinking about getting your own place since you're now a family man and all?"

I hadn't actually thought about that, but while we're on the subject..."Your shit in LA had Layla asking if I've had threesomes." Braxton barks out a laugh, but I don't join in. "Maybe it would be for the best if I find my own place."

"What?" Declan asks. "We've always lived together. We write together, make music together..."

"That won't change. But Brax isn't wrong. My endgame is Layla and Felix, and I don't want to cramp everyone's style by bringing them around. I guess I could go to her house, but..."

"We get it," Braxton says. "That was her house with her ex. No man wants to fuck a woman in the same bed she was fucking another man."

"I wasn't thinking about that, but now I am. Thanks," I say dryly.

Braxton shrugs.

"I'm getting ahead of myself. If Layla and I decide to one day live together, we can discuss the details then. For now, there's no reason we can't get a place together."

"Whatever you want, man," Braxton says. "You know we have your back." Declan and Gage both nod in agreement.

"All right, then it's settled. We need to find a place to live here."

"It'll have to be after we get back, though," Declan points out. "We leave for Florida in two days."

"What?" And then I remember. "Shit, we have the Disney parade. I completely forgot." We were invited by Disney to be part of their yearly Christmas parade. Ride on the float and sing a mix of some of our kid-friendly songs and the few Christmas songs we put out last year. Since it's recorded prior to Christmas, it's taking place this coming weekend.

"You've been a little preoccupied, but yeah, Jill sent us the info this morning."

While the guys are sitting around bullshitting, I call the real estate agent my family uses in New York to let her know what we're looking for. She says she'll get working on it and have places for us to see when we get back from Florida.

As we're hanging up, I get a text from Layla: **Felix is refusing to go to dance class. His dad made him feel like shit about it when he was with him over the weekend, and the other boy who attends the class isn't here, so it's only girls. We'll be home whenever you're ready to pick us up.**

Like hell he's going to give up what he loves because of that asshole.

Me: Text me the address, and I'll be right there. Don't leave yet.

"Hey guys, how would you feel about going to dance class with Felix?"
They all glance up at me with different levels of confusion on their faces.

"His dad gave him shit, and now he doesn't want to go."

"Fuck his dad," Gage says, standing. "I'm in."

"Same," Braxton and Declan both agree.

Since we don't know the situation we're heading into, we take security along with us. When we arrive at the studio, Felix and Layla are sitting inside, where the parents sit and watch.

"Hey, heard someone is starting dance classes today," I say, stepping in front of them.

Felix looks up, shocked to see me here. "I don't know," he says with a frown marring his features. "My dad said boys don't—"

"Your dad is wrong," Gage cuts in, making his presence known. Felix glances over and sees Gage, Braxton, and Declan all standing in front of him. "There's nothing wrong with a man dancing, and this class looks fun as hell. So if you don't want to go, fine. But we're going."

Layla's eyes go wide.

"You guys are going to dance class?" Felix asks.

"Yep, you coming or what?" Braxton asks, extending his fist.

Felix pops off the chair and fist-bumps him. "Yeah, I'm coming."

When the five of us walk into the studio, we garner the attention of everyone, including the instructor, who eyes us curiously. "Are you in a band?" she asks.

"Yep. Raging Chaos," I tell her. "My friend Felix here is new, and since he's the only boy, he asked us to join. Would you mind?"

She smiles softly. "Not at all. Welcome to beginners hip-hop dance."

"HOLY SHIT," DECLAN SAYS, WIPING THE BEADS OF SWEAT FROM HIS FOREHEAD WITH A PAPER TOWEL. "That was a damn workout."

"Yeah, it was," Gage agrees, still panting like he just ran cross-country.

"I had no idea dancing could use so many damn muscles," Braxton adds, flinching in pain.

"That was so much fun!" Felix says, completely unaffected. "Can we do it again?"

Layla laughs. "Yes, next week."

Since we came in separate vehicles, Layla and Felix head home, and the guys and I go back to our place so we can shower and get ready. When five o'clock rolls around, I head back out to pick them up. We're meeting everyone at Maya's, a Mexican restaurant Layla said Felix loves. I offered to pick up her mom as well, but she said she's riding with my parents.

It's nice going out to dinner in New York. Almost no security is needed.

We get a private room since there's a shit ton of us, but it's not like in LA, where you need one so people will leave you alone. It's a different vibe here, and I can see why my dad moved here years ago, leaving LA for good.

"Where are we all sitting?" Mom asks as the guys walk in.

"Oh, shit," Layla mutters.

"What?" I ask, confused.

"I didn't know they were coming to dinner. I didn't even—" Before she can finish what she's saying, Kaylee strolls through the door, running straight into Braxton.

"Oh, shit," I mimic.

"Oh," Kaylee gasps, her eyes going wide. Everyone turns to face them, no doubt holding their breath and waiting to see what'll happen. They haven't been in the same room in years, not since everything went down.

Kaylee's eyes meet Layla's, and Layla cuts across the room. "I didn't know. I'm sorry."

"It's okay. I can go," Kaylee says.

"Or you can stay," Layla offers.

"I can go," Braxton jumps in, refusing to look at Kaylee.

"Or you both can stay," Layla says.

"No, seriously, I can go," Kaylee insists. "I actually need to get home and pack."

"Where are you going?" Layla asks in shock.

"LA."

"What?" Layla shrieks. "Why?"

"The PR company that hired me has me going on tour with Sam York as his publicist." Sam York is a huge musician, sings mostly pop, and he's also a huge asshole with an even bigger ego.

Braxton snorts. "Of course they did."

Kaylee glares at Braxton, but as if remembering she's the reason for his bitterness, her features quickly soften, and she doesn't respond. "Anyway, I have like two days to pack, but I wanted to tell you in person and hug you." She wraps her arms around Layla, who sniffles in response.

"I'm going to miss you so much."

"I'll only be gone for a few months, and then I'll be back."

"You're going to be amazing!" Layla hugs her again.

"Thank you."

After Kaylee gives Felix and Layla's mom a quick hug, she takes off, and everyone finds their seats, none of us mentioning the huge elephant that still seems to be in the room, despite Kaylee leaving. Braxton is quiet for the entire dinner, drinking way too many beers, but everyone else is in good spirits. Layla thanks my dad several times for calling Daniel while he brushes it off like it wasn't a big deal.

"When do you guys leave?" Mom asks while we're eating dessert.

"Friday morning," Declan answers. "I've got my Mickey Mouse ears ready."

Mom snickers.

"Where are you going?" Layla asks me.

"*We're* going to Disney."

She frowns. "We? I can't…Oh, the parade. I forgot about that. I can't go. I actually need to talk to your parents about working for Blackwood."

"What? Why?"

"With David's visitation going down to two hours a week, that leaves me as Felix's only parent."

"And? Single parents work…"

"Yes, but I can't travel. Not without leaving him with my mom, and it's not fair to her to have to watch him all the time."

"*She* would love to watch him any time," Patricia cuts in, raising a single brow.

"And I was actually thinking we could take Felix with us to Disney," I add.

"Disney?" Felix screeches, overhearing. Shit, I thought I was talking low. Note to self: kids have bionic hearing. "I want to go!"

"I would be working," Layla points out.

"And when you're not, we have passes to all the parks."

"I can keep him with me," Bailey offers. "He can watch the parade with me."

"Perfect," I say before Layla can argue.

"And in the future," my mom says, "if Patricia can't keep Felix, he's always welcome at our house. Between Easton and Bailey and me…"

"And me," Phoebe, my younger sister, says.

"You have an entire room of support," I tell Layla, draping my arm around the back of her chair. "We got this."

Twenty-Two

LAYLA

"MY GOD, WOMAN, YOU'RE A WALKING, BREATHING TEMPTATION." CAMDEN EDGES ONTO THE BED, CIRCLING his arms around me and pulling me into his front. "I've been waiting all damn day to be able to touch you." His hand skates down my hip and goes between my legs, spreading my thighs.

We've been in Orlando for three days, and this is the first time we've been alone. The last fifty-plus hours have been a whirlwind of activity. Between the Disney parade on Friday and spending the last two days exploring four parks with a four-year-old who's never been to Disney—along with four grown-ass men who you'd think were four-year-olds—it's been nonstop. Friday night, the guys had a couple of radio interviews to do and got back late, then last night, we got back late from the parks because everyone wanted to watch the fireworks. Felix was tired and cranky from overstimulation and ended up falling asleep in my bed with me both nights. Tonight, though, he's in his own bed, and Camden has apparently snuck into mine.

"Does it bother you that you can't touch me all day because of Felix?" I ask, my insecurities of being a mom sneaking up on me.

"What? No." He turns me over to face him. "Your kid is fucking awesome, Layles. A mini you. I feel like I've gotten to experience my childhood all over again through him."

"Through him, huh?" I laugh. "I'm pretty sure you and the guys have experienced it through yourselves."

He grins, not arguing. "What I'd really like to do right now is experience *you*." He waggles his brows and cups my ass cheeks, pulling me close. His mouth seals over mine, and I groan in need. We've taken up an entire floor at the Disney resort we're staying in, each room having multiple bedrooms. Camden insisted Felix and I have our own room, not wanting to rush him seeing anything between us, for which I appreciate. Felix is going through a lot, and I love that Camden is aware and patient. But right now, I really want to experience him as well.

I turn over onto my back, and Camden climbs over me, deepening the kiss. His tongue delves past my parted lips, and his knees separate my legs, giving him access to my center.

"Fuck, you taste good," he murmurs against my mouth before moving to my ear. "I need to be inside you now." Our clothes come off, and once we're both naked, he dips his fingers into me to make sure I'm wet and ready—spoiler alert: I am.

Getting up on his haunches, he spreads my thighs wider, his thumb finding the spot that will bring me pleasure. He massages it with slow strokes while his other hand palms my breast, pinching my nipple.

When I moan in pleasure, he stops what he's doing. "I need a picture," he says, grabbing my camera from the nightstand and turning it on me. The camera clicks on, and he takes several pictures of me. "Do you have any idea how sexy you look like this? Your hair splayed out across your pillow, your cheeks flush. Your nipples hard and begging to be touched." He reaches out with the hand not holding the camera and pinches one. "I'm the luckiest guy in the fucking world." His words are like liquid heat straight to my core. I've never had a guy look at me like Camden does, like I'm everything he could ever want or need.

He sets the camera back down and then continues to stroke my clit and play with my breasts until I'm screaming out his name in pure ecstasy as my orgasm rips through me, sending shock waves through my body.

"Fuck, I love when you scream my name," he murmurs. Gripping the backs of my thighs, he enters me, his thick, hard length filling me to the hilt. His palms land on either side of my head, and his mouth crashes down on mine in a bruising kiss as he pulls back and thrusts roughly into me.

When I gasp into his mouth, he stills in place, removing his mouth from mine. "I'm sorry, shit. I didn't mean to be that rough. I wasn't thinking."

He's about to pull out, but before he can, I wrap my legs around him, holding him to me.

"Stop. You're good," I tell him. "I won't break."

He nods once, but he's obviously not convinced because instead of continuing the way he was, he's now slowed down.

"Cam, please," I beg, palming his face so he looks at me. He shakes his head, and I sigh, hating that he's holding back. Not wanting to ruin the moment, though, I let it go.

His mouth closes over mine, and he makes love to me slow and sweet. My climax builds higher and higher, and only once I've found my release does he let go, spilling himself into me.

"I can't get enough of you," he says, dropping kisses onto my lips, chin, neck..."Every time I look at you, I can't believe I finally get you all to myself, all the time."

"Well, not all the time," I joke. "Tomorrow morning, we have to go home to separate places."

"For now," he murmurs, locking his mouth with mine before I can ask what he means by that. Our kiss quickly turns heated, which results in us doing it all over again, leaving me sated and boneless and so damn happy.

"CAN WE GET A BIG TREE LIKE AT DISNEY?" FELIX ASKS, STRETCHING HIS HANDS OUT AS FAR AS THEY CAN go.

"We can get a tree that fits in our living room."

He pouts. "We need a bigger living room."

Declan laughs from his seat on the plane. "Yeah, Layla, next time, make sure the living room fits a Disney-sized Christmas tree."

"We're looking at places," Braxton adds. "We'll make sure the living room is big enough, then you can have two trees."

"Yes!" Felix whoops. "Can we put a million candy canes on it?"

"Of course, little dude," Declan says.

From the second the guys met Felix, they've taken on the role of pseudo uncles. Anything he wants, they give him, and Felix has quickly caught on. I've had to stop them from being had by my four-year-old on several occasions.

"We'll see," I cut in, giving them a side-eye that they ignore. "I didn't know you were looking for a place," I say to Camden.

"Can't live in a hotel forever." He shrugs.

"So you're going to be living here?"

"Where else would I be?" he asks, giving me a confused look.

"I don't know...LA."

He quirks a brow. "Are you moving there?"

"You know I can't," I mutter. While the court didn't mandate me to live in New York, I have to be available every Wednesday evening for David to meet with Felix so they can have dinner together.

"Then this is where we'll be living," Camden says like it's a done deal.

"And the guys are okay with it?"

"Yep, it's home. We still have our house over there for when we need to be there, but we can do everything we need to do here."

"Can we get a tree when we get home?" Felix asks. "It's almost Christmas. They're all going to be gone."

"We'll see," I say.

"That means no." He pouts, making the guys laugh.

"No, it doesn't," I argue.

"You always say it when you mean no." He crosses his arms over his chest and sinks into his seat, his sad face deepening.

"Well, if you act like that, it *will* be a no."

With a huff, he pulls out his iPad and sticks his earbuds in to watch something. Within minutes, his eyes close.

"Thank you for this weekend." I lean in and kiss the crook of Camden's neck. He smells like the comfort of home, and I wish I could bottle it up and keep it with me for when he's not around.

"You don't have to thank me." He tilts my face and kisses me on the lips. "Since Felix is off school today and we'll be home in the early afternoon, why don't we take the SUV and get you guys a tree?"

My heart skips a beat. "That would be amazing. Thank—"

"No thanking me," he says, silencing me with a kiss.

When we get home, the guys go back to the hotel while Camden joins Felix and me. Felix doesn't know we're stopping to get a tree, so when we pull up to the tree lot, he squeals in excitement.

"Can I get one for my room too?" he asks, eyeing the small trees that are only like two feet tall.

"Let's focus on getting the one for the living room first."

"Fine." He runs through the trees, stopping at each one and explaining why it's the best tree. When we finally decide on one—and Camden sneaks in the mini tree—the lot guys load it up so we can take it home. Since it needs a few days to drop before we can decorate it, we order in and put a movie on to watch after Camden sets it up.

Felix is out halfway through the movie, and Camden and I spend the remainder of the movie cuddling and flirting. I want to invite him to spend the night, but I also know we need to take things slow when it comes to that, for Felix's sake.

"We're going to be working on a couple of songs tomorrow in the studio," Camden says when I walk him out. "Can you come by?"

"Of course." I give him a chaste kiss. "Text me when you get home."

About twenty minutes later, my phone dings. When I open it, I expect to find a text from Camden, but instead, it's from unknown. There's a picture of Camden, Felix, and me bringing in the Christmas tree. Only the picture has been marked up with a huge red X over Camden.

Only one person would send something like this, so instead of responding, I save the picture and block the text. I'll show it to Camden tomorrow to see if we should report it so it's documented. At the courthouse, David was glaring daggers at me but was smart enough to keep his mouth shut. I knew he wouldn't stay quiet for long.

I'm about to click out of my messages when it dings again...another picture. Only this one has me smiling as I take in a bare-chested, smirking

Camden. **One day, instead of sending you pics of me in bed, you'll be next to me. Sweet dreams, Shutterbug.**

And with the image of him in my head, I fall asleep, pushing the thought of David from my mind—even if deep down my gut tells me this isn't close to being over.

She's like taking a hit of the strongest drug
She enters my veins, there to stay
I'm addicted, can't stay away

I STAND IN THE CORNER OF THE STUDIO, MY CAMERA IN MY HAND, FROZEN IN PLACE, AS I LISTEN TO Camden belt the words to a new song in the sound room. He told me he wrote a new song, but he didn't mention it was about me. And as I watch, with Camden's eyes locked on mine, heat radiating off his every word, the apex of my legs throbs in want, in need. If we were alone, I would be on him, begging him to be in me.

Earl—their producer who has flown to New York to work with them on recording their next album—presses a button and says, "Fuck yeah, that's what I'm talking about," but Camden isn't looking at him or really paying him any attention because he's zoned in on me, eye-fucking me. Liquid desire pools between my legs, and my blood boils like I'm on fire. My heart thrums in my chest.

"You wrote that about me," I breathe when he stalks over and pulls me into his arms.

"Damn near everything I do is about you," Camden murmurs, capturing my lower lip between his teeth. "Do you like it...the song?" He swipes his tongue along the seam of my mouth, sending a bolt of electricity straight to my core.

"I love it." I run my fingers through his hair and brush my lips against his. "And...I love you."

His eyes go wide at my confession. I didn't plan to say those words, but I one-hundred-percent mean them.

"Need ten," Camden chokes out, lifting me into his arms. My legs wrap around his torso, and his strong, supple lips collide with my own. I faintly hear one of the guys laughing, and I think Braxton makes a joke about being a minute-man, but I'm too caught up in Camden to really know.

The second we're alone, our clothes come flying off, both of us with one goal in mind: Camden inside me. Once we're both naked, he pushes me against the wall and devours my mouth. His hands go to my breasts, caressing them. Mine go to his dick, stroking it.

But that's not enough. I need more.

Without thought, I drop to my knees, ready to take him in my mouth, but before I can, he steps back.

"What's wrong?" I ask, glancing up at him.

"We should wait...until we're at your place...or mine."

"What?" I reach for him, but he shakes his head and pulls me up.

"We only have a few more hours. Afterward, we can go to your place before you have to pick up Felix."

I'm so confused. We were just ripping each other's clothes off, and now he's practically pushing me away.

And then it hits me...Every time we've had sex, it's been with him on top, or the one time in the shower, he let me ride him. He never lets me go down on him, and he never takes me from behind...because I told him what David did to me.

"Is it because you don't want me the way David had me or because you're afraid I'll freak out?"

His eyes widen slightly before they go soft. "I want to make sure you're comfortable. I don't want anything we do to trigger what he did...like the day on the helicopter."

I close the distance between us and, with one hand, cup his face. The other, I palm his now semi-soft length. "I can't promise anything we do won't trigger what he did. I don't know how it all works in my head, but I don't want what he did to affect us. I want to taste you, feel you, *love you.* I want you to fuck me every way possible. I want every bad memory with him to be erased and replaced with amazing memories with you. I want to be in the here and now with you. We already missed so much time. I just want to be with you."

"Fuck, I love you so damn much," Camden says before his mouth crashes down on mine. We kiss passionately for several minutes as I stroke his dick, getting it hard again. Then breaking the kiss, I drop back down onto my knees and take him into my mouth.

"Holy shit," he groans, his palm slapping the wall behind me as I go as deep as I can, licking and sucking on his velvety smooth flesh. His other hand goes to my hair, but instead of pulling it, he runs his fingers gently through it.

I have to admit, I was a little worried about how I would feel being in this position, but as I glance up at Camden, my mouth wrapped around his cock, and our eyes meet, I know I have nothing to be worried about because no matter what we're doing, Camden makes sure I'm comfortable.

"C'mere, baby," he says, pulling me up. My mouth pops off the head, and I pout because I didn't get to finish.

Camden chuckles. "I love your mouth on me, but I really want to be inside you." His lips capture my own, and he lifts me into his arms, pushing me against the wall. My legs wrap around his hips, and he enters me in one fluid motion. With his mouth never leaving mine, he works me over, hitting my clit in the most delicious way. That, combined with the way he's thrusting into me, hard and deep, sends me over the edge, taking Camden with me.

"Jesus," I mutter breathlessly, breaking our kiss and setting my forehead against his. "Every time I'm with you, I just want more and more."

"Well, that's good," he murmurs. "Because my hope is that you'll want me for the rest of our lives."

My eyes dart up, my head backing up slightly to meet his. "What...What do...?" I can't even finish my thoughts, my question. "The rest of our lives?" I finally say, swallowing the lump of emotion.

"That's my hope," he says, pressing his lips to mine. "Don't worry, Layles. I'm not proposing...yet. But yes, I want you forever."

His confession should scare me since I just got out of a crappy situation, but it doesn't. Instead, it feels as though the looming darkness has cracked open, exposing the most beautiful, bright light over us.

"Forever." I find myself smiling at the thought of spending every day for the rest of my life with Camden. "That sounds really freaking nice."

Twenty-Three

LAYLA

Camden: You, me, date tonight. Wear a dress.

Camden: And before you try to argue, your mom is keeping Felix overnight and taking him to school in the morning. She offered.

Me: Sounds good.

"WHAT HAS YOU SMILING?" BAILEY ASKS, TAKING A BITE OF HER SALAD. WE'VE BEEN WORKING ON THE YouTube channel all day, so she ordered in lunch so we could eat and work.

"Your brother." I grin when she playfully scrunches her nose up in disgust. "He's apparently taking me on a date tonight."

"Nice. Where are you going?"

"I don't know." I shrug. "But Felix is staying with my mom overnight." I waggle my brows, and Bailey fake gags.

"You guys are so sweet, it makes me sick."

"Like you and Cynthia aren't sweet?"

"Not like that. She's chill."

"Whatever." I roll my eyes. "I need to pick up something to wear and new lingerie. Want to join me?"

"Sure." She tosses her empty salad bowl into the trash. "I'm always down to shop."

While we're at the store, Camden texts to let me know he'll pick me up at my mom's since I have to drop Felix off there.

I end up getting ready at my mom's—going with a long-sleeved olive-green sweater dress with the front cut low and buttons running down the sides, paired with high heeled boots. It's recently snowed, and while I want to look good, I don't want to die. My hair is down in long waves, and my makeup is on point. Underneath, I'm wearing a new bra and panty set that is going to have Camden drooling when he sees them on me later.

"You look gorgeous," Camden says, stepping around the corner and startling me. I hadn't realized he was already here. He's dressed in a pair of dark denim jeans and a long-sleeved beige sweater with brown leather boots. His hair is gelled back, taming his usual messy do, and his facial hair is trimmed short. My thighs clench, imagining what his face will feel like between my legs later.

"Hey, bud, doesn't your mom look beautiful?"

"Yeah," Felix agrees, nodding.

"But I think she's missing something. What do you think, Felix?"

"Yeah." He giggles. "She's missing something."

"I am?" I glance down. "My jacket's by the door…"

When I look up, Felix holds a black box wrapped with gold ribbon and a large shiny bow on top. "For you, Mommy. I helped Cam pick it out."

I take it from him and unwrap and open the box, and nestled inside is a thin white-gold necklace with two charms hanging from it. The first is a camera charm—inside the lens is a beautiful sparkling diamond—and the other is a circle charm with a quote on it that reads: *She believed she could, so she did.*

"You guys," I breathe, looking up at Camden and Felix. "You got this for me?" I ask Felix, who nods proudly.

"I told Cam your favorite thing is a camera."

"Thank you, sweetheart." I pull him into a hug and kiss his cheek. "I love it."

I stand, and Camden takes the necklace from me. Lifting my hair, he puts it on me, then leans in and whispers, "So you always remember what your dream is."

"Thank you." I turn around and kiss him on the corner of his mouth. "This is the most thoughtful gift I've ever been given."

After saying bye to my mom and reminding Felix to behave, we take off to dinner in the SUV with Camden's driver driving us. On the way there, Camden and I can't keep our hands off of each other. By the time we arrive at the restaurant, the only thing I'm hungry for is Camden, but apparently, he has a hell of a lot more restraint than me because when I mention that, he simply chuckles and tells me he's taking me to dinner.

We're escorted into the restaurant by his security and brought back to a private room, where there's a comfy-looking circular booth with a round metal grill-looking thing in the center. Camden helps me remove my coat, then hands mine and his to the hostess, thanking her.

He has me slide in first, and then he slides in next to me, his hand coming down on my thigh. Pushing my dress up, he glides his hand over my flesh while the server introduces herself and explains that this is Korean barbecue and we'll be cooking the food ourselves. I've never done this before, but

Camden says he's had it a few times while they were on tour, so he orders for us both. The server lights the grill and then lets us know the food will be ready shortly. After she drops off our drinks, we're left alone.

"Thank you for my necklace," I say again, needing him to know how much the simple gift means to me.

"It looks perfect on you," he says, leaning over and kissing the crook of my neck. When he trails his nose along my flesh, I squirm in my seat.

"You can't do that." I groan. "I want you so badly, and you're making us eat instead."

When I pout half-playfully, Camden chuckles. "We have all night together, Shutterbug. I got us a room, and I plan to spend as much of the night as I can inside you."

The server drops off our food, explains each item, and then leaves us to ourselves.

"You're going to love this," Camden says, dropping a bunch of meat and veggies onto the grill. I watch as he cooks them, and once they're done, he captures a piece of meat between his chopsticks and brings it to my lips. The meat has a sweet taste to it and is full of flavor.

"What do you think?" he asks, taking a bite himself.

"Delicious."

The meal is spent with Camden feeding me, and once we've both had enough, he gets the check so we can move on to the next part of our evening.

Of course, the room he's booked is the penthouse suite, so we have the floor to ourselves. After he lets his security know we're good for the night, we head up to the room. Champagne and strawberries are waiting for us, and when I ask what the occasion is, he says, "There isn't one." He pops the top of the bottle and pours us each a glass. "My goal in life is to spoil you and Felix. To show you both every chance I get how special you are to me."

"If that's your goal, then you've already accomplished it," I tell him, taking a sip of my champagne.

"No, I haven't. I've only just gotten started." He sets our glasses down and encircles his arms around my waist. His mouth connects with mine, and the champagne and strawberries are forgotten as we get lost in each other.

When he unzips my dress, and I shrug out of it, letting it drop to the ground, Camden takes a step back, noticing my cream-color floral lace bra and panties complete with garters.

"Is this new?" he asks, licking his lips, his eyes locked on my body.

"Bought it today, just for you."

"Fuck yes," he growls, lifting and carrying me to the bed. He hovers above me, kissing along the seam of the delicate material. "Where did you buy these at?"

I quirk a brow. "Umm…why?"

"So I can buy you more because I'm about to rip these right off your fucking body."

Before I can protest, his mouth captures mine, the kiss so consuming that my mind goes blank. My only thought is that I don't care how Camden gets my lingerie off as long as he gets it off quick and gets inside me.

Twenty-Four

CAMDEN

social worker, walk with Felix to her vehicle. Since David can't be near Layla, the social worker will be picking him up from the house and driving him to meet with David every Wednesday. He's allowed two hours with him at a restaurant or park...somewhere public, and then she'll drive Felix back home.

"The social worker will be with him the entire time," I assure her, massaging her shoulders to try to calm her down. Once they've driven off, she sighs and walks inside.

I imagine this will be the longest three hours of her life, so when we're inside, I order us dinner and ask her to show me some of the video footage she's gotten so far, knowing when she's discussing videography, she's in her element and will be thoroughly distracted.

We spend the entire time Felix is gone looking over the footage—and I have to say, I'm impressed. I knew she had raw talent, but her vision for the channel and music video already goes beyond my expectations. As we're discussing our upcoming schedule and some of the shots she'd like to get, the door swings open, and Felix runs inside, his smile bright and excited.

"Daddy got me the best present ever!" he yells. "A PlayStation!"

"Wow," Layla says, sighing in relief that it seemed to go okay. "Where is it?"

"At his house. He said I get it when I go over there."

Beatrice walks in just in time to hear what he says and frowns.

"When can I go to Dad's?" Felix asks, his eyes begging.

"I'm not sure," Layla says, glancing at Beatrice.

"Hey, little man. Why don't we go play in your room? You can show me your Nintendo Switch."

"Okay." He shrugs, easily distracted.

We hang out upstairs, playing a few different games until Layla joins us. She's quiet, not wanting to say anything in front of Felix. I know she's worried, though, because she gnaws on her lip constantly, and I get it. It's clear what

David is doing. Felix is young and has a short memory. He's replacing the bad moments with the possibility of good ones while buying his trust. It's a shitty thing to do, and it doesn't surprise me that he's stooped to that level.

"Beatrice said she can't do anything about what David said," Layla says once Felix is asleep and we're on the couch, just the two of us. "He can tell him anything he wants as long as it isn't harmful. Saying he bought him something and that he'll get it once he can go over to his house isn't technically a lie. But she did say she'd add it to her report in case it's relevant later." She releases a harsh breath. "It just sucks because I know what he's doing, and there's nothing I can do about it. I feel so helpless."

"You're not helpless," I tell her, encircling my arms around her. "You're doing the best you can in a shitty situation. Many women in your shoes wouldn't have left him, filed for divorce, and then pressed charges. Every day, too many women stay in an abusive relationship out of fear of what will happen, scared for their kids. You're strong, and you have a good support system. All you can do is take it one day, one week at a time."

She nods against my chest, and I kiss the top of her head. "I was thinking about something you said before."

She looks up at me. "What is that?"

"About how many women have been hurt by their husbands, and more times than not, nothing happens to them. Every year, the guys and I donate to various charities, but I was thinking, what if we start one of our own instead of donating this year? One that focuses on helping women who have been in your situation but don't have the resources you have to get the help they need."

She sits up, her eyes locking with mine. "Are you serious? That would be amazing. You should've seen the horrible things I read when I was researching how many women every day are raped and abused by their husbands, and nothing happens."

"I was thinking you could be the spokesperson for it. Work with the organizer. We could host an annual charity benefit to raise money on top of what we donate."

Tears prick her eyes, and even though I know they're because she's happy, I still hate to see them. "I would love to," she says, wrapping her arms around me for a hug. "Thank you."

When she pulls back, she wipes her eyes and glances around the room.

"I'm thinking about moving," she says, shocking the hell out of me.

"Really?"

"Yeah, this place feels tainted." She means this is where David raped her, and it's hard to be here while trying to move on. "I think I'm going to look at some places. A fresh start of sorts."

She yawns and lays her head back on my chest, snuggling into my side.

We stay like this for several minutes until I feel her breathing slow, telling me she's fallen asleep. Careful not to wake her, I carry her to her bed, then after checking on Felix, I head out. I'm almost to the door when Layla's phone vibrates on the coffee table. It lights up briefly, and the picture on the screen has me curious.

I tap on the screen to make it light up again and find a picture of us standing on the front steps of Layla's house as Felix leaves. There's a red X over me with an accompanying text: **He doesn't belong, and soon, he'll be removed.**

It's from a random email sent through iMessage, but it's obvious who it is. I look to see if there are any more and find one other from a blocked number. He must've switched to email, so he could make up as many as needed to threaten her...or, I guess, me. I forward both to myself and then send them to Daniel, asking his opinion on the matter. I block the email and bring her phone over to her, so she has it, then head out, setting the alarm and locking up behind me.

As I get into my SUV, I glance back at her place and wonder if maybe Layla would consider moving in with me. We've only been together for a short time, but I'm not about to let some ridiculous societal norm dictate how our relationship flows. I hate having to leave her every night and want the two of them under the same roof as me.

"HOW LONG DID IT TAKE BEFORE YOU AND MOM MOVED IN TOGETHER?"

My dad glances at me, a knowing smirk quirking at the corner of his mouth as he takes a sip of his morning coffee from across the table. "A few months. She was pregnant, and I had bought a place to be near her and Kendall, and you, once you were born. She needed to find a place to live, so I forced her to move in with me." He grins, clearly proud of himself. "Planning to ask Layla to move in with you?"

"Thinking about it." I take a bite of my eggs that Mom made this morning when I showed up. "I need to find a place to live. I was supposed to move with the guys, but she mentioned finding a new place and…" I shrug. "I hate being away from her."

Dad laughs. "I get it. I'm the same way with your mom."

"You going into the studio today?"

"Tomorrow. I have a meeting I need to attend today. Earl said you already have half the tracks recorded. He thinks it might be your best album to date."

I smile at that. Every song, every instrumental, is written by us. From the beginning, we've said we would never sing someone else's words. Our music bleeds through our veins, and every piece of it comes directly from us.

"Although," Dad adds, "he did mention you're getting kind of soft."

I shake my head but can't deny it. "He's not wrong," I admit. "I can't help it. I'm in love."

Mom walks in, her eyes twinkling, having heard what I just said. "And it looks good on you," she says, kissing my cheek and sitting down.

"Gage and Brax have a few tracks they're working on. I'm sure their bitterness and hostility will even my happiness out."

Dad chuckles. "I'm sure it will. I can't wait to hear it all. Jill is planning out your next tour. The goal is to release this album after the holidays and do a summer tour."

The thought of leaving Layla has my stomach knotting, and my dad can obviously sense it because he adds, "We're thinking a shorter tour this year. Two months and only in the US. Felix will be out of school in June, so he and Layla can join you in a few cities."

I nod at that, thankful as hell to have a manager—and a dad—who has my back. Two months might seem like a long time, but our last tour was just over four months long. And as much as I don't want to leave Layla, it's not fair to the guys. They've busted their ass right alongside me every day to make us what we are.

"We're going to be leaving for Big Bear the day after Christmas and spending New Year's there," Mom says. "Patricia is going. You should ask Layla if she and Felix would like to join. Invite the guys. Kendall was supposed to come home for Christmas, but she's met a guy..." She rolls her eyes playfully, used to my sister flitting from one man to another. "She's going to meet us there."

Big Bear Mountain has been a family tradition since my parents first got together. My dad took my mom and Kendall there when Kendall was little, and we have gone every year since. Eventually, they purchased their own cabin that's damn near big enough to fit everyone.

"I'll talk to Layla about it. I'd bet Felix would have a blast on the slopes."

After we finish up breakfast, I meet with the guys and discuss getting my own place with the hope of Layla and Felix joining me. Just as I suspected, they're cool with it.

"Dad mentioned Jill's scheduling our next tour."

Braxton nods. "Figured as much since we're about to put out a new album."

"You going to be okay with leaving Layla?" Declan asks.

"Yeah, I have to be. This is our life."

"True," Declan agrees. "Unless you're thinking maybe this isn't the life for you anymore," he adds, no malice or accusation in his tone.

"This is the life I want. Do I want Layla as well? Yeah, but I can have both. My grandparents and my parents both did. Dad said the tour would be two months instead of the usual four. Would that be okay?" The longer the tour, the more cities we stop in, and the more money we make. Not that we're hurting for cash, but I don't want to be the reason the guys make less.

"Sounds good to me," Declan says.

I glance at Braxton and Gage, who both nod.

"I can't stand being on the road for too long anyway," Braxton says. "Two months sounds good."

We bullshit for a little while, and then I take off to meet with the real estate agent and go over several places. I consider asking Layla first but decide it would be better if I asked her once I found a place. What I can afford and what she can afford are in two different brackets. I don't want her to see the prices. I just want her to see the place I find and hopefully agree to make a home with me.

It takes several hours and virtual tours, but I find it. The home I can see us in. The real estate agent makes a couple of calls, and I get the approval to see it in person this afternoon.

Me: Can your mom watch Felix after school? I need to show you something.

Layla: I can ask.

A few minutes later, she texts back that we're good to go, and I tell her I'll meet her at her mom's.

"Where are we going?" she asks as we walk down the street, our gloved hands threaded together. "It's kind of freaking cold out, you know."

"You'll see. It's not that much farther." We walk a couple more blocks, and once we get to the address the real estate agent gave me, we stop.

Layla glances at me in confusion. "Are we lost? It's going to snow soon." She scrunches her nose up like she always does when she doesn't like something. Layla has never loved the cold or the snow. If it weren't for her having to live near her ex or the fact that I know she loves being close to her mom, I could convince her without any effort to move to the West Coast.

"We're here," I tell her, guiding her up to the gate. It's one of the few homes on the street with an actual wrought-iron gate in the front yard that can be locked. I type in the code the real estate agent gave me and unlock it. The driveway isn't big, but there's a garage on the ground floor with two staircases ascending from each side and meeting in the middle where the front door is. We take the stairs on the left, and once we're at the door, I unlock and open it, exposing the open space.

"Whose house is this?" she asks, stepping inside.

I ignore her question and instead take her through the house. It's four stories, including the garage, with five bedrooms and four bathrooms. A living room and family room, a gym, and an office. There's also a room next to the garage that could easily be turned into a studio.

"This place is gorgeous," Layla says when we get back down to the living room. "Are you thinking about moving here?"

She has her back to me, so I don't answer. That way, she'll turn around. While I wait, I drop onto one knee and pull out the ring I purchased. Bailey thinks I should've taken one step at a time—either propose or ask her to move in—but here's the thing: I want it all. Every-fucking-thing. And I want it with her.

The second she turns around and sees where I am and what I'm holding, she gasps, her hands going to her mouth. "Camden...what are you doing?"

"Hopefully, I'm moving in here with you...as my fiancée. I mean, if you don't like this place, we can find somewhere else—"

Before I can finish my speech, she runs toward me, wraps her arms around my neck, and pulls me up, yelling, "Yes," over and over again. "I want to marry you and live here with you. Yes!"

I kiss her and then take her hand in mine, so I can slide the engagement ring onto her finger.

"I love it," she says, admiring the ring with happy eyes. "And I love you."

Twenty-Four

BONUS SCENE

LAYLA

WHEN CAMDEN SAID HE NEEDED TO SHOW ME SOMETHING, I ASSUMED IT WAS RELATED TO WORK SINCE HE asked me to have my mom watch Felix, so I'm confused when he takes me to a neighborhood not far from where our parents live. When we step up to a gorgeous home with a double staircase leading up to the front door and a for sale sign hanging in the front, my stomach tightens. Camden had mentioned looking for a place to live, but this looks more like a family home than a bachelor pad.

He gives me a tour, and even though the place is empty, I can imagine decorating every room, every wall. The kitchen has been completely renovated with stainless steel everything, and though I suck at cooking, I can imagine baking with Felix in there. The dining room is huge and could easily hold a twelve-person dining table. The bedrooms are all a good size, and the bathrooms are elegant. The master bedroom has a spa tub, and Camden laughs when I jump into it and pretend to swim around.

"This place is gorgeous," I tell him when we get back down to the living room. "Are you thinking about moving here?"

I'm staring out at the fenced-in backyard, imagining a swing set for Felix along with a cute outdoor kitchen/grill on the back patio. We could put a table and chairs out there, and Camden could grill dinner when it's nice out.

I'm lost in my fantasy when I realize Camden never answered my question. I turn to see if he's still in the same room as me and find him down on one knee with an open ring box in his hand. I gasp in shock, my hands going to my mouth. "Camden...what are you doing?"

"Hopefully, I'm moving in here with you...as my fiancée. I mean, if you don't like this place, we can find somewhere else—"

I don't wait for him to finish whatever he was planning to say. I don't need to. I already know my answer. Cutting the distance between us, I encircle my arms around his neck and pull him up, chanting, "Yes," over and over again. "I want to marry you and live here with you. Yes!"

Camden kisses me passionately and then slides the gorgeous engagement ring onto my finger. It has a simple round diamond in the center with several tiny diamonds nestled around it on a platinum band.

"I love it," I tell him, admiring the way the ring sparkles in the light. "And I love you."

Camden lifts me into his arms and walks us over to the kitchen counter. He sets me on it and lifts my shirt off while I kick my boots off my feet and push my jeans down my legs.

After unbuttoning and unzipping his pants, I pull his hard length out and stroke it a few times, lining it up at my entrance while Camden trails along my jawline. Our mouths connect at the same time our bodies do. And as Camden makes love to me as his fiancée in the home where we'll be creating a future together, I can't help but wonder if it can get any better than this.

Twenty-Five

LAYLA

"Maybe," I say noncommittally.

"What about the bike?" he asks, placing two carrots on the plate for the reindeer.

"I'm not sure," I say this time.

"What about the Legos? Do you think I'll get them?" Felix asks. "I think I've been good this year."

"You'll have to wait until Santa comes to find out," I tell him, ruffling his hair.

It's Christmas Eve, and we've just gotten back from Camden's parents' house, where we had dinner and watched *The Grinch*, a tradition that's been part of their family for several generations. Camden brought us home and is here for the Christmas story—at Felix's request—but will leave afterward, coming back in the morning for presents. We've decided to wait and not sleep under the same roof with Felix until we're married and move into the new house. It seems a bit traditional, but Felix has been through a lot, and I want him to have stability. We discussed us getting married and moving in with him, and he's as on board as a four-and-a-half-year-old can be.

"I've been good, right?" Felix says, helping me pour the milk in the glass. "I'm not a brat, right?" A sharp pain slices through my heart at his question, at his insecurity because of his father, and my eyes fit to Camden, whose jaw is now clenched tightly.

"You most definitely are not a brat," I tell him, kneeling in front of him so I can look him in the eyes, "and your dad never should've said that to you. He was mad that day but not at you. You are a smart, sweet, amazing little boy."

"I'm not so little." His brow dips as he shakes his head. "I'm big enough for a sled, right?"

"Yeah," I choke out, a bout of emotion hitting me hard over how much I love my son and how quickly he's growing up. In August, he'll be starting kindergarten. Sure, he's in preschool part-time now, but kindergarten feels so…official.

"You're definitely big enough for a sled," Camden adds, ruffling his hair. "And when Santa brings you one, we're going to take it to Big Bear Mountain and ride it up and down the hill a million times."

Felix's face splits into a grin. "I can't wait!"

"Felix," I add, "please remember that Santa has to bring presents to a lot of kids, so even though you asked for a lot of toys, that doesn't mean you'll get them all, but that's not because you weren't good. It just means he needs toys for other kids too."

Felix nods in understanding.

After I read him a Christmas story, I tuck him in and kiss him good night. He goes right to sleep since he knows Santa only comes when the kids are asleep.

"I can't wait to see Felix open his presents from Santa," Camden says, walking me to the door. "I'm not even getting shit from Santa, and I'm excited." Since my vehicle is small, Camden went Christmas shopping with me, and we used his SUV to bring home the sled I bought for Felix. His list was long, and I couldn't afford all of it—and I refused to let Camden pay for the rest—but he got enough to know he's been good, and he's *not* a brat like his dad said.

"I'll call you when he wakes up," I tell him with a laugh, loving that he's excited and wants to be part of Felix's Christmas. "It'll be early, so get some sleep."

"Can't wait."

A couple of hours later, all the presents are set out under the tree. I send a picture to Camden with a cheesy sticker that makes it look like Santa is in the picture, with a caption that reads: **You've been replaced by a jolly old man in a red suit.**

Within seconds, Camden replies: **I don't care how jolly he is. If he touches my fiancée, I'll kick his ass straight back to the North Pole.**

I smile at the word fiancée.

Me: I like being your fiancée.

Camden: I'd prefer you to be my wife.

Me: Soon…

Camden: Not soon enough.

Camden: I wish I were there with you. 7 more weeks is too long.

We decided on a Valentine's Day wedding—well, the weekend after Valentine's Day since it's on a Thursday this year. It only gives us a short amount of time to plan the wedding, but neither of us wanted to wait long. I wasted too much time on the wrong man. Now that I've found the right one,

I don't want to wait longer than I have to for us to start our lives together. I want to be Camden's in every way, as soon as possible, and he's completely on board with that. We both agreed on something intimate with just our friends and family, so it shouldn't be too hard to plan on short notice. My mom is also going to keep Felix while we go on a short honeymoon.

A knock on the door has me jumping out of bed, a huge grin on my face. It's just like Camden to text me that he's missing me while he's on his way over here. He's not supposed to come over until after Felix wakes up, but there's no harm in having a little Christmas Eve quickie. Maybe I can hide him and have him come out and pretend he just got here.

Only, when I open the door, prepared to kiss my fiancé and sneak him in, it's not Camden on the other side...it's David.

"What are you doing here?" I ask in shock. I haven't seen him since court because he meets with Felix and the social worker due to the restraining order I have on him.

"Fuck, sweetheart, you're so beautiful," he slurs, eye-fucking me. In my haste, I came down in my tiny pajamas since the heat was on and it's warm in here.

"You need to go now." I try to slam the door on David's clearly drunk ass, but before I can, he catches the door.

"Wait, please," he begs. "I know I fucked up, but it's Christmas...Please, Layla. I miss you and our son. Please. I just want to see him for Christmas."

"You know the rules," I tell him. "You need to leave, or I'm going to call the police." I extend my hand to push him out of the doorway.

"Are you fucking serious?" he hisses, tugging on my left hand. "You're engaged?"

I pull my hand back. "Yes, and you need to stop this. You're drunk, and if I call the police, you're going to be arrested for violating a court order. Go home, David."

"You're engaged to *him*, aren't you?" he slurs, his eyes filled with heat. "I knew it. I knew he'd steal my wife."

"That's enough." I push on his chest, and he stumbles back, so I use the opportunity to slam the door closed before he can slip back through the crack.

When he starts banging on the door and doesn't stop, I call Camden.

"Hey, baby," he says, not sounding sleepy at all.

"Hey, umm...I have a little problem, and I'm not sure what to do."

"What's wrong? And...what's that noise?"

"That would be my problem. David showed up drunk, begging to see Felix for Christmas. I thought it was you since we were texting, and you said you wished you were with me. Then he saw my ring and freaked out. I got him out and locked the door, but he's still here, banging on it."

"I'm on my way," he says. "Call the police."

Just as he says that, the noise stops. I peek through the peephole, and David is gone. "He left."

"Call the police," Camden repeats. When I'm quiet, he adds, "I know you feel bad for him because you have a huge-ass heart, but he knows the rules, and if he gets away with this, he'll keep doing it."

I sigh, knowing he's right. "Okay, you don't have to come over if you don't want to. It's late—"

"I'll be there soon."

An hour and a half later, a police report has been filed, and Camden and I are snuggling in my bed. Because there are no cameras, it'll have to be investigated, and that will take some time because it's Christmas.

"I'm having better security installed in here," he says.

"I won't even be living here soon."

"Not soon enough. And I need to make sure you and Felix are safe until I can protect you under my roof."

I nod into his chest, knowing that it's pointless to argue. Camden will do anything in his power to make sure Felix and I are safe.

"I really like being in bed with you," I tell him, running lines up and down his chest over his shirt. "But you know what I like more? You *in* me."

He chuckles softly but stops abruptly when I climb over him and straddle his waist.

"This isn't a good idea," he says, gripping the curves of my hips as I rub my center along his groin to wake his dick up.

"Why not?" I lean forward and pepper kisses along his jawline and down his neck. "You're here anyway, so we might as well make the most of it."

"Because you don't know how to be quiet." He taps the tip of my nose. "And if you wake Felix up, he's going to know Santa came, and he won't go back to bed."

"I can totally be quiet," I argue. "You're the one who moans loudly when you come."

Camden scoffs. "That's all you."

"Let's make a bet," I say. "Whoever makes a noise first loses."

His brows kiss his forehead. "What do I get if I win?" he asks, interested.

I tap my chin in thought. "If you win...I don't know," I say with a laugh. "What do you want?" I know what it is *I* want, something I've been wanting for a while now, and once I win it, he'll have no choice but to give it to me.

Camden sucks in his bottom lip, his eyes twinkling. "If I win, you have to go out on a romantic date with me for New Year's."

I roll my eyes. "That's a win/win. There's nothing *you* want?"

He shrugs. "I have everything I want."

"Aw, you're so sweet." I kiss the corner of his mouth. "Well, I'm not as selfless as you. There's something I want, and if I win, I'm getting it."

"Oh, yeah? What is that?" He squeezes my hips.

I feel myself flush once I have to actually say what I want out loud.

"Your face is all red," Camden points out. "What is it you want?"

"I want to…" I swallow down the lump of emotion clogged in my throat. "I want to have sex my way." He quirks a brow. "In different positions and rough…rougher than what we do…No holding back or treating me like glass and…I want anal."

His eyes go wide, then soften. "Layles…"

"It's what I want," I say, making sure my voice doesn't crack. "You treat me like I'm going to break. How can I ever move forward if every time we have sex, I'm reminded of what happened because of the gentle way you make it a point to treat me?"

He releases a harsh breath and sighs. "Fine, it doesn't matter because you're the loud one, and there's no way you'll stay quiet."

"I only have to stay quiet longer than you," I point out, dragging myself down his body. Before he realizes what I'm doing, I hook my fingers into his belt loops and pull his pants and briefs down, exposing his dick. "And the bet starts…now." I take his entire length into my mouth and deep throat him as far as I can go. He groans loudly, and I pop off, laughing.

"You weren't supposed to make a noise."

"That's not fair!" he whisper-yells. "I wasn't mentally prepared. You just stuck my entire cock down your fucking throat."

I shrug. "I warned you we were starting. You lose. I win."

He sits up and pulls me close to him, so we're face-to-face. "That's where you're wrong, Shutterbug. *Nothing* about what just happened or is going to happen makes me a loser."

Before I can argue, his lips fuse against mine, and his tongue lashes out past my parted lips, tasting me, stroking me. We shed our clothes, and I expect Camden to flip me over, fuck me on my back like he always does, so I'm momentarily taken aback when I end up on top of him with his dick deep inside me. My fingers dig into his shoulders while I ride him to orgasm.

When I've barely come down from my high, he lifts me off him and drops me onto the bed. "On your hands and knees," he demands. I scramble into position, shocked that he's actually going to do as I said. "That's right, baby." He massages one of the globes of my ass. "One day, I'm going to take you here…" He runs his fingers down the crack of my ass, sending a shiver of both fear and need through me. "But tonight, I want in your tight pussy." He spreads my ass. "You sure this is what you want?"

I nod emphatically. "Yes, fuck me like you mean it."

"You better hold on," he warns. I've only just gripped the sheets when he thrusts roughly into me from behind, making me moan.

"You have to be quiet," he says, smacking my ass lightly. "Can you do that?"

"Yes," I breathe.

"If you make any noise, I'm going to stop. Understand?"

I nod, and he rams into me from behind, pushing me forward. Thankfully, I'm holding on. A moan threatens to escape, but before it gets out, I drop my face into my pillow to muffle it.

Camden fucks me how I asked—hard and deep and so damn good. With every thrust, it feels like he's replacing my past with our present and making a promise for the future.

As we both find our release, his fingers dig deliciously into my hips, and once he's filled me with his warm seed, he leans over and trails kisses down the center of my spine.

I love the way he makes me feel wanted and cherished in everything he does. It doesn't matter if he makes love to me or fucks me hard because he does it with his heart every single time. He pulls out, and I flip onto my back, pulling him to me for a kiss.

"Was that what you wanted?" he asks, searching my face to make sure I'm okay.

"It's exactly what I wanted," I breathe, my body feeling like Jell-O from the two orgasms he's given me. "Thank you."

"You don't have to thank me, Layles." He kisses me lightly on my forehead. "You should know by now I'll give you anything you ask for."

"MOMMY! SANTA CAME!" FELIX SHOUTS, RUNNING INTO MY ROOM. I SPRING UP, READY TO EXPLAIN WHY Camden is in bed with me. Only the spot where he was lying is empty. I glance around and wonder if I was dreaming, but when I move and feel the soreness between my legs, I know I wasn't.

"He did?" I ask Felix, focusing on him.

"Yep! And I was soooo good because he brought me a million presents."

I laugh at his exaggeration. "Wow, a million? You must've been the best kid in the world."

Felix nods, then runs out of the room. "C'mon, Mommy!"

"Give me a second," I call back, needing to go pee, brush my teeth, and make some coffee. I check the time on my phone and see it's only five thirty in the morning. It's going to be a long day.

Me: Where did you go?

When Camden doesn't respond right away, I assume he's back home and asleep. Once I'm done in the bathroom, I grab my robe to cover myself and pad downstairs to the living room.

I get to the bottom of the stairs and am halted in place by what I see. Presents...So many damn presents surrounding the tree and all over the floor. I blink several times in confusion. There's the sled I got him in one corner, but in the other is a...shit, there's a bike in the other.

"Mommy, this one has your name on it!" Felix shakes the box and runs it over to me. I read the tag, and sure enough, it's addressed to me, from Santa.

What the hell...

I pull my phone out and text Camden again: **What did you do?** He's the only one who could've done this. He's the only one with a key to my house and the alarm code. Well, my mom has one too, but this has Camden written all over it.

There's a knock on the door, so I put away my phone, checking the peephole to make sure it's not David. When I see it's Camden, I swing the door open, glaring. "What did you do?" I hiss.

"What?" he asks with a poker face.

"The presents...the millions of damn presents under the tree."

He steps inside and glances over at the presents, his brows furrowing. "Hey, Felix. Looks like you've been really good this year."

Felix nods, rummaging through all the wrapped presents. "I must've been so, so, so good."

Camden chuckles.

"When did you do this?" I ask, nodding toward the tree.

"Do what?"

"Bring all these presents over!" I whisper-yell so Felix doesn't hear.

Camden barks out a laugh. "The only thing I brought over are these donuts." He raises the box and then leans in and kisses my cheek. "Merry Christmas, baby."

With a smile on his face, he steps into the living room and sets the donuts on the table. "All right, Felix, which one of these presents are you tearing into first?"

Felix lifts a box—one I didn't wrap—and shakes it. "This one!"

"Oh, yeah," Camden says, winking at me. "I bet that's a good one."

Twenty-Six

CAMDEN

"YOU READY?" DAD ASKS, PATTING MY SHOULDER WHILE I STRAIGHTEN MY BOW TIE IN THE DRESSING room mirror at the church where Layla and I are about to get married.

"More than ready."

"He better be," Declan says with a laugh. "He's been dreaming of this day for the past eight years."

I don't bother to argue because he's not lying. The past two months since Layla agreed to marry me have been spent getting the house ready so we can move in after our honeymoon and counting down the days until I can make Layla my wife and give her my last name.

When I get to the front, our friends and family sit and wait. My mom is in the front row, next to Layla's mom. Both women are dabbing their eyes. I'm the first to get married out of my sisters and me, so Mom has enjoyed helping get everything ready.

Since Layla doesn't have a bunch of girlfriends, she didn't do a wedding party. She has Kaylee as her maid of honor, and my dad is my best man. Since her dad passed away, she's asked my dad to walk her down the aisle. The music starts, and Felix comes out first since he's the ring bearer. He's dressed in a sharp little tux, looking adorable as he carefully carries the rings down the aisle, stopping when he gets to me.

"That was scary," he says, making everyone laugh.

"You did a good job." I fist-bump him, and then he runs over to sit with Patricia.

Next is Kaylee. She flew in this morning for the wedding since she's traveling with Sam York on his tour as his publicist. When she gets to the front, she nods once at me and smiles softly. I hate that she broke my best friend's heart, but she's still Layla's best friend, so I'm going to have to get used to her being around.

The music changes, and Layla and my dad appear a beat later. She's dressed in some off-the-shoulder white dress with beads and shit all over it. Her hair is down in loose waves, and her makeup looks professionally done because she never really wears a lot of makeup. She's fucking stunning and all damn mine.

When her eyes lock with mine, her grin widens, and I swear to God, my chest cracks open, and my heart leaves my body. My dad gives her to me, and it takes everything in me not to kiss her right now.

The officiant reads us his speech, and we recite our vows, and the second he says the words I've been waiting to hear—*I now pronounce you husband and wife, you may kiss the bride*—my mouth is on hers. She tastes sweet, and I want to devour her, but I'll save it for tonight. I release her, and she laughs softly, her face glowing with happiness.

"YOU LOOK BEAUTIFUL, MRS. BLACKWOOD," I TELL HER AS WE DANCE TO "PERFECT" BY ED SHEERAN while everyone watches us. The reception is being held in the same hotel where we're spending the night before we take off tomorrow morning for our honeymoon. Layla hates the cold, and it's been a long winter, so I planned a week at an all-inclusive, adults-only resort in Mexico.

"I can't believe I'm Mrs. Blackwood." She shakes her head. "I can't remember the last time I was this happy. Thank you." She lifts up and kisses my lips. "How long until we can go to our room?"

I chuckle, loving that my wife is on the same page as me. "A few more hours."

The song ends, and the deejay welcomes everyone onto the dance floor. Layla seeks out Felix to dance with him while I ask my mom to dance.

"I'm so happy for you," she says, swaying to the music. "I always thought Kendall would be the first to marry." She laughs, glancing over at my sister, who's dancing with her newest boyfriend.

"She would have to stay with one guy long enough for him to propose and then for her to make it down the aisle," I joke. I love my sister, but she can't keep a man to save her life. And it's not them because she's the one always doing the dumping.

"One day, she'll meet the right guy, and she won't run," Mom says with a smile. "Not all of us meet the person we want to spend our lives with at fifteen."

I smile at that. "I didn't think it would ever happen."

"I know. But it did. Fate has a wonderful way of intervening. It's what brought your father and me together, and now you and Layla."

The song ends, and after kissing my mom on her cheek and thanking her for the dance, I find my way back to Layla. We spend the night dancing and socializing. The food is good, Felix loves the cake, and when it's socially acceptable, we thank everyone for coming and say good night. Layla tells Felix to be good for his grandma and that we'll be home in a week. She's nervous about not being there to hand him off to the social worker to see David, but her mom has assured her she'll make sure everything goes smoothly.

"Stop," I tell her when I open the door to our hotel room. "It's tradition, right? Good luck?" I scoop her up into my arms and carry her, bridal style, across the threshold.

"I think that's at the house," she says with a laugh.

"I'll do it then too." I shrug and place her on the floor in the center of the bedroom. Backing up, I take a good look at my wife before I walk up behind her and begin to undo the pearl buttons down her back. With each one I unfasten, her sexy back is exposed. When they're all undone, I flick the material, sending it into a pool on the floor.

"Jesus," I breathe, taking in her white silk corset and panty set. She steps out of the material, and my eyes go straight to her toned legs and fuck-me heels. I've got to be the luckiest motherfucker in the world. I want to send a thank-you note to David for being a dumbass and letting this perfect woman go, but he doesn't deserve shit.

Dusting her hair to the side, I press an open-mouthed kiss to the top of her shoulder, inhaling the vanilla and raspberry.

"I think I'm a bit underdressed compared to you," she says coyly, turning around and running her hands up my chest, then pushing my tux off my shoulders. Next, she unbuttons my shirt, kissing her way down my chest and torso. She bends down when she gets to my pants, squatting so she's eye level with my groin. The corset she's wearing plumps up her already full breasts, and I find myself running a finger across the swells of them.

She pushes my pants and boxers down and grips my shaft, stroking it up and down. It's already semi-hard from looking at her, so it doesn't take long for it to get as hard as granite. As much as I love her hands and mouth on me, the only way I'm coming with Layla as my wife is inside her.

"Come here, my beautiful wife." I pull her over to the bed, and she climbs onto it, giving me a show of her ass in the air, her heels still on her feet, and her tiny white lace underwear barely covering anything. When she stops and peeks over her shoulder through her lashes, I slap her ass playfully, making her moan.

"I've made a decision," she says, staying on her hands and knees.

I grip her hips and dip my head, giving the globe of her ass a kiss. "What's that?" I ask, massaging each round cheek.

"I want you to fuck my ass tonight."

Her words halt me in place. For most couples, a woman requesting that is simply kinky, but for Layla to ask is huge because the one and only time she's been taken there was when she was raped by her ex-husband.

I want to ask if she's sure, tell her there's no rush, we don't ever have to do it, but I know replacing the bad memories with the good is important to her, and if this is what she wants from me—*her husband*—I'll give it to her. I'll give her *any-fucking-thing* she wants if it makes her happy.

"You will, right?" she asks, her voice now shaky since I haven't said a word. "You said you would…"

I lean in and grip her chin, capturing her plump bottom lip with my teeth. "Baby, I'll fuck your ass so good that every horrible memory of that piece of shit will be wiped out." I kiss her hard, swallowing down the moan she releases.

"I brought lube," she says shyly. "In the luggage. I looked it up, and it said if you use it, it will hurt less."

My eyes stay trained on her for a few seconds, worried she's scared and doing this prematurely, but when she looks at me, I see the conviction in her gaze. She trusts me and knows I'll make sure anything we do together will be good for her.

"Go lie down on your stomach," I murmur, releasing my hold on her chin. She does as I say while I go to her luggage and pull out the lube she bought, along with the baby oil she uses when she gets out of the shower. I discard the last of my clothes, leaving me in only my boxer briefs, then pad back over to join her on the bed.

"You looked so damn perfect today," I tell her, straddling her legs and unclipping her corset that buttons down her back. "Walking down the aisle… standing at the altar…promising to love me for the rest of your life." I pull the straps off her arms, and she lifts slightly so I can remove the material from her.

I drop a kiss between her shoulder blades. "I swear I thought of a dozen love songs just watching you today, holding you, kissing you." I trail kisses down her spine, stopping at the sexy as fuck dimples just above her ass.

"The guys will think you've gone soft," she says with a laugh.

"They already know I have. You've heard our upcoming album." Damn near half the songs are about the way I love Layla.

I pull the silky material down her thighs and drop it onto the ground. "I can't help it, though. Every word, every lyric, is written with you in mind."

I squeeze some oil into my palm and rub my hands together to warm it up a bit. Layla is still on her stomach, her arms now above her head. Her face is to the side, her hair fanned out over her shoulder, and her eyes are closed. She looks like a damn angel. I'll never understand how anyone could ever want to hurt her, especially someone who claimed to love her. But I vow to make sure she's treated like she deserves every day for the rest of her life.

I start with her shoulders, massaging the tension out. She may trust me, but she's still nervous. He hurt her, and as strong as she is, she can't shake what he did. I knead her back and work my way to her peach of an ass, massaging the globes, working my way into the crack, but not yet going *there*. I skirt down, applying some oil to her thighs and giving them attention.

When I get to her heels, as much as I love the idea of fucking her with them on, I remove each one so she's comfortable, kissing the insteps of both of her feet.

"If you keep this up, you're going to put me to sleep." She sighs, clearly relaxed, just the way I want her.

"Then I'll just have to wake you up."

"We'll s—" Her words are cut off when I spread her cheeks and push a single oiled-up finger into her tight-ringed hole. "Ohhh," she half hisses, half groans.

"How does that feel, baby?" I ask, gently fingering her tight ass.

"It's...different."

I chuckle under my breath. "Get on your hands and knees." She pops up immediately, jutting her ass into the air. Reaching under her, I find her clit and massage it while working her ass with my finger. I can tell when the two combined begin to feel good because she starts to rock back and forth, helping me get her off.

"Oh, Oh...Cam," she groans. With a little more pressure on her clit, she explodes, her entire body shaking as she comes all over my fingers. I use the moment to add another finger to her ass, and she moans in pleasure.

"That's it," I murmur. "Fuck my fingers." I dribble a few drops of lube onto her ass, then add one more digit. Even though she's already come, she's turned the hell on, meeting my fingers thrust for thrust.

"It feels so good," she breathes, rocking back and forth. "More, please. I need more."

"So fucking polite. Begging me to fuck your ass."

"Please," she moans louder, taking my fingers deeper and harder. "Camden, please."

I pull my fingers out, and she whimpers, making me bite back a laugh. If that asshole had treated her right, she would've given him the damn world. Instead, he chose to hurt her. His fuckup is most definitely my gain. Because of his horrible choices, I'll get to spend the rest of my life loving and being with this woman. Something I never thought possible.

Grabbing the lube, I pour a generous amount on my shaft, then stroke it a few times, making sure to coat it nice and good.

"It might hurt a little," I warn her, lining my dick up to her entrance. "If at any point you want me to stop, tell me, and I will."

"Okay," she whispers, her voice shaky.

My fingers pull one of her ass cheeks to the side, and slowly, so fucking slowly, I breach the rim of her hole, watching as it swallows my dick inch by inch.

"Layles, you okay?" I ask when I glance up and find her face in the pillow, her body trembling. "Layla?"

"I...I don't—" The shakiness of her words has me pulling out and flipping her onto her back, not waiting for her to finish her sentence.

Twenty-Seven

LAYLA

I THOUGHT I COULD DO THIS, AND FOR A MINUTE, I WAS. HIS FINGERS IN ME FELT ODDLY GOOD. THE WAY they stroked my insides had me coming apart at the seams. But then I got too brave, asked for too much, and the second his cick pushed into me, the flashbacks hit me hard. I tried to close my eyes and get past them, but of course, Camden noticed. He notices everything. He's so attuned to everything regarding me. My moods, my body, my emotions, and my expressions. He pays attention, real attention. It's one of the things I love about him.

"I'm right here," Camden says, parting my legs and hovering above me. "It's you and me, baby." His lips brush mine, sending a shiver up my spine. "We don't need to do this," he says softly. "I can make love to you just like this."

I shake my head, not wanting to let David win. He doesn't deserve to be in our honeymoon suite with my husband and me.

"Can we do it like this?" I ask. "I think it's the position. I want to see you."

Camden smiles gently. "Baby, we can do anything you want."

His mouth captures my own, and we kiss passionately. He tastes like the champagne from our final toast before we said good night, and it makes my stomach do a flip-flop. I married Camden today, my best friend, and I want our marriage to be free of David, of my past. And the only way that can happen is for us to replace this final bad memory with a good one.

"Lift up," he says when he breaks our kiss. I do as he says, and he places a pillow under my butt, propping my lower half up slightly before his mouth is back on mine.

I'm so lost in our kiss that I don't realize what's happening until the slight pain hits me. One of my legs is hooked on the crook of his arm, and he's pushing into me slowly, his mouth never leaving mine. Because we're oiled up, he goes in easily, the burning sensation lessening the deeper he goes.

"I'm all the way in," he murmurs against my lips. "Tell me when you're okay with me moving, or I can stay just like this."

"You can move."

"You sure?"

"Yes, please move."

He backs up slightly, gripping my thigh, and starts to move in and out of my ass. With every drive into me, the burn turns into pleasure. The hand not holding my leg finds my clit, and he massages it, his eyes never leaving mine. My orgasm builds slowly until I'm dangling over the edge, begging Camden to make me come.

With a flick of his thumb, he pushes me over the edge. I'm still screaming his name when he pulls out and comes all over my belly.

"Fuck, you're amazing," he groans, kissing me hard. "Let's go shower. I need to clean you, so I can fuck you, this time in your tight cunt."

"I'M NOT READY TO GO HOME, YET I'M EXCITED TO GO HOME," I SAY, MAKING CAMDEN LAUGH WITH MY confusing statement. We've spent a week on the beaches of Mexico, and if it were up to me, we would stay forever. It's peaceful and sunny and relaxing, and did I mention it's peaceful? The only thing we're missing is Felix, who I've spoken to every day and has barely missed me since he's been too busy being spoiled by our moms.

"We can go back," Camden says, kissing my cheek. "Or we can go somewhere else. Aside from the next few weeks that are blocked off to finish this album and the tour that's scheduled, my calendar is wide open."

"When you're done with the album and we make the videos, my job will be done." I cuddle into Camden's side. "I was thinking of making a website and putting my name out there. Maybe get a few new artists to take a chance on me…"

I hold my breath, waiting for Camden to tell me there's no reason for me to work because he'll provide for us, the way David always did. Instead, he kisses the top of my head and says, "Baby, once our videos are out and your name is attached to them, opportunities will be flying in. You'll get your pick of who you want to work with."

I look up at him and smile, silently promising to stop comparing him to David and expecting the worst. Camden isn't David. He's already proven that over and over again.

"I know going on tour isn't the best situation for a kid, but I was thinking you guys can join us a few times. We'll be flying as well as using the tour bus, but we stay in hotels a lot. We can look at the schedule and see when I have days off, and we can explore the different cities."

"That sounds like fun," I tell him, leaning up and kissing his stubbled jaw. I'm going to miss the hell out of him while he's on tour for two months, but

I knew going into this that touring is part of his life. And I'd never want to make him feel guilty for following his passions. I know firsthand how shitty that can feel.

When we pull up to the new house, I look at Camden in confusion. We haven't moved in yet, and he knows I'm dying to see Felix. The car must have a scanner on it that Camden told me about when discussing security because the gate opens automatically when we pull up. Not many homes in the city are gated, but Camden made sure ours is.

We get out, and he scoops me into his arms. "Love getting to carry my wife over the thresholds," he says, kissing me as he walks us to the front door. With one hand, he pushes the door open, setting me on my feet once we're inside. I expected the place to still be empty, so I'm shocked when I find it completely furnished with everything I've bookmarked.

"How did you—?"

My question is cut off when Felix's voice booms through the house, and seconds later, he's running into my arms. "You're home! Wait till you see my room!"

He grabs my hand and pulls me upstairs, Camden following. The walls—painted the color I picked out—are all empty, so it seems he only had the furniture I picked out brought in.

When we get to Felix's room, I'm stunned. He had requested a Sonic the Hedgehog room because he's still obsessed with the game, and Camden made it happen. The walls are painted like the game's background, and his comforter matches. The two large beanbags in the corner both have Sonic on them. Even the curtains have Sonic on them.

"This is my room," Felix says as if it's not obvious. "Grandma said I get to sleep here tonight."

Speaking of which…"Where is Grandma?"

"Right here," Mom says, walking in and giving me a kiss. "Look at that tan you've got. You look beautiful." She presses her palms to my face. "And happy."

"I am," I tell her, wrapping my arm around Camden's waist. "Did you do all this?"

"No," she says with a laugh. "That would be your husband. Felix and I just arrived so we were here when you got home." She pats my shoulder. "I'm going to take off. I have book club tonight. Welcome home. Come over soon so you can tell me all about your trip."

Once she's gone, Camden shows me the rest of the house, which is exactly how I envisioned it when I was picking out stuff online, and then we order a pizza and watch a movie with Felix. Tomorrow is Saturday so he doesn't have school, which means we get to spend the weekend in our new home as a family. Life can't get much better than this.

"SHIT," I HISS, PRESSING END ON THE CALL.

"What's the matter?" Camden asks, startling me. He wraps his arms around me from behind and nuzzles his face into the crook of my neck. For a moment, I'm distracted, basking in his touch.

"I have to go to the doctor for my yearly checkup, and I completely forgot. My mom just left to go to The Hamptons with your mom for a girls' weekend, so I can't have her pick up Felix from school."

"You have me," Camden says, turning me around to face him. "I'm your husband, and while Felix might not be my son, he's part of you, which by extension is part of me."

"I know, but—"

"No buts. We're a family and in this together. If you need something, all you have to do is ask."

"Thank you." I wrap my arms around him and kiss him. "I'll let his teacher know you're picking him up."

"Sounds good. We do need to talk before you go, though."

The look in his eyes has me worried. "Did something happen?" When he sighs, I know something has. "Camden…"

"I ran into David the other day. He knows you've moved and that we're married. Before Simon could stop him, he made some threats." Simon is one of his main bodyguards. Several of them rotate, but Simon is Camden's personal bodyguard and tends to go where he goes when it's needed.

"What kind of threats?"

"He said he's not going to let me take his family from him, and if I think this is over, I'm wrong."

A chill races up my spine, and I step back, needing some space. "He threatened you…?" My thoughts go back to the images he sent—Camden had sent them to Daniel, and he advised us to report them as threats so they're documented.

"Layles…"

"He's snapped. He's not the same guy he was when we first got together. Or maybe he is, and I just didn't realize it. We need to take his threats seriously."

"And we are," Camden says, taking my hands in his. "I've added to my security team, and Simon will accompany you everywhere you go."

"But he's yours…"

"He's part of my team, and I trust him more than anyone else to keep you safe. As my wife, you should have security with you anyway. New York is quiet, but the paparazzi are still around. We've been going everywhere together up until now, but if you're leaving on your own, I want you to take Simon with you, and you need to always take the SUV. No taking the subway, even if you feel it's faster."

Shortly after we got back, Camden insisted on replacing my little car with something safer. I wasn't thrilled, but I understood and let him because I've seen the way the photographers linger, especially when we leave the house. Sometimes, I don't even notice them there, but later, I'll see pictures of us all over the internet.

"Okay," I agree. "I need to get going so I'm not late." I give him a kiss on his cheek, then head out, Simon meeting me outside.

"Ma'am," he says with a smile, opening the door for me.

Once I arrive at the doctor's office, I'm seen quickly. After I give a urine sample, they check my blood pressure, and I get changed into a gown, then the doctor comes in.

"Good morning, Mrs. Blackwood. How are you feeling?"

"I'm good." I grin, loving my new last name.

"Any morning sickness or tender breasts?"

"I'm sorry, what?"

She looks at me, confused. "Aren't you here for your prenatal appointment?" She clicks on the tablet in her hand. "Oh, this is your wellness checkup? I'm so sorry. Your urine test showed a higher than normal level of HCG, only found in pregnancy, so I thought…"

"Wait," I gasp, my hand going to my stomach. "I'm pregnant?"

"We'll need to do an ultrasound to confirm. I'm assuming, based on your reaction, you didn't know?"

"No," I breathe. "I'm on birth control. I take it every single day."

"Unfortunately, no contraception is one-hundred-percent effective. When was your last menstrual cycle?"

I think back. I get it every month at the same time. That's the plus side to being on the pill, but…"Oh my God. I didn't get it last month. This doesn't make any sense. I haven't missed a single pill. I've been so busy with the wedding and our honeymoon, I didn't even think about it when it didn't show up."

"Could you have missed some days?"

"No. My alarm goes off to ensure I take it every day at the same time. I know you probably hear that a lot, but I'm telling you, I haven't missed it."

"It's okay, dear." She pats my leg. "Lie back, and we'll check things out before we assume anything."

A few minutes later, a *whoosh, whoosh, whoosh* comes over the screen. It's a sound I would recognize anywhere. A baby's heartbeat.

"Based on the measurements, you're roughly five weeks pregnant, which is why you might not have experienced any symptoms yet. We'll say you're due October twentieth, but that might change. Everything looks good." She takes some pictures of the tiny little blob and prints them out for me. "Stop taking your birth control immediately, and since you struggle with anemia, I'm going to have you up your iron intake in addition to adding a prenatal vitamin. I'll send the prescriptions to your pharmacy on file."

I'm still in shock as I walk out of the doctor's office, staring at the sonogram pics of the tiny little thing that's growing in me. A baby...created by Camden and me.

"Oh! I'm sorry," I blurt when I run straight into another person. My eyes ascend, and I instinctually take a step back. David. Towering over me. I look around for Simon but don't see him anywhere, and then it hits me: when I checked out, I went out a different door. I was so wrapped up in the news that I forgot he was with me.

"What are you doing here?" I ask because there's no way this is a coincidence.

"I knew you had an appointment today. It was on my calendar. When you made it, you added it to our joint calendar."

"And you just took it upon yourself to show up?" I shriek. "You're not allowed to be near me. You know—"

"What the fuck is this?" David barks, cutting me off. He snatches the sonogram pictures out of my hand. "You're..." He glances down at my belly. "How far along are you?"

"Not that it's any of your business, but only five weeks." I grab the pictures back. "Now go away."

"No." He shakes his head. "No. No. No. Fuck!" His face turns red, and I take a step back in fear. We're on a crowded street, but it doesn't do anything to make me feel safe.

"This was not supposed to happen! You were supposed to get pregnant by me!" He stalks toward me. "It was supposed to be my baby! Not his! Of course he would take this away from me too. He's taken everything else! My wife, my son, and now he's taken my baby."

"David," I say slowly, my heart beating erratically in my chest. "This wasn't supposed to be your baby. We agreed to wait. I was on birth control." He isn't making any sense. This was an accident. When David and I were married, he asked me to have another baby, and I told him no repeatedly.

"Yes, it was! I knew once you were pregnant, you'd be okay. Just like you were with Felix. I just had to make it happen, and then you'd be on board." He now has me backed up against a wall and slams his hand against it in anger. "That baby was supposed to be mine, not his!"

An ice-cold chill flows through my veins at his words. He can't be saying what I think he's saying. There's no way he would..."David, what did you do?"

Before he can answer, he's ripped away from me by Simon, who shoves David against the wall. "Get away from her, now," Simon says, menace laced in his tone. "Let's go, Layla." He glares my way, and I go with him, feeling bad that I put myself in this situation because I didn't wait for him.

"I'm sorry," I tell him once we're in the SUV. "I left out a different door and completely forgot. David was outside waiting for me and...I'm so sorry."

He nods once. "I can't do my job if I'm not with you. Please remember that."

The ride home is quiet. I had planned to meet Camden at the studio, but I need to do something first. I have Simon wait for me in the vehicle while I run into the house and grab what I need. He takes me to the pharmacy I use, and once it's my turn, I hand the pharmacist the pills.

"Can you please confirm these are the pills for my birth control?"

A few minutes later, my suspicions are confirmed. "I'm sorry, ma'am, but these are placebo. They are not your birth control. Were you given these? I can investigate..."

"No," I say, shaking my head. "That's okay. Thank you."

There's nothing to investigate because I know exactly what happened. My ex-husband switched out my pills, not once but twice, to ensure I would get pregnant.

Twenty-Seven

BONUS SCENE

CAMDEN

"I WAS THINKING WE COULD DO A COUPLES MASSAGE." LAYLA GLANCES UP FROM READING THE BROCHURE the resort leaves on our doorknob every morning with what's happening that day. We've been here for five days, and if we didn't need to get back to reality, I would convince her to stay another few weeks. Getting to wake up every morning with her in my arms, spend the morning sightseeing, the afternoon lying out by the beach and pool, and the night getting lost in her is the best way to spend the day...Hell, it's the best way to spend my life.

"I've never gotten a massage," I admit. "And the thought of some guy rubbing all over me doesn't really sound appealing."

Layla rolls her eyes. "I can make sure it's a woman…"

I pull her toward me. "Let me rephrase...The thought of anyone but you rubbing all over me doesn't sound appealing." I nuzzle my face into her neck and playfully growl into her ear, making her giggle.

"Cam, please." She pouts. "I'm dying for a massage, and I think it would be cool to do it together. I read in a magazine that it's a huge turn-on."

"Sure," I tell her.

"Really?" she asks, shocked that I gave in so quickly.

One day, Layla will realize there's nothing I wouldn't do for her. She and Felix are my entire world, and I'd gladly give them everything I could if it means they're happy.

"Yep. Book it."

"Yay!" She squeals, reaching for the phone to call the spa.

An hour later, we're lying in a private room, the lights dimmed, a scented candle lit, and soft music playing in the speakers. With only my boxers and her panties keeping us from being completely naked, we're facing each other on our tables, a thickish blanket covering our bodies as the masseuses massage our backs. I must admit the way the woman kneads my shoulder and back feels amazing. I never realized just how tense I was until now.

As if Layla can feel my eyes on her, her lids flutter open, her gaze meeting mine. A small smile spreads across her lips, and my heart swells. I love seeing Layla happy.

"I love you," she mouths as the masseuse tells us both to turn over onto our backs, letting us know they'll be back in a moment.

As Layla sits up, her blanket falls, revealing her perfect breasts, and my mouth waters, wanting to taste them. She smiles knowingly, then covers herself back up.

I flip onto my back, and a minute later, they knock, so we know they're returning. The rest of the time we're massaged, my eyes stay on Layla, and hers stay on me. When the massages are over, Layla's masseuse brings us each a small cup of water and says we can take our time getting dressed.

The moment the door closes, I lock it, and then I'm on her, my mouth crashing against hers. She's silky smooth from the lotion, and I waste no time gliding my hand across her flesh and over to her pussy. One finger in and I find she's soaking fucking wet.

I finger-fuck her hard and deep as she strokes my cock. We don't have a lot of time before somebody notices that we're still in here, so once I've made her come, I spread her legs and enter her.

"Oh, God," she groans, holding on to my neck as I fuck her with abandon, not stopping until she's coming again, taking me along with her.

"Maybe massages aren't so bad after all," I murmur against her mouth

"I think we should make them a monthly thing," she says, licking across the seam of my lips.

"Done."

Twenty-Eight

CAMDEN

The guys and I hold back our laughter while Felix sings the song he wrote for his mom. When we arrived at the studio, he was fascinated with the music equipment, so I told him if he wrote a song, he could sing it, and I'd record it for him. Since Layla's birthday is in a few days, he said he wanted to sing her a birthday song. The kid is completely tone deaf, but he's cute as hell.

"You're the best mom ever 'cause you let me stay up late and watch movies. Happy Birthday."

When he finishes singing, he takes off his headphones and grins at us. "Did I do good?"

"You fucking rocked it," Gage says.

"Watch your mouth." I punch him in the arm. "The last thing I need is him going home and using words like that around his mom. She'll never trust me with him again."

Gage ignores me, walking into the sound booth and fist-bumping Felix.

"Can I hear it?" Felix asks, hopping up onto the stool.

Earl snorts out a laugh, and I glare at the asshole.

"Soon," I tell him. "First, we have to edit it." And add a shit ton of Auto-Tune to it so it doesn't break his mother's eardrums.

"Okay, I'm hungry," Felix says.

"Let me see where your mom is at." I grab my phone and find several missed calls and texts from Layla. Shit, my phone's been on silent. The last one asks if Felix and I are okay, so I call her back.

"Hey," she breathes. "I've been trying to get ahold of you."

"Sorry, my phone was on silent. We're still at the studio."

"Okay, will you be home soon?" Something in her voice has my hackles rising.

"Yeah. Everything okay?" She hesitates, and I know something is wrong. "Layles…"

"I just need you to come home, please."

After we hang up, Felix and I say bye to the guys and head home, stopping at Layla's favorite restaurant to pick up food on the way—and then a drive-through for Felix since it's his least favorite.

When we get home, she pulls Felix into a tight hug, making him screech in surprise. "Mom, you're going to choke me to death," he says dramatically.

"I'm sorry, sweetie. I just love you so much."

"I brought food." I hold up the bag.

"Thanks." A fake smile stretches across her face, making my stomach sink.

"Can I go watch TV?" Felix asks. "I ate chicken nuggets."

"Yeah," Layla chokes out. "Go ahead."

Felix hightails it up the stairs, leaving Layla and me alone.

"You want to tell me what's going on?" I ask, laying the food out on the table.

Layla doesn't say anything right away, so I give her time and focus on my food even though I've pretty much lost my appetite. Layla pushes her food around her plate but doesn't actually take a bite.

Finally, she sets her fork down and speaks. "Our freshman year of college, David cheated on me." I set down my fork, giving her my full attention.

"We were living in separate dorms, and I was spending a lot of time with Kaylee. She was a mess after...everything. David was always complaining I wasn't paying enough attention to him. We were fighting all the time. He got drunk at a party one night and messed around with another girl. He swears they didn't have sex, but I didn't care. I broke up with him the second I found out."

She releases a harsh breath and shakes her head. "A few weeks later, I found out I was pregnant. I didn't understand how it happened. I was on birth control and never missed a day. I was eighteen and scared, and David begged me to stay with him. I took him back, and we got married, moved off campus into our own apartment his parents helped him pay for, and I never looked back."

She sucks her bottom lip into her mouth and rolls it out slowly before continuing. "I told the gynecologist, and after I gave birth to Felix, I got an IUD, but it caused a negative reaction so I went back on the pill. They gave me a different one, in case the one I was on didn't work with me for whatever reason."

I'm trying to follow what she's saying, but I'm not quite sure where she's going with this.

"Last year, David asked me for another baby, and I said no. From the beginning, our marriage was rocky, and it only got worse over the years. He worked a lot but was also controlling. He didn't pay attention to Felix and me but didn't want us around anyone else. I think, in a lot of ways, I stayed with him for Felix, and he knew that. Our marriage was barely hanging on by a thread when we moved here. With Felix going to school, it was only a matter of time until I got a job and became independent. That's why, even though I said no to having another baby, he went behind my back again and switched out my birth control pills for placebos."

Her eyes meet mine, and it takes me a second to wrap my head around everything she just said. "Wait, again?"

"Again." She nods. "I ran into him today. Well, not ran into him since he knew I had an appointment and made sure to *run* into me."

"What?" I bark. "Where the fuck was Simon?"

She holds up her hand. "I'm fine. It was my mistake. I left out the wrong door. When Simon realized I was gone, he found me and jumped in and got David away from me, but before he did, David confessed to messing with my pills then *and* now."

My head is spinning. "Now? What do you mean now?"

"I mean, David took it upon himself to switch out my pills without me knowing, so this entire time we've been having sex, thinking we're protected, I wasn't. And now, I'm pregnant."

She slides a black-and-white image over to me. I don't know what the hell I'm looking at, but I've seen it in enough movies and shit to know it's a sonogram photo. "You're...you're pregnant?"

"Five weeks." Tears fill her eyes. "I'm so, so sorry, Camden." She releases a harsh breath, and a couple of tears fall.

"You're pregnant," I breathe. "Holy shit." I pull my chair out and pull hers toward me, so I can see her belly. "You're pregnant with my baby?" She nods, and I lift her shirt, exposing her flesh. I drop to my knees and kiss just above her belly button. "Holy shit," I repeat. "I can't believe it. We're having a baby."

When I glance back up at her, she's looking at me with tears streaming down her cheeks. And then I remember the part about her not wanting to have another baby. David tricked her, and thankfully, she didn't get pregnant until we were together, but that doesn't change the fact that she wasn't given a choice. I'm almost positive that doing something like this is a crime, and he could be charged. Hell, if it's possible, I'm going to make sure he is charged.

I sit up and take her face in my hands. "Do you want to have this baby?" I ask slowly. If she says no, I'll be devastated, but I won't argue. What David did was fucked up. No woman should be tricked or forced into having a baby, so I sure as fuck won't guilt her into having this baby. If she decides not to keep it, I'll support her decision one hundred percent.

"I do," she says. "I really do want this baby."

I sag in relief. "Then why are you crying?"

"Besides feeling betrayed, I wasn't sure how you'd feel. I know you love me, but we're young, and this is still all new, and you're already taking on a stepson..."

"Whoa." I pull back slightly. "I'm not taking anything or anyone on. We're a family."

She nods. "I know but still..."

"We take it at our pace, do whatever feels *right*," I tell her, repeating the very words she said to me in California when she told me she wanted to be with me. "I don't care that we've only been married for a short time. I love you. And while I hate what David did, I fucking love that you're carrying my baby."

A smile cuts through the tears, exposing those twin dimples I love. "I do too."

I take the sonogram picture and glance at it. "I think it looks like a girl. What do you think?"

She laughs, the sound melodic. "I think it looks like one of Felix's drawings."

"YOU'RE HAVING A BABY?" MY MOM SQUEALS, THROWING HER ARMS AROUND ME AT THE SAME TIME Layla's mom hugs her. We're not announcing anything until she's in her second trimester, but we had to tell our families. She was worried they would feel like we're rushing, but of course, they're all ecstatic.

"How long until we find out the sex?" Patricia asks.

"Umm...a couple of months," Layla says.

"I can't wait to go shopping!" Mom adds.

"I hope it's a boy," Felix says. "Then he can play *Sonic* with me."

"If it's a girl, she can play too," Layla tells him.

He looks at her like she's crazy and shakes his head. "Is it time for birthday cake yet?"

"We have to eat dinner first," Layla says, ruffling his hair.

"We could eat cake for dinner." Felix shrugs.

"You know what?" Layla says. "That actually sounds like a really good idea."

Felix's face lights up. "Really?"

"Yeah, why not? It's my birthday, and cake sounds good."

"Yes!" He runs straight into the kitchen and jumps on a chair to check out the cake we bought for Layla's birthday. We're barbecuing outside since it's actually on the warmer side, and we've picked up a bounce house/water slide for Felix to play on.

I light the candles, and everyone sings "Happy Birthday," then Layla makes a wish, blowing them out. My mom cuts slices and dishes them out to everyone.

"Here, Mom." Felix scoops his chocolate cake onto her plate while Layla does the same with her vanilla. I watch them, feeling so damn blessed.

"Mom," Felix says, shoveling his cake into his mouth. "Is the baby in your belly?"

Layla smiles and nods. "Yep. That's where you were too when I was pregnant with you."

Felix's eyes go wide. "When I was in your belly, did you eat cake?"

Layla laughs. "A lot of cake. All chocolate."

Felix cringes. "That's not nice. You know I don't like chocolate cake."

Everyone listening to them laughs.

"Wait, Mom. Stop!" Felix drops his hand over hers before she can take another bite. "If the baby is in your belly, and you're eating cake…" He takes his finger and drags it from her throat down to her belly button. "Does the cake fall on the baby's head?"

Layla stifles her laughter when she sees he's dead serious. "It's a different part of my belly," she explains. "The baby is here…" She points at one area. "And the food goes here." She points at another area.

Felix nods. "Like when I'm full, and my belly still has room for dessert?"

"Yeah," Layla says with a laugh. "Just like that."

After eating the cake, Felix insists we give Layla her birthday present because apparently, we're not doing anything in order. So we pile into the living room since Bailey helped me turn it into a video. I went on to her social media accounts and saved a bunch of photos and videos of her and Felix over the years, and we made it into a digital collage of sorts.

"I made it for you because I love you," Felix says proudly.

The second the song starts and Felix comes on the screen, with his headphones on and grinning as he sings the lyrics he wrote himself, Layla's eyes water. I have to admit, with the Auto-Tune shit we did to the song, it doesn't sound half bad. Okay, I'm lying. The sound is cringeworthy, but it's still cute as hell. As the song continues, it switches from Felix to the various photos and videos of them. Layla starts to sob, and I notice her mom also tears up.

When it's done, Layla scoops her son into her arms and peppers kisses all over his face. "Best present ever," she tells him as he squirms and laughs, begging her to stop.

"Thank you," she says to me once she's set him down. "I love it."

"And I love you." I give her a hard and long kiss, not giving a shit that we have an audience. It might be Layla's birthday, but she's given me so damn much.

"AND...THAT'S A WRAP," LAYLA SAYS, BEAMING AT US AS THE FILM CREW STARTS SHUFFLING ABOUT, getting everything organized and cleaned up. For the past two days, we've been shooting a music video that Layla's producing. When she pitched it to us, we all agreed it was perfect. The song is called "Ghosted," and it was written by Declan. It's about unrequited love and will be the single we release as a teaser to our album. The video is about a guy following a woman around. He appears like a ghost to emphasize the fact that she doesn't return his feelings. She's going about her day and feels him around but can't actually see him. In the end, he vanishes into thin air, and she's left feeling unsettled as if his presence alone was enough to make her feel safe. It's sad as fuck, and our fans are going to eat it up. I can't help but wonder if it's about my sister, but I'm not going there.

"How soon can we have it finalized?" Dad asks Layla. "I'd like to get it released in the next couple of weeks.

"I think I can have it done by this weekend." She glances at her phone. "Shoot. I need to grab Felix and get him to Beatrice." She's referring to the social worker who takes Felix to meet with his dad.

"No worries. Go," Dad says. "I can't wait to see the finished product. You did a great job."

Layla blushes. "Thanks." She gives me a chaste kiss. "See you at home?"

"Yeah, I need to swing by the studio for a bit. Want me to pick up dinner on my way home?"

"Sounds perfect." She takes off with Simon while the guys and I head in the opposite direction. We're wrapping up the album today, and Earl asked us to come by to get it all finalized.

We're all deep in the music when my phone rings. "Give me a second," I tell everyone, hitting answer. "Hey, Shutter—"

"He's gone!" she cries over the phone.

"What? Who?"

"He's gone! David took him. He took Felix. Beatrice has called the police, but he's gone. He took him to the bathroom, and they never came back. Simon and I have looked everywhere, but we can't find him."

"I'm on my way," I tell her, jumping out of my seat. "Where are you?"

She gives me the name of the restaurant, and after telling the guys what's happened, they insist on going. More eyes can mean locating him quicker. On the way, I call our parents and fill them in. When we arrive at the restaurant, a few police cars are there, and an officer is talking to Layla. The second she sees me, she throws herself into my arms.

"I should've known he would do something like this. He's made so many threats." She sobs into my chest while I rub her back, wishing I could magically make Felix reappear. Of course he doesn't own any electronics like a phone, so there's no way to track him.

Because of the situation and the restaurant footage, we're able to get an emergency missing child alert sent out as well as file a missing person's report. The police promise to follow up on any leads, and then we're sent home since it's clear they're no longer in the restaurant.

A little while later, the police let us know David isn't at his house or at his parents'. Layla asks about his assistant, and they confirm she hasn't seen him.

"They have to be somewhere!" Layla cries. "I just don't know where to look." The look of helplessness in her features damn near kills me. She wants to be out scouring the streets, but we live in New York. They could be any-fucking-where.

I hold her all night until she finally cries herself to sleep. And then I hold her until I pass out, praying for Felix's safe return.

Twenty-Nine

LAYLA

It's been two days. Two days without hearing my little boy's voice or seeing him smile. Since David walked him to the bathroom and they never returned, instead, going out the emergency exit. It's been two days of the police looking for leads, our family and friends searching anywhere we can think of. Even Kaylee came home to be with me.

But Felix and David are nowhere to be found. I've cried to the point that it feels as though my tear ducts have dried up. And of course morning sickness has decided to rear its ugly head, so between crying and searching, I've spent my time with my head in the toilet.

"Here, try this," Kaylee says, handing me a lollipop. "It's for morning sickness."

I'll try anything at this point, so I pop it into my mouth. "Thanks."

"We're going to find him," she says, her eyes meeting mine.

"I know." I nod, hoping my positive thinking will make a difference. "If you need to get back to work…"

"No." She shakes her head. "I don't need to be anywhere but right here with you."

"Thank you."

The day is spent with us being spoon-fed information on leads that don't seem to ever pan out. Camden suggests offering a cash reward for any leads, but the police are wary it will only make their job harder by causing a lot of false leads.

By day four, Camden insists we put out a cash reward, saying he's not leaving any stone unturned. He posts a picture of Felix on his social media and offers a million dollars to the person with the tip that leads to us finding him, along with a phone number they can call so we can weed them out.

It's late, three in the morning on day five, when I pass out from exhaustion, still not any closer to finding my son. I've tried calling and texting David, and Camden had a guy he knows try to track him, but his phone must be off or dead because it's untraceable.

I get up, groggy and in need of having to pee. When I glance at the time, I see it's seven in the morning. Camden left me a note that he's gone out to get breakfast. Through all of this, he's made sure I'm fed and taken care of, knowing I'm not in a place to do it myself.

I hear some shuffling, and assuming Camden is back, I go downstairs. Only it's not Camden...it's David and Felix.

"Oh my God!" I cry, running toward my son, but before I make it to him, David raises a gun, stopping me in my place. "What are you doing?" I screech. "Put that thing down!" Faintly, I hear my phone ringing upstairs, but I ignore it, focusing on David with a gun in one hand and my son, standing in front of him, sobs wracking his little body.

"He won't stop crying!" David yells. "The fucking kid won't stop crying for you." He shoves Felix forward, and he goes straight into my arms. I hold him tight, inhaling his scent.

"He can't have him," David barks. "And he can't have you! He took everything! My wife and my son and now he's having *my* baby!!" David says, his eyes manic while he waves the gun in the air. "If I can't have you, he doesn't get you either!"

His words seep into my pores like gasoline. "David..." He can't mean what I think he means.

"You're supposed to be mine!" he hisses. "Felix is supposed to be mine. That baby in your belly is mine! He took it all, and now he's going to lose everything."

"Please don't do this," I beg. "Please. I'll do anything!"

"It's too late." He takes a step forward, and instinctually, I take one back. "It's okay," he says, his voice now soft. "Because soon we'll all be together, happy again."

He raises his gun, aiming it directly at me, and I shove Felix behind me, hoping to at least save him. Then I close my eyes and do the only thing I can do: pray.

There's a scuffle, some shouting, and then a gun goes off. And when I glance up, what I see causes both relief and heartbreak deep inside me.

Thirty

CAMDEN

EARLIER…

"ANY NEWS?" I ASK MY CONTACT AT THE NYPD AS I GET INTO MY SUV AND PULL OUT OF THE GARAGE.

"Nothing. Not a damn peep." I can hear it in his voice. He's concerned. It's been days, fucking days since they've disappeared. If David did it for money, he would've made contact by now. Every day they're gone means they have the chance to get farther away. At this point, they might not even be in the state. We know he hasn't left the country since Felix doesn't have a passport, but anywhere within driving distance is game. And every day we don't find him statistically decreases the chances of ever finding him. Daniel was able to get a warrant to search David's accounts, but nothing has been flagged, which means he's using cash.

"All right, thanks. If you hear anything…"

"Of course."

We hang up, and after making sure the gate is closed behind me, I head toward Layla's favorite deli so I can get us breakfast. Traffic is a bitch, like always, and it takes me a good twenty minutes to get there. As I'm parking in front of the deli, my phone pings with an alert: **gate access granted.** That can only happen if someone knows the code.

A few seconds later: **front door open.**

This can't be right. I click on the camera mode and damn near lose my shit when I see Felix…and David inside the house. Somehow, David must've found out the gate code, which wouldn't be hard since he's been stalking the hell out of us based on the threatening images he's sent. And Felix knows where we keep the spare key because he was with us when we hid it after Layla got locked out by accident.

There's no Layla, which means she's either upstairs sleeping or somewhere else other than the foyer since that's the only part of the house with a camera. I dial her number, but she doesn't answer. I call again. Still no answer. I send a quick text to Simon, letting him know the situation since he's closer, then call the police, giving them all the info I have—all while driving like a bat out of hell back to our house.

I'm almost home when I get a text from Simon: **deactivated all alarms. He's armed. Come around back.**

What the fuck. My heart pounds behind my rib cage the rest of the drive, praying to fucking God that David isn't crazy enough to actually use the gun. I park outside of the gate and jump it so I don't make any noise. The cops aren't here yet. When I spot Simon around back, he puts a single finger up to his lips, and I nod once in understanding.

He's got his gun in his hand, and I trust he knows what he's doing. He knows his only priority is to protect Layla and Felix—at all costs.

With the door cracked open, we can hear David speaking.

"You're supposed to be mine! Felix is supposed to be mine. That baby in your belly is mine! He took it all, and now he's going to lose everything."

"Please don't do this," Layla begs. "Please. I'll do anything!" The fear in her tone has me stepping forward, but Simon shakes his head, stopping me.

"It's too late," David says. "It's okay...because soon we'll all be together, happy again."

His words aren't just a threat. They're a promise. He's going to kill Layla and Felix and then end his own life, and there's no way I'm going to stand out here and wait for the fucking police to get here while that happens. They might be dead if we wait much longer.

Before I can make my move, Simon knocks the door open, making it bang against the wall. I'm not sure what the fuck he's thinking until I glance inside, and see that by doing so, he's distracted David, making him look this way. Without waiting, Simon aims and fires, hitting David in the chest. The force of the blow sends him flying onto his back.

I don't know if he's dead or not, and I don't care. Simon goes straight for him, making sure he's disarmed while I pull a shaking Layla and a crying Felix into my arms, needing to get them out of the room and out of the house.

As we're stepping outside, the police pull up, and I tell them where they can find David. A few officers head that way while two others stay with us, asking me what happened. I give them a quick overview, then ask if the details can wait, nodding toward my family in my arms, clearly distraught.

The officer insists they go to the hospital to get checked out, and thankfully, Layla agrees. Since neither needs immediate medical attention and I'm not about to let them out of my sight, I let them know I'll drive them myself. On the way, I call our parents, letting them know we have Felix back and they're okay. Layla and Felix are quiet for the entire drive, and I worry they've gone into shock. Layla sits in the back with Felix, holding him.

When we arrive, the nurse brings us back right away, having been told to expect us. Thankfully, they let them both stay together. The nurse asks questions, and Felix nods and shakes his head. When they've determined he's physically okay, they check out Layla. Since she's further along, they can do an abdominal ultrasound.

"And that's the baby's heartbeat," the tech says softly.

"That's the baby?" Felix asks, finally speaking. He's lying next to his mom, against her side, but he sits up to check out the monitor.

"It is," the tech says, explaining all the parts.

"How does the baby get in there?" Felix asks, curious as ever, making Layla smile.

"It's science," the tech says.

Once the ultrasound is done, the tech leaves us alone.

I'm about to ask Layla how she's doing when there's a knock on the door. "Yeah?"

Simon steps inside the doorway. "Layla." He nods. "You both okay?"

"We are," she says, tears filling her eyes. "Thank you."

He nods then looks at me. "I need to talk to you for a second."

"I'll be right back," I tell Layla, leaning over and kissing her forehead, then kissing Felix's. "If you guys need anything, I'll be right outside the door."

"He's alive," Simon says once we're in the hallway and the door is closed. "At least for now. He's in surgery. I hit him in the chest, and they saved his fucking life."

"They were doing their jobs."

Simon glares. "A little more to the left and I would've hit his heart."

"You don't want that blood on your hands," I tell him, as much as I would've loved for him to have killed David. He sure as fuck deserves it. "If he survives, he'll be going to jail. Kidnapping a minor, attempt to commit murder. We heard the shit he said."

Simon nods, but I can tell the only way he'll be satisfied is if David's heart were to stop beating. And that's why I trust him with my family's lives.

After suggesting they both speak to someone about what they went through, the doctor discharges Layla and Felix, and we head to a hotel since our house is a crime scene.

Felix, like the four-year-old he is, snaps out of it the second he sees our room has a private one-lane bowling alley. After our parents visit, giving Layla and Felix love and affection, we spend the afternoon bowling, going swimming, and playing in the arcade while Layla stays close, watching but not participating.

When it's time for bed, Felix asks to sleep with Layla, and she of course tells him he can. I kiss them both good night, prepared to sleep in another room, when Felix says, "You can sleep with us. The bed is big enough for ten people."

I glance at Layla, making sure it's okay, and she nods once. I keep my clothes on and climb into bed behind her, pulling her into my front, so I can feel her warm body against mine. Felix lays his head down on the pillow, and within minutes, he's passed out. I assume Layla is asleep as well, but then she carefully turns over to face me.

"Hey," I say softly, tucking a few loose strands behind her ear.

"Hey," she says back.

We lie in silence for several minutes, and then, like a dam at capacity, her lids fill with tears, and they spill over. Not wanting to wake Felix, I pull her face to my chest and hold her tightly. "It's okay," I whisper, kissing the top of her head while she quietly cries into my shirt. "Everything is okay."

Epilogue

LAYLA

TWO MONTHS LATER

"WOW, THIS PLACE IS BEAUTIFUL." I GLANCE AROUND AS CAMDEN PULLS MY CHAIR OUT FOR ME, AND I have a seat. Life can get busy, especially with his line of work, so he insisted on weekly date nights. I wasn't about to argue since it meant my amazing, handsome husband was taking me out and spoiling me at least once a week. I mean, what woman would say no to that?

But tonight is a special occasion because, after two months of wondering what would happen to David—since the bullet didn't kill him—it's all over. He was charged with several crimes, including kidnapping and endangering a minor and attempted murder on two counts—since his plan was to kill Felix and me and end his own life—and found guilty of all of them. He lost all his parental rights to Felix, and today, he was sentenced to life in prison. It's been hard on Felix since he's young and doesn't understand everything, only knowing his daddy was mean to him, so we're seeing a therapist every week, which I think is helping.

"You look stunning," Camden says, sitting next to me and rubbing my small bump. The guy can't keep his hands off me, and it's only gotten worse since I started showing. His mom warned me the Blackwood men loved pregnant women, but I didn't fully get it until I experienced it.

"I was thinking, before you go on tour, we can do a weekend getaway since Felix is still in school," I suggest as we look at the menu.

"That sounds perfect," he says, taking my hand and kissing the top of it. "Where were you thinking?"

"I don't know. Somewhere we can relax since I can't really do much being pregnant."

"We'll figure it out." He lets go of my hand and moves his hand down my belly to my thigh, massaging the flesh. Since I'm wearing a dress that's on the short side, he's able to glide his fingers easily under the material and tease me.

"Not here," I hiss, glancing around. You never know who's watching or taking a picture.

He chuckles softly. "C'mon, I'll make it quick. You know I can get you off in like five seconds."

I glare at him. "I don't want to get off in five seconds. I want to fully enjoy it."

He backs off slightly, but the entire time we're eating and talking, he makes it a point to still touch me...everywhere but there, and by the time we get home—Felix is spending the night with my mom—I'd be completely okay with him making me come in five seconds. But of course, that's not what he's going to do.

He lays me out on the bed, undresses me so I'm completely naked, and then starts working me over slowly, sucking on my neck, tweaking my nipples, massaging my thighs. Not once, though, does he touch my clit, and I know it's because he's going to draw it out and make sure I can't say he got me off in five seconds.

When his fingers dip into my warmth, I wiggle my ass, silently telling him I want some ass play. He grins and grabs the lube, squirting some onto his finger. His tongue licks my center—everywhere but my clit—and his fingers push into my ass, deliciously filling me.

"More, please," I beg when he uses his other hand to finger my pussy.

"I'm not sure if you're ready for more," he murmurs, kissing my belly, just under my belly button.

"I am," I breathe. "Please."

"Hmm...I don't know. I need to make sure you're *fully* enjoying this."

He dips his face between my legs and laps straight up my seam, brushing softly against my clit. It vibrates in need, and I squeeze my legs together, making Camden chuckle.

"Please," I whine. "I need to come."

He laughs against my pussy, but does as I say, taking the swollen nub between his lips and sucking on it. Sparks go off behind my lids, but then he stops.

"Camden, please," I moan, riding his fingers that are still in my ass.

His tongue glides back and forth along my clit, taking me higher and higher until I'm dangling off the edge. Then like the perfect lover he is, he takes me right over it, sending me flying as I experience a mind-blowing orgasm.

Once I've come down, he removes his shirt, using it to wipe his fingers and face, and undoes his pants, exposing his long, thick cock. I take it in my hand and stroke it a few times before I guide it into me. The moment we become one, we both sigh in contentment. He makes love to me, switching between soft and sweet and hard and rough. It'll never get old, being with

Camden. I'll never have enough of him. I'll always want and need more, and he'll always give it to me.

When we've both come, we take a shower together and then climb back into bed. I love the moments after sex when it's just the two of us. We talk and laugh and just *be*. Camden is so great about simply being in the moment with me. Life can be crazy and chaotic, but when we're together, it's as if all the chaos is under control, even for just a moment.

"I'm going to miss you while you're on tour," I tell him. They take off in a couple of weeks and will be gone for two months. He made sure they'll be back long before my due date, not wanting to chance me having the baby and them having to cancel any shows.

"You and Felix should just come with us," he says for the millionth time, even though he knows it's not happening. I'm planning to visit him—with and without Felix—but being on tour full time with a rock band is not a place for a child or a pregnant woman.

"We'll visit…"

"I don't want to go more than a week without seeing you," he says, pulling me into his arms, his face resting on the top of my head that's laying on his chest.

"We'll video chat, and I'll visit. It's only a couple of months. It will fly by."

"I already miss you, and I haven't even left yet."

I smile at his sweet words. "We'll make it work. We were apart for five years, and we found our way back together."

Camden takes my chin and lifts it slightly, so I look at him. "I'll always find my way back to you." He presses his lips to mine, and I sigh into the kiss, getting lost in him.

When the kiss ends, I lean forward and press my lips to his tattoo, located right over his heart. He always said he wouldn't get one until he had something worth putting permanently on his body. So I was shocked when he told me he wanted to get a tattoo one day. I went with him to Forbidden Ink, the tattoo place where the guys always go when they're in New York to get their work done.

He wouldn't tell me what he was getting, but I was in tears once it was done and he showed me. It's the same tattoo I got: a camera. Only his isn't shattered like mine is. Instead, it's perfectly intact, and where I had written "Shattered," the title of his song he sang about me all those months back, he has "Pieced Back Together," the title of the new song he once again wrote about me—only this time, it's about our love putting all the shattered pieces back together. It might not be perfect, but it's ours, and I wouldn't have it any other way.

CAMDEN AND I ARE CUDDLING IN BED, BETWEEN ASLEEP AND AWAKE, WHEN MY PHONE BUZZES WITH Kaylee's name on the screen.

"Hey, Kaylee. How are you?" There's sniffling over the phone, and my hackles rise. "Kaylee…"

"I need you, Layla."

"Where are you?"

"At home…in New York."

"I'll be right there." I'm already jumping out of bed and getting my clothes on. "Kaylee needs me."

"I'll drive you," Camden says.

"Thank you."

When I get to Kaylee's apartment, the one she shares with her mom and stepdad, Camden kisses me and tells me to text him once I'm inside and to let him know when I'm ready to come home.

I haven't even knocked when the door swings open and Kaylee's standing there, her face splotchy from crying. "What happened?" I ask as she throws her arms around me and buries her face into my neck, sobbing heavily.

"I was fired from Evolution." Evolution is the PR company that hired her.

"What? Why?"

"Sam fucking York accused me of trying to sexually assault him. It's so ridiculous, but they, of course, took his word over mine and fired me on the spot. Four years of college all down the drain," she cries.

"You don't know that," I tell her.

"Yes, I do. Once it gets out what he's accused me of, no PR company will hire me. I'll be blacklisted everywhere."

"We'll figure it out," I tell her as I hug her tightly, trying to rack my brain with ways to help her. "There has to be something we can do."

Bonus Epilogue

LAYLA

CHARITY GALA

soaking it up. "Thank you. This truly means the world to me."

When Camden told me he wanted to start a nonprofit charity that raises money to help women who've been abused by their husbands and don't have the money to get out, I was in awe. And then he told me he wanted me to be the spokeswoman for it, and while I had no idea what that entailed, I knew it was something I had to do. Too many women are afraid to speak up when their husbands hurt them. And I might only be one person, but if telling my story means helping one other woman who's afraid to speak up, it'll be worth it.

Since I had no idea what I was doing, Camden hired a professional to handle all the details for Every Woman Has a Voice. She sat down with me, and we went over everything we needed to legally get our vision turned into reality.

And tonight we're holding a gala to celebrate that Every Woman Has a Voice is up and running. Between the Blackwoods' and Raging Chaos's pull, the most elite, wealthy celebrities and philanthropists with the deepest pockets have been invited. The donation cost per person is twenty-five thousand, and there will be auctions up for bidding to raise additional funding.

"I didn't do anything," Camden says, resting his hand on my protruding belly. "It was all you." He leans in and kisses my cheek before whispering into my ear. "Have I told you how beautiful you look tonight?" I'm in an elegant emerald dress that shows off my slight bump, and Camden can't seem to keep his hands off me.

"Only a couple of dozen times," I joke, loving how much my husband wants me.

"Dance with me." He steps back, extending his hand, and I take it, letting him pull me into his arms. We spend the night dancing and socializing. He introduces me to several celebrities that I have to force myself not to fangirl over, and after dinner, he gets up in front of everyone to talk about the motto of the charity before asking me to come up and speak.

"When I was married to my ex-husband, he raped me…" I begin, refusing to hold back, wanting every person in this room to understand why this cause is so important to me. Felix is at home with a sitter, so I don't have to worry about him overhearing.

I tell my story, allowing the tears to fall, and when I'm done, I end it by saying, "When you donate to Every Woman Has a Voice, every cent will be used to give a woman a voice because no woman should ever feel like she's alone and helpless and stuck when her husband has hurt her. Thank you for being here tonight and for supporting this cause."

As I walk off the stage to go back to my seat, a young woman stops me. I recognize her as a popular country singer who recently got divorced. "I just wanted to say thank you," she says softly. "I read your story online that you posted, and it's what gave me the courage to walk away from my husband. He was abusing me, and I knew I needed to get out, but I was scared. Your words gave me the courage I needed."

After we speak for a few more minutes, she excuses herself, and I find Camden. "I'm so proud of you," he says, kissing me sweetly. "I just got the initial numbers in, and we've already raised over six million."

"What?" I gasp in shock. "Seriously?"

"Yep. That's a lot of money to help women in need."

I throw my arms around him. "Thank you. I know you keep saying it's all me, but this couldn't have happened without you." I pull back and pepper kisses all over his face. "Can we go somewhere private?" I ask, suddenly horny as hell and wanting to thank him properly.

"We really shouldn't disappear."

"Wasn't it you who said you can get me off in five seconds flat?" I sass. "I need you to do that…now."

With a growl that tells me he's up for the challenge, he guides me to a private room where he does, in fact, get me off in five seconds flat.

Silent Chaos

A LOVE & LYRICS NOVEL

Your gray eyes
Your sweet smile
You fucked me over
And now I wanna forget

– Braxton Lutz, *Raging Chaos*

One

BRAXTON

THE PRESENT: HIGH SCHOOL PRE-GRADUATION PARTY

"TELL ME THIS ISN'T REAL. TELL ME YOU DIDN'T JUST FUCK THE CAPTAIN OF THE GODDAMN FOOTBALL team in his bedroom...in his fucking bed."

I step toward my girlfriend, my body vibrating with a mixture of pain and anger and confusion. When I received several texts from different people telling me what happened, I thought it was a sick joke, a misunderstanding, until I got on Instagram and found the post myself.

A picture of Kaylee in her bra and underwear lying on the bed. A selfie of the two of them—him not wearing a shirt and her still in her bra. And the last one...the one that hurt the most—them kissing. His goddamn lips on hers. Touching what's supposed to be mine. The caption read: **No better way to end high school than scoring with the cheer captain. #touchdown**

"Tell me!" I bark, making her jump. Fresh tears well in her lids and fall over, coursing down her cheeks as if she's the one who's been hurt and betrayed. As if she isn't the one who just destroyed everything. "Tell me the pictures are a joke." I step toward the only girl I've ever loved, the only girl I've ever given my heart to, and palm the side of her face, needing to feel her soft skin for what I know will be the last time. Because I can forgive a lot of things, but I can't forgive cheating.

"Kaylee," I choke out. "Please, baby," I beg, not wanting any of this to be real. Wanting to go back to my house, go to sleep, and wake up with all of this being nothing more than a fucking nightmare. "Tell me what I saw isn't true."

As I stare into the red-rimmed gray eyes of the girl I've spent the past ten months giving my heart to, I can't help but wonder where the hell it all went wrong.

Two

BRAXTON

SUMMER BEFORE SENIOR YEAR

"IT'S SO FUCKING HOT OUT," GAGE SAYS, DROPPING INTO A SEAT OUTSIDE THE COFFEE SHOP WHERE DECLAN and I are already sitting and drinking our iced coffees. We have a bunch of papers strewn everywhere—lyrics, songs, sheets of music. The three of us, along with Camden—who's out of town for the summer with his pop star sister who's on tour—are in a band. I know, I know…Who hasn't been in a band? Well, unlike most teenage bands, we're actually damn good, and thanks to Camden's family, who owns Blackwood Records, one of the largest record labels in the country, we'll be getting signed after we graduate in June.

"It's too damn hot," Declan agrees. "I think I saw it's going to be in the hundreds today." He lifts the paper and reads over the most recent song I wrote. It's called "Cheater" and is an ode to my piece-of-shit mother who cheated on my father, saying she wasn't meant to be a mother or a wife, then walked out the door, never looking back.

"Fuck, it's too hot to work on music." Declan drops the paper and takes a sip of his coffee.

"It's too hot to move," Gage bitches. "Who in the hell can even think in this heat?"

We live in New York, and there's a heatwave coming through. When most think of New York, they think of the frigid as hell winters, but if you live here, you know firsthand that the summers are a bitch. The humidity can shed ten pounds off you just by walking outside.

"You know what we should do?" Declan says, turning his phone around and showing us his screen—a picture of a bunch of kids from our school at the beach.

"I'm in," Gage says.

"You don't even like any of those assholes," I say with a laugh. Gage is literally the least social person I know—unless it's with someone in our very small circle.

"I don't need to like them to get in the water and cool down." Gage stands. "It's too hot to even smoke. Fuck it, let's go."

Declan chuckles, and I glance at him, raising a brow in question. "He saw Tori in the picture. He's been eyeing that cheerleader for months."

"Tori?" I say with a laugh. "Actually, I can totally see it. She's all cheerleader meets emo with her short skirts, black lipstick, and fishnet stockings. She's like the least peppy cheerleader on the squad. It's the perfect match made in hell."

Declan nods, and Gage punches me in the arm. "Fuck you, asshole. Let's go."

A couple of hours later, we're walking onto the beach wearing our board shorts with towels tucked under our arms. I immediately spot Layla, one of our good friends, lying out with her two best friends, Tori and Kaylee, and they're surrounded by a bunch of jocks. When Layla glances up, her lips pursed together in obvious annoyance, she nudges Kaylee, who then looks our way, her gray eyes meeting mine.

This gets Tori's attention, whose gaze seems to go straight to Gage. Something is said among the girls, and then a second later, the three of them saunter our way. I assume they're coming over to say hi, so I'm confused as shit when they head directly toward each of us individually.

"Quick, pretend you're in love with me and kiss me," Kaylee murmurs. Before I have a chance to ask what the hell she's talking about, her arms wrap around my neck and her mouth encloses over mine. Her lips are soft and supple, and when her tongue slips into my mouth, she tastes like the sweetest goddamn strawberries I've ever tasted.

Without thinking, I deepen the kiss, reaching down and lifting her off the ground. Her legs go around my torso, and her fingers drag through my hair, gently tugging on the ends. Our tongues collide with each other, stroking, caressing. I've kissed countless girls. It's one of the perks of being in a band in high school. Girls flock to you. They want a taste of the bad boy. I don't know what it is about the sight of a guy with a guitar in his hands, but they want it—want me. But never have I felt like this when kissing a girl. My heart thumps against my rib cage, my body's on fire, and my dick is as hard as a rock.

And then she ends the kiss. Her hypnotic gray eyes meet mine, and I force myself to suck in a harsh breath, having to remind myself how to breathe.

"Thank you," she says with a soft smile on her face and a hint of blush on her cheeks. "The football players were begging us to go out with them tonight, and Layla said we already had plans. They were asking who with, and then you guys walked up, and..." She shrugs, dragging her teeth across her bottom lip until it pops out, making me want to capture it with my own mouth. "I owe you one."

We stay like this for a couple of beats—Kaylee in my arms, her thighs pressed into my sides—and then I do something that shocks the hell out of us both. My mouth ascends, and my lips capture hers again. When her tongue finds its way back into my mouth, I suck on it, tasting her sweetness, getting lost in everything Kaylee Thomas. I grind her center against my dick, and she moans into my mouth. I have no clue what's happening, but I never want it to stop. I was just giving Gage shit about having eyes for a cheerleader, and now here I am, standing in the middle of the beach, making out with the head fucking cheerleader.

"Wow," Kaylee breathes when the kiss ends. "That was incredible. I don't think anyone will be asking me out now." It takes me a second, but then I remember that's why we were kissing in the first place.

"Go out with me," I blurt out, aware of the irony in my request. She throws her head back in a laugh, thinking I'm fucking with her. "I'm serious. Go out with me."

Her gorgeous eyes lock with mine. "You're serious?"

"Yeah, tonight...tomorrow...go out on a date with me."

"Okay."

"Yeah?" I didn't think it would be that easy. She was just complaining about guys bugging her, so I kind of assumed she'd turn me down. Layla, Tori, and Kaylee have been on a self-imposed anti-boyfriend kick all year—since Layla caught her boyfriend cheating, and it broke her heart.

"Yeah."

"Well, damn," Declan says once I put Kaylee down, and we walk over to join everyone. The jocks are all gone now, and only Gage, Tori, Declan, and Layla are sitting where the girls' stuff is. "How come you didn't kiss me like that, Layla, huh? I want a do-over."

Layla laughs and shoves his chest playfully. "Funny."

I notice Gage is staring at Tori like he wants to eat her alive, so I wonder how their kiss went. If it was as amazing as the one I just experienced with Kaylee.

"Have you guys heard from Camden?" Layla asks, pulling out her phone to I'm sure text him. "I think he's in Nashville." Camden and Layla met right before our sophomore year when she moved in next door. Camden's been in love with her ever since, but she has no clue. We've all told him to tell her how he feels, but he's too damn chicken.

"I'm going in the water," Tori says, standing and shaking the sand off her body. She glances at Gage. "Wanna join me?"

Gage shrugs, playing it cool. "Sure."

"I wanna go too," Layla adds, shoving her phone in her bag.

Declan stands to join them as well, leaving Kaylee and me.

"You guys coming?" Layla asks.

"Nah, you go," Kaylee says, her gaze darting over to me. "Braxton and I have to discuss where he's taking me out tonight."

Layla's eyes go wide. "What? When did that happen? While you were kissing?" Kaylee laughs. "What happened to our anti-boyfriend pact?" Layla pouts.

"It's officially summer," Kaylee says, "which means it's over."

Fuck yes.

Layla side-eyes her. "Whatever." She steps off the beach blanket. "Oh, shit! The sand is hot!"

"Jump on," Declan drawls, and Layla does so, laughing as he runs toward the water with her on his back, not stopping until they're completely submerged. Gage and Tori follow, stopping before they get to the water.

"Now, about that date," Kaylee says once we're alone. "What time are you picking me up?"

Three

BRAXTON

OCTOBER: SENIOR YEAR

"THIS IS CRAZY!" KAYLEE YELLS, HOLDING ME TIGHTLY AS WE DRIVE DOWN THE ROAD TOWARD THE Hamptons. It's our four-month anniversary, and to celebrate, I stole my dad's motorcycle and asked Camden for the keys to his parents' beach house since nobody's there this weekend. I texted Kaylee to pack a bag and to tell her mom she's spending the weekend with Layla.

With the cool breeze whirring around us, Kaylee snuggles up to me, her head resting against my back. Her hands find their way under my shirt, and she presses her cold fingers against my hot stomach. We've been taking it slow for the past few months. Going on dates, hanging out. Kaylee's a virgin, so I didn't want to rush her. But when she told me she was ready, I wanted it to be perfect. We might be young, but that doesn't mean I have to fuck her in the back seat of a car. I want tonight to be memorable for us both.

Two hours later, we step into the beach house. We've been here before for barbecues and shit, so we both know our way around. Camden's dad's one rule is no one is allowed in the master bedroom, so we go straight to the guest room that houses a queen-size bed and an en suite bathroom, and set our bags down.

"I'm going to take a shower," Kaylee says, suddenly sounding nervous.

"You hungry? I was thinking we could go out to dinner."

"Okay, that sounds good."

While I wait for her to get ready, I look up restaurants in the area and make reservations at one that looks good. I'm checking out the menu when Kaylee walks out in nothing but a towel wrapped around her. Her face is clean from all the makeup she was wearing earlier, and her blond hair is wet. She's never looked so beautiful.

She stops in front of me, nervously sucking her bottom lip into her mouth. I open my legs, and she steps between them, dragging her fingers through my hair. She tugs on the strands, and I glance up at her. Our mouths collide, and she moans as she climbs onto my lap, straddling me. I planned to make tonight special by lighting some candles and shit, but the moment she undoes her towel, dropping it to the floor, nothing matters but being with her.

Every man's wet dream, Kaylee has an athlete's body, lithe and toned, tits that fit perfectly in the palm of my hands, and an ass that's just thick enough to grab handfuls of. Every man can look all they want, but she's mine...all fucking mine. And I'm the only one allowed to touch her, kiss her, caress her.

We kiss for several minutes as I work her body to get her off. We've done this part several times, and at this point, I know her body as well as, if not better, than she does. Once she's orgasmed, screaming my name as her body trembles in pleasure, I lay her in the center of the bed. We've talked about it, so I know she's on birth control, and we're both clean. I kiss my way along her neck while she strokes my dick. It doesn't need any help getting hard, but I love the way she touches me and loves to explore my body.

After ensuring she's wet enough, I push slowly into her tightness. Her face scrunches up in pain, and I kiss her softly, gently, wishing I could take it away. Once I'm all the way in, I stop, giving her a second to breathe. I've had sex a couple of times before Kaylee, but none of the girls were virgins, so I looked it up online to be prepared and make it as good as it could be for her.

"I'm good," she breathes after a few seconds. "I'm okay."

With our eyes open and locked on each other, I slowly pull out and then push back in. She's tight and warm and so fucking perfect. I don't stand a chance at lasting, so before I blow my load, I find her clit and massage the already sensitive nub to get her off again. When she climaxes, her entire body shakes, and her pussy chokes the hell out of my dick, sending me straight over that cliff with her.

As we both take a moment to slow our breathing, I look down at her. Her eyes are slightly glassy, looking sated, her cheeks are flush, and her lips are swollen from our kissing. She's gorgeous, so goddamn perfect, and I don't care how young we are because I know she's the one for me. I've felt it from the moment she kissed me that day at the beach, and every day we spend together only strengthens my feelings toward her.

"I love you," I tell her, pressing my lips to hers. When our mouths connect, it's as if the entire world disappears, leaving just the two of us in our own little bubble.

"I love you too," she says when the kiss ends, palming my cheek. "And I totally think we should do that again before we go to dinner."

While Kaylee rinses off and then gets ready, I find my way out to the back patio. It's a cool night out, so I light up the outdoor firepit and have a seat in one of the Adirondack chairs, getting lost in my words. Being with Kaylee brings out so many emotions in me that I find myself constantly writing lyrics.

Most of them never amount to much, but some end up as songs.

"Whatcha got there?" Kaylee asks, plopping onto my lap.

"A possible song." I hand her the paper, not caring that every word on it is about her.

"Gray eyes, smile as bright as the sunrise. Her love is better than the best high." She turns and kisses me gently on the corner of my mouth. "I love when you write about our love. It makes it feel so...concrete. Permanent."

"It is." If I have it my way, we'll be together for the rest of our lives.

"That's what my mom thought about my dad too," she says sadly. "Before his accident."

She never talks about her dad, so I simply nod and wait for her to continue.

"He used to work for Empire," she resumes. "It's a marketing and advertising company. Every night when I was little, he would come home and work. I craved his attention, so I would bring my toys into his office and play while he worked. One day, he was struggling with a marketing pitch and asked my opinion. We spent hours working on it together. His pitch went over so well he was promoted, and that night, he brought home dinner and a cake, saying I was his good luck charm."

Kaylee's smile turns watery. "Every night after that, he would let me help him. It became our thing. Until his accident. He was stepping onto the street to grab a taxi when he was hit and dragged several yards. They had to perform surgery on his back, and while it was successful, he was left in permanent pain."

She swallows thickly, and I have a bad feeling where this is going. "They warned him the drugs could be addicting, but he said he had it under control." She shakes her head. "He didn't. One minute, he was my dad sitting with me in his office working, and the next, he was an addict, alcoholic stranger who would take his anger and pain out on my mom. It got so bad that he almost beat her to death. Thankfully, she left him."

"Where is he now?" I ask.

"I'm not sure. He lost his job and disappeared after she left him." A single tear slides down her cheek, and I catch it with my thumb, hating to see her sad. "I miss him...the *him* before the accident. I miss sitting in his office and working with him."

She's mentioned before that she plans to major in marketing and advertising, and now that makes sense. She wants that piece of her dad back.

"That won't be us," I tell her, cupping her face. "We're concrete, permanent, and nothing can change that."

Four

BRAXTON

DECEMBER-SENIOR YEAR

"MERRY CHRISTMAS!" KAYLEE SAYS, JUMPING INTO MY ARMS AND PEPPERING KISSES ALL OVER MY FACE.

"Merry Christmas, Crazy," I murmur, using the nickname I've dubbed for her as I walk us through her apartment. Being with Kaylee is as easy as breathing. She's carefree, always happy, and never gets mad. But she's also crazy as fuck. It's like riding the most exhilarating roller coaster. You know you're safe, but your heart still races with every dip and turn. It's both exciting and scary.

I try to set her down, but she clings to me like a koala bear, so with a laugh, I sit on the couch with her legs wrapped around my waist.

"I got you something," I tell her between kisses.

"Oh, a present?" Her eyes light up in excitement.

If you didn't know her, you'd think she's materialistic, but the truth is, I could give her a hand-written note, and she'd be just as excited. Kaylee just simply loves being thought about. I think it stems from her childhood. Her dad was—well, still is—a druggy alcoholic, who always puts his addiction before everyone and everything else.

Her mom was a victim, and once she was out of the shitty situation, she put herself first, needing to make herself happy again. She serial dated until she found herself a new husband, and they started a new family.

Meanwhile, Kaylee was ignored and left to her own devices. She told me once that her parents have forgotten countless holidays and birthdays, including her recent one when she turned eighteen. Layla and I threw her a huge party. So when she's given attention, she soaks it up like sunrays on a cold day.

I pull a small box out of my pocket and hand it to her. Her forehead wrinkles in confusion, and when she opens it, displaying a small white gold ring with two infinity symbols interwoven, she looks up at me in shock.

"It's a promise ring," I tell her, taking it out of the cushion it's nestled in.

It's not big or flashy, but I played my guitar for hours on the street corner by the coffee shop, singing the songs I've written that Camden usually sings to earn enough money to buy it.

"I want you to know that you're the one for me. I love you and want to spend my life with you. I know it's kind of small, but—"

"Stop," she rasps, tears filling her eyes. "It's perfect. I love it. I love you." She lets me slide it on the finger that I hope will one day house an engagement and wedding ring and beams down at it like it's a million-dollar ring.

"It's probably cliché as fuck," I say, "but it's two infinity symbols, symbolizing you and me never ending."

She smiles a watery smile and nods. "I love that."

"One day, when the band takes off, I'll replace this with something better, more expensive," I vow.

"I don't want anything else," she says, tears sliding down her cheeks. "I want this ring forever." She palms my face. "I want *you* forever."

Five

BRAXTON

MARCH-SENIOR YEAR

Kaylee: Come pick me up. I have the best idea!

Me: Where are you?

Kaylee: I just got home from cheer camp. Come over!

"GOTTA GO," I TELL THE GUYS, WHO ARE DISCUSSING A SONG CAMDEN RECENTLY WROTE. IT'S SPRING break, and we're hanging out at Camden's house since he's got a state-of-the-art studio in the basement of his house. Before his dad became the president of Blackwood Records, he was a huge musician—hell, his songs are still popular all these years later.

"Where are you going?" Declan asks.

"Girls are back from camp."

That has Gage standing. "I'm out."

"Damn, c'mon," Camden whines. "We've almost got this song on lock."

"Later," I say as Gage and I climb the stairs.

I faintly hear Camden muttering that we're pussy whipped, but I ignore it because he isn't wrong. One day, if he actually gets the balls to tell Layla how he feels and they finally get together, he'll get it. But until then, he'll continue to watch Layla from afar while she dates David the douche.

Since Tori lives in the opposite direction of Kaylee, Gage and I bump fists, then go our separate ways. I jump on the train and get off at her stop a few minutes later, practically sprinting to her place. It's been seven days since I've seen her, and I'm dying to kiss her, touch her, taste her.

I've barely knocked on her door when it swings open, and Kaylee pulls me inside by the front of my shirt, kissing the hell out of me. I'm assuming by the way she's attacking me in her foyer that we're alone, so I lift her into my arms and walk us to her bedroom, where I can properly welcome her home.

Our clothes are quickly shed, and I'm on top of her, kissing my way down her body until I get to her pussy. Spreading her legs, I devour her, licking and sucking on her clit until she's writhing under me and coming apart.

"God, I've missed you," I murmur as I crawl back up her body. My mouth crashes against hers, and she moans, loving her taste on my lips. I enter her in one fluid motion, and she groans. I would love nothing more than to fuck her for a long-ass time since being inside her is my favorite place in the world, but it's been a damn week, so all too soon, I'm coming deep inside her.

"I missed you," she says, kissing the corner of my mouth. Her legs are wrapped tightly around me, and even though I'm now semi-soft, I can feel her walls tightening around my dick from her orgasm.

"I missed the hell out of you," I tell her. "Now, tell me about this *best idea*."

When her face lights up, I know she's about to say something crazy, but I'll go along with it because like Camden said, I'm pussy whipped and completely okay with it.

"You still have your fake ID, right?"

"Yeah..." Since my birthday isn't until June, I'm younger than everyone, still seventeen.

"I was thinking," she says slowly, "we should go get tattoos."

"What?" I say through a laugh. Don't get me wrong. I'm down for it. I plan to get plenty once I'm old enough, but Kaylee has never mentioned wanting to get anything more than the sexy naval ring she got when she turned eighteen a couple of months ago.

"Something to commemorate our time together," she says with a soft smile. "I know you gave me this promise ring, but you don't have anything like that. I was thinking we could get matching tattoos, so when you're in LA and I'm here, every time you look at it, you can think of me."

My heart drops at her words. "I won't need anything to think about you because I'll be with you." We've talked about this, and we're in this together. I'm not going anywhere without her. She knows this.

Her smile turns sad. "I didn't get into U of C. I was waitlisted."

"But there's still a chance, right?"

She shakes her head. "I talked to my mom, and even if I were to get in, she doesn't have the money to help me with college, and any assistance from my dad is out of the question. I applied for financial aid, but because my mom is married to Peter, they count his income, and he makes too much, so I didn't qualify."

"Then we can take out a loan," I point out, refusing to give up.

"And graduate hundreds of thousands of dollars in debt?"

"We'll figure it out." I meant what I said. I'm not going anywhere without her.

She nods but doesn't look convinced. "Regardless, I thought getting matching tattoos would be the perfect way to link ourselves to each other forever."

I want to tell her the perfect way is for us to get married in June when I turn eighteen, but instead, since I'll give her whatever she wants, I agree. "What tattoo are you thinking of?"

"The same symbol as my ring. Two infinity symbols woven together.... never ending." She pulls my face down to hers. "Because no matter what, we're forever."

Six

BRAXTON

JUST BEFORE THE PRE-GRADUATION PARTY

"YOU'RE MAKING A MISTAKE!" DAD BARKS, FOLLOWING ME THROUGH OUR HOUSE AS I GET READY TO HEAD to the pre-graduation party. "Why the hell can't you see that?"

I groan, sick of this same argument we've had countless times over the past several weeks since I mentioned I might not be going to LA with the guys after graduation. It's not that I don't want to be part of the band...I do. But Kaylee can't afford to go to college in LA, and even if she could, she didn't get in. If I leave, we'll be living over three thousand miles apart, and while she's told me we can make it work over the distance, I don't see how, when neither of us can even afford a plane ticket to visit each other.

"I don't care what you think," I say. "Kaylee isn't Mom, and I'm not you. We're forever, and I'm not about to put the band before her." Everyone who has ever supposedly loved her has put her last, and I'm not going to do that to her. She deserves to be put first.

Dad backs up as if he's been punched in the face, and I feel bad about what I said. "I'm sorry," I say. I didn't mean to hurt him, but I know that's what he's thinking. He followed my mom to LA, giving up a huge opportunity, and in the end, she left him—*left us.* So I get why he's cynical, but Kaylee and I aren't them.

"I don't want to see you make the same mistakes I made," he says. "You're young. You don't get it, but there'll be a million girls like her."

"I disagree." I grab my phone from the nightstand and check to see if Kaylee has messaged me back. We were supposed to go to the party together, but she hasn't responded. "I'll be back later," I tell my dad as I walk out the door.

When I get to Kaylee's place, her mom—Ginny—opens the door, with Kaylee's three-year-old brother peeking out from behind her leg. "Hey, Braxton," she says. "Kaylee isn't here."

Damn, where the hell is she? "All right, thanks," I tell her. "If you see her, can you tell her I'm looking for her, please?"

"Of course, and have a safe trip to LA."

I freeze in my place at her words. "I'm not going to LA," I correct her. "I'm staying here, in New York." My phone goes off in my pocket, but I ignore it to focus on our conversation.

Ginny frowns. "Oh, I must've misunderstood. Well, New York isn't too far from Boston."

"What's in Boston?" My phone continues to vibrate, but I ignore it.

Her frown deepens. "Where Kaylee is going to school. She didn't tell you? She got into the same college as Layla and received a scholarship for her grades. They're going to be sharing a dorm."

Dread clogs my throat. "It must've slipped her mind," I say, my blood running cold.

My phone vibrates for what feels like the millionth time, and I pull it out as I quickly say bye to her mom. I have several missed calls and texts and some notifications from Instagram.

I open my messages and find some from Declan saying we need to talk, it's important, and to call him, a couple from Camden saying the same thing, and a few from some random people.

Confused as hell, I pull up the texts from the random people.

Kaylee is such a bitch. If you need a rebound fuck, call me.

Fuck that ho.

I can't believe she fucked Jack.

What the hell is going on? One of the messages includes a link, so I click on it. It takes me to a post on Jack's page and what I see damn near brings me to my knees.

No. No. No...Fuck, no. She wouldn't do this. She wouldn't cheat on me. I glance down at the tattoo of the infinity symbols on the outside of my hand. No, this can't be right. We're forever.

Seven

BRAXTON

THE PRESENT: HIGH SCHOOL PRE-GRADUATION PARTY

"BRAX..." KAYLEE CHOKES OUT, AND THAT ONE WORD, THE WAY SHE SAYS IT, TELLS ME EVERYTHING I NEED to know. It's not a mistake or a sick joke. She cheated on me with the goddamn quarterback. She gave him what she swore was mine, what she promised would be mine forever.

She reaches out for me but then quickly stops herself, pulling her hand back as a fresh round of tears fills her lids. I hate to see her cry, and any other time, I'd be pulling her into my arms and promising her anything in my power to make the tears stop. Only right now, there's nothing that can fix her tears. Because they're self-inflicted. She did this to us. I don't know why, but she did.

My phone buzzes like crazy in my pocket, so I pull it out to tell whoever is calling that now isn't a good time. But when I answer Declan's call, his words silence me. "Tori's dead. Gage is at the hospital. You need to meet us at Camden's place as soon as possible."

We hang up, and I look at Kaylee. "Something happened to Tori." Her brow furrows in confusion, telling me she has no clue. Of course she doesn't because she was too busy fucking that jock in his bed while destroying my damn heart. "She's dead."

The next few days that follow are a blur...

Layla gets engaged to David—Camden never did tell her how he felt.

We bury Tori—Gage checks the fuck out.

Camden's dad suggests we leave for LA immediately—we all agree.

And just like that, we step onto the private plane and never look back...
At least not for several years, that is.

Eight

KAYLEE

SIX YEARS LATER

"C'MON, BABY...YOU'VE BEEN TEASING THE HELL OUT OF ME WITH THOSE SEXY OUTFITS ALL DAMN TOUR. Just give me one taste."

I glare at Sam York, my first client since I graduated from NYU with my public relations and marketing/advertising degree and got hired by Evolution PR, and scoff. "Sexy outfits?" I glance down at my professional dress pants and button-down blouse that shows zero cleavage. I couldn't be dressed any less sexy if I tried. "You're drunk and delusional." The guy has been hitting on me since the tour began, but I've carefully managed to steer clear of him, counting down the days until the tour ends.

I didn't even want this job. I want to do marketing and advertising for the PR company, but they insist their employees get hands-on experience to learn about the people and brand they're marketing. I imagine not all employees are stuck going on tour with a musician, but my graduation lined up with his tour, and the fact that the original publicist backed out at the last second led to me being on tour with one of the most popular—and asinine—pop stars. My hope is once this tour is done, I'll be able to get into a position of my choice. Of course he'd pull this shit the day before it's time to go home.

Sam steps toward me, backing me up against the wall of the tour bus, and I extend my hand, refusing to allow him any closer. "You need to go sleep it off," I warn. "Sexual assault is a real thing, even for a pop star like yourself."

"Baby," he slurs, pushing past my hand and getting all up in my personal space. "Stop playing hard to get." He reaches for a breast and squeezes it hard, and I lose my cool.

"I'm not playing!" I wind my hand back and slap him in the face.

Because he's wasted, he stumbles back. "Bitch," he murmurs, coming at me hard. He pushes me against the wall and cups the area between my legs. "Stop being a fucking cock tease."

My fight-or-flight instincts kick in, and I lift my knee into his groin, making him stagger back in pain. "You're going to regret that." Without waiting for him to make his next move, I run off the bus and over to the other bus, where my bunk bed is. Once I'm safely there, I release a harsh breath, thankful I go home tomorrow. Fucking loser probably won't even remember the way he acted tonight. Assholes like him, who think they're above everyone else, always get away with shit like this. Not this time. Tomorrow morning, I'm going to tell my boss what he did. I'm not letting him get away with it.

"KAYLEE, YOU NEED TO WAKE UP," IRIS, THE TOUR MANAGER, SAYS. I OPEN MY EYES AND FIND THE BUS IS filled with light. It must be morning.

"Are we back in LA?"

"Yeah," she says, her lips pursed. "Pack up your things quickly. There's a car waiting to take you to the airport."

The ride to the airport is quick, and a few hours later, I arrive back in New York. Another car waits to take me to Evolution. When I enter the lobby, Evelyn is waiting for me, her face devoid of all emotion.

"Please have a seat," she says once we're in her office with the door closed.

I've been preparing what I'm going to say and how I'm going to word the way Sam behaved, but before I can begin, she speaks first.

"It's been brought to our attention by Sam York's team that you behaved inappropriately during the tour. He said last night you went as far as to sexually assault him, and when he refused your advances, you got physical—"

"He said what?" I hiss. "*He* was inappropriate. *He* tried to—"

Evelyn raises her hand, silencing me. "It doesn't matter. It's your word versus his. You never should've been on his bus alone with him. He's upset and making threats."

"What an asshole," I breathe. "So what do we do?"

"*We* don't do anything," she says. "In exchange for him not running my company into the ground, I agreed to let you go."

"You're firing me?" This is insane. "What do I do now?" My heart is racing in my chest. I busted my ass for this degree. I worked hard on that tour and didn't do anything wrong.

"I suggest you find a new career. Once it gets out how you behaved..." I open my mouth to correct her, but she shakes her head. "Whether it's true or not, you'll be blacklisted from this industry." She stands, making it clear this conversation is over. "Your last paycheck will be direct deposited. I wish you the best, and I'm sorry it didn't work out."

Nine

BRAXTON

"THAT'S IT, BABY. TAKE MY ENTIRE COCK DOWN YOUR THROAT." I PAT THE WOMAN'S HEAD AND CONTINUE reading through the group messages. I don't remember bringing this chick home with me last night, but when I woke up to her slurping on my dick, I wasn't about to stop her. It's the perfect parting gift—meaning as soon as I come down her throat, we'll be parting ways.

Camden: You're late to the meeting.

Me: Take notes for me.

Camden: We need a new publicist since you and Gage tag-teamed the last one...Nobody wants to work with us.

Gage: <shrugs>

Me: Such a waste...she wasn't even good in or out of bed. We have Jill...

I glance down at the woman still sucking my cock like a champ. She's been doing it for a while now, so I imagine her mouth is sore, but she still hasn't given up. "You're doing good," I praise her. "Maybe take me a little deeper."

She does as I suggest, gagging when my head hits the back of her throat. She's not the best dick sucker, but I'd give her an A for effort.

Camden: Jill is the tour manager. She has enough going on. She doesn't have time to babysit you guys. We need a new publicist before we go on tour. I need you here so we can discuss it.

Declan: Speak for yourself. I don't need a babysitter. That would be the other two dumbasses.

Gage: <shrugs>

The heavy breathing of the woman sucking my cock has me looking down. She's going to town on it, licking and sucking it like a lollipop, but it's doing nothing for me. She's not the first woman who hasn't been able to bring me to a release...not since...Fuck, I'm not going there.

Me: I don't care what you decide. I'm in the middle of something important.

Gage: I'm good with whatever you decide.

Declan: I'm almost there. I'm not getting stuck with another airhead on this tour.

Camden: Brax, I think you should be here...

Me: If you're worried about me fucking her, send a pic and I'll let you know.

Camden: GET THE FUCK DOWN HERE!

Me: No can do. Gotta go.

I chuck my phone onto the nightstand and focus on getting my dick sucked, refusing to believe that I'm broken. When the woman takes me deep again and nothing happens, I sigh in frustration. "Hey, babe, sorry to cut this short, but I gotta go."

She looks up, her mascara dripping down her cheeks. "But you haven't come yet." She pouts.

"It's not happening, but I appreciate the effort." I stand and tuck my dick back into my pants. "There's money in the bowl near the door for an Uber."

Once she's out the door, I head into the bathroom so I can shower, feeling dirty as fuck. I turn the hot water on to full blast and step under the spray. I squirt some body wash into my hands, lather it up, and clean my body. When my hand lands on my soft dick, I stroke it up and down, getting it hard, needing to prove that I'm not broken and just having a dry spell of sorts.

My eyes close, and I focus on getting harder and harder. I try to imagine the woman from earlier on her knees, sucking my dick, yet thoughts of someone else appear instead: blond hair, gray eyes, red lips, perfect tits, toned thighs, an ass I can grab on to, and—

I come hard all over the shower wall—proving that I'm okay and pissing me off at the same time. Because *she's* the last person I should be thinking about when I come, but ever since I ran into her a few months ago when we were having dinner with our friends, I can't get her out of my head. I hate her. I loathe her. But fuck if I don't still want her.

I tell myself it's because we're in the same city. I haven't seen her in years, so it's fucking with my head. She's all over the gossip sites for trying to fuck that pop musician. That's all it is. Seeing her face everywhere and hearing about her is messing with me. Once we're back on tour and I'm away from her, shit will go back to normal.

"IT FEELS LIKE WE WERE JUST ON TOUR," I WHINE AS I DRAG MY HUNGOVER ASS UP THE STAIRS AND ONTO the plane.

"That's because we were," Declan agrees. "Less than a year ago."

"I think after this one, we should take a long break," I say, fully aware I sound like an ungrateful asshole, but my head is pounding, and I'm already dreading living the next two months on the tour bus, on planes, and in hotels.

"I'm down for that," Camden says. "I'd like to be home for a little while after the baby is born anyway." A small smile spreads across his face, and even though I think love is bullshit, I can't help but be happy for my friend. Because he finally got the woman he's loved and wanted for years. It might've taken them awhile to find their way to each other, but they're now married, expecting a baby, and fucking happy. I hope it works out for them better than it did for me.

"Is Layla here?" I ask Camden, referring to his wife. He'd mentioned that she and her five-year-old son, Felix, would be joining us for a few days since our first stop on the tour is LA.

"Yeah, she's laying Felix down for a nap in the bedroom," Camden says. "Listen, I need to talk to you real quick. I've been trying to tell you something but—"

Before he can finish his thought, a blur of blond catches my attention. I glance over at the door of the plane and what I see has my heart picking up speed, my palms sweating, and my already pounding head throbbing in pain. This can't be happening. I'm seeing shit, I have to be. There's no way she's here on this plane. I close my eyes and then reopen them, but she's still there, standing in the doorway.

"What the fuck are you doing here?" I ask as Kaylee steps onto the plane.

"She's our new publicist," Camden says, shocking the hell out of me. "I told your ass to come to the meeting."

I swing my glare over to him. "You didn't say it was *her.*"

"Should've come down." He shrugs. "Nobody wanted to risk their career coming on tour with you and Gage. She was willing. We had to make a decision, so it was made."

"Look on the bright side," Declan says, humor in his tone. "You won't be sleeping with our publicist on tour."

His words hit me like a punch to the gut. I look over at Kaylee, who's still standing at the door of the plane, waiting to see how this all plays out.

My thoughts go to our past, to how much I fucking loved her, to how much she hurt me, took my heart and put it through a shredder. Then I remember the shit I've heard about her online. The rumors running rampant about what happened between her and Sam York.

With a smirk I hope relays how much I hate her and how much she disgusts me, I look her dead in the eyes. "Wouldn't put it past her to try. I heard she practically raped Sam York. Better keep my door locked just in case." Then I glance over at Camden, who's glaring daggers my way. "You sure Layla is okay with her going with us? She might try something on you."

Camden sighs, and Declan groans. Kaylee...She growls. Legitimately fucking growls.

"Fuck you!" she hisses. "I didn't touch him, and I sure as hell wouldn't touch you with a ten-foot pole."

I step over to her, ignoring her intoxicating scent—the same pink rose shit she used to wear when we were together, that I used to spend hours inhaling and getting lost in—and drag my gaze over the full length of her body. She's dressed professionally in a black button-down shirt and slacks, her heels low. Her shirt is on the tighter side, clinging to her breasts, which are perky and peeking out from the top where a few buttons are undone. The material of her pants molds to every perfect curve. She might be fully dressed and not showing a single inch of skin, but I've already seen her body, memorized every inch of it, so I can imagine what's underneath. What used to be mine...until she gave it to someone else.

Pain roils in my stomach at the thought, and it doesn't take much to muster up a look of disgust. "Pretty sure you already did, sweetheart."

"Yeah, before you became a manwhore. All those groupie sluts you've been sleeping with...you probably have a dozen STDs."

So it's going to be like that, huh? Okay...Game on.

"Let's not forget who the head slut is," I say, feigning nonchalance like a pro when the truth is, my body is vibrating in anger. Because who the fuck does she think she is pointing fingers? "Who fucked another man while we were still together?" I say, making her flinch. "I might be a manwhore, but you're just a fucking whore."

"Enough!" Camden barks. "I'm not going to play referee this entire tour."

"Then you should've thought about that before you hired the woman who fucked me over."

"What's going on?" Layla steps out from where the bedroom is and sighs, her hand going to the bump she's sporting. She and Camden are expecting a baby in October. A little girl. "Felix is sleeping."

Her gaze goes to me, and while I don't want to stress her out, I have no doubt Kaylee being on tour with us was Layla's doing. They're best friends and have been since our sophomore year of high school. "We're screaming because someone thought it would be a good idea to hire *her*." I don't bother saying her name since we all know who I'm referring to. "I get she's your best friend, but..."

"Can I talk to you alone?" Layla says, giving me a look that I can't say no to. Like she and Kaylee, we've been friends since Layla moved here, and I love her like a damn sister.

I nod, and we head to a secluded area of the plane.

"I know this is hard," she says softly, "but I need you to be okay with this for me, please."

"Layla...you're asking a lot." She knows what went down all those years ago. She knows how much I loved Kaylee, how much it hurt to find out that she was all too willing to spread her legs for the asshole jock who was after her for years, who she told me she couldn't stand. We were supposed to be forever, yet she so easily discarded me like yesterday's trash.

"I know," Layla says. "But she worked so hard in college to get her degree. You know all she's ever wanted to do is marketing and advertising." I do know that, which is why I was shocked she was a publicist and not working in the marketing/advertising department.

"Why the hell is she working as a publicist?"

"She took a job with Evolution, and they said they wanted her to get hands-on experience first, so they sent her on tour with Sam York to learn about marketing during a tour. She didn't do what he accused her of, and now she's been blacklisted everywhere. Nobody wants someone who's been tainted working on their team. If she's able to be your publicist for an entire tour, she'll have a better shot of getting another job because everyone knows your publicists never make it." She looks at me with her damn puppy dog eyes. "Please, Brax. She needs a clean slate and a good recommendation, and you guys need a publicist for the tour."

"Fine," I relent. "But don't think I'm going to make it easy on her."

She nods solemnly. "I understand. Thank you."

We walk back out, and everyone—including Kaylee—has found their seats. Gage and Declan are sitting next to each other discussing the details of the tour Jill sent over—she's meeting us in LA since that's where she's located. Camden is sitting across from Kaylee, talking low. Layla goes over and sits next to her husband, snuggling into his side. He kisses the top of her head, and not for the first time, my heart squeezes in my rib cage.

It was easy to tuck my heart away for the past six years. None of us were interested in settling down. Our only focus has been on making music. But then Camden saw Layla again, and the dynamic changed. He's become a father and a husband, and watching them, mixed with seeing Kaylee again, has the hurt and resentment I felt all those years ago rising to the surface.

Kaylee glances over at me, realizing the only seat left is next to her, and smiles sadly, as if silently asking for a truce. Well, fuck that shit. She's not getting one. She wants to be on this tour to save her ass? Fine. But I meant what I said to Layla. I sure as shit won't make it easy on her.

Ten

KAYLEE

THIS WAS A MISTAKE. A DESPERATE, STUPID MISTAKE. WHEN LAYLA SUGGESTED IT, I TOLD HER SHE WAS out of her mind. Me spending two months on the road with Braxton? She couldn't be serious. But she insisted it would also benefit the band because while they have Jill, they need a publicist to help with the promo of the tour as well as keep the guys organized and in line and make sure they're where they need to be. Jill can't do it all. Since Braxton and Gage apparently screwed the last woman who went on tour with them, Easton—Camden's dad, the band's manager, and the president of Blackwood Records—said it would help him out since the PR companies they use won't allow anyone to go on tour with the guys.

I suggested a male publicist, and Easton laughed humorlessly, saying the last guy they hired ended up all over social media after being recorded with strippers while they were in Vegas. Apparently, no one is immune to their charms.

So like the masochist I apparently am, I agreed to go. The pay is damn good—although I have a feeling it's more than what they usually pay. It probably includes hazard pay for all that I'll be dealing with. I should've requested *that* when I took the job with Sam York, but at the time, I didn't know what I was getting myself into. Between his drug problem and constantly hitting on me, I should've known it would end with him fucking me over. But even working with him didn't prepare me for going on tour with Raging Chaos.

The first two concerts in LA were easy. I handled the radio giveaways, organizing the meet and greets for the winners, and it all went smoothly. Gage and Braxton both behaved. Camden and Declan were social and chatty. The guys took pictures and signed merchandise, and for a minute, I thought, *I can totally do this*. But I should've known there was a reason for the obedience: Layla and Felix. They were there with Camden—celebrating Felix's birthday—and that kept the guys in line. Then she and Felix got on a plane, and we got on the buses, and everything changed.

We've been in Vegas for less than eight hours, and as I stand in my doorway to my hotel room, watching as Gage and Braxton stumble down the hall with multiple women in tow—who look to be hookers or at least dressed like ones—I'm not sure I can do two months of this. I know I have no right to feel the way I do. If anything, I deserve it. But holy shit, my heart hurts watching Braxton, his lids slightly droopy from being drunk and maybe high, being draped by two women who are all over him like fleas on a stray dog.

When I heard the noise, knowing we were the only ones on this floor, I opened my door to make sure everything was okay. Big mistake. My door creaked loud enough to grab Braxton's attention. His gaze met mine—a mixture of anger and indifference—and I had no choice but to stand in place and watch them walk past me. The alternative would've been to quickly close my door, which would've shown Braxton I was affected. The last thing I need to do is lower my guard and risk him using it to fuck with me.

Gage and the women go in first, but Braxton stops just outside the doorway. His eyes meet mine, and I hold my breath, waiting for the blow to come. He stares at me, and my heart thumps in my chest, wondering what's going through his head. If he's thinking about how much I hurt him. It's been six years, and he still hates me so much. Not that I blame him, but I thought time healed all wounds and all that...

"Brax, c'mon!" a woman yells. "I'm naked and waiting!"

"Coming," he says, his eyes not leaving mine. "We're going to need some lube...and condoms. I prefer Trojan."

For a second, my brain doesn't comprehend what he's saying...*that he's saying it to me.* Until he adds, "Learned a while back that condoms are a must. Never know who else the person you're fucking has fucked." And then it hits me like a train going full speed without any working brakes—he wants *me* to go get him the lube and condoms. And he's referring to me being the person he was fucking and not knowing who else I was fucking. The accusation stings, but I refuse to let him see that.

"I'm not your errand girl. If you want that shit, go get it your damn self."

He releases a sharp laugh, then stalks toward me, stopping so close I can smell the liquor on his breath and the smoke from the casino. But beneath the liquor and smoke, there's another scent, one I would recognize anywhere. It's the cologne I bought him for Christmas—our one and only Christmas together. It smells fresh and masculine and brings back memories of every time he would wear it when we were together.

Images of me snuggling against him, inhaling his scent, and kissing his flesh surface, and before I can stop myself, I blurt out, "You're wearing the cologne I got you."

Braxton flinches but quickly composes himself, his glare intensifying. He reaches into his pocket and pulls out a hundred-dollar bill, reminding me of his request. When he extends his hand, trying to give it to me, and I don't take it, he steps closer, invading my space. "Condoms and lube...*now.*"

"I'm not your errand girl," I repeat, jutting my chin out in defiance.

His finger and thumb pinch my chin, lifting my face to look at him, and my breath hitches. It's been six years since we've been this close, since he's touched me, and I've missed it...*missed him*...every single day.

"If you ever want to get another job in this industry," he says, his mouth mere inches from mine, "you'll be whatever the fuck I want you to be." He reaches around and slides the bill into my back pocket. "Don't make this shit harder than it needs to be."

Without waiting for me to respond, he releases my chin and turns his back on me, sauntering back to his room while I stand, frozen in shock, wondering what the hell happened to the man I used to know. Was it the fame? The fortune? And then, I'm overtaken with a bout of guilt as a thought occurs to me. Was it me and what I did to him...*to us* that's caused him to be like this? Am I the reason he's now a cold, heartless, womanizing bastard?

Tears prick my lids. It's one thing for me to hurt—it's nothing less than I deserve—but the thought, that after six years, Braxton's still hurting because of me, because of my actions, is like liquid guilt being injected straight into my vein, spreading through my bloodstream like acid and burning me from the inside out.

I let a couple of tears fall before I inhale a deep breath and swipe them away. I don't deserve to cry, and doing so is a waste of time anyway. What's done is done, and there's no going back.

With my head held as high as I can manage, I head down to the hotel store and get the items he's requested and then take them up to him. Thankfully, he's not the one who opens the door. Gage is. He's clearly high and maybe drunk, but that doesn't stop him from giving me a look of sympathy before he thanks me and closes the door.

Instead of going back to my room, I make my way downstairs, needing to get some air. I'm not really dressed for the Strip, but it doesn't matter. Nobody will be paying attention to me anyway.

I step outside, and the pungent smell of smoke combined with the sound of loud music assaults my senses. I'm halfway down the sidewalk when I hear my name being called. I turn around and find Declan walking over to me.

"Hey, did you need something?"

He shakes his head. "Nah. I was having a drink at the bar and saw you. Thought I'd join you."

We walk alongside each other for a few minutes before he finally speaks. "He still loves you."

"He hates me."

We keep walking until we're in front of the famous Bellagio fountains. It's in the middle of a show, so we stop and watch it in silence.

"He hates what you did," Declan says softly but loud enough for me to hear over the show. "But he doesn't hate you. Maybe you can fix it. It's been six years. You made one bad choice, but you can make things right. I can see it in your eyes that you still love him."

I smile sadly at Declan. He's always been such a romantic. Every song he writes is sweet, filled with hearts and flowers. He doesn't discuss his home life often, but I know it's not a good one. Yet he still believes in love and happily ever afters.

"It's too late," I tell him truthfully. "I hurt him too badly."

"I don't believe that," Declan says, pulling me into his side and kissing my temple. "It's never too late for love."

MY ALARM SOUNDS PROMPTLY AT SEVEN O'CLOCK, AND I SERIOUSLY CONSIDER TURNING IT OFF, COVERING my head with my blanket, and remaining in bed. But I can't do that because the guys have an interview this morning for a local radio station, then a soundcheck afterward, and a concert tonight, followed by a meet and greet the local radio station is hosting as a contest on their social media.

After taking a shower, blow-drying my blond hair straight, and getting dressed in a pair of black dress slacks and a blouse that's just as black—because these days my life feels equivalent to attending my own funeral—dramatic, much? Maybe—I head over to the guys' room. I have a key card, but I knock first before I enter.

I'm expecting the place to look like a porn studio—no, I've never seen one, but I can imagine—with naked bodies strewn about, but the place is clean. Since the suite has several bedrooms, I go to the first door I see and knock. Camden opens the door—fully dressed. "Morning."

"Morning. We have to get going to the radio station."

"All right, thanks," he says with a slight frown marring his features.

"You okay?"

"Yeah, just missing the hell out of Layla and Felix."

My heart swells, loving that my best friend found such an amazing man. After everything she's been through, she deserves nothing less. "When are they meeting up with us again?"

"Back here, next week, for the Billboards, but only Layla. Felix is staying with her mom."

I forgot about the upcoming award show. While the guys and I will be coming back here for the award show, Jill and the rest of the team will be heading to San Jose. After the show, we'll be flying to meet up with them at the next tour stop. "Not too far off."

"We agreed we wouldn't go too long without seeing each other." He shrugs. "They're meeting us in Tampa after that. We're going to take Felix to the theme parks there and in Orlando."

"And that will lead up to the Fourth of July." The guys took the week off for the holiday. I have no idea what I'll be doing. Layla invited me to join them, but I'm not in the mood to play the third wheel to their love fest. The problem is, I'm kind of homeless until I find a place to live once we get back from the tour. Maybe I'll rent a cheap room somewhere and spend the week relaxing. It's been a while since I've done that.

"I can't wait," Camden says, a real smile stretching across his face. "The last leg of the trip will suck. Two weeks without seeing them, but then we'll be home."

"It'll fly by," I tell him, praying I'm right because we're only on day five of the tour, and it feels like it's going to last a lifetime.

"Morning," Declan says, coming out of the room he must've shared with Camden and kissing my cheek. "Did you give any thought to what we talked about last night?"

I actually did think about it for hours until I finally fell asleep. I considered what he said—that deep down through the hurt, Braxton still loves me and I, him—and I've decided I'm going to talk to him about it when we have time. I'm not expecting us to be together again. I'm not Declan with his rose-colored glasses, but I do think if we talk—something we never got a chance to do—maybe we can find common ground and be friends...or at least be friendly with one another.

"I did," I tell him, not giving him anything more since I'm still not sure how I want to handle it.

"Good. What time do we leave?"

I glance at the itinerary on my phone Jill sent me. "Twenty minutes, and we won't be back. We're leaving straight from the show to head to Sacramento."

Turning on my heel, I head straight for the other door, knocking and opening it without waiting for someone to give me the okay. Big mistake. I was so lost in my thoughts, thanks to Declan, that I didn't consider what would be behind the other door.

I take in the scene in front of me, refusing to cry or throw up. Braxton is naked from the waist up, passed out on the queen-sized bed. With him are two very naked women. One is sprawled out across his stomach, and the other is lying across the foot of the bed. There are empty liquor bottles and the box of condoms and bottle of lube I brought him last night on the nightstand.

I step slowly into the room, unsure if I should be mature and gently wake

Braxton up or scream like a five-year-old when my eyes land on the book in his hand, sending me back six years.

"I can't believe you did this." I snuggle in close to Braxton, laying my head on his chest. It's our six-month anniversary, and he somehow booked us a gorgeous hotel room so we could spend the night together. He ordered us room service, and after eating, we spent time in the private hot tub before he made love to me.

"I'd do anything for you," he murmurs, kissing the top of my head.

We lie in silence for a few minutes before I remember something. "I have something for you."

I reach over and grab the gift bag I brought with me, second-guessing what I got him. "It's nothing as lavish as this"—I wave my hand in the air—"but I saw it in the store, and it made me think of you."

He opens the bag and pulls out a black notebook with gold script on the front that reads: **Write the words that pour from your heart.**

"It's for your words," I explain. "And to remind you to always write from your heart." He doesn't write half the music Camden does, but when he does write a song, it's always beautiful, powerful, and filled with such emotion.

"I love it," he says, flipping through the blank pages before he sets it down and cups my face. "And I love you. Thank you."

He has the notebook even now. Six years later, and he's still using it.

"Kaylee," Camden says, sympathy evident in his tone. "I can wake him and Gage up."

"Okay, thanks," I choke out, emotion clogging my throat. Without looking back, I run out of the room and out of their suite. I keep running as the traitorous tears spill down my cheeks until I get back to my room. I need to grab my stuff, but instead, I pull my phone out and call Layla.

"Hey," she says. "How's it going?"

"I can't do this," I rush out through my sobs. "Watching him with all these other women...I can't do it." I know what I did all those years ago was horrible, but seeing him like this is too hard, and it hurts too much. Declan was wrong. It is too late for love...It's too late for a lot of things.

Layla's quiet for a second before she speaks. "Do you still love him?"

Dammit, here we go again with the love shit.

"It doesn't matter. I don't have the right to. Not after everything. After the way I hurt him." Declan may believe Braxton would be willing to forgive me, but he's wrong. There's no going back from what I did, and thinking we could be friends was just stupidity on my part. I made my decision all those years ago, and now I have to live with the fallout.

"That was six years ago. Did something else happen?"

I give her a quick recap of last night and this morning.

When I finish, Layla sighs over the line. "I wish I were there so I could hug you."

"I don't deserve it. I did this." I swipe away my tears. "I need to pull up my big girl panties and stop getting emotional. This is a job...possibly my last chance, and I need to handle it professionally."

"True," she says, "but you're still human, and you have feelings."

"Camden's missing you like crazy," I say, changing the subject.

Layla laughs softly. "I swear he's texted me every five minutes since we left LA."

"You love it."

"Yeah, I do." We're both quiet for a moment. "Kaylee, one day you'll find your *Camden.*"

Too bad it's not a Camden I want...It's a Braxton.

I'm sitting here high
I can't forget
You wanted my love
I gave it to you

You wanted my heart
I handed it over
You took and took
Sucked me fucking dry
And now I'm sitting here high
I can't forget

After every hit I take
Every memory that surfaces
I wanna forget

Your gray eyes
Your sweet smile
You fucked me over
And now I wanna forget

I watch and listen as Braxton sings a song from their first album. It's not on the set for this tour, yet he's singing it. Camden is the lead singer. Gage is the drummer. Declan is the bass player. And Braxton is the guitarist.

But every once in a while, Braxton and Declan will sing. Braxton's voice is different than Camden's. It's raw and husky, and when he graces the world with it, women go crazy. Like they're doing right now as he sings "I Wanna Forget," a song about me and how much he hates me for what I did to him. I can still remember how people speculated when this song came out. They love to analyze the lyrics and put a face to the words. It makes it more personal when they can point a finger. But Raging Chaos is great about keeping their private life private, so only a few select people know this song is about me.

"You okay?" asks Bailey, Camden's sister and the head of Blackwood's media. She flew into Portland to watch the show and handle a couple of things for the band with Cade, who's on tour with us to film the guys and is working with Layla to create a web series. The fans love it because they get to see below the surface—put a face to the name. Feel and see and hear all the emotions.

"It's nothing I don't deserve," I say, my eyes trained on Braxton as he belts the lyrics with such emotion goose bumps prickle my flesh.

"Nobody deserves to have their dirty laundry aired out for all the world to see."

"Maybe." I shrug. "But that's the risk you take when you date a rock star, right?"

Just as I finish my sentence, the song ends. I expect Camden to take back the microphone, so I'm shocked when Braxton starts to talk. "How about one more?"

The crowd screams, and Braxton laughs, but I can see it on his face that he's not happy. "This one I wrote recently. It hasn't even been recorded yet."

Bailey glances at me in confusion. At the same time, Jill speaks into her headpiece in a rushed whisper, telling me this wasn't planned. I glance around at the other guys, all showing various looks of annoyance.

"It's called 'Unforgivable,'" Braxton says. Gage shakes his head but starts on the drums, and Camden, who took over Braxton's guitar, starts strumming it. I hold my breath, waiting for the lyrics to come, knowing they're going to hurt.

And I'm right because as Braxton opens his mouth and the words flow off his tongue, wrapping tightly around my heart, it feels as though I can't breathe. Declan was wrong. So wrong. Braxton doesn't just hate what I did. He hates me, and this song proves it.

> *Young love*
> *Dumb love*
> *Cheating love*
> *Unforgivable love*
> *It was love but the wrong kind*
> *The fucked-up kind*
> *The kind that sets your soul on fire*

Leaves you burning with desire
And in the end, all you're left with is heartache and regret

Young love
Dumb love
Cheating love
Unforgivable love

Unable to listen to any more of his words, swallow any more of his truths, or feel any more of his heartbreak, I run, and I don't stop until I get to my hotel room. Then I climb into my bed, throw my blankets over me, and cry. I did this. I created this. I deserve this. But I also really fucking hate this. And my heart...it's not sure if it can take much more of this.

Eleven

BRAXTON

"HOW LONG ARE YOU IN TOWN FOR?" ALYSSA ASKS, HER VOICE DRIPPING WITH SEXUALITY AS SHE RUNS her long-nailed finger across my thigh. When Gage and I ran into her and a couple of her friends backstage and they suggested we find somewhere more private to chill, we agreed and came back to our hotel room. We're all lounging in the living room, smoking and drinking and listening to some music. Declan and Camden took off, pissed at the shit I pulled earlier. They've known about the song I wrote, that's why we have the instrumentals for it, but it didn't make the cut when we put out our first album.

I don't know why I felt the need to sing it tonight. Actually, that's not true. I know why. Because every day I'm on tour with Kaylee, I'm softening a little more, my hate lessening. It's so easy to get lost in her beautiful gray eyes and pouty lips. In her melodic laugh. When Declan reamed into me about making Kaylee get the condoms and lube and then told me she ran out in tears when she saw me in bed with two other women, I had to remind myself what she did. She did this. She set the dominos in motion. And if I want to sing a thousand songs about what she did, I will. Because she deserves it. She deserves to hurt like I hurt and feel the pain the same way I felt it. She deserves to be reminded of what she ruined. I gave her all of me, and she destroyed me from the inside out.

"Tonight's our last night," I tell her, taking a shot of the whiskey we're drinking. Tomorrow, we'll be heading to another state, another city, singing at another show. It all kind of blends after a while.

"We should play a game!" her blond friend says.

"Oh, yeah!" her other friend—this one brunette—adds. "How about *Never Have I Ever?*"

"Isn't that the shit teenagers play in high school?" I ask, praying to fucking God these women are not in high school.

"Yeah, so? It'll be fun," Alyssa says. "And if you're a good boy, I'll let you take your shots off my body." When she says that, my eyes drag down said body, and I can't help but compare her to Kaylee. Where Kaylee is all real, from her blond hair to her pert tits, Alyssa is all fake. She's the type of woman I usually go for, but now, as I take in her burnt tan, bleached hair, and caked-on makeup, which is doing nothing for me, I can't help but wonder if I go for women like her because she's the complete opposite of Kaylee—perfectly real. And then I shake myself from my thoughts because the last person I should be thinking about is Kaylee. She might look real, but she's a damn cheater, which makes her fake as hell.

"We need more liquor," the brunette says with a pout, holding up the almost empty bottle.

"I'll go grab one," Gage offers, taking a hit of his joint and then snuffing it out.

"Actually, I'll send for a bottle," I suggest, already grabbing my phone to call the woman who's at our beck and call.

Gage does his version of an eye roll but doesn't argue. Instead, he relights his joint. My friends might hate the shit I'm doing to Kaylee, but they're loyal enough to keep their mouths shut—except apparently Declan, who seems to be trying to play mediator. But after the show tonight, I imagine he'll have gotten the hint—that I have no desire to ever forgive Kaylee for what she did—and will hopefully leave it alone.

"Hello?" Kaylee says breathily when she answers the phone.

"You asleep?" I ask, hoping I woke her ass up.

"No." She clears her throat. "How can I help you, Brax?"

I pause, wondering if she's been crying and if it's because of the song I sang about her. And for a brief second, I almost consider asking her if she's okay. But then I remember why I sang the song I did and nix that thought.

"We need a bottle of whiskey brought to our room."

While we wait for the new bottle, the girls start the game with the bottle we already have, mentioning stupid-ass shit like, "Never have I ever kissed a girl" and "Never have I ever had a threesome," all three of them giggling and drinking as they admit they've done each sexual thing.

When there's a knock on the door, I yell for Kaylee to come in instead of getting up since she has a key to our room. She walks in, dressed in a loose T-shirt and a pair of yoga pants that show off her curves.

"Here you go," she says, thrusting the bottle toward me. One look at her, and I can see she's been crying. Her eyes are puffy and red, and her cheeks are tinged with tear stains. My natural inclination is to pull her into my arms and hold her close. I always hated when she'd cry. But I don't because she doesn't deserve it. She deserves every single tear she sheds and much more.

"Stay," I suggest when I take the bottle. "Have a drink with us."

She scoffs. "I'm good."

"We're playing a game," Blondie says, oblivious to the tension Kaylee brought with her into the room. "*Never Have I Ever...*Heard of it?"

Kaylee's brow furrows. "The high school game?"

"Yep," I say, opening the bottle and pouring her a shot. "Whose turn is it?" I glance around. "You know what, I'll go." My eyes lock on hers. "Let's see..." I think for a second before the perfect one comes to me. "I got it. Never have I ever...cheated on the person I claimed to love."

"Oh, no, I've never done that," one of the women says.

"Real fucking mature," Kaylee hisses.

"Drink up, sweetheart." I smirk. "Hell, maybe you should have two shots for that one."

Kaylee throws the shot in my face and stalks out, slamming the door behind her.

"How long are you going to punish her for?" Gage asks as soon as she's gone.

"Until she's hurting as much as she hurt me."

"I'M TAKING KAYLEE WITH ME TONIGHT," GAGE SAYS, SHOCKING THE HELL OUT OF ME. WE'RE BACK IN Vegas at the MGM Grand for the award show since we've been nominated for several awards and are performing.

"She's the *help*. You can't find a fucking date?"

"I can." He shrugs. "I'm choosing to take her."

Jesus, first Camden hires her ass, then Declan tries to talk me into forgiving her, and now Gage is taking her as his date. So much for my friends having my back.

"With friends like you guys, who needs enemies?" I grumble, sounding bitter as fuck.

"Layla and Kendall are going," Declan points out as if the fact that her friends will be there is enough of a reason for her to join us.

"Well, she is an easy lay," I say, the words coming out sour.

Gage shakes his head, not bothering to respond.

Because I knew this event was coming up, I asked a friend of mine to join me, not wanting to bring some random chick to the event. She's a musician as well and will be performing.

Since we're all going in one vehicle, we pile into the stretch limo. Kaylee and Gage are the last to slide in, and I can't help but check her out. I seem to be doing that every damn time I see her. She's dressed in a strapless gold shimmery number with a thick shiny belt wrapped around her middle. The dress is tight up top, pushing up her already generous-sized tits, and loose on the bottom. Her hair is down in waves, her makeup light, and when she sits down, the slit in her dress parts, exposing her toned leg and showing off her matching gold heels. She looks fucking gorgeous. She always does, though, and I hate it.

"You okay?" my date, Adrianne, asks.

I glance down and notice my fists are clenched tight. "I need you to do me a favor," I whisper into her ear, my eyes locking on Kaylee.

Twelve

KAYLEE

THIS WAS A HORRIBLE IDEA—I SEEM TO HAVE A LOT OF THEM LATELY. WHEN GAGE ASKED ME TO JOIN HIM at the Billboards, saying he wasn't up for being the only guy without a date, I couldn't say no. The night we all lost Tori still haunts me. While I was ending my relationship with Braxton, Tori needed me, and I wasn't there. Something I will always regret. And now, Gage is alone, lost and sad, and I would do anything he asked even though I know nothing will bring her back or make it right.

But that doesn't change the fact that this was a horrible idea. I'm sitting in a limo with Camden and Layla, Declan and Kendall—Camden's older pop star sister who Declan is here with—Gage, and Braxton and his date, Adrianne, an up-and-coming pop star who's on tour with Kendall as her opening act. Everyone is chatting amongst themselves, but I can't take my eyes off Braxton, who's looking at me with a mixture of contempt and disgust while he whispers in his date's ear.

She giggles at whatever he's saying, then sits up, taking his hand in hers. "I love your tattoos," she says, playing with his fingers. "What do they mean?"

His eyes leave mine so he can look down at what she's looking at. He goes about explaining each tattoo in detail while she soaks up his attention like a sponge. When she takes his left hand in hers, I hold my breath, waiting for what he's going to say about the tattoo he got with me. I was honestly shocked when I saw that he never had it covered up.

"And this one"—he points at the infinity symbols inked on the outside of his hand, the same one I have in the same spot, and locks eyes with me—"was a mistake."

At his words, I suck in a harsh breath as tears prick my eyes. The shit he's pulled with having me bring him condoms and lube and liquor sucks, the song he sang hurt like hell, and the time he called me a cheater in front of his fuck-buddy groupies was embarrassing, but calling us a mistake…That just about kills me.

"Ignore him," Gage murmurs, leaning in so no one can hear. "You hurt him, yes, but now he's just being spiteful."

"I deserve it," I admit, trying to wipe my tears before anyone else notices.

His glassy eyes meet mine—because he's high...he's always high—and he shakes his head. "No, you don't."

"Aren't you the woman who sexually assaulted Sam York?" Adrianne says, making my head jerk up.

"Excuse me?" I ask in shock as the limo turns quiet, everyone stopping their chatter to listen to us.

"I thought you looked familiar." She eyes me up and down with disdain. "Your face is all over the internet as the woman who made a fool out of herself with Sam."

"That's not what—" Layla begins, but I shake my head to stop her. She's five months pregnant, and the last thing she needs is the stress from coming to my rescue.

"It's fine. I was taught to never defend a lie, and I'm not going to defend myself to her or anyone else." I jut my chin out, hoping to display the confidence I don't feel.

At that moment, the limo stops, and the door is opened. Everyone edges out, leaving Gage and me for last. I take a moment to calm myself before we get out and then put my arm through his, willing myself to make it through the night.

The rest of the evening goes smoothly. The guys win in almost every category they were nominated in, and their performance is on point. They're so talented, and despite how much Braxton's hurt me, I'm so proud of them. They've followed their passion, and it's paid off. The guys are all smiles when they return to their seats after performing, and everyone around them congratulates them while I sit in my seat watching, feeling like an outsider as my thoughts go back to six years ago, before everything went to shit.

"Condo or mansion?"

I roll my eyes. "A regular-sized house."

Braxton rolls onto his back, annoyed that I'm not playing along. "Mercedes or BMW?"

"I don't know." I laugh. "Something to tow our three kids around in."

"You want three kids?" he asks, propping himself up on his hand and elbow.

"Yeah, I'm thinking two boys and a girl. The girl last so her brothers can protect her."

"I like that. A little girl with blond hair and gray eyes like you." He runs his fingers through my hair that's splayed out around me. We're lying on a blanket in the grass in the middle of Central Park. Today was senior skip day, but instead of going to the beach with everyone else, I packed us a picnic basket and took Braxton out on a surprise date.

"Beach house or ski cabin?"

I shake my head and push his chest playfully. "It doesn't matter as long as I'm with you. I don't care about what car I drive, or how big our house is, or where we vacation. I just want to be happy and be loved by you."

"And you are," he says, touching our tattoos together. "Forever. But our band is going to blow up, and when we do, I'm going to make sure you have everything you could ever want."

"Just you," I insist. "I just want you and me...and a home," I add at the last second. "I want us to have a home that's filled with love."

Braxton nods in understanding, knowing how much I feel like an outsider in my own home, like I don't belong there.

"We'll have that," he promises. "And more. It's going to be fucking awesome. The guys and I will record our album, and then when it blows up, we'll go on tour. You'll come sometimes, right? Join me in different states."

The solemn look in his eyes tells me that even though he's been playing around, he's also serious, so instead of rolling my eyes or laughing, I go along with it. "I will. When I don't have classes, I'll join you."

This makes him smile. "I can't wait." He rolls onto his back again and tucks his arms under his head, staring up at the sky. "I was watching the Billboards the other night, and I just kept thinking, one day that'll be us. The guys and I will be on that stage accepting our award, and you'll be in the audience, cheering me on. And then..." He jumps up and hovers over me, his strong arms caging me in, not caring that we're in a public place. "I'm gonna steal that award and put it next to us in bed while I make love to you in our expensive-ass suite that we'll be able to afford because we'll be rich."

I can't help but laugh at the picture he's painted. "I can't wait," I tell him. "I've always wanted to have sex with a Billboard Award."

I've made sure to watch every award show they've attended, and even though Braxton isn't aware and wouldn't care, I was cheering him on from wherever I was—so damn proud of him for accomplishing his dreams—and wishing I were there with him, wanting the life we talked about and hating myself for being the reason we'd never have it.

After the award show is over, the guys are interviewed, and then we head to the after-party. Gage finds some guys he knows and takes off somewhere I'm sure to get high—or in his case, keep it going. Not wanting to play the third wheel with Camden and Layla, I head out to the back of the monstrous mansion to check out the pool.

I'm turning the corner when I run straight into Sam York.

"Shit, I'm so—" His words are cut off when he realizes it's me. "Well, well, well, if it isn't my cock tease ex-publicist." He smirks, eyeing me up and down. When his eyes meet mine, I can see he's already blitzed out. The guy could seriously put Gage's drug problem to shame.

"Excuse me," I say, attempting to go around him. Only he sticks his hand out before I can get away, stopping me in my tracks. He backs me up against the wall, and I glance around, wishing I would've stayed inside. It's dark out here, and there are no witnesses. I can scream, but I doubt anyone will hear over the loud music.

"You know, it would be easy for me to fix the problem you created for yourself," Sam says, his voice dripping with slime. "Make it all go away." He runs his hand down the side of my body and I shudder in response, hating his touch on me.

Of course, he mistakes my response for liking it and smiles cockily. "What do you say, baby? Wanna convince me to remember the situation differently? I bet your warm, wet mouth can convince me of anything..."

"Get your fucking hands off her."

I hear him before I see him, but I would recognize his deep, gruff voice anywhere. Braxton grabs Sam by the back of his suit and yanks him off me, slamming him against the wall. "Don't ever touch her again. You hear me?"

"What the hell, man? I don't know what your problem is, but she was coming onto me."

"Yeah, that shit might work with the dumbasses who like to kiss your ass, but I know better, and I heard what you were saying. Now, unless you want your pretty boy face to end up all mangled and fucked up, I suggest you walk away. And if I ever hear you speak Kaylee's name again, I'll be coming for you. Got it?"

"What-the fuck-ever." Sam shoves Braxton back. "The bitch is a fucking cock tease anyway. You want her? Good fucking luck." He adjusts his lapels and stalks off, leaving Braxton and me alone.

"You okay?" Braxton asks once he's gone.

His voice is soft, reminding me of the guy I once knew, and all I want is to run into his arms and beg him to hold me so I can inhale his comforting scent. But I lost that right six years ago, so instead, I simply nod. "Yeah, I didn't know he was out here. I was coming to get some air."

"You don't have to explain yourself to me." His tone is back to being cold and distant, and I already miss the warmth from a moment ago.

"I know, but..." I clear my throat and step toward him. "Thank you. You didn't have to do that."

"Yeah, well..." He shrugs and steps around me. "The only person who has the right to make your life hell is me."

I open my mouth to say something—what, I don't know—but before I can put the words together, Adrianne appears.

"There you are," she says, sauntering over. She wraps her arm around

Braxton and eyes me curiously. "Everything okay here?"

"Yeah," he says. "I need a drink." Then he glances at me. "You should go back to the hotel. You don't belong here." And with that, he turns his back on me and walks off without once looking back, reminding me that despite him saving me, he still hates me and probably always will.

I need to talk to you.

It's important.

It's about your father.

Kaylee, please call me ASAP.

I STARE AT THE SLEW OF TEXTS FROM MY AUNT, KNOWING WHAT SHE'S GOING TO SAY. I'VE BEEN WAITING for this day for years. Honestly, I'm surprised he lasted this long. Your body can only take so much before it finally shuts down, after all. And my dad's body has taken too much.

I change out of my dress and into something more comfortable and then head out of the hotel and down the Strip. I call my aunt on the way, and she confirms what I already knew. My dad is dead from liver failure. There won't be a funeral because it would be a waste of money. It would be expensive, and nobody would go anyway. She only found out because she's his emergency contact. The hospital called to inform her. He was found without any clothes on in an alley. Some other homeless people must've found him and taken his clothes. Dead people don't need clothes after all.

"A shot of JD, please," I tell the bartender. I've ended up in a trashy, hole-in-the-wall bar, but that suits me just fine. I wasn't looking for anywhere flashy, just somewhere I could drown myself in the alcohol for a little bit.

The bartender comes back with my drink, and I down it in one go, asking for another and then another. I lose track of how many shots I've had, but when I see Braxton taking a seat next to me, I assume I've had so much I'm seeing shit.

"Another shot!" I yell to the bartender.

"You sure that's the best way to mourn a man who lost his life to alcohol and drugs?"

I glare at Braxton and throw back my shot, slamming it on the bar top. "What better way to honor him than to get lost in the only thing he ever truly loved?"

I expect Braxton to argue, but he doesn't. I'm not sure what he's doing here or how he found me, but I'm guessing someone told him about my dad.

"Did you need something?" I ask him as the bartender places another shot in front of me.

"Nope," he says, then proceeds to order a Jack and Coke.

We sit next to each other for several minutes, drinking, neither of us saying a word. I don't know what to think or what to say. I have so many thoughts running through my head, and I can't make sense of any of them. Which is why I came out to drink. But now, with Braxton sitting next to me, I almost wish I were sober.

My phone buzzes in my pocket for the millionth time, and I pull it out, finding several missed calls and texts from Layla, my mom, and my aunt. All asking if I'm okay and to call them.

"Layla send you?" I finally ask, figuring she probably wanted to go after me herself, but Camden wouldn't let her since she's several months pregnant and Vegas isn't the safest place at night.

"Draw the short straw?" I add with a humorless laugh. When Braxton doesn't answer, I down another shot and glance over at him. He's still in the same outfit he wore tonight—an all-black suit sans tie—and he looks so damn good, it almost hurts to look at him. "I don't need you here. You can let Layla know I'm fine, and I'll be on the bus, ready to go on time. I'm sure Adrianne is waiting for you."

I slide off the stool, stopping for a second when the room spins, and then make my way onto the dance floor, where people are dancing to an upbeat song. I join in, getting lost in the music and making it a point not to look for Braxton. The alcohol runs through my system, numbing my body and mind, and I sway to the beat, letting myself go for the first time in a long time.

At least that's what I think I'm doing. Only my head is running, and my thoughts are all over the place. I don't realize I'm close to losing my shit until a pair of strong hands grips my hips and spins me around. My eyes meet Braxton's for a quick beat before he pulls me against him. My head rests against his chest, and I inhale his comforting scent. And then I let go, sobbing into his shirt while he holds me tight as I mourn the father I lost a long time ago. The man I used to look up to and have spent years loving and hating and missing.

In my moment of weakness, Braxton becomes my strength, silently holding me together. At some point, my legs give out, and he lifts me into his arms, carrying me out of the bar and down the street while I continue to cry into his neck, holding him like he's my only lifeline. I vaguely hear him talking to someone, and then we're in the hotel room in his bed, and he's still holding me.

"Shh, it's okay," he murmurs as he rubs circles on my back, trying to calm me. But I can't stop crying. I've worked myself up, and I can't control it—

the sobs, the hiccups, the lack of breath. It's all become too much to handle. Everything is a mess. Nothing is going right. I have no one, and I've never felt so alone in my life. And I only have myself to blame.

"I'm sorry," I mutter into Braxton's chest. "I'm so, so sorry."

Now probably isn't the best time to finally apologize, but I can't help it. For years, my dad hurt me and never once apologized. He did whatever he wanted to do and hurt whoever he wanted to hurt without any remorse. And I don't want to be him. I hurt Braxton, and I need him to know how sorry I am.

He places a kiss on my forehead, and I sigh into him, relaxing for the first time. My eyes flutter open, and I find him staring at me. After everything I've done, it's him who's here for me, holding me and making sure I'm okay. I don't deserve him or his compassion, but I don't have it in me to push him away. I've spent six years missing his touch, his love, wishing for a do-over. I know I'm not getting one, and come tomorrow, it'll be as if this never happened. But tonight, I'm going to close my eyes and pretend that all is right in my world. I'll deal with reality tomorrow.

Twelve

BONUS SCENE

BRAXTON

"FUCK THE SHOT, JUST GIVE ME THE BOTTLE."

The bartender shrugs and hands it over, and I chug several shots worth, craving the burn.

"So she never cheated?" Gage asks, taking the bottle and pouring himself a glass.

"Nope. She planned the whole damn thing." I take another swig and slam the bottle on the counter. "Had that asshole Jake go along with it."

"Damn, man, I'm sorry."

"The worst part is that instead of trusting me, instead of coming to me and telling me that my dad had cornered her, she took it upon herself."

"Wait, your dad set the whole thing up?"

"Yep. Guilted her into pushing me away."

Gage whistles and shakes his head. "Doesn't surprise me. Your dad's always been about your career."

"Yeah," I agree, "but Kaylee…? Fuck!"

We finish off the bottle, and I'm ordering another one when two women, donning dresses that barely cover anything, approach us.

"Aren't you Gage and Brax from Raging Chaos?" the blonde asks, running her long red fingernail along my arm seductively. The brunette grins at Gage, sidling up next to him, but he barely gives her any attention.

When I raise my brow in a so what? gesture, the blonde moves closer, giving me an eyeful of her perky, fake tits. "I'm Sonia, and this is Lorainne. Why don't you buy us a drink?"

I barely contain my eye roll. "Feel free…" I slide the bottle over to her, and she looks slightly taken aback, but since she's out for my dick and wallet, she keeps her mouth shut.

While the women flirt, Gage and I drink, and when I'm finally drunk enough that I might be able to stand letting Sonia suck my dick, I pay our tab and take her back to the hotel.

Only when we're walking in, I spot Kaylee sitting in the lobby in a reading chair, curled up with a book, and suddenly, everything feels wrong.

I'm mad as hell at her, but I still have feelings for her, so until I figure my shit out, I can't be with someone else...I don't want to be with someone else.

"Something came up," I tell...whatever the hell her name is.

She pouts and steps toward me, the look on her face determined, but before she can make it to me, I stop her in her place, pulling out a hundred-dollar bill. "Here, use this to get a ride home."

She glares but snags the bill. "Your loss," she hisses as she stomps away.

Gage chuckles, shaking his head as he walks to the elevator minus the other woman. "Where is she?"

He shrugs. "Not in the mood. I'm going to crash." He glances over at Kaylee who's still reading. "Why don't you talk to her?"

"I want to," I admit. "I'm just not sure yet what I want to say."

Gage nods. "You'll figure it out. Just don't wait too long." He frowns. "You never know what the future holds."

Thirteen

BRAXTON

It's been two days since Kaylee's dad died. Since her aunt called Layla concerned and I offered to find her, ignoring the looks everyone gave me. I probably should've been the last person to comfort Kaylee, but when I heard about her dad, all the times she spoke about him came back to me, and I needed to make sure she was okay. Her dad was always a hard issue for her. She loved him, but he wasn't capable of loving anything other than the numbness he craved. I found her grieving, drinking her weight in alcohol, and I put all our shit aside to be there for her.

While she cried and I held her, I imagined us together—her in my bed, in my arms—and I knew once reality hit, it would hurt all over again, but I couldn't stop myself. She's spent two days in my arms, crying, mourning, lost in herself, and I've spent two days soaking her in, rememorizing her scent, the softness of her body. Sometimes, I just want to say fuck it and forgive her so I can be with her because as much as I hate her, I still love her.

But that isn't what she wanted. If it was, when she cheated, she would've asked for forgiveness. She would've begged and pleaded and apologized. She wouldn't have let me walk away. She wouldn't have gone six goddamn years without saying a word to me.

And then it happened. The moment I imagined over and over again. She apologized. For cheating? For hurting me? I don't know. I guess it's one and the same anyway. I always thought when she finally did say she was sorry, I'd tell her to go fuck herself, but at that moment, all I could do was forgive her. Because the truth is, I'd probably forgive her for anything, and that's not a good thing. But it doesn't change the facts.

"Hey," Kaylee chokes out, looking up at me as if she's just now realizing, after two days, she's lying in my bed. We were supposed to fly to San Jose yesterday, but Camden insisted we stay for Kaylee since we don't have a show until tomorrow night. We had a radio interview to do, but Camden handled it over the phone so we wouldn't have to cancel.

"Hey." On impulse, I tuck several strands of her blond hair behind her ear and then palm the side of her face. She leans into my touch and flutters her eyes closed, sighing contently. I wish we could stay like this, suspended in time, but reality is waiting for us outside. As if needing to remind me, my phone buzzes on the nightstand. I remove my hand from Kaylee's face and check it.

Happy Birthday, son! See you tonight at Henry's...7:00.

For a moment, I consider canceling just so I can stay in bed with Kaylee a little longer, but I stop myself. My dad's been there for me when Kaylee wasn't. When I was hurt and struggling, he had my back. No matter where we are, he always meets me for my birthday, and I'm not going to choose her over him.

"We have to get going," I say, pulling back and climbing off the bed. I reply to my dad, thanking him and confirming I'll see him tonight, and then go into the bathroom to take a shower and escape the temptation lying in my bed. When I get out, she's gone. The buses are waiting for us, and I go straight to mine, not stopping to see if she made it on hers okay. It's not my problem, and I need to distance myself. She's hurting, and I feel for her, but I can't let her back in. I just fucking can't.

"Hey, man!" Declan pulls me into a hug. "Happy Birthday."

"Thanks. You guys coming to dinner tonight?"

"Of course," Camden says, giving me a one-armed hug.

The drive to San Jose is long as fuck, but I use the time to get caught up on my sleep since I've been up the past couple of days making sure Kaylee was okay. The guys don't mention her, and I don't bring her up. Nothing's changed between us, so there's no point in discussing it.

When we arrive, we get checked in to our hotel since we'll be here for a couple of days. We have shows the next two nights, and then we'll be heading to Denver.

"Are you inviting Kaylee to dinner?" Camden asks as we walk downstairs. It's always been just the four of us and my dad—not even Jill goes, and she's been our tour manager for every tour—so I know it's his way of asking what's going on with us.

"No," I say before we get into the SUV. Simon, one of the bodyguards we take almost everywhere with us, drives us to the restaurant and drops us off at the front. My dad is already seated, so we head straight back. When he sees me, he stands and gives me a hug.

"I can't believe you're twenty-four years old," he says. "I can still remember when you and Camden were twelve, singing karaoke to Nickelback. Now look at you guys."

Camden chuckles and shrugs. "Eh, we're still singing karaoke. Just our own songs and on a bigger stage."

"I saw all your shows are completely sold out," Dad says, pride in his tone.

He's always supported us and encouraged me to follow my dreams. While some parents would view their kid being in a rock band as a bad thing, I'm lucky that my dad never saw it like that. All he ever wanted was for me to put my dreams and goals and passions first.

"Yeah, we're damn lucky," Declan says with a smile. "I think a few dates even got added."

My phone buzzes, and I glance at it even though I know it's not Kaylee. She hasn't contacted me in years, and I doubt she has my number. Pulling up my messages, I send a quick text to Jill, asking her to check on Kaylee. Losing her dad hit her hard, and she doesn't have anyone on the tour she can lean on. Layla is back in New York, and her mom couldn't give a shit about her dad—or how his death is affecting her daughter. She's too busy living her perfect life and pretending he never existed.

"Everything okay?" Dad asks.

"Yeah, Kaylee's dad passed away a couple of days ago. Just making sure she's okay."

I regret the words as soon as I say them, but it's too late to take them back.

"Do not let her back in," Dad warns. "The last thing you need is a woman coming between you and your future."

"Some women are worth it," Camden says, taking my dad's comment personally.

"You're still young," Dad says. "Just make sure you think twice before you make any rash decisions. Your music should come first. Women come and go."

"I beg to differ," Camden replies, his jaw ticking in anger. "Layla is forever, and I'll always put her first."

"Ahead of your friends? Your band?" Dad shakes his head as if he can't fathom such a thought.

"Luckily, I'll never be put in the position of having to choose," Camden remarks. "We have each other's backs and make decisions as a group. Like our decision to move back to New York. The guys—"

"New York?" Dad barks, cutting Camden off. "I thought that was temporary."

"It's where Layla lives..."

"And Kaylee," Dad points out, glaring at me.

I sigh, not bothering to argue because clearly, this isn't about me. It's about him and his fear of me ending up like him. Despite how he sounds, I know he means well and is coming from a good place. When I got on the plane to LA after everything went down, he told me countless times how proud he was of me for choosing my future. But what he didn't get—or refused to understand—was that I didn't *choose* it. I was left with no choice. *Kaylee* made the decision for me—for us—when she cheated on me.

"Look, Michael," Declan says, jumping in. "Tonight is about Brax's birthday, so how about we just focus on that."

Dad nods, thankfully dropping it, and the rest of dinner goes smoothly. The guys are assholes and have people come out and sing "Happy Birthday." After we've eaten the dessert and my dad's paid the bill—he always insists on it when we meet up—the guys and I head to a club in the area to get a drink. I invited my dad, but he said he'd leave the partying to us "kids." He has an early morning flight out and will never wake up on time if he isn't in bed before midnight.

When we arrive at the club, we're taken straight back to VIP, and Gage orders us a bottle. The women flock to us like they always do, and I try to get into it, but for some reason, I'm just not feeling it at all. So after we toast to my birthday, we go back to the hotel.

As we're walking inside, I notice Kaylee coming out of the elevator. She's dressed in gray sweats and a matching hoodie. She's staring down at her phone, so she doesn't see us. I should keep walking, but something pulls me toward her instead. I tell myself I just want to make sure she's okay. Her dad only died a couple of days ago, and Jill never got back to me.

The guys tell me they'll see me later and get on the elevator. If they saw her or know that I'm going to talk to her, they don't say anything.

I'm about to call her name and go after her, but what I see stops me in my place, leaving me confused as fuck and speechless. My dad approaches Kaylee and guides her over to a secluded corner of the hotel. I walk around the outer perimeter, hiding behind the fake trees so I can get close enough to hear. My dad never cared for Kaylee while we were dating, and once she cheated, he made his feelings of disdain abundantly clear, so for them to be meeting up makes no sense at all.

"That's not how this was supposed to go down!" my dad hisses. "You were supposed to let him go, not follow him all over the damn country."

The fuck?

"I didn't plan this. But things happened, and the band…They're my last chance if I want to save my career before it's even started." Kaylee huffs and crosses her arms over her chest. "I didn't even want to be on that damn tour. I only took the job to get my foot in the door, and instead, I was shot in the foot. Now I'm just trying to save my ass. Camden offered me a lifeline, and I took it."

"You're so damn selfish. Just like every other woman," my dad says.

"That's not fair! I haven't even spoken to Braxton since that night." She turns slightly, and I catch a glint of liquid in her eyes. She's tearing up…but why? None of this makes any sense. I hear what they're saying, but I can't help thinking that I'm missing a vital piece.

"What will it take?" my dad asks, standing up straight. "Name your price. What will it take for you to walk away and never look back? Whatever they're paying you, I'll double it."

What the hell? My dad makes a good living, but why would he offer that? All because my ex-girlfriend is our publicist? I know he hates her, but this doesn't make any sense.

"You know what? Fuck you!" Kaylee cries. "I'm not the damn problem here. I did as you said, and he left like you wanted, but he's not happy. Can't you see that? He drinks and smokes and sleeps around. Sure, he has money, but he's not *happy*," Kaylee chokes out. "Don't you want that for him?"

"Don't you fucking go there." My dad steps toward Kaylee, and she takes a step back. My hackles rise, not liking the way he's cornering her. "My son is happy. Don't you dare ruin his future because you're jealous. You did the right thing, now do it again, and walk the hell away."

"And what if I can't?" she asks, jutting out her chin. "What if I want to tell him the truth?"

"Then you're more stupid than I thought," my dad says, "because he's never going to forgive you."

"Maybe...maybe not. But at least he'll know the truth."

"He doesn't need the truth! What he needs is for you to leave him the fuck alone."

"Actually, I would like to know the truth," I say, stepping out from where I've been hiding.

"Brax," Kaylee breathes, her eyes going wide in shock.

"Son...I thought you were going out for your birthday."

"Changed my mind." I shrug. "Now, tell me." I lock eyes with Kaylee. "What the hell is going on?"

"I can explain," Kaylee says.

"Please do."

"Can we go somewhere and talk?" Her eyes flit between my dad and me.

"Nah." I shake my head. "You can just say it right here."

"Okay..." She nods slowly as if she's psyching herself up.

"Braxton, listen—" My dad starts to cut in, but my glare shuts him up.

"Kaylee, talk. Now."

"I never cheated on you," she blurts out, her words making me take a step back. Because what in the actual fuck?

"What in the hell are you talking about?" I bark.

"You weren't going to go to LA, and I didn't want to be the reason you gave up your music career, so I lied." Tears fill her lids and spill over as she looks at me, silently begging me to understand. "I knew you wouldn't leave unless I pushed you away...did something unforgivable."

"So you cheated on me."

"But I didn't. I had Jack take the pictures and post them, so you would think I did. I couldn't do it, and he didn't care because everyone thought we did it anyway. So he took it as a win."

"Why the fuck would you do that?" I mean, I know why. I heard what she said, but I don't understand. That's not the kind of person she was back then...to purposely hurt me. If I hadn't seen the pictures with my own eyes, I wouldn't have believed she cheated.

And then it clicks. "You did this." I look at my dad, who's been quiet this entire time since she started confessing. "You told her to do this."

"I didn't tell her to cheat on you...or pretend or whatever." He waves his hand in the air like there's an annoying fly he can't get rid of. "But I did tell her to let you go." He steps over to me and puts his hand on my shoulder. "I did it for you, son. Because I love you. I didn't want you to make the same mistakes I made. You would've regretted not going to LA to be a part of the band. Look at the success you've achieved. You would've given it all up for *her*."

"That wasn't your choice to make." My fists are clenched at my sides, my body vibrating in anger. Everything I thought I knew was a fucking lie. I was manipulated, tricked...

"You were young and not thinking clearly," my dad says like he's talking to a child. "I had to do what was best for you."

"Fuck that!" I bark. "You knew how much I loved her. She was young and impressionable, and you used that to your advantage. You knew she would do anything to make sure I was happy because I would've done the same for her."

"Women come—"

"No." I step into his face, cutting him off. "Don't you fucking say it. You need to go now. I need time to think. I can't believe you did this."

"Braxton, please..."

"Go!"

With a sigh, Dad does as I demand and walks away, leaving Kaylee and me alone. Realizing we've made a scene, I head to the elevators, and she follows. The ride up is filled with a silent, stifling tension. I can tell she wants to say something, but she keeps her mouth shut, which is good since I have a million thoughts whirring around in my head, and I don't know where to go from here.

When we get up to her room, she stands in the corner, remaining quiet while I pace back and forth, trying to figure out what to say first. When my anger and frustration finally boil over, I stop and lock eyes with her, settling on the one thought that keeps circling around in my head. "You fucked it all up. You should've come to me and talked to me. Instead, you fucked everything up."

I stare at the woman who was my entire world, wanting to shake her, wanting her to make me understand why she would do this to me...to us. She didn't have the right to make that decision for me. I loved her and wanted to spend my life with her. And she pushed me away.

"You wouldn't have listened," she whispers, her voice clogged with emotion. "You wouldn't have gone to LA."

"That's not how relationships work!" I pick up a vase and throw it against the wall, making it shatter into pieces. Kaylee jumps in fear, but I don't have it in me to care. The anger and betrayal running through my body has nowhere to go. Somehow, this feels worse than her cheating. Because at least then there was a valid reason we broke up and went our separate ways. Why I spent the past several years hating her, missing her, forcing myself to live without her.

"Braxton," she cries, tears pouring down her cheeks. "I'm sorry."

"You're sorry?" I scoff. "*Sorry?* Fuck being sorry. We were supposed to be a goddamn team. Trust each other!"

"I know, I know," she sobs. "But I just...I didn't want to be the reason you lost everything."

"That's what you don't get," I say, walking over to her. I palm her cheek reverently, needing to feel her. She's the best and worst addiction I've ever had. "You were my everything, and because of your choices, I lost every-fucking-thing."

"So where does that leave us?" she asks, her voice shaky.

I back up, dropping my hand, needing to distance myself from her. "First, I didn't trust you because you cheated. Now, I don't trust you because you lied and hid shit from me." I sigh, mentally and emotionally exhausted. "Guess that leaves us right where we were...absolutely fucking nowhere."

And with that, I turn my back on the only girl I've ever loved and walk away.

Fourteen

KAYLEE

"WHERE'S BRAXTON?" I SEARCH THE DRESSING ROOM. "HAVE YOU SEEN HIM?"

The guys shake their heads while they quickly change into clean shirts. When they're on stage, they sweat, and by the end of the show, they're soaked. So before they head to meet the fans for the meet and greet, they always change. But Braxton is nowhere to be found, which is a problem since the winner of the radio contest picked to meet him.

"Dammit, I need to find him," I mutter, racing out of the room and down the hall in search of him. I ask everyone I come in contact with if they've seen him, and of course, nobody has. Honestly, even if they had, I doubt they'd tell me. I'm the bitch who broke his heart, and he's the guy who signs their paychecks. Well, technically the label does, but you get my point.

It's been several days since Braxton found out I didn't cheat, and while I hate to admit it, Michael was right. He's pissed. I mean, I knew he wouldn't be happy that I lied, but I thought he'd at least be less mad that I didn't actually cheat. Nope. If anything, he's madder.

When it's clear I'm not going to find him, I head back to where the meet and greet is being held so I can make up a lie and give the girl who won extra gifts in hope she won't be too upset that she won't be meeting Braxton.

Declan, Camden, and Gage are accommodating and spend a little extra time with her to make up for their fourth bandmate being a dick. Once we get through them taking pictures with everyone, we head back to the hotel since they have another show tomorrow night.

"Is he going to miss the meet and greets for the rest of the tour?" I ask. He's missed every one since the night he found out I didn't cheat on him. Aside from him showing up to perform, he hasn't been around at all. He doesn't even go out.

"He just needs time," Camden says. "He spent years thinking you cheated, and that gave him a reason to hate you. Now...it's all just fucked up." He blows out a harsh breath.

"Maybe I should leave the tour," I suggest, hating that Braxton is hiding out on his own tour because of me. The morning after everything went down, I heard him tell the guys he wanted me off the tour, but Camden told him it wasn't happening.

The guys don't argue, and I know it's because they're stuck between a rock and a hard place. They've told me countless times I'm doing a good job at keeping everything organized and promoting the hell out of this tour. But I'm also the woman who hurt their best friend.

We arrive at the hotel and go our separate ways. Since they don't need to do anything in the morning, we're all off until tomorrow afternoon for the sound check. Needing to clear my head, I change into my bathing suit and cover-up and head up to the private indoor pool that's only available to the band. After undressing and dropping my towel onto a nearby chair, I dive in and swim laps while I think about what I need to do.

As much as I need this job, it's not fair to Braxton that I stay. I was already selfish enough, between lying to him and taking this job. He's been hurt so much. I was stupid to think I'd tell him the truth, and he'd magically forgive me.

A movement out of the corner of my eye stops me in the water, and I see Braxton. Dressed in a pair of board shorts and T-shirt, he's standing against the pillar watching me.

"Sorry," I say, swimming to the steps to get out. "I didn't know you'd be using the pool tonight."

"You don't have to leave on my account."

"It's fine." I climb out and grab my towel, drying my hair and body off. When I look up, Braxton's standing right in front of me, so close I can smell the fresh scent of the cologne I originally bought him.

"Camden said you suggested you leave the tour."

"I did." I flip my hair up and wrap it in the towel so it's not dripping everywhere.

"I think that would be for the best."

My heart drops, and I nod, refusing to make eye contact with him. I know I set all of this in motion, but it doesn't mean I'm not hurt by it. Pushing Braxton away was the hardest thing I've ever had to do. I threw up for hours afterward and spent days crying, my heart feeling as though I reached into my chest and ripped it out myself. There were times I wanted to run to him and tell him the truth, and moments I didn't think I could move forward without him. But I watched as the band took off, and even though it hurt like hell, I thought deep down I did the right thing. And that's what got me through every day.

"I understand," I tell him as I reach for my cover-up to put it back on since I'm only in a tiny bikini. As I'm finding the sleeves, a hand pulls it away, and I'm forced to look at him, confused.

"What the fuck is this?" he breathes, his fingers wrapping around...*Oh, shit.* I forgot to take it off. "You still have this?"

He fingers the promise ring he gave me all those years ago, and I nod robotically, praying he doesn't rip it from my neck. I took it off the day he left since I didn't deserve to wear it, but I put it on a chain and have been wearing it around my neck ever since.

"Why do you still have this?" he asks, his eyes meeting mine.

"Because you gave it to me."

"And then you cheated." He shakes his head, growling under his breath in frustration. "Dammit, Kaylee. Why did you do it?" He tugs on the ends of his hair, his gaze pleading with me to give him the right answer. But I don't know what he wants or needs to hear. What will make this better.

"I didn't cheat—"

"Lie! Why the fuck did you *lie?*" he asks, his voice raspy and filled with so much emotion that all I want to do is wrap my arms around him and hold him tight.

"I thought I was doing the right thing." That's the only explanation I have because despite it sounding like a cop-out, it's the truth. In my head and heart, I thought I was doing what was best for Braxton and his future.

"You wouldn't have left." Traitorous tears fill my eyes, but I quickly blink them away.

Braxton grips my chin, raising my face to look at him, and the look of hurt in his eyes damn near sends me to my knees. I would do anything to make this right, but there's nothing I can do. The damage has already been done.

"It wasn't your choice to make."

"But your choice was because of me." I palm his hand that's holding my face. "I couldn't let you give it all up for me. What if we didn't work out? What if you regretted it? I know you don't agree with it, and maybe your dad and I handled it wrong, but I did it because I loved you," I choke out. "I still love you." I step closer. "I never stopped loving you."

He steps back slightly, breaking our connection, then his fingers go back to the ring, stroking it gently. "It could've been amazing." He looks at me, his hazel eyes so intense, it's as if they're reaching deep into me and squeezing my soul. "You and me...we could've had everything." He says the words as if they each were once living and are now dead. As if he's mourning the loss of the idea. "All you had to do was believe in us the way I did. I would've done anything for you, *for us.* All I wanted was forever."

He drops his hand and walks away, leaving me staring after him, wishing I would've made so many different choices. Once I know he's gone, I drop into the chair and cry. I hate how often I cry, but I can't help it. It all just hurts so damn badly.

I spend the next several minutes balled up, letting out my emotions, and once I'm all cried out, I wipe my face and head to my room to pack. It's the least I can do so Braxton isn't in pain having to see me every day.

After booking a flight home for tomorrow morning, I go down to the bar, needing a drink. I find Gage sitting there, drinking straight from the bottle.

"Mind if I join you?" I ask, sliding onto the seat next to him.

His eyes meet mine, and I notice they're bloodshot and puffy. *Has he been crying?*

"Hey." I place a hand on his forearm. "Are you okay?"

He tilts the bottle back, downing way too much alcohol, and then without looking at me, he says, "It's been six years...today."

He doesn't have to say anything else. There's only one thing he could be referring to, the only thing that would have him sitting alone in a bar, drinking himself into oblivion, and I feel like shit for not remembering the date.

Since nothing can be said, I don't bother talking, and instead, I sit next to Gage quietly while he drinks more liquor than can be good for his liver. When he's finally so wasted that he can barely keep his eyes open, I text Camden and Declan so they can help bring him up to his room.

"I'm worried about him," I say to them once they've delivered Gage to his room. "It's been six years, and every day, he's getting worse. Drinking more, smoking more. And we all know he's doing other shit behind closed doors."

"I know," Camden says with a sigh. "I've talked to him about going to rehab, but he's not having it."

"Well, maybe you need to make him."

"It doesn't work like that," Declan says. "We can convince him to go, but once he's there, he can check himself out. He has to want to go, and he's not there yet."

"So you're just going to pretend he's fine? For how long?" When the guys don't say anything, I sigh and walk to the door. "He needs you. You may think you're being his friend, but you're only enabling him. And at the rate he's going, we'll be burying him right next to Tori."

BUZZ. BUZZ. BUZZ.

I wake to the sound of my phone going off on the nightstand. It's Easton. When I see it's only five in the morning, I know something is wrong. That's the only reason he'd be calling me this early.

"Hello."

"Sorry to wake you. It's eight in the morning here."

"It's okay."

"We have a problem."

I should probably tell him that I'm leaving, and my flight is scheduled for this morning, but if it's about the band, I'll do everything in my power to help fix whatever I can as long as they'll let me help.

"A woman posted on social media that she's pregnant with Braxton's baby. She hasn't made any demands, but they never do on social media. They first post to get a feeler out there."

While my head wraps around what Easton's just said—a woman is possibly carrying Braxton's baby—my heart squeezes in my chest as I imagine a completely different scenario.

Braxton and me getting married.

Buying a home together.

Finding out we're expecting a baby.

Filling our home with lots of babies and love...

"What do you need me to do?" I ask, shaking my thoughts from my head. All of those dreams went up in smoke the second I pushed him away, so daydreaming about the what-ifs will only make it hurt that much worse.

"Braxton isn't answering his phone. I need you to find him and ask him if he was with her. I'll send you the info and her picture. Keep him from getting online, please. His initial response will be to lash out at her, which we don't want him to do. Once we know whether her accusation is plausible, we'll go from there."

We hang up, and I quickly shower and get dressed. It's still early, so I can handle this before I need to get going. Technically, this is still my job since I haven't been fired yet. I'd imagine if I was, Easton wouldn't have called me, or he would've at least let me know.

I find Braxton in his bed alone and sit on the edge, watching him for a few seconds before I wake him up. He looks so calm in his sleep, and I would give anything to be lying in bed with him, snuggling against his warm, hard body. When we were together, the times we got to spend the night together were few and far between, but those were some of the best nights of my life. Not just because of the sex, even though that was damn good, but because I always felt safe and at home in the comfort of his arms.

I glance over at the nightstand and see the journal I gave him. Despite the way he feels about me, I love that he still uses it to write his words in—even if some of those words are written with the intent to hurt me. It makes me think that in some way, even though I hurt him, he still cares about me the way I care about him. Otherwise, wouldn't he have thrown it away and gotten a new one that wouldn't make him think of me?

When I shake him, he turns over, and his eyes meet mine in confusion.

"What are you doing?" he asks, his voice gruff from sleep.

"We need to talk." I pull up the social media account that Easton sent over and click on a picture of a beautiful woman. "Recognize her?"

Braxton barely gives her a once-over. "Yeah...so?"

"She's claiming to be pregnant—"

"Good for her..."

"—with your baby."

"Not possible," he says matter-of-factly.

"Condoms break."

"True." He slides up the bed, and the blanket falls, exposing his naked, muscular, tattooed chest and six-pack abs. I can't help but look. It's been a long time since I've seen him up close, and when we were together, he was still more boy than man. Now...he's all fucking man.

"Like what you see?"

My eyes ascend to his face and find him smirking. He lifts his arms, crossing them behind his head, and I swallow down a groan.

"You've gotten a lot of tattoos," I say stupidly.

He chuckles, and the sound wraps around me like a warm blanket on a cold night. I can't remember the last time I heard him laugh, and especially not with me.

"She's not pregnant with my kid."

"Huh?" And then I remember what we were talking about. "How do you know? Condoms aren't one-hundred-percent effective. And we don't know how far along she is."

"It's not possible—"

"Braxton..."

"—because I didn't sleep with her."

"What? But you said..."

"I recognize her, yeah. Did we fuck around? Yeah. But I never stuck my dick in her." His tongue darts across the seam of his lips, and flashbacks of how well he used that tongue on me hit me hard.

"Maybe you were too high or drunk to remember."

"Doesn't matter how much I smoke or drink, I always know who I'm sticking my dick into. And I know I haven't stuck my dick into her."

"Maybe—"

"Kaylee," he says, stopping me from finishing my sentence. "I haven't fucked her or anyone in months."

His admission has me rearing back. "Months?"

He nods. "Months."

"But..." I've seen the women in his bed. He even asked me to get him condoms.

"Months," he repeats.

"I don't understand."

"That makes two of us." He throws his blanket off his body and stands. "Call her bluff. She isn't pregnant with my kid. And then can you order breakfast, please? I'm starved."

He says it so nonchalantly that I can't help but believe him.

BRAXTON WAS RIGHT. AFTER I REACHED OUT TO FIONA—THE WOMAN MAKING THE ACCUSATION—AND TOLD her that Braxton would gladly do a paternity test once she was seven weeks pregnant, she tried to go around it, saying she wasn't going to risk harming her precious baby. I was expecting this, so I explained science has come a long way, and a noninvasive test can now be done.

She immediately went on alert, saying if he didn't want to be part of the baby's life, he could pay her off.

Could she be any more cliché?

"Actually, he's excited. He's always wanted a baby," I lied. "Once we run the DNA test and get it confirmed, he'll reach out and discuss the custody details."

A few hours later, her account had been deleted, proving what Braxton said was true—he didn't sleep with her—and leaving me with a shit ton of questions I'm dying for the answers to, starting with...Was his dry spell because of me? And if so, what the hell does that mean?

I push my thoughts away, though, because it doesn't matter. It doesn't change anything. In a few hours, I'll be back on the East Coast, looking for a job. As I pull my stuff out of the small closet I was given on the bus I share with several other tour employees, I can't help but think about how off course my life has gone. Six years ago, I was about to graduate high school and had my entire future ahead of me. I was happy and in love and couldn't wait for what was to come. Now, I'm alone and jobless, and I only have myself to blame.

"There you are," a masculine voice says from behind me. Expecting everyone to be at the venue already, I jump, knocking my suitcase to the floor. The entire contents spill out, and I sigh in defeat.

"What are you doing?" Braxton asks, bending to help pick my stuff up.

"I got it." I grab my panties from him and shove them back into my luggage. "Thanks."

"Going somewhere?"

"Flight is for noon." I stand and set the suitcase back on my bunk. It's tight in the hallway, and when I look up, Braxton is close...too close to me. "Did you need something before I go?"

"Easton said you handled that woman like a pro. She disappeared, deleting all her accounts and shit. And the statement you made on my account was worded perfectly. Thanks."

"Of course. It's my job." I reach down to grab my suitcase to zip it up, but Braxton stops me in my place, his fingers wrapping around my bicep.

"I don't want you to leave." His words come out raspy, almost sounding desperate, and I have to force myself not to read too much into them.

"I think we both know my coming on this tour was a mistake."

"Maybe," he says. "But you're here now, and...the band needs you."

My stomach drops at his admittance. *He* doesn't need me. The band does. I wasn't expecting him to say he needs me, but a small part of me was hoping he would.

"We still have more than half of the tour left," he adds. "And next week, we'll be in Florida at the theme parks." His lips quirk into a half-smile, and a flashback from our past hits me hard.

"Paris."

"Why Paris?"

Braxton shrugs, and I roll over to face him, wrapping my arm around his torso. We started this game of "If you could..." months ago, and whenever we're bored, one of us will throw one out there. Mine was, if you could go anywhere in the world, where would you go? *Braxton's answer was Paris.*

"Tell me," I say, kissing his flesh.

His gaze darts to mine, and he clears his throat. "My mom used to say when you can afford to visit the Eiffel Tower, it means you've made it. I was young when she left, but for some reason, I always remember her saying that."

The mention of his mom leaves me momentarily stunned. In the years I've known Braxton, including all the months we've been together, he's never once mentioned his mom. Layla once said Camden told her she left him and his dad years ago. She was some huge actress, but I don't know who she is. I'm assuming she doesn't use the same last name as Braxton's, which is Lutz.

"How about you?" he asks, breaking the silence.

"Florida."

"Florida?" He laughs and rolls us over so he's on top of me. "Why Florida?" He kisses the corner of my mouth, and I shiver in anticipation.

"Specifically, Tampa and Orlando. I've never been to a theme park." I shrug nonchalantly. "My dad always worked too much. And then the accident happened, and my mom didn't have the money. I've always wanted to go to Disney and Universal and Busch Gardens. Ride the roller coasters and take pictures with the princesses."

Braxton chuckles. "We'll go together. You and me. Once we have the money, we'll ride every damn ride there is and take a million pictures."

"And then we'll go to Paris," I add. "Take a picture in front of the Eiffel Tower."

"Damn right, we will," he says, pressing his lips to mine.

"I can't wait."

"Have you been?" Braxton asks, shaking me from my memory.

"Nope. How about you? Make it to Paris yet?" They've been on several tours, some taking them to other countries, so it would make sense.

"Not yet." He glances down at my open suitcase. "Stay on the tour. Come to Florida with us."

"You going to ride all the rides with me?" I half joke.

"Yeah, I will," he says seriously.

"Brax," I breathe. "What does—?"

"I don't know, Kaylee." He cuts me off, knowing what my question is without me finishing it. "I don't fucking know what anything means anymore. All I know is, when Camden said you were leaving, I had to stop you. I don't know what that means or where we stand, but I'm not ready for you to leave this tour yet. So I'm asking you to stay."

Fifteen

BRAXTON

I ASKED HER TO STAY, AND SHE SAID YES. I DON'T KNOW WHY I DID IT. I'VE SPENT WEEKS WANTING HER OFF our tour, and when Camden said she was leaving, I should've felt relieved. Instead, my heart pounded against my rib cage, and without thinking, I went in search of her. I wasn't sure what the hell I was going to say until I saw her standing on the bus, packing her shit, and then the words just slipped out.

Maybe it was finding out that she never cheated, or seeing her wearing my goddamn ring around her neck, or perhaps it was admitting out loud that I haven't had sex since she came back into my life. It could be a combination of all of the above—but I just couldn't let her go...not yet.

"You asked her to stay?" Camden asks, dropping into the seat next to me. We've just finished our show in Tulsa and are about to leave for Atlanta, where we've got two back-to-back shows before we head to Florida. "She said you asked her to stay."

"She didn't cheat on me."

His gaze swings over to me, and I notice Declan glances up from the magazine he's reading. Gage is passed the fuck out from whatever he's on, but he already knows since I told him the other night while we were at the bar getting drunk.

"What do you mean?" Declan asks.

"She lied to push me away. My dad told her if she didn't let me go, she'd be the reason for my future being fucked, and she knew the only way I'd walk away was if she did something fucked up. So she staged it all."

Declan whistles, and Camden curses under his breath. For the past six years, I've made a damn career out of hating Kaylee because of what I thought she did. And yeah, I'm mad as fuck that she lied, but without her having cheated, it's making it really hard to hate her the way I did.

"So what now?"

"No clue." I drop my head back and scrub my eyes. I'm so damn tired. I hate being on tour, and I've spent years fucking and drinking my way through my heartbreak. And now, to find out it's not true. It's like my life, my anger, was all based on a lie.

"You know she still loves you, right?" Declan says.

"Doesn't matter. It's not enough. She pushed me away, and we can't go back. Too much has happened." I slam my fist into the sofa. "I'm just so pissed. She fucked it all up...and for what? Nothing!"

"For us," Camden says. "For Raging Chaos. We wouldn't be the same without you."

I appreciate his words, but..."I'm not the same without her."

Camden's gaze follows over my shoulder, and when I glance back, I find Kaylee standing in the doorway. Based on the look on her face, she heard what was said.

"And I'm not the same without you," she whispers, her tear-filled eyes meeting mine. It's at that moment that nothing else matters. Not our past or the present, or whatever the fuck the future holds. Nothing else matters but Kaylee and me. I need her in ways I've never needed anyone. From the moment she kissed me on the beach, she's owned every part of me—mind, body, and heart. Our souls are entwined. And when she pushed me away, I might've gotten on that plane without looking back, but my heart and soul stayed with her.

"I, um..." She clears her throat. "I have your schedules," she says, walking over with papers in her hands. She gives Declan his, then Camden. She leaves Gage's next to him. When she steps close to me, extending her hand, I catch a whiff of that sweet, intoxicating rose scent, and something in me snaps, just fucking snaps.

Without thinking, I grasp her waist, throw her over my shoulder, and stalk back to the main bedroom in the back of the bus. I ignore Declan and Camden laughing as I slam the door closed and then drop Kaylee onto the center of the king-sized bed.

"What are you doing?" she gasps as I climb up her body until I'm hovering directly above her.

"I'm about to fuck you. We have a sixteen-hour drive, and I'm planning to spend every fucking minute of it inside you, making up for the past six goddamn years I've been without you because of what you did to us. You got a problem with that?"

"I..." She swallows thickly. "I thought you were mad at me."

"I am," I growl, tugging on her hair so she's forced to look at me. "You fucked everything up." But I also miss the hell out of her, and I need her. I wasn't lying when I said she was the worst and best addiction. I've been craving her for six damn years, and I need my fix.

"I did it for you," she whispers.

"You should've come to me."

"We can't do this. I said I wouldn't sleep with you while I'm your publicist."

"Fine. Then you're fired." Problem solved.

Before she can argue, my mouth connects with hers in a bruising kiss. Her lips are pillow soft, just as I remember, and she tastes as sweet as the most decadent fucking candy. When I try to deepen the kiss, she bites down on my bottom lip, making me groan. I do it back, nipping at her flesh, and she moans into my mouth.

The chemistry between us was always like sparks flying on the Fourth of July. We were young and wanted each other like mad. But now, as she grinds her center against my hard cock, and I devour her mouth, tasting and caressing her, it's as if something stronger has replaced those pretty fireworks, and with one flick, we'll explode.

I break our kiss and yank her shirt off her body, exposing her powder-blue lacy bra. With her tits spilling out the tops, I take a moment to appreciate the sight in front of me. Her smooth, tanned skin. The freckles scattered sparsely across her shoulders. When she goes into the sun, they become more prominent. She hates them, but I love them—have spent too many hours kissing and counting each one.

A glint catches my eye, and nestled between her perfect tits is the ring— the one I gave her. My mouth goes to where the swells of her breasts meet, and I place an open-mouthed kiss to her flesh, making it a point to kiss the ring as well.

Kaylee sucks in a harsh breath, her legs tightening around me, and I pull one of her cups down, revealing her pale-pink nipple. I swipe my tongue across the tip, and it hardens, creating a point. I wrap my lips around it, sucking it into my mouth, and she arches her back, silently begging for more. When she walked onto the bus and admitted she's not the same without me, I imagined taking her back here and angry fucking the hell out of her, but now that I have her in my bed, all I want to do is reacquaint myself with every inch of her.

Pulling the other cup down, I swirl my tongue around the pointed tip. Kaylee's entire body shivers, reminding me how responsive she is to my touch. After removing her shoes, I unbutton and unzip her pants, pulling them down her thighs. Her underwear is the same color as her bra, and it brings me back to when we were together. She always made sure they were matching. She said if she was ever killed or hurt and had to be undressed, she didn't want to be caught in ugly undergarments. I didn't get it, but I loved that it meant she always looked sexy as hell under her clothes.

"Brax," she breathes, her voice husky. "I need you in me." She reaches up to grab my cock, but I swat her hand away.

"Soon, baby."

I turn my attention back on her, kissing my way down her soft, flat torso until I get to the top of her underwear. With an open-mouthed kiss to the hood of her pussy, I inhale her scent through the thin material. Of course she smells like goddamn roses, making my dick even harder.

"Brax," she groans, wiggling impatiently.

"Patience," I chide. "I've waited six years, and I'm not going to rush it."

I hook the sides of her underwear and drag them down her legs, leaving her completely exposed. Unlike when we were younger and she had curls of blond hair down there, she's now neatly trimmed. I spread her legs and have the perfect view of her pink pussy. It's already glistening with her arousal, so I dip down and lick up her slit, needing her on my tongue.

"Fuck, you taste just how I remembered," I mutter between licks, tasting and smelling her arousal. I push a digit into her tight hole, then two. She rocks against me, trying like hell to get herself off, so I stop. Her pleasure is mine. All mine.

Hooking her legs over my shoulders, I dip my face between her thighs and eat her pussy, licking and sucking, devouring it like it's the first sweet I've had after a six-year diet. I flick her clit softly—just enough so she feels it but not enough to get her off. I work her up higher and higher until she's begging and pleading for her release, and then I give her what she wants. She screams my name as she writhes under me, shaking as she orgasms all over my face and fingers.

I've been with a lot of women over the years, but Kaylee is the only woman I've ever gone down on. Those other women were about losing myself in and getting off. This is intimate, personal, and she's the only person I've ever wanted to be this close to.

When she comes down from her high, she sits up and reaches for my pants. "Now, it's my turn," she says, leaving no room for argument as she pushes me onto my back and tugs my pants and boxer briefs down. When my dick juts out, her eyes go wide.

"You're..." Her gaze flicks from my dick to my face and back to my dick again.

"Pierced? Yeah." I smirk, knowing it's one of her favorite things in a book. When we were together, she'd read raunchy as fuck romance and always said she loved when the guy was pierced. She begged me quite a few times to do it, but it would've meant going weeks without being inside her, and no way was that happening.

She glides her hand gently over my shaft where the piercings are. There are two horizontal bars pierced through the bottom of my shaft. They're not big, just enough to add pleasure to sex.

"Will I be able to feel them through the condom?" she asks curiously, but my mind stops on the word condom. Kaylee and I never used condoms, ever.

She was on birth control, and I wanted to feel every part of her. But now, she's implying we're going to use one?

"You don't really think I'm going to use a condom with you, do you?" I ask, taking her hand and tightening it around my dick. I stroke it up and down, showing her that she doesn't have to be gentle. I've had these piercings for years, and unless someone were to tug hard on them, they're good.

"You've been with other women..."

"And you've been with other men. But I've been tested, and I'm clean. And I know damn well you wouldn't risk fucking anyone without a condom but me."

Without giving her a chance to argue, I pull her on top of me to straddle my thighs and then lift her onto my dick. She takes me in, inch by inch, moaning as the piercings rub against her inner walls. When she's completely full, I close my eyes, needing a moment to get my shit together because regardless of all the pussy I've had over the years, nobody, and I mean *nobody*, feels the way Kaylee feels—like motherfucking home.

Her hands rest on my chest, and she starts to move up and down, using me to find her pleasure. I open my eyes, watching as her blond hair curtains around us, and her mouth parts slightly, releasing the sexiest damn moan.

"You're a greedy little thing, aren't you?" I ask as she grinds her pelvis against me, stroking her clit while riding me. With her bra still intact, her tits are trussed up, bouncing up and down in tandem with her movements.

She smiles down at me, not denying it, and I grab the back of her neck, pulling her face to mine for a hard kiss. I fuck her mouth with my tongue while she fucks me. And as we both find our release, I know that despite how fucking mad I am at her for what she's done, for all the years we've lost, there's no one like her, and there never will be. Now I just have to decide what to do with that.

Fifteen

BONUS SCENE

BRAXTON

I WAS JUST INSIDE KAYLEE...TWICE. I SHOULDN'T BE THIS HARD, THIS SOON. BUT AS SHE WRAPS HER mouth around my shaft and sucks me like she's starved, my cock gets even harder for her. If you'd have asked me how I would be spending the eleven-hour bus ride to the next venue, I never, in a million fucking years, would've thought it would be spent in the bedroom with a naked Kaylee.

I move her hair to the side, so I can get a better view as she takes me all the way down her throat, not giving a shit about my piercings. When the head of my cock hits the back of her throat, her eyes water, causing a trail of mascara to race down her cheeks.

Fucking beautiful.

She licks and sucks, and what doesn't go into her mouth, she pumps, working me over. Sex has always been about getting off and escaping reality for a short time, but with Kaylee, it's about the connection. The way she makes me feel. The woman owns every goddamn part of me.

Releasing my cock with a pop, she takes it in her hand and licks down my shaft to my ball sac. She sucks one into her mouth, and I damn near explode. Precum seeps from the tip, and she swipes her tongue across it, moaning in pleasure.

"Get over here," I demand, needing to touch her.

She raises a defiant brow, not wanting to give up my dick, so I grab her hips, flipping her so she's sitting on my face. Without giving her a chance to argue, I spread her pussy lips and go to town on her swollen clit, sucking and fucking her with my tongue.

With a loud moan, she takes me back into her mouth and sucks me down. I focus on her, on making her come, and all too soon, her legs are shaking as she comes all over my tongue. The taste of her juices sets me off, and seconds later, I'm shooting my load straight down her throat.

After showering again, we climb back into bed, and I pull Kaylee into my arms, wanting to feel her body wrapped around me. I grab the container of fruit I brought in earlier and pop the top, snagging a grape so I can feed it to her. She parts her lips, and I place it in her mouth, watching as she slowly chews.

When she's done, she smiles softly up at me. "Tell me about the past six years...about the band. I want to know everything."

My heart clenches at her question. I want to tell her she'd know everything if she wouldn't have pushed me away. She would've been by my side. But I don't want to ruin the moment. So I push my anger and bitterness aside and tell her.

We spend our time talking and laughing, and like old times, the conversation flows with ease. And when we're not talking and laughing, we're fucking. I can't even tell you how many times we've gotten off.

At some point, Kaylee passes out with her face toward me and her arms wrapped around the pillow. I use the moment to rememorize her features. The way her naturally thick lashes rest on the apples of her cheeks. Her plump, pouty lips are parted slightly, her mouth forming an O shape.

When we were together in high school, she was still growing into herself and trying to find her place in life. Now, she's grown—one-hundred-percent woman—but she's still searching, and I can't help but wonder if that's because of the choices she made. I know she did what she felt was best, but I knew back then she was my soul mate, and the fact that neither of us has settled down only proves my point. Since the day she stepped onto the plane, she's looked tense, but right now, she looks...content. And as I watch her sleep, I feel the same way.

Sixteen

KAYLEE

ONE MINUTE, BRAXTON WAS GLARING MY WAY, AND THE NEXT, HE WAS THROWING ME OVER HIS SHOULDER, full-on caveman style. I expected the sex to be selfish and for him to take. God knows I wouldn't have blamed him. What I wasn't expecting was for the old Braxton to appear, the one who always made sure I was taken care of several times before he even considered getting off. Unlike when we were younger, when we were learning our own bodies as well as each other's, he played mine like the strings of his guitar with such expertise, it made every guy I've been with over the years look like amateurs.

I should be resentful that part of the reason he's so fluent in the body language of a woman is because he's been with other women, and I am to an extent, but as he pulled me on top of him and I rode him while he fucked my mouth, I felt it, that spark, that chemistry, and I know he did too. I could see it in his eyes. He can fuck as many women as he wants, but none of them will replace what we have.

"Fuck," Braxton curses under his breath as I climb off him. Without a condom, his cum drips out of me and down my leg. I run to the bathroom that's connected to the bedroom and turn the water on while I go pee. I expect him to stay where he is, so I'm shocked when he joins me in the shower. On the bus I ride, one person can barely fit in the shower, but the bus for the guys is custom built with the two bedrooms, two bathrooms, a kitchen, and a living room all bigger than the average New York apartment.

We're both quiet as we wash our hair and bodies. I don't know what to do or say. The ball is in his court. He's the one who's mad at me. It's not that I'm allowing him to string me along, but I don't know where his head's at, and since it's been six damn years, and so much has happened and come to light, I'm giving him a moment to breathe.

When I go to step around him so I can rinse off, he stops me, pushing me against the wall. One hand slaps the tiles next to my head, and the other squeezes the curve of my hip.

"I hate you," he says, and my stomach drops at those three words.

I close my eyes, unable to look at him while he says whatever it is he needs to say, but when he pinches my chin, forcing me to look at him, I have no choice but to make eye contact with him.

"I hate you," he says again, his eyes alight with silent chaos stirring in his hazel orbs. "I hate that you lied. That you didn't talk to me. I hate that you let me go instead of holding on. That it took six years to learn the truth, and it was only because I overheard you and my dad. That you didn't believe in us. I hate that the moment my mouth was back on yours, that I was back inside you, it felt so damn right…"

His admissions cause me to choke up, and I thank God the water is spraying over us, so he can't see the tears racing down my cheeks.

"I fucking hate that no matter how much I hate you, I still fucking love you." He grabs my chin a bit tighter, and I release the sob I can no longer keep in.

"Fuck, I love you so damn much." He releases my chin and strokes the side of my cheek with the backs of his knuckles. "I never stopped. And I don't know what the hell to do about that. So yeah, baby. I hate you…because no matter how much I don't want to, I can't stop loving you."

His mouth crashes down on mine, and the taste of him, of his tongue plunging into my mouth, sends me into an emotional frenzy. My arms lock around his neck as he lifts me and slams my back against the wall. He breaks our kiss, and when his eyes meet mine, they're filled with a myriad of emotions—love, hate, confusion, desire. And I feel every one of them down to my marrow.

My legs cup his hips, and he drives into me, his thick, long, pierced shaft massaging my vaginal walls in the best way possible. As he bottoms out in me, he releases a pained groan, telling me he's battling with himself. He both loves and hates me. Likes and loathes me. He wants me but wishes he didn't—and I don't blame him. I did this. I hurt him, and while there's a chance whatever we're doing won't leave this room, this bus, I'll take Braxton any way I can get him if it means I simply have a piece of him.

I fist the chocolatey strands of his hair and bring his face to mine for a passionate kiss as we lose ourselves in each other. And as we both find our release, I tell myself that I'll accept whatever this is, for however long it is. As much as I've longed for this day—never thinking it would ever come—I know I have no right to make any demands. So I'll just roll with it and see where it goes.

When Braxton pulls out of me and I slide down the wall to my feet, he's silent. We finish showering, and he hands me a towel so I can dry off. I stay in the bathroom while he goes out to the bedroom to get dressed. I towel dry my hair and brush my teeth with an extra toothbrush I find under the sink, all while obsessing over what's going to happen next. I literally just told myself whatever it is, I'll go along with it, but it's hard when I don't know where Braxton stands.

Needing my clothes, I step into the bedroom but find it empty. He must've gotten dressed and gone back out with the other guys. I search for my clothes, which I know were scattered all over the floor, but I can't find a single article. What the hell? Since I can't leave naked, I pull open a drawer that I know is Braxton's and find a pair of boxer briefs and a T-shirt to throw on.

I stand in front of the closed door for several seconds, trying to get up the courage to do my mini walk of shame. The guys are going to know what we did, especially since I'm sure Braxton walked out there before me with wet hair.

Once I've formulated my plan—run through the bus as fast as possible without making eye contact and go straight to the other bus—look, I didn't say it was a good plan, just a plan—I grab the doorknob, ready to bolt, when the door pushes open, making me stumble back.

"What are you doing standing in front of the door?" Braxton asks, eyeing me up and down. He's in a pair of basketball shorts sans shirt, and I wonder, not for the first time, what all the tattoos mean. He explained a couple to his bitch of a date, but he has several she couldn't see under his shirt that are all exposed right now.

"Crazy," he says, using my nickname to get my attention, "what are you doing?"

"I was getting ready to leave. I, umm, couldn't find my clothes, so I borrowed these." I run my fingers over his Rolling Stones shirt. "I'll give it back."

"You can't go anywhere," Braxton says with a smirk. "The buses already left. We have an eleven-hour drive."

"Oh, shit," I breathe. "I can..." I glance around, unsure what exactly I can do.

"You can get your ass back in the bed and take those clothes off," he finishes for me, shocking the hell out of me. "I threw your clothes in the hamper to be washed."

I do as he says—climbing onto the bed but keeping my clothes on—while he follows, slamming the door behind him and then stopping on the side of the bed.

"Grabbed us some sustenance." He holds up a couple of drinks in one hand and what looks like a Tupperware bowl of food in the other. "Figured we should hydrate and replenish some of those calories before I take you again."

He drops the items he's holding onto the nightstand and climbs onto the bed. "Shirt off," he demands, lying next to me and tugging on the hem of his shirt to help me pull it over my head.

"I don't have my bra," I screech as the shirt comes off, exposing my breasts.

"That's the point." Braxton dips his head and latches onto my nipple, biting and then licking the pain he just caused away.

I moan, and he backs up, chuckling. "Food and drink first."

"Or..." I push him onto his back and scoot down, turned on all over again and intent on using every minute we have to my advantage. "I can just eat and drink you." I tug his shorts down, and his pierced dick pops out, semi-hard.

I wrap my fingers around his shaft and lick the tip, making Braxton groan. "Yes," I murmur. "This seems like plenty of sustenance to me." And then I proceed to suck him down like the best tasting lollipop.

"LET'S GO!" CAMDEN SHOUTS THROUGH THE DOOR. "WE'RE HERE!"

I roll over, completely spent, refusing to open my eyes. How the hell did eleven hours fly by that quickly?

And then I remember how they were spent.

Braxton in me. On me. All over me.

I stretch my limbs and wince at the slight pain between my legs. It's been a while since I've had sex and to the extent we had last night. I'm pretty sure we fucked in every position and on every surface in the bedroom and bathroom.

And when we weren't fucking, we were touching and talking. Our topics were scattered—going from what his tattoos mean to what rides I'm excited for when we get to the theme parks to the songs he's been writing—but neither of us seemed to care. We never broached the subject of us, and I didn't push. Instead, I just enjoyed the night for what it was.

"Brax, Kaylee, we gotta go!" Camden yells, annoyance laced in his words. "We have a radio interview."

His words have me sitting up since I'm in charge of that part of the tour. The blanket covering me slides down, and I quickly remember I'm still naked—and have no clothes on this bus.

"Brax..." I shake him gently since he's still passed out next to me, equally naked.

"Guys!" Camden says again.

"We're coming!" I yell back. "Just, uh...give us a few minutes."

There's grumbling on the other side of the door and then footsteps leading away.

"Brax," I say again. This time when I say his name, he groans and rolls toward me, pulling me into his arms. I'm not expecting it, so I screech in shock, and he covers my mouth to silence me.

His other hand slides down my hip and cups my pussy, and his mouth latches on to the side of my neck, nipping and sucking on my flesh.

"We have to go," I mumble from under his hand.

"What? I can't hear you," he says, humor in his voice. "Did you say you need some morning sex?"

He pushes two fingers into me, and I moan, my eyes rolling back. "We have to go," I say again even though my words are indecipherable.

"I agree," he says, a mischievous grin on his sexy face. "A good morning dicking is exactly what you need."

He uncovers my mouth, and I snort out a laugh. "We need to—"

My words are cut off when his thumb goes to my clit, massaging it gently. "Maybe...we can be a few minutes late."

"WE HAVE ONE MORE QUESTION TO ASK BECAUSE IF WE DON'T, WOMEN ALL OVER THE CITY WILL COME after us."

We're at the radio interview—and shockingly—I have no idea how—we actually arrived on time. After Braxton gave me two orgasms and a "good morning dicking" as promised, we showered, and then he ran to my bus to grab my clothes so I wouldn't have to do the walk of shame from one bus to the other. We parted ways once we were dressed since I needed to work and met back up in the SUV to grab breakfast and go to the scheduled interview. We haven't spoken a word about last night, and thankfully, although they know what went down, the guys haven't said a word either.

"Are any of you off the market, aside from Camden, since we know he's officially taken?"

The questions are always the same and have to be preapproved by the guys, so nothing pops up unexpectedly. I've listened to them answer this question a dozen times over the course of the tour, but now, as I wait for Braxton to answer, because he's always the one who answers it first, I can't help but hope his answer will be different than his usual.

"The only woman warming my bed is Melanie," he says, referring to his customized one-of-a-kind guitar.

Despite telling myself not to expect anything to change between us after last night, my heart sinks. It's not like I expected him to announce that he spent the night inside me, but I guess I hoped he'd make some kind of comment indicating something had changed.

Gage and Declan both give their standard responses, and then the interview ends. Since the first of the two shows aren't until tomorrow, the guys have the rest of the day to themselves to do what they want. Jill's already checked everyone into the hotel, so I grab the keys and give them to the guys, reminding them that we'll be leaving early in the morning and then take off to my own room.

As I'm pressing my key to the door, a warm body comes up behind me, sending butterflies scattering around my belly. "How many orgasms do you think I can give you in eight hours?"

"I don't know," I rasp, freezing in place.

Braxton plucks the key from my fingers and presses it to the door, unlocking and then opening it. "There's only one way to find out."

Guess *Melanie* won't be warming his bed tonight either.

Sixteen

BONUS SCENE

KAYLEE

THE SECOND WE'RE BACK AT THE HOTEL, BRAXTON HAS MY DRESS OFF MY BODY, AND MY BRA AND PANTIES ripped off, leaving me in only the red-soled heels he promised to fuck me in. His mouth goes to my neck, and he trails open-mouthed kisses down to my breasts.

Taking one in his hand, he roughly massages it before dipping his head and sucking my nipple into his mouth. My chest juts out, and I moan at how good it feels.

Everything Braxton does feels good.

After giving my other breast the same attention, he drops to his knees and lifts my leg over his shoulder, diving straight into my pussy like it's his dessert. He eats me until I'm coming all over his face, my juices dripping down my inner thigh, and then he stands and crashes his mouth down on mine.

"You taste yourself?" he murmurs against my mouth, running his tongue along the seam of my lips. "Your pussy is my addiction, and I'm so fucking hooked."

The way he says it—with such reverence and yearning in his tone—I can't tell if it's a good or a bad thing, but it's probably a bit of both.

Without waiting for my reply, he pulls his cock out of its confines and lifts me against the wall. I wrap my legs around his waist, my heels digging into his back, and in one swift motion, he enters me.

"Jesus, fuck," he growls, nuzzling his face into the crook of my neck as I encircle my arms around his neck. "An addiction...You are a goddamn addiction."

One I hope he never quits, I think but don't voice out loud.

Braxton fucks me against the wall, rough and hard, hitting that spot deep inside me in the most delicious way, then he moves us over to the bed, never breaking our connection.

With our bodies wrapped up in one another, he cages me in his strong arms and slows his movements. I close my eyes, getting lost in the moment. Lost in the thought that this suddenly feels a whole lot more like making love.

"Open your eyes, baby," he murmurs. When I do as he says, a soft smile graces his lips. "There they are...those beautiful gray eyes." His words have butterflies swarming in my chest.

His groin grinds down on my clit, and within seconds, I'm exploding around his cock. My walls tighten, and his dick swells, and a few thrusts later, he's filling me with every drop of himself.

While I'm cleaning up, Braxton turns on the tub and pours some bubbles into the water. "Join me," he says, extending his hand once the water is almost to the top. I take it and step inside, and he folds himself in half, settling behind me.

As he massages my shoulders, peppering kisses along my heated flesh, I sigh into him, wishing we could stay in our own little bubble like this forever but knowing it's not possible. Soon enough that bubble will pop, exposing us back to reality.

Seventeen

BRAXTON

 room at the venue, about to go on for our first of two back-to-back shows. It's the first time we've been alone since I hauled Kaylee over my shoulder and spent the next several hours inside her—only stopping long enough to do a scheduled interview.

"Like you didn't hear what happened on the bus over and over again," Declan says with a smirk.

"And on the other side of the wall in the hotel," Gage adds dryly, taking a hit of his joint before offering it to me.

"So what, you two are back together?" Camden asks.

I shake my head at Gage, not in the mood to get high, and think about Camden's question. I'm unsure what to say because despite spending the last day and a half in Kaylee, I don't know what's going on between us. Do I want to get back together with her? Yeah. But at the same time, the shit that went down is fucked up, and I need time to process it all. Should I have fucked her before figuring my shit out? Probably not. But our chemistry was never the issue, and when she told me she wasn't the same without me, something in me snapped, and I had to have her, consequences be damned.

When I don't answer him quick enough, he glares my way. "Great, so should I tell my dad we need to start looking for a new publicist now?"

A gasp from behind me has me turning around. Kaylee is standing in the doorway, a pained expression written all over her face.

"You're really firing me?" she asks softly.

"You told her she's fired?" Camden barks. "What the hell, man?"

"I thought you were joking." Tears fill her eyes, and before I can stop her, she runs out of the room.

"Dammit!" I'm about to go after her when Jill pops inside to let us know we have to go on. "I need to find Kaylee."

"Not now, you don't," she says. "You need to get your butts on the stage in two minutes."

I consider ignoring her and going after Kaylee, but I can't let the guys down. She can't go anywhere right now anyway, so I know she'll still be here after the show. She might be upset, but she takes her job seriously, and she wouldn't flake on her duties—even if she does think she's been fired.

"What the hell were you thinking firing her?" Camden says as we walk down the hall leading to the stage.

"I didn't fire her...well, not seriously." I wave him off, not wanting to explain it all right now. We have a show to get through, and the last thing I need is to fuck up because Kaylee is all up in my headspace.

The venue is dark so we can get situated, and a few minutes later, the lights come down on us. The crowd screams in excitement when Camden speaks, and then Gage starts in on the drums. The next couple of hours fly by, one song after the next, but the entire time, I can't get Kaylee off my mind and the hurt look on her face when she thought I'd actually fired her. I might be a dick, but I wouldn't do that to her. Sure, I mentioned I didn't want her on the tour, but that was before the past couple of nights. And even when I made the comments before, I never acted on them. It was just me talking shit out of hurt and anger.

The misunderstanding reminds me that despite how perfectly I fit inside her, we haven't been around each other for several years. We've both grown up and changed. While we know each other, we also don't. And I have to figure out what I want because the last thing I want to do is hurt Kaylee. She might've hurt me, but I wouldn't do it back just to spite her. I meant what I said. I love her. I always have and always will.

But a part of me is still pissed at what she did, so I need to figure out if I can let that go and whether we have a chance at a future. Hell, I don't even know what she wants. Maybe she just needed a good dicking, and now that she's gotten it, she's done with me. The thought pisses me off. She was upset about the possibility of her being fired, but she hasn't once asked about where we stand.

By the time Cam is thanking Atlanta for being amazing, I've worked myself up and am desperate to find Kaylee. Without waiting for the guys, I push past the crew in search of her. I don't find her in the dressing room or anywhere backstage. Figuring she must be on the bus, I head outside, but before I get there, I find her talking to Jill. Her eyes meet mine, and I'm about to drag her somewhere private, but she plasters a smile on her face and says, "Ready for the meet and greet?" Dammit, I forgot about that.

"We need to talk."

"We need to get you to where the fans will be waiting shortly."

"We have time," I argue. "It always takes a good half hour."

"Then you should probably use that time to change your shirt."

Without waiting for me to respond, she turns on her heel and leaves me standing there stunned silent. So it's going to be like that? Fine. I'll wait until we're done. Then I'll lock her ass in her hotel room until she's ready to talk.

Since I've already missed a couple of the meet and greets recently, when I let my emotions get the best of me, the last thing I want to do is miss more of them. So I go through it with a smile stuck on my face. The fans pay good money to meet us. They're the reason we get to do what we love and are able to make a damn good living at it.

But the second it's over, I'm out the door and off to find Kaylee. Since I was in her room last night, I already have a key. I storm inside and find her in bed, acting like she's already asleep.

"That's cute," I say as I lift her into my arms.

"Brax!" she shrieks. "Put me down!"

"No," I say, suddenly feeling a hell of a lot calmer now that I have her in my arms. "You're not going to run away when you hear something you don't like without even having a goddamn conversation."

Needing to have this discussion out of bed so I can focus, I carry her into the living room and set her down on the couch, then sit a few feet away from her on the same couch.

"If you would've asked before you ran away, you'd know that Camden was only asking if he should ask his dad to find a new publicist because he assumed you'd be quitting after we had sex."

"And why would he think that?" she asks, jutting her chin out in a challenging manner. Fuck, I've missed this woman so much. I love everything about her. How she can be both soft and hard and give me shit while still showing how much she cares.

"Because he asked if we were back together, and I didn't answer him."

"And...?" she says, throwing the ball straight into my court.

"And..." I tug her over to me, pulling her onto my lap to straddle my thighs. She's soft and warm and smells amazing. "I don't think we should rush shit. It's been a long time, and we've both changed, but I want to see where things go. I wanted you all those years ago, and I still do."

"I want you too," she agrees. "But you're right. It's been a long time, and things have changed."

I cup the side of her face and kiss her supple lips. "I can't wait to get to know you all over again."

"WHAT IS THIS?" KAYLEE GLANCES AT ME.

"A box."

She playfully rolls her eyes. "For me?"

"Open the damn thing."

She doesn't need to be told twice as she undoes the ribbon and tears the box open to reveal a shimmery black dress with matching heels. Since we were on the road to Jacksonville, I couldn't go to the store myself, so I had the hotel concierge handle it, but I made sure he sent me pictures so I could pick which one I wanted.

"It's beautiful," she says, awe in her voice. "What's the occasion?"

"I'm taking you out."

The smile that spreads across her face, along with the hearts in her eyes, makes it worth the effort. She's always been one to appreciate a thoughtful gesture. It's as if she's never expecting it, so when it does happen, she's that much more excited about it.

"Go get ready. I'll be back to pick you up at six o'clock."

Technically, we're sharing a room since I have no desire to sleep in a separate bed than her—regardless of us taking shit slow—but all my stuff is in my room, so I head over there to get ready. I made reservations at a Japanese restaurant since Kaylee mentioned she loves it. After taking a shower and shaving, I get dressed then go out to the main room to wait until it's time to pick up Kaylee. Camden and Declan aren't there, but Gage is sitting out on the private balcony.

"What's up?" I say, sitting in the chair next to him.

He offers me a hit of the joint he's smoking, but I shake my head, not wanting to be high when I pick up Kaylee. He shrugs and takes another hit before he takes a sip of his drink. While we sit in silence, I glance at him. He's the same age as the rest of us, but he looks older, more tired, and I'm worried about him. We all smoke and drink, but Gage is intoxicated more than he's not. We all know why that is, and because of it, we've looked the other way. But I can't help wondering if we're only hurting him by not forcing him to deal with his shit.

"See something you like?" he finally says when he catches me staring.

"I'm worried about you."

He chuckles humorlessly and shakes his head. I expect him to argue, to defend himself, tell me I'm a dumbass and to mind my own business, but all he does is take another hit of his joint.

"Where are you off to tonight?" he asks after a few minutes.

"Taking Kaylee out on a date."

A small smile graces his lips. "That's good, man." He takes a swig of his drink and then stands. "You both deserve to be happy."

"So do you," I say as he walks inside. The slight tenseness in his shoulders is the only sign that he heard me.

At six o'clock, I walk over to Kaylee's room and knock on the door. When she opens it, donning the dress and heels I bought for her with her blond hair down in waves and her face full of makeup, I consider saying fuck it to going out and taking her straight to bed instead.

"Don't even think about it," she says with a playful smile as if she could hear my thoughts. "I didn't get this dressed up not to be taken out." She steps toward me, patting my chest. "And if you're a good boy, I might even let you take the dress off me at the end of the night."

"And what about the heels?" I ask, glancing down and admiring the way they make her legs look even longer and more toned. "Can I take those off too?"

She shakes her head. "I think those will stay on," she murmurs. "I've always had a fantasy of being fucked with heels on. Like in the romance books... digging them into the guy's ass. Maybe you can help me fulfill that fantasy."

"I'm the *only* one who'll be fulfilling any fucking fantasy you have," I growl.

"We'll see." She shrugs and walks around me, the door shutting behind her.

Since we're not in LA, the chance of me being recognized is less, but since there's always the possibility, I have Justin, my personal bodyguard, drive us to dinner and escort us into the restaurant. The sight of the big, burly guy might draw more attention than if he weren't here, but I can't take the risk, especially with Kaylee.

As promised, we're seated outside in a private area overlooking the river, and the server has signed an NDA so nothing will get posted—seems like overkill, I know, but it's necessary if I want our date to remain private.

After taking our drink order, the server disappears, leaving Kaylee and me alone. She's quiet, clearly lost in thought, and I watch her for several beats, admiring how beautiful she is.

"What's going through your head?" I eventually ask, wanting to know all of her thoughts.

"I never thought we'd be here."

"In Jacksonville?" I joke, making her side-eye me.

"I spent so many nights wishing you would show up in Boston, and then when I got kicked out of school and ended up back in New York, I would constantly look for you...at the coffee shop we used to go to...at the beach. When I would visit Layla's mom, I would look for you at the Blackwood house even though I knew you were on the other side of the country."

The day she "cheated," I found out she was attending Boston, and I thought maybe that was why she did what she did, to push me away, but a few months later, Camden mentioned she was back in New York, and I always wondered what had happened.

"Why did you switch from Boston to NYU?"

"When I let you go, it was the hardest thing I'd ever done," she says quietly. We talked about what happened, but we've yet to discuss it in detail since we went from me hating her to being pissed at her to fucking the hell out of her.

"I knew it would be hard, but when Layla and I got to Boston, I missed you so much." Her eyes meet mine. They're glassy and filled with raw emotion. "I messed up. Drank too much, partied too hard to hide the pain, and I failed out."

The server drops our drinks off, and we both order. Once he's gone, she continues. "I tried to get a job working for a marketing firm, but nobody would take me seriously without a degree, so after I worked and saved up enough money, I went back to school. It took a little while, which is why Layla graduated before me."

"But you still graduated."

"Yeah, but it all felt like I was just going through the motions. I would see you on tour, in pictures on social media, laughing and having the time of your life, and it felt like my heart was being stomped on...but it also made me so happy because even though it hurt to let you go, every time I saw those pictures, I felt like I did the right thing."

I'll never agree with what she did, but I also get it. Because she's right. Had she not done what she did, I wouldn't have gotten on that plane to LA. I had already told the guys I wasn't going, and Easton was searching for a guitarist for the band.

"Anyway," she says, perking up slightly and plastering a smile on her face. "I just can't believe, after everything, we're here on a date, getting a fresh start." She smiles softly—a real one this time that has my heart pounding against my rib cage. "I'm really glad we're getting this second chance."

When our dinner arrives, our conversation takes on a lighter tone as we flit from topic to topic, catching up on the years we've been apart. You'd think since we haven't spoken or seen each other in so long, it might be awkward, but it's not. As Kaylee tells me about her time in school, some of the places she's worked at, and the various concerts she's attended—which leads to us debating over what good music sounds like—it's as if time has never passed.

After dinner, we take a walk along the river, holding hands while talking about our upcoming time off. We'll be going to the theme parks between shows in Tampa and Orlando, and then the entire band and crew will have a one-week break for the Fourth of July.

"I was planning to go back to New York," she admits sheepishly. "At the time, we weren't talking and..." She shrugs.

"Well, now we are." I guide her over to a darkened area that leads to an alley between two buildings. I can see Justin's following us, but he keeps his distance, so we have our privacy. "Gage, Declan, and I rented a place next to Camden. His parents and sisters are coming down as well, and so is Layla's mom. It'll be fun."

"I don't know," she says cheekily. "I'd hate to intrude and ruin your fun..."

I back her against the wall and, with our fingers threaded, lift her hands over her head. "Ruin the fun?" I part her legs with my knee and rub my thigh along her center. "I plan for you to *be* the fun." I bring my lips to the curve of her neck and suckle on her soft flesh, making her moan.

When she pulls her hands out of mine, I release her, kissing my way up to her earlobe. Her arms snake around my neck, and she hops up, making me catch her as she encircles her legs around my waist, her heels digging into my back. "I say we start the fun now," she murmurs, grinding herself against me.

"Not here," I say, nipping at her lobe. "When I fuck you, I want you in nothing but those damn heels."

"Well, then what are you waiting for?"

Eighteen

KAYLEE

"UNCLE BRAX!" FELIX YELLS, RUNNING OVER AND LATCHING HIS LITTLE ARMS AROUND BRAXTON'S LEGS. While Camden grabs Layla's and Felix's bags, giving his wife a quick kiss, Braxton carries Felix over to the SUV waiting for us. The bodyguards surround us so nobody can get close, but several people stand around taking photos that will end up on social media within minutes. I'm already messaging Bailey to warn her so she can keep an eye out for anything that shouldn't be posted. Camden and Layla are big on not allowing pictures of Felix to be posted, and if anyone does post them, they demand them to be taken down.

"I'm so excited!" Felix shouts as Braxton buckles him in. I can't help smiling as I watch the two of them together. Braxton might be this badass, tattooed, and pierced rock star to the world, but the second Felix is in his arms, he turns into a complete softy.

Layla's eyes meet mine, and she smirks, having caught me staring. "Bet he'd make a great dad," she whispers.

"Don't get any ideas. We're taking things slow."

"Yeah, okay." She scoffs. "I was on the phone with Camden and heard you guys taking things slow."

My face heats in embarrassment, which has Layla cackling. The drive from Jacksonville was only three hours, but it was spent with Braxton inside me the entire time. I tried to be quiet...I swear I did. But the guy has made it his personal mission to pull as many orgasms out of me as possible every time we're together, and despite the bus being luxurious and worth millions, it's still just that...a bus. And when I try to remain quiet, Braxton takes it as a challenge to make me scream that much louder.

"Mommy said we're going on fifty hundred rides!" Felix announces, and I've never been so thankful for a subject change in my life.

"Fifty hundred rides, huh?" I say. "That's a lot of rides."

"Uh-huh," he agrees. "You gonna go on the rides with me?" Felix asks, flashing his expertly staged puppy dog eyes that he knows I don't stand a chance against. "Mommy can't 'cause she's too fat."

Braxton snorts out a laugh, then quickly schools his features. "She's not fat, buddy. She's pregnant...with your little sister."

"Her belly is super fat," he argues. "She won't fit on the rides."

"Well, that's true," he concedes. "But it's not nice to call her fat. She's pregnant."

Felix shrugs. "Okay, but you and Kaylee will go on the rides with me, right?"

"Of course we will," I tell him. "I've never been on the rides either."

"Where's Gage?" Layla asks, looking around.

"At the hotel. He's not feeling well," Camden says.

The truth is, he went out on a bender last night and nearly got alcohol poisoning. I was afraid we were going to have to take him to the hospital, but thankfully, we didn't need to.

Layla sighs. "We need to—"

"You don't need to do anything," Camden says, cutting her off. "You're pregnant and shouldn't be stressed."

"But—"

"But nothing." He gives her a kiss. "You're here to have a good time. It's our last trip with Felix before we bring our little girl into this world." He rubs her belly, and her shoulders visibly lower. "Gage is at the hotel room, sleeping it off. He had a rough night, but he's fine."

Nobody in the SUV believes a word he's saying—not even himself—but until the guys do something, there's nothing any of us can say. Gage is functioning and performing, but he needs help. Unfortunately, until he hits rock bottom, I don't think the guys will interfere. Damn men...so stubborn.

"OKAY, SPILL," LAYLA SAYS, GLANCING OVER AT ME WITH A DOPEY SMILE ON HER FACE.

We've spent the day at the theme park, riding every ride with Felix until that cute little Energizer Bunny's batteries finally died. He passed out in the stroller, not waking when he was put in the vehicle or when Camden carried him up to the room. We're all sunburned and exhausted, but it was a great day.

After everyone got settled in their rooms, Layla dragged me down to the hotel spa for some pedis and "girl talk"—her words, not mine—leaving Camden and the guys to keep an eye on a sleeping Felix.

"That sounds messy," I joke, inwardly moaning at how good it feels to have my calves massaged.

When she glares my way, I laugh. "I don't know what to say."

"How about starting with how the hell Braxton went from hating you to acting like you two are in high school all over again?"

I flinch, hating that Layla isn't caught up to speed. I wanted to tell her everything, but I felt like it would be best explained in person since Braxton wasn't the only person I lied to. I thought maybe Camden would tell her, and I was half expecting a pissed-off phone call, but I should've known he'd leave that to me. Camden is the least gossipy person I know.

"Kaylee, talk to me," she says softly, her voice laced with hurt.

"I never cheated on Braxton."

Her brows dip in confusion.

"I lied to push him away so he would go to LA."

Her eyes go wide. "Kaylee..."

"While Tori was..." I swallow thickly, unable to finish my sentence. Even all these years later, I get emotional just thinking about her—we all do. "I was pretending to cheat on Braxton."

"Oh, Kay..." She sets her hand on mine. "I get it, I do. But..." She releases a harsh breath. "So he found out the truth?"

"Yeah, he overheard his dad and me talking. I was threatening to tell him the truth."

"His dad?"

"It was his idea. He has this issue with women. I guess he gave up a huge opportunity for Braxton's mom, and she ended up leaving him. He doesn't really talk about her, but his dad didn't want him messing up his future for a woman."

"So where do you guys stand? It's clear, you guys are..." She waggles her brows playfully, making me laugh.

"We are," I admit. "We're taking things slow."

She quirks a brow.

"I mean, not slow...I don't know. We're just seeing where things go. We're on this tour, and I think it's easy to get lost in each other while we're sharing a space. But once we're back at home, we'll be able to figure things out. For now, I'm just enjoying reconnecting with him."

"You've always loved him."

"Yeah, but I never thought I'd be given this second chance, so honestly, I'm just going with the flow. Getting to know him all over again."

"I'm happy for you." Layla squeezes my hand. "Look at us finding love. Did you hear the news about Camden's sister?"

"Kendall?"

"Nope, Bailey." She grins. "She's getting married to her fiancée, Cynthia, at the beach."

"Stop! That's awesome."

We spend the rest of our pedicures catching up, and it feels good to be able to relax and talk with Layla. For years, before she was with Camden, she was married to a grade A asshole who didn't let her do shit, so it's nice getting to spend time with her again.

"When I get home from the tour, we need to make this a weekly thing."

"I agree." Layla smiles. "I've missed you. Maybe we can go on a double date."

"We'll see. Let's not get too far ahead of ourselves."

"Ahead of ourselves?" she says. "I was watching you guys all day. Braxton is just as obsessed with you as he was all those years ago."

"Maybe." I shrug, not wanting to get my hopes up because I feel the same way about him, which scares the hell out of me. I already lost him once—completely my fault—and I don't know if I could go through that again.

After our toes are pretty and our feet are soft, we head back up to our rooms for the night. The guys have a show tomorrow, and then we're heading to Orlando for a show, spending the day at Disney, and then driving down to Miami for their final show before their much-needed break.

When I step into the room I'm unofficially sharing with Braxton, I find him sitting outside on the balcony, scribbling words into the journal I gave him years ago.

"Writing anything special?"

He glances up and smiles at me before he puts the pen down and pulls me into his arms. "I'm writing something I haven't written in a long-ass time...a love song."

"OH, WOW, THIS PLACE IS GORGEOUS!" I BREATHE, STEPPING OUTSIDE WHERE THE INFINITY POOL overlooks the beach. When Braxton said they were renting a place on the beach, I had assumed they were staying in a hotel of some sort—taking up an entire floor. I didn't realize they were renting an entire freaking house. And not just any house, a damn mansion, complete with a private beach.

"Camden's place is to the left, and his parents and sisters are one more over. Between the three houses and all the property they're on, we're completely secluded from everyone else."

Braxton wraps his arms around me from behind, and I sigh into him, excited for the next several days. No buses or meet and greets or radio interviews. Just Braxton and me and our friends and the beach.

"Too bad we're sharing this house with Declan and Gage," I say, grinding my ass up against his front. "This pool would be the perfect place to go skinny-dipping in."

Braxton groans. "I can totally make that happen." He fists my hair, tugging my head to the side, and suckles the side of my neck. "As a matter of fact, I can make it happen right now."

"How?" I gasp when he nips at my lobe.

"We're alone." He licks the curve of my ear, sending a chill down my spine. "They left as soon as we got here. A friend of ours opened a new strip club and invited the band to the opening. They'll be gone for hours. It's just you and me."

"You didn't want to go?" I ask since he implied whoever it is, is his friend as well.

"Why the hell would I want to spend the night with a bunch of strippers when I have you?"

His words cause my heart to swell and give me an idea. "Sit here." I direct him to one of the chairs near the table on the expansive patio that houses an outdoor kitchen complete with a massive grill.

When he drops into the chair, confusion marring his features, I grab my phone and quickly hook it up to the Bluetooth speakers, then scroll through my music until I find the perfect song—"Problem" by Natalia Kills.

I click play, and as the instrumentals start, I saunter over to Braxton, stopping just out of reach. He frowns, and I smirk. And then when I begin seductively rocking my hips from side to side, his eyes go wide.

As the woman begins to sing about a couple dripping in sweat as they fuck, I slowly pull my shirt over my head, then unbutton and unzip my shorts, sliding them down my thighs. Instead of kicking my Vans off, I make it a point to bend all the way over, my breasts damn near spilling out of their confines as I unlace and tug each shoe off.

"Jesus, fuck," Braxton hisses, grabbing his crotch and rearranging himself. "Get over here, Crazy."

"Nuh-uh." I shake my head. "You aren't allowed to touch the strippers," I tease, making him groan. "Pull your dick out. I want to see how hard it is."

He does as I say, undoing his pants and tugging them down enough to pull his dick out. It's dark outside, but thanks to the floodlights, I'm able to see everything. His shaft is hard and veiny, and the metal piercings glint in the light. My mouth waters, remembering what he tastes like…what he feels like.

The music picks up, and I sway my hips as I glide my hands down my neck, along my collarbone, and over my breasts. I reach behind and unclip my bra, letting the material slide down my arms. With my eyes locked on Braxton, I reach up and squeeze my tits, making it a point to pinch my nipples.

"Kaylee," Braxton growls, fisting his cock and stroking it roughly. I can tell he's losing his patience, so I pick things up, removing my panties and then bringing my hand to my mound, teasing myself as I walk closer to him.

"I could be persuaded to give you a private lap dance"—I lean forward, making sure not to touch him—"if the price is right."

"How much?" he asks, playing along when I step back and continue to dance slowly to the beat of the song.

"I don't know if you can afford me." I pinch my nipple some more, and his gaze turns molten with lust.

"I'm a rich fucking man," he says, his voice gruff. "Name your price."

"You," I say, stopping in my place. "I want you."

"Done." He reaches out and grabs the curves of my hips, pulling me toward him to straddle his thighs. Our mouths connect in a searing-hot kiss at the same time his dick enters me. I ride him to the beat of the song, hard and rough, while he fucks my mouth the same way until we're both coming apart in each other's arms.

"Wow," I gasp, out of breath. "It's hot out here." My hair is sticking to my neck, and I can feel droplets of perspiration dripping down my skin.

"I think I can fix that for you," Braxton says, settling his hands under my ass and standing. I assume he's going to carry me back inside, so I'm stunned in shock when he heads straight for the damn pool instead.

"Brax—" I start, but before I can finish my warning, he's jumping into the pool with me clinging to him. The water is cold as fuck, but with it being a hundred damn degrees out, it feels good.

"Now, we can go skinny-dipping," he says with the sexiest boyish grin on his face.

"I WANT TO GET A TATTOO."

"What?" Braxton asks, setting his writing journal down and laughing.

For the past hour, we've been lying on the oversized couch, our legs entwined while Braxton writes, and I read. But at some point, I got distracted and have been eyeing his ink instead. He's explained what each one means, and I love that he's gotten one to symbolize or represent milestones in his life over the years. When the band recorded their first album, when they went platinum, when they went on their first world tour...For every occasion, he's gotten inked, like a photo book of memories that people can see but only he understands.

"A tattoo. I want to get another one...with you."

"What do you want to get?"

"I was thinking a daffodil. I read that they represent new beginnings, a fresh start. And I feel like with this job and getting a second chance with you, it's sort of like that. You don't have to get the same thing. You can get whatever you want."

"I like it," he says, pulling me into his arms. "And I love that we're getting a fresh start."

"So you'll get one with me?" I perk up in excitement.

"Of course. I'll have to think about what I want to get—"

"Yay! Let's go."

"Wait, now?" He laughs, and I pout playfully, nodding. "Some things never change," he adds with a chuckle, standing and pulling me up with him.

"What's that supposed to mean?"

"You're still as crazy as ever." He shakes his head and pulls his shirt over his head, covering his sexy body. "And I'm still just as pussy-whipped."

"Is that a bad thing?"

"Nah." He grips the curves of my hips and tugs me toward him, so our bodies are flush against each other. "It's not a bad thing at all." He drops a kiss to my lips and then to my nose before he backs up and smirks. "Let's go get some ink."

I thought we'd have to find a place, but it turns out Braxton already knows someone and when he calls and asks if we can come by, of course the guy says he's available. You'd be stupid not to be when someone as famous as Braxton says he wants to come in.

When we get there, we're taken back to a private room, and Braxton and Guy bullshit for a few minutes catching up—apparently, he's done a few pieces for Braxton in the past—before he asks what brings us in today.

Braxton explains I want to get a daffodil inked, and I show him what I'd like. Since he specializes in freehand ink, I agree to let him do his thing. I get it on my hip, and when he's done and shows it to me, I'm in awe of how beautiful it is. Instead of one, he inked three and explained they reminded him of the past, present, and future when I told him daffodils represent a fresh start. They couldn't be more perfect. And Braxton agrees when I show them to him.

"What are you getting?" I ask when Braxton has a seat and lifts his shirt.

"You'll see." He winks and lies back while Guy gets the station cleaned up from my tattoo and ready to do Braxton's.

While he gets tattooed, Guy gives me free rein to his music, so I play deejay, going from song to song while Braxton bitches about my taste in music.

"We used to have similar taste in music," he points out.

"I've evolved. You should try it."

Guy shakes his head, and Braxton laughs.

When Guy announces he's done, I pause the music so I can see the ink. Braxton gets up and steps in front of the mirror to check it out, and I join him so I can see too. My eyes go straight to his rib cage where the fresh ink lies. There are several roses, shaded in black and gray, with the stems and thorns inked as if they're being woven under and over his skin. It's so lifelike, it almost hurts to look at them. I can practically feel the irony in the beauty and pain between the roses and thorns. My eyes sting, remembering that he would constantly tell me that he loved the way I smelled like roses, my signature lotion scent.

"*She's under my skin,*" I read out loud the words that are etched along the outline of the roses.

"She's under my skin, like the thorns of a rose. You know loving her is going to hurt, but you're blinded by the beauty of the rose." Braxton's eyes lock with mine in the mirror, his hazel to my gray. "It's from a song I've been writing..."

"About me."

"Yeah."

"I hurt you."

He turns to me, and it's then I realize we're alone. Guy must've left to give us privacy. "Love hurts, but the beauty that comes with loving you is worth the pain."

Nineteen

KAYLEE

"MOMMY, COME MAKE A SANDCASTLE WITH ME!" FELIX YELLS, SCOOPING UP AND THROWING SAND EVERY which way.

We're hanging out at the beach, lounge chairs under us and umbrellas above us. It's hot as hell outside, the sun as unforgiving as a woman scorned, but the guys have armed us with cold drinks and snacks that will quench our thirst. It's been like this every day since we arrived, and I'm dreading when the vacation is over. A woman could get used to this.

"I have to get up, don't I?" Layla groans, half-joking, her hand going to her very big bump—which makes sense since she's six months pregnant.

Before I can answer, she's already standing, looking adorable. From the back, you wouldn't even know she's pregnant since she's all belly, but from the front is another story.

"Layles, go lie down," Camden demands. "I got this." He jogs over to where Felix is and drops down next to him. If you didn't know their story, you'd think Camden was Felix's biological dad—that's how good he is with him.

"You heard the man. Lie back down." I pat the chair next to me and sip my delicious fruity alcoholic beverage Bailey made me. The woman was probably a bartender in another life.

Layla slowly lies back down, situating herself so she can get comfortable. "It's probably for the best. Had I actually gotten down in the sand, I'd probably never get back up."

We all laugh at her dramatics even though she's dead serious.

"You all ready for tomorrow?" I ask Bailey, who's cuddling on a blanket with Cynthia. They decided on a small ceremony, just close friends and family, and since Cynthia's family doesn't condone her choice of partner, that makes the party even smaller.

"Yep, my mom handled everything. All we have to do is get dressed and show up."

"Do you think Kendall will get here in time?" Layla asks, concern etched in her features.

"With my sister?" Bailey scoffs. "You never know. I love her, but she's so damn flaky."

"She's not flaky," her mom chides. "She just beats to her own drum." Sophia says it nonchalantly, but I can see a small amount of sadness there, and I briefly wonder what that's about. But before I can give it much thought, there's a commotion behind us, and as if speaking her name has summoned her, Kendall appears.

Sophia jumps up and runs over to her daughter, hugging her tightly as she jokingly reprimands her for being away for so long. While Sophia is obviously older than Kendall, the two look more like sisters than mother-daughter. They both have the same thick blond hair and creamy complexion. The only difference in their features is while Sophia has emerald eyes, Kendall's are a bright blue.

"I can't believe you made it," Bailey says, getting a bit choked up. I imagine getting ready to be married will do that to a person.

"I wouldn't miss my baby sister's wedding," Kendall retorts, wrapping her arms around her sister. Phoebe, their other sister, joins them, and then their dad does as well. When Camden sees his entire family is together, he gets up and goes over to them. Layla joins them next, along with Felix and Cynthia.

I watch as they embrace each other, kissing each other's cheeks while they smile and laugh.

"Why the frown?" a masculine voice asks. I look over and find Braxton sitting on the edge of my lounge chair. He had run up to the house to use the bathroom.

"I want that." I nod over to them. When Braxton quirks a brow, not understanding, I explain, "I want a family."

I don't have to say anything more because he gets it. He listened to me when I was younger talk about how much I missed my family. Sure, I still have my mom, but when she looks at me, I think she sees my dad, which makes it hard for her to be around me.

"Sometimes, I think having had a family and losing it is worse than never having had one at all," I admit softly.

"I get that," he says, squeezing my leg.

"What's going on?" Declan asks, joining us.

"Kendall's here," I say. "Flew in for Bailey's wedding."

Declan's gaze darts over to where the Blackwood clan are talking. "She, uh, here with anyone?"

Braxton rolls his eyes. "Man, when the hell are you going to ask her out? It's obvious you like her. Have since you were a damn kid. You guys hang out all the time. I know you write music together. Your ass has been friend-zoned, and if you don't speak up soon, it's where you'll remain."

Well, that's something new. I mean, I get it. Kendall is freaking gorgeous. But she's also Declan's best friend's sister and several years older. When we were in high school, Camden would talk shit about Declan having a crush on his sister, but I never knew it was more than that.

Declan doesn't say anything back. He just punches Braxton in the arm before walking over to where everyone is and wrapping his arm around Kendall, drawing her into his side. She smiles up at him and kisses his cheek. He must say something funny because she throws her head back with a laugh that has Declan grinning like a fool.

"Declan likes Kendall?" I ask even though it's obvious now that I'm watching them together.

Braxton laughs. "He's had it bad for years. Started out as a crush, from what Camden said, and eventually turned into more."

"So why doesn't he ask her out?" Declan is hot. With his long dirty-blond hair, midnight-blue eyes, and scruffy face, women practically cream themselves when he graces them with his presence. He's not my type. I prefer someone more rugged—i.e. Braxton with his tattoos for days and dick piercing—but Declan definitely isn't hard on the eyes.

"He's a romantic." Braxton shrugs. "And Kendall is a heartbreak waiting to happen."

"True." You'd have to be dead or living under a rock not to know about the dozens of men she's dated, dumped, and then wrote songs about. "But maybe she just needs to find the right guy."

"THERE'S A MUSIC FESTIVAL UP THE BEACH. WE SHOULD TOTALLY GO." KENDALL IS LYING OUT IN HER teeny-tiny bikini while Declan remains near but not too close, drooling from afar. I can't help but laugh at how obvious his feelings are now that I know, and I wonder if Kendall realizes.

"Really? Which one?" Declan asks.

"The Miami Summer Music Festival. It's mostly up-and-coming artists, but I bet it'll be rocking."

"And which *artist* are you interested in?" Camden says dryly.

Kendall laughs. "Can't I just be *interested* in the music?" Her parents snicker, and she rolls her eyes. "Whatever."

"I'm down," Easton says. "We actually have a few people performing there. We can check out the talent. I bet there'll be a few unsigned artists."

"You up for it?" Camden asks Layla.

"Sure." She shrugs. "But I'm not sure Felix will be." She glances down at her little boy, who's curled into her side and sleeping soundly, the sun having knocked him out.

"I can stay with him," Patricia, her mom, offers. "I'm wiped."

"Can I stay too?" Phoebe asks, looking up from her phone.

"Sure, sweetie," Patricia says, smiling at her.

After agreeing on when to meet, we head back to the house, shower, and get ready. Since it's an outdoor festival, I dress in a pair of denim cutoff shorts with one of Braxton's *Chaotic Tour* shirts that's a bit too big, so I've knotted it at the corner to show off a bit of my skin, and a pair of Vans.

Braxton was using the other bathroom, and when he comes out dressed in his ripped to shreds skinny jeans, a Raging Chaos shirt, and the same damn Vans as me, I can't help but laugh.

"What?"

"We're matching."

He glances down at himself and then takes me in. "You look hot in my shirt."

I roll my eyes playfully. "Of course that's all you'd notice."

He shrugs unapologetically and hooks his arm around my neck. "Let's roll."

We meet up with the others and walk down the beach to where the festival is being held. It's completely sold out, but of course, between the Blackwoods being who they are and the band being mega famous, we get in without a problem.

We spend the next hour or so checking out the various bands from the VIP section since the guys and Kendall can't exactly hang out with the rest of the crowd without being mobbed. They range from rock, like Raging Chaos, to R&B and pop, similar to Kendall. Most are newer in the music industry, but they're all extremely talented.

Of course, when you're famous, you're never really off, so when we go backstage, because Easton wants to find out about the possibility of signing a couple of the artists, and one of the guys mentions it would be awesome if Raging Chaos would surprise everyone by jumping on stage and performing a couple of songs, the guys agree.

Since it's the perfect opportunity to promo them, I pull out my phone and quickly log into their social media, clicking to go live. Fans love when musicians show up and do shit like this. They play one song and then start in on another, making the crowd go insane.

Wanting to zoom in on them, I walk over to the side of the open stage where I'll have a better view. I'm not paying attention, solely focusing on the band, so when I bump into someone, I'm a bit taken aback.

"Well, look who it is," Sam York slurs. He's too big to be performing tonight, so he must be in Miami partying for the Fourth of July weekend. He stumbles toward me, and I immediately retreat, not at all comfortable with being around him alone.

"C'mon, baby doll," he says, getting me into a corner before I can get away. "We can take this somewhere private, and I can make all of your problems go away." With his bloodshot eyes and slow movements, it's clear he's drunk and high—so, pretty much the norm for him.

"Not happening," I say, glancing around and wishing someone would walk over here. That's what I get for stepping away from everyone to get a better video of the band performing.

"Ahh, so I see you're still the same cock tease you were while you were working for me," he hisses.

Realizing my phone is still in my hand—and live—instead of shutting him down, again, I take the opportunity to set shit straight. The phone isn't facing him, so nobody can see us, but they can hear what we're saying.

"Really, Sam?" I say, making a point to speak his name. "Thought I was the one who sexually assaulted you? Now I'm a tease? Which is it? I can't be both."

And...like the drunk and sloppy dumbass he is, he falls right into my trap. "You're such a fucking cock tease little bitch. I've seen the pictures of you and that trashy rocker. Is that what gets you wet? A guy like—"

Before he can finish his accusation, he's being shoved against the wall by Braxton.

"Who the fuck do you think you are talking to her like that?"

Shit! They must've finished performing. "Brax, stop!" I say, pulling him by his arm. "Don't do this. Not now," I plead.

With my phone still live, we can't chance that being recorded. Thankfully, he listens and lets go of Sam, who cackles like an idiot, thinking he's won.

Wrong. So fucking wrong.

"Hey, Sam," I say, pointing the phone at him. "Say hello to everyone... We're live. And thousands just heard everything."

"You fucking bitch!" He steps forward like he's going to come after me, but Gage steps in front of him.

"Back the fuck up before I fuck you up."

And with that, I end the live.

"Sorry," I say to Braxton once we're away from Sam. "I didn't mean to use your page..."

"Hey, fuck that." He puts his arm around me and pulls me into his side, kissing my temple. "I'm glad you got that shit on camera. He deserves it."

"Yeah, he does," Declan agrees. "And now that the truth is out, your reputation will be cleared."

"Working with musicians is exhausting," I say half-jokingly. "After this tour, I'm planning to find a nice boring office job in marketing and advertising."

Since it's almost nine thirty, we make our way out of the festival and go back to the house so we can watch the fireworks from there. We have the perfect balcony overlooking the water, so Braxton and I say good night to everyone and head up to our room.

Just as we open the French doors, the first firework goes off, bright reds and blues exploding in the dark sky. I step up to the railing, and Braxton cages me in from behind, his arms wrapping around me and his hands landing on top of mine. I glance down as he threads our fingers together, and for the first time in a while, I feel content.

It feels like the past several years have been a constant uphill battle, a mountain that I've been climbing on my own—my own doing, of course—but tonight, right here in Braxton's arms, it feels like I'm no longer alone. I have friends who care about Braxton and me. We might not be officially together, but what we're doing is a step forward. When I'm with him, I feel complete.

"What's going through that beautiful head of yours?" Braxton asks, leaning to the side so he can look into my eyes.

"Nothing. I'm just happy."

He nods once, then dusting my hair to the side, he places a soft, open-mouthed kiss to my sensitive pulse. I try to focus on the beautiful fireworks, but my attention is half gone when his kiss turns into sucking. He quickly strips my shirt and bra off, then undoes my shorts, pushing them down my legs along with my panties. The warm breeze hits my overheated body, and a chill races through me, dotting my flesh with goose bumps.

His mouth goes back to my heated skin, licking and sucking, nibbling to the point I'm squirming in want with my lady parts aching. A gorgeous heart-shaped white firework bursts into the sky as Braxton separates my legs and drives his fingers into me.

"Oh, fuck," I groan as he pumps them in and out of me, working me up into a frenzy. All too soon, his thumb flicks my clit, and I'm spiraling over the edge.

As I come down from my orgasm, I hear his belt jingle and his fly lower. His shirt lands on the ground next to our feet, and a second later, he's entering me from behind. My body thrusts forward, my tits hanging over the railing. One of Braxton's hands digs into the curve of my hip and the other wraps around my front, pinching my nipple as he drives in and out of me. His mouth latches onto my neck, and I moan in pleasure, loving the way he knows exactly how to turn me on and get me off.

As our bodies connect in the most intimate way, our flesh hot, our skin dotted with sweat, the fireworks continue to light up the sky—gold and silver flecks raining down and disappearing into the black ocean.

"It's never been like this," Braxton murmurs into my ear huskily. "Never felt like this...*Fuck,*" he growls as his thrusts turn savage, hitting me deliciously deep.

I should probably be upset or jealous that he's comparing me to the other women he's been with, but I don't have it in me to be. Because right here, right now, he's with me. He wants me. And regardless of all the other women he's been with, I'm the one who does this to him.

"Only...Fucking...You," he growls as he lets go, his warm seed shooting inside me and coating my walls, sending me into another climax that's so strong, my knees damn near buckle.

He stills, his body still connected to mine, and drops a soft kiss to the top of my shoulder that somehow feels more intimate than the sex we just had. "Only you, Crazy," he whispers, pulling out as the fireworks finale lights up the sky. "Only fucking you."

Twenty

BRAXTON

THE MUTED SUNLIGHT SLIPS IN THROUGH THE BLINDS, MAKING KAYLEE BURROW HER FACE INTO MY NECK, her pillow-soft breasts pressing against my side. I don't move, not wanting to wake her up, just simply enjoying the quiet moment. In a rock star's world, quiet isn't something we get a lot of, especially not on the road, so when we do get it, we tend to soak it up and revel in it as long as we can.

When her stomach rumbles, her eyes pop open, and she giggles. "Morning."

"Morning." I kiss the tip of her nose. "Hungry?"

"How'd you guess?" She sighs. "I can't believe this is our last day on vacation. I say you quit your job, and we buy this house and never leave." She cuddles into my side, and I wrap my arm around her tighter. I know she's only joking, but the idea sounds damn good.

"Can't leave the guys hanging," I say, pinching her chin and raising her face to look at me. "But we can definitely come back soon." And if she wants me to buy a fucking beach house, I'm not opposed to doing so. The thought has me taking a deep breath because it's the first time since we've been doing what we've been doing that I've thought about us as more than just right now and at the moment.

I know I love the woman, always have, but I meant what I said at the time, that we needed to take shit slow. I didn't think having sex would affect us, but I should've known that sex with Kaylee isn't like sex with those groupies. Every time I fuck her, my heart is part of it. I can't simply think with my dick where she's concerned, and that's scary as fuck because even though I love her, she still hurt me—hence, the thorn-covered roses inked into my side.

Kaylee lied, pretending she cheated on me to push me away. She let me believe for six goddamn years that she fucked another guy. She knew it broke me, but she never tried to put me back together. I want to forgive her, want to move forward, but it's hard as hell to do that when her putting me first meant putting my feelings last.

"Hey, you okay?" Kaylee asks, snapping me out of my thoughts.

"Yeah." I sit up, gently moving her off me. "Wanna go get breakfast? Then we can figure out what we want to do today."

"Sure." She nods, her smile forced because she can sense my tension. She knows me as well as I know myself. It doesn't matter how much time we've spent apart. "We have to be ready to go to the airport tomorrow at five o'clock."

Since we're in Miami for the week, the buses drove to Tennessee, where we'll be performing next, and we're taking a flight there instead of having to endure the fourteen-hour drive.

After we both take showers, we head downstairs and find Declan sitting at the bar, drinking a cup of coffee.

"We're going to breakfast," Kaylee says. "Wanna go?"

Declan shrugs, making Kaylee frown. "Okay, you're going. I'm not leaving you here to pout." She grabs his cup and sets it in the sink. "You don't get to be upset about Kendall when you refuse to tell her how you feel."

Declan glares. "And risk her *stiffing* me? Fuck that. This guy will be gone soon enough." He's referring to the real reason Kendall wanted to go to the music festival—the guy she's recently started talking to was playing there.

"And then will you tell her?"she asks.

Declan shrugs."I don't know...maybe."

"Where's Gage?" She glances around, looking for him.

"Probably in his room." Declan stands. "I'll get dressed and then we can go."

"Drag Gage out too. He shouldn't be holed up in his room. He's sinking into a depression."

Declan's eyes meet mine because she isn't wrong. We've all noticed him getting worse, but he usually does around the anniversary of Tori's death—although it doesn't usually last a damn month—and it doesn't help that we're on vacation, giving him too much time on his hands. Hopefully, once we're back on the road playing, he'll snap out of it. We only have a few weeks left on tour.

I know it sounds like we're choosing to play over getting Gage the help he needs, but the guy is stubborn as fuck, and he'll never stay in rehab if he feels like he's letting down the band. It's all he has, all he lives for, and taking that away from him isn't the way to get him to focus on getting clean.

Once Declan and Gage are ready, we head out. Since we're in a busy city and Kaylee wants to walk, we have my bodyguard, Justin, with us. He mentioned a while back that he could use the money, so we offer him overtime to join us whenever we're going somewhere that's out of his contractual time.

"I read this place has the best Cuban coffee," Kaylee says, walking up to some hole-in-the-wall place.

"We're eating here?" Declan says, sounding like a stuck-up prick. The guy has probably eaten pussy dirtier than this place.

"Places like these always have the best food," Kaylee argues. "Besides, I'd rather give my money to a small business than some chain."

Without waiting for Declan to reply, she pulls the door open and goes in. If the smell of the place is anything to go by, I'd bet my left nut the food is delicious. We order iced *café con leches,* a bunch of pastries Kaylee wants to try, and some sandwiches, then we find a picnic table at a park near the beach.

"Damn, this is good," Declan says, taking a sip of his drink and then stuffing a bite of his sandwich into his mouth.

"Of course it is." Kaylee mock-glares. "It's like New York. You have to find the hidden gems. Once I—"

"Braxton? Is that you?"

The feminine voice calling my name has all of us turning our heads. Nobody's noticed us yet, so if someone did, shit's about to get crazy. But the way it's said, it's not like the fans usually say it. It's more like she's unsure, startled.

"Ma'am, I need to ask you to please …"

Whatever Justin is saying becomes a buzz in my ears as my gaze lands on the person who called my name. She's several years older than the last time I saw her, than the pictures I've seen her in. Crow's feet line her eyes, but she's still beautiful with glossy brown hair and bright hazel eyes. Everyone used to say I was my dad's twin, from our hair to our facial features. Even our body type is similar. But my eyes, they're not my dad's…they're my mom's. She's dressed in a flowy floral sundress, her skin a bit red from the sun.

As I take her in, I notice she's not alone. Standing with her is an older gentleman, a boy who looks to be in his teens, and two girls, identical, several years younger. When my eyes scan over them, trying to figure out what I'm seeing, I land on the boy's eyes: hazel, like mine…like my mom's.

"Braxton," my mom breathes, making me focus back on her. "It's been so long…"

"Nineteen years." I was five when she walked away and never looked back.

She winces, almost as if she's ashamed of how long it's been. "This is my husband, Scott, and our children. Shane is eighteen, and Julia and Jessica are—"

"Eighteen?" I hiss, cutting her off. "He's eighteen?" It's not difficult to do the math in my head. "You said you didn't want a family, that you weren't cut out for being a mom. You left!" I bark, making her flinch.

"Now, son…" her husband starts to say, which has me turning my glare on him.

"Fuck you. I'm not your son. Hell, I'm not her son either." I turn my attention back on her. "It's been nineteen years since I've seen you or heard from you. You left and immediately started a new fucking family? Why?"

Tears well up in her eyes, but I don't give a fuck. She did this, not me. "Why?" I repeat.

"I left for you," she whispers. "Your dad and I—"

"For me?" I cut her off, a humorless laugh escaping. "You left for me?"

"Braxton...maybe let her explain," Kaylee says softly, her hand going to my arm. It's meant to be comforting, but all I can think about is how when I found out she lied to me, she said the same shit. *I did it for you.*

"Fuck you," I hiss, shaking Kaylee's hand off me. "You didn't do it for me. You did it for you. You left and got yourself a whole new family."

Denise—because fuck that, I'm not calling her Mom—shakes her head, liquid spilling down her cheeks, and I can't be here another second. My body buzzes with pent-up aggression, my heart pumping with raw emotion. I need to get the fuck out of here before I do something, say something...

I turn on my heel and stalk away. I hear voices murmuring behind me, but my head is too fuzzy to know what they're saying.

"Brax, wait!" Kaylee yells, trying to catch up to me. "Talk to me, please."

"Not now, Kaylee," I bark. "I need some space."

When I get to the house, I grab the bottle of liquor sitting on the counter and take it up to my room, slamming the door behind me. Seeing my mom and her perfect little family and hearing her tell me that she left for me is just too much.

My dad told me why she left—she didn't want to be a wife or a mom. She wanted to act, wanted to live that life, and we were only holding her back. She broke his heart, so he moved us back to New York to get away from her.

Yet soon after, she remarried and had three damn kids. Not once, in all the years since she left, did she ever reach out. I never looked her up because I didn't want to face what I might find. I was afraid I would find her happy, living her life without a single regret of walking away from Dad and me, but I never thought for a second I would find out she moved on so quickly and started a whole new life.

Fuck, my dad. I wonder if he knows. If he did, it would probably gut him.

I take a swig from the bottle, the alcohol burning as it slides down my throat and warms my insides.

"Braxton!" Kaylee yells through the door, banging on it.

I ignore her. I know she didn't do anything, but hearing another woman who I loved tell me that she did what she did *for me*, something that hurt me, tore me up inside, has me raging, and I can't be around her right now.

"Braxton, please," Kaylee begs. "Open the door. Your mom is here and wants to explain."

Well, that gets my attention. I don't want to talk to the bitch who walked away, but maybe I need to hear her excuses so I can have all the facts when I tell her to go the fuck away for good.

"Where is she?" I ask when I swing the door open.

"Downstairs."

Pushing past Kaylee, I take another swig from my drink and go downstairs, finding Denise sitting on the couch alone.

"Where's your perfect little family?"

She flinches, wiping her eyes. "I wanted to talk to you alone."

"So talk." I sit on the coffee table across from her.

"When I met your dad, I was young, barely eighteen. I came from a poor family, and he was older. I wanted to go to LA to pursue acting, but then I got pregnant. While he was finishing law school, I stayed by his side, focused on raising you, but I had dreams too..."

"Dreams that were more important than your son?"

She shakes her head. "You were my entire world. A friend of mine told me about a film doing auditions in Manhattan. I didn't think I'd get the part, but I still went for the heck of it. Weeks went by, and I assumed I didn't get it, but then I got the callback. They wanted me. One movie turned into two, and the next thing I knew, I was being offered the chance of a lifetime to star in a huge production. The only problem was they needed me in LA...

"Your dad wasn't happy. He was up for partner at the firm he was working at, but I needed this...for me. So we agreed I would go, and we'd visit each other when we could. I wanted to take you with me, but he said no, said that living on set wasn't the life for a child, and I agreed. So you stayed with him. I was supposed to come back after filming, but then I was offered another role in another movie. The pay was more than your dad made, and I told him I would be a fool not to take it."

She sighs and shakes her head. "I think he resented that I was making more money than him. Anyway, after I told him I wanted to take the job, he agreed to move to LA, giving up his chance at making partner. And for a while, things were good. He found a law firm to work at, and I thought we were happy.

"And then one day I came home and found him with the nanny. I lost it. Told him I was going to file for divorce. I kicked him out and told him we were done."

What the fuck? Nothing she's saying makes any sense. This is nothing like what my dad has told me over the years.

"I had a friend of mine pick you up from school while I was looking for a new nanny, but when she got there, she was told you were already picked up. Your dad had taken you back to New York. Because I was contracted to finish the movie, I couldn't go after you, and before I could file for divorce, your dad filed first, claiming I abandoned you and was an unfit parent."

Fresh tears spill from her lids, and just as I'm about to reach for her and comfort her, she says the words that have me stopping in my tracks.

"I let him have you." Her admission causes my heart to drop. I always knew she walked away, but her confirming it makes it feel real.

"You gave me up without a fight?"

She sniffs. "I did it for you. A long-drawn-out custody battle wouldn't have been good for you. I was young, and your dad was a lawyer—a damn good one. I met with an attorney, and he told me the chances of me winning were slim."

"And I wasn't worth it to you to fight for..."

"No," she gasps. "I regretted it every day. I asked him several times to reconsider, but he was so mad. He said he cheated because I was never home. He blamed me. He was so angry and wouldn't let me near you."

"So instead of trying to fight for me, for your kid you gave birth to, who you were supposed to love and raise and protect and mother, you walked away and started a new family."

I stand, not wanting to hear another word. "Glad we got the facts straight."

"I never stopped thinking about you," she cries. "I just...I didn't know how to fix it. I missed you every day. I had planned to come to you once you turned eighteen, and then your band hit it big, and I'll admit, I was too scared. I thought you would think I was only coming to you because your band was successful."

"You seem to have excuses for everything," I say dryly. "You claim to have loved me, but it wasn't enough to fight for me. You missed me, but it wasn't enough to seek me out. You said you walked away for me. Well, I claim bullshit. You did it for you. Because you were scared and weak, and you didn't love me enough."

"Braxton, please," she pleads, but I raise my hand. I'm done. Just fucking done.

Without another word or sparing her another glance, I walk away from her, the same way she walked away from me all those years ago.

I'm back in my room, one bottle emptied, another half gone, when there's a knock on my door, followed by Kaylee begging me to let her in.

Knowing her ass isn't going to stop until I open the door, I stumble over to it, unlocking and opening it.

"Finally...I—"

"I said I needed space earlier, and I meant it."

"That was before your mom—"

"Doesn't change shit," I slur. "I need fucking space."

Her face falls, and I almost feel bad. "What does that mean?"

"That means what I said. I need time...space to figure my shit out."

"Let me be here for you, please." She places her soft hand on my arm, and I catch a glimpse of the tattoo she got when we were together.

"You said forever..."

"Huh?"

I grab her hand and twist it so she can see the ink. "You said forever, but the second shit got rough, you lied and pushed me away. Just like my mom did."

"That's not the same thing."

"Really? How is it any different? She walked away...for me. You pushed me away...for me. You both promised forever, and as soon as the first bump in the road hit, you forgot the promises you made."

"Braxton..."

"I don't wanna hear it. I've heard enough fucking excuses for one day. What I want is to be by myself and drink until I'm so drunk I forget about today."

Before she can argue, I slam the door in her face and head back onto the balcony, where I do exactly what I said—drink until I'm so drunk I can't remember anything but the porcelain toilet I spend half the night throwing up in.

Twenty-One

KAYLEE

Declan shrugs, closing the hotel room door behind him. "He passed out."

"I'm worried about him."

It's been several days since Braxton ran into his mom and lost his shit, and he's spent every waking moment drunk or high—or both. I've tried to talk to him, but he keeps pushing me away, refusing to let me in. Not that it would matter if he did, because he's always so drunk, he wouldn't be able to have a conversation anyway. But I can't imagine all this drinking is good for his liver.

My thoughts go to my dad and how his drinking led to his death.

"We need to get him help."

"He needs time," Camden says, walking over and joining us.

"Like Gage? You guys keep saying that about him, and it's been six years. I get you guys are rock stars, but that doesn't mean you have to go out like them."

Camden sighs. "They're grown-ass men, Kaylee. We can't make them do anything they don't want to do. And Braxton isn't Gage. He's hurt right now and lashing out, but he isn't going to be like this forever. He just needs a damn moment."

"Fine." I shrug, walking away from them.

When I get to my room, I call Layla, needing to vent.

"How are you?" she asks when she answers the phone.

"Better than Braxton."

"That bad, huh?"

She saw the aftermath the next morning when we all had to go to the airport. Braxton was still drunk, and she had to keep Felix away from him, telling him that Uncle Brax was sick.

"It's been days, and he's only getting worse. And the guys are enabling him."

"They mean well," she murmurs.

Since I don't want her caught in the middle, I change the subject.

"Evolution reached out."

"The PR company?"

"Yep. They wanted to apologize. They're probably afraid now that the truth is out, thanks to me going live, I'll throw shade their way."

"Which they would totally deserve."

"True, and I'm not interested in working for them anyway. Working with musicians is not my cup of tea. But at least it seems my reputation has been somewhat restored."

"And with the pay from working on the tour, you'll have money in the bank so you can look for the job you want."

"Exactly."

There's a crash and then, "Mommy!"

"Shoot, Felix just knocked the lamp over doing some new dance. I gotta go. Hang in there. Braxton loves you. He's just struggling right now. We'll talk soon. Love you!"

"Love you more."

We hang up, and since I have the entire night to myself, I pull out my laptop to search for jobs in New York to apply for. Life's too damn short to settle for something you don't love doing.

"HAVE YOU SEEN BRAXTON?"

Camden flinches and shakes his head. "I'm sure he's around here somewhere..."

"Well, he needs to be around here now," I say, irritation evident in my tone. He almost missed a show because he was passed out and nobody could find him. He's skipped two meet and greets and blew off a radio interview. This is quickly becoming an issue.

I get it. His mom messed up. I messed up—although I was hoping we were moving past that, I mean, we even got tattoos that symbolized a fresh start—until he compared me to her, saying we both promised him forever, only to walk away while claiming we were doing it for him. She hurt him...I hurt him. I one-hundred-percent get it. But instead of him dealing with it, he's choosing to avoid it all by remaining drunk and high twenty-four seven. I imagine he's even pissed at his dad since he lied as well, but as far as I know, he hasn't confronted him yet.

"Let's just do it without him," Declan says.

"Again? Fans have posted, calling him out. It's supposed to be all of you. Rumors are going to start circulating."

"We'll talk to him on the bus. But right now, they're waiting for us."

"Fine!" I throw my hands in the air and stalk off, determined to find him. As I'm checking out each of the rooms, I see Gage come out of the room all the way at the end.

"Hey, the meet and greet is starting. Is Braxton in there?"

Gage's bloodshot eyes meet mine. "Yeah," he slurs, "but—"

His words are cut off by the sound of giggles. Fucking giggles. "Motherfucker!" I storm into the room and find Braxton sitting on the couch with a bottle of JD in his hand, taking a large swig while two women are sitting on the other couch, making out like they're in a damn porn film.

"Are you fucking serious right now?"

Braxton glances at me, and then his gaze goes to the women who are still kissing and feeling each other up. His eyes go wide for a split second before he schools his features.

"They're with Gage," he says nonchalantly, looking around. "Speaking of which...where is he?"

"Going to the meet and greet, like you're supposed to be."

"Don't feel like it." He shrugs.

"So they're not here for you?" I nod toward the women still going at it.

"Nope."

"Then you won't mind me doing this..." I stalk over to them and fist each of their manes. "Get out. Now."

They both screech but stumble off the couch. "We were invited!" one whines.

"And now you're uninvited." I push them toward the door, open it up, and shove them out before I slam it closed again.

"What part of space did you not understand?" he says, glaring at me over the bottle.

"Seriously?" I walk over to where he's sitting and grab the bottle from him, the liquid sloshing out over my hand. "It's enough already. I get you're upset, but it's been days, and all you're doing is getting drunk."

Up until this point, he hasn't moved, his features completely devoid of any emotion. But the second the bottle leaves his hand, he jumps up in my face, grabs the bottle from me, and sends it flying across the room. It smashes against the wall, glass and liquid exploding under the pressure.

"It's enough? What are you, my fucking mom?" he half barks, half slurs since he's three sheets to the wind. "Although, I'd bet you two would get along really well. Both of you fucking martyrs."

When he gets in my face, the scent of the alcohol sends me back to when I was a kid...when my dad would get so drunk, he'd start throwing shit, which would lead to him beating the shit out of my mom.

The flashbacks have me stumbling backward, the reality of the situation hitting me like a slap to the face. "You asked me to communicate," I say to him slowly, my eyes locking with his. "Well, this is me communicating loud and fucking clear. I will not be with someone who uses drugs and alcohol to deal with the shitty parts of life. So figure your shit out, and then get back to me."

I open the door, but before I can make my escape, he makes sure to get the last word in. "That's right, Kaylee. Run. Run like you always do. I wouldn't expect anything less. Not from you or from my *mother*."

I want nothing more than to turn around and hug him, comfort him, because I know he's lashing out. He's been hurt. But I can't and won't ever be someone's punching bag. I watched my mom do it for years. I don't believe Braxton would ever put his hands on me, but when people are under the influence, shit gets twisted. My mom never thought my dad would hurt her either. She made excuse after excuse until she was in a hospital bed. She was fighting for her life after having been beaten and finally had no choice but to admit that the man she loved, who she swore would never hurt her, did just that.

So I do what I have to do and walk out the door.

Back at the bus, I pack my stuff and then book a flight to New York. I find Camden as they're coming out from meeting with the fans and pull him to the side.

"I have to go. If that means I'm fired—"

"Whoa, stop," he says. "Did something happen?"

"He threw a bottle of alcohol across the room. I just...with my mom and dad..." I choke out, my throat filled with raw emotion so thick I'm unable to finish my thoughts. This isn't how I saw Braxton's and my relationship progressing, but I should've known nothing in life is ever that easy. And the worst part is that I had finally got him back. Felt him, smelled him, touched him, kissed him...We made love under the stars while fireworks went off, and then the next morning, it all went to shit.

"I get it," Camden says, squeezing my shoulder in a comforting manner. "Honestly, I think it's probably for the best."

"You think I'm making it worse."

"I think as long as you're here, he's going to keep doing this. Maybe if he sees you're gone, he'll wake the hell up."

"Or he'll think I ran." Like he accused me of doing earlier.

"You're not running. You're walking away from a situation you don't deserve to be in. Braxton had a bunch of shit dropped on him, and he's got to wade through it on his own. He never actually dealt with what happened with you two, and now with his mom...I think space will be good for you both."

My heart aches at his words, but he's right. Braxton went from hating me for cheating to being pissed that I lied to pulling me close and us almost acting like it never happened. It was easy to do because when things are good between us, they're damn good. The problem is we've never dealt with the bad. I want to deal with it together, but I can't do that if he's not in a place to be with me.

"And don't even worry about a recommendation or your pay being deducted. You'll be paid in full, and Blackwood will give you a good rec. You did good on the tour. You kept us organized and in line. The promo for the tour exceeded everyone's expectations. It was a success, and we only have a couple of weeks left."

"Thank you. I'll type up everything that's coming up and email it to you and Jill."

"Sounds good. Give my wife a kiss for me when you get home, yeah? I hate not being there while she's pregnant."

"Since I'm between places, I'm actually planning to beg her...and you to let me crash." I wince, making Camden laugh. Since I was going to be gone for a couple of months, I gave up the room I was renting, throwing all my stuff into storage. I thought I had another couple of weeks to get it all figured out, but I guess not.

"I'm sure she'll love having you crash. And it'll make me feel better knowing she's not all alone with Felix. She won't admit it, but I know she's been doing too much and pushing herself. She's acting like she isn't less than three months away from giving birth."

My heart swells at the love shining in through the annoyance in his tone, proving that while my best friend drives him nuts, he loves her crazy ass.

"You might not be saying that once you're home and I haven't found a place yet."

Camden laughs. "You're welcome any time. Besides, our bedroom is on its own floor." He winks and then envelops me in a hug. "Give him time...he'll come around."

"Maybe," I say back, noncommittedly.

I call Layla on the ride to the airport, and of course, she's ecstatic about me staying with her temporarily. I could stay with my mom, but we haven't been close since she remarried. I actually get where Braxton was coming from when he learned his mom had a whole new family. Our situations aren't the same, but the feeling of your parent starting a new life, one that you feel like you're an outsider to, is something I've felt for years and can completely relate to.

While I wait for the plane to take off, before we're required to turn off our phones, I check my messages no less than a dozen times, hoping Braxton will text me. Of course he doesn't, and as I switch it off and the plane starts its takeoff procedures, I can't help but feel like maybe I made a mistake by crossing over that imaginary line with him. The past six years sucked, for sure. Watching him from afar, wishing we could have another chance, hoping for the opportunity to make things right, wanting to be with him again. But now, I almost wish I was still on the other side, hoping and wanting, because now that I've had him again, it hurts worse, knowing what we might never have.

Twenty-Two

BRAXTON

THE FLORAL SCENT LINGERS...EVEN AFTER DAYS...MAYBE WEEKS. I HAVE NO CLUE WHAT FUCKING DAY IT IS of her being gone, but I can still smell her. The fragrance of fresh roses clings to the pillows and sheets. If I had allowed the linens to be washed, the smell would disappear, but I've refused. It probably makes me a masochist, getting lost in the scent of a woman I pushed away, not wanting the smell to go away. And during the few minutes when I wake up and am faintly sober, I regret not having the sheets burned, but as soon as the alcohol flows through my system, I crave her scent. It's like the sweetest, most addictive drug—one sniff and I'm hooked.

"Yo, we're here," Camden yells through the door. Usually, the guys and I take turns in this room, but they let me have it when Kaylee was here, and I've continued to sleep in it since she left.

Fuck, she left.

Sometimes, my heart fucking aches. I miss every damn thing about her— the way she would run her fingers through my hair, lightly scraping her nails on my scalp. When she would wake up and smile softly, all sleep drunk and happy. The sight of her in my shirts that weren't long enough to actually cover anything, so when she would walk, her peach of an ass would peek out.

That same ass I'd spend hours squeezing and grabbing and fucking. She loved to be fucked, slow, fast, hard, soft. She would take me any way I wanted. Unlike some insecure women, she's comfortable with her body, with me seeing and touching her body. And after we would have sex and both of us were sated, she'd cuddle up next to me, and we'd talk until she'd eventually pass out.

Other times, I hate her...for the same reasons that my heart hurts. Because she came back into my life, gave me all of herself, and then walked away.

Because I'm not enough for her.

Not enough to fight for.

To stick around for.

Just like I wasn't enough for my mom.

She left. Didn't fight. Moved forward.

Just like Kaylee.

And they both did it for me.

The thought has me reaching for the almost empty bottle and downing what's left, not giving a shit that it's still morning. I have no idea where we are or what city we're in. And I don't give a shit. It's all the same anyway. Drive to a new city, perform the same songs, and then move on. And I could play in my sleep.

"Brax! Let's go!" Camden beats on the door harder, so I roll off the bed and stumble to my feet. I unlock the door, cracking it open slightly. The light filters in, and my skull pulses against my brain.

"We have an interview with NiteLife," he says, pushing the door farther open. "Let's go. You need to shower and"—he grabs the bottle that's apparently still in my hand—"quit drinking! Fuck, man. It's been nearly two weeks, and you've spent it drunk and high. We get it. Your mom fucking sucks, and Kaylee hurt you." He grabs my face and forces me to look at him. "You're making a big mistake, and when you realize it, it's going to be too late."

I snap my head out of his touch and back up, too hungover and not drunk enough to deal with him. "The only mistake I made was letting her back into my life."

"Oh, what-the fuck-ever," Camden spits. "You forgave her until your mom showed up. Now, instead of dealing with your shit, you're taking it out on everyone." He walks back toward the door. "You better figure your shit out soon before she moves on without you. Women will only put up with a man's shit for so long."

"Who the fuck said I want her back? I'll be ready to go in a few minutes."

Instead of arguing, he rolls his eyes and leaves me to get ready. Once I've showered and gotten dressed, I grab my wallet and phone to stuff into my pockets when my phone lights up with an incoming call from my dad. I've been avoiding him since I saw my mom, knowing if I answer, words are going to be said. He fucked up getting Kaylee to help get me to LA, but I forgave him—for the most part. Now, I find out the shit he pulled with my mom. If he tells me he did it for me, I might lose my fucking head—more than I already have.

When it rings again, I send it to voicemail and then type out a text, letting him know I'm in the middle of something important and I'll call him soon.

The drive to the studio is short, and once we arrive, we're taken to a waiting room that looks similar to a hotel living room. It has a few plush couches and a table and chairs with a spread of food and drinks. There's a bathroom off to the side and a vanity with a shit ton of makeup and hair products.

While we wait to be called out, Gage sprawls out on the couch, closing his eyes since he can't drink or smoke without the other guys giving him shit.

Camden sits at the table texting his wife, and Declan sits next to me on the other couch, writing away in his notebook.

Since we left the beach, he's been quiet lately, and I'd bet it has something to do with Kendall kissing that guy she was there to see at the festival. He gets moody every time she starts dating someone new.

I glance over, and sure enough, words like *asshole, heartbreak,* and *never mine* are scribbled on the page.

"It might not seem like it now, but you not telling her how you feel is for the best," I mutter.

He glances up at me. "What?"

"Women are nothing but a heartache waiting to happen, and Kendall is no different." She may be chill as hell and fun to hang out with—coming across like one of the guys—but she's still a woman who has no problem stringing men along before she drops them like flies.

"You're only saying that because you're half drunk and hurt."

"No, I'm saying that because it's the truth. Look at Tori..." Declan glares in warning, one I don't heed, and I feel Gage's eyes on me, but I don't care. "What she did to Gage was selfish as fuck. Did she give a shit about him when she destroyed him? No."

"Shut your fucking mouth," Gage barks.

"No. It's the truth, even if you don't like it. She claimed to love you and look what—" Before the rest of the words are out of my mouth, Gage storms over to me and grabs me by the front of my shirt, pulling me up.

Because I'm still half drunk—as Declan pointed out—and hungover, I'm slow to realize what's happening, so before I can block, his fist meets my face, knocking me back on my ass. My face stings from the brute force of his punch, and I can taste blood in my mouth.

"Punching me won't change anything," I point out. "She was a fucking liar, just like—"

"Braxton, stop!" Declan barks, jumping between Gage and me.

"—my mom and Kaylee."

"Enough!" Camden yells, pushing Gage back while Declan remains in front of me.

"Why?" I say, standing and walking over to where the alcohol is. I grab a bottle, crack it open, and chug it down. "It's the truth. Women want love and affection. They lure us in and make us dependent on them. They want loyalty and the promise of forever, and for what? So they can string us along and then fuck us over? Fuck that and fuck them."

I don't know what comes over me, but suddenly, everything feels like it's been built to the highest point and placed on my back. I can't stand, can't walk, can't carry all these fucked-up feelings anymore. The pain, the anger, the resentment. It's all become too much, too heavy, and I need it off me, off my back.

And before I realize what I'm doing, I'm swiping everything off the table, as if all that shit is the weight on my shoulders and in my heart. Fruits and bread go flying every which way. Glass bottles shatter when they hit the floor. Realistically, I know what I'm doing isn't helping in any way, but the release feels good, so I continue destroying everything around me.

At some point, my vision goes blurry, and then hands are on me, pushing me against the wall.

"Brax, chill out," Camden says, his voice calm as always.

"I..." I open my eyes and look around at my best friends, who are more like brothers. They're staring at me with genuine concern and sympathy in their eyes. "I feel sick." I push Camden out of the way and just barely make it to the toilet to throw up the entire contents in my stomach, which is mostly liquid since I've been drinking more than I've been eating.

"You can't keep going like this," Camden says, keeping it real like he always does. "We can't." His gaze swings over to Gage, and my heart plummets into my now empty stomach because his tone makes me realize I'm only adding to the stress Camden carries since he's the person who handles everything for the band, and that's not fair.

"I'm sorry," I choke out.

He nods. "We need to get your face covered before we go out there."

Declan grabs a makeup artist, who quickly covers the bruise that's already forming on my cheek, and then we go out and handle the interview like the pros we are.

On our way to the hotel, I consider calling Kaylee, but I don't know what to say or where we stand. We'll be home soon, so I decide it would be better if I wait until we can talk face-to-face. I'm not sure what I want at this point, and I know I need some time to figure it out. Even if it means we go our separate ways—a thought that feels like my heart is being squeezed by barbwire—I don't want to have that conversation until I'm sober and thinking clearly. Camden was right. I did forgive her—at least I thought I did—until the shit with my mom happened, and then I lumped her into the same category with my mom.

When we arrive at the hotel, we all go our separate ways. I head to the gym to get a much-needed workout in, hoping to sweat some of the lingering alcohol out of my pores and work on getting back into shape—not that I've fallen too far, but up until the past couple of weeks, I'd been working out once, sometimes twice a day for years.

While I'm running on the treadmill, Fallout Boy's "Sugar, We Goin' Down"—yeah, I prefer old school music, sue me—blares in my ears, forcing me to think about shit. The song cuts off for a second, indicating I have an email. I slow down to check it, since only work and personal shit go here, and press the stop button when I see it's from Easton with the subject: Denise Cohen.

When I was drunk and curious one night, I learned through a search of my mom that she met her husband, Aaron Cohen, while on the set of a movie he was producing—while she was still with my dad. They were married shortly after my parents' divorce was finalized, and soon after came Adam, my apparent half brother. Her husband is worth millions, and after she got pregnant, she took a few years off to be home with their son. She appeared in a few more movies before she got pregnant again with the twins, who I guess I'm also related to. It's crazy...I went from thinking I was an only child to finding out I have three half siblings. She's since remained out of the public eye, her husband the sole provider.

> Braxton, a woman named Denise Cohen has reached out to Blackwood in search of you. She's claiming to be your mother and would like a way to get ahold of you since all your social media and email is through us. Would you like me to give her your info?
>
> -Easton

I stare at the screen, unsure what to think. The woman went years without reaching out, and now she wants to, what? Keep in touch? I'm not sure what she can possibly have to say after our last chat. I thought I made how I feel pretty damn clear. I can't imagine anything she has to say will change my mind, but at the same time, the masochistic part of me wants to know.

> Easton,
>
> Yeah, that's the woman who brought me into this world and then walked away...You can give her my personal email. Thanks.

I'm lifting free weights when my phone goes off with another email. This time, it's from Denise. Not wanting to read this in the middle of the hotel gym, I go back to my room, take a quick shower, and then open it.

> Braxton,
>
> Thank you for allowing me to contact you. First, I would like to say I'm sorry. I know it's years too late, but I am truly sorry for not fighting harder. I have no excuses except that I was wrong. I took the coward's way out, and I will always regret not fighting harder. I could've contacted you so many times over the years, but I allowed my fear of rejection to stop me, and that's completely on me.

I'm not writing you today to ask you to forgive me, but for Adam. You see, while my husband, Aaron, knew about you, offering many times to help me reach out, I never told our kids about you. I used to tell myself it was because it hurt too much, but the truth is, I didn't want to have to admit what I did...I gave up my son. Because then my kids would ask questions, and my guilt couldn't handle that.

After Adam found out about you, he was upset that he had a brother I never told him about. My hiding the truth about you hurt him, and I don't know how to make that right. I know finding out about having siblings was a shock to you, but I just want you to know that if the day ever comes that you want to get to know them, I know they would love to, and it wouldn't have to have anything to do with me. Although I hope we can talk some more one day, but I'll leave that up to you...

She goes on to give me Adam's contact info as well as hers and then signs it: With love, Denise.

My first thought is the kid only wants to get to know me because of who I am, but at the same time, I have an eighteen-year-old brother who isn't at fault for what went down. Since I'm nowhere near ready to reach out to him, I store his info in my phone and then turn it off, needing to go for a walk so I don't end up getting lost in the bottom of a bottle. I have no desire to email Denise back. She's had years to reach out, so she can wait until I'm damn well ready to respond, if I ever do at all.

Right now, I only have one person I need to focus on: myself. Everybody else can fucking wait.

Twenty-Three

KAYLEE

"Cam!" Felix yells as the front door opens, and in walks Camden, dropping his bag onto the ground.

"Oh my God!" Layla gasps, springing to her feet and waddling her cute butt over to Camden. "You're home early!"

"Only a day," he says, wrapping his wife and stepson up in a hug. "The bus was having issues, so we ended up flying in instead."

"I missed you so much." She sighs into him, and he drops his arm around her shoulders as they walk back into the living room.

"I made up a new dance," Felix tells him, not giving him a second to get inside and decompress. But if Camden is annoyed, he hides it well, smiling at Felix and giving him his attention, despite, I'm sure, wanting to give his attention to Layla.

"Well, c'mon and show us," Camden says, dropping onto the couch with Layla still stuck to his side.

"Welcome home," I say, standing and hooking my purse over my shoulder.

"You're not leaving on my account..."

"No, I have somewhere I need to be."

"Where?" he presses.

"Café Latte. If you want some alone time later, I can watch Felix for you guys."

"Thanks," Camden says. "Maybe another night. Tonight, I just want to be home with my family."

Layla beams at him like he's hung the moon while Felix starts up the song I've watched him dance to no less than a hundred times in the past week. As I walk out, quickly glancing back at them, I make a mental note to find a place as soon as I find a job. They might have said I can stay as long as I need to, but after Camden being gone for two months, and Layla about to give birth soon, they need this time alone, as a family. Which means it's important I find a damn job.

When I arrive at the coffee shop where Ralph Martinez, the owner of Evolution PR, asked me to meet him, I look for him before grabbing a cup of coffee. I immediately spot him from his pictures on the company website and walk over to him.

"Mr. Martinez?"

"Please, call me Ralph. Kaylee?"

"Yes."

"What would you like to drink?" he asks, standing like a gentleman and pulling my seat out for me. He's dressed in a sharp suit that probably costs as much as the rent here in Manhattan.

"Iced vanilla latte is good," I tell him, keeping it simple.

"Anything to eat? Those chocolate chip muffins are calling my name." He smiles wide, and a single dimple pops out of his left cheek. He's cute in a wholesome way, but he does nothing for me...not like Bra—

I inwardly sigh and shake *him* from my thoughts. It's been over two weeks since I walked away, and he hasn't once tried to reach out.

"What the heck, I'll take one," I say, suddenly in need of something sweet. Emotional eating is a real thing.

"Sounds good."

While he's at the counter ordering, I check my phone for any messages or emails, telling myself that I'm not looking for anything from Braxton.

When a throat clears, I glance up, thinking it's Ralph, only, instead, it's the man who's been in my every thought.

"Brax," I breathe, shocked to see him standing here. "What are you doing here?"

"Camden said you were here."

"You asked him where I was?"

"He said you were staying with them, and I went by there to talk to you."

"Why didn't you call me?"

"Thought it would be better to talk in person."

My insides knot, unsure if that's a good or bad thing. I take him in, and despite Layla mentioning he was drinking heavily after I left, he looks good—sober and well-rested. He's dressed in a simple T-shirt and jeans, Vans donning his feet and a hat covering his head.

"Here you go," Ralph says, making me dart my eyes from checking out Braxton over to him. "One vanilla latte and a chocolate chip muffin." He sets them on the table in front of me, not realizing that Braxton is standing next to our table, staring daggers at him.

"Brax—"

"Are you serious right now?" Braxton says, not giving me a chance to explain. "You're on a fucking date?"

I shake my head, but he's already jumped to conclusions. "This is Ralph—"

"I don't give a damn who he is. Is this what you're into now? *Suits?*" he spits, making it clear a man in a suit is not a good thing.

Ralph's brows rise at the dig. "Something wrong with a man in a suit?"

"Nope." Braxton shrugs as I quickly stand and grab his arm, needing to haul him away before things get worse. "Just wasn't aware Kaylee was into guys with sticks up their asses."

I know damn well he doesn't feel that way since many of the people he works with at the label wear suits, but it's the only thing that he can think of to talk shit about since he doesn't know who this guy is.

"Braxton," I hiss. "Stop it. You're embarrassing me."

"I'm embarrassing you?" he barks out with a laugh. "It's only been, what? Two weeks and you've already moved on? You're embarrassing your damn self."

"Please give me a moment," I beg Ralph, who's now frowning.

"Nah, you don't need to give her anything. Go sit and enjoy yourself. We're done here." Braxton shakes my hand off his arm and stalks out, leaving me stuck wondering if I should stay where I am or go after him.

"I'm not sure what's going on," Ralph says, standing, "but maybe you should go handle that. The last thing I want is to get in the middle of..." He waves his hand, unsure of what exactly he just walked into the middle of, and I don't blame him. He's an important man, who has no time for immature shit.

"I'm really sorry."

"It's okay. Really, I just wanted to apologize on behalf of Evolution. When I heard about what happened, I wanted to clear the air myself. If you need a letter of reference, please contact my secretary, and she can get something for you."

In the emails, he mentioned the possibility of a job opportunity in their marketing department. While I wasn't even sure I would take it if it were offered, having not wanted to work for the company who didn't have my back when all that shit went down with Sam York, the fact that it's now off the table because of Braxton has me fuming.

"Take care, Ms. Thomas."

He leaves without taking his drink or muffin with him, and after I throw it all away, I head out, dialing Braxton's number so I can bitch him out. The first couple of times, he sends my ass to voicemail, which only makes me even madder.

On the third attempt, he answers. "Date over so soon? Hope it didn't end on my account."

"Where are you?" I hiss.

And that's when my eyes land on him, leaning against the black SUV with his bodyguard, Justin, standing next to him.

"Don't you move!" I hang up and stalk over to him, watching as he pockets his phone, and his eyes jump up to meet mine.

"What the hell is your problem?" I say once I get over to him.

"Maybe you should've mentioned you moved on, then I wouldn't have intruded." He shrugs, all cockily, like he's got this all figured out.

"For your information," I say slowly, "that was the owner of Evolution PR."

His mouth pops open slightly.

"For a guy who's so big on *communicating*, you're seriously the shittiest communicator there is." I poke my finger against his chest. "That was a potential interview, and you just ruined it because you wouldn't listen to me. So maybe, the next time, before you bitch at other people for not communicating, take a look at yourself."

I back up and hit him with one more glare. "Because of you, I lost a job opportunity, so thanks." And because this seems to be our thing, I walk away without waiting for him to respond.

Not wanting to intrude on Cam's homecoming, I go for a walk through Central Park, stopping and sitting on the bench so I can search for job listings on my phone. I apply to several places, even some I don't really want but will take if it means getting my foot in the door, and then send an email to Ralph's secretary, asking for the recommendation letter I was promised since it can't hurt to have.

Once I've sent it, I turn off my phone and people watch, trying to get lost in the beauty and craziness of the city so I can forget about how messed up my life is. When I was growing up and imagining what my life would be like, I never thought I would be so lost at my age.

When I was little, I imagined becoming a wife and a mom. When I got a little older and would sit with my dad, working with him for hours, I imagined going to college and becoming a marketing badass. When he got injured and turned to drugs and drinking, I imagined escaping to college and eventually following in his footsteps—pre-injury. I wanted to make him proud and show him what he was missing out on.

And when he left and my mom found new love, starting a new family, I imagined starting my own. Creating a life and a home that I felt happy and welcome in.

Yet here I am, about to turn twenty-five years old, living in my best friend's home, and once again feeling like an outsider. It's not her fault, and if Layla knew how I felt, she would do everything in her power to make me feel at home. But the truth is, there's nothing she can do because when I see her and Camden and Felix, I don't want to be a part of their family. I want what they have. I want my own house and my own husband who loves me. I want our own kids, our own family. I want a kick-ass career, to go to work and then come home and have someone to discuss my day with.

The problem is, every time I imagine it—the husband, the children, the house, the love—I only see it with one man: Braxton. So many times over the years, I attempted to move forward, went on dates, tried to envision it, but nobody ever fit into that picture but him.

I want him, in the house, with the kids. I want little hazel-eyed babies running around. I want date nights and rides on the motorcycle he told me he bought because he loved his dad's. I want family trips and hot sex...God, sex with Braxton is so damn good. And the way he loves to hold me afterward like he can't get enough...

I don't realize tears are running down my face until the liquid slides down my chin and along my neck. I swipe them away, hating how emotional I am when I did this to myself.

When the sky looks like it's going to burst with raindrops, I reluctantly head home, where I find Layla and Camden cuddling on the couch with Felix spread out on the floor, all of them watching a movie—like the cute, perfect little family they are.

Because Layla didn't fuck everything up like I did.

"Hey, you're home," she says, sitting up slightly. "Wanna watch the movie with us? It just started."

"I have jobs to apply for," I say, plastering a smile on my face.

As if she can sense my unease, she simply nods. "Okay, well, if you change your mind..."

"Thanks."

"Did, umm, Braxton find you?" she asks carefully.

"Yeah." I want to tell them that the next time they think it's a good idea to tell my...well, whatever he is...where I am, they should warn a girl. But then I'd have to explain all that went down, and I'm not in the mood, so instead, I let it go and go to my room so I can continue my pity party for one.

I'm lying on the bed scrolling through social media when my phone goes off with a text from Layla saying everyone is going out to dinner and that I'm invited. Because I know she'll give me shit if I say no, and because, at some point, I'm going to have to face Braxton since we're friends with the same people, I agree to go.

"WHERE'S GAGE?" I ASK DECLAN, GIVING HIM A HUG AND IGNORING THE TENSION BETWEEN BRAXTON AND me that's so thick, it would be hard to cut with even the sharpest knife.

"At home." He shrugs. "Probably sleeping the tour off."

We find our seats, and I'm shocked when Braxton comes over and sits on the other side of me. We obviously didn't leave things on good terms earlier, so I'm not sure why he's not sitting on the other side of the huge table.

To keep it from getting awkward, I make it a point to talk to various people throughout the meal, afraid if it goes silent, Braxton will find a way in, and the last thing I want is to argue with him here in front of everyone.

"Hey, Kaylee," Easton says, grabbing my attention. "We received your résumé from a recruiter."

"Oh," I breathe. I filled out a form with an online recruitment company, hoping they might be able to find places hiring that I couldn't. Since the companies are the ones who pay their fee, if they hire someone they find, I figured it couldn't hurt.

"I must've selected the wrong info, or our wires got crossed," I explain. "I'm actually not looking to do anything in PR. My goal is marketing and advertising."

"That's where we're hiring." He smiles. "With so much changing with social media, YouTube channels gaining more popularity, and platforms like TikTok and interactive apps, we're doing a complete overhaul. When I took over, I was focused on the artists and let the marketing side of things go, so our aim this coming year is to bring Blackwood into the twenty-first century, so we stay relevant and on top. We saw a huge increase in Raging Chaos's following when Layla took over and created the YouTube series, so we're planning to take that approach with some of our established clients as well as the new ones we're in the middle of signing."

"That's smart," I agree, having learned a lot about marketing and advertising through social media while in school. "The days of simple television, magazine, and radio ads are long gone. Now, it's all about social media. Look at Kylie Jenner. She's created a billion-dollar empire from her Instagram. Obviously, there's more to it than that, but one of her posts will bring in like a hundred-thousand dollars. People think she's simply posting, but it's all a marketing gimmick."

"Exactly," Easton agrees. "A few of Blackwood's marketing execs aren't on board, wanting to keep it traditional, so when I spoke to the team, a few made the decision to retire early, opening up positions."

"People hate change."

"And change is necessary." He shrugs. "I'm sure you have a few interviews lined up, but we'll be calling you on Monday to schedule one. Bailey will be running the department since she's familiar with the social media aspect, but she needs a team of marketing and advertising experts to work with her. And before you think it's a pity interview, it's not. I'm looking for young employees who are tech-savvy and willing to learn."

He's right. That was my first thought, but I know Easton doesn't do pity. He owns a multibillion-dollar recording label that houses some of the top artists in the world. You don't get to that level without making smart decisions. Which means if he's considering me, it's because he believes I might be a good fit, and I would be a fool to turn down an interview with his company. "That sounds really good. Thank you for considering me."

The rest of the meal is spent with everyone getting caught up since the guys have been gone. Bailey and Cynthia tell everyone about the week in Hawaii they spent for their honeymoon, alternating between the pool, beach, and spa.

When the check comes, Easton, of course, insists on paying. We walk out to the front, and after everyone says their goodbyes, I start heading to Camden's SUV when a hand grabs my wrist.

"Can we go somewhere and talk?"

Layla glances back, then quickly turns around, pretending to give us privacy.

"Please," he says softly, so he doesn't cause a scene. "I just want to talk."

I stop and look at him for a moment, wondering if that's smart, since every time we *talk*, it ends in us fucking or fighting, but I decide he's right. We do need to talk. We both have things we need to say, and it might as well happen now so we can get it over with. Neither of us is going anywhere, so it will be good to clear the air.

"Okay, sure. We can talk."

Twenty-Three

BONUS SCENE

BRAXTON

Braxton: You get home okay?

Kaylee: You already know I did...you walked me to the door.

Braxton: Just making sure you're safe inside.

Kaylee: I'm safe, lying in bed...

Braxton: I think I need proof. It will make me feel better...you know, to know you're home safe.

Kaylee: <Inserts picture of herself lying in bed, looking at the camera>

Braxton: Fuck, you're beautiful.

Kaylee: <<blushing emoji>>

Braxton: I can't stop thinking about the way you came on my leg.

Kaylee: I wanted to come again...with you in me, but you said no. <<insert pouty face>>

Braxton: How badly do you want to come again?

Kaylee: Really badly. Badly enough that I'm considering fingering myself...

Braxton: Take two fingers and push them inside you.

Kaylee: Done...

Braxton: How wet are you?

Kaylee: I'm soaked.

Braxton: Slowly run your fingers up and down your slit, gathering your juices, and then massage your clit.

Kaylee: I wish you were doing it…

Braxton: Me too, baby. Pretend they're my fingers. Rub that clit.

Kaylee: It feels so good.

Braxton: With your other hand, pinch your nipple.

Kaylee: I can't type and do both.

Phone rings

"Braxton," Kaylee breathes, her gorgeous face appearing through the screen. Fuck, I already miss her, and I was just with her not that long ago.

"Show me that sweet pussy, baby. I want to see the way you're pretending it's my fingers thrusting in and out of you."

She groans and turns the screen around so I can see her neatly trimmed pussy with her fingers slowly moving in and out of her.

"That's it, baby. Finger that pussy…Give your clit attention too."

I can tell when her thumb lands on her clit because her breathing picks up. "Spread your legs wider so I can see…"

"I want you to do it too. I want to see your hard cock getting stroked."

I flip my own screen around and pull my cock out. It's already hard, so I fist it and start stroking it up and down, using the bit of precum that's seeped out as lube.

"God, Brax, I want that inside me so badly."

"Soon. And I promise when we fuck, it's going to be so rough, you won't be able to walk for days."

She groans, and I smirk to myself, loving how rough my woman likes it. "Pretend I'm there, baby. You're bent over on all fours, and I'm grabbing your hair and fucking you from behind."

"In my ass?" she breathes.

"Yeah, I'm fucking you in the ass. Stroking your tight hole with my piercings."

"Oh, yes," she moans, the sound taking me to the edge. "I'm so close. Fuck me, Brax, please."

"I'm fucking you, baby. My cock is bottoming out in your tight ass, and I'm pinching those perfect pink nipples. Stroke your clit. Come all over your fingers."

"Yes, yes, yes! Oh, God," she moans, her fingers working her clit as her legs shake and she comes hard. Watching her sends me straight over the edge and ropes of cum spurt out all over my stomach.

"Oh, shit, that's so hot," she murmurs. "If you were here, that would all be in my ass."

I groan, wishing like hell I was there.

We both leave our phones on our beds so we can clean up, and once we're done, we turn our screens around so we can see each other.

"I miss you," Kaylee says, snuggling into her blanket.

"I miss you." I lie down, the same way she is. "Tell me your plans." I want to know everything about Kaylee. She wasn't just my girlfriend before. She was my best friend, and I want more than anything to get back to that, to who we were before everything changed.

"Plans for what?"

"Work, life...Talk to me."

She smiles softly and nods. "Well, my plan for work is..."

And that's how we spend the rest of the night and well into the morning—talking about life and our future, what we want and don't want—until, at some point, we both fall asleep on the phone. When I wake up, I find Kaylee still asleep, and for a second, my heart is happy, until the fog clears, and I remember we're on the phone. And it's at that moment that I know I have to find a way to truly forgive her so we can move forward because the only future I see is with her...in my bed, in my arms...in my life.

Twenty-Four

BRAXTON

WHEN KAYLEE AGREES TO TALK TO ME, I SIGH IN RELIEF. WE'VE BOTH FUCKED UP, DONE SHIT NEITHER OF us is proud of, but being without her these past couple of weeks has proven one thing: I can't be without her—and I don't want to be.

Since it's hard to go anywhere without being spotted, we go back to my place, but instead of taking her to my bedroom, we go out onto the balcony. I flip on the lights and guide her over to the lounge chairs. Neither of us says a word for several minutes, both of us lost in our thoughts. So much has happened. It would probably be easier for us to walk away from each other, but I can't do it. I love her and always have.

Just as I'm about to tell her what I'm thinking, she speaks first.

"Without trust, we have nothing. And it's clear you don't trust me. For you to think after everything we've been through, when you were inside me only a couple of weeks ago, I would run to another man without so much as talking to you first proves that.

"And if I'm being honest, I don't know if I trust you either because every time you get upset, you end up drinking and getting high, and I can't be with someone like that.

"What you did at the hotel, the drinking and yelling and throwing shit? It's what my dad did before he started to get violent..."

Her sad gray eyes meet mine, and I've never felt like more of a piece of shit than I do at this moment. I was so caught up in my anger, my hurt, I didn't even stop to think about how it would affect her because of her past. In my drunken head, it was just a fight. I was pissed and reacted, but for someone who was raised in an abusive household, it went deeper than that for her.

"Kaylee, I'm—"

"You're what? You're sorry? That's what he would say, the morning after... he would apologize and beg my mom for forgiveness. Sometimes, he would bring her roses and breakfast, and she would fall for it every time...because she loved him."

I hate that she's comparing me to her father, but I get it, so I don't argue.

Instead, I nod in understanding.

"I can't be her," she says, her words cracking with emotion. "I *won't* be her." The decisiveness in her eyes and in her tone fills me with pride. I have no doubt she loves me, but I believe she would walk away before she would allow what happened to her mom to happen to her, and I love her that much more because of it.

"I don't want you to be her." I edge closer and take her hands in mine, kissing the tops of her knuckles.

"So where do we go from here?"

"We fight." I lock eyes with her. "We fight for each other because we love each other. And we'll get through this." I entwine our fingers and tug her into a standing position, guiding her back into the house. I head straight for the kitchen and, with her hand still in mine, use my other one to open each of the cabinets, pulling bottles of liquor from them and dumping them into the trash. Next, I clear out the fridge.

Once that's done, I take us upstairs to my room, where I grab the few bottles and a couple of joints on my dresser and drop them into my garbage.

"I'm not an addict," I tell her. "But I do use it as an escape, and I will never do that again. If I have to see a therapist or go to AA to prove it to you, I will." I grab her other hand and pull her close to me. "I won't lose you over alcohol and drugs."

"It's not that easy," she argues.

"No, it's not," I agree. "But I love you, and you love me, and I'll fight for you, for us, every damn day if you fight right alongside me. And some days, when you don't feel like you can fight, I'll fight for us both." I release her hand and cup her face. "And I know you'll do the same."

"We fight," she breathes, tears welling in her eyes.

"We fight."

Our mouths come together at the same time, ravaging each other, needing the connection. Her arms encircle my neck, and I pick her up, twirling us around and setting her on top of the dresser. Her legs part, and I step between them, deepening the kiss. I've missed her so damn much, her lips, her touch, her scent.

Her hands glide down the sides of my neck and over my shoulders. She makes her way under my shirt, her cool hands sliding up and down my abs before she moves down to my pants. It feels so good, being with her, kissing her...I want more, but if we're going to make shit work, we have to change how we handle shit. What's that saying? *Doing the same thing over and over again while expecting different results...*

I pull back, breaking our connection. "I want this, and I want you, but I don't want to fall back into our usual pattern of having makeup sex."

Her eyes widen slightly in shock, and trust me, I get it because I've never imagined saying those words, but I don't want her for now. She's my goddamn forever, which means we need to make different choices.

"You said we need trust, and I agree. I think we should work on that. Getting to know each other without the sex."

The gorgeous smile that spreads across her face tells me I made the right suggestion.

"Okay," she says, leaning forward and giving me a chaste kiss before dropping onto the ground, her body rubbing against mine on the way down. "So I guess I'll see you later?" She steps around me, edging toward the door.

"Now, wait a second…" I snag her hand and pull her back to me. "I didn't say we couldn't hang out. We have a perfectly good hot tub…"

She laughs. "Which will end with us fucking in it."

True. "Okay, we could go out."

"Where?"

I think for a moment. It's hard for a person like me to just go out without being bombarded. New York is better than LA, but it can still get crazy if you're spotted. "Lush." A friend of mine owns the club, and he caters to people like me who are in the spotlight.

"Oh! I've been wanting to check out that club, but it's super hard to get into."

"Let's go. We can go dancing and—"

"Drinking?" She raises a brow.

"I was going to say dancing and have a good time."

She winces. "Sorry."

"Don't be." I wrap my arms around her. "I'm not an addict, Kaylee. I know those are just words, and it'll take time for you to see that, but I'll show you. I want to take you dancing. We never got to have that."

"Have what?"

"Dating. We did it when we were younger, but not once we were adults. We've been on tour for months. Now that we're home, I want to date you… woo the hell out of you."

She giggles, the sound so damn beautiful. "You've been hanging out with Camden for too long."

She isn't wrong. Camden and his dad love that damn word, and we always give them shit for it, but look at them, both happy and in loving relationships with families of their own. Maybe they're onto something.

"I'm gonna woo the fuck out of you, baby," I tell her, kissing her roughly.

"I can't wait."

AFTER TEXTING JUSTIN TO LET HIM KNOW I'LL NEED HIM TONIGHT, I GET DRESSED AND THEN WE HEAD TO Camden's place, so Kaylee can get dressed. Camden and Layla end up joining us because her mom took Felix for the night, so we pile into the SUV and head to Lush. I text Declan and Gage to let them know where we're going in case they want to join, and then shoot Brody Fields, the club owner, a message, letting him know we'll need a VIP table if that's possible. I probably should've asked first, but it was all last minute. A few minutes later, he replies that he'll have it taken care of.

Clubs like his are already popular, but they know that once we're in there and post our location on social media, it's free advertisement for them. It's why celebs can go anywhere and do anything for free. Why famous people get stuff sent to them in the hopes they'll post about it. I can't even tell you how many guitars I've been sent by various companies, hoping I'll post about their products.

When we arrive, it's after ten o'clock, and the line to get in is around the damn corner. With two of our guards flanking us, we walk straight to the bouncer, who immediately recognizes us and lets us through with a single nod.

The hostess takes us directly upstairs to a roped-off area and lets us know our server will be by momentarily to take our orders.

Without waiting for her to arrive, I snag Kaylee's hand and pull her over to the dance floor. She's dressed in a tight little shimmery dress with tall as fuck heels, her blond locks down and messy. Her fingers delve into my hair, and my hands grip the curves of her hips, grinding against her. This club isn't like most. It's not as loud and crazy. The clientele is a bit older and on the wealthier side. The music is more sensual, the lights lower.

The song transitions from one to the next, and I tighten my hold on Kaylee as our bodies sway to the beat. My knee is nestled between her thighs, so close to her cunt that I can feel her warmth. I drop my face into the crook of her neck and suckle on her heated flesh, then kiss my way across her exposed skin. My hands skate down to the swell of her ass and give it a slight squeeze.

She shivers in my arms, and I chuckle, loving the effect I have on her. The fact is, it doesn't matter what we do—our attraction, our chemistry, is so goddamn potent that the possibility of it ending in sex is always present.

When she sighs into me, squirming a bit, my lips meet the shell of her ear. "Are you turned on?"

"You know I am." Her thighs tighten around my leg, squeezing it like her pussy does to my dick when it's inside her. I lift my knee slightly, rubbing it against her center. When she moans, I know I've hit the right spot, so I keep doing it. Her moans get louder the closer she gets to her orgasm, and when she detonates around me, I crash my mouth to hers, muffling the sound, just in case. The music is loud, but I don't want to chance it. Her body trembles, and

I can feel the wetness between her legs even through my jeans.

When she comes down, sagging into me, I end the kiss, and her sated eyes meet mine. "I want you now."

I grin at that, loving that an orgasm isn't enough for her. She wants *me*. "Not tonight."

"Yes, tonight," she argues. "I bet there's a bathroom somewhere..." Her gaze darts around the area.

"I'm sure there is, Crazy, but we're not finding out." I palm her neck and kiss her softly. "No sex...not until I woo you."

We spend the next few hours dancing and hanging out with our friends. Declan shows up but doesn't stay for long, saying he's not in the mood to play the fifth wheel. When Layla says she's tired and ready to go home, we all head out. I want to ask Kaylee to come home with me, but I don't, wanting to mean what I said. Instead, when I kiss her goodbye, I thank her for tonight and tell her I'll text her later.

Twenty-Five

KAYLEE

"WOW! YOU DID ALL THIS?" TEARS FILL LAYLA'S EYES AS SHE TAKES IN THE PRIVATE ROOM FILLED WITH pink-and-white balloons and streamers. There's a three-tier pink-and-white cake with a princess-crown topper, dozens of matching cupcakes and cake pops, as well as several kinds of pastries.

Tables with pink linens and comfy chairs are spread out throughout the room, and a couple of servers are walking around, offering everyone coffee and tea since the shower is being held at The Tea Room.

"When you were pregnant with Felix, you didn't get a shower." I shrug. "You deserve to be spoiled a little."

She nods in understanding, wrapping her arms around me. "Thank you."

"That's what best friends do, especially ones who take over their best friend's guest room."

"Oh, stop it," she chides. "You know I love having you close to me."

It's been almost a month and a half since I've moved in with Camden and Layla, and while they keep saying I'm welcome to stay as long as I want, I need to seriously find my own place. I've started working at Blackwood, and with the pay they offer, I'll be able to afford rent without a problem.

"I know, but my plan is to be out before the baby comes."

She pouts slightly but doesn't argue.

"This all looks so great," Kendall says, giving us a hug. "I can't believe I'm going to have a niece soon." She rubs Layla's belly since she doesn't mind. She actually encourages it. "Have you thought of any names?"

"A few," Layla says, "but we haven't decided yet."

"Well, whatever you don't use, you can use for the next baby," Sophia says with a laugh.

"Funny," Layla says back. "Don't say that in front of your son, though. He's already asking how long we have to wait for me to get pregnant again." Everyone cracks up even though we know she's not kidding.

"Saw you were spotted out with Declan last night," Bailey says to Kendall when we're all seated with plates of sweets and cups of coffee and tea.

"Yeah, so?" she says, taking a sip of her coffee. "We're good friends."

I groan inwardly at the word friend and glance at Layla, catching her wince as well. The last thing Declan wants is to be Kendall's friend, but unfortunately, he's been friend zoned.

"We've been writing together," Kendall adds. "I think I'm going to pitch one to Dad."

"That'd be cool," Bailey agrees. "Won't be the first time a pop and rock star collaborated."

"Exactly." Kendall's phone goes off, and when she looks at it, she smiles.

"Declan?" Bailey pushes, clearly on a mission. Her wife, Cynthia, nudges her, but she ignores her.

"No." Kendall types out a message, then looks up. "I've started seeing someone. He's an attorney here in New York. It's not serious or anything, but I really like him."

That's what she always says...until she finds something wrong with him and dumps his ass. It's why Declan won't speak up. He's afraid he won't be able to hold on to her. From the outside, Kendall looks like the perfect pop star. She's beautiful and sweet, but underneath, there's something imperfect, something that eats away at her. Nobody goes through men like one changes their underwear unless they have a hidden insecurity. The problem is, until she deals with it, she'll keep doing what she's been doing for years.

"Does that mean you're sticking around for a while?" her mom asks.

"Yep. I was actually meaning to tell you. I've rented a place near the studio. Since everyone is here, and Layla is about to give birth to my niece, I should be here too."

"That makes me so happy," Sophia tells her daughter even though you can see it in her features that she won't believe it until she sees it.

After we finish eating, we play a few baby games, and then Layla opens her presents. I watch as she oohs and aahs over every outfit and item she unwraps, imagining what it will be like one day when I'm pregnant.

My thoughts go to Braxton and how amazing things have been lately. He meant what he said about wooing me. We've been going on dates almost daily, but since the night at the club—when he got me off with his damn thigh— we haven't taken it any further than that. He picks me up and drops me off like a gentleman, and while we're out, we talk and get to know each other all over again. I've already known I love Braxton, but with every day we spend together, I find myself falling for him all over again.

As if he can sense me thinking about him, my phone pings with a text from him: **So I was thinking...What would you think about going away, just the two of us, this weekend?**

Butterflies attack my belly, knowing what he's asking—implying. And he's leaving it up to me.

Braxton: Nothing has to happen...

I love that he's added that, that he made the decision for us to focus on us and has stuck to it. It's been a month, and not once has he had a drink or smoked. We haven't fought at all, and while I know it won't always be perfect, it's been nice getting to know each other all over again without the drama. We've talked about the past, about his mom and dad, and we've agreed to put it all behind us. This is our fresh start, and even though we'll always have history, we don't want it to taint our future.

Braxton: Kaylee...did I fuck up?

Shit! I never messaged him back, lost in my thoughts.

Me: You didn't mess up. I would love to go away with you, and it's the perfect time since I won't want to go anywhere after Layla has the baby...at least for a little bit.

I don't mention anything about his *nothing has to happen* comment. There's nothing to say. If it happens, then it happens—and really, I think at this point, if it does, then it's okay.

Braxton: Pick you up at 8:00. Pack light and a bikini.

"What's got you smiling like a crazy person?" Layla asks, nudging me.
"More like who...Braxton."
"Well, duh, but what did he say?"
"We're going away for a couple of days, so you'll get your house to yourself."
Layla rolls her eyes. "You know I don't care about you being there, but good for you."

"ARE YOU SERIOUS RIGHT NOW?" I SQUEAL, RUNNING OVER TO THE MOTORCYCLE PARKED IN THE DRIVEWAY. "I haven't been on one since..."

My eyes meet Braxton's, and he smiles. "Good. You don't belong on the back of any man's ride but mine."

He takes my bag from me and stuffs it into the saddlebag, then hands me a small helmet. He gets on and then helps me as I wrap my body around his. Once we're situated, and my arms are wrapped tight around his torso, he takes off down the drive and onto the road, going slow until we're out of the Blackwood's community. Since they live just outside of the city, it doesn't take long to get on the main road and away from the crazy traffic. The second I see the sign, I know exactly where we're going: The Hamptons.

The ride there takes a couple of hours, but it flies by. The wind is too loud to talk, but we don't need to speak to enjoy each other's company. While he drives, I cuddle up against his back, my hands finding their place under his shirt and resting on his muscular stomach. Every once in a while, he finds my thigh and squeezes.

When we pull up to the gorgeous beach house, I notice it's not the Blackwood's, which makes sense since Easton and Sophia use theirs a lot during the summer.

Braxton grabs our bags, and I follow him up to the house. He types in a code on the door, and then we enter. The house is as beautiful on the inside as the outside, decorated with a nautical theme in various shades of blues and whites. I immediately spot the pool and hot tub outside and know we'll be spending a good amount of time out there. With it being close to fall, this will probably be our last trip where we'll be able to hit the pool and beach. Soon, it will be cold as hell, and instead of a bikini, I'll be stuck sporting my snow jacket and UGGs.

After exploring the house, we settle in the master bedroom and quickly change into our bathing suits. Braxton is wearing a pair of board shorts that hang off his hips in that delicious way that only guys with sexy abs can pull off.

I packed a couple of suits but go with the risqué one since we're alone. Braxton's gaze goes straight to me when I walk out of the bathroom in a light pink bikini with cherries peppered all over the fabric, but it's when I turn around, and he sees the way the bottoms curve between my cheeks, leaving nothing to the imagination, that I hear the sharp intake of breath.

"Tell me you don't wear this fucking thing in public," he murmurs, his voice husky. The heat from his body radiates against me from behind, his hands roaming my exposed flesh.

"It's my tanning suit," I admit. Every woman has one...the one that gives us the least number of tan lines, but we'd never wear it while walking around—unless we're alone and want to turn our boyfriends on, that is.

"Fuck, Crazy," he mutters. His mouth lands on my naked shoulder, biting down playfully. His tongue darts out to soothe it while his hand reaches my ass cheek, taking a handful and squeezing it. "How are we supposed to take shit slow when you wear shit like this?"

"I think we've taken things slow enough." I reach behind and cup his cock through his board shorts. "I'm ready to speed this up a bit."

He dusts my hair to the side and trails open-mouthed kisses up my neck until he gets to the tie in the back holding my top on. With a kiss, I feel him tug, and the material falls away. My breasts hit the cold air, and a shiver scatters through my body, causing my nipples to instantly harden.

"Your tits are so perfect," he says, his hands coming around and cupping both of them. I glance up, just now realizing there's a mirror on the back of the door, giving us the full view of what he's doing to me.

As his thumb and middle finger pinch and pluck my nipples, I take us in through the mirror. His inked to my not, his hard body to my soft. Without heels on, he towers over me by almost a foot, something I've always loved because it makes me feel safe and protected in his arms.

His heated gaze meets mine, and I squirm in my spot, wanting nothing more than for him to take away the ache that's now throbbing between my legs.

"Are you ready to go swimming?" he asks, stopping his ministrations and tying my top back on.

"I'm ready for you to fuck me," I say, not caring how crass I sound.

He chuckles softly. "Not yet." He twists me around, so our fronts are flush against each other. "Once I'm inside you, I won't want to leave."

"I'm completely okay with that," I breathe, fully aware of how desperate I sound. But really, can you blame me? It's been a long-ass time, and my vibrator has got nothing on this man.

"Soon." He brushes his lips against mine, then bites down on my bottom lip, sucking it into his mouth before he lets go. "It's a beautiful day and probably one of the last before the cold weather moves in. Let's enjoy it." He kisses the tip of my nose and then takes my hand, guiding us downstairs and out the back.

Braxton hooks his phone up to the dock, and a second later, music is playing around us. He's right, it is beautiful outside, and as much as I want to be holed up in bed with him, I love spending time with him. We head straight for the pool, both of us diving underneath and immersing ourselves in the water. It feels good, the perfect temperature.

When I'm swimming from the deep end to the shallow end, Braxton hooks his arm around me and pulls me into him, his mouth connecting with mine in a passionate kiss. My legs encircle his waist, clinging to his muscular torso like a jellyfish, and for several minutes, we make out, our tongues dancing and our bodies grinding against one another. It feels good to just be with him.

When we both come up for air, he pushes the wet strands of my hair out of my eyes.

"Hey, beautiful," he murmurs with a smile. I love seeing him happy, alcohol and drug free. His hazel eyes are bright and filled with love. He hasn't said the words since we've been back together, but I can feel them in everything he does and every look he gives me.

"Hey back." I run my fingers through his messy, wet hair. "This is nice... being away. Between planning the baby shower and my new job, it's been kind of crazy lately." Good crazy, but still crazy.

"No matter how busy life gets, we'll make time like this." He kisses the corner of my mouth. "How was the baby shower?"

"It was good. That little girl is going to be so spoiled. I can't wait to give her all the lovin'."

Braxton chuckles. "Do you still want three kids? Two boys and a girl, so they have each other and will be protective of their little sister?"

My heart swells that he still remembers what I said even after all these years.

"Yeah, three kids would be perfect. What about you? How many do you want?"

"I want whatever you'll give me," he says, wading us through the water until my back hits the wall.

"So what if I wanted seven?" I joke.

"Then we better get to it." He winks. "But seriously, though, I'd be good with however many you want. I agree having two or three would be perfect, so they never feel alone. I always had the guys, but it would've been nice to have someone in my house I could talk to and get into trouble with." He hits me with a gorgeous smirk that has me tightening my legs around him.

"Speaking of which...How's Gage?" Ever since they returned home from the tour, he's been acting weird. We've always been close. Even during the years I didn't see them, we would keep in touch, but every time I text him, he gives me one-word answers, which has me worried.

Braxton frowns. "He met someone..."

"What? Who?"

"We don't really know much. A few days after we got home, she showed up and hasn't left. They're usually in his room, only coming out to eat, and sometimes they go for walks, I think. I've seen them hanging out on his balcony a lot. She doesn't really talk much, but she seems nice. Kind of...sad, though. I feel like there's a story there, but we're trying to give him his space. It's the first woman he's hung out with since..."

"Yeah," I breathe, my heart clenching at the thought of Tori. She was one of my best friends, and her death...fuck, it was just so tragic. "Is he still using?"

"I'm not really sure. He's been so wrapped up in her that he's rarely around. I can't imagine him not smoking, but if he's doing anything harder, it hasn't been in front of us."

"Kendall's dating some new guy...A lawyer."

Braxton shakes his head. "Poor Dec."

"It's his own fault for not telling her how he feels. He should've learned from Camden not to do that."

"True." He presses his mouth to mine. "I knew the moment you kissed me all those years ago that you were the one for me."

"And do you still feel that way?" I ask, knowing the question shows my insecurities, but in my defense, we haven't talked about our future, aside from fighting for each other—and now, when we were talking about babies...

"I do," he says without hesitation. "I know what it feels like to be with you, and without you, and I know you're the one for me." Pinning me to the wall with his body, he brings his hand up and cups my face. "I love you, and any future I see has you in it."

I can't help the smile that splits across my face at his words. "I love you too, and I feel the same way."

Braxton's lips glide against mine, and I sigh into him, feeling like I'm finally content for the first time in a long time.

Twenty-Six

BRAXTON

"You're going to get it," I warn, wiping my face and swimming toward her. We've spent the past two days between the pool, the beach, and the bed. We have to leave tonight so she's back for work tomorrow, but she wanted to spend the afternoon at the beach one last time before we go.

"I'm sorry!" She laughs, obviously full of shit.

While we were lounging under the cabana on a large beach blanket, I fell asleep and woke up completely covered in sand. She thought she was funny, but I had the last laugh when I grabbed her and carried her out to the water, throwing her ass in it.

"You're not, but you will be," I taunt, pouncing on her. She tries to swim away, but she's not fast enough, and before she can escape, I grab her and lift her into my arms.

"Brax, please. I really am sorry." She's laughing so hard her words come out in a breathy gasp. I fucking love it. The melodic sound. All I want is to listen to her laughter every day. See her smile. Her face light up. I can't get enough of it...of her.

"Nope. You should've thought about what you were doing." When I get to an area where I can stand, I haul her over my shoulder, smacking her ass as I walk us out of the ocean and back over to where our blanket and cabana are, dropping her onto the ground once we're there.

Holding her so she can't run, I lie on my back and haul her on top of me, kissing her lips while I shove her bikini bottoms off her, leaving her completely bare.

"What are you doing?" She gasps when I grip the backs of her thighs and haul her up until her legs are on either side of my face, hovering over me and giving me the perfect glimpse at her pink lips and swollen clit.

"Doling out your punishment. Now sit on my face."

We're on a private beach and haven't seen more than a handful of people walk by in the two days we've been here, so I'm not too concerned about getting caught. Besides, if someone does walk by, nobody will know it's me anyway since her pussy is covering my face.

"You want me to...?"

"Sit." I pull her down so her pussy is almost suffocating me and inhale deeply, loving the scent of her arousal mixed with the ocean.

When I start to lick her, she's shy at first, but then her hands come down, her fingers separating her lips, so I have better access. As I suck her clit, she rocks back and forth gently, working in tune with my tongue. And then, her fingers delve into my hair, and she uses her grip to grind herself against my mouth, finding her pleasure. She comes long and hard all over my tongue, moaning through her release as her juices flow into my mouth and down my face.

"Fuck, baby, you taste so good." I give her pussy an open-mouthed kiss, and she trembles around me, coming down from her orgasm.

She lifts up, and I'm not sure where she's going—maybe to clean off, maybe to ride my dick, I don't know—but I'm not done with her yet. So grabbing her hips, I flip her around so she's back on my face, only this time, her hands land on my thighs, as if she's on all fours, giving me a different view of her pussy and now ass.

"Braxton," she breathes, ready to argue that she already came, but before she can finish her sentence, my mouth is back on her pussy, licking her juices. She shocks the hell out of me when she once again starts riding my face, this time bouncing up and down while I fuck her with my tongue. She moves forward and back, and when she moves forward again, my tongue slides to her puckered hole to give it some attention.

"Oh, shit!" she screams. "Do it again."

This time, I thrust my tongue into the tight hole, making her moan. "Yes! Yes, that feels so good. More, please," she begs. "I want it in my ass."

She sure as hell doesn't have to tell me twice. I haven't been with her in over a month, so I'll take her any way she'll let me have her.

"Flip back over," I demand, slapping her ass a couple of times.

She does as I say, her legs coming back around to straddle my face. My finger swipes at her juices from behind, and I push it into her asshole, making her moan in pleasure. Her hands go to her tits, plucking and pinching her nipples, while I eat her pussy and finger-fuck her ass. Her moans get louder, her body jerking up and down, and then I feel it. Her pussy tightens and then releases, and she gushes, motherfucking gushes all over my goddamn face.

"Oh, fuck!" she screams, her head tilting back in ecstasy as she rides out another orgasm.

When she looks down and sees the mess she's caused, her eyes go wide, her cheeks tingeing pink as she scrambles off my face.

"Nope, don't you get embarrassed." I grab her hips so she can't go far. "That was the hottest thing I've ever seen in my life."

She drags her bottom lip between her teeth, and I grab her nape to pull her down for a kiss. I expect her to be disgusted by her orgasm all over my face, but instead, she moans, deepening the kiss. Since she's already in position, I reach down and pull my dick out, then thrust up into her sensitive pussy.

She moans into my mouth, taking every inch as I try like hell not to nut too soon. It's been too long, and she feels too good. I could stay right here in her for the rest of my life.

"Fuck me, please," she begs, so I do. I fuck her deep and fast. I would love for her to come again, but she's already come twice, and I'm not sure if I can pull off a third. But still, I try. I rock into her, my piercing hitting her walls in the way I know she loves, and minutes later, she's gripping me like a vise, coming for the third time, and this time, she drags me along with her.

When we've both come down, she opens her eyes and sighs, wearing a sated smile on her beautiful face. "I think we should say 'fuck the world' and move here. You can give me orgasms all day while we lie out by the pool and beach."

She drops down next to me and cuddles into my side, and even though she's only joking, a part of me wishes we could do just that. Because right here, with Kaylee in my arms, is all I fucking need.

The thought both excites and scares the shit out of me because the last time I lost her, I lost a big piece of my heart. And while I'm now older and stronger, my heart a bit tougher, when it comes to Kaylee, I'm still weak as fuck. I have no doubt if she walked away again, a huge part of my heart would go with her. And I'm not sure if there'd be enough left for it to function properly.

"What's going through that head of yours?" she asks, running her nails down my torso. She stops where my newest tattoo is—the one I got of the roses and thorns to symbolize our love—and gently brushes her fingers along it, tracing the outline of the roses.

"That I'm not sure I can handle losing you again," I admit truthfully.

Her fingers still, and she props herself up so she can look into my eyes. "You'll never have to worry about that. I love you, Brax. You're my forever, and nobody is going to come between us again."

Bailey: Pictures leaked of you and Kaylee on the beach.

I read the text, my mind going straight to her sitting on my face earlier and quickly hit call.

"What pictures?"

Bailey laughs. "Hello to you too."

Bailey, Camden's sister and our social media guru at Blackwood, handles everything for the band, monitoring what gets posted and making sure nothing pops up that can cause us to be seen in a bad light. Image is everything in our business, and with social media being so huge, it's easy for a simple picture to be taken out of context.

"What pictures?" If there are any of Kaylee naked, I will kill whoever invaded our privacy—even if it's my fault for dropping my guard so I could give her several orgasms on the beach under our cabana.

"You guys at a restaurant in The Hamptons..."

I release a breath of relief. "Oh."

"You've been spotted, so don't be surprised if you're accosted anywhere you go."

"We're about to leave, so it's all good."

"The paps are speculating, saying with two out of four band members with hearts in their eyes, this might be the band's undoing."

"They're fucking dumbasses." I scoff.

"True, but we should probably put out some kind of press release. I'm going to talk to the PR department and see what they think."

"All right, well, let me know. We'll be home tonight, and Kaylee will be at work tomorrow morning."

"Sounds good."

We hang up, and I'm about to join Kaylee in the shower when my phone pings with an incoming email to my personal account from Adam Cohen, my half brother.

I click on the email and read it once, then again, unsure how I feel about it. I'm reading it for a third time when Kaylee comes up and wraps her arms around me from behind.

"Whatcha doing?" she asks, kissing the side of my neck. "I thought for sure you'd have joined me in the shower."

"I was planning to, but then I got a text from Bailey saying that pictures were taken of us." She stills, and I know she's thinking what I thought. "Of us having dinner." She sighs in relief.

"People are talking shit, saying the band's going to split up because two of us are in relationships."

"Like what your dad was afraid of."

I pull her around so she's draped across my lap. "My dad was wrong."

"Have you spoken to him?"

"No, I've been avoiding him, and before you try to shoulder the blame, it's not because I found out he guilted you into pushing me away. He lied about my mom, and I'm not sure how I feel about that."

Kaylee nods. "I get that. But maybe you two should talk. Throw it all out on the table. He's still your dad."

"Yeah." I scrub my hand over the side of my face. "I also got an email from Adam."

"Your half brother?"

"Yeah, he's going to college in New York and would like to meet up to get to know me."

"And how do you feel about that?"

"I'm not sure." I stare down at the email. "Just yesterday, we were talking about wishing we weren't only kids so we would have siblings to connect with. Now I have one who wants to get to know me. On the one hand, it's not his fault, but on the other..."

"He's part of the person who hurt you."

"Yeah."

"Well, you don't have to do anything now. If he's here for college, he'll be around for a good four years."

"True. If I wanted to meet him, would you go with me?"

"Of course." She frames my face and kisses me. "We're in this together, Brax."

"STOP FIDGETING."

"I'm not fidgeting. Chicks fidget."

"Then I guess you're a chick because you're totally fidgeting." Kaylee grabs my hand and entwines our fingers, bringing them to her lips. She softly kisses my knuckles, and I instantly calm. I shouldn't be this nervous to meet a stranger. I mean, I meet fans every day. I take pictures with them, sign shit during the meet and greets while on tour, and converse with them. But this is different. Because this stranger is my flesh and blood.

"Hey, sorry I'm late," Adam says, stepping up to the table. "My class got out, and I had to ask the professor a quick question, which turned into a twenty-minute conversation, and then I took the wrong train and....Fuck, transportation is nothing like in LA. I mean—"

"Breathe," Kaylee says, smiling at Adam. "It's all good. We only just got here. Please, sit."

Adam does as she says and takes a deep breath. "Sorry, when I'm nervous, I ramble."

"That's okay. Braxton fidgets like a chick."

She winks at me, reminding me why I love her so damn much.

"I'm Adam," he says, extending his hand toward her.

"I'm Kaylee. It's nice to meet you."

He smiles warmly at her, then has a seat and glances at me, his features turning nervous. I take a moment to look at him, to see if we look alike, but aside from both of us having hazel eyes, nothing would prove we're siblings without a DNA test.

"So Adam," Kaylee begins, breaking the awkward silence. "What are you majoring in?"

"Umm..." He clears his throat, his eyes darting over to me. "Well...music. But please know me reaching out has nothing to do with that. I'm not like trying to start a band or anything. I'm double majoring in music therapy and education, so it really has nothing to do with what you do.

"I wanted to meet you because, up until recently, I didn't know who you were. I knew I had a brother out there, but Mom wouldn't say who you were. I mean, I knew your name, heard the whispers, even though she thinks she hid it from us, but not your last name. And shit, I'm totally rambling again." He sighs, sounding utterly defeated. "If you don't want to get to know me, I'll completely understand. I just thought since I was here and you're here...I have two sisters, but they're a pain in my ass. Well, I guess technically, they're your sisters too. They're cool, but I've always wanted a brother..."

"Breathe," Kaylee says again with a soft laugh.

"Sorry." He winces.

The server walks over and takes our drink orders, and then disappears. We're in a semi-private room at a bistro Kaylee loves. If I decide to pursue a relationship with Adam, I'll choose who knows and when. I'm not leaving that shit up to the damn media.

"You have nothing to be sorry about," I say, finally speaking. "Music therapy sounds awesome. When I was in school, music was cut out due to lack of funding, and it sucked. We actually donate to quite a few charities that work with schools who use music as therapy.

"As for Denise, I'm not ready to discuss her. I'm not sure I'll ever be ready. I know she's your mom, so if that's an issue for you, I get it. I'm here because, like you mentioned, we're brothers, and until I saw you guys in Miami, I had no idea you existed, but now that I know, since you're eighteen and living near me, if you want to pursue a relationship, I'm open to it."

Adam nods in understanding. "For the record, she used to tell my dad how much she missed you and—"

I put my hand up, halting whatever it is he's about to say. I can't go there. I just fucking can't. He doesn't get it because he was raised by two parents, and neither of them walked away. "I appreciate you trying to make shit right, and I get you wanting to defend her, but she walked away when I was a kid, *by choice,* and I'm not sure if I can ever forgive her. If you'd like to get to know each other, I'm down. But it needs to be separate from anything you have with her."

"I understand. And I do." After a beat of awkward silence, he asks, "So where do we go from here?"

I squeeze Kaylee's hand because fuck if I know where the hell we go from here.

"You guys can text, call, hang out, get to know each other," Kaylee says, saving me. "It doesn't have to be overnight. Just take it day by day." She glances at me. "Sometimes, taking it slow is the best way."

Twenty-Seven

BRAXTON

Dad: Tell me this isn't real...<insert link>

Bailey: Call me ASAP

Camden: You met your brother?

Adam: Please call me...

I CLICK ON THE LINK MY DAD SENT AND FIND SEVERAL PICTURES OF KAYLEE, ADAM, AND ME AT LUNCH. Based on the location of the pictures, somebody working at the bistro must've taken them and sent them to the media. And based on the in-depth article, they did their research and aired all our dirty laundry. It's been a couple of weeks since we met up, so it must've taken them that long to put all the pieces together.

"What's wrong?" Kaylee asks, walking out of the en suite bathroom wrapped in a towel.

"The entire world knows about Adam...and my mom."

Her brows kiss her forehead. "Adam...?"

"No, I don't think so. Looks like one of the servers must've snapped a couple of pictures."

"I'm sorry." She walks over and steps between my legs. "Is there anything we can do?"

"Nah, I gotta call Bailey. Also, my dad saw..."

"Shit."

"Yeah, but honestly, he has no room to say anything, not after all the lies he's told. I'm still pissed at him. My mom might've walked away, but he had a hand in it."

"Which is why you need to talk to him."

"I will." I stand and rest my hands on her hips. "Later. Today is apartment hunting day. Unless I can convince you to just move in here..."

"Not happening." She pecks my lips. "I have no desire to live in this bachelor pad." I open my mouth to argue, but before I can speak, she adds, "And we agreed to take it slow. Moving in together is *not* taking it slow. Besides"—she cups my face with her soft hands—"I need to do this on my own. I've never been independent. I've either lived with my parents, or in a dorm, or with Layla, or had roommates...I want a place to call my own."

I already know this since we've had this conversation before, and I get it, but you can't blame me for trying one last time. Waking up every morning with Kaylee in my bed, in my arms, is the best damn way to wake up, and we both know, even if she gets her own place, there's no way I'm sleeping without her.

But I also get that she needs to do this for herself. Because if she moves in with me, she's not proving that she can do it on her own, and if we get a place together, it's taking a huge step forward in our relationship. So for now, I'm going to let her do what she needs to do, support her independence, and in time, if I have it my way, enough of my shit will be there that she'll realize I'm not going anywhere.

"All right, Crazy"—I smack her peach of an ass—"get dressed and let's go find you the perfect place to live."

While she gets dressed, I call Adam to let him know I'm aware of the situation. We've been talking and texting almost daily, getting to know each other, and we have a lot in common. He even asked me for help with a project he's working on in music appreciation, and I was able to help him.

"What do we do?" he asks.

"That's up to you. I can make an official statement, sweep it under the rug, or deny the claim." When he goes quiet, I say something I never thought I'd say, "You're my brother, and I don't want to hide you. If you're okay with it, I'd like to make a statement that we're brothers. Generally, once the rumors are put to rest, the media calms down, but it will mean you'll be in the spotlight. People who recognize you will ask questions. This will affect you more than it will me, so if you want me to deny it, I'm okay with that. It won't change anything between us."

While I'm waiting for him to respond, Kaylee comes out dressed, wearing a knowing smile. Her ass heard everything I said.

"If you're okay with it, I am too. I mean, I don't want you to think I'm trying to—"

"Stop," I say, cutting him off. Too many times, he's mentioned not wanting to take advantage or use me. I practically had to beg the kid to let me help him with his homework. Sure, there's a chance he has a hidden agenda, but if I thought that about everyone, I'd drive myself insane. "It's all good. Just don't be surprised if you get people trying to talk to you who normally wouldn't."

"What are you saying? I'm not cool enough without my famous big bro?"

"Uh…"

"I'm kidding, man," he says with a laugh. "I know I'm plenty cool without you."

I snort out a laugh. "Yeah, okay, cool guy. I gotta go. Kaylee is making me go apartment hunting with her but won't let me move in." I jokingly glare her way, and she rolls her eyes.

Adam laughs. "Good luck with that."

We hang up, and I call Bailey next, letting her know how we're going to move forward. She tells me she'll speak to our in-house PR team and type up something for me to post.

Since the paps have been acting like fools lately, I have Justin join us. We spend the morning checking out several apartments in Kaylee's price range. When I see the places she can afford to rent based on her salary, it damn near kills me not to beg her to let me help her, but I keep my mouth shut—while I text Easton and tell him he needs to give my woman a fucking raise, even if he needs to take it out of my earnings.

Easton: What's wrong?

Me: Kaylee's looking for a place to rent. It's all shit, and she won't let me help.

Easton: Give me a few minutes.

I was only joking, but hell, I'm not going to stop him if he can make something happen.

"What do you think about this one?" Kaylee asks, standing in the kitchen of the fifth, maybe sixth place we've seen. The place is small, everything is outdated, and it smells like fucking mothballs.

"It only matters what you think."

She frowns, hating that answer, but in my defense, I'm not going to lie to her, and there's nothing I can do to help.

"I'm going to look around." While she does that, my phone goes off again.

Easton: Who's the real estate agent?

I give him the info, and he gives me a thumbs-up—if he weren't my boss, I'd send him a middle finger. Everyone knows you don't thumbs-up people unless you want to piss them off.

Kaylee is checking out the kitchen for the fourth time—I'd bet trying to convince herself it's not as bad of a shithole as it is—when the real estate agent says, "I actually found another place that's in your price range. It just became available."

"Oh, really?" Kaylee asks, hopeful.

"Yeah, let's go check it out."

As we're walking out, Easton sends me another text: **It's been handled.**

I don't know what he means by that, but ten minutes later, when we walk into a luxury apartment building, complete with a guard on duty, I figure it out.

We step inside the place, and it's not big—two bedrooms, two and a half baths, with a kitchen, living room, dining room, and a nice-size loft upstairs that can be used as an office—but everything is up to date with hardwood floors, stainless-steel appliances, and a balcony where you can put a couple of chairs and a table and enjoy the view.

"Are you sure this is in my price range?" Kaylee asks, sounding unsure. I don't blame her, especially not after seeing the places we've seen all morning.

"It is. The owner bought it as a write-off and just wants to get it rented."

While they talk, I text Easton: **What did you do?**

Easton: Do you really want to know?

No, I don't. Because if I know, I'm an accomplice, but if I know nothing, then I can honestly say I have no idea.

Me: Nope.

Easton: Didn't think so.

After Kaylee asks a dozen times if the real estate agent is sure the rent is what it is, and the real estate agent assures her it is, Kaylee has no choice but to say she wants it. There's no way in hell she's going to find anything half as nice as this place on her budget. I don't know if Easton owns this place, knows someone who knows someone, or if he paid the difference, but I'm thankful as fuck to him because with my hands tied, I couldn't do shit, and the thought of her living in some of those places had me considering kidnapping her ass and locking her in my bedroom so I'd know she's safe.

Me: Thank you.

Easton: Don't know what you're talking about ;)

"She said I can move in any time," Kaylee says with a huge smile on her face. "And the price is locked in for the entire year lease." She twirls around, grinning from ear to ear in excitement. "I can't believe this place is all mine."

I should probably feel guilty about whatever strings Easton pulled, but as I watch her face light up in pure happiness and pride, knowing she'll be safe, I don't give a shit. Kaylee is mine to take care of. She can have her independence, but she's still *mine*.

"HE'S CALLING AGAIN?"

"Every day."

"Brax, please answer him. If you don't want to talk to him, fine, but tell him that. Stop ignoring him."

I sigh, staring at the phone, knowing Kaylee is right.

"Dad."

"Braxton, finally. What the hell is going on? You're claiming that kid as your brother, and you won't return my damn calls—"

"He is my brother," I say, getting out of bed and walking away from Kaylee, who's lying there. We were in the middle of searching for furniture for her place since she's moving in this weekend. She wants to be out before Layla gives birth so the Blackwoods have their home to themselves.

"I ran into Denise. She has a husband and three kids."

"I'm well aware." Of course, he knew and never said a word to me.

"She had some things to say about you, about what happened when you guys split up."

"Braxton, let me explain."

"Explain what, Dad? That you lied to me about how shit went down? That you cheated on her with the fucking nanny and then took me away, filing for divorce and refusing to give her any custody?"

"She didn't want us! She chose her career over us. I gave up everything for that bitch, and I knew she was cheating. That piece of shit she's married to... She was cheating with him. It was all over the gossip rags. She wouldn't admit it, but I knew she was."

"Or maybe you let yourself believe it because you resented the fact that she was making more money than you."

"She didn't even fight for you," he says, switching gears.

"And you put her in that position."

We both go quiet, and I wonder if we'll be able to get past this. If I can forgive him for what he did. I thought I could talk to him about this, but I realize I'm too bitter to have this conversation.

"Look, Dad, I need some time."

"For what?"

"To deal with all this. You're saying one thing, and she's saying another..."

"And who the fuck has been there for you all these years? Who's had your back? Not her!"

"I know, but I just need some time."

"Fine," he says harshly. "I see you're back together with Kaylee..."

"Dad," I groan, not wanting to do this with him.

"Just remember when she fucks you over the same way your mom did to me that I warned you. Don't do anything stupid, Braxton. I've seen the rumors about the band breaking up. You've worked too hard to—"

"Dad, enough. I said I need time. I'll talk to you soon."

We hang up, and I head back inside the condo, where I find Kaylee right where I left her—lying in bed and searching for furniture.

"How'd it go?" she asks, genuinely concerned. She has every right to hate my dad after what he did when we were younger, but she puts it aside because he's my dad.

"His story doesn't match hers."

"Most breakup stories don't."

"True. I told him I need some time." I shrug, and Kaylee nods in understanding, not needing me to say anything more.

"Wait until you see the couch I picked out," she says, changing the subject. "It's so big, it's practically a bed."

"Good." I pull her into my arms, tossing her phone to the side. "That will make it easier when I'm fucking you on it because you know damn well we'll spend the first week at your place christening every inch of it."

Just as our mouths are connecting, my phone goes off. I quickly check it, seeing a text from Bailey: **You're keeping PR busy LOL**

Attached is a picture of Kaylee and me standing outside an apartment complex with the real estate agent with the caption: **With the lead singer recently married and about to have a baby, and the guitarist (see image) settling down, we have to wonder what this means for Raging Chaos's future. What are your thoughts? Comment below...**

Kaylee looks over my shoulder and sighs, shaking her head. "They're vultures."

"It's how they make a living," I say, refusing to let that shit get to me. "The bigger you get, the more they feel entitled to know, and the higher you get, the more they want to see you fall."

"Yesterday when I was coming out of work, they practically attacked me with questions."

I whip my head to the side. "What? Why didn't you say anything?" It's one thing to have pictures taken, but for them to go after her. Fuck no.

"I honestly forgot. I got stuck on the train, and then we met Declan for dinner. It slipped my mind."

"What did they do? Say?"

"They were just asking questions about us, but now, seeing that photo, it makes sense. I had to set all my social media stuff to private because women started sending me messages threatening me." She shrugs like it's no big deal when it's a damn big deal. "Apparently, they don't like that the notorious playboy Braxton Lutz is off the market." She rolls her eyes playfully, not taking it seriously.

"From now on, until I hire a guard for you, Justin goes where you go."

"What?" she gasps. "Why? I can handle some nosy-ass paps."

"You don't get it because you haven't seen it, but they can be crazy. Especially the fans. For the most part, when we're in New York, they leave us alone, but since shit is new, they're out for dirt. I'm not taking any chances." She opens her mouth to argue, but I keep going. "Even Layla has a guard, so I don't want to hear it."

"Only because they're married, and she has a kid."

"Because Camden wants to make sure they're safe, and I'm going to do the same. Shit will calm down, but for now, Justin goes with you when you go out."

"And what about you?"

"I'm fine. I'm here or at the studio for the most part, and I'm usually with one of the other guys who has security with them anyway."

I can tell she's about to continue arguing, but I give her a look that says I'm dead serious about this, and she sighs, knowing I'm not going to bend. She wants to be independent? Great. But I will *not* risk her safety, ever.

Twenty-Eight

KAYLEE

"THIS PLACE IS AMAZING!" LAYLA WADDLES HER CUTE BEHIND THROUGH MY NEWLY FURNISHED apartment, checking it out. It's been nearly a month since I signed the lease, and I've used the spare time I'm not working to decorate and furnish it. I love it, and for the first time, it's mine. All freaking mine.

The only downfall is that Braxton isn't living here. Because I was stubborn. I had it in my head that I needed to do it myself, and after giving me a little bit of shit, he respected that. But now I'm regretting it. I've quickly realized a home, a *real* home, is the place filled with the people you love. It's not about the dwelling, but who's inside it.

It hit me last night. Since the day I moved in, Braxton's spent every night with me, having dinner together at the dining room table, watching our nightly show we're currently bingeing while making out, showering in my shower, and sleeping in my bed, wrapped around me. Then last night, he had to fly to California for a business meeting for a couple of days that Camden asked him to handle since Layla is about to pop any day, and my home felt empty. And that's when I realized that I don't care about being independent and proving myself—about saying the place is mine—because without the person I love here, it means nothing.

"I'm going to ask Braxton to move in with me," I blurt out to Layla, who's checking out the gorgeous state-of-the-art kitchen.

"Yeah?" She glances back at me.

"Yeah. It might be too soon—"

"Stop." She walks over and presses her hands to my shoulders. "We only get one life. How we spend it is up to us. It doesn't matter what you choose to do as long as you're doing what makes you happy." Her voice cracks, and I know she's speaking from experience. "You deserve to be happy, Kaylee. Fuck anyone who thinks or says otherwise."

I hug her tightly—albeit a bit awkwardly since her big belly is in the way. "Thank you for being my best friend," I choke out.

"Always." She pulls back. "Now, what do you say we go out tonight? I know Braxton is gone for the night. Camden's at home with Felix, and Bailey, Cynthia, and Kendall are all on board. I can't drink obviously, but with me due soon, I want one night with my besties before things get crazy."

"Before you're a mom of two." I grin because despite her sounding like her life is about to be over, I know she's excited...just nervous.

"I'm a little scared," she admits, just as I thought. "The last time..."

"Camden is not *him*," I say, referring to her ex-husband.

"I know, but what if having a kid changes Camden?"

"That's not going to happen. What that asshole did and how he behaved is not normal. And you know better than to compare them to each other. Camden is amazing with Felix. He treats him like he's his own son. And he loves you more than I've seen any man love someone. You're just super pregnant and even more hormonal. You're right. We need to go out. You need yourself a virgin something and to relax because your life is damn near as perfect as it gets, and you're just having a moment. One that will pass."

"You're right," she says. And then, as if her husband can sense her struggle, her phone goes off. It's a text from Camden, with a video of him and Felix dancing to a new song. They're both laughing while they bust a move. And when it's over, they both look at the screen and tell Layla that they love her.

By the time the video cuts off, Layla is in tears. "God, I love them so much."

"And they love you. Camden is going to be an amazing dad to this little girl, just like he is to Felix, so take a deep breath, stop thinking the worst, and let's go out and have one last drink before you become a family of four."

"LET ME SMELL IT."

"What?" I crack up.

"Just a little sniff..." I pass the lemon drop shot under Layla's nose, and she inhales deeply. "God, I'm not even a drinker, but it smells sooo good."

Kendall laughs. "Just close your eyes and pretend you can drink."

Layla does as she says, taking another whiff. "When I'm back to myself, we're totally having a real girls' night, one I can properly participate in."

Kendall, Bailey, Cynthia, and I down our shots at the same time as our server arrives with another round. Thanks to Kendall's status, we were able to get into Lush and are partying VIP style. We have our own server, a private dance floor, and bottle service. Our bodyguards are standing in the corner, chatting quietly, watching us in case of anything, but it feels good to be somewhere the media can't document our every move. After the pictures came out about Braxton having a half brother and then us apartment hunting, the paparazzi have been relentless, hell-bent on getting the scoop on the status of Raging Chaos.

Around this time is when they usually announce a teaser for their next album and their upcoming tour dates since they go on sale months and sometimes a year ahead of time, but for the first time, they've been quiet. Braxton goes to the studio during the day to hang out with Declan and write, and I know they've been messing around with some possible songs, but Camden's been focused on Layla, and Gage has been MIA. I've seen the woman he's been hanging out with a couple of times, and she seems sweet and very pretty but, like Braxton mentioned, kind of sad looking. Gage won't willingly bring her around to hang out, but she doesn't look to be held against her will, so we're all just giving Gage some space since he doesn't look to be doing any hard drugs for the first time in years. Braxton has said they have no concrete plans to record at this time, and he seems to be completely okay with that.

"Oh, I love this song! Let's dance!" Kendall yells when "I Don't Mind" by Usher comes on.

"You down?" I ask Layla.

"Hell yes! Maybe I'll dance Marianna right out of me."

We all stop in our places, and Layla's eyes go wide. They weren't giving the name until the baby comes, but she totally just gave it away.

"Marianna?" Kendall asks.

"Yeah." Layla nods, giving her a watery smile. "We wanted to include Maria in her name..."

"Oh." Bailey sighs, her hand going to her chest over her heart. "It's so beautiful."

Maria was the Blackwoods' nanny when they were growing up. She was especially close with Camden, and when she passed away last year, he was absolutely devastated.

"It's perfect, Layles. What's her middle name?"

"Hope. It's not after anyone. We just thought it was pretty.'

"Marianna Hope Blackwood," I say. "It's beautiful."

"It is," Kendall agrees. "Now, let's get our dancing on."

We spend the next several songs dancing and drinking, only stopping once Layla announces that her feet can't handle another second standing.

"Guess I didn't dance her out." Layla pouts jokingly, rubbing her belly.

"Nope, but she'll be here soon enough." I give her a kiss on the cheek. "Love ya, girlie."

"Love you more."

After saying goodbye to everyone with the promise we'll do brunch soon, I get in the SUV with Justin.

"Here you go, Miss Thomas." Justin reaches back and hands me a bottle of water.

"Thank you." I sigh, grateful. It's nearly one in the morning, and between the dancing and drinking, I'm exhausted and sweaty and dying of thirst.

I twist the cap and down half the bottle in one gulp, take a deep breath, then drink the rest, already feeling slightly more hydrated.

My phone goes off with a text from Braxton asking how it's going. I had sent him a few pictures of us drinking and dancing, and he messaged me back that he wished he were dancing with me.

Me: Heading home. Miss you.

Braxton: Miss you more.

Me: My bed will be lonely without you...

Braxton: I'll be back in it tomorrow night.

Me: I was thinking...

Braxton: About?

Me: You moving in with me...

Braxton: Are you drunk?

I laugh and am about to type back that I'm nowhere near drunk, but as I try to find the right letters, my vision goes a bit fuzzy, and I wonder if maybe I am drunker than I thought. Regardless, I came to the conclusion that I wanted him to move in with me before I had any drinks. However, now that I'm thinking about it, it's probably for the best if we talk face-to-face and not through text messages after I have been drinking.

"Miss Thomas, we're here," Justin announces, pulling into the garage that's connected to my building.

He opens the door for me, and when I try to grab the handle as support, I stumble forward, almost doing a face-plant into the concrete before Justin catches me.

"Thank you," I say, my words coming out a bit slurred. "My alcohol must be catching up with me."

"It's okay," he says. "I'm going to walk you up to your place."

"Oh, it's okay, I can..." But before I finish my sentence, I trip over my heels, and Justin grabs my arms to stabilize me.

"I've got you," he says.

Since I don't want to die, and I'm clearly drunker than I thought, I let him help me up to my apartment. We're coming in from the garage, so we head straight into the elevator. Justin has a key for emergencies, and he uses it, pressing the correct number for my floor.

As the elevator ascends, my body seems to heat, and my limbs begin to tingle. I find my phone in my clutch, where I dropped it, and send a message to Braxton.

Me: I miss yu

Braxton: You already said that, Crazy.

Me: Yeh but I realllllyyyyy mis yu

Braxton: You okay, baby?

Me: I want u send me a pic

While I wait for him to respond, the elevator doors open, and Justin helps me out and down the hall to my place. As we walk, it feels as though the floor is bouncy, making it hard to take each step.

"Is it hot in here?" I ask when he unlocks the door for me, and we walk inside.

"Not really."

"I'm so...hot." My body is on fire, my heart pounding behind my rib cage. "Maybe I just need to get naked. Thank you for bringing me home." I drop my clutch on the table and then stumble to my room, lifting my dress over my head as I go. Next, my bra and panties come off and finally, my heels. I'm so warm and my body buzzing. I can't decide if I want to take a shower or go to bed.

Needing to cool down, I turn the shower water on. But before I make it in, a masculine voice comes from behind. "I think you should go straight to bed."

I twirl around—at least in my head, I do—but since my body isn't cooperating, it's more like a stumble. I'm not sure why Justin's still here, but my head is too fuzzy to give it much thought.

Justin enters the bathroom and reaches around me to turn off the water. When his arm rubs against my front, the material brushes against my nipple, and it hits me...I'm naked in the bathroom with Justin.

"I think you need to go," I say, glancing around for my robe. As my eyes scan the bathroom, everything goes blurry. My legs feel like Jell-O, and it's hard to focus. I think Justin says something, but I can't concentrate enough to make it out. My skin is scorching hot, and I just want to get cold. It's hard to catch my breath. I need to call Braxton. Something is wrong. Very wrong.

I hear more words being said, but it now sounds like I'm underwater. How is that possible? My apartment is on the eleventh floor.

And then I'm lifted. *Oh, thank God. I didn't want to drown.* Someone is carrying me. I try to open my eyes to see who it is, but the room is spinning.

I'm hot and drowning and floating all at the same time.

I'm set on something soft.

More words.

I can't hear anything, though.

And then a warm breath is on me. "It's okay, Kaylee. Just close your eyes, and everything will be okay."

Braxton? Is that Braxton? I don't think it is. He's across the country still...I think. But maybe he came home.

I try to call his name, tell him I'm feeling funny, but the words...they just won't come out.

Twenty-Nine

BRAXTON

Bailey: Call me ASAP.

Bailey: There's no way this is real.

Camden: Call me.

Declan: As soon as you land, call me. Don't do anything stupid.

Easton: Call me.

Layla: I know Kaylee, and she wouldn't do this. I'm going over to see her now.

I STARE AT THE ONSLAUGHT OF TEXTS THAT HIT MY PHONE THE SECOND I TURNED IT BACK ON. NORMALLY, when we need to go somewhere, we take the Blackwood jet, which means we have cell service, but since the meeting was scheduled at the last minute, the jet was already being used, so I had to fly commercial, and my phone has been off for the past four hours.

When Kaylee never texted me back last night, I assumed she drank a bit too much and passed out. Since Justin was with her, I knew she was safe—which was confirmed when he texted me that she arrived safely at her apartment. But now, as I read the texts in utter confusion, my stomach roils in fear of what could've happened while I was without service. Clearly, something happened with Kaylee, but what? What the fuck could've happened from the time Justin made sure she got home to now? It's only been six damn hours. None of this makes any sense.

Ignoring everyone's texts, I call Kaylee first, but her phone goes straight to voicemail. I try again and again, but each time, it doesn't even ring, telling me it's either turned off or dead.

With my phone blowing up with notifications from social media, I click on one of them, which takes me to Justin's Instagram page—where I've been tagged in one of many comments.

@BraxtonLutz fuck that bitch is the first one I see. Maybe it's the jet lag, but I'm not sure what the hell is going on until my eyes move to the pictures in the post.

And then the comments and texts make sense...*perfect* fucking sense.

Because right there in front of me are several pictures of Kaylee and Justin in her bed.

She's naked.

He's without his damn shirt on.

Kissing her neck.

Grabbing her tit.

Her head is thrown back.

Eyes closed.

I swipe through them until I get to the end, and then I swipe back, refusing to believe what I see. My initial thought is déjà motherfucking vu. But then I remember she never cheated back then. It was all a lie to push me away, to get me to go to LA. So what the fuck is going on now?

I swipe through them again and again, analyzing each picture. His lips on her neck, his hand covering her nipple.

Why the fuck is my bodyguard touching my woman's nipple?

I swear to God when I get ahold of him, I'm going to break his hand, along with every single fucking finger that touched my woman.

My woman. She's mine. She told me so over and over again. We were supposed to be fighting for each other. *And this is how she fights?*

No, fuck that. She wouldn't do this to me. She wouldn't hurt me like this. I know Kaylee. She loves me. And Justin...why the hell would he fuck my woman and then post that shit for all the world to see? It makes no goddamn sense. He's about to lose his job. He'll never work in security again. That's if I don't kill him first.

I try to think back to the past several months. They've never shown a single sign of liking each other like that. Sure, they get along, but Kaylee gets along with everyone. But to jump in bed with each other?

She was drunk last night, but he sure as fuck wasn't. And I don't believe for a second she would ever be drunk enough to cheat on me.

But fuck, the proof is right in front of me. I want to trust her and believe this is all somehow a fucked-up misunderstanding.

But. His. Hand. Is. On her motherfucking tit.

His goddamn mouth is touching her flesh.

His body is pressed up against hers.

And fuck! I can see the fluffy body pillow she sleeps with at night.

Unable to look at the photos any longer, I close out the app and have my driver take me straight to Kaylee's apartment. I considered going to Justin's, but the pictures were taken at her place, so he's either there with her still—in which case that motherfucker is dead—or she's there alone, and I want to hear from her what happened. I want her to look me in the eyes and tell me why the hell she's in photos with another man touching her when she's mine.

I'm using another guard from the security company we have on retainer. If he's heard anything, he doesn't say a word, just drives me to where I need to go. When we arrive, I tell him to stay here, and he simply nods.

I get up to Kaylee's apartment and use the key she gave me to get in—expecting the worst but hoping for the best—although I'm not sure exactly what the best is.

The place is quiet, *too quiet*, and as I walk through the apartment, checking each room—living room, kitchen, bathroom—I'm holding my breath, praying she's alone. That the images were a figment of my imagination. That I'm jet-lagged and seeing shit, and everyone has lost their damn mind.

Like the wuss I am, I save the master bedroom for last. The door is closed, so I slowly turn the knob and open it. A part of me is expecting Justin to be in here, in her bed, tangled up in her sheets with her. His hand still on her tit, his face nuzzled into the crook of her neck—my favorite position to sleep with her.

But when I finally get the courage to look at the bed, she's sleeping alone. The blanket covers her bottom half and shows her bare body from the waist up.

I check her bathroom just to be sure, but it's empty—no sign of another man having been here. I open the app up again, just in case I was seeing shit, but the pictures are still there. Comments are multiplying, and I'm being tagged left and right. I wasn't seeing shit. They're still there for all the world to see.

I close out of the app again and stop at the edge of the bed, watching her for a few minutes sleeping, her chest rising and falling. She never removed her makeup from last night, and it's created dark circles under her eyes. Her blond tresses are a mess, fanned out across her pillow, and her beautiful plump lips are slightly parted.

My phone is going off in my pocket, but I ignore it, focusing my attention on the woman I love more than life itself. I try to convince myself that the images were a joke even though I know damn well she would never think that's funny. Photos, just like those, tore us apart once before, and there's no way she would pose for those photos, let alone allow someone to post them as a joke.

As I sit and watch her sleep, I wonder why I'm so calm after seeing those photos. I should be freaking the fuck out, yelling and screaming, going after both of them. But I'm not, and I know why. Because deep down, I know, *fucking know*, my woman wouldn't betray me, which means someone else has—Justin being my main suspect—and once I get to the bottom of this shit, once she tells me what happened, I'm going to act accordingly. But I won't freak out yet because the last time I did that and took off for LA, I lost Kaylee—and I'll be damned if I'm going to let history repeat itself.

Maybe this makes me a pussy, or maybe it makes me a dumbass, but I just can't find it in me to believe she cheated on me. I know what the pictures look like, but I also know her, and until I hear her say the words, I'm not going to believe she cheated.

"Brax," she croaks, her voice tiny and rough. Her lids are hooded, and her eyes are bloodshot. "You're..." She glances around, then drags her body up—either not noticing or remembering or caring that she's naked—leaving her soft breasts on display. "I...don't feel good."

She clambers off the bed, and I jump to help her, but before either of us can do anything, she vomits all over the hardwood floor. And when she's done, she does it again and again. I kneel next to her, holding back her hair while she gags and sobs between throwing up. The smell is rancid as fuck, but something is wrong with her, so I block it out.

Once she seems to be done, she tries to stand, but her legs are shaky. She's barely on her feet before she collapses back onto the ground.

"Let's get you to the shower," I offer, picking her up and carrying her to the bathroom—ignoring the fact that she's not just naked from her waist up but completely naked. Like without a single piece of clothing on her body.

In response, she snuggles into my chest, her eyes closing. Not giving a shit about my clothes or phone or anything, I turn the shower on warm and step inside, sitting on the bench with her laid out across my lap and in my arms. I wash her the best I can while she stays where she is, not saying a word, not moving or helping at all. As I wipe her face and wash her hair, her eyes remain closed. I want to demand answers, but I first need to make sure she's cleaned up and is okay.

"Kaylee, can you stand?" I ask, needing her to get on her feet so I can clean the rest of her.

Her eyes flutter open, meeting mine, and her gray orbs appear lifeless. "I think so," she whispers softly.

I gently set her on her feet, not letting go, and she uses the wall to hold herself up. I wash the rest of her body and rinse out her hair while looking for any signs she had sex—hickeys, bruises, I don't fucking know. I'm confused as hell and have no idea what I'm doing, so I turn off the water. Grabbing two towels, I quickly strip out of my wet clothes and secure a towel around my waist, then use the other one to dry her off and wrap her up.

When we get back to her room, it smells like vomit, so I quickly set her on the bed and slip into some clothes I have here, then help her get dressed. She's barely moving, reacting, and in my gut, I know something is very wrong. She either did what those pictures implied or something worse happened—and at this point, I'm not sure what I'm hoping for.

When she's in a T-shirt and sweats, I carry her out to the living room to get away from that smell and lay her on the couch. I grab her blanket and tuck it around her, then prop a pillow up under her head.

Figuring she's in pain and probably dehydrated, I snag a cold water bottle from the fridge and two pain pills from the cabinet. After she's taken them and drunk half the bottle of water, I sit across from her so we can talk.

"I know you're not feeling well, but I need you to tell me what happened last night."

Her brows knit together in confusion, so I pull out my phone—thankfully, it's waterproof—and click on the post, turning it to face her. She stares at each of the photos while I swipe from picture to picture until I get to the last one.

"Can you tell me what happened?"

A single tear wells in her eye, then skates down her cheek, and my stomach tightens in anticipation.

"Kaylee...You didn't sleep with Justin, right? There's a reason you're naked in bed with him and he's touching you."

More tears fall down her face, and then finally, she speaks, and I almost wish she wouldn't have. "I...think..." Her face scrunches up in agony, and she bites her bottom lip hard as if the words hurt too much to come out, and I know whatever she says is going to kill me. "I think I did...sleep with him."

And just like that, my entire world is blown apart for the second time by this woman.

"You had sex with him?" I choke out, needing a verbal confirmation.

"I think so."

"What do you mean, you think so?" I ask, staying calm even though I want to lash out. My blood is boiling beneath my skin, and my heart is racing behind my rib cage. I have so many thoughts running through my head, and the only reason I can think as to why I'm not freaking out is because I'm numb.

"I didn't think I drank a lot, but I must've," she says, making no fucking sense. "I thought I was alone, and then he was there. I...I think I wanted to take a shower. I was naked, and he helped me to my bed." She swallows thickly, and a fresh wave of tears fills her lids and falls over. She drops her chin to her chest and shakes her head. "I don't really remember," she whispers, refusing to look at me. "I think he kissed me...maybe. I'm so sorry. I wish I could tell you more, but I don't remember. I must've drunk more than I thought, but I swear..." She glances up at me, her eyes rimmed red in devastation. "I wouldn't cheat on you, and I wouldn't let someone take my picture. I don't know what happened, but..." She chokes on a sob and covers her face. "I'm so sorry."

We sit in silence—her crying and me trying to figure out what the fuck happened—and finally, after several minutes, I come to a conclusion. She didn't do this. She *wouldn't* do this. I don't care how drunk she was. And since she doesn't remember—and yes, I believe she really doesn't fucking remember—I'm going to need to get my answers from the only other person who would know anything, who has absolutely no reason not to remember.

"I need to go talk to Justin," I tell her gently, making her eyes pop open in shock. "Will you be okay here while I'm gone?" Layla had said she was coming over, but she never showed up. I don't want to leave Kaylee, but I need answers, and I'm not going to get them here. There are pictures all over the goddamn internet that make it look like my girlfriend cheated on me, and I need to know what the hell happened.

Kaylee nods, and I lean forward, kissing her forehead. "I'm going to find out what happened," I promise. Before I go, I find her dead phone and put it to charge near her on the couch, then help her get situated, so she's lying down. She's still crying softly, and I hate that. Fucking hate it. "I'll be back soon," I tell her, then head out, locking up behind me.

Thirty

BRAXTON

 find a text from her: **My freaking water broke! Camden is driving me to the hospital. I can't get ahold of Kaylee. Please call me! I know she wouldn't do this.**

I press call, and she picks up on the first ring. "Have you seen her?"

"Yeah, I just left her apartment. She was sleeping, and when she woke up, she threw up everywhere." Speaking of which, I need to call someone to clean that shit up because there's no way I'm touching it.

"Is she okay?" The worry in her tone is evident.

"Yeah, I helped her shower and gave her some pain pills. Layla...did she drink a lot last night?" I ask, flinching when the question comes out sounding accusatory.

"What? Why? She didn't do this, Brax. She loves you so much! She was just saying she wants to live with you. None of this makes any sense."

"I know, I know, but she said she doesn't remember what happened, so I'm just trying to piece it all together. I'm going to find Justin."

"I mean, yeah, she drank. So did Kendall, Bailey, and Cynthia. But when we said goodbye, she wasn't obliterated. She was walking and talking and laughing. She wouldn't cheat on you. Something is wrong."

"I agree."

"Please call me once you know anything and tell Kaylee to call me. Her phone is off..."

I hear Camden in the background grumbling about her needing to focus on giving birth, so I quickly agree to keep her updated and wish them both luck, promising to come by the hospital as soon as the baby is born.

When I get to Justin's apartment, I knock on his door, half expecting him not to answer. With the images flitting through my head of him kissing her neck and grabbing her tit, the calm I forced myself to have with Kaylee gets thrown out the window the second Justin opens the door, his guilty as fuck eyes meeting mine.

My fist hits his jaw so hard, he flies sideways, his head bouncing against the wall. "What the fuck did you do?" I bark, grabbing him by the front of his shirt and dragging him backward until his ass hits his couch. I don't wait for him to answer, though, instead decking him in the face again. This time, blood spurts from his mouth, and he groans, not even trying to block me.

"What happened?"

He licks the blood on his lip, his gaze meeting mine. "What do you think happened?" he says dryly. "We fucked."

"Wrong fucking answer." I hit him again and again, and when I'm about to hit him a third time, he stumbles off the couch to get away. "Let's try this again. And this time, tell the truth. What the fuck happened last night?"

He stares at me for several seconds, and just when I think I'm going to have to punch him again, he speaks. "I already told you. We fucked. If you don't want to believe me, that's on you."

"So you're telling me that while I was paying you to keep Kaylee safe, you let her get drunk, then you brought her home and fucked her?" I stalk toward him, shoving him up against the wall. "She says she doesn't remember shit! Are you telling me you raped her?" I grab his throat and bang the back of his head against the wall, wanting to kill him but knowing I can't.

When he doesn't answer me right away, I tighten my grip on him, slowly cutting off his airway. "Answer me."

"No, no, fuck, no! I didn't rape her," he chokes out as I tighten my grip.

"You're saying she consented? The woman who woke up this morning throwing up everywhere and swearing she can't remember shit. You're saying she agreed to fuck you?" I don't believe it for a fucking second, but I want to hear it from him. Something is off, and I'm going to get answers. "Because if she didn't consent, it's rape, and I'll use every dollar I have to make sure you're put away."

"Nothing happened!" he yells. "I didn't touch her."

"Bullshit! I saw the pictures." I slam his head back. "And I'll use them to prove you raped her."

"We didn't have sex. Nothing happened, I swear! I just made it look like it did. I drugged her so she would let me, and once she was pliable, I took pictures to make it look like we were together. I swear, I didn't rape her. Nothing happened."

I step back, and he sucks in a sharp breath, thinking I'm letting him go. Just as he releases his breath, I punch him straight in the face. Blood flies from his nostrils, and a cracking sound indicates I broke his nose. He cries out in pain, trying to get away, but I'm not done with him, not even close.

Dragging him to a chair, I throw him into it, so I'm standing over him. "Why the fuck would you want it to look like you and my woman had sex?"

Blood's pouring down his face, and his eye and mouth are both swelling up. He closes his eyes and shakes his head as if trying to decide what to say.

"If you even think about lying, I'm going to add a broken jaw to your nose."

He sighs, his eyes opening back up. "My brother is sick, and his meds are expensive. They were covered by insurance until my mom lost her job and her insurance. He needed them, and they didn't want to tell me. Without them, he got really sick and ended up in the hospital. They would make sure he's comfortable, but in order to treat him, they needed to move him to a different hospital...a private one. You have to pay up front or have insurance.

"I tried to get him insurance, but because he has a preexisting condition, they make you wait six months before covering anything. I didn't know what to do. And then..." He swallows thickly. "Your dad came to me."

Motherfucker.

"What did he do?"

"He said he'd pay me to seduce Kaylee, but the problem was I couldn't do it because she's so in love with you. I told him that, but he wouldn't take no for an answer. So I drugged her and took pictures so it would look like she cheated. But I swear, nothing happened. I sent them to him, and he told me once I posted them, he would wire me the money."

He has the decency to at least look like he feels bad for what he's done, but that doesn't make it all right.

"How much?" I ask. "How much was destroying Kaylee's reputation and our relationship worth?"

"Two million."

I laugh humorlessly. "That's it? If you would've come to me, I would've given you double that just for being honest."

I step back, done with this piece of shit. "I'll speak to Kaylee and find out if she wants to press charges. Hopefully, you have some money left over if she does because I meant what I said before. I'll spend every dime of my money to drag your ass through the mud, and guess what? I have way fucking more than your measly two mil."

Without waiting for him to respond, I turn my back on him and walk out the door. When I get downstairs, Paul is waiting for me.

"Where to, boss?" he asks, opening the back door for me.

"To my dad's office."

Forty minutes later—thanks to the city's fucked traffic—we arrive at Lutz, Burger, and Goldstein, the firm my dad is a partner at. Once again, I have Paul wait in the SUV since this won't take long. Unlike the beating I gave Justin, I would never hit my dad—even if he deserves it.

His secretary isn't at her desk, so I walk straight back to his office, not bothering to knock before entering. Of course, once I open the door, I find his secretary with her face between his legs, sucking his dick.

"Real nice, *Dad*," I say, making him jump. "Next time, try locking the door."

The woman's head pops up, looking like she's young enough to be my sister, and scrambles to her feet, righting her dress and attempting to wipe the smeared lipstick off her lips.

"We need to talk."

Dad tucks his dick back in his pants and zips them up. "Jewel, please hold my calls."

She nods, scurrying out and closing the door behind her. Once we're alone, my dad stands and walks over to me as if to hug me, but before he gets close enough, I raise my hand.

"I'm going to ask you something, and I suggest you not lie about it."

His brow furrows in confusion, and if I didn't already know what I know, I would believe he genuinely has no idea why I'm here.

"Did you have anything to do with the pictures posted of Kaylee and Justin?"

He must realize that I already know because, unlike Justin, who tried to follow through with the lie, he nods. "I did. I asked him to seduce her, but only because I was afraid she wasn't loyal, and based on those pictures, I was right."

"You were right?" I bark out a humorless laugh. "You were right? I guess the man you paid two million to didn't explain what happened?" I cross my arms over my chest and shake my head. "He didn't seduce my girlfriend. He drugged her."

Dad's eyes go wide in shock. "No, I...What are you talking about? Is that what she's saying? That's her excuse for cheating on you? That she was drugged?"

"That's not her excuse." I drop my hands and stalk toward him, shoving him against the wall behind him. "It's what happened. Justin was desperate. He needed the money to pay his brother's medical bills, but I bet you already knew that, didn't you? It's why you targeted him. Why you thought it would be easy. Dangle a couple of million in front of his face, and he'd fuck my girlfriend, proving she's like Denise."

I slam my hand against the wall next to his face, wanting so fucking badly to punch him but knowing it's not worth it. Because if I do, I'm sinking to his level. No, I'm going to say what I need to say and then walk out the door. "He couldn't figure out a way to get in her pants while she was sober because she's fucking loyal, so he drugged her. Then after she was naked, he staged it to look like they fucked, posted the pictures, and collected his money."

Realizing he's been had, he scrunches his face up, and it turns red in anger. "That's not what was supposed to happen!"

"I'm sure." I step back. "I hope it was worth it. Paying two million and in exchange you lost your son."

His brows hit his forehead. "Braxton...Son, I did this for you. I didn't know—"

"You didn't do this for me. You did it for you. Just like you did all those years ago. You're so determined to prove that all women are deceitful like Denise that you're willing to fuck over your own son in the process. I loved Kaylee, I still love her, and by trying to break us up to prove your point both times, you not only hurt her, but you also hurt me."

I slam my fist into my chest. "It sucks you chose Denise over some job, and she let you down. It *sucks* that you guys had different visions of what life should look like, and in the end, it tore you guys apart. It *fucking sucks* that you felt betrayed and were hurt by her actions. Although, now, I know you weren't the completely innocent bystander you led me to believe all these years."

I shrug, done with this shit, done with him. Just. Fucking. Done. "But you are not me, and not every woman is *her*. And if you truly loved me, you wouldn't be trying to manipulate me. You wouldn't be trying to take the one person who makes me happy away. And you sure as hell wouldn't be okay with putting her in danger."

"Braxton, please. I fucked up. You have to understand—"

"I don't have to understand shit," I hiss. "You've lied to me, manipulated me, and fucked with me for the last time while using the excuse of having my best interests at heart. You and me..." I grab the knob and yank open the door. "We're done. And if you ever contact Kaylee or me, I'll run your ass right through the mud. I don't know the legal terms, but I'd bet paying and soliciting someone to seduce and fuck someone else, then paying them to post the pictures online is illegal. And even if I can't sue you, I'll tell everyone what you did until your name is so dirty, nobody will want to touch you or this law firm."

Without waiting for him to respond, because I don't give a fuck what he has to say, I walk out the door, slamming it behind me.

When I arrive at Kaylee's, she's still where I left her, wrapped in a blanket on the couch. She's passed out, and not even me opening the door and walking in wakes her. I want to go to her, pull her into my arms and hold her tight. What my dad did is unforgivable. Had Justin decided to take advantage, she could've been fucking raped. And my dad didn't give a shit. All he cared about was proving his point—that women can't be trusted and you should never put them first.

For years, I felt sorry for him, but now that I know the truth and have witnessed the shit he's pulled, I don't have it in me. He made his bed, and now he has to lie in it.

The longer I sit here, thinking about what he's done, the more worked up I get. I told him I would leave him alone as long as he left us alone, but when I click on Instagram and see all the posts about Kaylee, calling her names and accusing her of cheating, my blood boils, and I know I have to do something. Because if it's between my dad and Kaylee, I'm going to choose her every damn time.

Not wanting to leave her, I take my phone to the other room so I can make a call without waking her up. "Hey," Easton says, answering on the first ring. "How're you doing?"

"Not good, man. I don't want to leave Kaylee, so I'm going to conference the guys and tell everyone what happened at once."

I add Gage, Declan, and Bailey to the call—leaving Camden out since he's at the hospital with Layla—then start talking.

"She didn't do it, what everyone is saying. She was set up." I explain everything, from the deal my dad made to Justin drugging her and staging the pictures so he could get his money, and once I'm done, the guys are damn near as pissed as I am.

"Are we taking legal action?" Gage growls.

"I want to, but I don't think taking this to court, dragging Kaylee through all that, will be worth it. I told my dad if he didn't leave us alone, I would destroy him, but..."

"But you're not going to let him get away with this, right?" Declan says. "We're going to do something. Kaylee could've been fucking raped! And what the fuck...Justin? His ass is never working in security again."

"I agree," I say. "I thought if he deleted them, it would go away, but it all blew up so fast, and the only way to clear Kaylee of what she's being accused of is to throw them under the bus."

"Then that's what we do," Bailey adds. "We publicly set the facts straight."

We're discussing the details when footsteps sound, and a second later, Kaylee appears in the doorway, looking like the most beautiful hot mess.

"Hey, guys, Kaylee just woke up. Let me call you back."

We hang up, and my eyes lock with Kaylee's. She doesn't move closer, just stands in the doorway. "You're here..."

"Of course I'm here. Where else would I be?"

"I just figured...since I..." She swallows thickly, and tears fill her eyes. "Since I had sex with Justin, you wouldn't want anything to do with me anymore."

"One, you didn't have sex with anyone," I tell her, walking over to the couch. "And two, there's nowhere I'd rather be than here with you." I pull her into my arms and settle her on my lap, needing to hold her.

Thirty-One

KAYLEE

I DIDN'T SLEEP WITH HIM.

I was set up.

Drugged.

Framed.

Pictures were staged.

I'm torn between being angry as hell, disgusted, and relieved. I knew Braxton's dad was shitty, but to take it to that level takes some serious balls. When Braxton finishes telling me everything, I settle on relief. The disgust and anger can wait. Right now, I'm just so damn relieved that I didn't cheat on Braxton. He's my entire world, the love of my life, my home. I don't know what I would do if something tore us apart again.

My phone goes off in the distance, and I have every intention of ignoring it until Braxton says, "You better get that. It might be Layla. She's in labor at the hospital."

"What?" I shriek, jumping up and running to my phone. Sure enough, there's a picture of a teary-eyed Layla holding the most beautiful baby in the world—after Felix, of course—in her arms with the caption: Please welcome Marianna Hope Blackwood. 7 lbs, 3 oz. 20 inches.

"She had the baby! We have to go." Instead of texting her back, I call her, hating that I'm not there.

"Hey," she says, sounding exhausted in the best way possible.

"I'm on my way. I'm so sorry—"

"Stop, it's okay. How are you? I was coming to check on you, and my water broke, but Braxton kept us updated, so I knew you were okay."

"Don't worry about me. How are you?"

"Of course I'm going to worry about you. You're my sister from another mister." I can hear her smile through the phone. "She came so fast. My water broke, and when we arrived and got settled, the doctor said she was ready. I was in shock since I was in labor with Felix for damn near two days."

"She was ready to meet her mommy and daddy and big brother. Has Felix met her yet?"

"He's on his way over with my mom."

"Should I wait to come over? I don't want to crowd you guys." With Felix, her ex left to go home and sleep because he said he needed a bed to sleep on, so I stayed with her until her mom arrived. But now she has Camden who, unlike her dumbass ex, is amazing and would never leave her or that baby's side.

"Kaylee, you're family. Get your ass over here."

We hang up, and I let Braxton know I'm going to take a shower. I took one earlier with him, but I want to take a real one to wash my hair properly and shave.

As I step under the hot water, flashes of last night come back to me—of Justin offering me a bottle of water, me feeling light-headed, then disoriented shortly after. Stumbling out of the SUV, him offering to help me up to my place...Him—

"Hey, what's wrong?" Braxton asks, stepping into the shower, still fully clothed. "Why are you crying?" I have no clue what he's talking about until my hand goes to my chest in shock from him appearing out of nowhere, and I realize I'm sobbing, my chest rising and falling in quick succession.

"Talk to me, baby. Are you hurt?"

"He drugged my water." Braxton tightens his hold on me. "He wasn't anywhere near me all night. But when I got in the SUV, he offered me a bottle of water. He's never done that before, and really, why would he keep bottles of water in there? I drank the entire bottle and that's when I started to feel weird. He helped me to my place, and I thought he was gone, but when I was about to get in the shower, he appeared, telling me I needed to go straight to bed."

I told Braxton some of this earlier this morning, but I was still out of it and unsure what happened. But now that my head is clear, I remember everything until I blacked out in the bed.

"He saw me naked," I cry. "Took pictures of me. What if he took more? What if there's ones of me completely naked?" I feel invaded. I know Braxton said we never had sex, but he still saw me...every part of me.

My eyes meet his, and I find them burning with intensity, his jaw clenched. "I'll handle it. I promise you. By the time I'm done with him and my dad, they'll wish they never fucked with us." He kisses me softly, tenderly. "Let's get you showered, so we can go meet the little Blackwood princess."

Once we're both showered and dressed, we head to the hospital, stopping at the store to pick up a couple of little gifts on the way. When we get up to the room, Declan is there, holding the baby, but everyone else is gone.

"Where is everyone?" I ask, giving Layla a kiss on her cheek.

"You actually just missed them. They went downstairs to get breakfast.

My mom and Felix are on their way. He insisted he make a card for the baby first, so she said they'll be a little while."

"Where's Gage?" Braxton asks Declan.

"He must've fallen back asleep after we got off the phone. I knocked, but he wouldn't answer. I'm sure he'll be by later."

"My turn!" I wiggle my fingers, indicating for Declan to hand the baby over. He rolls his eyes and steps toward me as the door swings open and in walks Kendall and—

"Oh, my God! Is that a ring on your finger?" Layla squeals, waking up Marianna, who starts to whimper. I glance at Kendall, who's sporting a massive shimmering diamond on her left hand.

"It is!" Kendall gushes. "We're engaged."

Camden's eyes go wide. Kendall has dated a lot of guys, but none of them, and I mean none of them, have managed to put a ring on her finger. She's been proposed to a handful of times, but every time she's said no, ending their relationship.

"Congratulations," Layla says, giving her a hug.

"Thanks. He literally proposed this morning. I wasn't going to say anything until later. I figured, with you having a baby and all, you wouldn't even notice."

"Not notice that ring?" Layla laughs. "You'd have to be blind not to notice that thing." She takes Kendall's hand and admires the ring. "It's beautiful."

"Thanks."

"Congrats," Camden says, giving his sister a hug. "Congrats, man." He shakes her fiancé's hand.

The baby whimpers again, and I glance over at Declan, who's quiet, staring down at the baby. Everyone—besides Kendall, who has no idea—knows how he feels about her, and now she's engaged.

"Hey, want me to hold the baby?" I ask quietly.

"Yeah." He clears his throat. "I should get going. Congrats, guys," he says to Layla and Camden, kissing her on the cheek and hugging him.

He walks toward the door, and I swear all of us—well, all of us who know how he feels about Kendall—are waiting with bated breath to see what happens next. He stops in front of Kendall, and she smiles, oblivious as hell. "Congratulations," he says, his gaze aimed at her fiancé. "You're a lucky man."

Then without another word, he walks out the door. I notice Kendall frowns slightly, but she doesn't comment on it. Instead, she walks over to see Marianna up close. "She's beautiful," Kendall coos, giving her a kiss on her head. "And she smells so good."

"Right?" I say with a laugh, having just smelled her myself. "Want to hold her?"

"Oh, yes." Kendall beams. "I can't wait to have a cute little bundle of joy."

"You're pregnant?" Camden asks, not even caring about blurting it out in front of everyone.

"What?" We all look over and see Sophia and Easton standing in the doorway. "You're pregnant?"

"What? No." Kendall laughs. "I just meant one day…" She side-eyes Camden, who just shrugs. "But there is something I need to tell you…" She hands the baby back to Layla and shows her mom her ring. "We're engaged!"

Sophia and Easton both blanche but quickly recover, congratulating their daughter and soon-to-be son-in-law.

A few minutes later, Layla's mom and Felix arrive, and I tell her we're going to get going so they can have some time with Felix. "Call me if you need anything," I tell her before we go.

Since neither of us has eaten, we stop at a deli and pick up some food and drinks, then go home. We spend the day lounging around the condo, watching movies, cuddling, and kissing. When it's dinnertime, we order in Thai and eat while we watch my favorite movie, *Save the Last Dance*. Braxton lets me know that Bailey handled the announcement that will destroy Justin's and Michael's reputations, but I stay off social media, not wanting to see anything being said about me.

Around ten o'clock, my eyes start to flutter closed, and Braxton says I need to go to bed, that I've had a long couple of days and need my sleep.

"You're staying, right?" I ask, which is stupid since he's been here every night, aside from when he had to fly to LA for that business meeting. But for some reason, I'm suddenly insecure even though he's given me no reason to be.

"Are you serious?" he asks. "I'm not leaving until you make me."

"And what if I said I didn't want you to ever leave?"

A small smile quirks at the tips of his lips. "Are you asking me to move in with you, Crazy?"

"I know I said I wanted to live on my own, that I needed to do this on my own, but…I love waking up and falling asleep with you."

He encircles his arms around me and kisses my forehead. "I never planned for you to live here long on your own anyway. You've been here for less than a month, and half my clothes are in the drawers."

I laugh at that because he isn't lying. Every time he comes over, he brings a bag full of his stuff. I knew what he was doing, but I didn't stop him because I love his stuff being here.

"We wasted too much time being apart." I snuggle into his side. "I don't care what's right or wrong, or if this is too fast. I just want to be with you every day." I wrap my arms around his neck and kiss his lips. "I want to love you and be loved by you."

"You have me, baby," he says, pecking my lips. "Forever."

"So is that a yes? Will you move in with me?"

"Damn right, I will," he says with a melodic laugh, tightening his arms around me. "I'm actually glad you asked because I had no intention of ever leaving anyway. At least now, I can say it was your idea."

He presses his mouth to mine again, this time harder. "Now, how about we head to bed? You're tired, and tomorrow, we have plans."

"We do?" Tomorrow is Sunday, and I don't recall making any plans.

"Yep. We're going to spend the day christening every inch of this place and making it ours. We have years to make up for, so you're going to need to be well-rested." He waggles his brows and lifts me into his arms, carrying me to bed...*to our bed.*

Once there, he reaches around my neck. I have no clue what he's doing until the necklace holding the infinity heart promise ring lifts off my chest.

"What are you doing?" I breathe.

"Something long overdue." He takes the ring off the chain and slides it onto my finger. "There," he says, kissing my finger and the ring. "It's back where it belongs."

He pulls me into his arms, where he holds me tight as I drift off to sleep, feeling safe and protected and loved. For the first time in a long time, I feel like I've finally found my home.

Epilogue

KAYLEE

THREE MONTHS LATER

"I CAN'T BELIEVE YOU BOUGHT THIS PLACE." I TWIRL IN A CIRCLE IN THE MIDDLE OF THE BEACH HOUSE IN The Hamptons, the same beach house where Braxton and I came to reconnect. It's right down the street from the beach house that Camden bought recently, so his family can vacation together since his parents have one nearby as well.

"I know how much you love it here," Braxton says, gripping the curves of my hips and tugging me toward him. "I tried to buy Easton and Sophia's since it's where I took your virginity..." He smirks, and I slap his chest playfully. "But he wasn't having it, so I figured this was the next best thing."

"I love it." I kiss him. "And I love you."

"Good. I'm glad you love me because I have a question for you, and I think you loving me will help tip the odds in my favor."

I bark out a laugh at that. "You already know I love you. What do you want?"

"To marry you." His words are so simple and said so softly that it takes me a second to wrap my head around them, and while I do that, he drops to one knee and pulls a ring box out of his pocket, popping it open.

"I've loved you for the past seven years, and I plan to love you for the rest of our lives. You're not only my girlfriend and my lover, but my best friend, and I would love it if you would become my fiancée, and soon...like, as soon as possible, my wife."

I can't help but laugh through my falling tears at his little declaration. We've spent the past three months falling in love all over again. It hasn't been easy, especially after the posts were made, throwing Justin and his dad to the wolves. People had things to say, not all of it nice, but we got through it together. Justin disappeared, his social media accounts deleted, and from what Braxton told me, his father was forced to resign from the firm where he was partner. His brother's been there and they've been growing their relationship, which is hard for Braxton because while he loves his brother, he still wants nothing to do with their mom. But he's taking it day by day...we both are.

The band has been on an unofficial hiatus since they returned, and no decisions have been made about when they'll be releasing their next album or scheduling their next tour. A lot has happened, but through it all, we've remained strong, united, and I love him more now than I did before. So as he looks at me, waiting for me to speak, there's really only one answer to give him.

"Yes. Yes, I'll marry you."

A beautiful smile splits his face, and he stands, pulling me into his arms and lifting me off the ground, kissing me hard and passionately. When he sets me down, he takes my left hand in his and slides the infinity promise ring off my finger, replacing it with the engagement ring. The platinum band has two encrusted infinity symbols intertwined around one another, framing the circle diamond on top.

Once the ring is safely on my finger, Braxton's mouth descends on mine, kissing me reverently, passionately, silently telling me how much he loves and wants me. He lifts me, my legs encircling his waist, and carries me to our bed—I never get sick of saying that—then he lays me on the center of the mattress.

Our mouths stay connected, kissing, caressing. Our tongues swirl and dance together. We only break apart long enough to shed our clothes, and then we're back to kissing, touching, feeling.

I love how Braxton tastes sweet with a hint of warmth. The way he smells fresh and masculine from the mixture of the cologne I bought him all those years ago and his own scent. I'm obsessed with the way he feels hard and smooth. But what I love the most is the way he fits perfectly with me. The way, as he spreads my legs and enters me, our bodies connect and align as if we were made for each other.

And I truly believe we were. Braxton is my soul mate, my other half. The yin to my yang, one-half of the infinity symbol in our forever. He makes love to me, devouring me, stroking me, working me up, up, up until I'm falling off the ledge and taking him with me.

When we've both come down from our high, he doesn't let me go clean up. He pulls me into his arms and holds me tightly, kissing me, massaging me, loving me. We stay like this for several minutes, reveling in the silence and the peace we bring each other.

"I don't want to wait," he says when he finally speaks. "Do you want a big wedding?" I know if I say yes, Braxton will ensure I have the wedding of my dreams, but the truth is, I have no desire for a huge wedding.

"Nope, I don't even care about a wedding. I just want to be yours as soon as possible."

He nods in agreement, his eyes sparkling in excitement. "Then it's settled. Tomorrow, we're applying for a marriage license, and as soon as we're allowed, we're saying I do."

Butterflies attack my belly at the thought that Braxton could be my husband by the end of the week. "That sounds perfect."

He rolls me onto my back and kisses me softly. "I can't wait to make you mine."

"I'm already yours...I've always been."

He kisses me again, this time harder, deeper, and that's all it takes for us to get lost in each other once again—in the beautiful, silent chaos of our love.

"I'M GOING TO POST A TOTALLY CLICHÉ PICTURE OF MY RING," I WARN BRAXTON AS WE WALK TO THE kitchen, both of us showered and somewhat dressed. Hours of sex have left us starving, so we agreed to eat before continuing our engagement celebration.

"Nothing cliché about telling the world you're going to be *legally* mine," he says with a laugh, playfully smacking my ass.

I grab my phone from the counter and am about to pull up the camera app when I notice several missed calls and texts. Something must've happened.

"Hey, Brax," I say, my heart in my stomach. "Did you get...?"

Before I can finish my question, a voice speaks from his phone. I don't know if it's a voicemail or what, until the woman says, "This is Evelyn from *Hollywood Gossip*..." And then I know he's watching or listening to something. "According to our sources, Gage Sharpe, the drummer for Raging Chaos, was brought in to New York Medical after he was found in his home unconscious. While we don't know the specifics, our—"

Braxton cuts off the video and dials someone, putting it on speakerphone. "Is he okay?" he asks, not giving whoever is on the other end a chance to even say hello.

"I don't know..." It's Declan. "They're not telling me anything, but it's not good, man. I think...I think he tried to kill himself."

Total Chaos

A LOVE & LYRICS NOVEL

Haven't touched a single drink all night
But I'm drunk as fuck
On your scent, on your touch
Hand it over, baby
And you'll never know what it's like to be without
love

- Declan, *Raging Chaos*

One

DECLAN

The bitch yapping on the screen is cut off by an incoming call from my mom. I hit ignore, but it immediately starts up again.

"Another, sir?" the bartender asks, nodding toward my empty glass.

"Yeah, and you can keep 'em coming," I tell him as my phone rings again. "As a matter of fact, if you could just bring me a bottle, that'd be great." Since the bar I'm drinking at is located in the building I live in, they have my card on file. Normally, I'd just drink in my apartment, but right now, it's empty and lonely, and I hate being there more than I have to be.

The bartender nods and grabs me a new bottle, opening and placing it on the bar top, along with a larger glass.

"If you need anything else, let me know," he says before he walks away to help someone at the other end of the bar.

My phone starts up again, and since she's clearly not going to stop until I answer, I hit accept and bring my phone up to my ear. "Yeah." I pour myself another double shot of Johnnie Walker Blue Label—my go-to—and throw it back.

"Hello? Who is this?"

"You called me, Mom," I say dryly.

"Declan, I wasn't sure if it was you. Is that how you answer the phone for everyone who calls? It's rather rude. I know you're in a band, but—" The word *band* comes out sounding like a curse word, and I sigh, already exhausted by this conversation.

"Mom—"

"What if it were someone important? A business—"

"Mom!" I bark, having zero fucking patience for her shit today.

"What in the world is wrong with you?" she asks, sounding as if I've offended her. "Have you lost all respect for your elders? I'm your mother, not one of your trashy friends. Don't—"

Fuck, I've had enough. "Is it an emergency?"

"Excuse me?"

"Your reason for calling incessantly. Is it an emergency? Because I'm really not in the mood to talk."

"Yes, it is, actually. Your father and I saw the news. That...*friend* of yours almost died, and they said your band is over. Why didn't you tell us?"

"Because one, you don't like my friends, so I didn't think you would give a shit that he almost died." Since the day I became friends with Camden and Braxton, who asked me to join their band—later, recruiting Gage—she and my dad have been negative as hell, trying everything in their power to get me to "stop messing around with the wrong crowd." It's been over ten years, and they still don't take my career seriously.

"And two," I add, "our band isn't over. We're taking a break, so if you're calling to gloat or whatever, save it."

I know I sound disrespectful as hell, and normally, I try a lot harder to be the son she and my father want me to be—the son I'll never fully be. Since I refuse to give up being part of the band, I make it a point to speak properly and dress nicely. I don't have any tattoos or piercings, but I do have long hair, which drives them insane—but in my defense, I had long hair before the band—so when I'm at home or at a function they've guilted me into attending, I make sure to wear it up and out of my face. But she's called me at the wrong time, at a moment when I just don't give a fuck about being nice or proper or respectful, especially to the woman who has done nothing but talk shit about the band since we started it over a decade ago.

"I don't know what's wrong with you, Declan, but I would appreciate it if you would not speak to me that way. I was simply calling to see how you're doing and talk to you about your future." And here we go..."You're only twenty-five years old, so it's not too late to go to college, and if you're in need of a job—"

I laugh. Fucking laugh. Because she's lost her damn mind. And if I don't laugh, I might snap at her because I don't have it in me to refrain from doing so.

"Mom, I am *never* going to work for you and Dad. I'm a musician, not a hotelier. I play the bass guitar and sing, and even if the band never produced another album, we're worth millions, so please fucking stop. I love you, but I can't deal with you today. Let's call this a loss and try again tomorrow. Goodbye."

Without waiting for her to respond, I pull the phone away from my ear and hit end on the call, throwing it onto the bar top, facedown. I pour another double shot and am bringing it up to my lips when a feminine voice, one I would recognize anywhere, says, "Drinking alone?"

"Got no one to drink with."

I swallow down my shot, set the glass on the bar top, and glance at the gorgeous woman occupying the seat next to me. Her naturally blond hair is pulled around to the side in a braid that would make most women look young and childish, but it looks sexy as fuck on her. With her hair swept up, leaving her face completely visible, the light makeup she's sporting makes her bright blue eyes pop and her lips look glossy and plump. She smiles softly at me while she removes her jacket, hanging it over her chair and revealing a long-sleeved white shirt that shows off the swells of her breasts, skintight jeans that, if she were to stand, would showcase her toned legs and ass, and those fluffy boots women always wear.

My gaze ascends back to her face, and I notice her eyes are a bit glassy and the area under her eyes a tad swollen, like she's been crying and did a good job of covering it up.

"You okay?"

Scrunching up her adorable button nose that, when she's not wearing makeup, houses a cluster of freckles, she waves me off while she grabs the bottle and pours herself a shot, slinging it back. "How's Gage?"

"Alive."

Her eyes flit over to me. "Because of you."

"No, he almost died because of me."

I reach for the bottle, but she pours the shot for me, then hands me the glass. "You saved his life, Dec." Her words are soft and matter of fact, but they don't change the guilt I feel about everything that went down.

"His life never should've needed saving in the first place." I down the shot and slam the glass on the table, glaring at her.

"It wasn't your fault," she insists.

"Yeah, it fucking was."

Two weeks ago

"I love this. It's sexy and sweet and so perfect." Kendall reads over the slight changes to the lyrics and music I made and grins, nodding in excitement. "This is it. It's going to be amazing."

"Yeah? You sure?"

"Definitely. There's no way my dad won't be all over this."

Her dad is the owner of Blackwood Records, the label both she and I are signed with. Kendall is a pop princess—think Taylor Swift meets Ariana Grande—and I'm the bass guitarist for the rock band, Raging Chaos—think Maroon 5 meets OneRepublic. We couldn't be any more different if we tried, but that's precisely what Kendall wants—to shake shit up a bit. And since the band is on a bit of a hiatus, with our lead singer—her brother—Camden and his wife, Layla, having a baby, I had some time on my hands, so I said, fuck it, why not? We had written a few songs together while we were messing around, so all we had to do was figure out which one would be the best and make it perfect. Then we could pitch it to her dad, Easton.

When we first discussed it, we were both on tour, so it got thrown on the back burner, but now that she's living in New York, she brought it back up, saying it would make the perfect single—and I agreed.

The truth is, even if I didn't agree, I'd still say okay because I can't say no to Kendall. I've been in love with the damn woman for as far back as I can remember—even though she has no clue—and would go along with whatever the hell she wanted.

"We should totally record it, so he can listen to it when we pitch it to him."

"Sounds good."

We spend the next hour singing our hearts out until we agree it's as good as it'll get without having the professionals produce it.

"I'm going to play this for him tomorrow." Her stomach rumbles, and she giggles, covering it with her hands. "We've been at this forever. I'm starved. Wanna grab some dinner?"

"You don't have plans?" I glance at the huge rock on her left-hand, trying to keep the bitterness and jealousy out of my words, but it's hard, so damn hard, *wanting a woman I can't have.*

"Kyle's working late." She forces a smile, and I want to ask if she's sure he's really the one, but I bite my tongue because it's not my place to ask. Because we're only friends. Because I've been friend-zoned.

"I'm not in the mood for being in the public eye tonight, but if you want to come over, I can cook us something."

She beams, and it takes everything in me not to beg her to dump the fool who'd rather spend his night at work than with the woman he's supposed to be in love with. "That sounds perfect."

Since it's late, we lock up the studio behind us and head out. Gage and I are renting an apartment just up the street, which was our goal when finding a place, but Kendall and I can't go anywhere on foot without security. So we jump into her waiting SUV, and her driver takes us to my place, leaving us at the elevator in the underground garage.

We're talking about the snowstorm that's supposed to be arriving in the next couple of days as we walk into my place. It's quiet, and I assume Gage is sleeping since I don't hear any of his loud music playing.

"I'm going to light the grill and see if Gage wants to join us. Want to pour us some wine?"

Kendall nods, and I hand her the bottle and opener, then search for Gage, hoping he'll agree. He's sunk low lately, and I'm worried about him.

I knock and, when he doesn't answer, crack the door open so I can check on him—

make sure he doesn't just have his headphones on and can't hear me. Sometimes, unless I force him to eat, he doesn't give a shit enough to feed himself.

He's lying on the bed, and I'm about to assume he's sleeping as I originally suspected, but then the light hits him in such a way that I do a double take. He's still, too fucking still. The worst feeling comes over me, and I rush over to him, my heart pounding in my chest.

"Gage. Gage!" I shake him, but he doesn't move. "Fuck! Kendall!" I yell. "Call for an ambulance."

Everything from that point on is a blur. The paramedics, ambulance, hospital, doctors, nurses. They manage to save him but make it clear it was a close call. Too close. Had Kendall not been hungry...had we not gotten to the apartment when we did...had I not checked on him...He'd be dead.

But she was, and we did, and I did, and he's alive...If you can call it that. Thankfully, there was no brain damage or long-lasting effects. He's been an addict since the summer after our senior year, and we've ignored it. We should've forced him to get help sooner, but he was functioning, and when we brought up him getting help, he shot us down. We didn't want to push him away, so we let it go until he almost died.

Now he's agreed to get help, so that's where he is...getting help.

And Braxton's living with his girlfriend, Kaylee.

And Camden's married with two kids.

And that leaves me here, alone. Well, not alone. Right now, Kendall's here with me...But later, she'll go home to her fiancé, and then I'll be alone again.

"What are you doing here anyway?"

Kendall's gaze shifts, and she pours another shot. "Same thing as you." She throws her drink back and shakes her head, wincing as the whiskey goes down. "Trying to drown my problems at the bottom of a bottle."

My eyes stay trained on her for several seconds, and when it's clear she isn't going to talk about whatever is wrong, I shrug because I know how she feels. The last thing I want to do tonight is talk. So instead of pushing the topic, I grab the bottle, pour us both a double shot, and raise my glass.

"To drowning our problems."

She clinks her glass against mine. "To forgetting the world exists."

We swallow back our drinks, and then I pour us another one. We do this a few more times before the bar music turns up—the game on the television has finished—and Kendall slides off the seat.

"Let's dance!" She's loud in the quiet bar, but since it's not too busy, only a few people glance over before minding their own business.

Nobody's dancing...There's not even a dance floor, but Kendall doesn't seem to care as she extends her hand and bats her long lashes at me, waiting for me to join her.

And that's exactly what I do...Song after song, we dance our drunken hearts out in the corner of the bar. Well, Kendall dances her drunken heart out while I watch her sway her luscious hips to the beat as she throws her head back, exposing her slim neck. The entire time she belts out the lyrics to each song like she's performing, I imagine what it would be like for her to be mine. To do more than dance with her. To be able to pull her closer, to kiss and touch her...

I'm lost in my fantasy, so I don't realize she's stopped dancing and is looking at me like she's waiting for me to say something.

"What?"

She cracks up laughing, and I join in, having no idea what we're laughing about but loving the sound of her laughter when she lets herself go.

"What?" I say again.

"I said, the bar is closing."

I glance around, and she's right. Everyone is gone, the music has been silenced, and the lights have been raised. "Well, shit..."

"I don't wanna go home yet," Kendall says. Stepping into my space, she wraps her hands around my neck. The smell of her perfume—Dolce & Gabbana Light Blue—mixed with the sweet scent of the whiskey on her breath sends my head into a tailspin.

"Let's take that bottle up to your place and continue drowning." She places a soft kiss on the corner of my mouth, and shivers, motherfucking shivers, race down my spine.

A throat clears in the distance, and I look over at the bartender, who's trying to silently convey he'd like to go home. His disruption is enough to help clear the fog clogging my drunken brain.

"What about Kyle?" She's engaged, which means she shouldn't be kissing me, and she most definitely shouldn't be giving me a look that says drinking isn't the only thing she wants to do once we're at my place.

"We're over."

This gets my attention. Kendall got engaged a little over three months ago, and their wedding is next month. She insisted on fast-tracking the hell out of it, so her saying it's over is a huge one-eighty.

"What happened?"

"I don't wanna talk about it." She drags her nails up my nape, stopping at my bun, and tugs on it gently. "I just..." She swallows thickly. "I just wanna forget." Her blue eyes, filled with so much sadness, bore into mine, begging, pleading. "Please, Dec," she breathes. "Help me forget."

I want to ask questions and find out what the hell's going on...But remember when I mentioned I would do anything for this woman? I wasn't kidding. So instead, I simply nod. "All right. Let's go up to my place."

Two

DECLAN

THE VIBE BETWEEN US SHIFTS THE MOMENT I AGREE TO TAKE THINGS UP TO MY PLACE. SHE'S QUIET ON THE elevator and stays that way when I unlock the door, and we go inside. I set the bottle on the counter and grab us both a water while she stands in the kitchen, looking around and not saying a word.

"Nobody's here." I hand her the water. "It's just me."

Her eyes meet mine, and she steps into my personal space, bringing her warmth into my cold, lonely existence. "You can't blame yourself for what happened. You didn't force the drugs down his throat."

"I knew he was struggling. I should've forced him to get help." It never should've fucking come to Gage almost dying. We should've done something, said something.

"He wouldn't have listened," she argues as if she can hear my silent thoughts. "He needed to hit rock bottom. Now he'll get the help he needs. And whether you want to believe it or not, he's alive because of you."

"I don't want to talk about it," I say, slinging her earlier words back at her. "Want another drink?"

She nods, so I grab two glasses from the cabinet and pour us each a shot. We throw them back, slamming the glasses on the counter. I'm about to ask if she wants another when I'm silenced...by her mouth.

Her supple lips glide against my own. Her tongue, coated with whiskey, delves into my mouth. My tongue swirls against hers, and then I capture it, sucking the liquor off and making her groan.

"Fuck me, Dec," she whispers against my mouth.

"You sure? We've been drinking and—"

"I'm sure." She palms my face, and I sigh into her embrace. "I want you to fuck me so long and hard, the rest of the world will cease to exist."

I stare into her eyes, making sure she means what she says, and when I don't see even the tiniest hint of uncertainty, I grab her ass and lift her into my arms. "You're about to get the goddamn fucking of your life."

The second we're in my room, and I drop her onto the bed, she starts peeling off her clothes. After tossing her winter jacket to the side, she kicks off her boots, each landing somewhere on the floor. When she grabs her shirt, I stop her, removing her fingers from the material. I want to take this slow, worship every inch of her, and memorize every second so when she's gone—and she will be gone because she's a runner—I'll be able to remember what it was like to have her in my arms, for her to be under me, to be inside her. When I'm alone again, I'll be able to close my eyes and remember everything about tonight.

"Dec, why are you stop—" Her soft voice snaps me out of my thoughts.

To keep her from finishing her question, I capture her mouth with my own, tasting her lips and caressing her tongue. I devour her, memorizing her taste, her scent. How soft her lips are and how strong her tongue is as it swirls with mine.

Her fingers delve into my hair, yanking on my hair tie. My hair creates a curtain around us when it falls, shutting the rest of the world out until it's just Kendall and me.

Breaking the kiss, I drag my lips across her heated flesh, suckling on her neck until I get to her collarbone. Then I pull back, admiring how beautiful she looks. Her lips red and puffy from being kissed. Her cheeks slightly flushed. Her eyes a bit glassy. And her hair fanned out across my pillow.

I take the hem of her shirt between my fingers and lift it over her head. Then I unbutton her jeans and tug them down her legs, pulling her socks off along with them.

Once she's undressed, I spread her legs so I can kneel between them, stopping for a few moments to soak her in. If I wouldn't look like a goddamn creep, I'd ask if I could take a picture of her just like this.

"I didn't plan for anyone to see under my clothes," she says, a hint of embarrassment tingeing her cheeks. I love that she's not in fancy undergarments, just a simple black and white polka-dotted bra and underwear set—both cotton and matching. It's the real her. The woman she doesn't let the world see. I follow her on social media and laugh when she posts pictures, acting like she just woke up, yet her hair and makeup are perfect. It's all part of the game. Only a select few get to see the real Kendall Naomi Blackwood, who loves to sing karaoke and bakes when she's stressed but enjoys eating the batter more than the final product. Who enjoys Sunday football, family get-togethers, and playing in the rain.

"You look perfect," I tell her, meaning it. I can't decide which part of her I want to taste first, so I start where her ample cleavage is peaking out the top of her bra. I place an open-mouthed kiss to the swell of her breast, then pull the cup down, exposing her dusty-pink nipple. Closing my lips around the hardened tip, I suck on it, tugging gently. I'm rewarded with the sexiest moan as her hands come around to the back of my head, silently indicating she wants more.

I bite down instead of sucking this time, and her moans get louder, reverberating straight to my dick. I bite harder, and the proof of her pleasure increases several octaves. Slowly, I swipe my tongue across the tip to soothe it, and she squirms under me. I do the same to her other breast, nipping and licking before I work my way down her toned belly, stopping at her navel ring—a multicolored music note. I give it a quick kiss and then continue my descent, kissing each of her hip bones and ending at the area between her thighs.

Lifting her leg, I slide one side of her underwear down, bending her knee so I can get it off, then lift the other leg, removing the other side, so her pussy is on display for me. It's trimmed neatly, and when I spread her thighs to get a better look, her lips are glistening with want.

My gaze flits from her pussy to her face, and our eyes lock. She's watching my every move, her bottom lip sucked between her teeth. I want to devour this pussy, but before I do, I need to make sure…"You definitely want this?" We've both been drinking, and the last thing I want is for her to wake up tomorrow and regret this.

She nods once, but that's not enough. "I need to hear the words, Kendall. Tell me you want this."

"I want this," she breathes, her eyes sad and pleading. "Please…today sucked. I need you to make me forget."

I'd like to think I'm a good man and that I wouldn't step into the middle of a relationship, but this is Kendall, and as much as I want to get the specifics as to whether they're really done, I don't have it in me to ask. I've waited years to be with this woman, for her to notice me, and when she finally did, she only saw me as a friend—as her brother's best friend and bandmate, and eventually one of her best friends. So while it might make me sound like a pussy, I'll take what she's willing to give, knowing this is all I'm going to get.

I drop to my stomach and part her lips, licking my way up her slit. She tastes just as I imagined—sweet with a hint of zest, just like her. I lick up and down slowly, inhaling her scent and memorizing her taste on my tongue. The more my tongue glides between her folds, the wetter she gets. I could do this all night, but she's panting, her chest rising and falling in quick succession. She's tugging on the strands of my hair and begging me to get her off. So I give her one last good lick, burning her taste into my brain, and then move on to her clit. The second my tongue lands on it, she jumps slightly, her hips jerking up. I tug it between my teeth playfully, sucking it into my mouth, then release it, so I can focus on getting her off.

With the flat of my tongue, I massage the swollen nub slowly, gently, giving it just the right amount of pressure to make it feel good. One hand ascends to her breast, tweaking and pulling on her nipple, and the other pushes two fingers inside her tight hole. The trifecta of pleasure is too much, and before long, she's flying high, her legs trembling as she comes all over my tongue and fingers.

"Oh, wow," she breathes, her eyes meeting mine. "That was...just...wow."

I smirk at the fact I've left her so sated that she's unable to form a complete sentence, and then pull off my shirt and unbutton my pants, needing to be inside her. She stays where she is, watching as I undress until I'm naked, and then, just before I'm about to drop over her, she sits up, taking my dick into her delicate hand.

With our bodies so close that our heat radiates between us, she darts her tongue out and runs it up my throat and over my Adam's apple. When she gets to my chin, she nibbles on it playfully, then presses her lips to mine as she strokes me up and down. The feeling of her touching me sends a rush of pleasure through me, and I have to force myself to calm the fuck down before I make an ass out of myself. In my defense, it's been a while...a long fucking while. And it's Kendall...touching my dick.

She falls back onto the bed, taking me with her—our kiss never breaking, her hand still stroking—and then guides me into her. The moment I enter her tight heat, I groan into her mouth, wondering if this is all a damn dream but praying it isn't.

Once she's stuffed full of my cock, I take over, slowly thrusting in and out, continuing to kiss her. Memorizing every moment of being inside her until we're both finding our release.

As we break apart, and I glance down at Kendall softly smiling at me, her lids fluttering open and closed, I have no idea how I'll ever go back to being without her. But I push the thought away, not wanting to ruin tonight. Tonight is all I have...

"What are you thinking about?" she asks, pulling my face toward hers for a quick kiss.

I consider lying, but then figure *fuck it. If tonight is all I have, I might as well give it all I've got.* At this point, what do I have to lose? "How I've been in love with you for years, and I can't believe you're finally in my bed, spending the night with me."

Her eyes fly open, popping her orgasm-induced bubble. "What? What are you talking about?"

"Just what I said...I've been in love with you for years."

"Why didn't you say anything?"

I laugh at that. "Until a couple of years ago, you didn't even know I existed."

"That's not true!"

"Oh, it definitely is…"

Three

DECLAN

NINE YEARS AGO

"GRAB ME A SODA WHILE YOU'RE UP THERE," CAMDEN YELLS AS I JOG UP THE STAIRS FROM HIS FAMILY'S private recording studio to their main house. Usually, the fridge is stocked with drinks and snacks, thanks to Camden's nanny, Maria, but we've been down here all weekend, writing and fucking around—even though Camden's dad won't officially sign us until we graduate high school—so it's damn near empty.

"Me too!" Braxton adds.

"You want anything?" I ask Gage since he's the only one who hasn't said anything.

"Nah, I'm good," he says from behind his drum kit.

I'm grabbing several drinks and snacks from the fridge and pantry when a soft noise comes from behind me. When I turn around, Kendall is walking toward where I am, staring at her phone. She doesn't notice me until I close the fridge, and her head snaps up.

"Oh, God, you scared me." Her hand that's not holding her phone goes to her heart, but my gaze is stuck on her face, on her red-rimmed eyes and blotchy cheeks.

"Sorry," I say, setting the shit in my hands down.

"Deacan, right?" she asks, slicing my heart in two. It shouldn't shock me that she doesn't even know my name. She's seven years older and mostly lives in LA when she's not touring. I might've been crushing on the woman hard for the past two years—since I came over for New Year's, and she was singing her heart out to old-school songs on the karaoke machine—but that doesn't mean she knows I exist.

"Declan."

"Oh, right. Sorry." She sniffs, sitting on the barstool.

"You okay?" I grab a tissue from the container on the counter and hand it to her.

She takes it with a watery smile and dabs the bit of makeup that's running under her eyes. "Do you ever feel...like you don't belong?" she asks, avoiding my question with one of her own—or maybe she's answering it...I don't know.

As she waits for my response, I can't help but see the vulnerability in her features. Every time I've seen her, she's always so put together. Her makeup and hair are done, and a smile is plastered on her face. But right now, something about her is different, like without everyone watching her, she's able to unveil her mask and simply be herself.

"Every day of my life," I tell her honestly.

She nods in understanding. "Did you know Easton isn't my real dad? It's why I have blue eyes, and everyone else has green and hazel."

"I didn't." I've been friends with Camden for a couple of years, but guys don't tend to gossip like girls do. Despite their age difference, I know they're close, but aside from me saying she's hot and him pointing out I don't stand a chance, she's not mentioned often.

"My real dad," she says softly as if she doesn't want to chance anyone hearing her, "was a piece of shit. A rapist and a corrupt politician. I never knew him, but from what I've read and heard, he was heartless." She sniffs and wipes her eyes. "Sometimes, I wonder if I'm screwed. If nature will win out over nurture, no matter how hard I try."

"You're afraid of becoming a rapist, corrupt politician?" I ask. "Because the last time I checked, you're a pop princess who sings about love and shit, and I don't think you'll be running for office any time soon." I'm half joking, hoping it'll cut some of the tension she's brought into the kitchen with her.

I know it works when she snorts out a laugh and rolls her eyes. "No, smart-ass. But..." She sighs and closes her eyes as if needing to get her thoughts together. Finally, she opens them, and her blue orbs lock with mine. "If you think about it, I don't *actually* sing about love. I sing about heartbreak because...I've never experienced love."

She swallows thickly, and it takes everything in me not to move toward her. "I'm afraid I'm more like my sperm donor. Cold, heartless, incapable of love. Every song I write comes to me once I've been hurt, or I've done the hurting."

Her words have me gravitating toward her—even though she couldn't remember my name a few minutes ago—and pulling her into my arms. Surprisingly, she lets me, dropping her head against my chest and releasing the sob she was holding back.

"What if I'm broken?" she whispers.

We stay like this for several minutes, in the kitchen, me holding her while she sits on the barstool crying into my chest, and every second that ticks by has me falling harder and deeper for her. Because every time I saw her, she was beautiful, talented, always smiling, and putting on a front for the camera and the fans, but now, she's real and broken, and in the world we live in, that's worth more than the fakeness we're surrounded by.

I lift her chin gently, forcing her to look at me, and then tell her the only thing I can think to say. "I think we're all a little broken, and that's okay."

"YOU'RE RIGHT," KENDALL SAYS WITH TEARS IN HER EYES. "I DIDN'T NOTICE YOU...AT LEAST NOT UNTIL that day. But that conversation was the only time I told anyone how I felt, and what you said glued several of my broken pieces together. I was so down. I had just broken up with a guy who told me I wasn't capable of more than a good time, and I was feeling low.

"And then I found out some stuff about my bio dad...And it all just hit me so hard." She reaches around and takes her bra off, and I'm confused about what she's doing until she lifts her arm, exposing a small tattoo covered by her bra.

I edge closer and read the words inked on her skin: *It's okay to be a little broken.*

"I got it that night after we talked. I cover it up in public, when I'm wearing something that could show it, not wanting the paps to psychoanalyze me, but when I'm standing in front of the mirror, naked, I look at it a lot...to remind myself what you said: we're all a little broken, and that's okay."

Finding out that she's been wearing my words for the past nine years has me grabbing her face and kissing her passionately. I roll us over, caging her in my arms, and enter her smoothly, her legs locking around my waist. I've never been this turned on in my life, knowing that she looks at that tattoo every day and thinks about me, about what I said to her. If I wasn't already head over heels for this woman, this would've sent me right over the edge.

I kiss her the same way I fuck her, with slow, methodical movements, hoping to convey how much she means to me and how much I want her. Praying that tonight is only the beginning and not the end of what we could have together.

With my pelvis grinding against hers, she comes hard around my cock, moaning her pleasure into my mouth, and I follow, draining every drop into her.

When we've both gotten our breathing under control, I carry her into the bathroom, and we shower together. I wash her hair, and she washes my body. After two back-to-back orgasms, my dick shouldn't be able to stand at attention, but when she drops to her knees, wraps her fingers around the shaft, and licks my head, I'm a fucking goner.

My back hits the wall, and I watch as she takes me in as far as she can go, stroking and licking and sucking until I'm coming down her throat.

"Fuck, woman. I think you've drained me of my soul," I tell her as I help her to her feet. She throws her head back with a laugh, and I grip the curves of her hips, pulling her toward me so I can kiss her slim neck. I pepper kisses along her wet flesh and over to her ear. "Spend the night," I whisper, praying she'll agree.

When she looks up at me, our eyes locking, I hope I haven't pushed my luck.

"Okay," she breathes. "But I'll need something to sleep in."

I have no idea how the hell we got to this point—fucking and spending the night together—but I'm sure as hell not going to question it.

After we're showered and dressed, Kendall crawls into the bed, and I join her. For about a second, I consider giving her some space, but then I remember that tonight is all I have, so instead of keeping to my side of the bed, I tug her toward me, tucking her into my side. And that's how we fall asleep—with her snuggled against me and our legs intertwined.

PRYING MY EYES OPEN, I FIND THE OTHER SIDE OF THE BED EMPTY AND WONDER IF LAST NIGHT WAS A dream. And if it wasn't, does that mean she left?

I climb out of bed and go in search of her, hoping like hell she's still here. I find her in the kitchen, cooking. She's still wearing my clothes, and she's shaking her ass to the music playing on the living room television. Instead of alerting her to my presence, I take a few moments to watch her. Since she asked me to make her forget last night, I've spent every moment trying to memorize every detail, not wanting to forget a single second of my time with her. Knowing all too soon that our time will come to an end.

"Hey, you," she says, turning around. "Hungry?" She reaches into the oven and pulls out a pan. The scent is sweet, and my stomach rumbles. "I ran to the corner store early this morning and whipped up some homemade cinnamon rolls and bacon."

She baked. It's what she does when she's stressed.

"They smell delicious."

She smiles softly and turns off the stove, removing the pan. She lifts the lid, and the scent of bacon wafts in the air, overpowering the cinnamon.

"Try a piece," she says, picking up a slice and extending her hand.

I step toward her and lift her onto the counter, stepping between her legs. Her eyes go wide, but she doesn't stop me as I grip her thighs and lean in, opening my mouth so I can take a bite.

She feeds me the bacon, alternating between giving herself and me nibbles, and then she moves onto the cinnamon rolls, forking us each a bite.

"This is delicious. Sweet…" I kiss the corner of her mouth. "Just like you." I swipe my finger across the top of the rolls, scooping up some icing, and then run my finger along the seam of her lips. Once they're covered with icing, I dip my head and lick across her lips, making her moan.

"The rolls are good, but I think I'd rather have you for breakfast."

Food forgotten, she wraps her legs around my waist, and I take her back to my room, where I eat her until she comes, and then I fuck her until she comes again. And the entire time, I wish for time to freeze and for this moment, this morning, to never end.

"MY PHONE WON'T STOP VIBRATING," KENDALL GROANS, NUZZLING HER FACE INTO MY NECK. "MAKE IT stop." After I had her for breakfast, we fell back asleep for a little while, but the sound of her phone going off must've woken her up.

I reach over and grab her phone from the nightstand, ready to turn it off, but then I see the name Kyle on the screen and freeze.

"It's your fiancé," I tell her, moving her arm and giving myself some distance. With the bubble we created last night that continued this morning, it was easy to pretend that Kendall's mine, but seeing his name on her phone is enough to pop that bubble and throw my ass back into reality.

"He's not my fiancé," she says, taking the phone and turning it off.

"You're still wearing his ring," I point out, glancing at the huge rock on her finger. I was too distracted by the rest of her to notice it…until now.

She looks at it and grimaces. "I'm ending things with him today. I just didn't have a chance to take it off." She shrugs and rolls off the bed, standing. She's in nothing but my white shirt, and I can make out her perky tits through the thin material and the swells of her ass underneath. All I want to do is pull her back into bed and spend the day devouring her over and over again, but what she said stops me from dragging her back to bed.

"You're still engaged?"

"Technically, but only because he doesn't know it's over yet."

"And why is it over?"

She sighs and shakes her head. "I don't want to talk about it. It's embarrassing, and I'm just not ready yet, but as soon as I leave here, I'm ending things with him."

"And where does that leave us?"

Her eyes meet mine. "I'm a mess, Dec…"

"I don't care."

"You're best friends with my brother."

"Still don't care. You know how I feel about you, and nothing you say is going to change that, so stop fighting this."

"It would be irresponsible to jump from one man to another. People would think I'm a—"

"Life's too short to give a fuck about what anyone thinks. I want you." I grab the front of her shirt and pull her toward me. "Last night, the chemistry was there, and this morning...still fucking there." I nip at her jaw, and she groans. "Tell me you felt it too."

"Of course, I did," she says softly. "I do...And I'd love to spend more time with you, to see where this could possibly go. But I have to end things with Kyle and call off the wedding first. It's all a clusterfuck, and I don't want to drag you into it. I just need a little bit of time. Tell me you understand." She palms my cheeks, and I nod.

"I get it. I'll be here. Take all the time you need."

Her shoulders drop in relief. "Thank you." She presses a chaste kiss to my lips. "I better get going."

I fist the back of her hair and crush my mouth against hers, coaxing her lips open and sucking her tongue into my mouth. My kiss is done with a dual purpose: needing to leave her wanting and remembering, so she'll come back to me, but also, if this is the last kiss I ever get, I want to make it count.

When I break the kiss, her eyes are glassed over, her lips are bee stung, and she looks as if she wants to climb on top of me—just how I wanted.

"I'll see you soon, beautiful," I tell her before I kiss her one last time, praying like hell she comes back to me.

Four

KENDALL

Kyle: Where are you?

Kyle: I'm sorry. Please let me explain.

Kyle: I've called everyone in your family, and nobody knows where you are.

Kyle: I'm worried about you.

I ROLL MY EYES AT HIS TEXTS, THEN DELETE THEM ALL, WONDERING HOW I EVER ALLOWED MYSELF TO BE fooled by him. I'm smarter than that, and the fact that I fell for his bullshit pisses me off.

Since I'm not in any rush to let him know I'm okay, and the only conversation I plan to have with him involves me chucking my engagement ring at his head while telling him we're over, I click into the family chat—since everyone texted me several times last night—to let them know I'm okay. Then I send a text to my parents only, asking if we can talk. They both respond instantly that they're home and I can come over any time.

After letting them know I'll be by in a couple of hours, I glance out the window of the Town Car I'm in, watching the city pass me by as I think about how quickly everything's changed in the past eighteen hours...Jesus, has it only been that long since I found—?

I push the thought out of my head, replacing it with Declan. Over the past couple of years, we've grown close. He's become someone I can talk to and have fun with. When we were both still living on the West Coast, we would have barbecues, go to the gym, and spend hours writing music together. And once we were both living on the East Coast, it continued—the hanging out, going out, writing music...

But not once did I ever look at him as anything more than a friend. Not because he isn't boyfriend material, because he totally is. The guys have been ragging on him for being a hopeless romantic for years. He isn't known for hooking up with random women, and he hasn't been seen with many over the years anyway. Still, when he is, it's clear he's spending time with them, getting to know them, and not just using them as a hole to fill like the other guys did before Camden and Braxton settled down...and Gage—my heart clenches when I think about everything he's been through. I hope he's getting the help he needs.

My point is, I never viewed Declan as being anything more than a friend, and I think it's because I knew he was boyfriend material. He's sweet and caring and selfless. Take last night—he asked me multiple times if I was sure I wanted to cross the line, knowing we'd been drinking. And when we crossed that line, he made sure my pleasure came first, something most guys don't consider—at least not the ones I've been with.

Which leads me to my very long-winded point. I never considered Declan an option because I think I knew deep down he would be the perfect boyfriend, and if my track record is anything to go by, I would mess it all up, like I always do...Because I'm not capable of loving anyone or being loved. At least not with anyone outside of my family. And even when I'm with them, I feel like an outsider, as if I'm missing a certain chromosome that allows me to simply feel happy and content.

But then I spent the night with Declan—and this morning—and for a little while, it felt like that chromosome wasn't lost. I wasn't the broken pop star, known for *stiffing* men—a stupid name I was given after a few—okay, a lot—of my relationships ended with me running, and then a few months later, releasing songs that may *or may not* have been about our time together.

I smile to myself, remembering the way my heart beat a bit faster in Declan's arms. The way I felt adored and cherished. And holy shit, the chemistry. I've been with quite a few guys in my thirty-one years, and none of them, and I mean none of them, could make me orgasm the way Declan did. But it wasn't just about the sex. It was the way he looked at me like I was more than Kendall Blackwood, pop princess.

When he told me he's had feelings for years, my first thought was nope, no way. I'm not going there. He's my brother's best friend and signed to the same label as me. He's been a family friend for years. But when he looked at me and said he didn't care what anyone thought, that life was too short and he wanted a chance to be with me, I couldn't help but imagine what it would be like to be with him. To be happy and content. To create a family, to love and be loved...

It's why I said yes to Kyle even though I knew he wasn't the one. I'm thirty-one years old, and the only thing I have to show for it is my musical success. But I want more than that. I looked up my shitty bio dad, and while he created a family, he wasn't a successful husband or father or human. And I don't want to be like him. I want to be like my mom: a loving wife and mother. I want to know what it feels like to be in love and love someone else. I want to have a family and create a life outside of music. One I can be proud of.

Before spending the night with Declan, I didn't think it was possible. I thought I was broken, damaged, and destined to settle or be alone. But now, everything looks different, like the sky is bluer, the sun is brighter. I'm capable of more with him.

But first, I have to break things off with Kyle and get my shit together. Once I do that, I can go back to Declan so we can see where this will go.

The car is about to pull into my condominium complex to drop me off in the underground parking lot when a loud siren rings out—a police car or ambulance. My driver is stuck in traffic—fucking NYC—and tries to get out of the way, but before he can, an SUV turns the corner like he's part of one of those reality programs that shows car chases. He's not paying attention to everyone trying to move over for the siren, and that's when the siren appears. Then it dawns on me that the SUV is in a car chase, and that siren is after him.

And before my driver can move out of the way, the SUV plows straight into the car.

Everything shifts and tumbles.

The car begins to roll.

And then there's a loud crunching sound.

And everything goes black.

Five

DECLAN

I STARE AT MY PHONE, PACING THE ROOM AS IF WILLING IT TO GO OFF WILL BE ENOUGH TO GET KENDALL TO text or call. It's been hours since she's left here. She said she was going to end it with Kyle and get her shit together. Logically, I know that isn't going to take hours. It could be days or weeks, but fuck, I really should've asked for clarification before she left so I wouldn't be over here, wondering how long is long enough before I can contact her. A part of me knows it's because I'm scared. Because Kendall is a runner. It's what she does. She lets men get just close enough to fall for her, and then she runs. Where they all went wrong was when they saw this beautiful, wealthy pop star and didn't know what to do with her. But I do. I'm going to love the hell out of her, and when she tries to run, I'll catch her ass and drag her back. Okay, that sounds a little creepy, but you get my point.

My phone rings, and I jump since it's currently in my hand. The name on the screen says Camden, and I can't help wondering if maybe Kendall spoke to him and told him about our night together. "Hello," I say cautiously, preparing for anything.

Well, I think I'm ready for anything until he speaks. "Kendall's been in an accident. We're all heading over to the hospital now. New York Medical."

And with those words, my entire world implodes.

Having zero patience to call for a car, I throw on some clothes and rush downstairs to flag down a taxi. Thankfully, there's already a car available, so I hop in and tell him I need to get to New York Medical. The twenty-minute ride feels like it takes hours, but finally, he pulls up to the entrance. Camden had texted that the hospital gave them a private room to wait in so they didn't draw attention. I head straight toward it, finding Simon, one of our bodyguards, standing outside the door.

He nods at me and opens the door to let me in, where I find Kendall's entire family. Her brother, Camden, and his wife, Layla, their baby daughter, Marianna, and son, Felix, are on the couch huddled together. Her sister, Bailey, and her wife, Cynthia, sit together on another couch. Her other sister, Phoebe, cries softly in the corner with her mom and dad holding her.

And then I lock eyes on the final person in the room: Kyle Sanford. His presence means either she never got a chance to break it off or he cares that much he's here even though they're no longer together.

When the door opens and shuts, everyone glances over, expressions hopeful for information, but then shut down when they see it's only me. Camden texted me on my way over that they don't know anything yet. Sophia is her emergency contact, so they called her when Kendall was brought in, but the hospital hasn't given the family any information about what happened yet.

"This can't be good," Phoebe cries. "If it weren't that big of a deal, we would be able to see her. Why can't we see her?"

"Shh, stop," Sophia coos. "We don't know anything. All we can do is think positive thoughts and pray. The nurse said as soon as they've finished assessing her, they'll be back to let us know what's happened."

I walk over and give Camden a hug, then go around hugging everyone else, avoiding Kyle, and just as I'm sitting on the couch next to Bailey, Braxton and Kaylee burst through the door. Kaylee hugs everyone while Braxton asks if there's any news. They tell them the same thing they told me. And then we wait for what feels like hours.

Finally, there's a knock, and in walks a young man, who looks no more than thirty, wearing a white lab coat, along with a woman in blue scrubs. "Good afternoon, my name is Dr. Babki, and this is Dr. Kerns. We're the doctors who assessed Miss Blackwood."

Introductions are quickly made, and then he continues telling us about Kendall. "When the vehicle flipped, she wasn't wearing her seat belt, and her head hit the ceiling, causing a transient disturbance to her brain, creating a—"

"Doctor," Easton says gruffly. "Can you please tell us in layman's terms? Is our little girl okay?"

The doctor winces. "Sorry, this is a teaching hospital, so we tend to use medical terms. When Miss Blackwood hit her head, a blood vessel burst, causing bleeding in her brain. We were able to go in and stop the bleeding before any severe damage occurred. It helped that she was brought in immediately."

"So she's okay?" Sophia asks.

"She's stable. We'll keep her in a medically induced coma to give her time for the swelling to go down while her brain heals. We'll monitor her closely, and once the scans come back clean, we'll decrease the medication to slowly wake her up."

"And what about side effects?" Easton asks.

"Unfortunately, we won't know until she wakes up. I won't scare you with all of the possibilities, and I suggest you don't google them as it won't do you any good. Once she's awake, we'll reassess and take it one step at a time. But for right now, she's doing okay. The bleeding has stopped, and she's stable. All very good signs, especially for the hit she took."

"What about the driver?" Sophia asks. He's been with the family for years, so it makes sense she would ask.

"I can't give out any information to non-family," the doctor says, but the way he frowns tells me it's not good. "His family has been contacted and should be here shortly."

"When can we see her?" Bailey asks.

"I'll have a nurse come and get you once she's been situated."

"We would like a private room," Easton says. "I don't care about the expense. Whatever it takes to make sure she has the best medical treatment and is comfortable."

"She'll get that here," Dr. Babki assures him. "If you have any questions, I'll be on for another few hours. I'll find out who'll be treating her once I leave and let you know."

"Thank you," Sophia says, shaking his hand.

The moment he leaves, the girls all fall into a fit of cries, and their significant others hold them. I watch, wishing I could hold Kendall, wondering if I would've pulled her into my arms and made love to her one more time... if I would've insisted that we eat the cinnamon rolls she baked...if this never would've happened.

While we wait for the nurse to let us know Kendall is ready for visitors, a pair of police officers come in and introduce themselves, telling Easton and Sophia that they were two of the officers on the scene and called the ambulance.

"What happened?" Easton asks.

"A convenience store robbery gone wrong," one of the officers explains. "He was armed and when the owner refused to give up the money, he shot him. The panic button was pressed, and the perpetrator took off. It turned into a car chase, which took them into the city. Not wanting to lose him, the officers followed him until the helicopter could take over, but by the time it arrived, the man was in the thick of traffic. Tire tracks indicate he tried to slam on his brakes, telling us he must not have been expecting the traffic to be at a standstill, but it was too late. He hit the driver-side of the vehicle your daughter was in, but luckily, she was sitting on the opposite side in the back seat, so she didn't take the brunt of the impact."

"We want to press charges," Kyle says, finally speaking up like the lawyer he is.

"He didn't survive," the officer says. "And, off the record, neither did her driver. We're waiting for the family to arrive to tell them. A few others were injured when the vehicle rolled, but nothing serious."

Everyone goes silent at that, realizing the weight of the officer's words. Out of the three most affected, two of them died. Kendall could've died. But she lived. We could've been having an entirely different conversation with the doctor and police officers, but somehow, an angel was looking down on Kendall, and she survived.

"Mrs. Blackwood," a female nurse says. "Your daughter can have a visitor now."

Sophia and Easton glance at Kyle, unsure who should go first, telling me they either have no idea that Kendall has broken the engagement off, or she never made it to tell Kyle. Either way, I have to keep my mouth shut. The only important thing right now is concentrating on Kendall's healing. Everything else can wait.

"You should go," Kyle says. "You're her mom. Please...umm, give her a kiss for me." I could be wrong, and maybe it's just me overthinking shit, but he sounds off. The words make sense, but his tone is weird, almost as if it's riddled with guilt. Could she have been coming from seeing him when she was in the accident? Did something happen from the time she left my place to when she was hit? At this point, it doesn't really matter, but it also doesn't stop me from wondering what the hell happened.

Sophia nods, then kisses her husband quickly and follows the nurse out.

"Should we tell Gage?" Braxton asks, breaking the silence after a few minutes.

"No," Easton says. "The last thing he needs is unnecessary stress or to feel like he should be here. He's where he needs to be." He glances around the room. "I appreciate everyone coming, but as the doctor mentioned, Kendall won't be awake for some time, so if you want to go home and get some rest, I can text everyone and keep you updated." He walks over to Layla, who's rocking her sleeping baby girl, and tears fill his eyes. "Life is so damn precious," he murmurs, bending slightly and kissing her forehead.

"I'm going to take Layla and the kids home, and then I'll be back," Camden says to his dad. "If anything changes..."

"I'll keep you informed."

One by one, everyone hugs Easton, telling him if they need anything, to let them know, until it's only Kyle, Easton, and me left.

"I left without showering," Kyle says awkwardly. "I'm going to go home and shower and change, and then I'll be back up. Do you need anything?"

"No, I'm good," Easton says, giving him a small smile, "but thank you."

With a nod, Kyle leaves, and it's just Easton and me.

"If you want to get going..."

"Actually, I think I'll stay, if that's okay," I tell him.

He nods. "Of course, I know you and Kendall have grown close. She's been so excited about recording that song. She made us all listen to it over a dozen times at dinner."

"It's going to blow the hell up," I say with a small laugh to lighten the mood. "It's a side of Kendall her fans haven't seen...raw...real."

Easton chokes out a watery laugh. "She's an expert at putting on a good front, isn't she?" He laughs a little harder, fresh tears filling his eyes and falling. "I remember when I first met her. Her mom was soft and sweet, but Kendall... She was all mouth and sass." He chuckles softly. "We argued for hours over the lyrics of 'I'm Looking for a Love.'"

It takes me a second to place the song, but once I do, I give him a brow up in confusion. "Isn't that your song?"

Easton full-blown laughs. "Yeah, but she swore the lyrics were *looking for a dove,* and nobody could tell her any differently. 'Doves fly, so obviously, it flew away, and he's looking for it,' she argued, hand on her hip, brows dipped in determination. 'Why would anyone be looking for love?'"

I can't help but think about the irony in his words—Kendall's spent half her life looking for and running from love...

A few minutes later, Sophia comes back, looking a mixture of relief that her daughter is alive and distraught that she's in a coma.

Since Kendall's been moved to a private room, they're both able to go visit with her, so while they do that, I go to the gift shop to pick up a couple of things for her room. I pass on the flowers since they're cliché as fuck, and instead, I grab some candy since she has a huge sweet tooth, playing cards since she loves to play solitaire when she's alone and Rummy with her family when they're hanging out and bullshitting, and a stuffed puppy holding a huge heart. It's cheesy as fuck, but I've been in Kendall's room and know she loves stuffed animals, especially dogs. She would love to have a real one, but with her traveling, she can't. She once told me that she wants to get a puppy whenever she finally settles down.

I'm waiting in the private waiting room when Camden returns, saying his dad texted and said the room is big enough for a few more people to go in.

When we walk in, my eyes go straight to Kendall. I imagined she'd look rough since she was in an accident, but aside from the monitors attached to her chest and arms, and the bandage covering her head, she looks like she's simply asleep.

"She didn't break or bruise anything," Sophia says. "It was just horrible luck that she wasn't wearing her seat belt and her head hit the ceiling."

I place the stuffed dog on the nightstand, along with the candy and cards. I glance over, and her parents and Camden are talking about something the doctor said, so I take the moment to lean over and kiss her forehead. "Come back to me, Kendall," I plead softly. "We haven't even gotten started yet."

KENDALL

THERE'S A *THUMP, THUMP, THUMP* IN MY HEAD AS IF SOMEONE WITH THE WORST RHYTHM IS DRUMMING against my skull. I attempt to open my eyes, but they're heavy, like a pair of weights have been set on my lids. A constant beeping has me questioning where I am and why I feel like death warmed over.

Inhaling, the scent of antiseptic assaults my nostrils. *What the…?*

"Kendall, you can do it. Wake up, sweetheart. Just open those beautiful blue eyes and come back to me."

The sound of Declan's soothing voice has me sighing in contentment and wanting to open my eyes so he knows I'm awake. *Where does he think I went? I'm right here…*

With all the strength I possess, I take a deep breath and pry my lids apart. At first, it's blurry, and with the constant drumming, it hurts. But I can see. White walls. A whiteboard with writing on it. A sink…cabinets…machines. *What the hell? Why am I in a hospital?*

I swallow thickly and wince when it feels like sandpaper is being shoved down my throat. I glance over at Declan and take in his appearance. His brows are knitted together in worry, there are dark circles under his eyes, and his hair is up in a messy bun. He looks how I feel: like he's been to hell and back. But even as distressed as he appears, he still looks delicious, with his blue eyes that have the ability to see beyond the bullshit, his full lips, pouty and pink and kissable, and his face full of scruff that I have no doubt would leave burn tracks between a woman's legs.

Whoa, where the heck did those thoughts come from?

With more effort than it should take, I part my lips to ask where I am and what's going on, why he looks so upset and was just begging me to *come back to him*, when the sound of a door swinging open and then voices speaking distract me.

My gaze flits over to where the noise is coming from, and my eyes land on my parents and…Kyle—my fiancé.

"Oh my God!" My mom gasps. "She's awake?"

"She was just opening her eyes," Declan explains as he stands and steps back so my mom can take his spot. "We were so worried," she breathes, a watery smile spreading across her face.

"I'll, uh, go tell a nurse she's awake," Kyle says, glancing at me oddly.

"How are you feeling?" Mom asks, running her fingers gently through my hair. "You gave us quite a scare, Sunshine." She takes my hand in hers and threads our fingers together.

Confused and disoriented, I don't say anything. It feels like everyone is talking in riddles. It's clear I'm in the hospital, but I don't know why. I want to ask, but my throat hurts, and I'm too tired to speak. I try to smile at her to let her know I'm okay, but the action is too exhausting, so instead, I squeeze her hand the best I can and close my eyes, wanting to rest them for a few minutes.

"Miss Blackwood." With my name being called, I force my eyes back open, and standing in front of me is an older gentleman dressed in a suit with a white jacket. "I'm Dr. Oswald. You're in New York Medical because you were in a car accident and hit your head pretty hard."

His admission has me trying to recall the accident he's referring to, but when I think too hard, the drumming in my head switches to downright banging, and I stop trying to remember.

Dr. Oswald has me go through various exercises to test my sight and touch, and then he asks if I can speak. The room is quiet—the only sound coming from the incessant beeping—and I want to say something to break the silence, but I can't find it in me to speak. It should be so easy...I've been speaking for over thirty years. All I have to do is part my lips and release the words, but I can't.

"It's okay," the doctor says. "You've been through quite an ordeal. Would you like something to drink?"

I nod, suddenly extremely thirsty, and my mom rushes to the counter to pour me something to drink.

She brings the cup to my lips, and I open my mouth just enough to swallow down the cool water. It feels like heaven sliding down and softening the feel of sandpaper in my throat.

Once my throat isn't so dry, I release a deep breath and attempt to speak. "I..." I croak out.

"Take your time," Dr. Oswald says gently.

"I don't know what happened."

In my peripheral, my parents both frown, and Kyle raises his brows.

The doctor smiles softly. "That's okay. Sometimes when we hit our heads, our brains go a little haywire. Can you tell me your name?"

"Kendall."

"Good," the doctor says. "Do you know the people in this room?"

I nod, then clear my throat. "My parents, Declan, and Kyle."

"Good," the doctor repeats. "And do you know what year it is?"

I think for a moment, but it's a bit fuzzy, so I go with the year that pops into my head.

"That's right. Now, I want you to tell me the last thing you remember."

I think for a few moments, trying to remember this supposed accident he mentioned, but my last memory is...laughing, drinking..."Declan and me..." I try to place where we are, what we're doing...And then it hits me. "Dancing on New Year's Eve." I glance at Declan, and his features are etched with concern. "We were talking about the song we were working on, and then you asked me to dance. We danced to..." I think hard, trying to recall the details. "I can't remember." I shake my head, then wince at the pain radiating into my skull.

"It's okay," the doctor says. "So New Year's Eve is the last memory you have?"

I nod. "Did something happen?" A flash of Declan and me getting into a limo has me looking at him. "Did we get into an accident?" I rake my gaze over him, but he looks okay. No bumps or bruises. "Are you okay?" I ask, just to be sure.

Declan clears his throat. "I'm okay. No, we didn't get into an accident. You did a few days ago, but I wasn't with you."

"Oh," I breathe. "That's good." But then I'm confused. "Where were you? You were with me in the limo, right?"

"I was. The limo dropped you off first and then me."

"Okay, so then what happened?"

"Kendall, can you tell me what month it is?" the doctor asks, ignoring my question.

"Umm..." If my last memory was on New Year's, and the accident, as Declan said was a few days ago, that would make it..."January?"

Declan curses under his breath. "What?" I ask, getting annoyed. "What's going on?"

"You were in an accident a few days ago," the doctor begins. "but it wasn't on New Year's. It's February sixteenth."

I think about what he's said, but I don't remember anything past New Year's. Declan and me dancing, the ball dropping, and him kissing me softly, me wondering where Kyle was. After several texts, he replied, apologizing that his emergency meeting ran late but that he would meet me at my place. The limo took me home, and I fell asleep waiting for him.

"I can't remember anything after New Year's," I tell the doctor. "What does that mean? Is there something wrong with me?"

Dr. Oswald shakes his head. "Losing your memory isn't uncommon with brain injuries. We'll need to run some tests now that you're awake to make sure you're healing properly, but I wouldn't worry about it. You also just woke up, so your brain is still fuzzy." He pats my shin. "I'm going to put an order in for those tests. Take it easy and let the nurses know if you're in any pain. I'll be by with the results to discuss this further."

With a gentle smile, he exits the room.

"We were so worried," Mom says.

"What happened?" I ask, wanting to know since I can't remember.

"There was a car chase in front of your building," Dad explains. "Your car was hit and rolled, and because you weren't wearing your seat belt, you hit your head."

"Is my driver okay?" We use a car service, so it could be various people, but the same handful tend to rotate.

"It was Greg," Mom says solemnly. "Unfortunately, he didn't make it."

My heart sinks in my chest, a contradiction of emotions hitting me hard: sad that a good man lost his life yet grateful I'm still alive.

"Can you please text Marcia and tell her I want to make sure his funeral is covered and his family is taken care of?" Marcia is my assistant back in LA. Since I moved here after my tour ended, she works remotely. With my brother and Layla having a baby, I wanted to spend some time at home and take a little break of sorts. With Kyle and me getting married in a few months...Oh, shit! "It's February sixteenth?"

"Yes," Mom answers, her brow popping up in concern. "What's wrong?"

"Well, we're supposed to get married in a few weeks," I say to Kyle, who flinches. "How are we supposed to do that if nothing is planned? Maybe we should postpone it," I blurt out.

"Actually," Mom says, smiling softly, "it's all planned. You can't remember, but you've only been out for a few days."

"Oh, right," I breathe. "Yeah, okay..."

My head throbs, and I'm suddenly tired. "I think I need to rest," I mutter.

"Okay," Mom says, giving me a kiss. "We'll be by tomorrow. Camden, Phoebe, and Bailey have been coming by every day. I texted them you're awake, and they wanted to come by, but I told them to wait until tomorrow, so you're not overwhelmed."

"Thank you," I tell her. "I love you."

"Love you more, Sunshine."

"Your phone was recovered," Dad says, pulling it out of his pocket and setting it on the nightstand. "I made sure it's charged. If you need anything, call or text us."

Declan says goodbye next. He looks at me oddly, like he wants to say something, but instead, he sighs and kisses my forehead before retreating and leaving Kyle and me alone.

When a sharp pain radiates through my skull, causing me to wince, Kyle asks if I'm okay.

"I think I need more pain meds."

"You can press the button here, and the nurse will come," he says. A few minutes later, the nurse has upped my pain reliever, and we're alone once again.

"I can—"

"You should—"

We talk at the same time. I have no idea why it's so awkward between us, but something feels off.

"You go first," I insist.

"I was going to say I can stay if you want."

I nod. "I'm just going to sleep. I'm sure you have tons of work to do. Have you been here this entire time?" Kyle works for Berg, Weiss, and Ross—a law firm specializing in creative professionals and businesses. He's a junior partner and is working hard to make partner. One of the partners has announced he's retiring soon, and Kyle hopes to fill his position. This means he works more than he's home, something I can understand since I've spent the past thirteen years working my ass off to get to where I am.

"Of course, I've been here," he says. "I had these delivered for Valentine's Day." He points to the beautiful red roses sitting in a vase on the bedside table. "Once you're out of here, we'll celebrate properly."

"Thank you." My eyes move from the roses to the adorable stuffed puppy, and I reach out and grab it. "I've always wanted a puppy," I say, petting his soft fur. If it weren't for how busy I am, I would already have one. But I can barely take care of myself most days...

"Oh, uh…" He clears his throat. "That's actually not from me."

"Oh, who's it from?"

"Declan."

At the mention of his name, butterflies try to attack my belly. But before I can think too hard as to why that is, Kyle scrapes a chair across the linoleum floor and has a seat next to me, changing the subject. "So, uh, you really don't remember anything after New Year's?"

I shake my head. "Not that I know of."

He nods and takes my hand in his, bringing it up to his lips. "I'm so glad you're okay, Kendall. When I heard you were in an accident...Fuck, I was so scared."

"When did it happen?"

"Sunday morning."

Normally, we spend the day together. Even with his busy schedule, he makes it a point to spend time with me during the weekend. We go to dinner

Saturday night, and then I spend the night. We spend all day Sunday together, and then I go home Sunday night so he can do some work before he returns Monday.

"I was on my way home on Sunday morning? From your place?"

Like earlier, Kyle flinches, and the hairs on my arms rise. "What aren't you telling me?"

"We, uh…" He clears his throat. "We got into an argument Saturday night. I was supposed to meet you for dinner, but I got caught up at the office. We didn't spend the night together Saturday night. You don't remember any of this at all?"

"No…So where was I coming from Sunday morning?"

Kyle shrugs. "I don't know. I was texting you all night, asking you to talk to me, but you wouldn't respond. And then your brother called me and said you'd been in an accident."

Something niggles in the back of my mind, but I can't quite grasp it. "Are we…okay?"

"Yeah." He bobs his head. "Of course. I shouldn't have stayed at the office, and I'll forever regret it. Had we gone to dinner and then back to my place, you would've been in bed with me instead of getting hit by a piece of shit criminal."

"People fight. You can't blame yourself for that." My head pounds, and I wince in pain. "I don't mean to be rude, but I'm exhausted."

"I can stay…"

"No, it's okay. Go sleep in a comfortable bed."

"I'll be back in the morning."

"What's today?"

"Wednesday."

"Then you have to work…"

"They know what's happened."

"I'm okay," I tell him, needing some space but not wanting to say that to him. "Go to work. You can't do anything for me here, and you heard the doctor. They'll be running tests tomorrow."

"If you need anything…"

"I'll let you know."

He stands and leans over, kissing the corner of my mouth. "I love you, Kendall, and I'm so sorry this happened to you." With his kiss, accompanied by his admission, I expect to feel a spark of some sort, for my heart to beat a little faster, for butterflies to take over my belly, to feel *something*—I'm engaged to this man and marrying him in a few short weeks—but I feel…nothing.

I smile up at him, unable to say anything back, and tell myself what I'm feeling—or the lack thereof—must be linked to my head injury. Once I'm back home, feeling better, things will get back to normal. I'm just feeling off right now.

Seven

KENDALL

"YOU'RE SURE YOU'LL BE OKAY HERE?" KYLE ASKS FOR THE TWENTIETH TIME. I WAS RELEASED FROM THE hospital yesterday after several days of being monitored and every test coming back perfect. Aside from not remembering the past six weeks, I'm thankfully okay. The doctor warned me that headaches will be common, but if they become unbearable or lead to dizziness, vomiting, or blacking out, I should go to the hospital immediately. He also referred me to follow up with a neurologist.

My parents wanted me to go home with them, and Kyle wanted me to move in with him, insisting I'll be moving in once we're married in a couple of weeks anyway. But I turned them down, wanting to go home to my own bed. I know my parents mean well, but my mom will hover, and Kyle...well, I still feel off. I keep hoping I'll feel something with every kiss, every touch, but instead, I keep questioning why I'm marrying him. I must've loved him, right? Or I wouldn't be marrying him. And I didn't completely lose my memory, so I remember him proposing.

It was six weeks after we'd been dating. I had gone out with Kaylee, Layla, Bailey, and her wife, Cynthia, for a girls' night before Layla was due to give birth.

I stepped into my foyer, and the only sound was the humming of the refrigerator. I set my purse on the counter and stripped off my clothes, throwing them into the hamper before washing my face and changing into my pajamas.

After checking my social media accounts, I went through my photos from that night to make sure I could post a couple. As I was swiping through the pictures, I stopped on the one of Layla and me. She was glowing, her hand on her big belly. Instinctually, my hand went to my own, and I wondered what it would be like to be pregnant. To carry a life inside me for nine months and then after giving birth, hold a precious little miracle in my arms that I get to spend the rest of my life loving.

My thoughts went to my mom and how close we used to be. For the first several years, it was just me and her—and my aunt Naomi—against the world because my bio dad didn't want us. And even when Easton—the only dad I've ever known—came into our lives, and she had three more kids, she always made sure to make time for me. Our relationship had always been special, and we were always close, until I found out that my sperm donor was a piece of shit rapist who made her life a living hell for years. I don't know why finding that out changed things, but it was the start of me pushing her away. Maybe it was the guilt I felt for being the reason she suffered, or because I wondered if when she looked into my blue eyes—the same ones as my sperm donor—she saw him in me. If she would've had a better life if it weren't for her getting pregnant by him with me. She's never once made me feel that way, but it didn't stop me from thinking those thoughts anyway.

After that, I spent more time in LA than New York, insisting on going on long-ass tours and avoiding my family. I no longer felt like I was one of them, like I belonged. I felt like an outsider, dirty and tarnished.

And that's when it all started—me *stiffing* guys. At first, I didn't realize I was doing it. I would date someone, and when it didn't work out, we would break up. But with every breakup, the media speculated. I would write a song, and they would tie it to one of the guys. So I started paying attention, trying to figure out where it was all going wrong...I would nitpick them. They weren't neat enough, not ambitious enough, or they were too ambitious. I didn't see the same future they saw, didn't fall in love when they did. I didn't want to take the next step when they did. They would say I love you, and I couldn't say it back.

As I sat in bed, staring at the photo of Layla and me, I realized I was broken. I pushed everyone away, from my parents to my siblings to men. So instead of going to bed, I called Kyle and asked if he was up for company.

"I'll come to you. I'm still at the office anyway."

He showed up a little while later, and I clung to him, not wanting to be broken. Wanting to have what my parents have, what my siblings have. We spent the night together, and the next morning, when he shocked the hell out of me by proposing over breakfast, instead of running, I said yes.

"Kendall," Kyle says, snapping me out of my thoughts. "I can stay here with you. They don't mind me working from home."

Home...this isn't his home. This is my home. And in a couple of weeks, I'm supposed to give it up to move into his. The thought causes a bout of anxiety to rush up my spine and neck, landing in the dead center of my head, where I've been getting frequent headaches.

"I'm okay," I insist. "I'm just going to rest. I'll text or call if I need anything."

He frowns but nods. "All right. I'll see you later."

"Call first, please. In case I'm sleeping. I wouldn't want you to come here for no reason."

He looks like he wants to argue but just nods again. "Okay."

Once he's left, it feels like I can breathe again. I spend the morning resting, scrolling social media, and when the afternoon rolls around, I'm so bored that I take a shower so I can get out of the house. I'm not on bed rest or anything.

As I'm considering where to go, I spot my writing journal on the counter. I open it up and find the most beautiful lyrics. I remember writing some of this with Declan, but this song looks damn near complete, so we must've worked on it some more during the time I lost my memory.

I'm on a break, but I don't see why I can't go to the studio and mess around, maybe put some instrumentals to it. I text my dad, asking if there's an open studio, and he replies that there's always one available for me.

Thirty minutes later, I'm walking into Blackwood Records. Everyone knows who I am and what happened, so they all greet me with smiles and tell me they're glad I'm okay.

I go in search of my dad, but when I can't find him, I end up in an empty studio that the receptionist said he booked for me. Just being here, with the equipment and sound booth, makes me feel ten times better. I plop onto the comfy couch and am reading through the lyrics again when the door opens and in walks Declan.

He's dressed in a simple white Vans T-shirt that's taut across his chest, showcasing the hard body hidden underneath, ripped jeans that mold to his muscular thighs, and clean white Vans don his feet. His dirty blond hair is up in a man bun, and his midnight blue eyes are wide, having not expected me to be here.

"Shouldn't you be in bed resting?" His deep, masculine voice sends shivers down my spine, and I squirm in my spot, the apex of my legs clenching in... want. *What the hell? Since when do I get turned on by Declan?*

"I got stir-crazy," I say, inwardly cringing when my words come out breathier than intended.

"Gotcha. I didn't know anyone was in here. I'll just..."

He's about to back out when I blurt out, "You can stay...if you want. I was reading through this song I wrote. Actually, it's the song we worked on together. I don't remember finishing it, but it turned out so beautiful. I'm thinking of asking Johnny to help me put some music to it."

Walking over, Declan takes the notebook from me and reads the words before handing it back to me. "The song is already done."

"What?"

"We finished it...*together* and put the music to it."

"Really?" *Jesus, how much happened during the six weeks that I can't remember?* "Did we record it?"

"Kind of. We recorded it so you could pitch it to your dad, but we'll have to have it redone properly." He pulls out his phone and pulls up the file, then hands it to me so I can press play. The instrumentals start, and then I begin singing about finding myself and love. About halfway through the song, Declan's voice comes on, and I suck in a harsh breath at his words...

I've been watching you all night
Memorizing your every move
Know exactly what you need
To cure that chaos in your heart
Hand it over, and I'll fix the broken
Turn the chaos into calm
Make that heart of yours mine
And you'll never feel alone
All you gotta do is say yes
And I'll handle the rest
Haven't touched a single drink all night
But I'm drunk as fuck
On your scent, on your touch
Hand it over, baby
And you'll never know what it's like to be without love

Butterflies erupt in my belly, chills race down my spine, my heart... *my freaking heart* flutters in my chest as if it was dead inside and has been resuscitated. The song continues, but my focus is on Declan, on his words...

"This is a love song." I don't write love songs. I write about heartbreak. I knew it was a love song when I read the words in my notebook, but it didn't click until I listened to them.

"Yeah," he says, his voice devoid of all emotion.

"We wrote a love song together..." I glance at my notebook, reading the lyrics as I listen to the emotion bleeding through every word we sing. The song can't be about Kyle because we started it before I met him...*So who is it about?*

For some musicians, writing a love song isn't a big deal, but for me, it's huge. I think back to when we started writing the song. We were hanging out, and Declan was scribbling words. I read them, looked into his eyes, could feel every raw emotion in every word, and added words of my own. We went back and forth until our friends showed up, and we put the notebook away. At the time, I didn't realize we were writing a love song—not until I just heard it finished.

"It's just words, K," Declan says, snapping me from my thoughts. "Doesn't mean anything."

I glance up at him, confused, as he takes his phone back and turns off the song, but he won't look at me. It's as if he's looking *past* me. We wrote this beautiful, emotional song together, yet he's acting like it means nothing.

My thoughts go back to the day I woke up in the hospital. *"Kendall, you can do it. Wake up, sweetheart. Just open those beautiful blue eyes and come back to me."*

Something is off, but I can't pinpoint what it is, and the harder I try to reach into my brain and figure it out, the more my head hurts. I'm about to ask him, no, *beg* him, to tell me what's going on, but before I can get the words out, he says, "I need to get going." He leaves me alone, wondering what the fuck is going on and why it's suddenly freezing in here. It's as if he took all the damn warmth with him.

And I'm still sitting here, confused as hell, when my mom walks in. "There you are!" She sits next to me and wraps her arms around me. "I was texting you."

"Sorry," I say, sighing into her comforting embrace. "My phone is on silent."

"That's okay. You look good," she says, sitting back slightly to assess me. "How're you feeling?"

Confused, frustrated…"Okay."

"The seamstress called to confirm your appointment for your final fitting tomorrow. I was thinking we could make a day of it. Go to lunch, do some shopping. We had talked about buying you some bridal lingerie."

"How did you know Dad was the one?" I blurt cut.

"Umm," she says, a bit taken aback by my change in topics. "Well, I think I knew he was the one when, even though I put up walls made of concrete, he tore them down like they were nothing more than paper."

When I don't say anything for a few beats, she takes my hand in hers, squeezing it softly. "What's going on, Sunshine?"

"I don't know," I admit. "Were you nervous when you married Dad?"

"Well, no…" She flinches. "But we're different."

Yeah, I know…

"Hey." She cups the side of my face. "Talk to me."

"I just feel different…*off*," I say, tears filling my eyes.

"Are you having headaches? Any vomiting or—"

"No," I cut her off. "I'm not talking about the accident. I mean, me. I know I can't remember the past six weeks, but it's more than that. I can't…" I sniffle back the sobs bubbling up. "I don't feel grounded, put together."

Mom's brow furrows, so I explain. "For a long time, I've felt like I was flying above the Earth on my own, lost and searching for something to ground me. I don't feel like I belong. I'm not like you or Dad or Camden or Bailey…I suck at love."

Yet I wrote a damn love song with Declan.

"Oh, sweetheart," Mom coos. "You don't suck at love."

"Yes, I do. I thought marrying Kyle would ground me and make me feel less...lost, but the thought of marrying him, living with him...*having kids with him* is doing the opposite."

"Maybe you're just having a moment," she says gently. "When I met your dad, I was lost. I was in school and working at the bar. Naomi and I were raising you the best we could. And then I met your dad. It wasn't love at first sight, but it was definitely lust." She smiles softly, probably remembering their first encounter, and my heart clenches, wanting to feel the way she looks—in utter love.

"We hooked up." She shrugs unapologetically since I already know the story. She and my dad have shared it many times over the years. "And I ended up pregnant with your brother. When I found out I was pregnant, I was so scared, felt like you, like I was soaring above the clouds, lost, but Easton brought me down and grounded me. In the chaotic world, I found myself, my place, my calm, through his love."

My thoughts go to the lyrics of the song I listened to earlier:

> *To cure that chaos in your heart*
> *Hand it over, and I'll fix the broken*
> *Turn the chaos into calm*
> *Make that heart of yours mine*
> *And you'll never feel alone*

"What if...What if Kyle's not the one?"

Mom's eyes go wide before she quickly schools her features. "Only you can know that."

Eight

DECLAN

"It's just words. Doesn't mean anything."

I can't get the conversation with Kendall out of my head. The one where she was shocked we wrote a love song together, and I told her it didn't mean shit...even though those words meant everything. While we were writing it, I thought she would catch on and realize she was writing her first love song, but she never said a word if she did. She acted like the queen of heartbreak wrote love songs every damn day, when the truth was, she'd never written one before...until now.

And while one might say it's because of her relationship with Kyle, I refuse to believe that because when we started to write it, he didn't exist. It was just Kendall and me and a notebook.

Now, it's Kendall and Kyle...getting married. Fuck. When she finally woke up and was talking, I hung on to every word, hoping she would kick Kyle out and tell me that once she got out of the hospital, she wanted to pick up right where we left off. But then, through the doctor's questioning, we learned she has no recollection of the past six weeks. Which means she not only doesn't remember saying she wants to end her engagement but she also doesn't remember the night we spent together.

"Dammit." I swipe the canister off the counter, sending it crashing to the floor. The only thing worse than spending the night with Kendall and her not remembering is knowing it will never fucking happen again. She might not be able to remember a damn thing, but I still remember everything. Every touch and kiss and fucking caress. The way she came on my fingers and cock over and over again.

And now, in two motherfucking days, I have to go to her wedding because it's still on. A reminder was sent to everyone, letting us know Kendall is doing better, completely healed, and the wedding will be taking place as planned. Two days. In forty-eight hours, she'll be married to a man who she can't remember not wanting to marry.

"It's such bullshit." I knock the other canister off the counter and grab the bottle of Jack I've been guzzling for the past hour since I got that stupid event reminder in the mail.

"Tell us how you really feel," Camden says as he and Braxton walk into the kitchen. Since Braxton used to live here, he still has a key and the code.

"What's got you drinking and cursing…?" He glances at the floor, where the shattered pieces of canisters are. "And throwing shit."

"I called Gage." I needed my friend, needed someone to vent to. "The receptionist said he's not accepting calls at this time. It made no sense. It had to be a mix-up, so I called your dad since he's Gage's point of contact, and he told me there wasn't a mix-up. Gage isn't accepting any phone calls."

Camden and Braxton glance at each other. "What do you mean he isn't accepting phone calls?" Braxton asks slowly. "Who the fuck is he trying to avoid? Because the only people who would be calling him are us, so why the fuck isn't he taking our calls?"

I shrug, at a loss. "I don't know, man." I've tried to think about why Gage wouldn't want to talk to us, but I can't think of one damn reason. We've always had each other's backs. Always. And when he agreed to get help, no one forced him.

"What are you guys doing here anyway?" Between Camden having a five-year-old and a four-month-old, and Braxton obsessed with Kaylee, we haven't hung out much, aside from the obligatory holidays or when we were all at the hospital visiting Gage and then Kendall.

When Camden's brows kiss his forehead, I realize I asked the question a bit too harshly, so I backtrack. "I just know you guys are busy," I mutter.

"What does that have to do with anything?" Braxton asks, taking the bottle from me and pouring it down the drain. "We've been trying to get ahold of you, and you haven't returned a single call or text."

"I've got a lot of shit going on." Like getting drunk and wallowing like a little bitch.

Camden picks up the reminder card and glances at it. I can already see the pity in his eyes, so before he can speak, I shake my head. "Don't go there."

"You saying the reason for you getting drunk has nothing to do with my sister getting married?"

"I'm saying it doesn't matter because like you've said on several occasions, she doesn't even know I exist."

"Not according to that song you guys wrote."

I snap my head up. "You heard it?"

"Was at the studio with my dad earlier. He needs the band to sign off on you releasing it with Kendall since it will be considered a solo, and it states in our contract if one of us wants to release without the rest of the band, we all have to agree."

"And?"

"Of course, we all agree. You think we'd hold you back?"

"No...I don't know." I shrug. "Just feels like the band's falling apart. Maybe releasing a song without you guys isn't the best idea."

"You know you saved his life, right?" Camden says, understanding what I'm upset about without me having to say it.

"And now he won't even answer my calls."

"We're going to get through this," Braxton adds.

"Yeah." I sigh. "So what were you trying to get ahold of me about?"

"Just wanted to check in. The ladies are, uh, doing a girls' night. Layla's mom is watching the kids, so Brax and I were thinking we could do a guys' night. Maybe play some poker and shoot the shit like we used to."

"Girls' night?" I raise a brow. "You mean they're at her bachelorette party? Why aren't you at your future brother-in-law's bachelor party?"

"He decided against one. Said some shit about not wanting to party." Camden snorts out a laugh. "I didn't question it since I can't stand the guy. I wasn't in the mood to party with him anyway."

"You don't like him?"

"He's a kiss-ass workaholic. One of those guys always looking for ways, or people, to help him climb the ladder. I honestly thought my sister would call this shit off before she made it down the aisle."

"So why the fuck haven't you said that to her?"

He raises his hands in a placating manner. "Ain't for me to say. If you think she's making a bad decision, why don't you say something?"

I sigh and shake my head, debating if I should admit to them what happened between Kendall and me...at the very least, tell them what she said to me. Don't I at least owe her that much? What if what the guy did was something horrible, and now, she's marrying him.

"Before Kendall lost her memory, she told me something..." Camden's brow furrows, and he nods for me to continue. "She said she was going to end their engagement."

"When?" Camden asks.

"Right before she got into the accident." I decide not to mention what happened between us because it might look like I'm jealous. If she does decide to go through with the wedding, I don't want her knowing she technically cheated, especially since she can't remember ever being with me.

"Did she say why?" Braxton asks.

"No. Just said it was over."

"Probably just cold feet," Camden says. "Everyone knows my sister is afraid of commitment."

"Yeah, maybe," I agree even though that night it felt like a whole lot more than her being afraid of saying I do.

"C'mon." Braxton stands. "We need a night out. Shit's gotten too real lately, and we need a night to let loose, let off some steam."

Since I've been missing my friends and I'm down for drinking, I tell them to give me a few minutes to get changed, and then we head out. With our security detail tagging along, we end up at Lush, our go-to place. Instead of getting a table, we go straight for the bar in the VIP lounge.

The great thing about Lush is that the people here are just as wealthy, if not wealthier than we are, and many are famous in their own right, so we don't have to worry about being accosted. The bartender doesn't even bat an eyelash when she comes over to take our orders.

"I don't know what to do," Braxton says once she's dropped off our drinks. "Kaylee and I were supposed to get married, and then all that shit went down with Gage, and now…"

"You don't want to do anything while he's not here," Camden finishes for him, taking a sip of his drink. "I say you get married. You weren't planning a wedding anyway, right?"

Braxton shakes his head. "We just wanted something small, with just us, since our families suck. My brother said he'd be our witness." He shrugs. "But I don't know…It just kind of feels wrong, doing anything while he's…there."

"There's no way Gage would want you to wait on him. I mean, he could've changed since he left, but I can't imagine him ever getting upset over you wife-ing Kaylee up. He knows how much you love that woman. We all do," I tell him, patting him on his back.

"Yeah, you're right. I think after Kendall's wedding, we'll plan something. Maybe have a little dinner with everyone afterward. Since we're on a bit of a break, I'm going to surprise her with a trip to Paris. We talked about going there when we were younger."

"Nice," Camden says. "With spring break coming up, Layla and I are taking the kids to The Hamptons. Put the place we bought to use."

We're all quiet for a few minutes when Camden adds, "If you wanna go…"

"Bro," I say dryly. "I'm not about to play the fifth wheel with your family vacay. I'm good. I was actually thinking of taking off for a little while."

Both guys' faces swing toward me.

"Where?" Braxton asks.

"When?" This time Camden.

"I don't know. I just think I need to get away for a bit. Clear my head."

"You do what you need to do," Braxton says, putting his hand on my shoulder. "Just know that we're here for you. Any time. I don't give a fuck if I'm across the damn pond. You got me?"

"Yeah," I say, downing my drink. "I got you."

We spend the next couple of hours drinking and bullshitting. It's been a while since we've done this, so it's nice to spend some time with the guys, minus everyone else, even if it's bittersweet as hell since Gage isn't with us.

When it's late, and their women start to text that they're back from their girls' day/evening, we call it a night. We all grab separate cars since we're going in different directions. Instead of going home, I find myself at the studio. I text Easton to let him know I'm here so he's not confused when he gets a notification from his security company that someone's entered.

I assume the place is empty, and I'll have it to myself, but when I step into the room we tend to favor, I find someone already there, sitting on the couch, scribbling away in a journal.

"What are you doing here?" I ask from the doorway.

"Oh, my God!" Kendall jumps, clutching her chest. "You scared me. I thought this place was empty."

"It is...well, it *was*. I just got here, thinking the same thing." I step into the room and notice she's writing lyrics in her journal. "Shouldn't you be home with your fiancé? You're getting married in less than two days."

It's a dick question because I know she's refused to move in with him until after they get married, and she's mentioned on several occasions that she only spends the night on Saturdays because he works a lot.

"I've been with him since I got out of the hospital," she says. "I just needed a moment to myself."

"I'll leave you to it then."

I'm about to step out of the room when she says, "Or you can stay." She shrugs. "There's plenty of room in here for two."

I want to stay so fucking badly, but I'm torn because as much as I want to spend time with her, doing so only hurts, knowing I'll never have her. Knowing in less than two days, she'll bear another man's last name. She'll be his wife, one day give birth to his children, and the only thing that will be left of us is the memory of the night we shared—a memory she doesn't even have.

"Please," she says softly. "I'm writing a new song. Maybe you can...take a look at it."

Because I can't say no to her, I nod and walk all the way in, sitting down next to her and taking the journal so I can read what she has so far.

The words are both beautiful and heartbreaking, a story of a woman who's lost and begging to be found. She wants to love and be loved, but she doesn't know how to go about it. It's raw and gritty and so fucking Kendall. It reminds me of our conversation the night we spent together when she confided in me about her biological dad and how broken she feels. These aren't lyrics of a woman happily in love, excited about getting married and starting her life with someone. She might not remember that night, but it's clear in her words that she can still feel what she felt.

Maybe she just needs a little nudge to jog her memory.

"What do you think?" she asks, her eyes meeting mine.

"Are you sure you want to get married?"

Her eyes go wide, and I open my mouth to backtrack. That's not how I wanted to word what I wanted to say...at all. But before I can think of what to say, she answers my question.

"I'm not sure."

Nine

KENDALL

I'VE BEEN HIDING OUT, SPENDING MY DAYS AT THE STUDIO WRITING, DOING WHAT I DO BEST: GETTING LOST in my thoughts while shutting out the rest of the world. Today was my bachelorette party, so I had to leave my bubble. I wanted to enjoy going to dinner and dancing with my friends and sisters and Mom, but the entire time, I felt too much like a fraud.

Every time they spoke of their own weddings, of them finding love, gushing about how beautiful of a bride I'll be, how perfect my day will be, how they're so excited to be there and share what will be the best day of my life—their words, not mine—all I kept thinking was that I'm making a mistake. I don't feel what they feel. I'm not excited. I'm scared and nervous and freaking the hell out.

I keep telling myself that it's just pre-wedding jitters, and once I say I do, I'll be okay. I'm overthinking things and overanalyzing. I was in an accident that injured my brain, for crying out loud. That's bound to mess a person up, right?

But then why was it that the second Declan appeared in the doorway of the studio—like when he sat next to me while I listened to the song that I don't remember recording with him—butterflies attacked my belly, and my heart pounded against my chest? Shouldn't I be feeling that way toward my fiancé?

"Kendall," Declan says softly, snapping me from my thoughts. "What do you mean you're not sure?" *Huh?* Oh, right! He asked me if I'm sure I want to get married, and I blurted out the truth instead of lying like I've been doing to everyone, including myself.

"I..." I almost lie, tell him I didn't mean it like that, but something inside urges me to be honest. I can trust him. He's not just Camden's best friend. He's mine too. We've written a beautiful, intimate song together, and that doesn't happen unless you're close.

"I think something is wrong with me."

His brows kiss his forehead. "What's wrong? Is it your head? Are you having headaches?" His eyes skate over my face and body, assessing my features.

"No, I'm okay. I mean, I still have occasional headaches, but I was checked out yesterday by the neurologist, and everything came back clean."

He sighs in relief, and my heart clenches. I know we're only friends, but is it possible he's feeling the way I am? Like there's something more between us, something I'm terrified to explore, both as Camden's sister and Kyle's fiancée?

"What's wrong?" Declan asks, moving a stray hair out of my eyes and tucking it behind my ear. My body acts of its own accord, shuddering in response. When Declan sees, the corner of his lips tugs into a sexy smirk, forcing my legs to tighten. I haven't once felt turned on since I got out of the hospital. I even told Kyle I wanted to wait until our wedding night to be together, hoping by then whatever is broken in me would be fixed, but sitting here with Declan, it's clear I'm not as broken as I thought.

"I...I feel different. Kyle has been so sweet and attentive since I woke up, but I can't conjure up any feelings for him. I must've cared for him enough to be engaged to him, but I...I don't feel it. When I look at him, I feel nothing."

"Then why are you marrying him?" His question comes out thoughtful and not at all judgmental.

"I spoke to the doctor about it, and he said what I'm feeling isn't uncommon. With memories come emotions, and I can't remember almost half of the time we've been together."

"Maybe you're feeling that way for a reason. Like something happened, and you can't remember." His statement is one I've thought about many times, but asking Kyle would raise a red flag, and I wouldn't even know if he's lying or telling the truth.

Before I can answer, my phone buzzes on the table, Kyle's name flashing on the screen. I've been avoiding him all day, so I should probably answer, but as I stare at the screen, I can't bring myself to do it. It stops and then starts up again, and I inwardly sigh, knowing I need to answer. He could be worried about me.

"I need to take this," I tell Declan, who nods. "Hey."

"You okay? I've called you a few times."

"Yeah, sorry. I'm in the studio writing. Phone's on silent."

"By yourself?"

"No." I clear my throat. "Declan's with me."

There's silence on the other end, and then Kyle says, "When will you be home?"

"I'm not sure. Did we have plans?" I know we didn't, but I'm not sure why he's asking.

"No, we haven't had plans since you woke up," he snaps, then sighs into the phone. "I'm sorry. I just miss you. I feel like I never see you. Your mom said the bachelorette party ended a while ago."

I should apologize, tell him I'll come over or offer for him to come over. Make plans for tomorrow since I don't have any. But as I glance at Declan, the only thing I want to do is hang up and write music...with him. So instead of saying what I should say and doing what I should do, I say, "I'm sorry. I'm really tired and wouldn't be good company."

"So what? I'm not going to see you until at the wedding?"

"You'll see me at the rehearsal dinner. Besides, it's bad luck to spend the night together before the wedding."

Kyle releases a harsh breath, and I wince, hating myself for what I'm doing to him, but I don't know how to fix this.

"All right, well, I guess I'll stay at work. I need to get ahead anyway since we'll be gone for a week on our honeymoon."

I don't realize how tense I am until I sag in relief. "Okay, sounds good."

"Text me when you get home, so I know you're okay."

"Will do."

There's a brief pause, like Kyle wants to say something, but instead, he sighs and says, "I love you, Kendall."

He's said those three words a few times since I woke up, but I've yet to say them back. I already feel like the worst person ever for living this lie, for being on the fence and not telling him how I really feel, that I can't bring myself to say it back. The truth is, as far as I can remember, I've never said those three words to any man, including Kyle. Maybe I said them during the six weeks I've lost, but I just can't bring myself to say them now. Not when I don't feel them.

"Good night," I say instead, then hang up, tossing my phone to the side and glancing over at Declan. "So what do you think about that song?" I nod toward my journal.

"I think you're living in a state of lies and denial, and the only truth is on this paper." He sets the journal down and takes my hands in his. "If you're not one-hundred-percent sure you want to marry him, you shouldn't do it. He'll wait if he loves you like he says he does."

He's right, I know he is, but the thought of letting everyone down makes me feel sick. My parents have spent thousands of dollars on this wedding, countless hours making sure everything is perfect. They're so happy I'm settling down and have found a man to start a life with. I know they were worried, with me jumping from man to man, refusing to get serious or commit. My mom mentioned how excited she is to have more grandbabies. And what about Kyle? Pushing the wedding back would hurt him, and he's been nothing but kind to me since I woke up.

No, this is just a moment. The effects of my brain injury. I'm going to feel again, and everything will be okay.

A text chimes from Kyle: **I really do miss you, Kendall.**

No butterflies. No sparks. But it's the confirmation I needed.

"I want to marry him," I tell Declan. "He loves me." I grab my phone and journal and stand. "I should probably go."

"Kendall—" He starts, but I cut him off.

"I appreciate you listening to me. You're a wonderful friend, and even though I don't remember us finishing this song, I know it's special. I hope once I get back from my honeymoon, we can have Blackwood hammer out the specifics so we can release it. I have no doubt it will be a hit."

Declan clenches his jaw. "I won't be here. I'm going away. But I'll let your dad know I'm on board with however he wants to go about it. If he needs me to fly in to record it, I can do that."

His confession rattles me. "Going where? Will you be at the wedding?" The thought of him not being there affects me more than it should.

"I'll be at the wedding. Then I'm taking off on a road trip. With the band on a hiatus and…" He clears his throat. "I just need to get away for a little bit."

I nod in understanding, but a huge lump fills my throat. "I'm sure they'll want to do a music video as well. How long will you be gone for?" I don't give a shit about the video, but I'm too much of a wuss to ask outright how long he'll be away.

"I'm not sure," he says, his voice hard. "I'll keep in touch with Easton, though."

"Okay." I bob my head up and down, trying to appear nonchalant, while I'm freaking out on the inside. Which is ridiculous since Declan and I are only friends, and him going away has nothing to do with me since I'll be away on my honeymoon as well. "Okay," I say again.

"Okay," he repeats.

He walks me out, keeping his distance, and when I get in the car, he mutters a goodbye before shutting the door and walking away. I have no idea what's going on with me, my thoughts, my chaotic mess of emotions, but as the car takes off from the curb, I can't help feeling as though my heart is being ripped from my chest—which is crazy because Declan doesn't own my heart. Kyle does. Right?

My intention was to go to Kyle's, but instead, I find myself back at home, alone, where I stay curled up in bed, writing lyrics and pouring my heart out, all while the words Declan said run on repeat: *I think you're living in a state of lies and denial, and the only truth is on this paper.*

"WOW," MY DAD SAYS, HIS EYES FILLED WITH EMOTION. "YOU LOOK LIKE A BEAUTIFUL PRINCESS."

It's Saturday afternoon, the day of my wedding. The morning has been spent with everyone getting their hair and makeup done and the seamstress ensuring everyone's dresses fit perfectly.

As I stare into the mirror, I have to agree with my dad—I do look like a princess. My makeup is flawless, my dress is elegant, and my glossy golden locks are up in a tight bun, complete with a diamond-encrusted tiara. But unlike the Disney Princesses, I'm unsure if this is where I get my happily ever after. My heart is pounding against my rib cage, and I feel as though I'm about to pass out.

The music starts up, indicating the wedding procession is about to begin. I'm hidden behind the door, but I can picture everyone walking down the aisle. We practiced it last night—who would walk when and where they would stand. Then afterward, we went out to dinner, where we ate Italian food, and I faked having a headache to be excused early, so I could spend the rest of the night writing more songs.

"I can still remember the day I married your mom," my dad says, placing his hand on my shoulder and gently turning me to face him. "As I watched her walk down the aisle, I knew I was the luckiest man in the world. She was carrying Camden, and she said she felt fat and ugly so many times, but when I looked at her, all I saw was the most beautiful woman, the love of my life. And I couldn't wait to officially make her mine."

As he recounts his memories from the wedding with a content smile on his face, I'm brought back to when I was a little girl, dressing up in my pretend wedding dress so I could marry my pretend fiancé, and begging my mom to retell the story of her wedding day. She would put on their wedding video, and we would watch, as my parents, with hearts in their eyes, promised each other forever. As a young girl, it would give me butterflies, imagining that one day I would fall in love and put on a pretty white dress and make the same promises to the man I wanted to spend my life with.

Only now, as I think about that, butterflies don't attack my belly. Instead, anxiety roils in my stomach with the fear that I'm making a mistake. That while I'm dressed like a princess, Kyle isn't my prince. I keep telling myself it's my brain injury, but shouldn't I feel something...*anything* toward him? Shouldn't I be excited that in a few minutes, I'm going to walk down the aisle, exchange vows with him, and start our lives together?

"It was without a doubt the best day of my life," my dad says, snapping me out of my thoughts.

"Of course, it was...because you married your best friend," I say robotically, knowing how the story ends. I've heard this same story a million times over the years, and both my parents always end it the same way.

"Well, that, of course, but also…" He softly palms my cheek. "Because it's the day I became a dad."

"Camden always has the worst timing," I say, rolling my eyes playfully. Only my brother would decide he was ready to join the world the night of my parents' wedding while they were attempting to consummate their marriage.

"That he does," Dad agrees with a chuckle. "And yes, your mother giving birth was definitely part of making that day perfect, but what I was referring to was you."

"Me?" I ask dumbly.

"Yes, you," he says with a light laugh. "In case you forgot, you made me a dad first. Before Camden was born, I signed the papers to legally make you mine. It was also the first time you called me Daddy." His lips curve into a watery smile. "Camden had just been born, and you were so excited. You looked up at me, and you said, 'Wow, today is the best day ever. I got a daddy and a brother.' And I swear, my heart swelled so big, I wasn't sure how the hell it still fit in my chest."

A choked sob escapes at his admission, and tears course down my cheeks. He thumbs a couple, smiling down at me. "I'm so proud of the woman you've become, K. You're strong and independent, and your heart…fuck, it's so big and full. I'm going to sound like a selfish asshole when I say this, but giving you away is probably the hardest thing I'll ever have to do, but if it means you have with Kyle, what I have with your mom, I know I have to be okay with it. Because that's all I want for you, sweetheart. To find love."

Something in me snaps at his admission. "I…I…I don't think I do."

His brow furrows. "You don't think you do, what?"

"Have what you guys have." My sobs strengthen, and it's hard to see through my tears. "I keep telling myself that it's in my head, it's because of my injury, but I don't feel anything. I don't think…I don't think I'm in love," I cry out. "Oh my God, Dad. I don't *think*…I *know* I'm not in love with Kyle." It's the first time I've said the words out loud, and while they suck, I know deep down they're the truth. I don't love Kyle. I'm not *in love* with him. He's not my best friend, and I can't imagine spending the rest of my life with him. "I'm broken, aren't I? I'm broken, and now I'm going to break him because I can't marry him."

"What? No…No, K. You're not broken." My dad pulls me into his arms and guides us over to the couch. "Sweetheart, why would you think you're broken?"

"Because I don't know how to love anyone. I fuck up every relationship I'm in. I wanted what you and Mom have so badly, but I'll never have it because I'm broken." I cover my face with my hands and cry, hating myself and wishing I wasn't so messed up.

"You are not broken. Hey...look at me." Dad lifts my face and forces me to make eye contact. "Just because Kyle isn't the one doesn't mean you aren't capable of love. You love me and your mother and your brother and sisters... And you're the best damn aunt to Felix and Marianna."

"But that's different. You guys are family."

"Love is love, K. And you have a huge heart."

"Then why can't I find what you and Mom have?"

"Oh, sweetheart." He palms my cheeks. "You just haven't met the right guy yet. One day, you will meet him, and you'll know he's the one. You'll look at him and see your entire life in front of you with him by your side."

"Or maybe I'm not meant to be with anyone. Maybe...it's not in me."

I regret the words the second I say them, but it's too late to take them back. My dad's jaw clenches. "Tell me you're not referring to your genetics."

"It would make sense, wouldn't it? The only thing *he* was capable of was destroying everyone around him. How am I any different?"

"Don't you ever say that," Dad says, his voice commanding. "You are nothing like that man. You might carry his DNA, but you are every bit your mother's daughter. And you are not broken. You are perfect just the way you are."

"You have to say that because you're my dad," I say lamely.

"Damn right, I am," he says. "You might not carry *my* DNA, but never, for a fucking second, doubt that you're not the best part of your mother and me."

He pulls me into a hug, and we both go quiet as the music in the background bleeds through the walls, reminding me that I'm supposed to be walking down the aisle. They must be wondering where we are. I'm honestly shocked nobody has knocked on the door yet.

"What am I supposed to do?" I whisper even though I already know the answer to my question.

My dad pulls back and takes my hand in his, squeezing it softly. "You're supposed to follow your heart."

Ten

DECLAN

The day I didn't think would actually happen. Between Kendall being allergic to commitment, what happened with us, and then her getting into an accident and losing her memory, I honestly thought the wedding would be canceled at some point, but it's like a fireproof safe after a fire. The entire house has burned to the ground, but that damn safe is still standing.

I considered not going. It's not like I'm in the wedding. She probably won't even notice I'm not there. But something in me convinced me to go. Maybe it's my way of officially saying goodbye to the woman I've been pining after for the past decade. It's one thing to have feelings for her while she's jumping from guy to guy, but it's another to be crushing—for lack of a better word—on a married woman. And that's precisely what she'll be soon: *married.*

After I finish putting on my suit, I grab my suitcase and lock up since I'll be gone for several weeks. I don't have a concrete plan, but I'm thinking I'll drive down the East Coast and probably end up in the Keys. With it being March, Florida is the perfect place to chill for a little while. The beaches are beautiful, and the laidback vibe in the Keys is exactly what I need to lose myself for a bit.

When I get down to the garage, I pop the trunk to my Dodge Challenger I had shipped here from California and throw my bag in. She's not my favorite out of the vehicles I own, but she's the most practical to take on a road trip, and since I purchased her right before we moved to New York, I haven't put any miles on her.

I try calling Gage again on the way to the church, hoping something has changed, and he's now accepting calls. Only I'm told the same damn thing by the receptionist, who I'm sure is sick of hearing from me: *I'm sorry, but he's not accepting calls at this time.*

It's been over a month, and he still won't talk to anyone. Easton checks in with his doctor on a weekly basis, so we know he's okay, but fuck, if I don't want to talk to my friend myself. Hear him tell me he's okay. Since he'll be gone for at least ninety days, my plan is to be back by the end of April, so I'm back when he gets out. Until then, with the band on a break, there's nothing for me here right now.

I pull up to the church, and the parking lot is filled with vehicles. I check the time and see I'm about to be late, but instead of getting out, I don't move. I stay in the car, the engine rumbling under me, contemplating if I can do this. If I can sit in a pew and watch her promise herself to another man, one we both know isn't right for her. I have nothing against the guy. Don't even really know him. But from what I know, he works a lot, doesn't put her first, and for whatever reason, when she came to me that night, she was one-hundred-percent ready to end the engagement, which tells me all I need to know.

As I sit in my car, staring at the front doors where I'm supposed to walk through, I imagine how beautiful she'll look today with her hair and makeup done and wearing some expensive, gorgeous dress. Without a doubt, she'll be the most beautiful bride, but she won't be mine. Never will be. Because she belongs to someone else. She'll say I do to someone else, dance with someone else. Tonight, she'll go to a hotel room and make love to someone else. And tomorrow, she'll go on a honeymoon with someone else. Eventually, she'll give birth to beautiful blue-eyed babies, but they won't be mine. And she'll live happily ever after, like the queen she is, but it won't be with me.

Braxton sends me a text, asking where the hell I am, but I don't respond, unsure if I'm going in. I sit for a few more minutes, contemplating whether I should bite the bullet and just go in or say fuck it and take off.

I've almost convinced myself that the wedding has probably started by now, and I wouldn't want to walk in and disturb the service, when a blur of movement out of the corner of my eye catches my attention.

The window is open, and it looks as if a white blanket is being shoved through it. I turn the ignition off on my car and step out, wondering what the fuck is going on, when the white shit collapses onto the ground and then...

What the fuck? Is that...?

"Kendall?"

She pops her head up, exposing her flawlessly done-up face. Her blond hair is up in a bun, and a crown rests on top of her head. She huffs out a small laugh and shrugs, lifting her puffy dress and scurrying toward me.

"You, uh, going somewhere?" I ask, glancing around in confusion. The woman, who should be saying I do, just damn near fell out of a window.

"Yeah, away from here." She steps over to my car. "This yours?" Her eyes are wide and bright, a mixture of nervous and excited.

"Yeah, it's mine."

"Great. Mind giving me a ride? I didn't exactly think this part through."

"What part?"

"The getaway."

It takes me a second, but my brain finally catches up, realizing what she means. She's running away...from her wedding. And fuck me if I'm not going to help her.

"Hop in." I round the front and open the door for her.

"Thanks." She pops a quick kiss to my cheek and ducks in, gathering her enormous dress to fit in the vehicle with her. Once she's all the way in, I close the door, then click the fob to start the car while I head back over to the driver's side and get in. Music is thumping, my phone still connected, and when I get in, Kendall has already gotten her seat belt on and is changing the song.

"Does anyone know you left?" I ask, not giving a shit about Kyle but knowing her family will be worried if she just up and disappeared.

"Yep. My dad knows. He'll tell everyone."

"You told your dad?"

She nods, a giggle escaping past her lips, and fuck if it isn't the most beautiful sound in the world. "He told me to follow my heart." She glances over at me, her eyes filled with unshed tears. "So I did."

I know she isn't referring to me, her heart taking her straight to me, but I can't help but think about the fact that I was here when she escaped. I could've been inside that church, but I wasn't. And now, here she is, sitting in my car, in her goddamn wedding dress that she didn't get married in.

My screen lights up with a text from Braxton: **You wouldn't believe this shit. Kendall ran.**

"I think everyone knows."

"We should probably get out of here," she says, nervously biting the corner of her bottom lip.

"Where to?"

My phone goes off again with another text: **Enjoy your road trip, man.**

"That's right. You're going out of town." She flips her dress up, knocks her heels off, and plops her feet up on my dash. "Count me in. A road trip sounds perfect."

She looks over at me with a smile spread across her entire face, and I briefly wonder if I drank too much and am dreaming because...what the fuck? Did the woman of my goddamn dreams just agree to go on a road trip with me?

"We'll be gone for weeks," I warn. "Probably over a month."

"Perfect," she says. "That'll give everyone enough time to get over the fact I just left my fiancé at the altar." The door to the church opens, and Kendall's eyes bug out. "Oh, God, Dec, go!"

I put the car in drive and take off, dirt from the parking lot kicking up behind us as we peel out. The first few minutes are silent, but then her phone vibrates, and she pulls it out, cringing. "I better get this. It's my mom."

I turn down the music as she hits accept. It's a video call, so her mother's face takes over the screen. "Kendall Naomi Blackwood…"

"Oh, shit. All three names, Mom? Am I in trouble?" She sounds so adorable and apologetic, I want to pull her into my arms and comfort her, but I stay quiet, letting her talk to her mom.

Her mom sighs. "Of course, you're not, Sunshine. Are you okay?"

"I am," Kendall tells her with a soft smile. "I just couldn't…Dad told me to follow my heart and…" She sniffles. "I'm sorry."

"You have nothing to be sorry about," her mom says. "Your dad was right. You should always follow your heart. Where are you going?"

"I just need to get away for a bit. Clear my head."

"Okay, sweetheart. But please keep in touch so we know you're okay. I don't care how old you are, you're still our little girl, and we're always going to worry about you."

"I know. I'm sorry I left that mess for you to clean up."

"It's okay. Your dad handled it."

"And, uh…Kyle?"

"He's not too happy. I'm sure his ego is bruised, but he'll be okay."

Kendall nods. "I love you, Mom. Talk soon."

"Love you too."

She hangs up, and her phone goes off several times in quick succession. To give her some space, I turn the music up and drive while she texts everyone.

She sets her phone down a little while later and glances at me. "So, where are we going first?"

"The Jersey Shore."

She grins. "Nice." Then she looks down at her dress and frowns. "I don't have any clothes."

"We can pick some up once we get there."

"And where's there?"

"Not really sure. I didn't book any rooms, not wanting to be tied down to an agenda. I get enough of that with the tours."

"I feel that deep," she says, pulling something out of her clutch. It's a small silver flask.

I laugh as she opens it and raises it up into the air. "To road trips and freedom." She toasts the air and takes a quick sip before offering it to me.

"I'm driving." I shake my head.

"Just take a quick sip. It's like a contract. You have to drink to the road trip."

I do as she says, taking a sip of the vodka in it, and then hand it back to her. "To road trips and freedom."

She takes the flask back. "And whatever trouble we shall find along the way." After downing some more, she screws the top back on and drops it into her clutch. Then she turns up the music. "This is going to be epic."

Eleven

KENDALL

THE TWO-HOUR DRIVE TO JERSEY FLIES BY. THANKFULLY, DECLAN DRIVES IN SILENCE, GIVING ME TIME TO process what the hell just happened, and doesn't ask any questions. When my phone doesn't stop vibrating, and I turn it off, then turn up the music and sing the songs on his playlist at the top of my lungs, he only smiles, letting me let go.

At some point, I know I'll have to deal with what I've done. At the very least, I owe Kyle an explanation and apology, and I'm aware that running away is immature as hell, but right now, it's what I need to do. My dad told me to follow my heart, and I don't find it a coincidence that as I stumbled out the window, the person standing there was Declan. The guy I wrote my one and only love song with. The same guy I've been thinking about since I woke up in the hospital.

I've known him for years—he's been my brother's best friend for over a decade—and in recent years, we've gotten closer, hence us writing music together, but for some reason, it feels like more than that. There's an attraction there. A feeling I know I can't act on because he's too close to my family, too close to my brother, and I always fuck up the relationships I'm in. But maybe he's who I need right now. He was heading out on a road trip, and I was running away, so maybe in some crazy way, we were meant to be on this journey together.

We pull up to a gorgeous modern-looking resort, and when we step out of the car so the valet can take over, I inhale the salty ocean breeze.

"It's oceanfront," Declan says, taking my hand in his. "Let's go get our sun on." He waggles his brows playfully, and I can't help but laugh at how adorable he is. Don't get me wrong, he's sexy as hell, but he's also lowkey adorable, which is something you rarely see with rock stars. They're usually dark and broody and covered in tattoos. Braxton and Gage are the perfect example. My brother is more of a dark pretty boy. He's mastered the brooding, but his wife, Layla, brings out the softness in him. But Declan...he's always happy and smiling.

"I was wondering if you have a room available," he asks the woman at the front desk, proving what he said earlier, that he didn't book anything and was planning to just wing it.

"We do," she says, eyeing Declan in his suit and me in my wedding dress, which reminds me that I need to get out of this thing and into some regular clothes.

"We have the Presidential suite," she explains. "It's a two-bedroom, two-bathroom suite with an ocean view. It's the most common for honeymooners."

Declan's brow furrows, and then he laughs when he looks at me. "I forgot you're in your wedding dress," he says softly. To her, he adds, "That room will be fine."

"How many nights?"

"We're not sure," he says. "How many nights is this room available?"

She taps away on her keyboard. "At least for the next five nights, but—"

"Perfect. Book it for all five nights, and if we leave early, it's no big deal."

"We, um, if we do all five nights, you'll be charged for all the nights."

"Of course." Declan hands her his credit card.

After she goes over the amenities and gives us our room keys, he has her point us in the direction of the resort shop, so I can purchase a bathing suit and cover-up.

I end up picking out a few different bikinis since their selection is good, along with a cute romper, a couple of cover-ups, a pair of sandals, some sunglasses, and a hat to help keep anyone from recognizing me. We also purchase a couple of fluffy towels since hotels—no matter how luxurious the hotel is—never have good towels.

Declan reserves the cabana by the pool for the next five days, and then we head up to the room to get settled in.

The moment we step into the room, the energy changes. Maybe it's because of the bottle of champagne sitting on ice or the fact that we're now alone, but suddenly, I'm nervous, unsure of what I was thinking when I hopped in the vehicle with him without having a plan.

"I'll take this room," he says, pointing at the room to the left and leaving the one on the other side for me. "Wanna get changed and hit the beach? I'm sure they have a bar down there where we can get some drinks and food."

"Sure."

Closing the door behind me, I take a deep breath as the heaviness of the morning drops onto my shoulders. I set the bags from the resort shop on the bed and pull my phone out to check my messages. My brother and sisters left several, telling me they love me, and if I need anything, they've got my back. One from my dad, asking that I let him know I'm okay once I get to where I'm going, one from my assistant, asking if I need anything, and a *What the fuck, Kendall?* from Kyle.

I text my siblings back, thanking them; let my parents know I'm okay and will stay in touch; tell my assistant that I appreciate it, but I'm good, and she's off the clock—paid, of course—until I get back; and then text Kyle back two words: I'm sorry.

It's a cop-out, but I don't know what else to say. He deserves an explanation, and once I have one, I'm going to give it to him, but for right now, I'm doing as my dad said and following my heart.

After I hit send, I throw my phone onto the nightstand, wanting to check out for a little while, and pick out which suit I'm going to wear. I go with the two-piece burnt orange ombre number and the matching cover-up, but when I go to take off my dress, I realize I can't. It's formfitting up top with several dozen buttons down my back holding it together. I couldn't even put it on myself this morning—my mom had to help me.

I try several times to get it off, but when it's obvious it's not happening, I head out to find Declan. He's standing in the living room, staring out at the beach with his back to me. I stop in my place for a moment, taking him in. His hair is up in his usual bun, and he's changed out of his suit and is sporting a pair of board shorts. But what has me staring, and maybe drooling, is his shirtless, muscular back. He's tanned and fit from years of living in California and working out every day. I always assumed he didn't have any tattoos, but in the center of his shoulder blades is a single tattoo. I can't see what it is from here, so I step toward him, but before I can make out what it is, he turns around.

"I'm not sure that's exactly pool attire." He smirks playfully, and I roll my eyes.

He sticks his arms through the holes of his shirt and is about to put it on when I reach out and stop him. "What's your tattoo of?"

His brow furrows, and he quickly throws his shirt on over his head. "Just a quote." He shrugs it off, which has me that much more curious. I've known him for years, and I've never known him to have one, so it has to be new.

"C'mon. Let me see."

"It's nothing. I thought we were hitting the pool."

I let it go for now since we'll be together for the foreseeable future. I'll find a way to see what he's got inked on his back when he least expects it. The guy can't keep his shirt on forever.

"I need help." I spin around and glance over my shoulder. "Unbutton me, please."

It takes him a second to understand what I mean, and once he does, his eyes go wide. "You can't do it yourself?"

"If I could, I'd already be in my bathing suit." I back up, so I'm closer to him. "Please."

With his big hands, one by one, he unbuttons my dress, exposing my back. Every once in a while, his fingers brush against my skin, and the craziest shiver races down my spine as I imagine what it would be like if, as he removed each button, he pressed a kiss to my heated flesh. When he gets to the last few buttons, leaving almost my entire back on display, I imagine my dress falling to the floor and Declan scooping me up into his arms and making love to me. Worshipping every inch of my body.

A moan escapes my lips, and I clear my throat to cover it up, praying he doesn't notice. This is what I wanted to feel with Kyle, what I *wished* I could feel for Kyle but couldn't, yet all Declan is doing is helping me take off my dress, and I'm fantasizing about him doing naughty things to me.

"There you go," he says, his voice gruff.

Holding my front up so I don't flash him, I turn around to thank him, but my words are caught in my throat when I realize how close we are. So close, I catch a whiff of his masculine scent—earthy and warm with a hint of comfort. His eyes lock with mine for a moment before his gaze descends slightly, landing on my mouth. My tongue darts out, wondering what it would feel like to kiss him. Would his lips be hard like the rest of his body? Would the kiss be heated, similar to the way he's staring at me, like with his look alone, he has the capability of setting my entire body on fire?

"Declan," I breathe, stepping forward and throwing all thought out the window, ready to find out.

Only my speaking seems to snap him out of the trance we're in, and he takes a step back, blinking rapidly. "I'll, uh…" He clears his throat, averting his eyes. "I'm going to call down to make sure our cabana is ready while you finish getting changed."

He flees the living room, and I'm left wondering what the hell just happened. Not with him…I don't blame him for not kissing me. I'm in my damn wedding dress, for crying out loud. No, I'm wondering what the hell is going on with me. When did Declan go from being a friend of my brother's to a man I'm sexually attracted to? Because that's exactly what I am…attracted to him. I felt it when I woke up to him sitting by my bedside in the hospital, when he walked in on me in the studio, when I listened to the song we wrote and sang together. And when I saw him standing outside of the church, my first thought was that it had to be fate. My dad told me to follow my heart, and there Declan was as if he had been waiting for me.

Now the question is, what the hell do I do with this new information? I could tell him. I could act on it. But then what? I'm just coming out of a relationship—even if I can't muster up a single feeling for him—and on top of that, Declan is, in fact, my brother's best friend and one-fourth of their band.

And if my history is anything to go by, the only thing that will come from me acting on my feelings is me hurting Declan, and the thought of hurting him causes my heart to clench in my chest.

No...no way. Those feelings are staying bottled up, right where they belong. Declan and I are friends, and right now, what I need is a friend. I'm not going to risk losing him over some *feelings*.

When we get down to the pool where our cabana is set up, the server assigned to us introduces herself and takes our drink and food order. The cabana is so adorable, like a tiki hut but with three walls for privacy. A comfy-looking L-shaped couch stretches across two adjacent walls, and two equally comfy-looking lounge chairs face the crystal-clear infinity pool. There's a flat-screen TV hanging in the top corner, and directly underneath it is a mini fridge. If you want privacy, the front of the cabana can be closed.

After I spread my towel across the chair and remove my cover-up, I pluck the sunglasses and floppy hat out of my beach bag and put them on. Then I plop down, sighing in contentment. "I kind of feel bad," I admit as Declan removes his shirt, giving me another glimpse of his sexy as hell body. Unfortunately, he lies back quickly so I don't catch a peek at the tattoo, but I'm determined to find out what it is.

"About what?" he asks, crossing one ankle over the other. There's a portable speaker, so he sets his phone against it and clicks play on his playlist.

"I just left a guy at the altar with my family to deal with the fallout, and I'm relaxing at a beautiful resort"—the server sets my martini and Declan's scotch down and walks away, and I pick it up, taking a sip—"while drinking a delicious martini in a poolside cabana."

Declan takes a drink of his scotch, and I can't help but notice the way his Adam's apple bobs as he swallows. An image of me licking my way up his throat hits me so hard it's almost as if it's real. It can't be since I've never been with Declan, but the vivid picture—of my tongue gliding up his throat and across his stubbled jawline to his chin—has me squeezing my thighs together. I can't remember the last time I had sex or even got off. It was definitely before the accident since, despite him trying, I wasn't with Kyle at all from the time I was discharged and leading up to the wedding that obviously didn't happen.

I think I need to find some alone time to release some of this pent-up tension, and then maybe I'll stop fantasizing about Declan.

"Do you love him?" Declan asks, glancing over at me.

I don't even have to think about it. "No...I wanted to. I tried for weeks to conjure up some kind of feelings for him, but they weren't there. I don't know what happened, if it was the accident or what, but my heart wasn't in it." I sigh. "God, I'm such a shitty person."

"Nah, you're not. A shitty person would've gone through with the lie and led him on longer. You did the right thing by calling it off. Now you both can move forward."

"True, but my moving forward meant leaving my family to deal with everything."

"Your family loves and supports you, and Camden said your dad handled it all without issue."

"You told him I'm with you?"

"No." He quirks a brow. "But would that be a problem if I did?"

"I just think it would be best if no one knew we were on this trip together. They'll constantly try to check up on me and jump to the wrong conclusion. I don't want you in the middle of everything."

He nods in understanding. "I won't tell them you're with me, but if they ask..."

"You won't lie." I roll my eyes. "I get it."

"Where do they think you are?"

"I told them I needed to get away and promised to keep in touch. Honestly, they're kind of used to this." I take another sip of my drink, slightly embarrassed to admit what I just did.

"Used to what? You tumbling out of windows while running from your wedding?" He smirks playfully, so I know he's just kidding, but his tone is curious, asking me to explain.

"As you know, I suck at relationships." Everyone knows. It's not exactly a secret, what with my entire life being on display in the tabloids and on social media. "Whenever I break up with a guy, I tend to...escape. Well, hide. Let the media run me through the mud and then calm down."

Declan's lips tip down into a frown, and he swings his legs over the side of the chair to face me. "You don't suck at relationships." He reaches over and lifts my sunglasses, so I'm forced to look him in the eye. "You just haven't found the right guy yet. There's nothing wrong with dating until you find the person you want to spend your life with. You're not doing anything different than what most people do. The only difference is your life is on display for the entire world to see...*and*"—he chuckles softly—"you make a habit of writing music about your breakups."

"I don't write about *them*," I say with a huff, dropping my sunglasses back over my eyes and crossing my arms over my chest. "I write about my feelings. Anyway, my point is, they're expecting me to hide out for a bit, so they won't suspect anything."

"Unless we're spotted," Declan points out.

"If we are, then we are, but until then, please keep it between us. The last thing I want is to draw you into my circus of a life. One picture of us together and they'll be linking you to me, predicting how long it will take for you to get *stiffed*."

Declan snorts out a laugh and plucks my glasses off my face. "They can predict all they want, but it wouldn't happen." He pinches my chin and leans closer, so close I can feel his cool breath against my lips. "Those guys you dated got stiffed for a reason. They didn't know how to handle a woman like you."

His words cause my breath to hitch. "What are you trying to say?" I choke out.

"That if you were mine, I'd make sure you never had a reason to run."

Twelve

DECLAN

I REGRET THE WORDS THE MOMENT THEY'RE OUT OF MY MOUTH. NOT BECAUSE I DON'T MEAN THEM—I do—but because I told myself I wouldn't go there. At least, not yet. Kendall just ended her engagement. Dipped out on her wedding. I meant what I said: she has no reason to feel bad. She did the right thing. Her brain might not understand it, but her heart knows, fucking *knows* she wasn't supposed to marry Kyle. I don't know why she planned to call off her engagement the night she came to me, but it was clear she had no intention of going through with that wedding. When she woke up and didn't remember, I thought for sure she was going to marry him, but the heart proved it's stronger than the brain, and even though she couldn't explain it, she knew the feelings were gone.

But even knowing that, she still needs time because I don't want to be her rebound. If I have it my way, I'm going to be her goddamn forever. I can see the way she's eyeing me with interest. Earlier in the room, I'm almost positive a part of her was hoping I would kiss her. Because that heart...it knows what she doesn't remember. That it opened up and let me in. I have a long way to go, but I'm okay with that. I've always been a hard worker. And having her here with me, just the two of us alone, will make it that much easier to show her that I'm the one for her.

I meant what I said. Those other guys didn't know how to handle Kendall, and none of them have what we have...what we've been slowly building for the past couple years—friendship. Kendall's going to be mine, but I have to walk before I can run. She's like a scared doe, and I have to approach her slowly, carefully, so she doesn't flee. And I will.

Which is why, even though I meant what I said—that if she were mine, I'd make sure she never had a reason to run—I shouldn't have said it out loud. The last thing I need or want is for her to get spooked and take off. Which is why I didn't kiss her earlier in the room. She might've wanted it, but once it happened, there'd be a damn good chance she'd freak out and run. And one kiss isn't worth the risk of her running.

"It's hot as hell out here," I say, standing. "I think we need to cool off."

Before she can process where I'm going with this, I'm scooping her up and throwing her over my shoulder—her hat flying off her head and hitting the ground—then stalking toward the pool.

It takes her a second, but once all the dots connect, she shrieks, "Declan! No!"

"Shh, Kendall, don't yell." I give her luscious ass a quick smack. "We don't want to draw attention to ourselves."

At the edge of the pool, I slide her off my shoulder, ready to throw her in, but somehow, before I can complete the action, she clings to me. Her arms and legs wrap around me like a damn octopus, and instead of her going in, and me laughing, we both crash into the pool.

As we plunge into the water, she holds on to me, and when I come up for air, she's still wrapped around me, our bodies flush against one another.

"I can't believe you just did that!" She throws her head back with a laugh that rings out in the otherwise quiet area.

"That wasn't how it was supposed to go down." I mock glare, swimming us over to a private part of the pool tucked away in the corner with a large cluster of rocks. I push her against the wall, and even though she's holding me, I bring my hand down to grab her ass as if I'm holding her up.

With my other hand, I swipe a wet lock of hair from out of her eyes, tucking it behind her ear so I can get a good look at her face. It's free of all makeup—she must've taken it off while she was changing—showing off her sexy as hell freckles that are dotted across her nose. In the sunlight, her eyes are extra bright and filled with mirth. And her lips, full and pouty, are curved into a gorgeous grin.

"You look beautiful like this," I admit, unable to control the words spilling from my lips.

"Like a wet dog?" She laughs.

"Nah, you look...happy, carefree. I haven't seen you like this since—" I cut off my words, stopping myself just before I say *the night we spent together.*

"Since when?" she prompts.

"Since before the accident."

She nods even though she doesn't fully understand since she doesn't remember. "I feel different. I've been so frustrated lately, like someone trying to fit a square into a circle. I kept searching for the right size, trying other shapes, but this morning, I said fuck it and threw it all in the trash, realizing it didn't matter, and now, it feels like I'm free."

Kendall's legs tighten around my waist, and her center grinds against my crotch. Not wanting her to feel the hard-on that's undoubtedly to come, I back up and release her, thankful when she lets me.

"Wanna race?" I nod toward the other side of the pool.

"Sure." A small smile tugs at her lips, but I don't suspect she's up to anything until I count to three, thinking she's going to take off next to me, and she instead jumps onto my back.

"Giddyup!" she jokes, squeezing my sides and tugging on my hair like I'm a damn horse. "Let's go!"

"Keep it up, and I'm going to buck you off like a bull," I warn.

"Ha! What you don't know is, I've ridden one before and almost lasted the full time." She tightens her hold on me, and I twist around, determined to send her flying. When she doesn't budge, I hold my breath, submerging my body in the water to make her let go and swim to the surface.

Of course, her crazy ass never does what I expect, and she stays on while I swim from one side of the pool to the other. When I come up for air, she's still holding on for dear life.

"Better try harder than that to..." Her words trail off, followed by a gasp. "'Drunk on Your Love.'"

Fuck. My tattoo...

In her shock, she releases her hold on me, so I'm able to pry her from my back, but instead of getting off me, she slides around to my front, encircling her legs around me once again while she looks me dead in the eyes.

"You," she breathes. "You tattooed the title of our song on your body."

Since she didn't ask a question, I don't say anything.

"You don't have tattoos. All the guys have tattoos, but you always said..." She swallows thickly. "You said you wouldn't get one until there was one worth getting."

She still hasn't asked me anything, so I keep my mouth shut.

"Declan, say something."

"What do you want me to say?"

"Tell me why."

"It was worth getting."

"Why?"

I told myself I would wait and take it slow, but I'm not going to lie to her. Not when she's asking me a direct question. "Because the song means something to me."

"It's about two people falling in love..."

"It is."

"Are you...in love with someone?" she asks softly.

"I am," I admit truthfully.

Her eyes turn sad. "I didn't know." She shakes her head. "Do I know her? Is that why we wrote the song? For her?" Her brow furrows together in confusion, and for a second, I wonder what the hell she's talking about because everyone knows I haven't dated anyone in a long time. And in the past year, the only person I've hung out with is Kendall, but then I remember... *she* doesn't *remember*. She's heard the song, so she knows we wrote it. She can remember us writing the beginning of it, but she doesn't remember us writing the entire song together. She doesn't remember that when I wrote my verse, she was sitting across from me, smiling softly as I scribbled across the paper with only my feelings for her in mind. And even if she did remember, I never actually told her that every word I wrote and sang was about her.

She tries to scramble away, but I grip the curves of her hips, holding her to me. "There's no one else," I say, looking her in the eye. "There's only you."

Her eyes go wide. "Me?" she squeaks out.

"Yeah. Just you. Every word was written for you. There's only ever been you. You're the only person I see."

"You wrote that song for me?"

"*We* wrote that song together," I remind her. "You wrote about falling in love for the first time, and I wrote about falling in love with you."

"I..." She releases a harsh breath, and since I'm not ready to handle her rejection—where she tells me she had no idea, doesn't feel the same way, and only considers me a friend—I speak first.

"You don't need to say anything. It was a while ago, before you were engaged."

"Okay, but—"

"Please...Just drop it." The last thing I want is for our trip to be cut short because of this. I finally have her all to myself and a chance to show her what it would be like to be with me, but I can't do that if I send her running scared. I never should've taken my shirt off. I wasn't thinking.

I stare at her, silently begging for her not to reject me, not to cut me off before I've even been given a damn shot. I don't know what she sees when she looks at me, what's going through her head, but after several seconds, she sighs and nods. "Okay, it's dropped."

"Good. Because I'm starved. What do you say we eat and then head down to the beach?"

"Sounds good." I don't miss the way the corner of her lips tips downward slightly before she plasters on a fake smile.

"Hey," I say, feeling like something needs to be said before the trip is ruined, thanks to my damn tattoo and admission. "We're friends. We've been friends for years. Yes, I have feelings for you, but until you saw the tattoo, you had no idea. I promise I'm not going to attack you or anything. I know you just ended your engagement, and you're not looking to start anything new. I just want to have a good time and enjoy your company while you're here. Okay?"

She opens her mouth as if she wants to say something, and I internally flinch, hoping she isn't about to tell me she's out of here. But, after a few seconds, she simply nods in understanding before walking past me and up the pool steps. I stay where I am for several beats, watching as she saunters out of the pool, looking like a fucking wet dream as water slews down her tanned, toned body. My eyes land on her pert ass, which is barely covered by the scrap of material someone deemed to call a bathing suit, torn between enjoying the show and wanting to demand she cover her ass up—literally.

In the end, I tamper down the caveman in me and simply enjoy watching the woman in front of me own her beauty while mentally planning how to make every inch of her mine.

Twelve

BONUS SCENE

DECLAN

"DO YOU WANT TO GO OUT OR ORDER IN?" I ASK KENDALL WHEN WE WALK INSIDE THE HOTEL ROOM. WE'VE spent the day between the pool and beach, and if it weren't for the young couple who whispered that they thought they saw Kendall Blackwood, we'd probably still be drinking by the pool. It's almost seven o'clock anyway, and we have as many days as we want here, so when we heard Kendall's name mentioned, we called it a night.

"Order in," Kendall says. "I'm not picky. A burger and fries if they have it. I'm going to jump in the shower."

I laugh to myself. Kendall is most definitely picky, but that's cute that she thinks she's not, or she's trying not to be, for my sake. Either way, I know her better than that.

While she showers, I order us food, making sure her burger is medium well, cooked through but not burnt, swiss cheese instead of American, two slices because she loves cheese, only mayo and tomato on it, fries just shy of being overcooked—because she hates soggy fries—and the sweet tea is freshly brewed and not from the fountain—because she will know the difference. She usually prefers a glass of wine with her dinner, but when she eats pizza or a burger, she likes it with sweet tea. Once I've placed the order, I take a quick shower, throwing on a pair of sweats and a T-shirt.

The food arrives just as Kendall walks out of her room, with only a towel wrapped around her body. Her face is free of makeup, and her hair is up in a wet, messy bun, exposing her slim neck. She's a bit flushed from all the sun she got today, and when she glances at me shyly, her top teeth dragging across her bottom lip, I want to say fuck dinner and eat her instead.

But since she's not on the menu—yet—I ask if everything's okay.

"I didn't buy any pajamas."

Shit, that's right. She doesn't have clothes, and the resort shop only had beachwear. "I'll grab you a shirt and boxers, and tomorrow, we can find a store to buy you some stuff."

Once she's dressed in my clothes, we sit down at the table to eat. I watch as Kendall cuts her burger in half to make sure it's cooked through, then pops a fry into her mouth, no doubt to make sure they're not soggy, and lastly, takes a sip of her drink to...yep, check and make sure it's freshly brewed. When they've all passed her *I'm not picky* test, she glances at me knowingly.

"Thank you," she says with a smile on her gorgeous face. "Maybe I'm a little picky." She shrugs, and I crack up laughing as I take a bite of my mahi sandwich.

"MIND IF I JOIN YOU?"

I glance up at Kendall and shake my head. "Of course not."

After we ate, she excused herself to call her mom and dad to check in—probably to make sure everything *non*-wedding related was handled—so I grabbed my notebook and came out onto the terrace that overlooks the ocean to listen to the waves and write a little.

She sits in the chair next to me and pulls out her own notebook. For the next hour or so, we sit in silence. Kendall scribbles furiously while I watch her and occasionally write down some potential lyrics. Eventually, she stops, looks over at me, and says, "Wanna read what I wrote?"

I take the notebook from her and read over the words...and every single one is about love. I was expecting her to write about heartbreak, about her running from her wedding, but they're about falling in love. The words are raw and real and filled with so much emotion. And when I read over them again, I realize her song is about falling in love and the lyrics from our earlier conversation when I told her I'm in love with her.

Not wanting to call her out on it, I smile softly and hand the book back to her. "They're beautiful words," I tell her. "It's going to fit perfectly in your new album."

We move inside, and suddenly, the vibe gets a bit awkward. And that's when it hits me: I'm on a road trip with Kendall. Even with separate bedrooms, we're spending the night in the same hotel rooms for the next however many days and weeks.

"I'm gonna go…" I nod toward my door. It's only like ten o'clock, but I don't want her to feel like I'm crowding her. It's been a long day, and I imagine she probably needs some space.

"Oh, okay," she says, sounding almost sad. "I guess I'll go…" She nods toward her own room. "Or we could watch a show," she blurts out. "I'm kind of a night owl and love to binge-watch shows...But if you're tired—"

"A show sounds good."

We plop onto opposite sides of the same couch, and I hand the remote to Kendall.

"They have Netflix," she says, signing in. "Anything in particular you want to watch?"

Since I'm not really a TV person, I shrug. "Whatever you want to watch is fine."

"Don't say that." She laughs. "I'll make you watch *The Vampire Diaries* with me."

"The glittery animal eaters?"

"You've seen *Twilight*?"

"Kaylee, Layla, and Tori made us watch it one night when we were in high school." Mentioning Tori causes an ache in my chest. It's coming up on the seventh anniversary of her death. The thought reminds me of Gage…

"Hey," Kendall says softly, as if she can sense the shift in my mood. "He's getting the help he needs." She edges closer to me and places her hand on my arm, squeezing it.

"Yeah, I hope so," I murmur.

We're both quiet for a few seconds before she says, "*The Vampire Diaries* is not *Twilight*. It's better," in an attempt to shift the mood back. "We're watching this."

"Not happening."

"What? Why not? It's a damn good show."

"Do they eat animals?"

"No."

"Light up in the sunlight?"

She rolls her eyes. "No."

"Is there a human chick torn between two vampires who can't decide who she loves more?"

Kendall bites down on her lip, and I crack up laughing at how transparent she is.

"There is! I'm not watching that shit."

Please." Her puppy dog eyes meet mine. "If you just give it a chance, you'll love it. Camden watches it with Layla, and he's addicted."

"He's addicted to her, not the show." I roll my eyes. "The guy would watch anything she asks."

"True, but he really does like it." She flips her bottom lip, pouting, and I, of course, give in. Because, just like Camden's addicted to his wife, I'm addicted to Kendall.

"Fine. Put it on."

"Yay!"

We watch the first episode, and I have to admit, while it's a bit cringeworthy, it's not horrible. By the second episode, I'm hooked, and at the end of the third, when Kendall asks if I want to watch another episode or go to bed, I tell her to hit play.

Since the couch isn't comfortable before we start the fourth episode, we move to my bed and get comfortable. Sometime during the fifth episode, Kendall falls asleep, and instead of waking her up or moving her to her own bed, I lie next to her and watch her sleep until I fall asleep as well.

Thirteen

KENDALL

I just ended an engagement.
He's my brother's best friend.
I suck at relationships.

I keep repeating those four facts in my head every time I think about what it would be like to be with Declan, to get lost in him. When my brain goes haywire and tries to imagine how it would feel to be kissed by him, for him to be inside me. When I remember his confession—that he wrote his part of "Drunk on Your Love" for me...that he has feelings for me, it damn near throws those four truths out the window.

Since the night we talked all those years ago, I've thought about him. His words of wisdom—that we're all a little broken—took seed in my heart and have remained there, growing and flourishing, reminding me that it's okay if I'm a little broken. We've become closer the past couple of years, but I never allowed myself to go there...until now. Because now that he's confessed to having feelings for me, I can't stop thinking about him.

It's been several days since he told me he has feelings for me yet has no intention of acting on them. Every second of every freaking day has been spent with me thinking about him, watching him, and paying attention to every little detail regarding him.

Like when he wakes up, he walks out of his room all sleepy, his hair thrown into a sexy as hell messy knot, sporting no shirt and gray sweats—yep, motherfucking sweatpants—with his hand scrubbing his chest and abs lazily. I'm already awake, reading or writing on the couch. He glances my way with a sleepy smile and goes straight to the phone to order room service, his voice raspy in that sexy way from just waking up. He looks over at me when he's ordering to silently confirm I still want the same thing—coffee and French toast—and when I nod, he'll jerk his chin up in response, lifting his hand to his face and scrubbing his scruffy face that he hasn't shaved since the day we took off out of town.

Or when we're hanging out by the pool and beach and he goes into the water to cool off, swimming laps from one side to the other, his taut muscles flex in a way that reminds me of how strong he is—strong enough to pick me up and carry me like I weigh nothing.

And don't get me started on how well he knows me. It's clear that even though my paying attention to him is new, he's been watching me for a while. He knows how I like my coffee and what foods I love and hate. He knows I like a glass of wine at dinner and which ones are my favorites. He always orders dessert, knowing I won't do it but secretly want it, and shares it with me.

Every evening, after we both shower and are settled in for the night, we sit on the balcony together, writing and discussing music and life. I've written several songs for my next album, and he's written quite a few that he's said he wants to show the guys once he's back. He's worried about Gage since he still won't accept any of the guys' phone calls, and he's scared the band might not recover. For him, it's not about the money but the friendship. They've drifted, and he's not sure they will ever be the same.

Once I've had enough, yawning in exhaustion, we move inside and watch reruns of *The Vampire Diaries*. At first, Declan complained, but now he's as obsessed with the show as I am, wanting to know when Elena will finally figure out that Stefan is a vampire—which he only knows because he tricked me into telling him.

We're friends.

I just ended an engagement.

He's my brother's best friend.

I suck at relationships.

I chant the words again. I'm chanting them in my head as I watch Declan stalk out of the water with his board tucked under his arm, droplets of salt water sliding down his chest, with a huge grin on his face because he totally rode the hell out of the waves. I had no idea he could surf, but it makes sense since the guys spent several years living near the Pacific Ocean. I also had no idea how hot watching him surf would be.

"Damn, I'm beat," he says, planting the board into the sand and then dropping down next to me. Drops of cold water hit my warm flesh, causing me to jump and, in turn, make Declan laugh. Since he thinks he's hilarious, he shakes his hair like a wet dog and soaks my face and body.

"Stop!" I shriek, trying to get away from the water, which only has him laughing and shaking his hair and face harder. "Dec, I'm serious!" I try to push him away, but he grabs my wrist, and we both tumble over, his hard body landing on top of mine. For a second, our eyes lock, our faces so close all it would take is one of us to move forward slightly, and our lips would touch, but before I can contemplate if I'm brave enough to make the move, he backs up as if he's been burned, breaking the moment.

"I was thinking since it's our last night here, we could go check out the boardwalk," he suggests. "I know how much you love those carnival rides and games."

Of course, he knows because he knows everything about me. "And we can go on the Ferris wheel?" It's my favorite ride, and nobody ever wants to go with me because of how high up it is.

"Maybe…if you ask nicely." He winks, and holy hell, my lady parts tingle, wanting to know what else he'll give me if I simply ask nicely.

As if he can sense my thoughts, his eyes hood over slightly before he clears his throat and moves back slightly farther.

"So where are we going next?" I ask, not wanting it to get awkward. We haven't discussed anything other than whatever we're doing at the moment.

"It's a secret."

"What? Why?" I sit up. "Am I not part of this trip." I pout.

"You're a guest on this trip." He taps my nose playfully. "I'm in control, here. You're just along for the ride." His lips quirk into a sexy smirk, and I laugh, slapping his stomach, which hurts my hand more than it hurts him.

"Can I at least get a hint?"

"Nope." He rolls over onto his stomach and closes his eyes. "I'm going to take a nap. Wake me when you're ready to head up to the room to shower."

A few minutes later, he's snoring softly. I watch him sleep, wondering how much longer I'm going to be able to last without jumping his bones. Several times, I've considered making up an excuse to leave before I do something stupid like kiss him or, worse, have sex with him, but I can't bring myself to do it.

My phone pings with a text, and when I check it, I see it's my dad: **Hey K, just wanted to check in. I've been discussing your upcoming album with the team, and I think Drunk on Your Love would be perfect to promo the new album. I was thinking we could make it your first single. I know you're away and so is Declan, but I'd like to get the details sorted so we can get the ball rolling. Any chance you know when you'll be back? We'll need you here to finalize the song, make the video, and shoot the promo ads.**

I think about the best way to respond. On the one hand, I should admit I'm with Declan because otherwise, it's as if I'm lying by omission, but that will lead to questions I don't have the answers to, so instead, I snap a picture of the beach and go with vague: **Hey! I'm so glad you want to make it the first single. It might be my favorite yet. I'm good. Enjoying the sun. I'm not sure when I'll be back, but I'll ask Declan what his plans are, so we can figure it out. I've been writing a lot, and I think several songs will be perfect for the next**

album. I'd like to take it in a different direction. I was thinking I could call it: Falling.

I hit send before I second-guess myself. I knew the title the second it came to me, but I know it will lead to questions...ones I'm not sure I'm ready to face yet.

Of course, my dad catches on and asks the hard question: **Falling...as in falling in love?**

And because I can't lie...

Me: Yes, it's what I hope to do one day. Fall in love.

You didn't really think I was about to admit I'm in love with Declan, did you? That would be crazy, right? No, I'm not in love with Declan. It's too soon for that, but as I watch him sleep, his lids fluttering every now and then and his full lips parted slightly, I can't help but admit to myself that, no, I'm not in love with Declan, but for the first time in my life, I'm falling...hard. And it scares the hell out of me.

My phone pings with a new text from my dad: **You will, sweetheart. One day, you'll find the right guy, and you'll feel it. Your heart will beat a little faster, your smiles will get brighter, and butterflies will swarm your belly. And you'll know every wrong guy was simply leading you to the right one.**

As I read his words, I think about the past several days and how every action he mentioned I've experienced with Declan. From my heart picking up speed, to smiling and laughing more, to freaking butterflies attacking my belly—they all seem to happen more often when I'm around Declan.

I don't realize tears are leaking from my lids until Declan, who I didn't realize had woken up, asks, "What's wrong?" He goes from being asleep to wide awake, his features expressing his worry. He edges closer, and his thumb swipes across my cheek. "Kendall, talk to me."

"I..." I choke out. "I think..."

His brows dip in confusion. "You think what? Did something happen?" He glances at the phone in my hand. "Did Kyle text you?"

"No," I breathe. "I think..." *I think I have feelings for you.* I say the words in my head, but I can't make them come out because I'm a damn chicken. "I think I made the right decision by not marrying Kyle," I say instead.

Declan looks at me like I'm crazy for a moment, then he nods. "Yeah, I agree." He wipes another tear. "But why are you crying?"

Because I can't say what I really want to say, I give him a different truth. "I'm naming my next album *Falling*."

"*Falling*?" he repeats.

"Yeah, like falling in love. I've been doing a lot of soul-searching for the past few weeks, and I realized I said yes to Kyle because I didn't want to be alone. I wanted to prove I wasn't broken, so I went along with it when he proposed.

"Everyone in my family is in perfect love-filled relationships. And I wanted that…I *want* that. But Kyle wasn't the right guy, and coming to terms with that made me a bit emotional." *I'm also now realizing what it feels like to fall for someone, and the difference is like night and day.*

Declan smiles softly and tucks a wayward strand of hair behind my ear. "You just haven't found the one yet, but all the pieces will fit together perfectly when you do."

"I know that now. I think that's why the songs I've been writing recently all have a different vibe to them." Because every one of them is about how I'm slowly falling in love with the man lying in front of me.

"And those songs are amazing," he says. "*Falling* is the perfect title for your album, and I have no doubt it will be your best yet."

"It's so different…What if my fans don't like it?"

"They'll love it because every song you've written has come straight from your heart. I've watched you every night, putting your heart and soul into every one of those lyrics. They'll see that. See that you're evolving and growing, and they'll love that you're sharing your innermost thoughts with them. You've allowed them in, opened up every part of your life to them, which isn't something many people do."

"You're right," I agree, then change the subject, not wanting to risk blurting out that every song I've written lately has been with him in mind. "Speaking of which…my dad texted me. He wants to know when we'll be back so he can get things scheduled for the video and promo for 'Drunk on Your Love.' He wants to release it soon as a single and preview for my next album."

"You told your dad you're with me?"

"Well, no…I told him I'd speak to you, but he doesn't know that means in person instead of over the phone."

His lips tip down, but he quickly hides his displeasure. "I'm down for whatever. Since the band is on hiatus for the foreseeable future, my calendar's wide open."

"Well, not *completely* wide open," I say, shifting closer to him. "Right now, our calendars are marked as busy."

My eyes meet his before they dart to his mouth, wanting to kiss him, wanting him to kiss me. It would be a horrible idea to cross that invisible line. It doesn't matter that I'm falling for him. It would be irresponsible and selfish to act on my feelings. He's connected to my family, and with my track record, the chances of us working out are—

"Tell me what you're thinking about."

"How much I want to kiss you," I blurt out. "And how stupid I would be if I did."

He edges closer. "And why would that make you stupid?"

"The obvious reasons," I whisper. "I was just engaged…"

"And you said you never loved him." He sets his hand on my hip and squeezes softly. "Problem solved."

"You're best friends with my brother," I argue. "What if this ends badly?"

"You're worried about it ending"—he rounds his hand to my butt and pulls me closer, so our faces are only inches away from one another—"and nothing has even started."

He's right, but…"I suck at relationships."

He quirks a brow. "Who said anything about a relationship? I thought you just wanted to kiss me."

"I do, but—"

"Then kiss me," he says slowly. His lips are so close that all I'd have to do is lean in a little bit, and our mouths would connect. I want to, so damn badly, but I'm scared.

"What if—?"

"Kiss. Me." His warm breath carries a hint of the whiskey he's been sipping all day, and I wonder if he tastes how he smells.

He shrugs, his hand leaving my butt. His face starts to move backward, and I realize he's going to back away. The thought of losing my chance and not finding out what he tastes like, feels like, has me reaching over, gripping his neck, and pulling him toward me for a kiss.

Our mouths connect softly at first, our lips brushing against one another. I take his bottom lip between my teeth and suck on it gently, wanting to taste him, feel him. He groans, and the sound makes me gasp. He uses my action to slip his tongue past my parted lips, and in slow, methodical movements, his tongue caresses my own. He tastes perfect, sweet with a hint of spice, and something flashes in my head as if I've tasted him before. That can't be right since we've never kissed, but maybe it's because, unlike most first kisses, which can be awkward, kissing Declan is as easy as breathing.

When my tongue tangles with his, he sucks it into his mouth, deepening the kiss. As if his mouth is connected to an electric current, with every curve of his lips and every swipe of his tongue, my body is hit with the most delicious shock to my system, which goes straight to my belly, tightening my insides and then descending to the area between my legs. One kiss with Declan and my entire body is affected in the best damn way.

He ends the kiss, pulling back slightly, and I sigh at the loss of the connection, wanting to kiss him again. Wanting to strip him of his clothes and explore the rest of him. Wanting him to explore me.

"Did you feel that?" he asks, his lips brushing against mine.

"Feel what?"

"The connection...like your mouth was made for kissing mine."

Yes, I felt it..."Dec...I don't think—"

"No, don't think. Just feel."

And before I can argue, his mouth is back on mine, making me do nothing but just that...feel.

Fourteen

DECLAN

FUCK, THAT KISS. HER LIPS, HER TONGUE, THE WAY OUR MOUTHS MOVED IN PERFECT RHYTHM. EVERYTHING about her is addicting. Her taste, her scent. I want more. No, I *need* more. The last time I had her in my grasp, she slipped through the cracks. But not again. I can't go another month without kissing her, touching her.

Everything I tell myself, every decision I come to, I contradict. Since the day she showed up at the bar, and we spent the night together, I haven't been able to think straight. I keep telling myself to stand down, take a step back, and take it slow, but I can't help myself when I'm with her. I want her in every way possible.

So fuck it. I'm done trying to stay away. She's here, and it's clear she wants me, but she's scared. She has a dozen reasons we shouldn't jump, so my new plan is to show her how good it can feel to fly. No promises and no talk of the future. Once she sees how good we are together, she'll get on board. The risk will be worth the reward. She just has to feel it for herself. And she will. We have only kissed once, and I can see it written all over her face. She wants more. And I'm going to give it to her. Right after I tell her the truth about us…

"We need to talk."

She places her perfectly manicured fingers over my lips. "No." She shakes her head. "Nothing good ever comes from someone saying, 'We need to talk.' And I am not about to let you ruin that kiss. So for now, no talking. Please."

Her big blue eyes plead with me, and maybe it's because I can't say no to her, or because the last thing I want to do is ruin the moment or…maybe it's because I'm scared as fuck that once I tell her about our night together, everything will change, but whatever the reason, I nod back, agreeing not to say what I was going to say.

"Thank you," she says, leaning in and swiping her tongue along the seam of my lips. "Now where were we?" Her mouth curves around mine, and that's all it takes for all thought to fly out the window. *Later,* I tell myself. *I'll tell her later.*

"THIS IS SO AWESOME," KENDALL SAYS, HER FACE LIGHTING UP AS SHE TAKES IN THE SCENE. AS IT TURNED out, the boardwalk is hosting a wine festival this week, so on top of us checking out the rides, games, and shops during our last night here, we'll also be tasting wine. Kendall couldn't be more in heaven.

She threads her fingers through mine and drags me over to the booth, where we purchase wineglasses to use during our wine walk. We spend the next hour going from booth to booth, learning from the different vendors about the types of wines they make: cabernet sauvignon, merlot, pinot noir... They all taste different, but I couldn't tell you which one is what. Kendall, on the other hand, discusses the various flavors and notes that she tastes in each sip, purchasing a few of the bottles of the ones she loves. So she doesn't have to carry them, they offer to leave them at the main booth with her info on them.

By the time we reach the end, she's tipsy from all the wine she drank, and she's smiling and laughing, looking so carefree and happy. Music plays from the speakers surrounding us, and when a song she loves comes on, she wraps her arms around my neck and says, "Dance with me, Dec."

It doesn't matter that we're in the middle of a busy boardwalk with people all around us, or that someone might spot us—despite me wearing a baseball cap and her wearing an adorable floppy hat—I pull her close and sway to the music. The song picks up, and I take her hand, spinning her out and then back into my arms. She throws her head back, laughing, as I dip her low and then bring her back up, tugging her body flush against mine.

We haven't discussed the earlier mini make-out session, so I'm sticking with my plan of taking action—showing her how good we are together. And I do just that by dipping her again and, when I bring her up, connecting our mouths in a searing kiss that I know takes her breath away. She gasps at first, then moans when I gently curl my tongue around hers.

"Dec," she breathes against my lips, her lids fluttering open, and her azure eyes looking at me with *more.*

I give her one more chaste kiss before I pull back and wrap my arm around her shoulders, tucking her into my side. "What do you say we go check out the rides and games?"

We spend the next couple of hours playing the overpriced games—I win her a stuffed unicorn and a goldfish we give to a kid who squeals in excitement while the parent glares—then go on several rides, including the Ferris wheel, where I make it a point to kiss her at the top. I'm shocked when she pulls out her phone and takes several pictures of us: smiling, cheesing, making crazy faces, and the last one...us kissing.

Afterward, we grab a couple of hot dogs, candy apples, and cheese fries at a local vendor and chow down while Kendall begs me to tell her where we're going next, and I refuse.

"Pretend it's a wrapped present for your birthday," I joke, making her pout.

"Don't remind me how old I am. We're going to pretend I'm turning twenty-five all over again."

"Pretend all you want." I shrug. "But you're still the sexiest almost thirty-two-year-old I know, and I'm not telling you where we're going because it's a birthday surprise."

I end my statement with a kiss, and she drops it.

Once we've experienced all the boardwalk has to offer, we stop by the wine booth to grab her bottles and then head back to the room. We shower—separately—and then crawl into bed to watch another episode of *The Vampire Diaries*. The suite has two bedrooms, but we've been sharing a bed since the first night and falling asleep while watching the show. Tonight, though, Kendall changes things up a bit, and instead of staying on her side, she lays her head on my chest, snuggling up to my body. I wrap my arm around her, feathering my fingers up and down her back, and within minutes, she's passed out, with me following shortly after.

"YOU'RE SERIOUSLY NOT GOING TO GIVE ME A SINGLE CLUE?" KENDALL POUTS FROM THE PASSENGER SEAT of the vehicle. We've been driving on and off for almost twelve hours, and I swear she's asked this same question every hour.

"I'm seriously not," I say for the millionth time as I get off the highway. "What part of birthday surprise don't you understand? Besides, we're almost there." My original plan was to stop in North Carolina before heading to Florida, but when Kendall jumped on board, and I learned about her secret obsession with a certain show, my plans changed—and the fact that tomorrow is her birthday is the icing on the cake.

"We're almost there?" She looks around, trying to find a clue, but unless she knows what she's looking for, she won't get it. "What's in Covington?" she asks, scrunching her adorable, freckle-covered nose up in confusion when she spots the sign.

"You'll see."

We drive down a winding road leading to a bed and breakfast where I had to pull major strings to get a reservation. When we pull around and park, she still has no idea, but when we grab our bags—we went shopping while in Jersey and bought her some actual clothes—and walk around to the front, she eyes it curiously.

"This looks so familiar," she says, looking around. "It's beautiful." The bed and breakfast is a three-story colonial-style Southern mansion, complete with a second-story balcony, black shutters, massive, old-style pillars, and a wraparound porch.

"I'm surprised you don't recognize it." I pull out my phone and click on an image, then turn it around so she can see it. The moment she recognizes where we are, her eyes go wide, and she screeches so loud my ears ring.

"This is from *The Vampire Diaries*? Are you freaking serious?" She steps back and takes the mansion in with new eyes. "Oh, my God, Dec! This is the Lockwood mansion from 1864!" She walks over to the right side of the mansion. "This is where Damon and Katherine walk and…" She rushes up the stairs and swings the door open, stopping in her tracks. "Oh, wow," she breathes. "This is where Stefan and Katherine danced. This is amazing." She turns around and jumps into my arms, wrapping her legs around my waist as she plants a kiss on my lips. "Thank you for bringing me here. This is the best birthday present ever!"

"Then you're going to love what I have in store for tomorrow." I grip the bottom of her thighs to hold her up, not giving a shit that we're standing in the middle of the foyer of a bed and breakfast, where other people are walking around.

"Better than staying where they filmed several scenes of *The Vampire Diaries?*"

"Yep."

"Tell me!" She encircles her arms around my neck and forces my face closer to hers. "Please."

"It's another birthday surprise." I kiss the tip of her nose and then set her down.

After getting checked in, we bring our stuff up to our room, which has Kendall freaking out since it was the Salvatore brothers' study. With floor-to-ceiling mahogany bookshelves surrounding a working fireplace, a queen-sized antique bed, and—according to the brochure—original tile, tub, and shower, it feels as if we've stepped back into the 1800s. Since it's getting late, we head out and walk around the property, checking out all the areas they used for filming. Because Kendall is obsessed with the show and has seen every episode no less than a half-dozen times, she tells me about each scene without giving away too many spoilers.

Once we've covered every square inch that we're allowed to see and explore, we go back up to our room to get ready for bed. Kendall showers first, and once I'm showered, I find her lying in bed, typing away on her phone.

"Whatcha doing?" I ask, climbing into bed next to her.

"Sending my mom pictures of the mansion. She's so jealous I'm here. Did you know they do—" Her hands still, and her head pops up to look at me. "Declan…Did you get us Vampire Diary tour tickets?"

Whatever facial expression I make must give me away because a second later, she releases a loud squeal, drops her phone, and then tackles me. "Did you?"

"It was supposed to be a surprise," I mutter. "You suck."

"I can't believe it! This is seriously the best birthday ever!" Straddling my torso, she leans down to kiss me. At first, the kiss is soft, a silent thank-you, but it quickly heats when her tongue slips into my mouth. As we kiss, she grinds her center—which I realize quickly is only covered by the barely-there material of her underwear—back and forth along my dick. It perks up, not having been given any proper attention in over a month, and I groan, knowing as much as I want to sink inside Kendall's warm, tight as fuck pussy, I can't. It's too soon. It's one thing to kiss her and show her how I feel about her, but it's another thing to have sex with her less than a week after she ended her engagement. I don't know the rule of how long I should wait, but it's got to be more than a week, right?

So I'm not tempted to say *fuck it* and fuck her. I flip us over to put her under me. She wraps her legs around my waist and pulls on the hair tie holding my hair up, making it fall and create a curtain around us as I kiss my way down her neck, peppering kisses along her exposed collarbone and shoulder. When she uses the heels of her feet to force me closer, I stop kissing her flesh and sit up.

"Why don't we watch an episode of *The Vampire Diaries*?" I suggest. There isn't a television in the room, but I have my laptop, and right now, I need a damn distraction before I'm balls deep in her.

Her brow furrows in confusion. "You want to watch TV?"

Taking her feet, I untangle her legs from around me, then drop onto my side next to her. I lift her leg over my thigh so we're still partially connected.

"Do I want to? Fuck no," I admit truthfully. "But you only just walked away from your fiancé…and"—I look her in the eyes, so she knows how serious I am—"I don't want to be your rebound."

"Dec…" She sighs, and my heart drops, knowing from her tone that whatever she's about to say isn't going to be in my favor. "I want you…I'm attracted to you, and even though I can't remember the past couple of months, I feel something between us. I wouldn't have written a song like 'Drunk on Your Love' with just anyone. But we can't ever be anything more than friends."

"Because you don't think you're capable of more?"

"Because you're best friends with my brother, close to my family, and when I mess it all up, they'll be forced to choose sides, and while you're like family, I *am* family, which means they'll choose me…even though I won't deserve it."

"So what is it you want?" I ask, already knowing the answer but hoping I'm wrong.

"Well…" She shrugs, and her cheeks tinge pink. "I was thinking while we're on this trip we could…you know…" She smiles shyly.

"We could what?" I push, wanting to hear the words.

She huffs. "We could have fun."

"We are having fun." Yeah, I'm giving her a hard time—I'm not about to make this easy on her.

"You know what I mean." She slaps my chest playfully. "I like you, and as I said, I'm attracted to you, but I can't be who you want me to be. You're Mr. Perfect, Mr. Romantic. Everyone knows that. Even the women you've dumped have nothing but nice things to say about you. But I'm just not capable of more, and I don't want to lead you on. So if you don't want to have fun while on this trip, I completely get it, but if you do, I'm down. But that's all it can be…fun."

Fuck, this woman. I don't get it. She's gorgeous, rich, and has the most amazing voice. She's the music industry's pop princess, not just because of all that but because she's also sweet and sexy and funny. She's the spokesperson for several charities that focus on various issues like domestic abuse and music education. She's a hands-on aunt with her brother's kids and a wonderful older sister to her siblings.

She might be flaky and all over the place, but if anyone needs her, she's there and would do anything for anyone. I've literally watched her take the jacket off her back and give it to a woman who was freezing on the streets of LA during a cold night without thinking twice.

But beneath the surface, she has such low self-esteem and thinks so little of herself. She has it stuck in her head that since she hasn't met the right guy yet, it means something is wrong with her. She doesn't see what everyone sees. She doesn't understand how goddamn lovable she is. And I'm going to make it my mission to show her, but in order to do that, I need time with her. If I push the whole making her mine thing, telling her I want her forever, she's going to run. It's what she does. This means I will have to go along with what she *thinks* she wants…for now. Give her, her fun while showing her how amazing we'll be together. And hope, when we return to New York, it's enough for her to give us a real chance.

"Okay." I say what she needs to hear. "We'll do it your way."

"Really? You're okay with just having fun?" she asks speculatively.

I grip the curve of her hip and pull her over to me. "Yep." I press a chaste kiss to her soft lips. "But I still think we should wait a little bit. We have our entire trip ahead of us, and you did just get out of a relationship…Besides, half the fun is the foreplay." I shoot her a playful wink that has a shy smile stretching across her face.

"Just so you know," she says, hooking her arm around me and kissing my neck. "Kyle and I never had sex once after I woke up in the hospital."

I pull back slightly. "What?"

"It felt wrong. I knew he wasn't the one for me. He tried a couple of times to start things, but I pushed him away. I don't remember the last time we had sex since I can't remember anything before waking up, but it was before my accident."

If that's true, that means I'm the last person she had sex with. Knowing that—despite her being engaged to another man and almost marrying him—I was the last man she was with sexually has me smiling on the inside. And if I have it my way, I'll be the last damn guy she's with.

Fifteen

KENDALL

check in with the tour guide. "It's just us?"

"You wanted to make sure we're off the radar, and the only way to ensure that is to make sure no one is around us long enough to recognize us." Declan shrugs. "So I paid for a private tour."

"I take it back. Yesterday wasn't the best day ever...Today is!" I encircle my arms around his neck and my legs around his waist and kiss him hard, not giving a shit who's around. So far, nobody has recognized us—aside from someone our first day in Jersey, but we took off before it could be confirmed— and I might be getting lazy, letting my guard down, but I just don't have it in me to care. I'm having the best time on this trip, and if someone finds out, I can just tell everyone that Declan and I are on this road trip as friends, which would be the truth since he understands I can't give him any more and has agreed to just having fun on the trip and keeping complications like commitment out of it.

We didn't have sex last night, the mood a bit ruined by the talk about my ex and such, but we did make out, which was hot as hell, and then we watched another couple of episodes of *TVD* before falling asleep. Tonight, I hope Declan will give in, but if he needs more time, I'm okay with that too. As he mentioned, we have an entire trip ahead of us.

"Hi, are you Johnny and June?" a woman asks. Declan nods and sets me on my feet, taking my hand in his. "Yes, ma'am."

I side-eye him in confusion, wondering who the hell he's talking about, but I don't comment until we're checked in and on the golf cart, ready to get the tour underway.

"Johnny and June?"

"Yeah, I gave her different names so she wouldn't put two and two together." Ah, duh. Makes sense, but..."Who's Johnny and—" And then it hits me. "Johnny Cash and June Carter?"

He grins and nods while I think about the fact that he picked names of one of the most iconic couples in the music industry. I can't think too long, though, because a minute later, Tonya, our personal tour guide, is taking off and telling us all the fun facts about *The Vampire Diaries*.

We spend the next few hours touring the area. We get to take pictures where Damon and Elena shared a kiss in the pouring rain—and I totally have Tonya take a picture of us recreating the scene, minus the rain.

We stop and take more pictures in front of Elena's and Caroline's house, and then do a walk-through of the Lockwood mansion, where I make Declan recreate the image of Caroline and Klaus drinking champagne on the bench while on their date—yes, we totally stopped and bought champagne and glasses because I'm extra like that. I had no idea that scene was filmed in the backyard of the Lockwood mansion! Declan hasn't met Klaus yet, but he doesn't care.

He goes along with everything I want, acting like he's having as much fun as I am. Our last stop is in the town center, where we get pictures with the famous clock tower and in front of the Mystic Grill. While we're there, Declan tells me we'll be having lunch there later, and I damn near pass out.

Once we're back where we started, we thank Tonya and then head back to town. There's a cute little store that sells everything *TVD*, and I swear I buy everything in sight—from blood bags to a diary that looks just like Elena's. We even buy and put on matching Mystic Falls hoodies and hats.

After we take several more pictures, I send a bunch to my mom since it's her favorite show as well, telling her we're coming back soon and she's going to love it here.

Mom: I love these! You're with Declan?

Huh? What? Oh, shit! In my excitement, I included pictures of Declan with me.

Me: Please don't say anything to anyone. We're just friends. Nothing is going on. I needed to get away, and he was already going away. He surprised me with a trip here for my birthday.

Mom: I'm not judging, and I'll keep it to myself. Declan is a good man, and I'm glad you're with him. At least now I know you're safe and not alone on your birthday.

Me: Thank you, and yes, I am. Love you!

Mom: Love you more. Have a wonderful birthday. When you get back, we're having a belated birthday spa day.

Me: Sounds good!

"My mom knows I'm with you." Declan's brows rise to his forehead.

"I sent her pictures with you in them by mistake. She promised not to tell anyone. She's glad I'm with you. It makes her feel better, knowing I'm not alone, especially on my birthday." I'm sure she'll tell my dad since she doesn't keep secrets from him, but she'll make sure he doesn't say anything to anyone.

Declan nods in understanding, then changes the subject. "You ready to go have lunch at the Mystic Grill?"

"Hell yes!"

"OH, JEEZ...SERIOUSLY?" I SCROLL THROUGH THE COMMENTS, WISHING I NEVER WOULD'VE OPENED THE app in the first place. I knew what would be waiting for me, but no matter how thick of skin I have, I'm never fully prepared for the nastiness that is social media.

Like an idiot, I read a particularly hurtful comment and choke up, letting my emotions get the better of me. When I glance in the mirror and see my eyes are red and filled with tears threatening to spill over, I swipe out of the app and throw my phone onto the counter, not wanting to let that shit ruin the amazing day Declan and I've had.

"What's wrong?" Declan's baritone voice has me spinning around, my hand clutching my chest. "Way to sneak up on a woman." I glare. "Next time, knock."

"Door was open." He shrugs, leaning his shoulder against the doorjamb. "What's wrong?"

"Noth—"

"Nope, try again," he says, not even letting me finish my lie.

"I went on Insta."

"And?"

"And since I haven't made an official announcement about Kyle and me, he did the honors." I grab my phone and pull the image back up, showing it to Declan. It's a ripped-up picture of our wedding announcement with the caption: *Only give your heart to an ice princess if you want her to jab an ice pick through it.*

"He's an asshole." Declan hands my phone back to me. "And you don't owe anyone an explanation. It's your personal business."

"That I made public by picking the career I did. I need to post something, but I've been putting it off."

"I stand by my previous statement," he says, gripping the curve of one of my hips and pulling me toward him. He plucks the phone out of my hand and holds the side button down until it prompts to turn off, then he swipes it off and drops it back onto the counter. "When you're ready, if you choose to, then you make a post. But you don't owe anyone anything. Just because you sing music doesn't mean you're required to post about every personal detail of your life. The guys and I don't post shit. Aside from the overdose speculation, nobody knows what happened to Gage or where he is. Let them fucking speculate. It just makes them want you even more."

"Guys do that shit, and they're labeled as mysterious. Women do it, and they're frigid bitches."

"Fuck them," he says, lifting me into his arms. I wrap my legs around his waist and hold on as he walks us over to the bed. It's late, close to midnight, and I was in the bathroom taking a shower and getting my pajamas on. We spent the day in Covington, eating ice cream at the local place where the cast of *TVD* used to eat it and having dinner here at the B&B, complete with a cake for my birthday. Afterward, we explored more of the property since we leave first thing tomorrow to head to Oklahoma. For what? I have no idea.

With me in his arms, Declan climbs onto the bed, stopping once my head gently hits the pillow. "You're so damn beautiful," he says softly, moving several strands of hair out of my face. "And not just on the outside, but on the inside too." He palms my cheek, and instinctually, I lean into his touch. "Anybody who matters knows that you ending the engagement was for a good reason, and anybody who doesn't know that doesn't matter."

I get what he's saying, and I love how he sees me, the way he never judges me. "But—"

"No buts," he says, cutting me off. "I'm tired of listening to you second-guess every damn decision because you don't see yourself the way I do. You're not a frigid bitch or an ice princess. You're a warm, loving woman who almost married a man you weren't in love with because you were *hoping* you'd feel something for him so you wouldn't hurt him. Because you care about others.

"Haven't you listened to your songs? They're about heartbreak, about wanting to fall in love, about not finding the right guy, but you never say anything mean about a single one of them. Every one of them is about you. How you wish they could be who you need them to be. You wish you could be who they want you to be. You're not a bad person, Kendall. You just want to love and be loved."

His words hit the deepest, darkest part of my soul. I both hate and love that he sees beyond the surface, and he understands me on a deeper level. That somehow, along the way, he's been able to clear the fog and see the real me. The woman who, as he just said, wants to love and be loved.

"Dec," I choke out, a lump of emotion clogging my throat. "I want..." I try to think of what I want, what I need, but my head is a mess of emotions, and my heart feels like it's been cracked open.

"Tell me, baby," he says, leaning forward and brushing his lips against mine. "Tell me what you want, and I'll give it to you. Any-fucking-thing."

"I want...to feel..." *Loved* is what I want to say. I want to feel loved. I want someone to make me feel like I'm their everything, be the center of their universe, the way my family has found love. I want someone to look at me with hearts in their eyes and not just want me, Kendall Blackwood, the pop star, but actually want me, the insecure, vulnerable woman who secretly just wants to be loved. To know I'm not broken. But because fear stops me from saying any of this, I go with the next best thing. "I want to feel wanted."

"Done." That is all Declan says before he crashes his lips against mine with such passion it feels as though he's making love to my mouth. Our tongues connect, swirling with one another, tasting, coaxing, devouring. I can't get enough of him. I've been kissed by many guys, but none of them...not a single one...ever made my insides tighten and my heart beat faster the way kissing Declan does.

He breaks the kiss, only to pepper kisses along my jawline and down my neck, suckling on my sensitive flesh. He lifts onto his knees and pulls my shirt over my head, exposing my naked breasts. Then he stops and stares at me, his gaze filled with heat and lust. "You're so fucking beautiful," he says reverently, taking one of my breasts in his hand and pinching my nipple with his thumb and forefinger while he strokes the beaded tip with the pad of his other finger. "So damn perfect."

He dips his head and takes the nipple he's not playing with into his mouth. His tongue swipes the tip, getting it wet, and then he blows on it gently, his cool breath sending shivers down my spine. He does it again and again and then shocks the hell out of me when he bites it *hard.* A zap of pleasure shoots straight to my center, and I lock my legs around his waist, grinding myself against him.

"Fuck, this tattoo." He lifts my arms over my head and pins them against the headboard. "Keep them right there," he demands, giving me a chaste kiss.

"Do you have any idea what this tattoo does to me?" He glances at me for a quick moment before he spreads my legs and slides downward so he's eye level with my tattoo. "*It's okay to be a little broken.*" he reads, then kisses the first word inked into my flesh. "Every day, for the rest of our trip, hell, for the rest of our lives if you let me, I'm going to show you how perfectly broken you are," he murmurs, kissing each word. I ignore the *rest of our lives* part, refusing to think about what the idea of spending the rest of my life with Declan does to my insides.

Once he's kissed every part of my tattoo, he licks and nips my flesh as he works his way across my side, planting an open-mouthed kiss to my hip bones.

Taking the waistband of my boy shorts between his fingers, he pulls them off and then takes my foot, kissing the instep softly before he trails more kisses up the inside of my calf and thigh, stopping at the apex of my legs.

"I've dreamed and fantasized about this," he says, sucking his bottom lip into his mouth and releasing it. His tongue darts out, sliding along his lips as if he's about to consume his favorite food, and then he drops onto his stomach, parts my lips, and licks up the center.

"Oh, God." I moan loudly, not expecting him to just dive right in. "Dec…"

"Shh," he murmurs, blowing onto my center. "Just watch, baby." He glances up and licks his lips. "Watch me want the hell out of you." His face disappears between my legs, and a second later, the flat of his tongue is ascending up my middle again. He laps gently, from my hole to my clit, up and down, over and over again. He stops at my clit, flicks it softly, and then goes back to teasing me. My body is hot and needy, and with every flick and lap and lick of his tongue, he works me up higher and higher until I'm dangling off the precipice, begging for him to shove me off the edge.

"You taste so good," he mutters as he shoves a finger and then two inside me, stroking my walls. Between his tongue stroking my clit and his fingers fucking me, I fall off the ledge, getting lost in the strongest orgasm I've ever been given. My body trembles, and my pussy spasms in the most delicious way.

Declan continues his ministrations until I can't take it anymore and push his head away. He glances up at me with a sexy smirk on his face and his lips wet with my juices, and the need to kiss him hits me hard. I sit up and, gripping the back of his neck, run my tongue along his, tasting myself on him, before I press my mouth to his.

"My turn," I murmur, peppering kisses over his stubbled jaw. "I want you."

"And you will have me…soon, but not tonight." He places his hand gently against my chest, forcing me to lie back down. "Tonight is about you."

My eyes widen in a mixture of shock and confusion. He's already made me come. "But…"

"You," he repeats, crawling up my body and kissing me softly on the lips. "Only you."

And holy shit, he does exactly what he said he would do. For the rest of the night, Declan fucking Pierce shows me over and over again just how wanted I am.

Sixteen

DECLAN

She's referring to the two-story, four-thousand-square-foot log cabin I've rented on a lake in Oklahoma. Since Kendall wants to stay under the radar, I figured the best way to have a good time is by spending some time on a lake, where we can go on a boat, go swimming, or relax in the hot tub. There's also a ready-to-use bonfire in the backyard and wraparound porches on the first and second levels. This is the perfect way to go camping without dealing with all the camping shit.

"We have the place for a week, but we can leave whenever we want."

"Let's go see the house!" She squeals in excitement, grabbing her luggage and running up to the front door. I use the code I was given to open the door, and she gasps when we enter. It's identical to the pictures: an open floor plan with hardwood floors, walls, and ceilings. The furniture is rustic, giving the place a luxurious outdoorsy vibe, with a two-story brick fireplace used as the focal point.

"Oh, my God, Dec! Come look at this."

I already know where she is, what has her freaking out, but I join her, loving her excitement. When I find her, she's looking out of the floor-to-ceiling windows that make up the entire back of the house. Since it's late and dark outside, you can't see anything, but in the morning, no matter which room we're in or which floor we're on, nothing will block our view of the backyard and lake.

"I rented a boat for the week as well," I say, stepping behind her and wrapping my arms around her waist. She sighs into me, resting her back and head against my front, her hands landing on mine and threading our fingers together.

Ever since we've agreed to *have fun*, Kendall's allowed herself to let go and not overthink our closeness and connection. It probably also has something to do with the three orgasms I gave her last night. With each one, it felt as though I was cracking the hard exterior that she uses to keep everyone out, exposing little pieces of the softness she keeps hidden underneath. I know it was the oxytocin from the orgasms, but I'll use whatever I have to my advantage to break down her walls.

"That'll be fun." She turns in my arms, leaning against the glass wall. "Thank you for this. For making sure we're not in places where we'll get swarmed. I didn't realize how badly I needed this time away."

I dip my head and kiss the corner of her mouth. "Let's go check out the rest of the place."

"Or…" Her eyes lock with mine as she reaches down and rubs her palm along the front of my pants, waking my dick from its slumber. "We could stay right here, and you can fuck me against this glass wall."

With a smirk, she lifts her hoodie over her head and throws it to the side. Then she bends slightly and pulls her cotton shorts off and kicks her sandals out of the way. She pushes me back gently, and I'm able to take her in. A royal-blue lace bra barely covers her breasts, her rose-colored nipples showing through the see-through material while the swells of her breasts spill over the tops of her cups. The matching underwear is thin, covering only the important parts, and I have no doubt that her peach of an ass would be on display if she turned around. It makes me want to turn her around and see for myself.

"What are you thinking?" she asks, making me realize I've been staring at her for several long beats.

"How sexy you look like this." I run the tip of my finger along the swell of her breast and down to her nipple. She shivers slightly, and her nipple hardens instantly. "And…" I go with the truth because fuck it, why not? "I was wondering if I turn you around, will I get a view of your perfect ass?"

She sucks in her bottom lip seductively, then twirls around. Her palms smack against the glass, and her legs part slightly as if she's under arrest. And holy fuck, the sight is better than I imagined. With only a tiny, *so fucking tiny* string running up her crack, her entire ass is exposed. And then, because she's a goddamn tease, she peeks over her shoulder and wiggles that ass.

Unable to help myself, I step over to her until our bodies are almost flush against one another. One hand goes to hers, which is still on the glass, and the other goes to her pert ass, giving it a squeeze. "Keep it up, and instead of fucking that tight pussy, I'll fill your ass."

"Don't make promises you can't keep," she sasses.

I step back and give her ass a quick, hard slap, which has her squealing in shock. "You ever been fucked in the ass?"

She shakes her head slowly, and in the reflection of the glass window, I see her suck her lip between her teeth, her go-to move when she's turned on.

Gripping her chin, I turn her face, making her look at me. "You wanna be fucked in the ass?"

She shrugs. "I read it can be good, but I've never been with anyone I trusted enough to try it with." She says the words so nonchalantly as though we're talking about what we want to eat for dinner instead of anal play.

"You want *me* to fuck you *here?*" I ask, dropping my hand from her chin and sliding a finger along her crack.

She nods, and she might not realize it, but that's a huge step in the right direction. She trusts me. Something that doesn't come easily for her. But her nodding isn't enough. "I need the words, baby. Tell me you want me to shove my dick into that tight hole of yours."

She groans, her eyes fluttering shut for several seconds before opening them, her gaze locking with mine. "I want you to fuck me in *every* one of my holes."

God-fucking-dammit. This woman is going to be the death of me.

I grip the curve of her hip and turn her around, pushing her back against the glass. My fingers wrap around her delicate neck, and my mouth crashes against hers, kissing and devouring her. I've been waiting for over a month to be inside her again, and now that I've finally been given the green light, I can't go slow.

"This will be hard and fast," I murmur against her lips, silently vowing to go slower next time, to take my time and worship every inch of her.

"Yes," she gasps into my mouth, clearly on the same page. "Fuck me hard."

Without the patience I usually have, I wrench the scrap of material she calls underwear off her body, then quickly undo my pants and yank my already hard as hell dick out. In one fluid motion, I lift her and then enter her tight, warm pussy. Kendall's legs encircle my waist while her fingers delve into my hair, holding on as I fuck her deep and hard against the glass wall. Our heated bodies slap against one another, our mouths tasting and consuming. Our tongues duel as hard as we fuck, and despite Kendall's position, she gives as good as she takes, meeting me thrust for thrust, grinding her pelvis against mine.

She comes first, screaming out her orgasm, and when her walls grip my dick so tightly, I lose any remaining semblance of control. Letting go, I fill her pussy with every drop of my cum.

"Oh, wow." She sighs, dropping her forehead to my shoulder. "I need to clean up, and then I need you to do that again."

I bark out a laugh, loving that she's again on the same page as me. "You don't have to tell me twice," I say, kissing the side of her head. "If it were up to me, I'd spend the next week inside your perfect pussy."

"Sounds like a plan," she quips.

SINCE WE'VE BEEN SITTING IN THE CAR ALL DAY—DESPITE IT BEING LATE, NEITHER OF US IS TIRED—INSTEAD of going to bed, we end up on the back porch, lounging on the comfortable bed swing. It's in the fifties tonight, so we're in sweats and hoodies with a blanket she found thrown over us. Without the city lights, the sky is dark, and only the moon and stars shine any light on us. But it's enough that I can see her face as she stares up at the sky, inhaling the fresh air as she sips her wine from one of the bottles we bought in Jersey.

"Does this taste weird to you?" she asks, scrunching her nose and putting the glass up to my lips.

I take a sip, a hint of fruit hitting my senses. "I'm not really a wino like you, but it tastes all right."

She sets it on the table next to her and snuggles up against my chest, stretching her legs out over mine. "This is nice...I enjoyed Jersey and *loved* the B&B, but this is really relaxing. It reminds me of Big Bear minus the snow."

"I love Big Bear." Big Bear Mountain is a ski resort in California where Kendall's parents and grandparents own cabins. They've been vacationing there every winter since I've known the Blackwoods, and since Camden and I became friends, I've joined them damn near every year.

"It's a shame we didn't go this year. Maybe I'll try to convince my parents to go before the snow dries up in May."

I sit up slightly and look at her, confused because we did go to Big Bear. And then it hits me. She doesn't remember. "We went in January, right after the new year."

Her brow furrows, and then she frowns, realizing she doesn't remember. "Well, that sucks. I went and can't even remember if I had a good time."

"We did," I tell her truthfully. Kyle was busy at work, so we spent the entire trip together, skiing and chilling by the bonfire.

"I guess I'll have to take your word for it." She pouts and drops her head to my chest, and I wrap my arms around her. "I can't remember like six weeks of my life, and it feels like forever. I can't even imagine how I'd feel if I had no memory. Who knows what else I can't remember? I could've received life-changing news, and I'd never even know I got it."

I tighten my hold on her, then hold my breath, praying she didn't feel it. I've thought about telling her about us so many times, even came close a couple of times, but fuck, how do you *tell* someone you spent the most amazing night with them, a night they don't even remember? I keep hoping maybe one day she'll remember. Eventually, if she doesn't, I'm going to have to tell her, but I don't want her to be told how amazing the night was. I want her to *feel* what I felt.

"Oh, look!" She gasps. "A shooting star. Make a wish!"

I do as she says, figuring it can't hurt, and wish for Kendall to be mine forever.

"Did you do it?" she asks, glancing up at me.

"Yep."

"Me too." After a few minutes of silence, she says, "I'll tell you mine if you tell me yours."

I chuckle at how adorable she is. "You go first."

"No way! I just wanted to see if you'd do it. I'm not taking that chance." She huffs and cuddles closer to me.

Wanting to take advantage of the alone time, I decide to play twenty questions with her. "If you could travel anywhere in the world, where would you go?"

"Hmm...I'm not sure. I've been to so many places while on tour and on vacations. Honestly, I'm kind of tired of traveling," she admits. "I'm loving this road trip we're on, but I think once we're back at home, I just kind of want to stay put for a while. What about you?"

"Indonesia. There's a surfing spot I've always wanted to check out." Aside from making music and playing the bass, surfing is one of my favorite pastimes. I've missed it since we moved to New York. "Favorite food."

"Crème brûlée."

"That's not food. It's a dessert."

"Does it enter my mouth, go down my throat, and land in my belly? Then it's food, and it's my favorite. I know yours...empanadas."

Mmm...she isn't wrong. Her grandma's empanadas are the shit. When she comes to visit, she'll make double just for me. "They're the best. I miss Grandma Alicia's cooking."

"I know how to make them," she says with a shrug. "I can make you some one day."

My stomach rumbles at the thought. "I'm going to hold you to it."

"New York or LA?" she asks, catching on to my game and joining in. "And you can't say wherever the band is." Actually, my thought was wherever she is, but I don't tell her that.

"That's hard. I love both, but if I had to pick one, I'd go with New York. It's crazier, but people leave you alone there."

"True," she agrees. "But I'd want to live outside of the city in the 'burbs. That's one thing I love about Calabasas. The gated communities and a bit of property. One day, I'd like to live on a bit of land, maybe have some horses and four-wheelers."

"With a husband and kids?" I ask. As soon as the words come out and she tenses, I immediately regret it, thinking she'll retreat into her shell, but she shocks me by answering.

"Yeah, I'd like a husband and kids someday," she says softly. "At least two, so they have each other. And I'd want them close in age because as close as I am with my siblings, being so much older makes me feel like the odd one out sometimes. What about you? You're an only child. Does that make you want to have one or a bunch?"

"I want a few. I loved when I'd go to your house, and the place would be loud, filled with people. Growing up, I never had that. My parents are uptight and close-minded, so I always avoided bringing my friends over. I want my home to be open and inviting and for my kids to know everyone is welcome."

"Do your parents hate that you're in a rock band?"

"Of course. They're hoping this break means the end of Raging Chaos. They made sure to reach out and let me know that I have a job waiting for me if I want to go to school." I scoff. "I would rather do anything besides work for their hotel."

"They own a hotel?" she asks, sitting up and looking at me. "How did I not know that?"

"Because I keep it separate. The media knows about Pierce Hotels, but since it's not gossip, they don't really talk about it."

"Wait? What?" She gasps. "Pierce Hotels is your parents' hotel chain? They're huge."

I laugh. "No shit, and my parents feel their son playing in a rock band taints their pristine reputation." I roll my eyes. "It doesn't matter how successful the band is. They'll always view me as a failure. All they care about is money and their image. They're not even in love. It's all business.

"Growing up, I saw how fake their marriage was, and then every summer, I'd go visit my grandparents, who were in love. Even in their eighties, they couldn't keep their hands off each other. It gave me hope that I could have what they had and not be stuck in a loveless marriage like my parents. My grandfather died when I was sixteen, and my grandma followed shortly after. I believe she was so heartbroken without him that she followed him to heaven."

Kendall sighs. "I want that kind of love."

I said I'd give her time, but I can't help myself when I blurt out the following words. "You can have that." I tip her chin to look at me. "We can have that. You just have to stop being scared and give us a chance."

She swallows thickly, and I worry she's going to run. But instead, tears fill her eyes. "I want to," she whispers so softly, I almost don't hear her. "But you're right, I'm scared. So many things can go wrong."

"Or they can go right."

"But if they go wrong, it can ruin everything."

"Or it can be amazing," I argue. "We still have some time left on our trip. What if, instead of being hell-bent on just having fun, you give me a chance to show you how good it can be? Let me woo you."

She chokes out a laugh. In her family, the men always talk about how they woo their women. It's an old-fashioned term, but they believe in the old-fashioned kind of love. The kind where the man treats his woman like a queen and always puts her first, reminding her every day how blessed he is to have her in his life. And that's exactly what I want to do with Kendall. I want to woo the hell out of her.

"All right," she says, shocking me. "I'll give you a chance to woo me. But I don't want anyone to know yet. Just in case."

This is another gigantic step in the right direction, so I'm not about to argue. I started this trip with the intent of getting away from Kendall since she was marrying someone else, and now, here she is, willing to give us a real chance. I'll take it, and by the time this trip is over, she's going to be shouting it from the rooftops that we're together.

"Deal," I tell her, standing and lifting her into my arms.

"What are you doing?" she squeals.

"I'm about to woo the fuck out of you...*literally.*"

She throws her head back with a laugh. "Sounds good to me."

Seventeen

KENDALL

THE MOMENT MY BRAIN WAKES, I FEEL HIM BETWEEN MY LEGS, LICKING HIS WAY UP MY SLIT AND THEN sucking on my clit. For a second, I wonder if I fell asleep while we were in the middle of sex, but then I remember, after the third time Declan made me come, he carried me to the bathroom so I could clean up. Then he carried me back to bed, tucking me under the covers and spooning me from behind. I crack my eyes open and notice the rays of sunshine darting through the slats of the blinds, telling me it's morning.

Declan nibbles on my swollen nub, and I groan. He sucks harder, then massages it slowly. My orgasm creeps up on me, and before my eyes have even fully opened, I'm moaning out my release.

"Is this your way of waking me up?" I ask, lifting myself onto my elbows to look at him. "Because a girl can get used to this kind of wake-up call."

With lips glossy from my juices, he smiles wide. "By the time I'm done with you, you're going to need to go back to sleep." The corner of his lips curls into a sexy smirk, and then he flips me onto my stomach, giving my ass a slap. Grabbing the curves of my hips, he pulls me onto my hands and knees and thrusts a couple of fingers into my sensitive center.

"Dec," I groan as he fingers me slow and deep. I'm so wet from my orgasm, my pussy suctions his digits, making a sound that would be embarrassing if I wasn't so turned on.

"Fuck, this pussy," he murmurs. "This ass…" With my head against the pillow, I can't see anything he's doing, but when his fingers leave my pussy, dragging up my center and puckered hole, I don't need to see anything to know where this is going.

A few seconds later, my cheeks are being spread, and then Declan's tongue is sliding up and down my slit, stopping at the tight ringed hole and pushing inside. I've never let anyone near my ass before, so I have no frame of reference, but the way he's licking me from top to bottom feels so good. My juices are dripping down the inside of my thighs.

"You gonna let me fuck this sexy ass, baby?" Declan croons. "You gonna let me spread these perfect cheeks and stretch your tight hole?"

Jesus, his dirty talk. Most guys cut to the chase. Don't get me wrong, I've been with guys who aren't completely selfish in bed and make sure I get off first, but it's always as if it's a prelude. But Declan acts like making me come is the main act.

"Kendall, I need words," he says, reminding me that he asked me a question. "If you don't want me to, just say the word and—"

"I want you to fuck my ass," I tell him, cutting him off.

"You sure?"

"Yes." I push my ass back to drive my answer home. "Fuck my ass."

The sound of a bottle popping open echoes in the otherwise quiet room, and then cold liquid lands on my ass, dribbling down the crack.

"Is that...lube?" I ask as he runs his finger down the same line as the liquid and then pushes a single digit into my tight hole, making me groan loudly.

"Yep, got it at the store while you were sleeping. Also picked up coffee and breakfast." He pulls his finger out slightly, then pushes it back in. It feels odd... but not bad. Not good, though. I read that if it's done right, it can heighten an orgasm, and a lot of women find it pleasurable, but I'm not expecting to enjoy it the first time. I remember how badly it hurt when I lost my virginity, and that hole wasn't half as tight as this one.

"I also picked this up," he says, just as a vibrating noise hits my ears and then my ass. I jump slightly as the object pulsates against the ring of my ass before pushing in. It's thicker than his finger, and as he pushes it into me, inch by inch, I feel fuller and fuller.

"You...got...sex toys?" I breathe, trying to focus on my question, but the intrusion in my ass feels too good. It's hitting my insides in the craziest way, and if he keeps doing what he's doing, I'm going to explode.

"The store has a female pleasure section," Declan says. "Damn, baby. I wish you could see this. The way your ass is sucking the fake dick in. If I weren't afraid of my phone getting hacked, I'd record it so we could watch it later." My insides clench at the thought of lying in bed later with Declan and watching him fuck my ass.

"You'd like that, wouldn't you?" he says through a soft chuckle.

"Yes." I gasp as the toy almost completely leaves my ass, only to be pushed back in even deeper. I never thought I would ever feel comfortable enough to let a man this close. There have been guys who've asked, but I always said no. Couldn't imagine putting myself in such a vulnerable position. But with Declan, I didn't even think twice. And I know why that is. I trust him. He's more than just a man trying to catch me so he can say he had me. He genuinely wants to keep me. And the more time I spend with him, the more I'd really like to be kept by him.

"One day, I'll record us, but not on my phone and not today. I need to focus on this ass." His fingers plunge into my pussy, and within seconds, I'm coming the hardest I've ever come in my life. My ass tightens, my pussy clenches, and juices...Jesus, my juices slide down my thighs like a waterfall, no doubt soaking the bed.

"Fuck, yeah."

Suddenly, the toy is gone, and the head of Declan's dick is in its place. I hold my breath, expecting him to thrust into me, but instead, he goes slow, filling me little by little. He makes me promise to let him know if it hurts or is too much. It stings and is definitely uncomfortable, but thankfully, it doesn't hurt.

"Holy shit, this feels so good. So tight. I'm never going to last," he murmurs once he's stuffed me full of his cock.

When he doesn't move for several seconds, I wiggle my ass, needing him to do something. My pussy is sensitive, and my clit is throbbing. I've already come twice, but with him filling me, I want more.

He takes it as his cue to move and begins to slowly and gently fuck my ass. One hand grips my hip, and the other reaches around and under, finding my clit and massaging it. Between the fullness in my ass and the pressure on my clit, my climax builds fast, and then I come hard, screaming out Declan's name.

"Fuck, fuck," he grunts, then pulls out. I'm about to ask what he's doing when he flips me onto my back. His muscular thighs trap mine, kneeling over me, as he fists his cock, pumping a couple of times before ropes of white shoot out all over my belly and breasts. He doesn't stop until he's completely drained himself.

He releases his dick and reaches down, smearing his cum across my flesh and over my breasts. He stops at my pert nipple and swirls the sticky substance around the tip. "This is the most beautiful sight I've ever seen," he says, smiling softly, reverently, as if he's looking at a masterpiece and not at me, covered in his cum. "I need a Polaroid camera, so I can take pictures and remember you like this."

He drops his hands to either side of my head and locks eyes with me. "Thank you, baby."

"For what?" I mutter in confusion.

"For giving us a real chance..." He kisses the tip of my nose, and my heart picks up speed. "For trusting me." He plants a soft kiss to the corner of my mouth, and my head goes fuzzy. "For letting me love you." His lips brush against mine, and I suck in a sharp breath at the word love. He loves me? Declan Pierce loves me? As I'm trying to wrap my head around that, he kisses me again, this time harder, his tongue dipping into my parted lips and tasting me. "If you let me, I'll spend the rest of our lives showing you every day how much you mean to me."

The rest of our lives... The thought of forever should scare me. That was my cue to run—and run fast—with other guys, but as he trails kisses along my jaw, butterflies erupt in my belly, reminding me of the words my dad texted me.

One day you will find the right guy, and you'll feel it. Your heart will beat a little faster, your smiles will get brighter, and butterflies will swarm your belly. And you'll know, every wrong guy was simply leading you to the right one.

My heart is beating faster...My smiles are brighter...and fuck, it feels like I have an entire army of butterflies in my belly.

"Declan," I breathe.

"Yeah, baby?" he murmurs.

"I think...I think I'm falling in love with you."

He stops kissing me so he can look at me, his eyes filled with shock and happiness. "Say it again."

"I think I'm falling in love with you," I repeat, shocked as hell that I can even say the words a second time. "I know it's only been a couple of weeks, but I...*I feel it.*"

Declan dips his face and plants a soft kiss over my heart. "Time doesn't dictate your heart."

"I'm scared," I admit, feeling as though I've been cut open and exposed for the entire world to see. Aside from my dad and brother, I've never told a single man I loved him until now. "What if—"

"Stop," he demands, cutting me off. "No what-ifs. We're living in the present. I'm here, and I've got you, Kendall. It's okay to be scared. This is new for both of us."

"Both of us?"

"Yeah, both of us because you're the only person I've ever loved. And not to scare the shit out of you, but these feelings have been going on since I was a damn teenager"—he chuckles—"so I'm glad you've finally caught up to me."

His words nearly take my breath away. I'm unsure what to say, but I don't need to say anything because a moment later, his mouth is on mine, kissing me passionately, as if trying to prove the truth in his words through his actions.

He pulls me into his arms and carries me to the bathroom, never once breaking the kiss. For the next couple of hours, as we shower and then find our way back to bed, Declan shows me over and over again just how much he loves and wants me while I pray to God that I don't completely fuck this up. Because for the first time in my life, I can actually see my future, my life with Declan, and the picture is everything I've ever wanted and never thought I'd have.

Eighteen

DECLAN

lunchtime—and discussing what we want to do today when my phone rings. Kendall glances over and flinches slightly at the name on the screen—Camden.

"I'm going to take it in the other room," I tell her, standing and leaning over to peck her lips. I can see it in her eyes that she wants to tell me it's okay to take the call with her here, but I know she isn't ready to tell anyone about us yet, and I need her to know I'm okay with that. She needs time, and I'll give it to her. Knowing how she feels about me, that she's falling in love with me, is enough...for now. I don't want to overwhelm her with too much too soon. I'm still in shock that we went from being friends to giving a relationship a real chance in such a short amount of time. We have our entire lives, and if how long it took her to fall for me is any indication, she'll be ready sooner rather than later.

I step into the living room and click accept. Camden pops on the screen, along with Braxton, in a group video call. The only person missing is Gage.

"Well, look who it is," Braxton says with a smirk. "I was starting to forget what your ugly mug looks like."

I scoff. "Speak for yourself. What's up?"

"Hi, Dec!" Kaylee yells from behind, her head popping onto the screen and replacing Braxton. "How are you?"

"I'm good. How are you?"

"Perfect." She grins and holds up her hand, showing me her ring. "Braxton and I have some news...hence the video call. We got married! I'm officially Mrs. Braxton Lutz."

Fuck, I forgot they were planning to get married after Kendall's wedding. I left and haven't heard shit. Everyone's been giving me my space...Dammit, I should've been there.

She must see the look of guilt because she adds, "And before you think you weren't invited, we eloped. Went to Vegas and got married and then flew to Paris for our honeymoon. When we're all together again, we'll have a dinner to celebrate."

Braxton pushes her onto his lap so they're both visible and kisses her cheek. "We're in Paris now," he says. "Just arrived last night. We wanted you guys to be the first to know."

"Congratulations," I tell them both, happy that they found their way back to each other after all these years.

"Congrats!" Camden adds.

"Thanks," they both say, all smiles.

"Cam, how's the fam?" I ask.

"Good." He beams. "Marianna is trying to crawl and is stealing Felix's toys and driving him nuts. He said he's changed his mind and wants us to give him a brother instead. If she's this crazy at six months old, I can't imagine how she'll be when she's a toddler."

We all crack up laughing.

"Anyone talk to Gage?" I ask after a moment of silence.

"Nah," Camden says, his smile dimming. "My dad's been in contact, and he's still there but isn't talking to anyone on the outside. His ninety days are over at the end of the month."

"We'll be back before then," Braxton says.

"Same," I agree. There's no way I won't be there for our best friend when he gets out.

Camden nods. "Speaking of not talking to anyone. Have you heard from Kendall? Mom and Dad said she's contacted them, and they know she's okay, but she isn't posting on social media and hasn't reached out to anyone else. I'm worried. She's one of the strongest people I know on the outside, but deep down..." He sighs. "She's great at putting on a good front, but I think she's hurting and doesn't want anyone to see it."

"I haven't heard from her," Kaylee says with a frown. "But we're not all that close. She hasn't spoken to Layla? They're good friends."

Camden shakes his head. "Aside from a call to our mom and a few texts that she's okay, nobody's heard from her since she dipped out on her wedding."

"She's okay," I confirm.

"You've spoken to her?" he asks, his eyes wide.

"She's okay," I repeat, hoping he gets what I'm saying. I promised Kendall I wouldn't say anything, and I don't want to go back on that, but I can't just sit here and let her brother worry.

Camden looks like he wants to ask more questions, but thankfully, he doesn't.

We bullshit for a few more minutes, avoiding the topic of Raging Chaos since we've silently agreed not to discuss it until we have Gage back, and then everyone hangs up after saying we'll talk soon.

I throw my phone on the counter and go in search of Kendall, finding her lying out on a lounge chair on the expansive back deck. She's lost in thought, scribbling in her notebook, and doesn't notice I'm there until I drop down next to her.

"Your brother asked if I've spoken to you."

Her hand stills, but she doesn't look up.

"Said you haven't contacted anyone but your parents..." When she doesn't say anything, I continue. "I told him you were okay."

Her head pops up. "You—"

"Just said you were okay. Nothing more."

She nods.

"Why haven't you reached out to your brother and sisters?"

She shrugs, but I refuse to let her get away with that shit. Grabbing the notebook and pen from her, I drop them onto the end of the chair and then pull her into my lap so she's straddling my thighs. "Baby, talk to me."

Her gaze drops, refusing to look at me, so I lift her chin and kiss the tip of her nose. "Kendall..."

"I was embarrassed," she admits softly. "Still am...Bailey and Camden are both so perfect. They have the perfect relationships and make perfect decisions. They both told me I was rushing things, but I didn't listen. They probably think I'm such an irresponsible idiot."

"First of all," I say, meeting her eyes. "Nobody is perfect. And they might've said that to you, but it's only because they love you. You should've seen the look in his eyes. He's so damn worried about you. Nobody thinks you're irresponsible or an idiot. They only want you to be happy."

"I think this is the happiest I've been in a long time," she admits, making my heart swell. "I love our little bubble and didn't want to pop it."

"I love our bubble too," I tell her, kissing her pillow-soft lips. "But those people are a part of our big bubble, and in a few weeks, when we return, they'll be there because they're not going anywhere."

She nods in understanding. "How is he?"

"Good. Braxton and Kaylee got married in Vegas and are now in Paris for a few weeks on their honeymoon. Marianna is starting to crawl and driving Felix nuts. Camden said he wants to trade her in for a brother."

Kendall barks out a laugh. "I miss them." Her eyes water, and when a tear escapes, I wipe it away with my thumb.

"We can go home anytime you want."

"Not yet." She leans her head against my chest and wraps her arms around me. "I need a little more time with you. Is that okay?"

"Of course, it is," I tell her, kissing the crown of her head. "I just need to be back before Gage gets out."

We spend the rest of the day lounging outside. We write for a few hours, then hit the hot tub. When it gets dark out, we light the bonfire and roast hot dogs and s'mores.

One day at the lake turns into two, and before we know it, a week has passed, and we're packing up to head to our next destination.

"WHERE ARE WE GOING?" KENDALL ASKS AS WE DRIVE DOWN THE HIGHWAY TOWARD THE INDUSTRIAL airport, where a private plane is waiting to take us to our next stop.

"Surprise," I tell her. "Make sure you get everything of yours from the car."

"What? Why?" she asks as I pull into the airport.

"Someone's coming to pick it up and drive it back to Calabasas."

She glances around, her eyes going wide when she realizes where we are. "We're taking a plane?"

"Yep, it's too long of a drive where we're going." Technically, we could drive there, but with it being twenty-four hours by car, we'd have to stop a few times, and it's not worth it. Not when we have the money and means to get on a plane and be there in less than three hours.

The moment Kendall finds out where we're going, she squeals in excitement. "Big Bear Mountain?"

"You said you didn't remember skiing. Figured we could make new memories."

She wraps her arms around me. "Thank you, Dec. This has seriously been the best trip."

The ride from the airport to the mountain isn't too long. I hired a car service to pick us up and have security meet us there. The goal is to stay out of the spotlight, but Big Bear is filled with people, and anything can happen.

"There's a chance we'll get spotted when we go skiing," I warn Kendall as the SUV pulls up to the cabin I rented. I could've asked Camden or her parents to borrow theirs, but I didn't want to have to explain why. "We can hang back, stay at the cabin—"

"It's okay," she says, taking my hand in hers and lacing our fingers together. "If someone spots us, we can always say we're two friends spending time together. I'm planning to tell our family that we're together, but I'd like to keep our relationship out of the media for a little bit. Just in case…"

Her words trail off, but I can fill in the rest myself: *Just in case it doesn't work out.* I hate that she's so negative about herself and relationships, but over time, she'll see that I'm not going anywhere and what we have is forever.

We find the master bedroom and get situated. Kendall says she's going to shower the flight off, and while she does, I get Jose, our security, caught up to speed. He's just left—since we won't need him until we leave later for dinner—when Kendall walks downstairs in nothing but a towel, her hair wet and messy. Her eyes meet mine, and a seductive smile spreads across her lips.

"I was hoping you were going to join me." She reaches up to the knot holding her towel together and pulls it apart, the material falling to the floor and leaving her standing there naked and gorgeous.

"I had to speak to our security. He'll be back later so we can go to dinner."

"Or…" She saunters over to me. "We could have dinner here, and I could be your dessert."

"That would imply I have to wait until *after* we eat to eat *you*." I pull her into my arms, my hands landing on her plump ass at the same time as I crash my mouth down on hers.

We don't end up leaving the cabin, too lost in each other. Instead, I spend the rest of the day and night making her my dinner, dessert, and eventually my breakfast. The rest of the week pretty much goes by the same way. We never make it out of the cabin to actually ski. When we need sustenance, we order food and have Jose pick it up. Kendall has fast become my addiction, and while I want our relationship to be out in the open, I understand what she means about not wanting our bubble to burst. Because being in a Kendall-only bubble is the best damn way to live my life.

Unfortunately, that bubble can only stay intact for so long, and soon, we're going to have no choice but to pop it.

Eighteen

BONUS SCENE

KENDALL

"THIS BOAT'S ALL OURS?" I ASK, STEPPING ONTO THE BOAT FROM THE DOCK WITH DECLAN'S HELP. IT'S A beautiful, sunny day, so he suggested we take the boat out on the lake.

"Yep, it's ours for the week." Declan gets on and undoes the ropes, then turns the boat on, slowly driving it away from the dock. I had no idea he knew how to drive a boat, but it really shouldn't surprise me. He's a man of many talents.

When I glance around and don't see anyone in the vicinity, I remove my cover-up, leaving me in only my bathing suit that Declan's yet to see. From the front, it's a simple blue, two-piece bikini with bright pink flowers, but when I walk past him, and he gets a good look at me from behind, my entire ass on display, he grabs me and pulls me in front of him.

"New suit?" he murmurs, nibbling the shell of my ear.

"New to you." I push my ass against his front and wiggle it playfully. "I haven't worn it on the trip yet. You like?" Part of me is expecting him to tell me to get dressed. Most guys I've dated can't stand when a woman is comfortable with her body and has no problem dressing as such. So far, Declan hasn't said a word, but I also haven't worn anything this risqué.

"How am I supposed to concentrate on driving this boat when you're walking around like a wet dream?"

I turn around and wrap my arms around his neck. "I'm your wet dream." I give him a quick kiss on his lips.

"Damn right you are," he growls against my mouth, his hand squeezing my ass cheek. "Why don't you go lay out and relax while I get us to where we're going? And then I'll join you once I anchor."

With one more heart-racing kiss, I do as he says, setting up at the front of the boat. After getting comfortable and putting on some music, I lie out and close my eyes, relishing in the peaceful moment.

When I open my eyes, I'm not sure how long I've been asleep, but Declan is kneeling behind me, his muscular thighs trapping my legs as he massages my shoulders. "You have to put sunscreen on," he says, rubbing the lotion into my skin. "Don't want your perfect skin to burn."

He places a kiss on the back of my shoulder and edges downward, continuing to massage my body with the expertise of a masseuse. When he gets to my ass, he plants a kiss on each cheek before he spreads my legs slightly, focusing on each thigh and calf. Once he has me so worked up, I feel like I'm going to explode, he lies down next to me.

"Are we alone out here?" I ask, glancing around. The lake is huge, and I can see land in the distance, but aside from us, I don't see any other boats.

"It seems so," he says, lifting his shirt over his head and exposing his hard chest and abs. When he crosses his arms behind his head, his muscles flexing, I've had enough looking and need to touch.

"Are we alone enough that if I fuck you right here, right now, no one will ever know?" I glide my fingers down the hard ridges of his six-pack, stopping at the V that disappears beneath his board shorts.

"There's only one way to find out," he says with a playful smirk.

Crawling between his legs, I pull his shorts down, and his hard length pops out. I give it my attention, licking the head and then sucking it into my throat as Declan moans and curses under his breath.

When I've teased him enough, I pull my thong bikini to the side and climb on top of him, sinking onto his hard cock.

"Fuck," he groans, gripping the curves of my hips. "Your pussy was made for me." He pushes the triangles of my top to the sides and plucks my nipples while I start to ride him. Up and down, I swivel my hips, finding the perfect rhythm. Declan pulls my nipples, forcing me to shift forward slightly, and captures my mouth with his own.

As we both find our climax, our mouths and bodies connected in the most intimate way, I vow to never let Declan go. He's quickly become my entire world, and I can't imagine not being with him. Before him, it was as if I were going through life only seeing in black and white, only hearing in monotones. But with him in my life, it's like every color is brighter, every sound is sharp and beautiful.

Nineteen

KENDALL

her lips. "Where are you? How are you doing? Are you still with Dec?"

My heart swells at her concern. It's been over a month since I've seen my family in person, and just as long since I've spoken to my siblings, and I'm missing them like crazy. After Declan and I spent time in Big Bear Mountain, we went to my place in Calabasas, where we lost track of time, getting lost in each other. We only came up for air when my dad texted Declan, letting him know Gage is due to return next week and that he's scheduled time for us to record "Drunk on Your Love" in the studio the following week, then the video after that. He also let us know that our publicists have set up promo for the single since it's going to be marketed as a preview for my upcoming album.

"I'm at home. I'm good. And yes, he's here with me." I can't help the smile that stretches so wide, my cheeks hurt, and of course, my mom immediately notices.

"Are you two…?"

I nod, biting my lip to try to contain a bit of my happiness. It's hard, though, when these past several weeks have been without a doubt the best of my life. I not only found myself on this trip but I also found love. Real butterfly-inducing, heart-thumping love. And it feels so good. I haven't told Declan that I love him yet. I'm scared. But once we're home, I plan to. I just want to make sure we can make it in the real world first. He has all the faith in the world, and I'm definitely on board, but I can't help the niggling feeling that I'm going to do something to mess it all up.

"You look so happy," Mom says. "When will you be home?"

"Late tonight. Declan is going with the guys tomorrow to pick up Gage, so I thought we could have a lunch date and see if Phoebe and Bailey want to join. We could invite Layla and Kaylee too."

"That sounds perfect. I'll call them. Have a safe flight, and I'll see you tomorrow."

"Love you."

"Love you more."

I close my laptop and stow it away in my luggage that contains everything I've purchased during our road trip, including a few gifts for my family.

"You ready to jet?" Declan asks, walking into the living room. He's dressed in a plain black T-shirt, a pair of ripped jeans, and is sporting a pair of black Vans. His hair is up in his signature bun, and the only thing I want to do is devour him.

"Not happening," he says with a smirk, knowing me too damn well. "Once we're home, you can have your way with me, but we'll never make it on that plane if you touch me now."

I shrug, not caring, and he frowns, mistaking it for me being scared about going home. "I told my mom we're together." His brows kiss his forehead. "And tomorrow, while you're picking up Gage with the guys, I'm meeting her and my sisters for lunch. Layla and Kaylee too, if they're available. I'm going to tell them that we're together."

Declan walks over and rests his hands on my hips. "You have no idea how much that means to me," he says, kissing my lips.

"I'm not ready for the world to know," I admit, "but I don't want to hide us from our family and friends. Just promise me that if things don't work out, we'll go back to being friends." I frame his face with my hands. "I care about you so much, and I can't lose you. And I don't want you to lose my family. I know how important they are to you."

"You're never going to lose me," he vows.

"Promise?"

"I promise."

He seals it with a kiss, and then we take off to the airport. Since the private jet we're on is my parents', complete with a bedroom, the flight is spent with him inside me—because apparently, we can't even go long enough to make it home before we attack each other.

When we arrive in New York, Declan insists I go back to his place with him, and I don't argue. We could probably use a bit of time away from each other since we've been together for so long, but I have no desire to part ways.

His place is spotless, and he tells me that he had Camden let a cleaning crew in to clean it while we were gone. He also did a search for drugs and liquor, so it'll all be gone when Gage gets home. Exhausted from the flight and sex, we fall into bed, tangled up in each other, and pass out immediately, not waking up until Declan's alarm goes off the following morning. We shower together, but nothing happens. I can sense Declan's nervousness about seeing Gage for the first time since everything went down, so I simply hold him and tell him I'm here for him.

Once we're ready to go, we call for a car since he's meeting the guys at my parents' place so they can drive together to pick up Gage.

"You ready for this?" he asks, standing outside my parents' door. He's referring to us walking in together with our hands entwined.

"I'm scared," I admit, knowing it's okay to be honest with him. "I've hurt so many guys in the past. I'm terrified it's in my DNA, and not even loving an amazing man like you will prevent me from messing up. The last person I want to hurt is you. You're perfect in every way and deserve everything."

Declan grins. "You love me?"

"What?"

"You said not even loving an amazing man like me will prevent you from messing up."

"That's what you took from all that?"

"That's the only important part," he says, his grin growing wider. "Is it true? Do you love me?" He pulls me into his arms, and I sigh.

"Yes, it's true. I've fallen in love with you, and that scares the hell out of me because, as you know, I've never truly loved anyone before, and I'm terrified of what will happen when we hit the concrete."

"Say it again."

I playfully roll my eyes. "I love you."

"Again."

"Dec!"

"Say it," he insists.

"Declan Pierce, I love you."

"I love you too, baby." He connects his mouth with mine for a heart-stopping kiss that makes me wish we were back at his place instead of on the stoop of my parents' house.

"Nobody's perfect," he says once the kiss ends. "And while having *everything* sounds amazing, the only thing I want is you because to me, you loving me *is* everything. So stop worrying about the what-ifs and focus on us. Because I'll never..." He kisses the corner of my mouth. "Ever..." The other corner. "Let you fall without knowing I'm there to catch you."

He kisses me again, this time softly, then pulls back, his brow furrowed. "Speaking of not being perfect...There's something I need to tell you." He tightens his grip on my hips. "Before your accide—"

His words are cut off by the door swinging open and my little sister exclaiming, "I knew it!"

I try to scramble out of his hold, but he holds me close, turning to face Bailey while wrapping his arm around my middle.

"Admit it," she says, raising a brow.

"Admit what?" Camden asks, coming up behind her.

"Can we take this inside?" I mutter, worried someone will be spying and catch us on camera.

Bailey moves to the side. "I'll let our sister tell you."

"Tell me what?" Camden asks, his eyes going to Declan's hand, which dropped from my waist so we could walk inside and is now holding mine. "Oh, shit. Is this where you've been? With my sister?"

Declan glances at me, leaving me to answer. "Yes," I admit to my entire family—including Layla and Kaylee—who're all now standing in the foyer, staring at us. "Declan and I are...dating."

I wince, ready for my brother or my dad to lose it, so I'm shocked when everyone starts hugging and congratulating us.

"Welcome back," my dad says into my ear when he wraps me in his arms. "Happiness looks damn good on you."

"Thank you," I choke out.

"Dad's right," Camden says, hugging me next. "You look good, sis."

"You don't mind me dating your best friend and bandmate?"

"Maybe if he were anyone else," Camden says. "But I've known how much Declan cares about you for years, so I have no doubt he'll treat you right."

"You knew he liked me?"

"Everyone knew," Bailey says with a snort. "Everyone but you."

"Yep," Layla agrees. "While you were talking crap about me not knowing how Camden felt about me, you were completely blind to the crush Declan's had on you for years."

Everyone laughs.

"I didn't know."

"It's all good, baby," Declan says, kissing my temple. "It wasn't our time yet."

I snuggle into his side. "We're not telling anyone yet," I say to everyone. "I just want to keep this private for a little bit. It's only been a short time since I called off the engagement..." And a small—okay, maybe big—part of me is still scared, but some of my fear was tamped down by Declan's words outside.

My family and friends all nod in understanding.

"We better get going," Camden says. "Checkout time is noon."

The guys say bye to everyone, then take off, leaving the women and kids here. Instead of going out to brunch, Mom had food brought in so we could catch up in private. While we eat, I tell them about our trip. And once we're done, I spend some time with my niece and nephew, giving them the gifts I picked up.

Layla is about to take the kids home for a nap when Declan, Dad, Camden, and Braxton walk back through the door.

"What are you doing here?" Mom asks. After they picked up Gage, they planned to bring him back to his place and spend the afternoon making sure he had everything he needed.

"Where's Gage?" Kaylee asks. She and Gage are close, have been for years, and she hated not being able to go with them to pick him up.

Declan, Braxton, and Camden don't stop to answer, the three of them stomping down the stairs to where the studio is.

"What's going on?" Layla asks.

"Gage wasn't there when we arrived," Dad says. "He had already checked out."

"What?" Mom gasps. "So where is he?"

Dad shrugs. "We don't know. We were just told he checked out early."

"Oh, God." Mom tears up. "What do we do? How do we know he's okay? He has nobody. He needs us."

Dad pulls her into his arms to comfort her. Mom considers all of the guys to be her kids, especially since once they started coming around in middle school, they never stopped, practically living here. And when Gage aged out of the system, and the family he was living with made it clear they no longer wanted him, he moved in here, at my mom's demand. When Gage would have no one to attend his parent-teacher conferences, Mom would do it. And when shit went down at the end of their senior year, she and Dad helped him handle everything.

"There's nothing we can do," Dad tells her. "He's a grown man. We have to hope that wherever he's going, he's safe and will eventually contact us."

"IF YOU'RE NOT UP FOR THIS, WE CAN RESCHEDULE," I TELL DECLAN AS WE WALK INTO THE STUDIO. IT'S been a week since they went to pick up Gage, only to find out he wasn't there. The guys needed some time alone but eventually came up to tell us that Gage sent a group text, letting them know he's okay but needs some time. He insisted they move forward with the band without him, not wanting to hold them back, but the guys agreed that there's no band without him and told him they'll be here when he's ready to come home.

Ever since then, Declan's been on the quiet side. Still attentive and loving, but I can feel his hurt and worry. I wish I could make it better for him, but the only thing that will help is Gage coming home.

"I'm good," he says, bending and kissing my temple. "This song deserves to be recorded for the world to hear."

"There they are," Johnny, the producer handling our song, says, giving Declan a fist bump. We recorded it a while back—though, I don't remember—to show it to my dad, but he made a couple of changes to the instrumentals, and we'll be finalizing it today. I also gave him all the songs I wrote while we were on our road trip, and he said there's enough for an entire album there. He's having one of his staff writers edit and tweak them, and then next week, I'll begin recording my album. I was set on the title *Falling*, but the more I think about it, I think a more apt title might be *Fallen* because let's be real— I'm not falling for Declan...I've completely and utterly fallen.

"You guys ready?"

"Always," Declan says, heading straight into the sound room. Since we're in public, albeit my parents' studio, we're not holding hands or touching, and even though it's only been a few minutes and my choice, I already miss him.

I put the headphones on to start my part, and once Johnny gives me the go-ahead, I sing my heart out.

I've never been in love before
Never knew what my heart was capable of
Until you walked in and turned my life upside down
Now my heart's racing, my body's vibrating
I should run the other way, protect you from me
From what I'm capable of
But you make me weak, make me someone I'm not

Because…
You've got me drunk on you
Drunk on wanting you
Drunk on needing you
You've got me drunk on your love
And I'll never be the same

The moment you walked in, everything changed
My heart is filled with chaos, my head fuzzy
I want to be the one who makes you happy
Who gives you the world
I've spent too long pretending
Wishing, hoping, praying these feelings would go away
This might be the biggest mistake I've ever made
But it will also be the best

Because…
You've got me drunk on you
Drunk on wanting you
Drunk on needing you
You've got me drunk on your love
And I'll never be the same

I've been watching you all night
Memorizing your every move
Know exactly what you need
To cure that chaos in your heart
Hand it over, and I'll fix the broken
Turn the chaos into calm
Make that heart of yours mine
And you'll never feel alone
All you gotta do is say yes
And I'll handle the rest

Haven't touched a single drink all night
But I'm drunk as fuck
On your scent, on your touch
Hand it over, baby
And you'll never know what it's like to be without love

I'm handing my heart over to you
Keep it safe
Promise you'll never stray
I've fallen for you, I must admit
I'm flying high, not worried about the hit
That I'm going to take the day you walk away
Hoping and praying when I go down, you'll be there to catch me
I know it's a risk, but it's one I'm willing to take

Because…
You've got me drunk on you
Drunk on wanting you
Drunk on needing you
You've got me drunk on your love
And I'll never be the same

Declan and I spend the next couple of hours working with Johnny, perfecting the song, and with every word we sing, I wonder if deep down I maybe always knew how I felt about Declan.

My thoughts go to the day I woke up in the hospital. When I opened my eyes, Declan was the first person I saw, and all I could think about was how delicious and kissable he looked. I pushed the thoughts aside and told myself we were just friends, but the fact that I wrote my first true love song with him tells me that maybe it was more, and I just wasn't ready to admit it yet.

"What's going through that beautiful head of yours?" Declan asks, snapping me out of my thoughts. I look around and realize we're alone.

"Johnny said it's perfect," he says, giving me a chaste kiss. "He's going to finalize it after he grabs dinner and then send it to your dad and us to approve. Now tell me what's got you lost in your head."

"I was just thinking about when we wrote this song." I encircle my arms around his neck. "I think I knew you were the one for me back then, but I didn't want to admit it. I'm sorry it took me this long and almost marrying the wrong guy to realize my feelings for you."

Declan smiles. "It's all good. We're here, together, and that's all that matters. Now, what do you say we go home and celebrate 'Drunk on Your Love'?"

"And how do you want to celebrate?" I ask, knowing damn well how he wants to celebrate.

"By getting drunk on you, of course."

Twenty

DECLAN

"HOLY SHIT, IT'S COLD!" KENDALL LAUGHS THROUGH HER CHATTERING TEETH AS I PULL HER INTO MY ARMS, determined to warm her. We're on the set for the "Drunk on Your Love" video. It's been a crazy day, but we're in the final scene. The video starts off at the club, where I'm eyeing Kendall as she dances provocatively with a few of her friends, all for the purpose of seducing me. It goes to me asking her to dance and us spending the evening with her in my arms. When the night ends, she says goodbye, but I don't let her go. Instead, I follow her out into the night.

She tries to argue that the night is over, but I refuse to let her go, telling her that she's the one for me. While we're going back and forth, the skies open, and it starts raining. The water was supposed to be warm, but the water heater on the set is broken, so we had two options: wait for them to get it fixed, which won't be tonight, or finish the video tonight with cold as fuck water raining down on us.

"Don't focus on that," I tell her, rubbing her arms up and down in an attempt to warm her flesh. "Just focus on me." She nods once, melting into my arms. I lean in and whisper, "When we're done, I'm going to warm you up...in the hot shower at my place, then again in bed."

Kendall shivers as a groan escapes past her lips. "You're such a tease."

Layla, our videographer leading this music video, yells at us to get dry so we can do it again, forcing us to separate.

The hair and makeup artists get us sorted, drying our hair and clothes, and then we head back out to try this again.

"Try not to laugh this time." I mock glare at Kendall. "If I have to dry off again, I'm going to be coming after you." I point my finger in her direction, emphasizing my threat.

She playfully rolls her eyes. "Is that a threat or a promise?"

I'm shocked she just said that in front of everyone since we're keeping our relationship on the down low, but she doesn't seem to notice or care, so I don't say anything.

The music starts, so we can make sure it matches once they put all the pieces together, and Kendall runs out of the club and is about to get into the cab, when—at my cue—I run out after her and pull her to the side before she can get in. The driver screams for her to get in or he's leaving, and then he speeds off without her, leaving only me and her.

My hand goes to the side of her face, and she leans into my touch instinctually. Since the music is playing, our parts are played through our actions, letting the music speak for itself. I tug her closer to me, my other hand palming her ass, and our eyes lock, everything and everyone fading away. It's just Kendall and me...and the ice-cold rain. But not even the iciness of the water falling around us breaks our spell. Maybe it's because she's expecting it this time, but she remains in character, focusing on me like I told her to.

I push her drenched hair out of her face, and her tongue darts out, licking across the seam of her lips. And then my mouth is devouring hers. She tastes like love and lust rolled together to create the most perfectly sweet addiction. My hand glides from the side of her face to her nape, deepening the kiss. She moans into my mouth, then nips at my lips before sliding her tongue along my top lip, then the bottom.

Needing to be closer to her, to feel more of her, I reach down and palm the backs of her thighs, lifting her into my arms. I'm about to walk us to the bed when it hits me...Fuck! We're not at my place. We're on set, with over a dozen people watching us make out. Yeah, we were supposed to kiss, but it wasn't supposed to be like this.

I break the kiss, and Kendall's eyes go wide, realizing the same thing I just did. I expect her to freak out and demand I put her down—the fake rain has stopped, the music has been silenced, and nobody is saying a word—so I'm shocked as hell when the biggest smile spreads across her face, and she says, "Oops," followed by the most adorable snort-laugh.

When a couple of people snicker, she drops her head into the crook of my neck to hide her embarrassment and laughter. A second later, she lifts her head and meets my eyes, and fuck if I don't want to finish what we just started.

"We done?" I ask Layla, who laughs.

"Yep, that's a wrap."

Without giving a fuck who's watching—and knowing they'll have signed NDAs and have no electronics on them since it's not allowed—without a backward glance, I carry Kendall off the set and to my dressing room, which has been vacated. Closing the door behind us, I lock it and walk us over to the couch, dropping her onto it.

"Oh God, I want you," she groans as I lift my shirt over my head and then drop back down on top of her, crashing my mouth against hers. We kiss, hard and rough, only stopping to remove her soaked shirt and bra, and then again to get our shoes and pants off.

Once we're both naked, she pushes me back and climbs onto my lap, lowering herself onto me. I let her ride me, enjoying her tits as they bounce along with her sexy ass. Her hips swivel from side to side, her pussy gripping me like a vise. I take one of her tits in my hand and bring her nipple to my mouth, wrapping my lips around the tightened bud and sucking on it.

"Oh fuck, Dec..." Her eyes roll to the back of her head. "Suck harder."

I love how responsive she is, the way she lets any and all of her inhibitions go when we're together. To the world, she's one person—a prim and proper pop star who's constructed a wall to keep her feelings in and everyone else out—but with me, she lets that wall down, exposing her real self and allowing every emotion to be front and center. She doesn't even realize she's doing it, but I see it...I see *her.*

I do as she asked and take her nipple farther into my mouth, sucking on it until her back arches, and a loud moan escapes her parted lips. As if there's a direct line from her breast to her pussy, she squeezes the fuck out of my dick, and I take over, needing to make her come before I do.

With one hand curled around her hip and the other stroking her clit, I move her up and down, massaging the inside of her walls with my cock until she's screaming my name in ecstasy as she comes hard, taking me along with her.

"Jesus," she mutters once she's come down. Her head drops to the crook of my neck, and she places a soft open-mouthed kiss on my flesh. "I can't get enough of you."

I smile inside as I lift her face and kiss her lips. "That's my hope," I tell her honestly. "That you'll always want more."

"PASS ME THE SALT."

Kendall reaches behind her and grabs the salt, handing it to me. Before I can take it, though, she pulls her hand back and leans forward. "Kiss first."

She makes the most adorable kissy face that has me chuckling as I step between her thighs and plant my hands on the countertop on either side of her. My mouth connects with hers, and my tongue delves in, capturing hers and sucking on it.

"Dec, you're going to burn the food," she says, pushing me away with a laugh. "And it smells too good to waste."

"Hey, you're the one who asked for a kiss," I point out, taking the salt from her and stepping back in front of the stove.

It's been almost two weeks since we've been home, and every night has been spent with Kendall at my place. When she's not at the studio recording her next album—where I join her most of the time—we're here eating, fucking, or watching *The Vampire Diaries*. We've created a nice little bubble—yeah, we love those damn bubbles—but it's about to be popped because tomorrow is Mother's Day, and my father has requested my presence at dinner. It's not that I don't want to see my mom, but every time we're together, it ends with them teaming up against me in some ridiculous and pointless effort to get me to quit my job. And with the rumors running rampant about Gage missing and the band and label staying silent, they probably think their chance of convincing me has increased.

Which is why I almost told her no when Kendall offered to go and play the buffer...but then she looked at me with bright and hopeful eyes, and I didn't have it in me to say anything but yes. She had mentioned once that Kyle rarely brought her around his parents because they would snub her career choice, and I didn't want to chance her thinking I was doing the same thing. So I called my parents and told them my girlfriend would be coming and warned them that she's a singer and if they so much as make a rude comment, we'll be walking out the door.

They were both so shocked I was actually dating someone serious enough to bring home that they agreed without argument.

"Eww, what's that smell?" Kendall asks, knocking me from my thoughts. I glance over and see she's referring to the garlic I minced earlier and just added to the pan.

"Garlic."

"I don't like that." She shakes her head and gags, jumping off the counter and walking over to the cabinet to grab us a couple of plates.

"It won't be as strong once it's all mixed in." I've been cooking while Kendall bakes because we're hiding out from the media until Kendall is ready to go public. We've spent weeks eating out while on our road trip, and we both actually enjoy eating at home. I've been cooking for the guys and me for years when our meals aren't cooked for us, and Kendall has always enjoyed baking.

"What time do you want to leave tomorrow?" she asks, pouring us each a glass of wine. "Brunch at my parents' place is at eleven, but I like to get there early to hang out."

"Whatever time you want." I take the food off the stove and plate us both a good-sized portion. One thing I've learned about Kendall is that she loves to eat. In return, she busts her ass in the gym with her personal trainer, but she'd rather do that than miss out on all the tasty food.

I bring the plates over to the table and sit next to her, setting her plate down in front of her. I cut mine up and am just digging in when Kendall makes a gagging sound, then runs to the sink, throwing up whatever she had in her stomach.

"You okay?" I ask, grabbing a couple of paper towels so she can wipe her mouth.

"Yeah, I think it's the garlic. It's making me feel sick."

"Maybe you're coming down with something." I lift my hand to her forehead, and she feels a little clammy, but it could be from throwing up.

"Ugh, maybe." She groans. "Would you be super offended if I just ate a bowl of cereal?"

"Of course not. Go rinse off and take some vitamin C, and I'll bring it to you in bed in case you're coming down with something."

She smiles softly at me. "Thank you."

After putting the food away in the fridge for another night, I grab her a bottle of water, a vitamin C capsule, and make her a bowl of cereal—her go-to when she's not up for eating something heavy. I bring it to my room, setting it all on the nightstand for when she gets out.

While I'm waiting for her, my phone rings, and the name on the caller ID makes me hit answer immediately.

"Gage?" I breathe, walking out of the room.

"Hey, Dec." Those two simple words have me tearing up. The last time I heard his voice was months ago.

"Fuck, Gage. You okay?" I choke out, squeezing my eyes shut and praying the image of him lying in his room doesn't appear.

"I'm okay," he says back. "But..." he breathes out, and I hear the words he can't say. He's not ready to come home.

"It's okay. We're here whenever you're ready." I try to keep the emotion out of my words, but it's hard when all I want to do is beg him to come home.

"I just wanted to say thank you for saving my life."

Fuck, this guy. "Gage...You don't—"

"Yeah, I do," he says, cutting me off. "I need you to know how thankful I am for you. I'll never forget what you did. I...I gotta go," he chokes out. The line goes dead before I can argue and beg him not to end the call.

"Hey, what's wrong?" Kendall asks, framing my face with her delicate hands. She's freshly showered and smells like her signature scent. "Why are you crying?" She swipes a tear I didn't know had fallen, and I pull her into me, nuzzling my face into her damp hair. "Dec, you're scaring me."

"Gage called to thank me for saving his life."

She stiffens at my words. "Is he coming home?"

"He didn't say." I replay the quick conversation in my head, and it hits me. "He didn't say," I repeat. "He was calling to thank me, and it almost sounded like..." Fuck, no. It couldn't be. Gage wouldn't do this.

"Sounded like what?"

"Like goodbye."

Her eyes widen, on the same page, and I quickly call Gage back, only to be sent to voicemail.

Me: Your call sounded like goodbye...Tell me I'm wrong.

Gage: If you're worried about me doing something like I did before, don't be. That will never happen again.

His reply has me sagging in relief. He didn't say it wasn't a goodbye, but at least he's okay, and right now, that's all that matters.

Me: I'm here always.

Gage: Thank you.

"He'll come home," Kendall says. "He just needs time."
"I hope you're right." I kiss the corner of her mouth. "How are you feeling?"
"Better."
"Good, your cereal is in the room. Let's get you fed and full of vitamin C, and we'll spend the night watching some Damon and Elena."
Kendall rolls her eyes. "I can't believe you're Team Damon."
"What's that supposed to mean?"
"Nothing." She shrugs. "It's just...you're a good guy, so I figured you'd want the good guy to get the girl."
"It's not about good and bad," I tell her. "Damon is the right guy for her. Doesn't matter who he is or what he's done...When it's right, it's right."

Twenty-One

KENDALL

"JESUS H. CHRIST." I GROAN AS I SUCK IN MY GUT, QUICKLY BUTTONING MY PANTS BEFORE RELEASING MY breath. I've tried on several outfits, but none of them fit. And unless I want to go to my parents' place, and later, meet Declan's parents, in sweats, I need something to fit. I have a few dresses I could wear, but none of them are meant to be worn to Sunday brunch. The problem with living bi-coastal is that no matter which house you're at, the item you need always ends up being at the other one.

After I'm almost positive the button isn't going to pop off, I put on my heels, double-check my makeup and hair, and head out to meet Declan, who's been ready for the past hour—damn men have it so much easier than women.

"Ready?" he asks, standing and placing his phone into his pocket. Dressed in a white button-down shirt with the sleeves rolled to his elbows, a pair of gray linen pants that fit him perfectly, and a pair of white sneakers, he makes dressy-casual look so damn good.

"Women should really take a page out of a man's playbook." I shake my head. "Getting up, taking a shower, throwing on the closest items of clothing they can find, and dropping onto the couch, ready to go. This whole doing my hair and makeup and finding the right outfit takes up too much of my damn time. And after all that, I still don't come close to looking as sexy as you do."

With a lazy grin, he pulls me against him. "I love when you dress up in your tight little outfits and do your hair and makeup, but I can assure you, you're just as sexy when you wake up, with your hair a mess and your face free of all makeup."

On the outside, I roll my eyes, but deep down, I love every word he says. Especially since right now, I'm not feeling sexy at all.

"Thank you," I tell him, refusing to let my insecurities get to me.

The drive to my parents' place doesn't take too long, and when we arrive, since we're the last to do so, everyone is already in the family room chatting away.

"Auntie K!" my nephew Felix yells, running over to give me a hug. "I got the best dance! You gonna do it with me on TikTok?" Felix is almost six years old with the personality of a teenager and is one of the best dancers I've ever seen. He's appeared in several music videos and has millions of followers on TikTok—that his mom monitors and doesn't let him on, aside from doing the trending dances.

"Of course!" When I reach down to give him a hug, the button on my pants pops off, and the material attached to the zipper splits right open.

The button hits the hardwood floor with a clanking sound, and Felix grabs it. "Oh man, your pants just ripped!" he says, pointing out the obvious, loud enough for everyone to hear. "I bet my mom can fix it." He hands me back the button. "When I ripped my Justin Bieber Halloween costume, she fixed it."

"Thanks," I mutter. "Apparently, a couple of months of eating whatever I wanted and not going to the gym has caught up to me." I glance at my mom. "Can I borrow something?"

"Of course." She smiles sweetly. "Let's go to my room." She wraps her arm around me and kisses my temple.

"Happy Mother's Day," I tell her, leaning into her. "Dad spoil you?"

"Of course," she says with hearts in her eyes. I love that even after all these years, my parents are just as, if not more, in love than they were in the beginning. They are total relationship goals.

"You want another pair of pants?" she asks, turning on the light in her massive walk-in closet as we enter.

"Better go with a dress. We're the same size, and none of my pants are fitting." I groan. "Something Mother's Day appropriate since we're going to Declan's parents' place afterward."

"How about this?" She shows me a beautiful light pink flowy dress with wide sleeves. The neckline is a bit low, but it's the perfect mix of sexy and classy, and because it's loose, nothing should rip or pop open.

"Perfect. Thanks." I undress quickly and then grab the dress from my mom, unzipping the back and sliding it on over my head. "Zip me up?" I ask, giving her my back.

She attempts to do so, but when she gets to the top, it's too tight, and I wince at the way it adds pressure to my breasts.

"Dammit. I really should've been finding a gym while we were away."

"Let's try another dress," Mom offers as I take this one off.

After three dresses, we finally find one that fits me. I've just finished getting dressed when Bailey comes strolling in. "Hey, sis!"

She pulls me into a tight hug, and I gasp at my breasts' sensitivity. "Ow."

"What's wrong?"

"That hurt."

"Your breasts?" Mom asks.

"Yeah, I guess...a couple of months of eating whatever I want and not going to the gym, and I feel like I'm falling apart. Nothing fits, and my body is beyond sore. And I think I might be coming down with something because I threw up last night. We almost canceled today, but I woke up feeling a little better."

"Hey, Ken," Bailey says slowly. "When's the last time you had your period?"

"What?" I give her a confused look. "What does that have to do with anything?"

"Just humor me," she says with a tight smile.

I think for a second, but I can't recall. I never had one while we were away...and before that...Shit! "Not since the hospital."

"You had one while you were in the hospital?" Mom clarifies.

"No, I mean, not since before then. I can't remember." I think some more, and then it hits me. "In December. I had it the weekend of the Christmas parade."

"Sunshine," Mom says softly. "That was five months ago. Could you be pregnant?"

"No," I scoff. "I get the shot. You know this." I've been on it for years.

"When's the last time you got it?" Bailey asks. "It's every three months, right?"

I try to remember, but I can't because it would've been during the time I have no memory. But I had to have gotten it, right? I grab my phone and scroll through my calendar, finding where I input my last appointment: November 19th. Three months later would be..."Fuck! I should've gotten it in February."

"Do you know for sure you didn't?" Mom asks, taking my hand in hers and guiding us over to the loveseat. Bailey sits in the reading chair next to us.

"I would've put it in the calendar. I put *everything* in there." Oh my God. This can't be happening. It has to be some kind of a coincidence. The weight gain, sore breasts, feeling sick...It could be something else. Anything else. Right?

I dart my eyes back and forth between my sister and mom. "Between the accident and the non-wedding and then taking off, I didn't even think about it." Tears prick my eyes. "There has to be another explanation."

"There's only one way to find out," Mom says. "You need to take a test."

"Oh, jeez," I groan. "This is so crazy. Wouldn't I know if I were pregnant?"

"Everybody's body is different," Bailey says. "Cynthia didn't—" She slaps her hand over her mouth, her eyes going wide.

"Cynthia what?" Mom gasps. "Is Cynthia pregnant?" She and Bailey talked about using a surrogate. Bailey has no desire to carry a baby, but Cynthia wants to, so they were considering going to the sperm bank, but they haven't said anything.

"She is." Bailey's entire face lights up. "On the first try." Tears fill her eyes. "She's only eleven weeks, so we were waiting another week before we told anyone."

"Oh my God!" I leap into her arms. "I'm so happy for you guys."

"I'm going to be a grandma again?" Mom sobs, hugging Bailey next. "Congratulations, sweetie."

"What's going on?" Cynthia asks. "Why are you guys crying?" She walks into the room and closes the door.

"I slipped," Bailey admits sheepishly, making Cynthia laugh. "They know."

"Congratulations," Mom and I say, each giving Cynthia a hug.

"Sorry," Bailey adds, pulling Cynthia onto her lap. "Kendall was asking if she could be pregnant and—"

"What?" Cynthia gasps, her head swinging my way. "You're pregnant?"

"I don't know. They think I could be, but I feel like I would know if I were."

"Maybe not," Cynthia says. "I haven't had a single day of morning sickness." She reaches over and knocks three times on the wood. "Aside from my clothes not fitting, I haven't had any symptoms."

"You need to take a pregnancy test," Mom says again, giving me a sympathetic smile.

"Oh! I have one." Cynthia pops up. "I had a couple with us when we were traveling to test, and I never removed them. I'll go grab my purse." She scurries out of the room.

While she's gone, I scroll through my calendar. It's been roughly six weeks since the first time Declan and I had sex. It's enough time for me to have gotten pregnant, especially since we've never once used protection because I thought I was protected.

"Here you go." Cynthia hands me the stick. "It's digital, so it will read pregnant or not pregnant."

"Thanks."

I take it from her and head into the bathroom. Once I've peed on the stick, I wash my hands and then remain in the bathroom alone, waiting for the results to pop up on the blank screen. First, the word PREGNANT appears, but like an idiot, I keep watching and waiting for the NO to pop up as well. Only, after several minutes, it doesn't.

"Sunshine," Mom says through the door. "Are you okay?"

When I don't say anything, *can't* say anything with the ball of emotion clogging my throat, the door creaks open, and she comes in.

"You're pregnant," she whispers.

"Maybe the no just hasn't appeared yet," I croak out.

"Oh, sweetheart." She pulls me into a hug. "It's been enough time. If it were going to appear, it already would've. Do you want Declan here?"

"No." I shake my head, pulling back. "I don't want to get his hopes up. I can't be more than six weeks along *if* I'm even pregnant." Jesus, if my clothes are already busting at the seams at only six weeks pregnant, how big will I be at nine months?

"Does that mean he'll be happy?" Bailey asks.

"We haven't talked about me getting pregnant, but he said he wants a family." Although, that was just hypothetical. He never actually said he wanted to start a family *now*.

Oh, shit. He's still so young. What if he's not planning to start a family for several years?

"Kendall, you're breathing heavily," Mom points out.

"What...What if he doesn't want to start a family now?" I ask, my chest rising and falling in quick succession. I'm on the verge of having a panic attack, but I can't stop the freak-out that's building. "What if he freaks out like..." I swallow thickly. "Like Freeman freaked out on you. What if he doesn't want this baby the way Freeman never wanted me?"

Mom's eyes widen, and I immediately regret my words. She hates speaking about my sperm donor. "Don't you dare compare Declan to that monster. He might be shocked, but he would never treat you the way *he* treated me. Not every man is like that. Look at your father. When he found out I was pregnant with Cam, he was shocked but still excited, and he barely knew me. That boy has been in love with you for years."

Okay, yeah, that makes sense, but...

"What if I'm a shitty mom?" I blurt out, moving on to my next fear. Declan might not be anything like Freeman, but half my DNA matches that monster.

"Oh my God, Kendall, stop it," Bailey demands. "Take a deep breath." I try to do what she says, but I'm having trouble catching my breath.

"Sunshine, calm down," Mom adds. "Declan is going to be happy, and you're going to be an amazing mom."

She's right. I know she is, but I'm already chin-deep in freak-out mode, so I'm not thinking clearly. I'm drowning in what-ifs, and I can't come up for air. Suddenly, it all becomes too much. The room spins, and everything turns fuzzy.

"Mom," I mutter. "I don't feel so good."

And then everything goes black.

"THERE SHE IS," MOM SAYS WITH A TIGHT SMILE.

"What happened?" I rasp, my throat dry.

"You blacked out."

"What?" I gasp, my hand going straight to my belly. "Is the baby okay?"

Mom's smile widens. "It was only for a few seconds. You were sitting, so you didn't fall. You worked yourself up and passed out."

"You sure you don't want us to get Declan?" Bailey asks.

"No. I don't know for sure that I'm pregnant. I know the stick said I am, but I would rather have it confirmed by a doctor first. Then I'll tell him."

The women all give me various looks that say they don't agree, but I'm sticking to my decision. If this is just a coincidence or something is wrong, I don't want to get him worked up for nothing. Once I know for sure, I'll tell him when we're alone.

"Can I ask you something?" Bailey says after a few minutes.

"Of course."

"Is it possible that the baby could be Kyle's?"

"What?" I shriek. "No! We haven't had sex since...I don't know when. At least since before the accident."

Cynthia quirks a brow, so I explain, "After I woke up, I felt off. I knew in my heart I wasn't in love with Kyle, so even though he tried, I never once went there with him. The only person I've had sex with is Declan."

"Okay, good," Bailey says. "I'm sorry. I just had to ask."

"It's—"

I'm cut off by a knock on the door, followed by Declan's baritone voice. "Kendall, are you okay?"

"We better get out there," I say, walking over to the door. "Please don't say anything."

My mom and sister both pretend to zip their lips while Cynthia nods.

I take a deep breath, then open the door, plastering on a fake smile. "Hey, sorry. Girl talk."

Declan rakes his gaze down my body. "That dress looks beautiful."

"Thanks."

"Breakfast is ready," he says to the four of us.

"Great," Mom says. "I'm starved."

The rest of the morning goes by without a hitch. Breakfast is delicious, and I make several TikToks with Felix. We watch the music video—since it's done and will be released, along with the song, on Friday at midnight—and my dad suggests Declan and I make our relationship public because, according to him, that video is way too hot. No way anyone in their right mind will believe nothing is going on between us.

After we give Mom our gifts, Declan and I say our goodbyes so we can head to his parents' place for an early dinner. Unlike the warm vibe at my home, Declan's parents are ice cold.

We spend the entire meal with them judging us while acting like they aren't. I try not to let it get to me—I'm used to public scrutiny—but it's hard when it's clear they don't approve of what either of us does for a living. I come from a home where the music industry is in all of our blood, and every dig they make feels like it's aimed at not just Declan and me but also my entire family.

Finally, Declan must have enough because he tells his mom we need to leave, using the excuse that I haven't been feeling well. She gets upset, saying we haven't even had dessert yet, but he insists we go, promising to see them soon.

The ride home is filled with silence, and I expect him to push me away, obviously upset over the way the dinner went, so I'm surprised when the moment we step through the door, he attacks me.

"Thank you," he murmurs against my lips as he reaches around and unzips my dress.

"For what?"

"For putting up with my parents' shit. I love them, but sometimes, I hate them so damn much. Thank you for being there today. It's the first time I've ever had someone in my corner, and it made it that much easier. It sounds crazy, but it would've been twice as bad had you not been there."

God, I can't even imagine. Your parents, your family, should be your safe place. You shouldn't dread going there. It's the one place where you can be yourself and feel accepted. Despite all my insecurities and hang-ups, I know without a shadow of a doubt my family loves me and supports me. Knowing Declan doesn't have that at home makes me so sad.

"I'll always be there." I cup the sides of his face and look up into his blue eyes filled with love and awe. "*Always.*"

"Promise?" he says, placing a soft kiss on my lips before backing away slightly.

"I promise. You and me...always."

Twenty-Two

KENDALL

"THANK YOU FOR SEEING ME ON SUCH SHORT NOTICE." I SMILE NERVOUSLY AT DR. WEISEERG, THE OB/GYN Layla recommended I use since my gyno is back in California. She mentioned she's the OB to many celebrities who require NDAs to be signed, so her office would handle it without any hiccups, and she was right. Not even twenty-four hours after calling the office, NDAs have been signed and sent to my assistant. I'm sitting on the medical bed in the small yet inviting room in only a cotton gown, my entire body buzzing with anxiety.

"You're very welcome," Dr. Weisberg says, sitting on the rolling stool in front of me. "You mentioned you were in an accident that—"

Her words are cut off by the sound of the door opening as my mom walks in. "Kendall Naomi Blackwood." My eyes widen at her using my three names, wondering what she's doing here and why I'm in trouble. Even though I'm thirty-two years old, it scares the shit out of me when my mom uses my three names.

"Mom, what are you doing here?"

She closes the door behind her and walks around the side to stand next to me. "Marcia told me you were coming here alone. Why wouldn't you tell me so I could come with you?" she chides in her motherly tone that has tears pricking my eyes.

"I don't know," I mutter. "I guess I'm scared and…" I shrug, unable to verbalize how I'm feeling. Ever since Bailey mentioned Kyle could be the dad, I've been freaking out on the inside. I wanted so badly to tell Declan I might be pregnant and that I'm scared it might not be his, but I couldn't do that to him. He might've become one of the closest people to me—the person I share my thoughts and dreams with—but I couldn't be so selfish to tell him there's a chance the baby I may or may not be carrying is his. So instead of saying a word, after Declan and I made love Sunday night and then again last night, I lay awake, watching him sleep, wondering what our future holds.

"Oh, Sunshine. You don't have to take on the world by yourself," my mom says, knowing me well enough that I don't have to finish my thoughts.

"Whatever happens, you have an entire family who loves and supports you." She pulls me into her arms and kisses my cheek. "I love you, Kendall."

"Love you too, Mom," I choke out, feeling like shit for all the times I've pushed her away. It doesn't matter how many times I push because she always finds her way back in.

Once I've composed myself, the doctor greets my mom, already knowing her since she's Mom's gyno as well, and then I explain everything to her.

"Well, first things first," Dr. Weisberg says. "Based on your blood work, you have high hCG levels, telling us you are pregnant, but we want to do a scan to confirm and get an estimated due date. I'm going to have you lie back and cover you with this blanket. Usually, I would try transvaginal first, but I believe you are far enough along to use a Doppler."

She hands me the blanket to cover myself and lifts my gown to expose my belly. My mom stays next to me, taking my hand in hers, and I've never been so thankful to have a mom who cares enough to know that I would need her today.

Dr. Weisberg explains everything she's doing as she does it, and then the loudest *woosh, woosh, woosh* fills the silent room. From going with my mom to her appointments when she was pregnant with my siblings, I instantly recognize the sound.

"That's my baby's heartbeat."

"It is," the doctor confirms. "A good, strong heartbeat at 141. And…" She moves the Doppler over slightly, the sound fading and then increasing again. "A second heartbeat. Also a strong heartbeat at 135."

"What?" I gasp.

Dr. Weisberg laughs softly. "You're pregnant with twins."

Mom squeezes my hand and leans over to kiss the top of my head. "Congratulations," she murmurs, causing me to choke up in the middle of my state of shock. Holy shit! I'm not only pregnant, but I'm pregnant with twins.

"All right, so based on these measurements," the doctor says as she moves the Doppler around and clicks away on the screen. "You're fifteen weeks along. Due November third."

Her words have my heart stopping in my chest, my lungs depleting of all my air. No. No. No, no, no…This can't be happening. I did the math a million times and checked several pregnancy calculators. In order for Declan to be the dad, I could only be, at the most, six weeks pregnant. Yet I'm…

"Are you sure?" I blurt out. "Could they be measuring big?"

The doctor explains each measurement and the weight of the babies. Baby A is measuring at 6.47 inches and weighs 4.03 ounces, and baby B is 6.57 inches and weighs 4.12 ounces. They're not sharing a placenta, which means they won't be identical, even if they're the same sex. Everything looks good, and I'm in my second trimester of my pregnancy, missing the entire first one altogether. She shows my mom and me the hands and legs and head of each of the babies while my mom rubs my shoulder, and I push everything else aside, giving my precious babies my full attention.

"I can't believe I didn't know I was pregnant, let alone fifteen weeks along with twins," I say to no one in particular. Once she's done and has removed the Doppler from my belly, she hands me some paper towels to wipe the gunk off my stomach.

"It happens," Dr. Weisberg says, "especially if you don't have any morning sickness." She lifts the headrest and helps me sit up.

"I haven't had any," I admit, and then I remember something. "I've drunk wine…" Though, thinking back, I thought it tasted off and only had a sip. "Can that harm the babies?" My hand goes to my stomach, and now that I'm looking at it in a whole new light, it's protruding out and has been for a few weeks. I don't know if I was in denial or really thought I had just eaten too much, but now that my pregnancy is confirmed, my ill-fitting clothes make so much more sense.

"Everything looks good, and a little wine won't harm the babies. I want you to start on a prenatal vitamin as soon as possible, and we'll schedule your twenty-week checkup. It's an ultrasound, and generally, we can see the sex of the babies during that one, so if you have someone you'd like to bring, you can do so."

While she goes over a few more things and does an internal exam, I try to focus, but my emotions are all over the place: shocked, excited, scared, and the one I hate the most, heartbroken—because I know what I have to do, and it hurts so damn badly.

Once I'm dressed, the doctor gives me several pictures of the babies, who are labeled A and B. I make my next appointment, and then we head out. Since I didn't drive here, instead of calling my driver to pick me up, I go with my mom in her vehicle. The ride to her house is silent. We stop at the pharmacy to get the prenatal vitamins that Dr. Weisberg prescribed and then swing by the deli to grab lunch to take back to her house. When we get there, the place is quiet.

"Phoebe is at school," she explains. "And your dad is at work."

I nod, setting the drinks on the counter. Ever since I found out how far along I am, and what that means, I've gone numb. My mom let it go since we were at the doctor's office and then in the car, but now that we're home, I know she won't let it slide for much longer. I swallow down the vitamin, and then we eat in silence. The subs are from our favorite deli, but it tastes like cardboard today. While we eat, Declan texts me a few times, asking how it's going since he thinks I'm in a meeting with the label regarding my upcoming album. It's the first time I've lied to him, and it makes me sick to my stomach.

"Kendall," my mom says once we're both done eating. "Talk to me." She takes my hand and guides us over to the couch. "Tell me what's going through your head. You were given a lot of information today, so it's normal to be a bit overwhelmed, but I'm mostly worried about one piece of information in particular. How far along you are."

"Declan's not the dad." Saying those words, despite my mom already knowing, were probably the hardest, most gut-wrenching words I've ever had to speak, and as the last word leaves my lips, the numbness that was temporarily holding me together disappears, forcing me to feel every heartbreaking emotion.

Tears fill my lids, blurring my vision, as a sob rises up my throat and forces its way out. My mom pulls me into her arms, and I bury my face in her chest, crying for everything I'm about to lose. Deep down, I always knew that the elusive happily ever after my parents and siblings have gotten with their significant others wasn't in the cards for me. It's why I always chose to sing about heartbreak.

But the hardest part is knowing I came so close to having it, only for it to be ripped out of my grasp. And what's even worse is that, while I'm devastated that I'm about to lose the man I love, I feel guilty because I can't regret getting pregnant. My babies, despite being Kyle's and not Declan's, already own my heart. The moment I heard their heartbeats and saw their tiny bodies fluttering across the screen, I fell in love.

And it's at this moment I finally understand why my mom was able to love me despite me having half of that monster's DNA.

"I get it," I choke out. "All these years, I've wondered how you could love me when half of me comes from such a horrible person. When I found out the things he did to those women, I started to push you away because I didn't understand how you could look at me and not see that evil monster..."

"Oh, Kendall," my mom murmurs softly, lifting my face and pushing my hair out of my eyes. "Why didn't you say something? From the moment I found out I was pregnant, you became my entire world."

"I get it now," I say, crying in her arms. "Because despite these babies being Kyle's, I love them so much, and even though it breaks my heart that they're not Declan's, it doesn't make me love them any less."

"Of course it doesn't," she says. "That's called a mother's love. We love our babies unconditionally."

"I have to break up with Declan," I tell her through a sob that has my entire body shaking. "And before you tell me I'm being ridiculous, I'm not. Declan is the best guy I know. He loves with his entire heart, and I know he'll accept these babies if I ask him to, but that's not fair to him. He deserves to find a woman he can love and create a life with. He's so romantic and wants it all—the marriage and kids—and it's not fair to force him into a situation where he has to play stepdad and deal with Kyle."

Fuck, Kyle…"Ugh, I'm going to have to tell Kyle I'm pregnant." I would never keep a man from knowing his children, but what a damn mess this is.

"When I met your father, you weren't his, but you'd never know it," Mom points out.

"Yeah, but you were also pregnant with Dad's baby, and he went into it knowing about me. I'm pregnant with twins by another man. He deserves to have babies of his own, and at my age, I have no idea if I'll have more kids. So I what, string him along and force him to take on two babies who aren't his? No, I won't do it."

Mom's lips purse together. "I don't think you're giving him enough credit, nor do I think you understand how unconditional love works. What if the roles were reversed, and he found out he was expecting a baby who wasn't yours? Would you want him to break up with you?"

"It's not the same thing. I could still get pregnant, and Declan isn't the kind of person to just sleep around with any woman. He takes relationships seriously. He wouldn't sleep with another woman and turn around and be with me a few weeks later." *Pulling stunts like that and messing everything up is more my style.*

"It's for the best," I tell her, sniffling. "He shouldn't be drawn into my shit show of a life. It's not like I deserved a man like him anyway. Fate has a way of reminding us where we belong in this world, and I don't belong with a man like Declan."

"Oh, stop with the self-deprecation," Mom chides. "You're hormonal, and your emotions are all over the place. Please don't make any rash decisions until you've thought this all through."

"There's nothing to think through. I'm not putting Declan in that position. He's a good guy and would no doubt step up, but I'm not going to let him do that."

"And where does Kyle fit in?"

"I won't be with someone just for the sake of the kids. Kyle deserves to be happy and in a marriage for love. I don't feel that way about him. I'll let him know I'm pregnant, and if he wants to be in the babies' lives, we'll figure it out."

Mom sighs. "Maybe you should move home."

"Mom, I love you, but there's no way I'm living with you and Dad again." I lean over and kiss her cheek. "I have the money and means to live on my own. But I would like to find a bigger place, and I'll need to look for help with the babies. I was supposed to go on tour for the new album, but—"

"Breathe. You have plenty of time. Take a deep breath."

"You're right," I tell her as items mentally get added to my list of things I need to do...starting with breaking up with Declan.

As if he knows I'm thinking about him, a text comes through from the man himself: **Dinner tonight at my place. Six o'clock.**

My heart drops out of my chest and into my gut. Tonight...Tonight, I'm going to have to break both his and my heart. **I'll see you then.**

Twenty-Three

DECLAN

TULIPS—KENDALL'S FAVORITE—CHECK.

Korean BBQ—her favorite—check.

Crème brûlée for dessert—also her favorite—check.

I reach into my pocket and open the box for the dozenth time…

Engagement ring—check.

When I had Braxton go with me to pick out the ring, I looked at hundreds, but only one caught my eye. It's an eight-carat oval-cut diamond with a micro-pavé band. It's simple and classic yet elegant, and when I saw it, I knew it was the one—the ring that will sit on Kendall's finger for the rest of our lives.

I light the candles and dim the lights and am about to text Kendall to see if she's on her way since it's a few minutes past six when the alarm indicating she's here sounds.

She walks through the door, dressed casually yet beautifully in a flowy dress. She's been down about gaining some weight recently since she's gone off her usual strict diet and workout routine, but I have to admit, the extra pounds look good on her. She was already the sexiest woman I've ever laid eyes on, but she's even sexier with the bit of thickness added to her. The other night when we were fucking, I flipped her onto her hands and knees and took her from behind, loving the way my fingers gripped her full hips.

I shake the visual from my head, not wanting to be stuck with a hard-on, and walk over to greet her. "How was your day?" I ask, leaning in for a kiss.

She dodges it, and my lips land on her cheek. And that's when I notice her face is splotchy, and her eyes are rimmed red. "You've been crying."

She answers by saying the four words every man dreads. "We need to talk."

"Okay, I have dinner in the kitchen."

"I'm not hungry." She averts my gaze, and when her eyes land on the table, all done up, she flinches. "Shit, I didn't know dinner was a *thing*. I'm sorry."

"It's fine. We don't have to eat." I try to take her hand to walk us over to the couch, but she pulls away. Fuck, this isn't good. I can feel it down to my marrow. Something is wrong.

"I've decided to move home."

Huh? I'm confused. While she's been staying here often, she hasn't actually moved in, so I'm not sure why she's telling me this.

And then she finishes her sentence, making it make sense. "...back to California."

"What?"

"The album is done, and most of the PR will be in LA, so it makes sense for me to move back to my house in Calabasas. This was never supposed to be my permanent home anyway."

"Okay." My head spins. "I was hoping to be here when Gage is ready to come home, but Camden and Braxton are here, and I can always fly—"

"I don't mean us," she says, cutting me off. "I'm moving back to the West Coast...alone."

"What?" I say again like a dumbass. But I'm so confused, I don't know what else to say. "Why would you move, and I stay here?"

The answer hits me at the same time she speaks the words. "Because it's not working out between us."

"What?" Jesus, can't I think of anything else to say?

"I'm sorry," she says, her lids turning a brighter shade of red as if her eyes want to cry but she won't let it happen. "I tried, but I can't do it. I care about you, but I don't want to be with you anymore." She turns her back on me, ready to bolt like the runner she is, but before she can make it out the door, I gently grab her elbow and spin her around. Her eyes are filled with liquid emotion, and I'm baffled as to why she's doing this when she's clearly so upset about it.

"What's going on? Why are you doing this?"

"I told you," she chokes out. "It's not working out. Please don't make this any harder than it needs to be," she pleads. "I'm sorry, but it's over. I have to go."

She runs out the door, and I follow, refusing to let her get away. I don't know what the fuck is going on, but I'm not about to lose her without at least knowing why. Since I've known Kendall, she's been a runner. When shit gets rough, she runs. When she gets hurt, she runs. When she breaks up with a guy, she runs. Hell, she ran from her wedding, climbing out a goddamn window, for God's sake. You don't get into a relationship with Kendall without understanding that she's going to run at some point. The difference is, I'm always going to chase and catch her. Every single time.

"Stop," I demand, covering the button to the elevator before she can press it. "You want to run? Fine. But first, tell me why you're breaking up with me."

She shakes her head. "Let me go. It doesn't matter why. All you need to know is that we're over."

"Did I do something wrong?"

She scoffs through her tears. "You're perfect, Dec. You could never do anything wrong."

I roll my eyes, hating that she sees me without faults and flaws. She puts me up on a pedestal that nobody belongs on, let alone me.

"Okay, so you did something? Talk to me, baby," I say, palming the side of her face. "Whatever it is, we'll get through it together. I love you."

For a split second, she leans in, her eyes fluttering shut, and I think maybe she's going to talk to me. But then her eyes pop open, and I see her resolve and determination. I know it will take more than me begging to get through to her.

"There's nothing to talk about," she says, her back going straight. "I'm leaving, and I would appreciate it if you'd let me go."

"Fuck that!" It's the first time I've ever raised my voice at her, but I'm so damn confused and frustrated. "Tell me what the hell is wrong so I can fix it! Please."

"You can't fix it!" she yells back. "Nothing you say or do will fix this. So please just let me go." She moves my hand from the button and presses it. The damn thing must've been sitting on this floor because it immediately opens, and she gets in. "I'm sorry," she mouths as the doors close, whisking her and my heart away.

I consider chasing her, but whatever's going on with her is something she isn't ready to talk about, so instead, I go inside and blow out the candles, throw the flowers and food away, and then go down to the bar for a stiff drink while I contemplate my next move. Because despite what Kendall thinks, we're not over, and if she thinks I'm going to let her get away that easily, she has another thing coming.

Kendall: Congratulations on the release of Drunk on Your Love.

I STARE AT THE TEXT, TRYING TO FIGURE OUT HOW TO PROCEED. IT'S BEEN FOUR DAYS SINCE KENDALL walked out the door. Four days since I've seen her beautiful face or heard her melodic voice. It's been four goddamn days since I've kissed and touched and sunk deep into the woman who I know without a doubt is my forever. And unfortunately, I'm not any closer to finding out why she's run across the damn country to get away from me.

Despite me texting her several times a day, telling her I love her and this isn't over, this is the first text she's sent me. It's midnight my time, and our song and video have been released. Blackwood's social media team has handled everything, so there's nothing for me to do but watch the music video on loop since it's my only way of seeing Kendall. The way she dances in my arms and the passion behind the kiss we share reminds me that she loves me and wants me. She's just going through something, and instead of coming to me, she's run.

The good thing is, I'm going to be on a plane to LA later this morning since we have a few appearances lined up to promote the song as well as Kendall's upcoming album *Fallen*. Yes, *Fallen* because despite the bullshit she's pulling, she's fallen in love with me. And once I remind her of that, I'll get her to tell me what's wrong, and we'll sort out whatever it is together because nothing could push me away or stop me from loving and being with that woman.

Me: Congrats, baby. See you soon.

Several hours later, I'm on the West Coast, sitting beside Kendall as we're interviewed on the *Late Night Show*. When a video clip finishes playing—the part where we kiss in the rain—the host, Steve Barkin, fans his face dramatically.

"So guys, I have to ask, because holy moly, the chemistry in that video…" His eyes widen for the audience. "Is there something going on between you two?"

I've already been told by the label that I'm not allowed to say there is, and honestly, I wouldn't anyway. When the world finds out about Kendall and me, it will be because she's made it happen. Because she trusts in us enough to know that we're forever, and she's comfortable letting everyone know.

"Have you seen this gorgeous woman?" I point at Kendall. "She's way out of this rock star's league." I shrug, laughing and making the audience laugh as well. Kendall's face falls for a second, but she quickly recovers, laughing it off. She looks like everything is fine to someone who doesn't know her. But because I know everything about her, I can see the faint black circles under the makeup, the tension in her shoulders, and the way she sits stiffly in her spot on the couch. Clearly, something is going on with her, and after we get out of here tonight, I'm going to find out what.

"Right, right, I can see that," Steve adds, moving on to discuss the song and how our collaboration came about. Then he talks with Kendall a bit about her upcoming album. Aside from the evident sadness she works hard to hide, she plays her role perfectly.

Once Steve thanks us for coming, and it cuts to commercial, we thank him for having us and then head out. I follow Kendall, not about to let her slip away, and when we get outside where our security is waiting for us, I pull her to the side so I can talk to her.

"How've you been?"

She avoids my face. "I'm fine. I really need to get going, though."

"Get going where? To your house, to go to bed?"

She sighs. "Yes, to my house. It's late, and I'm tired and hungry."

"Let's go eat, and then you can go home and get some sleep."

"Dec, don't do this." The pain in her voice tears my heart to shreds. I don't know why she's doing this when it's obvious she's hurting as badly as I am.

"Do what? Ask you to get something to eat with me? You said if we broke up, you wanted to remain friends. This is me being your friend."

Her gorgeous blue eyes meet mine. "I appreciate that, but I'm not in the mood to go out."

"Then let me make you something," I offer, stepping into her space. "I get it," I tell her, saying what she needs to hear. "It didn't work out. Does that suck? Yeah, it does. But you were...*are* one of my best friends, so please don't shut me out. I'm trying to be your friend here, so let me."

I tuck a wayward hair behind her ear, and as my fingers skate down the side of her neck, I see her shiver from my touch. She wants to act like we're over, fine, but her body says otherwise.

"Please..."

After a long beat, she relents. "Okay, fine. You can come over and cook me something...as friends."

Since she had Gale, her housekeeper, restock the fridge upon her arrival, there's plenty of food for me to cook. While she showers and changes, I make a simple meal for the two of us I know she loves: breakfast for dinner.

I'm setting the plates of pancakes and bacon on the table as she walks into the kitchen, dressed in a pair of flannel pants and a loose pajama shirt that reads: World of Chaos—a shirt from one of our previous tours that she stole from me a while back. Her hair is in a messy bun on top of her head, and her face is free of makeup. She looks beyond beautiful, and it takes everything in me not to sweep her off her feet and take her to her room where I can get lost in her all night long. Not that she'd let me anyway since she's being all stubborn and shit and insisting we're over.

"This all smells so good," she moans, sitting at the table and grabbing a couple of pancakes. She snatches up a piece of bacon, breaks off a piece, and pops it into her mouth. The way she moans when the bacon enters her mouth has my dick twitching and begging me to reconsider taking her to the room.

Not wanting it to get awkward, I make light conversation about the numbers Easton sent us. The song has only been out for a day, and it is already topping the charts for being the most downloaded and streamed song in a twenty-four-hour period. The official video has over eighty million views.

"It wouldn't be what it is without you," she admits, forking a piece of pancake into her mouth. "Thank you for being a part of it."

I hate how formal she's speaking like we haven't been intimate, and I haven't stuck my dick into every one of her damn holes. But I bite the inside of my cheek and go along with it, hoping she'll say something that indicates why she's made this decision.

When we're both done eating, she insists I leave the dishes, then walks me to the door. "I'm really glad we can still be friends," she says softly, opening the front door. "I guess I'll see you tomorrow night for the interview with Larson?"

"Kendall…"

"Declan, don't…please." She shakes her head. "I don't have it in me to argue with you."

"Baby, I don't want to argue. I want to know how to fix whatever happened so we can go back to being us again." My eyes plead with her, but she doesn't give me a damn inch.

"I already told you it can't be fixed. I need you to leave, please."

"Ken…" I start to beg, suddenly feeling anxious. At first, I had it in my head that she was just freaking out, and as soon as I got her to talk to me, I'd be able to set her straight, but now, as I look at her defeated face, it hits me… It's really over. She isn't running or hiding. She let me in to her home and ate dinner with me. But she doesn't want to be anything more than friends.

For whatever reason, Kendall Blackwood no longer wants to be with me. The realization is damn near crippling, knowing the woman I want to spend my life with doesn't see or want the same future as I do.

"It's really over, isn't it?" I ask, needing her to say the words one last time.

"It is," she says softly. Her eyes flutter closed and then open, and a single tear slides down her cheek. "I'm so sorry, Dec," she says as more follow. "I'm so sorry for hurting you." She shakes her head, and I pull her into my arms, needing to feel her against me. Her signature D&G perfume hits my senses, and it takes everything in me not to break down.

Fuck! I don't know what to do. I'm at a loss. On the one hand, I want to lock her in the room and force her to talk to me, but that's not how this should be. It's not how a relationship should be. If she wanted me to know, she'd talk to me. Right? Deep down, I know she wouldn't. Kendall is sweet and funny and has the biggest heart, but she's also a little broken. There's nothing wrong with that. I stand by what I told her all those years ago: It's okay to be a little broken. But the problem is, whatever is broken inside her is preventing her from functioning, and I can't do it on my own.

"You don't have to apologize," I tell her, squeezing her a little tighter. "It was worth it…To have you in my arms, to be with you for that short time. It was worth the heartbreak."

She nods into my chest, then sniffles. "I agree," she murmurs. "I already miss you."

"Oh, baby. I'm here. I'm always here," I tell her, repeating the words she said to me not long ago. Needing her to understand that no matter what happens between us, I'm not going anywhere. "Always."

Twenty-Four

KENDALL

"HAVE YOU SEEN THE POST FROM *THE GOSSIP GAZETTE*?" LAYLA TURNS THE SCREEN TO FACE ME, AND I cringe at the headline—"From doing bump to a baby bump?"

"Ugh. I hate them so much. They should be sued for slander." I've never done drugs a day in my life, but once, over a year ago, I made the mistake of attending an award show with a musician who did—and I had no clue. One party, where someone got a picture of him doing lines of coke while I was in the restroom—and when I returned and sat down and saw what he was doing, I had my security team escort me out immediately—and they've turned me into a damn wannabe druggy.

"Truth, but that photo they snapped of you...you can't deny you look pregnant," Layla says, popping a piece of bagel into her mouth. We're all at my parents' house for Sunday brunch. The guys—minus Declan and Gage—are helping my mom move around some new furniture she bought for the house and isn't sure how she wants them placed, while Layla, Kaylee, and I eat and drink our coffee as we watch Felix dance to a new music video. Marianna crawls around, chasing his feet and driving him nuts.

"I know." I sigh. It's why I've flown in from California this weekend—to handle something I've been dreading. I need to tell Kyle about my pregnancy, which I've put off all weekend. Since it's Sunday, and I know it's his only day off, I'm going to drive over there this afternoon. I'd call or text him first, but when I tried, I quickly realized he blocked me. Not that I blame him... if leaving someone at the altar isn't reason enough to never want to speak to someone again, what is? But that means I'll have to awkwardly go over there and deal with this.

"How are you holding up?" Kaylee asks, flashing me a look of sympathy. Since our family knew about Declan and me, I had no choice but to tell them that we broke up. I also asked them not to mention I'm pregnant. I want to be the one to tell him, but I need to tell Kyle first. I should've told Declan when I broke up with him, but it was too hard. My heart was too broken to go there.

"I'm hanging in there." I shrug. "I miss Declan so much, but he deserves so much better than what I can give him. Have you seen him?"

Layla and Kaylee both shake their heads.

"No," Kaylee says. "He's been MIA the past couple of weeks. I think between Gage refusing to come home and then…" She trails off and clears her throat. "He just needs some time."

My chest tightens, hating myself for what I've done and wishing I could change the facts.

"After I talk to Kyle today, I'm flying back to LA for the rest of my pregnancy so he can have some space."

"What?" My mom gasps, making me turn around. "You're leaving again?"

Dammit, this is not how I wanted to tell her. I'm just messing everything up with everyone lately. "LA is my home. And with Declan here…I don't want to rub it in his face. It's not fair to him."

Camden and Braxton both nod in understanding, and I knew they would because they care about Declan.

"But Kyle is here," Mom points out. "I can't see him being okay with that."

"And I'm planning to come back before I give birth if that's what Kyle insists. But if he's okay with me staying in LA, and him traveling to visit, I think that would be best. The last thing I want is for Declan to have to see me all the time."

"Or you could stop being stubborn," Camden says. "Tell him what's going on and let him make the decision for himself."

I stand, not wanting to have this conversation for the millionth time. "We'll agree to disagree. I'm going to head over to speak to Kyle. I'll come back afterward. I'm not leaving until tomorrow."

"I actually need to speak to you regarding some business," Dad says. "Can you come by the studio in the morning before you go?"

"Of course."

"You're taking security with you, right?" Mom asks. "I don't like you going to Kyle's by yourself."

"Yep. I'm going to text Evan now and let him know I'm ready to go." I give my parents a hug.

"I really hope you'll consider staying here," Mom says. "Your family is all here, and selfishly, I don't want to miss my grandbabies growing up. Bailey and Cynthia's baby is due not long after yours."

"I agree," Layla adds. "Would you rather be alone in California or with your family and friends?"

I know they're all right, but it's just so unfair to Declan. Not only is he about to be surrounded by his married friends, who are all happily growing their families, but he's going to have to be around the woman who hurt him.

"I'll think about it," I tell everyone noncommittally. "I better get going."

After saying goodbye to everyone, I head out with Evan. When we arrive at Kyle's place, I quickly find out that he's not home. Not wanting to leave without speaking to him, I have Evan drive over to Kyle's office. It's really the only other place he would be since he's such a workaholic.

Since I know the code to get into the building from when we were together, I input it into the elevator and take it up to the floor his office is located on, telling Evan to wait in the lobby for me. He isn't thrilled, but I think it'd be better to tell my ex-fiancé that he's about to be a father to twins without an audience.

Leaving Evan standing by, I walk down the hall to where I know Kyle's office is located. I hear a voice, telling me he's here, which isn't all that shocking. The man would live here if he could. He's probably making calls, something he often did on Sundays if I didn't demand he take the day off.

As I get closer, the voices get a bit louder, and I wonder if maybe he's not alone. That or he's on speaker. Regardless, since I'm already here, and he has me blocked, I should still proceed, so I can at least ask him to unblock me so we can talk when he's alone.

Even though the door is partially open, to be polite, I raise my hand to knock when my eyes land on the inside of his office, giving me the perfect view of Kyle thrusting into a woman who's bent over his desk, begging him to fuck her harder.

Her eyes meet mine, and something in me snaps as visions and images flood my brain.

A little over three months ago

Kyle: I'm sorry I can't make it tonight. Ross gave me an important project to work on. I'll make it up to you tomorrow. I promise.

I toss my phone onto the table, annoyed. This is the same excuse he's given me the past several Saturdays. I'm sick of his job coming first. I get that he's ambitious, but I'm not sure I want to be married to a man who's married to his job. I understand it firsthand, as I've spent years married to my music career, but at thirty-one years old, I'm ready to settle down and start a family. Do I really want to do that with a man who can't give me one night a week of his time?

Deciding that the only way for him to understand where I'm coming from is to speak to him, I head to his office. On the way, I stop at the deli we both like and pick up dinner since he's probably been too busy to eat.

When I get up to his office, the place is quiet, save for a couple of voices coming from Kyle's office. I'll just knock and let him know I'm here in case he's in a meeting and will be a while.

Only when I get to his door, I find it ajar, and the important project he's working on is Britney, his boss's daughter and colleague. She's bent over his desk as he fucks her from behind. In shock from the visual in front of me, I gasp, which has both of them looking up. Britney smirks while Kyle flinches.

"What the hell?" I shriek. "If you didn't want to be with me, why didn't you just say so?" I chuck the bag at them, and it breaks open, the food flying everywhere. "Fuck you!" Unable to look at him and not wanting to cry in front of her, I fly out of the office.

"Kendall, wait!" Kyle yells, but I'm already in the elevator with the doors closing.

I should've known...Deep down, I think I always did, but I was so caught up in wanting to have what my family has that I chose to ignore all the red flags.

Only once I'm safely in the car do I allow the tears to fall. I can feel my phone buzzing in my pocket, but I ignore it since there's nothing Kyle can say or do that'll make this right. Honestly, he's done me a favor by saving me from entering a marriage that shouldn't be taking place.

So then why am I crying?

Because once again, I wasn't enough. I wasn't the woman Kyle wanted or needed. I tried to be everything he needed, even took time off work and put him first, but it still wasn't enough. I'm never enough. Just like I wasn't enough for my sperm donor. Because I'm broken. And unlike when you're little and can still play with the toys that aren't perfect, nobody wants to play with the woman who's damaged beyond repair.

Not wanting to go home, I have my driver take me to Declan's place. He's become such a good friend, and right now, I don't want to be alone. He's been down ever since Gage almost died, so I know he'll appreciate the company.

Before heading up to his place, I check the bar, where he seems to spend the majority of his time these days, and sure enough, I see him sitting there, throwing back a shot. "Drinking alone?" I ask, sliding onto the seat next to him.

"Got no one to drink with."

He downs his shot, then glances over at me with his hypnotizing blue eyes. He rakes his gaze down my body, and my heart goes haywire, something that's been happening more often. I ignore it because Declan is not only my friend but also my brother's best friend and bandmate. And while ninety-nine percent of the time, I make shitty decisions, I'd never do anything that would potentially jeopardize my brother's friendships or band.

"You okay?" he asks when his eyes land on my face—no doubt noticing my splotchy and tearstained cheeks. One thing about Declan is that he notices everything when it comes to me.

Not wanting to get into the details of tonight, I change the subject. "How's Gage?"

"Alive."

"Because of you."

"No, he almost died because of me."

When he reaches for the bottle, I pour it for him and hand him the glass. "You saved his life, Dec." I hate that he's drowning in guilt when he's the reason Gage is even alive.

"His life never should've needed saving in the first place." He downs the shot and slams it on the table, glaring at me. I don't take it personally since it's only because I'm the one who's here for him to take his guilt out on.

"It wasn't your fault."

"Yeah, it fucking was." He eyes me. "What are you doing here, anyway?"

I pour myself a shot. "Same thing as you…" I down it and cringe as the whiskey burns going down. "Trying to drown my problems at the bottom of a bottle."

I can tell he wants to ask questions, but thankfully, he pours us each another shot instead. "To drowning our problems."

"To forgetting the world exists."

We spend the next couple of hours pushing our problems aside and focusing on simply living in the moment. We drink and dance, and when the bar announces that it's closing, I'm not ready for the night to end or to walk away from Declan when all I want to do is get lost in him. This isn't the first time I've had these thoughts, but the liquor running through my veins is allowing me to go after what I want.

What about Kyle?" Declan asks when I tell him I want to continue the night upstairs at his place.

"We're over."

"What happened?"

"I don't wanna talk about it." I drag my nails up his neck, stopping at his bun, and tug on it gently, loving the way his thick hair falls around his face. "I just…" I swallow thickly. "I just wanna forget." Declan just might be the only person in the world that I feel like I can be somewhat honest with, who I know won't judge me. Because he gets it. Gets me. "Please, Dec," I breathe. "Help me forget."

And that's exactly what he does…helps me forget, over and over again.

I shake my head as several more memories hit me hard…

Declan telling me he's in love with me…and has been for years. Asking me to give us a chance. Me scared of hurting him, of tearing apart the band and my family. Scared of what people would think if I jumped from guy to guy.

But in the end, my heart wins out, and I promise him that once I get my shit together, we can see where things go. And Declan, the amazing man he is, tells me he'll wait however long it takes.

"Kendall, what are you doing here?" Kyle asks, forcing me to focus on him and the woman he was just balls deep in.

"You fucked her while we were engaged."

Kyle's eyes widen, realizing I know. Because of the accident and my memory loss, he thought he'd gotten away with it.

"Why would you continue with our sham of an engagement if you wanted her?"

"Because he pitied you," Britney snarks. "It would've looked bad if he dumped you after you'd just been injured."

"Can we talk alone?" I ask him, ignoring her. I should probably be more upset than I am about being cheated on, but honestly, I'm not. I realized a long time ago Kyle wasn't the one for me, and this whole time I felt guilty, thinking I was the one who hurt him. But now that I know the truth, that guilt has been washed away. But I do have some questions.

Against Britney's wishes, Kyle forces her to leave so we can talk. Once she's gone, I ask my first question. "Were you with her the entire time?" It doesn't matter now, but damn, if he wanted her, why go through the trouble of proposing to me? If he had just broken off the engagement, or hell, not proposed, it would've prevented us from wasting so much pointless time together.

"No. It just happened. She came onto me and…"

I roll my eyes. "Don't treat me like an idiot." I'm going to be dealing with this guy for the next eighteen-plus years. I'm not about to let him get away with that crap.

He sighs. "I fucked up. I wanted to make partner so badly. I bust my ass for this firm, and sometimes, it feels like I'm not getting any closer to my goals."

"So you slept with her, hoping to get an in?" It hits me that I really had no clue who this guy was. I was too caught up in wanting to settle down and prove I'm not broken that I didn't take the time to get to know the person I was planning to marry.

You took the time to get to know Declan, a voice in my head points out.

"I know it's too late," Kyle says. "But I didn't do anything with her again… not until after you left me at the altar and took off with Declan." He crosses his arms over his chest. "Speaking of which, why are you even here?"

I open my mouth to tell him that I'm pregnant when it hits me…I had sex with Declan the night before my accident—several times and without any protection. Which means…Holy shit! Declan could very well be the father.

I try to think back to when Kyle and I had sex, but my memories are spotty at best. I could ask him, but I don't want to raise suspicions.

"You know what…never mind. Coming here was a mistake." Kyle tries to stop me, but I'm now on a mission to find the man who I spent—from what I can remember—the most amazing night with and never told me.

The moment I'm back in the SUV, I text him: **Where are you? We need to talk.**

Declan: At home.

Me: I'll be there soon.

This entire time, I thought we weren't together until the road trip, but he knew...fucking knew that we shared a special night together, when we made love. I told him about my tattoo, and he confessed his feelings for me. The next morning, we made love again, and then I was in the accident, and when I woke up, I didn't remember. Except my body and heart actually did. Because when I opened my eyes, I felt it...the pull, the connection with Declan, but I didn't understand it because I couldn't remember it. So I pushed it away.

Oh, my God! Declan knew my engagement with Kyle was over, yet he was going to let me marry him!

Twenty-Five

DECLAN

MY PLACE IS A FUCKING MESS, AND I STINK. I'VE SPENT THE PAST COUPLE OF WEEKS DROWNING MY sorrows at the bottom of a bottle of Jack. Because I didn't want to see anyone, I canceled the cleaning woman who usually comes. And I can't remember the last time I showered because I haven't given a shit enough to.

After Kendall texts that she's on her way, I quickly jump in the shower and get dressed, then spend the rest of the time shoving garbage into cabinets to make it look like the place isn't as dirty as it is. Just as she knocks, I light a candle, hoping it will help the place smell a little better.

Figuring this is as good as it'll get, I head to the front door to open it, both nervous and excited to see her. I'm hoping she's changed her mind about us, but I'm not counting on it.

"Hey," I say when I swing the door open.

She glares and walks past me. "Hey yourself."

She stops in the center of the living room, and before I can ask what's gotten her so upset, she speaks. "When did you plan to tell me that we had sex *before* my accident?"

Oh, shit. Dammit, I knew I should've told her, but…"I wanted you to want me. To choose me. I wanted you to feel what I felt…what I feel. I didn't want to have to *tell* you that we spent the most amazing night together."

Her features soften slightly, so I walk over to her. "I tried to tell you a few times, but every time, I didn't know how. I mean, how do you tell the person you're in love with that the best night of your life is the same night she can't even remember?"

Kendall sighs. "You were going to let me marry Kyle, even after knowing I planned to end our engagement."

"Only because you never told me why, and when you woke up, you were acting like everything was fine. Again, how was I supposed to tell you that you shouldn't be with him because you told me you were going to end things? It was a shitty situation, and maybe I made the wrong decision by not telling you, but in the end, your heart told you, which is why you walked away."

"He cheated on me," she admits. "I caught him screwing a colleague of his. Walked in on them doing it again today, and it all came back to me."

"You went to go see him?" Fuck, if she tells me she planned to give him another chance, I'll lose my shit.

"Yeah, to tell him that I'm pregnant." She says the words so nonchalantly that I almost don't process them, but once I do, I stumble back.

"You're pregnant...with Kyle's baby?" Fuck. "You and him...after you broke up with me?" My heart feels as though it's been ripped from my chest, thrown onto the ground, and stomped on.

"What? No!" She bridges the gap between us. "No. I'm almost seventeen weeks pregnant."

I glance down at her belly that she's holding and see the bump there. With the baggy clothes she's been wearing, I couldn't see it before, but now, it's obvious.

"When I found out I was pregnant, I was scared and excited," she says softly. "I wanted to tell you, but I wanted to know for sure, and then Bailey pointed out that because of my memory issues and not getting my period since I woke up in the hospital, there was a chance the baby could be Kyle's. And since I couldn't remember the last time he and I had sex, I wanted to make sure I was pregnant and find out how far along before I told you..."

Her words trail off, but I can finish her sentence. *Before she told me Kyle's the dad...*Fuck, this sucks, and it also explains why she broke up with me.

"Kendall..." I pull her onto the couch and take her hand in mine. "Did you break up with me to be with Kyle because he's the dad?" She, of all people, knows that just because you have someone's baby doesn't mean you should be with them. Look at her mom and her sperm donor.

"No," she breathes. "I..." She swallows thickly and averts her gaze. "I broke up with you because I didn't want you to have to raise someone else's babies."

"What?" I heard what she said, but what the fuck. "Are you being serious right now? You didn't think I could love your ba—wait, did you say babies? As in more than one?"

She nods, and a smile lights up her face. "I'm pregnant with twins."

My eyes go to her slightly swollen belly. "Wow, twins? There are two of them in there?"

"Yeah." She laughs, and the melodic sound has me wanting to pull her into my arms. "You should've seen me when I found out."

My heart sinks. "I wish I could've been there." We're both silent for a beat before I continue saying what I had started to say a moment ago. "Did you break up with me because you didn't think I could love someone else's babies?"

She shakes her head, and tears fill her eyes. "No, I knew you could, but I didn't want to put you in that position."

"So, instead of coming to me and telling me you were pregnant, you decided for me?" The more I think about this, the more fired up I get. I understand Kendall has her issues, but to make decisions for me isn't okay. "Don't you think you should've asked me? Like 'Hey, Dec, I found out I'm pregnant, and it's not your baby. How do you feel about that?'"

Kendall's face falls. "I know. I messed up big time, but the thing is, based on the date of conception, there's a chance you could be the dad."

Wait, what? It takes me a second to wrap my head around what she said. I could be the dad...because we had sex during the time the babies were conceived. Holy shit.

"That's why you're here? Because you remembered our time together, and now there's a possibility I could be the dad?"

"No." She shakes her head, and tears fall down her cheeks. "Dammit, Dec. I suck at all of this. I'm sorry. I'm just all over the place. I thought I was doing the right thing. I love you so much, and I didn't want you to be stuck—"

"Stop saying that," I bark. "Stop thinking for me. Does your dad feel stuck? No. Does Camden feel stuck? Hell no. I get you have your insecurities, but instead of trusting how much I love you, you not only pushed me away but you also broke up with me. Had you not remembered what happened, you never would've come back here." I wait for her to disagree, and when she doesn't, I let out a frustrated sigh.

"So where do we go from here?" she asks, her eyes filled with tears. I want to pull her into my arms and tell her the only place we go from here is to the bedroom, so I can make love to her because I've missed the hell out of her. But I can't do that because I'm too hurt.

"Fuck, Kendall, I don't want to push you away, but I need some time." Her eyes flutter closed, and I hate that I'm hurting her. I palm her cheek, and she opens her eyes, sadness and regret filling them. "This all sucks. It feels like no matter what I do, it's never enough to show you how much I love you. That I want you, every broken piece of you, forever."

She chokes out a sob. "I'm so sorry, Dec. I know I messed up. I know you love me. I just...I really thought by letting you go, I was saving you, and I hear what you're saying, but I...I didn't see it like that. All I kept thinking is how you deserve better than this...better than me."

"I want to believe you, but at the same time, I think you used this as a chance to run. I know I fucked up by not telling you that we were together, but regardless, when you found out that you were pregnant, you should've come to me. Instead, you did what you always do...you ran."

"And I get it. Running is what you've been doing for years. But up until now, you were running from guys who weren't me. Who don't love you the way I do. We promised each other forever. You should've trusted in our love enough to know that no matter what, I would stand by you, and we'd make the decision together.

"The worst part is, you didn't just run. You left. I'm supposed to be your partner, your best friend. I chased after you, but you wouldn't let me catch you."

Sobs wrack Kendall's body, and I hate how upset she is. It can't be good for the babies. But I don't know what to do or how to handle this entire fucked-up situation.

"I guess I'll go," she says, giving me the saddest damn smile. Even through the worst of times, she tries so hard to keep that wall up so the world thinks everything is okay. I'll never fully understand how a woman could be so strong yet vulnerable.

With her hand on her belly and her head hanging, she turns on her heel, ready to leave. But something in me screams to stop her from walking out the door. Yeah, she hurt me, but she's hurting too. And it's during the moments when we think someone deserves to be punished that what they really need is to be loved.

And if I want her to let me in, to stop running, pushing her away isn't the way to do it. I have to show her that she's safe with me. Safe to fuck up. Safe to make mistakes. Because no matter what, I'll be here. Always.

"Stay."

She stops in her place and glances over her shoulder. "What?"

"Stay with me tonight."

Her eyes widen. "Are you being serious?"

"Yeah. Stay here, please."

"Wha…What does that mean?" she asks, her words filled with nervous hope.

"It means that I love you, and I want you in my arms and in my bed. We can figure everything else out tomorrow."

Tears stream down her face as she cuts back across the room. I wrap her up tightly in my arms and kiss the top of her head, inhaling her scent. Fuck, I've missed her so much. Maybe I'm a sap for forgiving her so easily, but I don't care. All I want to do is love Kendall, and staying mad over shit isn't the way to go about it.

She grabs one of my shirts and changes into it, then crawls into my bed. "I need to call my mom. She called while we were talking." She puts the phone to her ear, and a second later, she says, "Hey, Mom…Yeah, I'm okay." I can't hear what her mom is saying, but while she listens, she chews on her bottom lip, telling me she's nervous. "I'm sorry. I was in the middle of talking to Declan." A soft chuckle. "Can we talk about it tomorrow? Okay, see you in the morning. Love you, bye."

She hangs up and eyes me. "The last she heard, I was going to tell Kyle about the pregnancy."

"How'd it go?"

"I didn't tell him. After I saw him banging Britney and remembered everything that happened, I left and came here."

I nod in understanding and open my arms for her, silently telling her to lie with me. She scoots down and snuggles into my side, then lays her head on my chest, her arm encircling my torso.

"It's not bedtime yet," she murmurs, pointing out the obvious since it's still the afternoon.

"Yeah, but there's nothing wrong with having a lazy Sunday in bed."

She sighs into me. "I agree."

With the hand that's wrapped around her, I run my fingers through her hair, knowing it calms her. Sure enough, within minutes, her breathing has evened out, and she's snoring softly.

While she sleeps, I use the hand that's not playing with her hair to pull out my phone and search all things pregnancy. Obviously, we're going to have to get a paternity test done. Even though Kyle's a cheating dick, he deserves to know if he's fathered two babies—but regardless of the outcome, I'm going to be in Kendall and these babies' lives.

I'm reading about the decreased chance of giving birth full term with twins when Kendall stirs awake, stretching her body against mine. She glances up at me, her blue eyes meeting mine.

"Hey," she says, her voice raspy from sleep.

"Hey back."

"I haven't slept that well in a while," she admits

"I didn't sleep, but I get it. This is where you belong—in my bed and in my arms."

She sighs and lays her head back on my chest. "I like being here. If it were up to me, we'd never leave." Just as she finishes her thought, her stomach rumbles out loud as if to remind her that staying in bed forever isn't possible.

"How about I make us something to eat, and then we can come back to bed? We can stay here until tomorrow morning when we have to go to the studio."

She smiles up at me. "That sounds perfect."

While I make us a simple chicken stir-fry, I ask Kendall about her appointment, wanting to know everything.

"I really thought I was at the most six weeks," she admits. "When she told me I was fifteen weeks and there were two babies, I damn near died. Thankfully, my mom was with me."

I chuckle, imagining Kendall finding out and the look on her face she probably had. "When are you due?"

"November third. It's impossible to know exactly when the babies were conceived, but based on their measurements, the doctor said the estimated date of conception is February tenth."

"We spent the night together February twelfth." I know the date by heart. It's the night I confessed my feelings to Kendall, and the night before the accident.

"I can't remember when I had sex with Kyle, but if—"

"Hey." I set the spatula down and walk over to her, letting the veggies cook. "It doesn't matter. If he's the dad, we'll deal with it, but there's no point in worrying about what-ifs. I looked it up, and your doctor can do a paternity test that won't harm the babies." I lean over and kiss her lips. "The test will let us know, but regardless of the results, we're in this together, yeah?"

"Yeah."

After eating, we head back to bed, but instead of Kendall lying back down and snuggling into me, she climbs on top of me, straddling my thighs. With my back against the headboard, I grip her hips as she leans down and presses her lips to mine.

"I missed you so much, Dec," she murmurs against my mouth before darting her tongue out and silently asking for access.

"Missed you more, baby," I say, then part my lips, accepting her tongue into my mouth. I suck on the tip, which has her moaning and her thighs clenching.

"I want you," she whispers as she runs her hands down my chest and abs, then breaks the kiss to lift my shirt over my head. "I know we have things to figure out, but…"

"Kendall," I say, holding the side of her face. "Yeah, we've got shit to figure out, but do you want this? Us?"

"Yes." She nods emphatically. "I want you, always."

"Then you're mine, and I'm yours. *Always*. Which means you can have me any time you want."

I palm the nape of her neck and crash my mouth against hers, needing to feel her soft lips against my own.

She breaks the kiss again, this time to remove her own shirt, but when she does, exposing her bare breasts and stomach, I stop in my place because holy shit, she's a sight to behold.

"Baby…" I glide my hand over to the front of her swollen belly and admire the bump.

"I swear I popped this week," she says with a laugh. "I had to order maternity clothes because nothing fits. I can't even imagine how big I'll be when I'm ready to give birth." She smiles down at me, her eyes sparkling with happiness, and my chest expands. I love this woman so damn much, and in less than six months, we'll be having not one but two babies. I need to make her mine—officially—as soon as possible.

I sit up slightly and tilt her back a little, then lean down so I can kiss the protruding area above her belly button, which no longer houses the navel ring she usually has. "I can't wait to watch you grow. When's your next appointment? I don't want to miss another one."

Our eyes lock, and hers are filled with raw emotion. "I want to say I don't deserve you," she says, sniffling back her tears. "After everything, you let me back in so easily when I don't deserve it, but I won't say it because I know what you'll say."

"And what's that?"

"You'll say I do deserve it, that I do deserve you."

"Damn right." I capture her mouth with my own and flip her gently onto her back. Without breaking our kiss, I tug her underwear down her legs, then inch downward so I can get reacquainted with her pussy. Trailing kisses down her growing belly, I settle between her thighs and spread her lips wide so I can lick up her center.

"Fuck, I've missed this. The taste of your pussy."

She moans, bucking her hips as I tongue her, stopping at her clit. With slow and methodical flicks to her swollen nub, I make her come so hard that she screams my name while fisting my hair and holding my face to her pussy. Only once she releases my face and pushes me away, shaking her head and telling me she's had enough, do I stop.

With one hand holding me above her, I take my shaft into my other hand, and guide myself into her tight warmth. She's so slick my dick glides right in. I stop once our bodies are connected, taking a moment to appreciate what this feels like: home. I'm finally home.

"No more running," I murmur against her lips as I start to move in and out of her. "This is where you belong, with me inside you. Understand?"

"Yes," she pants, wrapping her legs around me.

"Say it," I growl, fucking her harder, deeper, needing to be as connected as our bodies will allow. I find her clit, and her body trembles as I massage circles, determined to make her come again.

"No more running," she breathes.

"Because you're mine." I suck on her heated flesh. "Always."

Just as she starts to repeat my words back to me, her orgasm rips through her, sending her over the edge and taking me along with her.

I drop my head into the crook of her neck, catching my breath, and she wraps her arms around me. "I'm yours," she murmurs into my ear. "Always."

Twenty-Six

KENDALL

"I KNOW IT'S LAST MINUTE," MY DAD SAYS FROM BEHIND HIS DESK, "AND IF YOU'RE NOT UP FOR IT, WE CAN absolutely tell them no, but with you and Raging Chaos being in the running for several awards, when they asked, I wanted to at least run it by you guys."

"What do you think?" I ask Declan since the decision whether we play at the iHeartRadio Music Awards isn't only mine to make. While we're both supposed to be attending, since Raging Chaos is on a break and I was as well, we weren't scheduled to perform. But when another artist broke her leg, they called my dad to see if Declan and I would be up for performing "Drunk on Your Love."

"I think that's up to you," Declan says, squeezing my hand. "The show is next week, which will put you at eighteen weeks pregnant. Will you be up for that?"

"I don't see why not. Since you're not a dancer, we can have a tamer performance choreographed. Nobody will expect you to bust out with any moves."

Matty, my choreographer, snorts out a laugh. "That's true. We can play off the video. Have it set up like the inside of a bar. Then switch to the outside. Throw in some fake rain, some pyrotechnics, yada yada"—he waves his hand in the air—"and call it good."

"You okay with that?" I ask Declan, just to be sure since Raging Chaos's idea of a show generally includes them, their instruments, and at some point, them taking their shirts off while women beg them to impregnate them.

"I'm good with whatever you want to do."

He smiles at me, and Bailey makes a gagging sound. "We could just forget all the rain and pyrotechnics and have them dry hump on the stage. I bet the viewers would prefer it."

"Ha-ha." I glare at her. "Don't you have somewhere else to be?"

"Actually, yes, I do." She stands. "We have a week to get ready for a performance that we usually have months to prepare for."

"I want you both in the rehearsal studio as soon as this meeting is over,"

Matty says, standing as well.

"Actually, I have an appointment afterward. Can we start fresh tomorrow?" I bat my lashes at him, hoping it will keep me safe from his wrath.

He growls under his breath but agrees before stomping out. "Love you, Matty!" I yell.

"Love you too, *Stiff*."

I roll my eyes at his annoying nickname for me. "How long will we have to be together before that dumb name goes away?"

"I think in order for it to go away, people would actually have to know you're taken," Bailey says with a laugh before fleeing.

I glance at Declan, expecting him to say something, but he stays quiet, and I know it's because he respects my choice not to make our relationship public. Every step of the way, he's done nothing but respect my wishes and go along with my choices. It's time I stop thinking about only me and take us into consideration, which gives me an idea.

"Everything okay?" Dad asks once it's only Declan, him, and me in the room. When I give him a confused look, he adds, "You mentioned you have an appointment."

"Oh, yeah." I take a deep breath, needing to hype myself up to tell him my truth. "Declan is going to take a paternity test."

"Declan?" Dad quirks a brow up. "I thought Kyle…"

"*Might* be the dad…yeah," I admit, my skin heating in embarrassment. "But, um…there's a chance Declan might be as well."

Dad's eyes go wide. "How…? What…?"

I spend the next several minutes explaining how Kyle cheated on me and how I turned to Declan. I hate having to admit that there's a chance I slept with two different guys in a close enough date range that either of them could be the dad, but when I get done, like the amazing dad he is, instead of making me feel bad, he simply smiles warmly and says, "It will all work out, sweetheart. And no matter the outcome, I can't wait to be a grandpa again."

"And regardless of the outcome," Declan adds. "I can't wait to spend the rest of my life with Kendall and these babies."

Dad gives him an approving smile, and I sink into his side, falling more in love with him by the minute.

The next week and a half flies by. Between the grueling practices during the day and getting lost in Declan at night, the next thing I know, we're on a plane heading to Vegas for the award show along with my parents, Phoebe, Bailey, Cynthia, Braxton, Kaylee, Layla, and Camden. I was shocked to learn that they were leaving the kids with Layla's mom and making it an adult-only weekend getaway.

"Have you heard from Gage?" Declan asks my dad—a question he seems to ask almost every time he sees him.

"He's okay," Dad says, patting him on the shoulder. "I spoke to him a few days ago."

Declan nods, then turns his head to stare out the window. He doesn't say anything for the rest of the flight, and I know it's because he's lost in his own head. Gage is an intricate part of Raging Chaos, and without him here, it's as if the guys are all lost, unsure of where to go and what to do. I get he needs time, but I hate that it's leaving the guys in limbo since they're refusing to make any music or plans until he returns.

When we arrive at the MGM Grand, we get checked in. Since Declan and I are sharing a room and need to get settled, then head to the venue to get ready for the show, we tell everyone we'll see them later.

The show begins, and shortly after, we're announced. Our performance is perfection. My outfit covers the fact that I'm pregnant, and at the end, when Declan kisses me, instead of ending it after the three count we rehearsed, I wrap my arms around him and deepen the kiss. The crowd goes crazy when Declan lifts me into his arms, my legs encircling his waist, and walks us off the stage.

He doesn't put me down when we exit the stage, nor does he release me when he walks us through my private dressing room door and kicks it shut behind us, pushing me up against it. Our mouths devour each other as he shoves my panties to the side and thrusts into me from below. Unlike the way Declan usually takes his time, he fucks me with abandon, not stopping until we both find our release.

"Not that I'm complaining," I pant, trying like hell to catch my breath. "But what was that for?"

"That was because you kissing me the way you did in front of all those people turned me the fuck on." He drops his forehead against mine. "It was so unexpected, K, but fuck, it meant so much to me."

"I love you," I tell him. "And I don't want how I feel about you to be a secret."

"Did you get the results back?" he asks, knowing they were due any day.

"I did, and they're in my purse, unopened. I needed you to know that I want forever with you, regardless of what the test results reveal. You're my forever, Dec. Always."

Tears prick his eyes, and my heart swells in my chest that something so simple as kissing him in front of the world could make him so happy.

"I want forever too," he says, setting me on my feet. The warmth between my legs leaks out, but I ignore it as I watch Declan reach into his pocket and pull out a...Oh, shit! It's a ring. "I've been carrying this around with me since the day you broke up with me. I planned that dinner to propose, but things didn't work out that way."

My hands fly up to my mouth, hating myself for what I did. "I'm so sorr—"

"No apologies." He takes my hand in his and kisses the top of it. "It might've taken a little longer to get here, but I can't ever regret a single part of the journey I'm on with you. My reason for telling you that is so you understand that I wanted to ask you to marry me before I knew you were pregnant. Whatever it says in that envelope won't change how I feel or what I want. Since I was a teenager with a crush, I knew you were the one for me, and all these years later, I know without a doubt, you're the woman I want to spend my life with.

"So Kendall Naomi Blackwood, will you do me the honor of marrying me?"

For the first time in my adult life, there's not a single doubt, a single niggling of a thought that has me questioning if I'm making the right decision, when I squeal, "Yes," and throw myself into Declan's arms. Because for the first time, it feels like all those broken pieces of me aren't so broken after all.

"AND THE WINNER OF THE FEMALE ARTIST OF THE YEAR AWARD GOES TO...KENDALL BLACKWOOD."

I jump out of my seat and hug my family and friends, who are all surrounding me. Everyone but Declan, since he's the one on stage. I had no idea he would be presenting an award, let alone one I was nominated for.

When I make it up to the podium to accept the award, he leans in and kisses my cheek. "Congratulations, baby." Butterflies erupt in my chest, and I can't help the grin I have splayed across my face as I turn to face the camera and audience. Unlike the outfit I wore on stage, the dress I'm wearing now shows my bump. People are going to speculate, but at this point, I don't even care.

"I'm not going to pretend I have a speech prepared," I begin, making everyone chuckle. "Most of the time, I don't know what the date is, what I'm doing, or where I should be. If it weren't for my amazing assistant, Marcia, and the team at Blackwood, I wouldn't even be able to function. My entire life has been about music, and because of my family at Blackwood, I've been able to follow my dreams. So thank you to everyone who makes it possible for me to do what I love.

"More importantly, thank you to my amazing listeners. Without you, I wouldn't be standing up here with this award in my hand. Your love of my music allows me to keep writing and singing."

I hold up my award, and everyone claps. "I would also like to thank my fiancé…" Gasps are heard throughout the stadium, and when I glance at Declan, he's shaking his head with a huge smile across his face. "*Go big or go home*," I mouth to him before I finish my speech. "Declan is not only my best friend but he's also my inspiration for my upcoming album *Fallen*…because for the first time in my life, I've fallen in love, and I can't wait to share my journey with you guys."

Everyone claps as Declan escorts me off the stage, and we head to the back so I can take a few required pictures and then hand the award off to my assistant before finding my seat.

"You realize you just told over two million people you're engaged to me?" Declan asks, pulling me into his arms. "There's no going back now." He smirks playfully.

"I don't want to go back," I tell him seriously. "I just want to move forward…with you."

"YOU WERE SUPPOSED TO PROPOSE AT DINNER!" MOM LAUGHS, SLAPPING DECLAN PLAYFULLY ON THE shoulder as we're seated at the table in the private room of the restaurant that Declan booked—to propose. "It's the entire reason we all came."

Declan flinches. "I'm sorry. It just kind of happened."

We find our seats, and the server immediately fills our glasses with iced water, then goes over the specials before excusing herself to give us time to look at the menu.

"How does proposing just happen?" Layla asks with a laugh. "At least tell us how it went down. Was it romantic?"

The memory of Declan fucking me against the door and then dropping to one knee as his cum dripped down the inside of my thighs has me choking on and spitting out the water that I'm taking a sip of.

With a knowing smirk, Declan calmly pats my back as he says, "I think she was *satisfied* with it."

"Oh my God," I breathe, glaring at him. "He proposed after we performed," I tell Layla. "It was perfect."

Since Declan was supposed to propose at dinner, the table is filled with gorgeous flowers, and at the end of the meal, a decadent dessert and delicious champagne are brought out, along with a bottle of sparkling grape juice since I can't drink alcohol. We take tons of pictures and videos, and Declan and I both post photos on our social media announcing our engagement. As I thought, several people comment asking if I'm pregnant since the pictures of my bump are going around, but I ignore them. When I'm ready, I'll confirm the pregnancy. Until then, they can have fun analyzing every photo and angle of me.

Exhausted and knowing I'm close to crashing, we head back to our room after we're done eating dessert, telling everyone we'll see them in the morning for breakfast before we check out to go home.

While I know it has to be the same room we left our luggage in before the show, I do a double take when we walk in because it's been transformed into the definition of romance. Bloodred rose petals in the shape of a heart adorn the bed and are scattered along the floor. There's a platter of chocolate-covered strawberries on the nightstand, along with several candles placed along various surfaces.

"You did all this for me," I breathe, turning to Declan, who's standing behind me.

"I'd do anything for you," he admits, pressing his lips to mine. "I love you, Kendall. You and these babies…" His hand goes to my belly. "You're my entire world."

Tears prick my eyes as a huge messy ball of emotion climbs up my throat.

"What's wrong?"

"Nothing," I tell him. "Everything is perfect."

"Then why are you crying?" he asks with a laugh as he swipes a tear from under my eye.

"Because you love me."

"Yeah, I do." He laughs again, giving me a look of confusion as I try to figure out how to word the million different thoughts and emotions hitting me all at once.

"You did all of this without even knowing if the babies are yours," I choke out. "But it's more than just this—the engagement and romantic night. You planned to go to my wedding knowing that you were in love with me."

He nods.

"And when I climbed out of the window, instead of telling me to go fuck myself, you were my getaway driver, when the fact is, that road trip was supposed to be your way of getting away after my wedding because you were so hurt."

Another nod.

"And then you made the entire trip about me. The wine walk and *Vampire Diaries* tour…the lake and mountain…" I encircle my arms around his neck. "For years, I was so caught up on the fact that half of my DNA comes from the shittiest human that I allowed it to dictate my life. Every mistake, every failed relationship, I blamed him.

"Yet you come from a home where they only care about money and reputation, and instead of allowing them to dictate your life, you love harder than anyone I know. And even if these babies aren't yours, I know you will make sure we're loved every day for the rest of our lives, just like my dad made sure I'm loved."

A sob escapes my throat as I realize I've had it all wrong this entire time. "I'm capable of being loved and loving someone else. My love might not be perfect, but it's okay if it's a little broken because we're all a little broken. The key is to find someone who can love all those jaded pieces."

Declan presses his mouth to mine tenderly. "And I love every single imperfectly perfect piece of you."

He loves me. Just the way I am.

"Marry me."

Declan laughs. "That's the idea, baby." He kisses the tip of my nose.

"No, now. We're here, in Vegas. Let's get married."

"You're serious?" he asks.

"Forever," I say. "Always."

Twenty-Six

BONUS SCENE

KENDALL

"YOU'RE GETTING MARRIED? TODAY?" MOM SQUEAKS.

"Today, and I would really love it if you guys would be there." I glance around at our friends and family, then stop on my dad. "And it would mean the world to me if you would walk me down the aisle...and this time, I promise to actually make it down the aisle."

Everyone laughs.

"There's nowhere else we'd rather be," Dad says.

"I'm on it," Marcia says, already typing away on her phone.

Six hours later, I'm dressed in the most gorgeous maternity bridal gown, standing at the end of the aisle of a beautifully decorated church next to my dad.

"You ready, sweetheart?" he asks.

"More than ready."

He hooks his arm in mine, and we walk down the aisle toward Declan, who's standing next to the officiant in his sexy black tux. When I try to walk faster, wanting to get to him sooner, my dad laughs. "Slow down, K," he says softly. "He's not going anywhere. Enjoy the moment, and take it all in. This is the only time you'll be getting married."

I take a calming breath and do as he says, slowing my pace as I look around me at my family and friends seated in the front row, watching us with smiles on their faces as we walk down the aisle.

When we get to the front, the officiant asks. "Who gives this woman away?"

With my dad's eyes locked on Declan's, he says, "Her mother and I do." He takes Declan's hand in his and shakes it. "You see that smile on her face?" Declan glances at me and smiles. "It's for you. Being with you has made her happier than I've seen her in years. And I know you will put that smile on her face every day. Love her and care for her, the way her mom and I do." He pulls

Declan into a hug. "I love you, and I can't wait to officially call you my son."

His words choke me up, and I will myself not to cry, but when he releases Declan and leans in to kiss my cheek, murmuring, "I didn't give you the gift of life, but life gave me the gift of you. I love you, K, and I'm so proud of the woman you've become," I let a sob loose.

"Thank you, Dad. I love you."

The officiant gives me a moment to gather myself, and then the service begins. Declan and I exchange traditional vows, promising each other forever, and once the officiant announces us husband and wife, he pulls me into a passionate kiss that leaves me breathless.

"All right, all right," Camden says when Declan kisses me for the second time. "Enough of that. It's time to celebrate."

Twenty-Seven

DECLAN

THREE WEEKS LATER

I roll over and hover above Kendall, giving her a peck on her lips. "That doesn't mean shit. She feels obligated to be with Stefan, but she wants Damon. Besides…" I roll onto my side, taking her with me so our bodies stay connected. "Klaus is the real MVP."

"What?" Kendall cackles. "He's a monster!"

"They should give him his own show." I shrug. "I'd watch that shit."

Kendall smirks. "He has his own show."

"What? Why aren't we watching it instead of this teen high school drama shit?"

She rolls her eyes. "You love this teen high school drama shit."

She isn't wrong, but I'll never admit it out loud.

"We have to watch them in order," she explains. "*The Originals* doesn't start until season five."

"Damn, that's like a million seasons away."

"Don't be dramatic." Kendall sits up. "We're almost done with season three."

"Does Klaus end up with Caroline?" That woman is without a doubt the most annoying character on the show, besides Bonnie, that is. "Maybe if she'd let Klaus hit it, she'd lighten up a little."

Kendall laughs. "I'm not giving you any spoilers."

I pout, hoping to get my way, but she isn't having it. "We need to get going so we're not late to my appointment." She edges off the bed and starts getting dressed while I stare at how goddamn sexy she looks carrying my babies. If I have it my way, I'll knock her ass up a couple more times, just so I can watch her belly grow.

"You going to stare at me all day or get ready to go?"

"I'd like to do more than stare, Mrs. Pierce."

Yeah, that's right. We not only got married the next day, at a small chapel in Vegas just off the Strip with her entire family there to witness it, but she also took my name—none of that hyphenated shit either—and I use every opportunity to call her by it—Kendall Naomi Pierce: my wife and soon-to-be mother of my children.

After we were married and celebrated with her family, we went back to our room, made love for damn near most of the night, and then opened the results, where we found out that I'm the dad—best wedding present ever.

"C'mon!" Kendall says. "I'm dying to see the babies."

Getting up, I throw my shirt on, then stuff my wallet, phone, and keys into my pockets. "If one of them is a boy, we should name him Klaus. That would be badass."

Kendall, who's walking toward the door, stops in her place and turns around to glare at me. "That's not happening. Baby-naming rule number one: no naming them after vampires...a horrible one at that."

"Klaus hater."

"BABY A IS A BOY!" DR. WEISBERG TYPES *BOY* ACROSS THE SCREEN AND CAPTURES A PICTURE.

"Oh my God, we're having a boy!" Kendall chokes out, squeezing my hand while keeping her eyes trained on the screen. We've spent the past thirty minutes with the doctor taking measurements and making sure everything is on point with Kendall being twenty weeks. As she pointed and clicked, she explained everything she was looking for. I couldn't tell you half the shit she said, but what I do know is that there are definitely two babies swimming around and growing in there. They both have perfect arms and legs and spines. They both have strong heartbeats, and everything is progressing as it should.

"We're totally naming him Klaus, baby," I whisper, kissing her cheek.

She snorts out a laugh and looks at me with tear-filled eyes. "I love you, Dec, but that's not happening."

"We'll see." I shrug.

"And Baby B is...a girl!"

"Oh!" Kendall breathes, glancing back at me. "We're having one of each." The tears that were piling up fall like the most beautiful twin waterfalls down her cheeks. "Thank you," she chokes out. "I wouldn't have any of this without you."

I lean over and press my lips to hers, thanking God for everything good in my life. For years, I prayed to find a love like what my grandparents had—and nothing like my parents' marriage—and every time I'd pray, I imagined Kendall by my side, her gorgeous blue eyes filled with love and happiness.

Recently, I thought maybe it wasn't meant to be. But now, as I look at my beautiful wife and our babies, I realize my prayers didn't go unanswered. It just wasn't our time yet. Kendall's and my path wasn't the shortest or the easiest, and at times, it's been total fucking chaos, but in the end, it led us to each other.

"It's me who needs to be thanking you," I murmur. "You've made me the happiest man in the world. Thank you."

Once the doctor finishes, she hands us several copies of the ultrasound pictures, then reminds Kendall to make her next appointment, and leaves us so Kendall can get dressed.

"I want to buy a house," she says, threading her fingers through mine as we walk out the back door of the office and straight to the SUV waiting with her security and driver.

"You already own a house."

"No, here. I want to live here, near my family."

"Then we'll buy a house here, near your family." I kiss her temple, then help her slide in.

"Can we buy a place before the babies come?" she asks.

"We can buy a place today if you want."

She beams up at me. "I'm so happy." Fresh tears fill her eyes. "I never thought I'd ever be this happy. I know our lives won't always be perfect, but I just want you to know, I'm really freaking happy, and it's because of you."

"It's because of you." I kiss the tip of her nose. "Because, despite being scared, you stopped running and let me in."

"I THINK THEY'RE TWO BOYS," FELIX SAYS, SIDE-EYEING HIS SISTER. "WE NEED MORE BOYS AROUND HERE."

"I think one of each," Easton guesses.

We've just arrived at Kendall's parents' house for dinner, and we're going to announce the sex of the babies. We considered doing some gender reveal shit, but Kendall was too excited to wait.

"You're right!" Kendall squeals in pure happiness, not even waiting for anyone else to guess. "We're having a boy and a girl."

Everyone congratulates us while Kendall shows off the ultrasound pictures.

"We're going to need to go shopping stat," Sophia says. "I can't believe you're going to have twins."

"I know," Kendall agrees. "Declan and I are going house hunting soon. I'd like to be moved in before the babies come. I'm sure it's going to be crazy having two newborns, so I'd like to be settled, and neither of our places is big enough for two babies."

"Have you thought about what you're going to do once the babies are born?" Easton asks. "Your album releases soon. You planning on touring?"

I look at Kendall, wondering as well. Whatever she wants to do, I'll support, but we haven't talked about the logistics yet, aside from her saying she wants to live in New York.

"Actually…" Kendall glances at me, smiling softly. "I've been thinking, and this album is going to be my last. Every album has been about the journey of my life, and like the ending of a book, the last one is about me falling in love." She shrugs. "I've been searching for love for so long that I just want to enjoy it. I'm ready to settle down. No more touring. No more traveling. I just want to be a stay-at-home mom and wife." She sucks her bottom lip into her mouth and then releases it. "If that's okay with you."

"Baby…" I pull her into my arms. "I appreciate you asking for my opinion, but you never have to ask my permission to do anything when it comes to your future."

"I don't know how this all works," she admits. "I just wanted to make sure it's okay. Don't couples discuss it when one person wants to quit their job?"

I chuckle at how adorable she is. "Yeah, they do. And I love you talking to me."

"What about Declan?" Easton asks. "They're going to go back on tour once the band is back up and running."

"We can't even get Gage to talk to us," I mutter, hating the bitterness I hear in my voice, but fuck, it's been five damn months since we've seen Gage. "Is there even a band anymore? We all agreed not to record without him, and based on his actions, I think it's safe to assume he's done, which means the band is done."

"He's not done," Kendall says. "He just needs a little more time, and then he'll be back."

"Speaking of which," Camden says. "What are you going to do about the condo?"

"Gage asked us to move forward." I shrug. "And while the band isn't doing so, I won't put my life with Kendall on hold. I'll keep the condo until the lease is up, so if—"

"Not if," Kendall says, cutting me off. "*When*…he will be back."

I wish I had her confidence, but a part of me is scared Gage may never return.

"He'll be back," Kendall says again. "And as far as the band goes…I'm completely supportive of you guys touring. I've been doing this for over fourteen years, and I've loved every minute of it, but I'm ready to focus on being a mom and a wife now. It's your turn." She frames my face and kisses my lips. "And when you're gone, I'll visit and travel with you. Whatever it takes. But do not give up on Gage. Raging Chaos is not over. Not by a long shot."

FIVE MONTHS LATER

"WE NEED TO GET GOING TO MY PARENTS' HOUSE SOON," KENDALL SAYS, PLACING OUR SON GENTLY INTO his bassinet before climbing onto the bed and kissing the top of our daughter's head, who's drinking the last of her bottle, as her eyes flutter open and closed, barely awake.

"Just one more episode," I tell her, clicking into *The Vampire Diaries*. "I need to find out if Elena forgives—" My words come to a halt as I, for the first time since we've been watching this show, notice the information in the top left corner.

"Are you serious?" I mock glare at Kendall, who scrunches up her nose in confusion.

"What?"

"You're such a damn cheater!" I whisper-yell. "Nina Doprev? Really? Who is she? If you tell me she plays Elena…"

"It's a human name!" She laughs, startling Nina—our daughter, not the actress. "I named her after the human, not the vampire. And anyway…" She glares back. "Don't act like you didn't cheat too when you named our son Morgan…after Joseph Morgan, the actor who plays Klaus!"

Because she isn't wrong, I close my mouth and shrug. When Kendall and I agreed that we'd each name one baby, with the other person's final approval of the name, I thought I was slick. Turns out my wife had the same thoughts.

After propping Nina up against my chest and burping her, I give her the pacifier—or as Kendall calls it, her pluggy—and lay her gently in her car seat since we actually do need to get going soon. Today is Thanksgiving, and since my parents are opening a new chain of Pierce Hotels in Colorado, the only house we're going to is her parents'.

Kendall takes Morgan from his bassinet and puts him in his car seat, and then we load them up into the SUV parked in the garage. Once they're both covered with thick blankets, since it's in the low forties today, we head out of the house. Once we're out, I hang a left and then drive three houses down…to Kendall's parents' house. Yep, you understood that correctly. We found a house only three houses down from her parents, and Easton and Sophia couldn't be more thrilled. So much so, Sophia has decided to retire so she can focus on being a grandma. Between Layla and Camden's two kids, our two, and Cynthia due in December, she wanted to be around more often to help out. Something Kendall and I are particularly grateful for. It's only been a little over a month and a half since Kendall gave birth, and we're both beyond exhausted. I can't even imagine how we'd function if we didn't have our support system.

The second we walk in, Sophia, Layla, Bailey, and Phoebe are on the sleeping babies like white on rice. I find Camden, Braxton, Felix, and Easton watching football and drop onto the couch with a tired groan.

"It gets easier," Camden says with a smile.

"It better," I say back with a laugh. "I feel like I haven't slept in a month." The sound of Nina crying catches my attention, and then Kendall walks in, holding her in her arms. My sweet baby's eyes meet mine, and I sigh, knowing every hour without sleep is worth it. Kendall sits next to me, laying her head on my shoulder, and I situate Nina between my thighs, where she loves to lay.

"Where's Morgan?" I ask, turning my head to kiss her temple. "He's still sleeping, so Mom put him in the guest room." She pulls the baby monitor out of her pocket and sets it on the table. "Would you mind keeping Nina so I can help with dinner?"

"Baby, you're supposed to be taking it easy." A few weeks before her due date, the babies went into distress and were delivered via C-section. They came out perfect and only had to be in the NICU for a few days, but because of the surgery, the doctor told Kendall not to do any strenuous activity for six weeks. Spoiler alert: she hasn't been following those orders at all.

"I will. Promise." She leans over and kisses my cheek, then scoops the monitor back up and takes off before I can argue.

With Nina sleeping safely between my legs, I close my eyes, needing a few minutes of rest. I don't know how long I'm asleep, but when I wake up, Nina is no longer between my legs, and Gage is standing in front of me. His hair is the same as it was the last time I saw him—chin length and curly—but that's the only thing that's the same. Unlike the last time I looked into his lifeless eyes, they're clear and lucid. His skin is no longer pale and pasty, and even through the shirt he's wearing, I can tell he's muscular and fit. He's been working out.

"Am I dreaming?" I ask groggily.

Gage chuckles. "As sweet as it is that you apparently dream about me... Nah, it's me, in the flesh."

I glance around but don't find anyone else in the room but Gage and me. "Where's everyone?"

"Giving us a minute." Gage sits on the couch next to me. "I wanted to say I'm sorry. I shouldn't have stayed gone as long as I did, but I needed time."

"What made you come back?"

"Your wife." He grins. "Congrats, by the way. Finally got the girl."

"Kendall?"

"Yeah, she came and saw me. Told me it was time to come home. Brought

Kaylee as backup.”

Fuck, I love that woman. “So where’ve you been? Why’d you stay away for so long?”

Gage drops back against the couch and turns his head to face me. “Where do I even begin?”

“How about at the beginning?”

Epilogue

KENDALL

FOUR MONTHS LATER

MY EYES POP OPEN AND I GLANCE AROUND, NOT HEARING A SINGLE SOUND. THERE SHOULD BE SOUNDS. With five-and-a-half-month-old twins, there are *always* sounds. And then it hits me...My parents kept Nina and Morgan overnight so Declan and I could have a night to ourselves.

"About damn time you woke up," Declan says, kissing his way up the inside of my thigh. "I was wondering if I was going to have to fuck you awake."

After dropping the twins off with my parents, Declan took me out for dinner and dancing. Since I hadn't had any alcohol for the past year, I passed out on the way home from the club, and Declan carried me inside, putting me to bed.

"I wouldn't be opposed," I say with a shrug.

With a light chuckle, he grabs the Polaroid camera I bought him for Christmas—since he always says he wishes he could take pictures without worrying about our phones being hacked—and takes a picture of me, shaking it until it appears.

"Fuck, you're so damn perfect," he murmurs. Since I purchased the camera for him, he takes daily pictures of us and puts them into a photo album I also got for him. I often catch him flipping through it, and as much as I want to be embarrassed that my husband has an entire album filled with naked images of us—well, mostly me—I love that he can't get enough of me.

After setting the picture and camera back on the nightstand, he places another kiss on my flesh, making my nipples harden from his touch.

Grabbing his shirt, I pull him up, so we're face-to-face, not giving a shit about morning breath. When you're raising two babies, you have to find time to be together, and in order to do that, you have to throw any and all perfect scenarios straight out the window.

Declan drops a sweet kiss to my lips before he drags his lips across my jawline and neck, trailing open-mouthed kisses along my flesh. Reaching between us, I pull his hard cock out and stroke it up and down, using the beads of precum to create the perfect amount of friction.

"I need you," I murmur as he lifts my shirt and takes one nipple in his mouth, sucking gently on the tip before biting down on it playfully.

"Careful, or you'll get more than you bargained for," I joke, referring to the milk he tends to get a taste of when he gets excited and forgets that I'm still producing and pumping milk for two babies.

"Eh." Declan shrugs. "Milk does a body good."

I throw my head back with a laugh, and he uses the opportunity to kiss the column of my throat. "I love you so damn much," he murmurs, working his way back up to my lips.

Since he already removed my panties while I was asleep, I spread my legs and guide him inside me, needing to feel him. In one fluid motion, he thrusts into me, hard and deep, as he slams his mouth against mine, pushing all thoughts but him and me out of my mind.

I love the way Declan fucks me—rough yet gentle, hard but sweet. He worships my body, making sure I come before he lets go, filling me with every drop of himself.

"I don't think I'll ever get enough of you," he says, kissing me one last time before he pulls out.

"That's good because you're stuck with me for life." I stick my tongue out at him playfully and roll off the bed so I can get cleaned up.

He comes up behind me and swats my ass. "Keep up with the smart mouth, and I'm going to fuck it right out of you."

"Promises, promises," I say as I saunter to the bathroom, making sure to add some extra sway to my walk.

Of course, that leads to him doing just that: fucking me from behind under the water while we shower.

"What are you up to today?" he asks once we're both dressed for the day.

"Felix is on spring break, so we're taking all the kids to A Latte Fun. Wanna go?"

"Hell no." Declan mock shivers as he presses start on the coffee maker. "That place is nuts."

I bark out a laugh at his dramatics. He went there with me one time, and after seeing all the kids running around, jumping all over each other, and acting crazy, he swore he'd never be back.

"Whatever. What are you up to?" I ask, handing him my mug so he can make me a cup as well.

"Actually...the guys and I are going to the studio...to practice."

"What?" I gasp. "Seriously?"

"Yeah," he says, hitting me with a boyish grin. "I'm excited. All the songs are written, so it's time."

"I'm so happy for you!" I jump into his arms and pepper kisses all over his face. "The album is going to be amazing."

"Who's all going?" he asks, setting me down.

"Layla and Kaylee," I say with a laugh. "Bailey and Cynthia are home with Matthew. He's got a bit of a cold."

"Why the hell would Kaylee want to endure that shit when she doesn't have to?"

"Maybe because she's hoping she and Braxton will be pregnant soon."

Declan's eyes widen. "They're trying?"

"Yep, have been for a little bit. Don't say anything." I grab my coffee and pour it into a to-go cup. "I'm off to my mom's." I lean up on my tippy-toes and kiss Declan. "Let me know how it goes."

Before I can get away, Declan grabs my arm and drags me back. He kisses me tenderly, making my heart pick up speed and the butterflies soar in my belly. God, I'll never tire of that feeling. Ever.

"Give the babies a kiss from me," he says. "I love you."

"Love you too...Always."

"YAY! YOU CAN DO IT, NINA," I CHEER AS SHE ROCKS BACK AND FORTH ON HER HANDS AND KNEES, attempting to crawl.

"Don't encourage it," Layla says. "Once they start moving, there's no stopping them." She nods toward Marianna, who's jumping on the trampoline that's level with the ground. She bounces up and down, gaining height and then does a flip into the foam pit.

"That child is going to give me a heart attack," Layla says with a grimace.

"Hey, do you see that woman?" Kaylee asks, nodding toward where Marianna is. "The one with the blue shirt."

"Yeah," Layla and I both say at the same time. She's kneeling next to a little girl who's stacking a bunch of blocks.

"You know her?" I ask.

"I'm pretty sure that's Sadie."

Layla and I both whip our heads around to look at her.

"Gage's Sadie?" Layla asks.

"Yeah."

"I never saw her," I tell them. Shortly before Gage overdosed and then went to rehab, he was hanging out with some woman. I don't know the details, only that one day she was there and the next she was gone.

"Me neither," Layla agrees.

"Well, I have," Kaylee says, "and that looks an awful lot like her."

She pulls her phone out and snaps a picture of the woman, then types on her phone.

"Are you sending that to Gage? Do you think that's smart?" I might not have seen her, but I've heard about her, and I'm pretty sure Gage made it clear that he doesn't want anything to do with her.

"How old do you think that baby is?" Kaylee asks, ignoring my questions.

"Maybe eight or nine months," Layla guesses.

Kaylee's phone goes off and she curses under her breath. "I was right…It is her. And Gage is on his way here."

"What? Why?"

"Because if Layla's calculations are correct, that baby might be Gage's."

"Oh, fuck," Layla and I say in unison.

Bleeding Chaos

A LOVE & LYRICS NOVEL

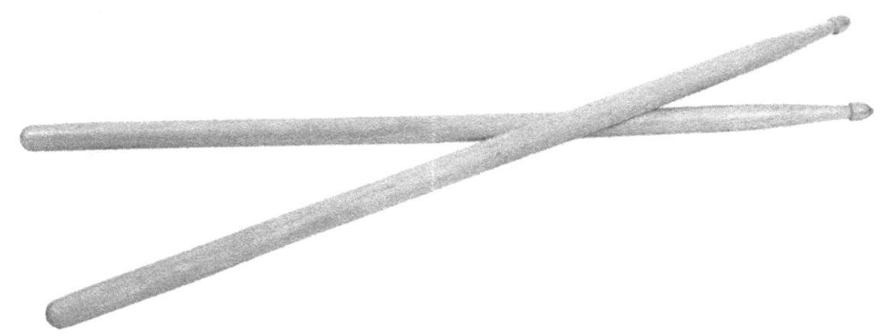

Someone like me doesn't deserve her time
But that doesn't stop me from wanting to take what's mine
From wanting her heart to be mine
Her body, her soul, all mine

- Gage, *Raging Chaos*

Prologue

GAGE

SUMMER
BEFORE SENIOR YEAR

"IT'S SO FUCKING HOT OUT," I SAY, DROPPING INTO A SEAT OUTSIDE THE COFFEE SHOP WHERE DECLAN AND Braxton are already sitting and drinking their iced coffees. They've got a shit ton of papers strewn everywhere—lyrics, songs, and sheets of music—since we spend most of our time writing or playing music. When we graduate from high school in June, our goal is to get signed by Camden's parents' record label, Blackwood Records.

When I was little and banging on the drums my uncle bought me for Christmas, I never imagined I'd have a chance to play professionally one day. Every night, when my mom would leave for work, I'd use our neighbor's Wi-Fi to watch YouTube videos on how to play. I never thought it'd go anywhere until I met Camden, Declan, and Braxton, who were hell-bent on starting a band and in need of a drummer. I played for them—and Camden's dad—and learned, according to him, I was damn good, and if I stuck with them, I'd make a living one day from beating on those drums.

My thoughts go back to my uncle. He was the only decent person in my life... until he died from heart disease only a few short months before my mom died, leaving me alone in this fucking world.

"It's too damn hot," Declan agrees, snapping me from my thoughts as he lifts a paper and takes a look at a song Braxton wrote. "I think I saw it's going to be in the hundreds today." He drops the paper and takes a sip of his coffee. "Fuck, it's too hot to work on music."

"It's too hot to move," I say, wiping the sweat beading across my forehead. "Who the hell can even think in this heat?"

I've lived in New York my entire life, and I'm still not used to the few months a year when the heat waves come through and knock us all on our asses. Thankfully, fall and then winter will hit in a few months, and this ridiculous weather will be replaced with snow and ice. I'd take that over the humidity any day.

"You know what we should do?" Declan says, turning his phone around and showing us an image of a bunch of our classmates at the beach. I'm about to tell him he's lost his mind when I spot one classmate in particular. Bright red hair, piercing green eyes, and the body of a damn goddess, Tori Spears is the definition of a teenage wet dream.

"I'm in," I say without hesitation. I've had my eye on her for months. The only problem is, she and her best friends, Layla and Kaylee, have been on a no dating kick the past year since Layla's boyfriend cheated on her and broke her heart. Since the school year is over and we're about to start our senior year, I'm hoping that shit will be over, and I can slide in and take my chance.

"You don't even like any of those assholes," Braxton says with a laugh, reading my mind.

"I don't need to like them to get in the water and cool down." I stand, down the last of my iced coffee, and chuck the cup into the trash. "It's too hot to even smoke. Fuck it, let's go."

Declan chuckles. "He saw Tori in the picture. He's been eyeing that cheerleader for months."

"Tori?" Braxton says with a laugh. "Actually, I can totally see it. She's all cheerleader meets emo with her short skirts, black lipstick, and fishnet stockings. She's like the least peppy cheerleader on the squad. It's the perfect match made in hell."

Declan nods, and I punch Braxton in the arm. "Fuck you, asshole. Let's go."

A couple of hours later, we arrive at the beach. The place is packed, and I almost consider turning around and going home, but then I remember home fucking sucks, and Tori's here somewhere. After a few beats of scanning the area, I spot her, along with Kaylee and Layla, lying out in sexy as fuck bikinis surrounded by a bunch of jocks.

Layla glances up, noticing us first, followed by Kaylee and then Tori, whose gaze goes straight to me for several seconds before she turns back to her friends.

They whisper back and forth, and then a few seconds later, the three of them head our way. They're all in tiny as hell bathing suits, but once my eyes land on Tori, she's the only one I see. Sporting an all-black string bikini, she saunters straight over to me and wraps her arms around my neck, whispering, "Go with it," before her lips lock with mine.

The kiss is intense as fuck. Our mouths and tongues devour each other. She tastes sweet like mint, and as our kiss deepens, the gum responsible for her flavor ends up in my mouth. When she realizes what she did, she pulls back and laughs. "I'm so sorry. That was not supposed to happen."

"The kiss or sharing your gum?" *Because let's be real...I'm okay with both.*

"The gum," she says, her cheeks turning an adorable shade of pink. "The kiss was planned...well, as planned as it could be during our three-second conversation."

I glance over at my friends and notice Kaylee and Braxton are making out, and

Layla and Declan are standing nearby laughing at whatever they're talking about.

"And to what do we owe the pleasure of getting kissed by the most beautiful cheerleaders on the squad?"

Tori snorts out a laugh. "The football players were totally trying to get in our pants." She scrunches her nose up in disgust. "We told them we had plans, and then you guys walked up, so when they asked with who, we said you guys. Perfect timing." She glances back and sees the guys have moved on to another group of women. "Seems like they bought it." She reaches up and kisses my cheek. "Thanks."

Just as she's about to turn and walk back to where Declan and Layla are now sitting, I grab her hip and pull her back toward me.

"You know what would be the perfect way to show your thanks?"

She quirks a single brow in response.

"Go out with me."

THANKSGIVING
SENIOR YEAR

"HOLY SHIT! YES, JUST LIKE THAT." TORI THROWS HER HEAD BACK AS I FUCK HER FROM THE BOTTOM, HARD and deep. The day after I asked her out, I took her to dinner and a movie with the only fifty bucks I had to my name. By the end of the movie, we were dry fucking in the corner of the theater. The next night, she snuck me into her pool house, where we actually fucked, and shortly after, I was calling her my girl.

She's my first girlfriend, and I was worried I would suck at it, but she makes it easy. I don't know if it's because she knows I'm broke, but she never asks for shit. Always wants to hang out at her pool house, and simply being with me seems to be enough.

"Oh, God," she breathes as she comes down from her orgasm and slides off me so she can get cleaned up. "How soon until we can do that again?"

"Aren't we supposed to join your parents for dinner?" Unlike me, who comes from a home without a dad and a mom who sold herself on the street corner to make ends meet until she was found dead in a motel room when I was twelve, where I was then placed in the state's care and thrust into several foster homes, Tori's family is somewhat normal.

Her parents were in love until her dad passed away from a heart attack. Her mom remarried Tori's stepdad earlier this year, and they all live in a nice house in the Upper East Side. Tori only goes to the same school as us because she already attended our high school when her mom married her stepdad. She begged to stay with her friends, and her mom gave in.

"I told them I'm not feeling well," Tori says with a clipped tone I don't understand. Every time I'm around her parents, they seem nice, but Tori, for whatever reason, hates being around them. When I ask her about it, she says they're annoying, but it feels like there's more to it than that. I would give anything to have two parents who actually want to be around me...Hell, I would give anything to have a living parent, period.

"Tor..." I meet her in the bathroom and wrap my arms around her from behind. "It's Thanksgiving. Isn't it a day to be with your family?" Until I was invited to Camden's house for Thanksgiving last year, I never experienced an actual Thanksgiving dinner filled with family and friends and delicious food, but now that I have, I can't imagine not wanting it. Yet Tori would rather stay here, just the two of us, and miss out on the family and food.

I'm watching her in the mirror, so I catch her flinch, but before I can ask what's going on, she turns around and hops onto the counter, wrapping her arms and legs around me. "I'd rather spend today with you," she murmurs against my lips, "inside me."

And because I'd do anything she wants, instead of questioning her, I give in and spend the rest of the day inside her, just as she wants.

JANUARY
SENIOR YEAR

I've just returned from spending a week at Big Bear Mountain with Camden's family. I wanted her to go with us, but her parents said no. I offered to stay, but she insisted I go, not wanting to ruin my trip. I've never been there before or stayed in some crazy-expensive mansion/cabin. The trip was unreal. The guys and I spent the week skiing and snowboarding. It was the first real trip I've ever been on, and I hope when the band takes off, I can come back with Tori one day.

The moment we got home, I came straight here to see Tori, only to find her tucked into bed in the pool house. Her eyes are puffy, and her cheeks are stained pink like she's been crying, but aside from saying she doesn't feel good, she won't tell me what's wrong.

"Do you need medicine?" I ask.

"No," she chokes out. "I need you to leave me alone and let me sleep, please."

"Or I can lay with you while you sleep," I say, refusing to give up. I climb into her bed and wrap my arms around her from behind. At first, she stiffens at my touch, but after a few moments, she sighs and lets me hold her until she falls asleep.

FEBRUARY
SENIOR YEAR

"I'D LET YOU LIVE HERE," TORI SAYS, "BUT GLEN WOULD NEVER ALLOW IT." HER WORDS ARE SLURRED FROM the liquor she's been consuming and the weed we've been smoking.

I turned eighteen a few days ago, and the people who foster me made it clear I need to move out sooner rather than later since the money is about to stop, and as long as I'm there, they can't take in a younger kid, who will bring in more money. The state spouted some bullshit about helping me transition, but the last thing I want is any help from the same people who stuck me with that shitty-ass couple.

"It's all good," I tell her, kissing the corner of her mouth. "I'll figure something out."

"We could get our own place," she says, perking up. "We could get jobs and find a small apartment..."

"While going to school and playing in the band?" I shake my head. "We'd never make enough money. Besides, you're still seventeen, so there's no way your parents will let you move out. They'd kill us both."

Despite Tori trying to keep me away from her parents, I've been forced into several situations where we're all together during the past few months. While they seem nice, I've learned they can't stand me—especially her stepdad—and are hella strict. And not just like with a curfew, but about everything. Tori wants to go to school for dance, but her parents told her she'll be going for business, or they'll cut her off completely. They have no idea she's a cheerleader or that I'm in a band. They'd probably lock her ass up and stop her from seeing me altogether if they knew.

"Yeah," Tori mutters. "So what are you going to do?" She looks at me with glassy, sad eyes, and I pull her into my arms to kiss her soft lips. When we first started dating, Tori didn't smoke or drink, but now, it seems like she's high and drunk more than she's not. But since I am too, I guess I don't really have any room to judge.

"I just need to get through the next few months, and then, if all goes well, we'll be heading to LA." Tori's made it clear that she has no desire to major in business, and since she turns eighteen at the end of July, I told her she should just follow us over to the West Coast once she's legal and her parents can't give her any shit.

"I wish we could go now," she says softly. "I hate it here."

"In your pool house that your maid cleans and stocks with fresh food?" I joke. "There could be worse living conditions..."

"Fuck you, Gage," she snaps, sitting up and pushing me away. "You don't know anything about my life, so before you talk shit, maybe you should know the facts."

"Then tell me," I say, not shocked by her attitude. Tori's been lashing out at everyone in her life lately—especially me, since I'm the one around her the most—but she won't tell me what's going on. She just smokes and drinks, and once in a great while, she'll fuck me.

"I need to go," she says instead of answering. "My mom's having a stupid dinner for her birthday, and if I'm not there..." She doesn't finish her sentence. Instead, she stands and stumbles toward the bathroom. "You can see yourself out."

I sigh, wishing she would speak to me but knowing she won't. After getting dressed, I head over to Camden's, where his mom tells me I can stay with them as long as I promise not to smoke or drink in the house. I respect Sophia and Easton too much to ever do that shit around them, so I have no problem agreeing.

MAY
SENIOR YEAR

"I'M WORRIED ABOUT TORI." I'M SITTING IN HER PARENTS' LIVING ROOM. IT'S THE MIDDLE OF THE SCHOOL DAY, but I took off so I could meet with them without Tori knowing. She's spiraling out of control, and I'm worried about her. She's stopped going to cheer, doesn't hang with her friends as much, and barely speaks to me. I don't know what's going on or how to help her. I know her parents can't stand me, but they love her, and I'm hoping they'll listen.

"We are too," Glen says. "She's been seeing a psychiatrist, who believes Tori has bipolar disorder. We've tried to put her on medications, but with her using drugs and drinking, they're causing her to lash out. Which is why we need your help."

I'm taken aback by everything they're saying since Tori has never said a word about any of this, but mostly, I'm shocked they actually want my help...until Tori's mom, Sandra, explains.

"We need you to break up with her, please," Sandra says. "We know you're planning to leave for LA once you graduate. We overheard you and Tori speaking, and if Tori goes, she'll never get the help she needs."

"Not happening," I say, realizing I made a mistake coming here.

"Please," Sandra pleads. "Tori is so lost, and as long as you're together, she won't let us help her."

"I love her," I choke out. "I can't just abandon her. She's my entire world. I get you don't like me, but I love her, and she loves me." I look at both of them, silently begging for them to understand. "I know we're young, but what we feel is real. I want her to get help, but please don't ask me to walk away from her. I can't do it. Not until she tells me that's what she wants."

Glen clenches his jaw. "Despite Tori trying to keep it from us, we know about your little band and how you're linked to the Blackwoods. If you want to pursue those dreams, I suggest you rethink your decision. End things with Tori and move on with your life. Otherwise, I'm going to be forced to make my own decisions that you're not going to like."

I stand, refusing to let this asshole threaten me. "Do what you got to do, but

I'm not walking away from Tori."

"Please," Sandra begs as I walk toward the door. "If you love my daughter. If you want what's best for her, let her go."

MAY
PRE-GRADUATION PARTY

Tori: I won't be able to make it to the party. I'm sorry, Gage, for everything. But please know that I love you.

I STARE AT THE TEXT, CONFUSED AS FUCK. THIS IS THE LAST PARTY BEFORE WE GRADUATE, AND THE GUYS AND I take off to LA. I asked Tori several times if she wanted to go, and she said she did. The more she pushes me away, the closer I pull her toward me. When I asked her about seeing a psychiatrist and being on meds, she lost her shit, telling me her parents were lying, and she wants to run away.

And when I told her I couldn't do that because she's still a minor, and I could get in serious shit, she accused me of being on their side. Despite me telling her she shouldn't smoke or drink, she got trashed, which led to us arguing until I ended up fucking the anger out of her. Since then, she's been quiet. Surprisingly, she hasn't been smoking or drinking lately, but she also hasn't been acting like herself. I just keep telling myself that once we're situated in LA, I'm going to bring her over there, away from her parents, and make sure she's taken care of. I love her and will do anything to make sure she's okay.

As I stare at her text, I consider texting her back but decide to just go over there. If I tell her I'm coming over, she'll argue and possibly leave. So instead, I pocket my phone and wallet, then head out.

Half an hour later, I arrive at Tori's house and head straight back to her pool house since that's where she spends all her time. I can't even remember the last time she actually spent the night in the main house.

Without knocking, since I never do, I enter the pool house. The first thing I notice is that it's quiet, which is unusual for Tori because, like me, she's one to blast music when she's alone.

"Tor!" I call out as I walk through the main room and down the hallway to the bedroom where she sleeps. "If you think I'm letting you stay home on the last night we have together, you have another—"

My words come to a halt, stuck in my throat, as I stare at the scene in front of me.

Tori.

Her lifeless body.

In the walk-in closet.

It takes several seconds for my brain to understand what I'm looking at, but once I do, I spring into action.

"Tori!" I shout as I quickly get her down and gently set her onto the floor. "Baby, what did you do?" Her body is cold...too cold, and her eyes aren't opening. "Tori, wake the fuck up!" I pat her cheeks, then drop my head to her chest to listen for a heartbeat. But there isn't one.

Refusing to give up, I call 911. While I wait, I try everything I can think of to bring her back to me. But she never wakes up.

When the paramedics arrive, they force me to step back, and when I do, my foot lands on something. I reach down and find it's a folded-up piece of paper with my name scrawled across the front. Needing to focus on Tori, I shove it into my pocket, praying to whatever fucking God there is that this is a mistake, a nightmare, that Tori will wake up, and I'll see those beautiful green eyes again.

Only she never wakes up.

And I never see her green eyes again.

When she's confirmed dead, it feels as though I've died right along with her.

One

GAGE

SIX YEARS LATER

"FUCK, TORI, I CAN'T BELIEVE IT'S BEEN SIX DAMN YEARS SINCE THE LAST TIME I SAW YOUR FACE, HEARD YOUR voice, felt you in my arms." I glide my hand across the marble and release a harsh sigh. "You would've been twenty-four years old last week." I place a dozen flowers into the holder. "Sorry, I couldn't be here on your birthday. We were still on tour, and I couldn't figure out a way to get here and back without missing a show."

I drop onto my ass and close my eyes, wishing for the pain in my heart to go away. After all these years, you'd think the heart would be able to heal. But I swear, as I sit here and think about the only girl I've ever loved, my heart bleeds as badly as it did the day I lost her.

I've been busy for the past six years. After losing Tori, Easton put us on a plane to LA, where the guys and I signed a contract with Blackwood Records. A few months later, we released our first album and it blew the fuck up. We've been on several world tours, sold millions of songs and albums, and broken numerous records, but nothing relieves the constant pain deep in my soul over losing yet another woman I would've given my life to save.

"Sometimes, I wonder—" I start to speak, but my words are cut off by the sound of someone crying. Since I'm sitting in a cemetery, it's not uncommon to hear someone crying, but this cry...it's gut-wrenching like someone is literally pulling the soul out of one's body.

When I look around, I see a woman a few gravesites down lying across the ground with her arms draped over a headstone. Her body is visibly shaking, and her cries are heartbreaking.

I'm usually one to mind my own business, but something draws me to her. Maybe it's recognizing a kindred spirit, feeling the pain she feels.

When I walk over to her, I find her eyes are closed, and she's actually sleeping. She's crying, sobbing in her fucking sleep. I consider leaving her alone, but the sky is gray, and based on the dark clouds, it's due to rain soon.

Leaning down, I gently press my palm to her shoulder to nudge her awake. It only takes a few times before she jolts awake and faces me. Her dark red hair is up in a messy bun, and when her big green eyes meet mine, bloodshot and glassy and sad, so fucking sad, I'm momentarily taken aback. Aside from the similar hair and eye color, she looks nothing like Tori, but something in her eyes reminds me of Tori. Maybe it's the deep-seated devastation, silently begging someone to take her out of this world. I didn't see it in Tori when she was alive because I was young and wasn't looking for it. But after she was gone, I spent hours upon hours replaying every conversation we had, analyzing every word she spoke and didn't speak, wondering if I could've prevented her from ending her own life. I was too close to the situation to see it at the time, but when I look back, there were so many signs that I didn't see or pay attention to.

"Are you okay?" I ask the woman, who's barely looking at me.

She nods and is about to lie back down when I point out the obvious. "It's going to rain."

She doesn't even bother to look up at the sky, just nods again, then lies back down, wrapping her arms around the headstone like it's a blanket. She doesn't make any sound indicating that she's crying again, but her body wracks with silent sobs. And since she isn't my problem or my business, I walk away from her, knowing there's no way I can save her.

I snag a cab back to the apartment I share with my friends and bandmates, Declan and Braxton, and go straight to my bedroom, so I can light up a joint and lose myself in the high. When the high isn't enough, I pull some powder out and do a couple lines. The pain doesn't dull, but my head goes fuzzy enough to block it out a bit. With my headphones on and music blaring, I tune the world out, refusing to think about the sad as fuck woman crying at the cemetery. I couldn't save my mom, couldn't fucking save Tori, hell, I can't even save myself...I have no business thinking about that stranger or the pull that has me wanting to save her.

ONE WEEK LATER

AS I WALK THROUGH THE GATES OF ETERNAL CROSS CEMETERY, I TELL MYSELF I'M HERE BECAUSE I MISS TORI. And that is partially the truth. When I miss her, which is a helluva lot, I visit her, especially when we're in town. But if I'm honest, my reason for coming here today isn't completely about Tori. For the past week, that green-eyed woman has been on my mind. The way she looked at me—like, even though she was visiting someone else's grave, her life was the one that was over—called to me. I don't know anything about her, but I could feel her pain. I told myself to let it go, but here I am, heading back to visit Tori, wondering if I'll see that woman again.

I'm several yards away when I spot the woman who's been on my mind...along with two police officers. She's facing me, so I'm able to see the tears skating down her cheeks, but I can't hear what she's saying until I get closer.

"Please," she begs. "I can't leave. Please don't make me leave." She drops to the headstone and holds on to it like it's literally her lifeline as one of the officers bends to grab her arm.

"Ma'am, I'm sorry, but you need to leave."

"Hey!" I bark, making them all turn their attention to me. "Don't fucking touch her."

The officer stops reaching for her and stands. "Excuse me, sir. Do you know this woman?"

"Doesn't matter. You have no right to touch her or make her leave."

"Actually, we do," the other officer says. "She's been here for three weeks, and the manager called, requesting she leaves."

What the fuck? She's been here for three weeks? When I glance at her, I notice her hair isn't just messy, it's greasy, and her clothes are wet and dirty as if she's been stuck outside for...as the officer said, weeks. But still...

"This is a public place. You can't stop her from visiting."

"During visiting hours," the officer says. "But she's been refusing to leave, even when the cemetery is closed. A few people have complained, and the manager has asked that we escort her out. She can come back tomorrow, during visiting hours."

"So you're making her leave now...during visiting hours?"

"Visiting hours end in twenty minutes. She was warned yesterday that she needs to leave, but she refused."

"I can't leave him," she cries out. "Please don't make me leave him." She clutches the stone as liquid trails down her already tearstained cheeks.

"Ma'am, if you have nowhere to go, we can steer you in the direction of a shelter, but—"

"No, please," she continues to beg, and for the first time in years, the strings of my heart are tugged, making me realize my black, broken organ still works. "I miss him so much," she sobs. "I can't go home without him. I promise to be quiet. Please."

"You're not allowed to sleep here," the officer tells her. "I really am sorry, but if you don't leave on your own, we're going to have to detain you."

The woman's cries worsen, and without thinking, I step toward her, putting myself between her and the officers. "You're not taking her anywhere." Without giving her a chance to argue, I lift her into my arms and walk past the gentlemen as they watch me take her away.

I expect the woman to put up a fight about me carrying her, especially since I'm a damn stranger. Instead, she clings to me, sobbing that she doesn't want to leave him—I'm assuming him refers to the person's grave she's apparently been sleeping at for the past few weeks, refusing to leave.

"I know," I tell her, walking us to the front of the cemetery, "but those officers were going to arrest you, and then you wouldn't be able to stay with him anyway. Once they're gone, you can go back, okay?" She nods into my shoulder, her body trembling in devastation.

I flag down a cab, and once we're in the confined space, heading to my place, I get a whiff of her body odor. It's rough and proves what they said is true. She's been there for weeks without showering or changing her clothes. She's obviously left long enough to use the restroom and eat—though, she's tiny, which has me wondering how much she's actually eating.

She falls asleep in my arms and stays asleep as I carry her up to my apartment. I hate to wake her up, but she needs a good shower and a meal, so once we're in my bathroom, I gently nudge her until she opens her eyes. They're tired and sad and damn near lifeless, but unlike Tori and my mom, she's still alive...*For how long, though?*

"You need a shower," I tell her. "If you don't want me to see you naked, you're going to have to stand so you can do it yourself."

She stares at me...No, stares *through* me, and I know, despite her body being here, she isn't really here. I set her on the counter and, without looking, undress her and then turn the water on. In her back pocket, I feel something hard, so I pull it out and find her license and a credit card. Sadie Ruiz, born June 26th. Based on the year she was born, she's twenty-eight years old.

I set the cards down on the counter, and with my clothes still on, I step into the shower with her and wash her from head to toe. I scrub her hair a couple of times since it's been a while and soap as much of her body as I can without touching the parts I shouldn't touch.

"Can you wash yourself?" I ask her.

With her eyes barely open, she takes the washcloth from me, spreads her thighs slightly and wipes between her legs, then hands it back to me, closing her eyes. Figuring that's as good as it's going to get, I turn the water off and get out so I can get out of my wet clothes and into dry ones. Then I grab a towel and wrap her up in it, carrying her to my bedroom, where I put one of my shirts on her, along with a pair of my boxers.

Since she's barely awake, I lay her on my bed and cover her with the sheets so she can get a good night's sleep. Once she wakes up, I'll feed her, and then she can be on her way.

"NO! NO! PLEASE, FIX MY BABY! HE CAN'T BE GONE!"

The screams of terror have me jumping up from my seat—where I was sitting on the balcony and smoking a joint—and sprinting into the bedroom.

Sadie's eyes are closed, but her body flails from side to side. Fuck, she's stuck in a nightmare. Knowing about them all too well, I pull her into my arms, holding her tightly so she won't hurt me, and whisper for her to wake up.

She jolts awake, her eyes meeting mine. She's only been asleep for a few hours, but she already looks better. The sadness is still there, but she looks a little less tired.

"Who are you?" she breathes, her brows pinching together. "Where am I?" She tries to scramble out of my hold, so I let her go.

"I'm Gage, and you're in my apartment. The cops were going to arrest you for sleeping at the cemetery, so I brought you back here to shower and get some sleep."

Her features fall at the mention of the cemetery, and her eyes glass over as she edges off the bed and stands. "Thank you," she mutters, glancing down at my clothes. "I need to go back."

"Not tonight. They'll arrest you. You need to wait until at least tomorrow. It's two in the morning."

She sighs, tears filling her lids. "Maybe they won't notice."

"Or they'll be waiting to bust you, and you'll spend the night in jail and be charged with trespassing."

Understanding flits across her features. "Yeah, okay." She nods. "I'll just, um, get going..." As she speaks, her stomach rumbles so loudly it fills the room.

"You're not going anywhere." Her eyes go wide, and I realize I said that a bit too harshly. "It's late, and I'm not letting you leave in the middle of the night. Let me feed you, get a bit more sleep, and once it's morning, you can go." She contemplates this for a few beats before she nods in agreement.

The kitchen has food, but not much, so I make us both a bacon, egg, and cheese sandwich, which she devours in only a few bites. When I offer to make her another, she shakes her head.

"That's okay. I'd like to get some sleep if that's okay with you. Do you...have a guest room?"

"Nah, it's a three-bedroom place, and I have two roommates, but I can sleep on the couch—"

"No," she says, cutting me off. "I can. I don't mind."

"Not happening." I walk us back to my bedroom and turn the blankets down. "Get in and get some sleep."

She listens, climbing into the bed, but once she's in, she doesn't lie down. "Do you think you could lay with me? I know we don't know each other, but..." Tears fill her eyes. "I just have a hard time sleeping."

"No worries," I tell her, getting in and sliding next to her. She doesn't come closer, but she faces me, looking past me for several minutes until her eyes drift shut.

Once I know she's asleep, I get out of bed and go out onto the balcony to smoke. I'm only out here for maybe a half an hour when a soft, feminine voice has me turning around.

"Hey," she says, standing in the doorway, eyes filled with tears.

"Bad dream?"

She nods, and I jut my chin, silently telling her to join me. She plops into the chair next to me, and I pass her my joint. For a second, she eyes it wearily, then takes a hit, choking on it slightly.

"First time?"

She glances over at me and shakes her head. "My husband used to smoke back in college, but it was never really my thing." She takes another hit, and her body relaxes. She hands it to me, and I take a hit before passing it back.

We take turns, silently passing the joint back and forth until her eyes are damn near closed, and I know the joint did what I was hoping it would do. It relaxed her enough to go to sleep.

I take one last hit, then pick her up and carry her to bed. As I watch her chest slowly rise and fall, I wonder where her husband is or if maybe he's the one she's mourning for. Then I push the thoughts away because Sadie isn't my business, and tomorrow, she'll be gone.

Two

SADIE

WHEN I WAKE UP WRAPPED IN SOFT SHEETS WITH A MAN SNORING SOFTLY NEXT TO ME, I FORGET WHERE I AM for a second. My brain automatically takes me back to before my entire world was taken from me, and for a split second, I imagine I'm in my bed, in my home. The man snoring is my husband, and it's only quiet because our son is still sleeping. My hand goes to my belly, and for a moment, I pretend there's a bump there, and my precious little girl is still growing safely inside. I lie still, enjoying a moment of reprieve, the escape, until there's a knock on the door, followed by, "Hey, Gage, I picked up breakfast. Get out here and eat...I miss you." My little escape is blown to pieces, and I'm back in reality.

No soft sheets.

No home.

No husband.

No son.

No baby growing in my belly.

I jolt up and glance at the guy apparently named Gage, but he doesn't stir at all.

"Gage, c'mon," the woman says. "I'm not letting you hide forever."

Making sure I'm dressed—which I am in clothes that definitely aren't mine—I drag myself out of the comfortable bed and quietly pad over to the door to make my escape. But before I open the door, I see my clothes folded in a neat pile in the corner with my license and bank card on top. I snag the pile and slip my sandals on, then open the door and step out, closing it quietly.

"Oh, hey," the pretty blonde says, still standing there. "I didn't know Gage had company. I'm Kaylee."

"Sadie," I murmur. "He's, um, still sleeping."

She gives me a once-over, and based on the look in her eyes, she's assuming I'm doing the walk of shame. I could correct her, but it doesn't really matter since I'll never see her again.

"There's plenty of food."

"Thank you, but I really need to get going."

"Okay."

Without another word, I leave as quickly as possible, not stopping until I'm outside the front of the building. I've lived in New York for the past ten years, since coming here for college, so I immediately recognize where I am and know which train I need to take to get back to where I belong.

Thirty minutes later, I walk through the gates of Eternal Cross Cemetery. I use their bathroom to change back into my freshly laundered clothes, and then I head straight over to where my entire world is.

"Hey, sweetheart, I'm sorry I left you." I choke up, something I do more often than not. "I can't promise I won't leave again since the mean people want to keep me from you, but I'll be here as long as I can be." I bring my two fingers to my lips, then place them on the headstone. "Mommy loves you so much."

Three

GAGE

Mind your own fucking business.

That woman is not your damn problem.

You're not some superhero, for God's sake.

I tell myself all this and more, yet nothing I say stops me as I walk through the gates of the cemetery less than a week after I woke up to find Sadie and her clothes gone. I told myself it was for the best, and for a few days, I stayed away. But then I ran into Kaylee, and when she asked about Sadie, that prompted my thoughts to go to her. No matter how high or drunk I got, I couldn't push her out of my head.

I don't visit Tori often. It hurts too much. But that's the excuse I gave myself as I got dressed and headed out to the cemetery—I was going for Tori. But the truth is, I'm going to check on Sadie because I can't stop fucking thinking about her.

I just need to make sure she's okay, I tell myself. Once I know she isn't still sleeping in the cemetery at the grave of...whoever's grave it is she's sleeping at, I'll go.

Before I'm at Tori's grave, I know she's not here. The grave she was sleeping on is empty, and I sigh in relief. Good. She was just having a few rough weeks. I get it. If I wasn't in LA after Tori died, I probably would've done the same shit. Since I'm here, I walk over to Tori's grave to say hello. I end up spending a few hours here, but Sadie never shows, so I take off at dusk.

The next morning, I wake up and find myself at the cemetery again, telling myself that I just need to make sure she's okay. Once I know she is, I'll stop showing up. Like yesterday, Sadie isn't here, and by the time nightfall rolls around, it's clear she won't be showing up.

I'm about to take off when an older man and woman walk over to the grave Sadie was at. The woman drops to her knees and sobs as the guy lays flowers on not one but three graves lined up next to each other. They stay for a few minutes, talking quietly before they start to walk away.

I don't know why I do it, but before they get too far, I call out to them, making them turn around.

"I'm sorry to bother you. I just...I wanted to make sure Sadie's okay. I met her while she was here." I nod toward the graves they were just visiting.

The woman's brows shoot to her forehead, and the man frowns. "We're not sure how she is," the man says. "She won't speak to us."

"Sorry," I say dumbly, unsure how else to respond.

"Do you know Sadie well?" the woman asks.

"Nah, just seen her here a couple of times."

"She, umm..." The gentleman clears his throat. "She's been detained at the NYPD. We tried to get her out, but aside from her not wanting our help, they denied her bail."

Fuck. "For sleeping here?"

The woman nods as fresh tears fill her eyes. "It was all my fault," she cries out.

"Stop, honey," the man says, pulling her into a hug. When the woman's cries deepen, he apologizes and says he needs to get her home.

As soon as they're gone, I go to the front office and demand to speak to the manager. "Did you have Sadie Ruiz arrested?"

"I cannot speak about this matter," the manager says, sticking his nose into the air like he's better than me. Well, we'll see about that...

I stalk out of the office and pull my cell phone out, dialing Easton.

"Gage, everything okay?"

"No, a...friend of mine has been detained at the NYPD. I'm on my way there, so I don't know the specifics, but I know you're good friends with that judge...I wouldn't ask but..."

"I'll give him a call now," Easton says. "Text me his name."

"It's actually a *her*."

Easton's quiet for a moment, but thankfully doesn't question me on it. "Text me her info and I'll see what I can do."

Two hours later, Sadie is released with a warning, thanks to Easton's friend, Daniel Maxwell. She has to promise not to sleep at the cemetery anymore, and despite not wanting to agree to that, she does, understanding that the next time she's arrested, she can be forced to serve ninety or more days in jail.

"Thank you," she says as we walk out of the courthouse and over to the car I have waiting for us. It's not often I use our car service, but it was easier than dealing with cabs, and since I was going to be in a public place, I had to take security with me to be on the safe side.

"No problem. Where do you want to be dropped off?" I ask, already knowing what she'll say.

"The cemetery please."

We arrive a little while later, and she gets out, thanking me again. But before I let her go, I ask a question that's been on my mind. "Are you homeless?"

She doesn't even look surprised by my question when she says, "I can't go home."

"So you do have a home then?"

She shakes her head, not giving me anything more.

"You can't sleep here anymore. Easton pulled a shit ton of strings to get you out, and if you get arrested again, he won't be able to save you."

"I know," she murmurs. "I'll figure something out. Thank you, again."

She closes the door, not waiting for my response, and I tell my driver to go. Sadie isn't my damn problem...

And that's what I'm still telling myself several hours later as I'm pulling back up to the cemetery to make sure she isn't doing anything stupid like trying to sleep here.

Of course, I find her doing just that. Lying across the middle of two of the three graves those people laid flowers on and crying softly. Since she only has a few minutes before the manager will no doubt be out here to make sure she's gone, I sit next to her and say, "You need to say goodbye."

"I can't," she says, "it's too hard."

"Just for the night, Sadie," I remind her. "You can come back tomorrow."

She nods, then sits up, wiping her tears.

Since this is the first time I've ever sat over here, I take a moment to read the headstones, noticing that all three have the same last name—the same last name as her.

Jesus, fuck. All of these are her family?

As if she can sense my question, without tearing her eyes away from the graves, she says, "In one day, I lost my entire world."

Four

SADIE

FIVE WEEKS EARLIER

"MOMMY, CAN WE GET LOTS OF FIREWORKS FOR THE FOURTH OF JULY?" COLLIN, MY FOUR-YEAR-OLD SON, asks, jumping up and down as I push the shopping cart down the grocery store aisle. His dark red hair, identical to mine, flops across his forehead, in need of a cut. I make a mental note to call to schedule an appointment.

"Of course," I tell him, pushing the strands out of his eyes. "But I'm going to let your daddy handle that."

Collin frowns. "Daddy's at work. Can't we get them now? What if they sell them all, and then there's nothing left?"

"He'll be off all weekend, and I promise they won't sell out." I reach on the top shelf for the pasta Collin loves as a sharp pain radiates through me, making me clutch my belly and take a deep breath. I'm twenty-six weeks pregnant, but I've been having annoying pains during the entire pregnancy. The doctor says they're growing pains, and when I mentioned I didn't get them with Collin, she pointed out that every pregnancy is different.

"Mommy, are you okay?" Collin asks, his features etched with concern.

"Yes, sweetie. I'm okay," I tell him, leaning over and kissing the top of his head. "What do you say we check out, and when we get home, I'll make some sandwiches to bring to Daddy's work? I bet we can convince him to leave early and go buy all the fireworks."

I wink playfully, and Collin's face lights up in excitement. "Yes!"

Once the groceries are brought in and put away, I go about making the sandwiches, with Collin's help, then text Vincent to make sure he's at work.

Vincent: I'm here and hungry. Can't wait to see you guys. Thanks, baby. Love you.

Since we found out I'm pregnant, he's been trying so hard to stay on the right track. Unfortunately, because of his track record, I'm reluctant to give him the benefit of the doubt, but I will say it's been close to four months since, according to him, he's touched a single pill. And he goes to his NA meetings several times a week. It's going to take longer than that to prove he's serious about staying clean, but I hope, for our family's sake, he does.

Me: Love you too. See you soon.

Because we live just outside of the city in the suburbs, it's too far to walk to the train station, and the investment firm Vincent's family owns is in the city, so we drive when we have to go into the city. It's annoying, with all the ridiculous traffic, but I try not to go as often as possible, preferring to spend my time in the quietness of the 'burbs.

An aching pressure pushes down on my bladder, and I hand the basket to Collin, telling him to put it in the car while I go pee. Only when I wipe myself and find a good amount of blood on the toilet paper, I know we won't be going to see Vincent today. I close my eyes and say a silent prayer that the baby is okay, but deep down, I know it's not.

Grabbing a pad, I line my underwear and then call my doctor, who tells me to go straight to the hospital. Next, I call Janice, my mother-in-law. "Something's wrong," I tell her. "I'm going to go to the hospital, but I don't want to take Collin."

"I'll be right there."

After hanging up, I call Vincent, who tells me he'll meet me there. It's not ideal for me to drive, but it would take too long for him to drive home, only to drive back out to the city where my doctor is located.

Less than an hour later, we find out our baby, our precious little girl has no heartbeat, and because I'm so far along, I have to give birth. It's the worst night of my life, and by the time we're leaving the hospital, we're both so filled with grief that neither of us says a word to each other. Usually, when you go to the hospital and give birth, you come home with a baby, but when we arrive, we're empty-handed. And because of how far along I was, decisions need to be made. Do we cremate or bury her?

Collin is asleep in his bed when we arrive at the house, so I tiptoe in and place a soft kiss on his temple. "I love you, baby boy," I murmur, the pain in my heart healing a tiny bit at the sight of my sweet boy.

He stirs and mutters, "I love you too," but he's too deep in his sleep to actually wake up. He was looking forward to having a little sister, and I dread having to tell him that we lost her before we even got her.

After thanking Janice for watching Collin, and her insisting on spending the night, I excuse myself, so I can privately mourn for the baby I've lost. As I pass Vincent's home office, I stop in the doorway.

"It's late. Come to bed, please." I could really use him right now. Holding me and telling me everything will be okay.

He glances up at me, his eyes bloodshot. "In a little bit. I need...a moment."

"Vince..."

"Sadie, just give me a few minutes."

I nod, praying our loss doesn't send him spiraling back down, and retreat to our room. I don't know how long I'm asleep, but when I wake up, I'm a bit disoriented. The first thing I notice is that light is shining in through the slats of the blinds, so it must be morning. Then I notice my mother-in-law is sitting on the edge of the bed, crying.

I assume it's because of the baby we've lost until she says, "I'm so sorry. I never should've left."

"Left to go where?" I ask, sitting up and wiping the sleep from my eyes.

"Oh, God," she sobs. "I'm so, so sorry. I can't believe this happened. I'll never forgive myself."

"What's going on?" I ask, my heart picking up speed in my chest. Like a mother's intuition, I can feel deep in my gut that something is wrong, very wrong.

"I left to take Henry some papers," she cries out. "I told Vincent I would be back soon. I don't know why he left...but he did...They're gone, Sadie. They're both gone."

"Where did they go?" I ask, somehow already knowing the answer but refusing to understand. "Where did they go?" I scream, jumping out of bed and ignoring the pain from giving birth only hours ago.

"I don't know," she says, shaking her head. "We don't know anything except that they're both gone. The police and the hospital tried to call you, and when you didn't pick up, they called me. I'm so sorry, Sadie. They were in a car accident and brought to the hospital. The doctors did all they could, but they didn't make it. I'm so sorry." She sobs. "They're both gone."

PRESENT DAY

"YOU LOST YOUR UNBORN BABY, YOUR SON, AND YOUR HUSBAND ON THE SAME DAY?" GAGE SAYS SLOWLY.

"Well, technically not all in the same day, but within twelve hours of each other, yeah." My eyes go to the three graves: my husband, my son, and my baby girl. "He swore he wasn't taking any more pills, but he lied. The autopsy report showed traces of them in his system. He knew better than to drive our son anywhere, but he wasn't thinking. We were both grieving. I'm not making excuses for him, but I'd like to believe that he wouldn't have left with our son if he was thinking clearly. They found breakfast and two coffees in the car. He must've taken Collin to get us all breakfast and thought he would be okay," I choke out. "According to the street cam, he ran a red light and hit another vehicle. It was a large truck, and the guy survived, but Vincent and"—emotion fills my throat, making it hard to speak—"Collin died on impact."

Gage pulls me tighter into his arms, and I cry into his chest. I don't know anything about this man aside from the fact that he seems to care about me enough to keep saving me, but I don't have it in me to care that I'm leaning on a total stranger.

"Sometimes, I wish I wasn't alive," I admit out loud for the first time. "My heart aches so badly, and I wish I could just turn it all off."

Gage's hold on me tightens. "I know exactly how you feel."

After I cry for a little while longer, Gage carries me to the SUV he drove here and takes me back to his place. He forces me to eat and then shower, and when I get out, I find him sitting on the balcony smoking a joint.

"Mind if I join you?" I ask, stepping outside.

He answers by taking a hit and then stretching out his hand in proffer. Because I have nothing left to lose, I accept it and take a hit, allowing the weed to calm my body. After several hits, my body is numb, and I can't feel anything. I know this is a dangerous game I'm playing. I watched Vincent suffer with addiction, but I just don't have it in me to give a shit. I've lost everyone I love, leaving me with nothing and no one to live for. For just a little while, maybe it's okay to allow myself to be numb, to turn it all off temporarily. It sure as hell beats the constant pain I feel.

We sit outside, passing the joint back and forth, until my eyes start to droop. Then Gage insists we head to bed. I snuggle into the sheets and close my eyes as he joins me, spooning me from behind. I'm just about asleep when I hear the sound of his drawer opening and closing. A pill bottle being opened, and then the distinct sound of him swallowing.

Pills...He's an addict. *Just like my husband* is my final thought before I allow myself to fall into a fitful sleep where I dream about my life before I lost everything.

And for the next several weeks, our routine seems to run on a loop. During the day, I visit the graves, refusing to leave my son and daughter. When it gets late, Gage comes and gets me. We eat and smoke and eventually pass out. Until the last week in September, when I wake up and see what the date is. Then everything changes...

"CAN WE STOP BY THE STORE?" I ASK ON OUR WAY TO THE CEMETERY. GAGE GIVES ME A CONFUSED LOOK, MOST likely because, aside from asking to pick up tampons last week, I never ask for anything since there's nothing I need.

"Today's...Collin's birthday," I tell him, hating that after all this time, I still can't say my son's name without my throat clogging with emotion and tears filling my eyes. "I'd like to get him a cake. His favorite is..." I clear my throat. "*Was* vanilla with buttercream icing."

Gage nods and takes a detour to the store. Using my card, I purchase a small cake and have *Happy Birthday, Collin* written on it.

"He would've been five years old today," I tell Gage as we sit on the balcony later that evening. We never talk about anything, but not talking about my son, the best part of me, on his birthday feels wrong. "He was so excited to start school, but because his birthday is after the cutoff date, he had to wait an extra year." A choked sob pushes up my throat. "He never got to go to school."

My eyes meet Gage's, and he nods in acknowledgment, not bothering to say anything since there's nothing for him to say.

"He loved Batman," I continue. Even though it hurts like hell to think about him, I'm afraid if I don't talk about him, no one will, and my little boy deserves to be thought about, spoken about, on his birthday. "And riding his bike. We would ride for hours along the streets of our neighborhood."

My sobs strengthen, but I can't stop. "He was so smart and caring and..." Fuck! "He should be here!" I slam my fist on the table. "He should be here! His father's job was to protect him, and instead, he killed him, and now, on his birthday, he's not here!"

Between my screaming and crying and despite being high as hell, I quickly spiral into a panic attack that has Gage picking me up and carrying me to the bed. But tonight, the weed isn't enough...

"I need you," I beg, wrapping my arms around his neck. "Just for tonight, I need you to make me forget."

"Sadie," he groans, shaking his head. "I can't be that person for you."

"I need you to help me escape," I beg. "Help me *feel* something other than pain. Please."

He stares at me for a long moment as if contemplating what to do, and just when I think he's going to reject me, his mouth crashes down on mine. He tastes a mixture of spicy like the alcohol he was drinking and smoky like the weed we were smoking, and I focus on that, allowing myself a moment of reprieve. The kiss isn't sweet or gentle. It's rough and hard, and everything, at this moment, I didn't even realize I needed. I've gone months without feeling wanted or needed or desired. My only emotion has been constant pain.

Needing to feel something else, something more, even if I allow myself to get lost in Gage for a short time. Our clothes are ripped off, and hands are everywhere, all over each other. Mine grab for his dick while his massage my breast. His mouth sucks on my neck, my throat, then wraps around my nipple, biting hard and making me squirm. Vincent was always gentle, loving...Most of the time, he was apologizing for messing up. But Gage is unapologetically rough, and it's exactly what I need.

He glides down my body, finding my center, and pushes a couple of digits deep into me. If I wasn't so wet, it'd probably hurt, but I'm soaked, and as he pumps in and out of me, that's proven by the sound of my slickness reverberating throughout the otherwise quiet room.

As my orgasm slams into me, I hold on to it for dear life, wanting to latch on to this moment of euphoria, where the short-lived bliss overpowers the agony and devastation I know are waiting for me.

I'm still flying high from my climax, panting unabashedly, when Gage spreads my legs and thrusts into me. His fingers wrap around my throat, and his mouth slants across mine, his tongue delving past my parted lips. He fucks me with abandon, siphoning pleasure from my body...pleasure I freely give him. I want him to temporarily feel as good as I do, knowing that once this ends, we'll both be right back where we were, in pain that shows no hope of letting up.

Gage shocks me by reaching between us and finding my clit once again. We both come long and hard, and between the high of the orgasms and the weed, I'm barely able to keep my eyes open long enough to see him pull out and grab a washcloth to clean me.

Still naked, we both fall asleep, our bodies wrapped up in one another, and for the first time since I lost my entire world, I sleep all night without a single dream or nightmare. And just like that, I've found my new escape, my own addiction.

And for the next couple of weeks, it works...until everything changes once again.

Five

GAGE

I glance over at Sadie, whose eyes were just closed but are now open. Over the past couple of months, I've learned that she has trouble sleeping. And since I know firsthand nothing can cure what we have—a broken heart—I do what I can to help. When she can't fall asleep, she likes to ask questions. So I answer them, and at some point, while I'm talking, she'll pass out. When she has nightmares, I'll pull her into my side to try to comfort her. She'll sigh against me as if my presence reminds her that wherever she was in her dream wasn't real, and within seconds, she'll pass back out. And when she wakes up early, she likes to take a warm bath. When she does this, I'll hear her crying from inside the bathroom, so I give her space.

Tonight, it looks like questions it is.

"You know you can," I tell her, pausing the TV and rolling onto my side to face her.

"Why don't you ever work?"

Until now, her questions have been about bullshit topics like my favorite color and food or my favorite subject in school. She's made it a point not to broach any topics that cause either of us to delve too deep. Until now...

But in her defense, this question isn't really deep. And since I live in a three-bedroom apartment in one of the nicer areas of New York and have yet to leave her side in the two months we've been chilling together, it's a valid question. But it's one I'm not prepared to answer. Telling her I'm in a band might change our dynamic, something I don't want to happen because...I like Sadie. More than that, I like her company. She doesn't judge or question shit. She just rolls with the flow.

For years, I've felt like an outsider with my friends, especially as of late—with Camden and Braxton finding their significant others and settling down. Declan's single, but he hangs out with Kendall—Camden's sister and Declan's love interest—a lot. And when we're all together, they look at me like I'm a broken toy they need to fix.

But Sadie doesn't see me like that. She knows I'm broken, but she accepts me the way I am. We could spend an entire day watching shows, laughing about nothing—something that's rare for her—to laugh that is—or we can go an entire day without saying a word, and both days she's content to just...be.

But I'm worried once she knows who I am, shit might change. She might not see me the same way as she does now, or she'll ask more questions that will lead to topics I don't want to touch.

When I don't answer quickly enough, she says, "Sorry, I didn't mean to overstep," and fuck if that doesn't make me like her that much more.

"You're not," I say, reaching out without thought and pushing a few strands of her dark red hair behind her ear that have fallen out of her messy bun. "I'm taking some time off." Not a lie since the band is taking a little break after our tour, and Camden and Layla just had a baby. "I have some money saved up, so I'm living off that until I figure out what's next." Also, not a lie.

Of course, she takes the answer at face value, nodding in understanding. "I've been thinking about the future," she says, shocking the hell out of me. While she loves to ask questions, she never usually talks about herself. "I got my degree in English and was working as an editor when I got pregnant with..." She swallows thickly. "When I got pregnant with Collin. Because Vincent made more than enough money, I decided to be a stay-at-home mom. But I'm thinking now, that...I have..." Tears fill her eyes, and she gets so choked up she's unable to finish her sentence. I pull her into my arms and hold her tight as she cries softly into my chest.

"You don't have to figure shit out right now," I say. "Just...let yourself grieve."

"OH, GOD, YES, JUST LIKE THAT."

I know I've hit the spot when Sadie's eyes roll up to the ceiling. Her back arches, and her tight cunt squeezes the fuck out of my dick, taking me straight over that edge right along with her.

I pull out and drop onto my back, needing to catch my breath. Fuck, I'm out of shape. I can't even remember the last time I worked out. Maybe it's because I've never been with the same woman more than once since...Well, I had no idea how insatiable women could be. At least Sadie is. Ever since the first time we fucked, she's wanted it on the regular. Since she's the one grieving, I don't want to take advantage and am never the one to start it, but to be honest, I don't even need to because she wants it all the damn time...Not that I'm complaining.

My phone dings with a text, and I glance at it, seeing Camden's name, along with a picture of his newborn daughter, Marianna. She was born a couple of days ago, and I was supposed to go up to the hospital to visit. I tried, but the moment the car pulled into the hospital parking lot, flashbacks of the worst fucking night of my life hit me so hard, I made the driver turn around and take us back to the condo, where Sadie and I spent the next two days getting high and fucking.

I text Camden back, telling him she's beautiful, but don't make any promise of coming to visit, knowing that shit isn't happening until they're back at home.

"I need to clean up," Sadie murmurs, sliding off the bed and stumbling to the bathroom, still high from the joint we shared earlier.

I open my bedstand drawer and grab the baggie of powder, dropping some onto the wood. Using the razor, I form a line and then lean in, taking a hit. The high is instant, but it's not enough, so I do one more line before I get up to get dressed.

"I'm gonna take a shower," Sadie calls from inside the bathroom, poking her head out. "Wanna join?"

"Nah, I'm gonna get a drink and make something to eat. You hungry?"

"Starved," she groans. "I'll just be a few minutes."

After taking a piss, I throw on my shorts and pad out to the kitchen to see what I can whip up. I'm scouring through the fridge when the front door alarm goes off, and seconds later, Braxton and Declan join me in the kitchen.

"'Sup," I say, grabbing some bread to make Sadie and me a couple of grilled cheeses.

"Just came from visiting the baby. They're back at home, so we stopped by to bring them some food. Have you gone by to see them?" Declan asks, his tone filled with accusation.

Without meeting his eyes, I shake my head, not wanting him to see the truth... That I couldn't fucking do it.

"Nah, I forgot," I lie. "But Camden sent me a picture. Cute kid. I'll go by and see them soon."

I can feel Declan glaring my way, but I ignore him, focusing on buttering the bread and heating up the pan.

"How's Kaylee?" I ask Braxton, referring to his girlfriend, who I'm friends with. Some bullshit went down the other night with his dad paying off Braxton's bodyguard to seduce her, which ended in her being drugged and a bunch of photos being posted that made it look like she was cheating on him—which was a fucking lie because she wouldn't do that shit to him.

"She's all right," Braxton says. "Still a little shaken up, but we'll get through it. She's actually why I stopped by. I wanted to talk to you both."

I set the sandwiches in the pan to cook and look up. "What's up?"

"I've convinced Kaylee to let me move in with her." Braxton grins, and my heart clenches in my chest, happy for him and Kaylee. They've been in love with each other for years, and I'm glad they're finally working shit out. They both deserve to be happy.

"Congrats, man!" Declan hugs him.

"Congrats," I add, flipping the sandwiches over.

"Thanks." Braxton smiles, looking happy as hell. "I had planned to give her space and let her live alone for a while, but—"

"But you can't stay away from her, so you're ditching this bachelor pad to move in with your girlfriend," Declan finishes.

"Yeah." Braxton shrugs. "Pretty much."

"It's all good," Declan says. "Speaking of which..." He turns his attention on me. "The lease is due to renew soon. You still want to live here, or are you planning to ditch me too?"

I scoop up the sandwiches and drop them onto the plates. "Where the fuck am I going?" I ask, confused as shit.

"I don't know," Declan says slowly. "You and Sadie have been chilling for a minute, so I wasn't sure if you guys were wanting your own space or if she's planning to officially move in."

When I glare at him, wondering where the fuck this is coming from, he raises his hands in mock surrender. "What? I'm just saying, if you want Sadie to move in, I'm okay with that. If you guys want your own place so you can fuck somewhere other than the bedroom, I'm not about to cock block." He shrugs.

"It's not like that," I mutter.

"Gage," Declan says softly. "You know it's okay to move on, right? It's nice seeing you with someone since Tori died. You deserve to be happy."

The mention of Tori causes a huge fucking ball of emotion to clog my throat, making it hard to breathe. One second, I was making a goddamn sandwich, and the next, I'm struggling to find my next breath. My heart picks up speed, pounding so hard behind my rib cage that it feels as though my entire body is pulsating.

"Gage, you okay?" Braxton asks, but I'm too lost in my thoughts to respond. My hands are clammy, and my body breaks into a cold sweat. Fuck! Did I have a bad hit? But even as I mentally ask the question, I know it's not the coke. It's me...

"Gage..." I vaguely hear Braxton and Declan talking, but the blood roaring in my ears drowns out the words.

Tori.

Moving on.

Sadie.

Happy.

No. No. No. Fucking no.

That's not what's going on with Sadie. She's grieving like me and needed a place to crash. We're smoking, chilling, fucking. It's nothing more than that. I'm not capable of anything more than that.

Sandwiches and friends forgotten, I stumble down the hallway, needing some space. Some fresh air. Needing to get high and make all these thoughts go away.

When I get in my room, I grab a joint from my drawer and am walking to my balcony when Sadie exits the bathroom, dressed in nothing but my shirt and some tiny as fuck panties.

"Hey," she says, smiling softly, her green eyes warmly meeting mine. She saunters over, wrapping her arms around my neck and kissing my lips. "Where's the food?"

My heart swells in my chest, and I push her away. "What are we doing?" I choke out.

Her lips turn down into a frown. "Umm...I thought we were going to eat. Are you not hungry?"

"No." I shake my head, stepping back. "What are *we* doing?"

She opens her mouth then closes it, unsure of what to say. "Umm, we just had sex," she says slowly. "I figured we would eat and then go to bed. It's late...Are you feeling okay?" She brings her palm up to my face, but I move before she can touch me.

Her worried tone. Her sad, confused eyes.

"Gage, talk to me," she says, and I can hear it in her voice. She cares about me.

I glance around, taking in my room. Her lotion is on my nightstand, her clothes are hanging over my chair. The TV is paused on her show. She's become a part of my life.

Our routine. The cemetery, the talking and fucking.

This wasn't supposed to happen.

I warned her. I told her I couldn't be that guy.

She said she understood.

"Gage, you're scaring me," she says, her voice cracking. "What's going on with you? Did something happen?"

This woman is grieving. She's lost her entire fucking world and has nothing left to live for. No reason to give a shit about anyone or anything. Yet here she is, worried about me. Caring about me.

My eyes lock with hers, and for a moment, my future flashes before my eyes.

Letting her in.

Letting her love me.

Loving the hell out of her.

Creating a life with her.

All I ever wanted was to create a life with you...

Tori's letter...

My hands hit my knees as her last words to me play back in my head.

Dear Gage,

Let me first start by saying how much I love you. If you're reading this, it's because I'm gone, and for that, I'm sorry. They say suicide is a selfish act, and I never understood that until now because even as I write this letter to you, the only guilt I feel about ending my life is that I'm hurting you. You're not only my boyfriend but also my best friend, which is why it's so hard to write this letter. There are some things you need to know., But before I tell you, I need you to promise that you won't tell anyone. I'm only telling you so you understand that my taking my life isn't because of you. If anything, the only reason I didn't do it sooner was because of you. Because of how much I love you. Every time I imagined my future, it was with you. All I ever wanted was to create a life with you. I thought I could be strong, but I'm not. I'm weak.

What I'm about to tell you needs to stay between you and me. Once you're done reading this letter, I want you to burn it. Then get on a plane and go to LA and become the best damn drummer the music industry has ever seen. Promise me, please. Do this for me. Nothing will bring me back, and I don't want you to ruin your life because of him.

Glen. For the past several months, he's been coming into the pool house when you're not here and raping me. I know what you're thinking. Why didn't I tell you?, For a couple of reasons. One, I was scared of what you'd do. I know how much you love me and would do anything to protect me, and I couldn't put you in that position. I went to my mom. I thought she would believe me and protect me like a mom is supposed to, but instead, she said that I'm sick and need help.

And then I heard them talking. You went to them and begged them to help me. God, I, love you for that, but there's no helping me because they don't want to help me. They want me gone. Glen is planning to run for mayor, and he sees me as a loose string. He's planning to send me away, and if you stand in his way, he's going to ruin you. He's rich and has connections, and I can't let him ruin you like he's ruined me...

"Fuck!" I bark out, fisting my hair. "No more!" I can't hear the words in my head anymore. Can't replay that fucking letter for the millionth time. I can't finish her thoughts. Her confessions. I can't finish the rest of the letter. For years, I've blocked the words out, and now they're rushing back, filling my head and heart, and I can't fucking do it.

I need to get high. I need to escape.

"Gage, what are you doing?" Sadie asks.

"I gotta go."

"What? Where?"

"Out!" I snap as I throw on a shirt, grab my wallet, and then stalk out of the room and the apartment. I faintly hear Sadie calling my name. She's confused since I've never gone anywhere without her, but I don't stop. Because if I do, I might lose the guts to do what I need to do.

I failed my mom, failed Tori, and I have no doubt if I let Sadie in, I'll fail her too. She's been hurt enough, has lost enough. The last thing she needs is to be dragged down into hell with me.

I repeat those words to myself over and over again on my way to the club. I keep repeating them once I'm there and the manager escorts me to the VIP loft. The words play on loop as I snort line after line of coke. And it's only once the needle enters my arm that the words as well as everything else finally go silent.

Six

SADIE

STARTLING AWAKE, I GLANCE AT THE WINDOW, THE DARKNESS REVEALING THAT IT'S EITHER STILL NIGHTTIME or early morning. My hands glide across the sheets. Cold. Gage never came to bed. As I press the button on the remote to flash the time, a noise from the living room grabs my attention.

4:00 a.m.

After Gage freaked out and left, I tried to stay awake to wait for him. Because I don't have a phone, nor do I know his number, I couldn't call or text him. But at some point, I must've fallen asleep.

Another noise has me sliding off the bed and padding out to the living room to see if it's him. His roommates, Declan and Braxton, are rarely home, and when they are, they spend most of their time in their rooms. I've only run into them a couple of times, but they seem like nice guys. When they've seen me, they smile and say hello, and despite feeling dead inside, I make it a point to smile and say hello back.

The noise gets louder, and I wonder if maybe someone is watching TV in the living room. I consider remaining in Gage's room, not wanting to intrude, but my throat is dry, and I could use a bottle of water. Really, I want to see if it's Gage. Maybe he came home and fell asleep on the couch. I don't know what got into him before he left, but it's so unlike Gage. During the short time I've known him, he's always been so calm and collected. Not once has he ever raised his voice or freaked out the way he did last night.

When the noise increases, I decide to take my chances and go out there. Worst-case scenario, I turn around and come back to the room. But if Gage is sleeping on the couch, I want him to know he can come to bed. This is his place, after all, and if I'm honest with myself, I like sleeping with him. He makes me feel a little less alone, especially when he pulls me into his side and holds me until I fall asleep in his arms.

The moment I step out of the room, I regret it. I wish I could go back inside and remain ignorant. Go back to sleep. Pretend I didn't hear anything. But that's the thing about life: there's no going back. If I could, I would've forced my husband to get more help. I wouldn't have accepted his word when he promised he would never pop another pill. And when we lost our daughter, instead of locking myself in my room to grieve, I would've pulled him and our son into my arms and held them tight, refusing to let them go. I would've made sure Vincent was okay instead of focusing on myself, on my mourning.

But that's not how it works. Every action has a consequence. And we can't predict how any situation is going to play out. But what we can do...is learn from our mistakes. Which is what I'm about to do right now.

As I stare at the scene in front of me, I take it all in. Gage is sprawled out on the couch, his pants unzipped and his head back, eyes closed, as a woman kneels between his legs, bobbing her head up and down while making the loudest slurping sounds I've ever heard. My stomach tightens and roils, and I worry I'm going to throw up right here, all over the floor.

The other woman—yes, there are two—sits next to Gage with her dress bunched at her waist. Her thighs are spread wide, showing everything between her legs as she fingers herself, making noises of pleasure. With the hand that she's not using, she drags her fingers through Gage's curly locks and fists his hair, pulling his face toward hers. His eyes remain closed as their mouths connect, and they both find their release.

My heart...my battered and bleeding heart feels as though it's stuck in my throat, blocking my airway as I continue to watch the scene unfold.

The woman who was just sucking Gage's dick stands and reaches into Gage's pocket, pulling out a small baggie. She spreads the powder on the table and then dips her head and does a line.

"Come on, baby," she coos, "your turn."

As Gage lifts his head, his hooded lids lazily flutter open, and our gazes clash. His eyes are lifeless and glassed over, and even though it seems like he's looking at me, it's almost as if he's looking through me.

"Gage," I breathe, tears filling my eyes as it hits me. As much as it breaks my heart to see him with other women, we're not together. We never made any promises to each other. Gage made it clear that he couldn't be that guy for me. He warned me, but I didn't want to listen, too caught up in my own grief.

But I have to listen now because as much as I care about Gage, as much as I appreciate him taking me in and helping me through the worst time in my life...I can't do this. I can barely save myself, let alone him, and I can't put myself in this position again. Unlike my husband who lied to my face, Gage has been honest. He doesn't hide the weed or the coke. He told me, flat-out told me, he couldn't be that guy.

Gage is a drug addict, and I learned the hard way that I can't compete with the drugs. I tried once, and I lost everything. So I can't do that again. This means I only have one option: I have to leave, so I can save myself.

Breaking our eye contact, I go back to the bedroom and get dressed. Since I don't have anything here but a few outfits and toiletries, I don't take anything with me. But before I go, I spot a journal on the nightstand. Gage writes in it sometimes...

Grabbing a pen, I rip a sheet out and pen a short note to him.

Gage,

Thank you for being there for me when I had no one else. You took a broken stranger in and saved me from myself. I wish there was some way I could return the favor, but I don't have anything to offer you. I hope one day you get the help you need. I know underneath the drugs and addiction, there's a sweet, beautiful, caring man fighting demons that are winning. Don't let them win, Gage. Fight harder and find happiness.

Xo, Sadie

IT'S BEEN OVER THREE MONTHS SINCE I'VE BEEN HOME. THE DAY OF THE FUNERAL, WHEN WE BURIED THREE lifeless bodies, I walked out the door and haven't been back. As I stand on the front porch, staring at the door with the American flag wreath hanging from the Fourth of July, my heart races in my chest at the thought of walking through the door. I consider turning around and running away. I have my bank card, so I could stay in a hotel, but for how long?

At some point, I'll have to go inside and deal with everything I left behind, so with a deep, cleansing breath, I type in the code on the handle to unlock the door and then enter the alarm code to shut it off.

When I walk through the door, the sight in front of me causes me to choke up: trains...all over the floor. Collin loved trains and would play with them for hours. Too many times, Vincent would come home from work and step on them. A watery laugh bubbles up as I remember the way he would bounce from one foot to the other, swearing the trains to hell.

I switch on the light and am shocked when it actually works since I haven't paid a single bill in months. I walk farther into the house, taking in the toys and folded clothes. Vincent's loafers are in the corner. I stop by Collin's room first, and the second I turn on his light, waves of emotions nearly drown me. He hasn't stepped foot in his room in over three months, but I can still smell his shampoo. More trains are on the floor. I pad inside and find his favorite train on the bed along with his stuffed train the Easter Bunny brought him. Needing to feel close to him, I slide onto his bed and pull the stuffed train into my arms, dipping my face into the plush material and inhaling deeply.

Memories from the past several years flood back. Vincent and I getting married. Buying this home. Finding out I was pregnant. Collin's homecoming. Vincent admitting that he had a drug problem and promising to get help...

Tears roll down my face as I remember the good and the bad: Collin learning to walk and talk, and Vincent surprising us with a trip to Disney. Finding out my husband was still addicted to pills. Learning I was pregnant again. Vincent promising that he would never touch drugs again...

I have so many regrets, but they're all pointless because none of them will change my reality. My husband and son are dead. The baby growing in my belly is gone, and I'm all alone.

I spend the rest of the day in Collin's bed crying, telling myself I just need some time, and then I'll figure out my next move. As I close my eyes, his scent creating a warm blanket around me, the image of Gage pops into my head—the way he would lie behind me and hold me close—and I pray to whatever God that's up there that he gets his life together. I meant what I wrote to him: beneath the drugs and addiction is a sweet, caring, beautiful man. And if I were stronger, I would try to save him, but I just don't have it in me. I tried to save a man once from himself, and I learned the hard way that the only person who can save you is yourself. Which is what I'm going to do—save myself. Because I'm the only person I have left.

Seven

GAGE

"GET UP!" THE BOOMING VOICE HAS ME SQUEEZING MY EYES AS I TRY TO BLOCK OUT THE HAMMERING IN MY head.

"Gage, now!" Declan continues, determined to make my head explode.

"Get out of my room," I groan, reaching over so I can grab Sadie and get a good whiff of her sweet, floral scent. Only instead of finding her, my body rolls over and hits the ground, chin smacking the hardwood floor. "Fuck!"

"Serves you right. Now, get up."

I roll onto my back, prying my eyes open, and the first thing I notice is the fan. It's not the one in my room, but the one in the living room. *What the fuck...?*

I glance around and realize I'm not in my room but in the living room. *How the hell did I get out here?*

"Gage, where's Sadie?" Declan asks, snapping me from my thoughts.

"What?" I sit up and close my eyes when the pounding in my head increases.

"Open your fucking eyes, bro."

I do what he says and find two women passed out: one on the loveseat and the other on the floor. And that's when everything comes back to me.

Braxton telling us he's moving in with Kaylee.

Declan asking if I'm moving Sadie in or if we're planning to get our own place.

Me freaking the hell out.

Going to Collided—the illegal underground club where I go when I want to get fucked up.

Bringing two women home.

Oh, fuck...Sadie.

I try to stand, but with the drugs still flowing through my veins, I stumble, crashing into the coffee table.

I faintly hear Declan calling my name, but I ignore him as I make a beeline straight to my room, which is empty. I check the balcony, but she's not there, so I try the bathroom. And that's where I see it...a note. I snatch it off the mirror and read the words.

She's gone.

She thanked me for saving her and then said goodbye.

The thought makes my stomach roil, and I drop to the toilet just in time to puke everything in my guts up.

"She leave?" Declan asks, his tone now cautious.

"Yeah," I choke out, grabbing a towel and wiping my mouth. "She's gone."

"Is there anything I can do?"

"Yeah, you can kick those women out," I tell him, my eyes going to the note on the floor.

Declan agrees and disappears, closing my door behind him.

Grabbing the note, I go back out to my bedroom and pull the baggie out of my drawer, pouring the powder onto the nightstand. As I bring my nose to it, snorting two lines—the high is almost instant—I tell myself that Sadie's leaving is for the best. Then I pop a few pills as I try to convince myself that's the truth.

THREE MONTHS LATER

BEEP. BEEP. BEEP. BEEP.

"Gage, c'mon, man, you can do it. Wake up, please," Declan says, his voice raw with emotion. I wrench my lids open, and our eyes lock. "Oh, thank God." Tears fill his lids, his worried features making him look like he's aged ten years, and my stomach knots, trying to remember how I ended up in the hospital with my friend and roommate sitting next to me and begging me to wake up.

"What happened?" I croak out when I come up with nothing.

"You overdosed. I found you half dead in your room. Kendall called for an ambulance, and they were able to save you." He exhales a harsh breath as I take in the dark circles under his eyes and the way his brow is furrowed in stress. I did this to him. I caused him stress because I can't deal with my shit.

"Gage," Declan says softly. "I have to ask...Did you try to kill yourself?"

His words, his question, triggers a memory...

"Hey, Tor." I stumble over to her grave and drop onto the ground. "Looks like it's just you and me today." I glance over at the three gravestones that have been without company every day since Sadie took off. The first few times I stopped by, I told myself I was visiting Tori. But when Sadie never showed up, and the manager said he hadn't seen her, I started to get worried that something had happened to her. So I kept showing up, hoping to run into her. I told myself that once I saw she was okay, I would stop. Only she never, not once, showed up.

The last day I was there, the couple I met before showed up...

"I was wondering if you've seen Sadie," I ask, trying to sound as casual as possible.

The woman smiles sadly. "She actually moved away a couple of months ago. Said it was too hard to be here...with the memories and all." She places a small bouquet into each of the holders. "Sadie asked that we come once a month and bring flowers since she's too far away to come herself."

"We talk to her occasionally," the gentleman says. "Would you like us to tell her anything?"

I shake my head as it hits me. I failed my mom and couldn't save Tori. Then I drove Sadie away.

"Yeah," I admit to Declan. "I did. I tried to kill myself."

They're the hardest words I've ever spoken, but they're also the most honest, and I owe him that—fuck, I owe all the guys that. After I left the cemetery, I was low...so fucking low. I was missing my mom and Tori...and Sadie. Fuck, I was missing Sadie so fucking much. Her touch and her scent and the way she just made everything more bearable. And I couldn't take it anymore. The pain in my heart just became too much. And I wanted it all to end. I wasn't thinking clearly and just needed a moment of reprieve.

"Dec," I choke out. "My heart...it fucking hurts."

Declan nods in understanding. "We're going to get you help, Gage. We should've gotten you help sooner, but we fucked up. We thought you just needed time, but we were wrong. I promise you..." He takes my hand in his. "We're going to get you the best fucking help."

"Damn right, we are," Camden says, walking in with Easton and Braxton. "We never should've let you get this bad." Camden leans over and kisses the top of my head, and tears fill my eyes. I don't deserve these guys. They've always been there for me, and in return, what do I do? Put them in the worst position possible.

"This isn't on you guys. It's on me," I tell them, needing to take responsibility. I fucked up. I let the drugs overtake my life. Instead of dealing with my shit, I chose to escape it, which not only hurt me but also hurt everyone around me.

"It is on you," Easton agrees. "But you're family, and we should've intervened sooner. We have everything set up. It's a ninety-day program, but once they evaluate you, they'll alter the plan to your needs."

Ninety days...Fuck. "What about the band?" We haven't recorded shit in months because I was too busy spiraling.

"It'll be here when you're better," Camden says.

"I can't ask you guys to put your lives on hold for me." They've been here for me for years, and all I've done is held them back every step of the way. I can't keep doing this to them. And what if I can't get better?

I glance down at my hands, which are shaking with need. Already craving the high. Even as we're discussing me getting help, I'm thinking about the drugs, the escape.

"You're not asking us to do anything," Declan says. "We're a band. The four of us. And unless we're all in this together, we're not doing shit."

I open my mouth to argue, but Easton speaks up before I can. "This is Roy."

He points at a gentleman I didn't notice was standing in the corner until now. "He'll hang out here until you're cleared by the doctor to leave." In other words, they're worried I might try to kill myself again, so they're making sure I'm not alone and given the opportunity.

I nod toward the man, who smiles sympathetically.

"And this is Bernadine Winters," Easton says when an older woman walks through the door, a warm smile on her face. She's accompanied by another woman, who's a bit younger and has a more serious expression. "She's from Changing Seasons, the private facility you'll be going to."

"Good morning," Bernadine says, stepping over to me and extending her hand to shake mine. "As Mr. Blackwood mentioned, I'm Bernadine Winters, and this is Pamela Finn, our resident psychiatrist who's been assigned to you. To get started, we have some questions we need to go over and paperwork that needs to be filled out. Are you up for that, Mr. Sharpe?"

"Yes," I tell her, ignoring the way my heart races in my chest because I'm craving the high I'm not getting at the moment. "I'm up for that."

After going over my situation with Bernadine and Pamela, I sign the papers, agreeing to voluntarily check myself into Changing Seasons mental health and drug rehab facility. They also go over the papers Easton's wife, Sophia, had them sign, such as NDAs and all the necessary shit to cover my ass. Once all the legalities are out of the way, I'm monitored for the next several days while the doctors ensure my overdose didn't create any issues with my kidneys, brain, liver, and heart. The cravings worsen, and thankfully, I'm given something to help curb them.

The day I'm cleared and discharged, my friends are there to see me off. With tears in their eyes, they hug and tell me they're rooting for me. But it's hard to look any of them in the eye, knowing I'm the reason for their stress. Without the drugs to fog my brain, the guilt I feel is stronger, more potent. They should be making music and enjoying their families, not dealing with my shit and my fuckups. And then a thought hits me, something Sadie mentioned when she was talking to me about her late husband. What if I get cleaned up, only to relapse? He swore several times he was pill-free when he wasn't. The thought of letting the guys down is too much, the weight nearly bringing me to my metaphorical knees.

"What's going through your head?" Pamela asks as we get into the Town Car.

I shake my head, and she frowns. "In order to help you, you're going to have to be honest with me. Otherwise, everything we're doing is pointless. So I'm going to ask you again. What's going through your head?"

"I'm afraid of letting them down." I nod toward my mini entourage of people watching us take off. So the paparazzi couldn't catch a glimpse of me, I was taken out through a private underground exit. "I'm afraid of failing them. I've failed so many damn people in my life," I admit. "I don't think I can handle failing them too...I mean, fuck, I already have, I guess." I think about my next words for a moment before I continue. "Can I make a request?"

"Sure," she says. "Can't be sure I can oblige, but you can always make a request."

"Aside from Easton being told I'm okay, I think it'd be best if nobody was able to call or visit." That way, they can move on the best they can. And if I fail them...I won't have to hear the disappointment in their voices...see it in their eyes.

Eight

SADIE

"JESUS EFFING CHRIST!" I THROW MY ARMS AROUND THE PORCELAIN BOWL, RETCHING INTO IT AS I CURSE bacon to hell. I love bacon and could eat it with everything. It's one of those foods that makes everything better. Mac 'n' cheese—yummy—but add bacon, and it's amazing. An egg and cheese sandwich is delicious, but add bacon, and it's perfection.

Bacon has only been my nemesis two times in my life—when I was pregnant. I've been avoiding it since the first time I threw up a few weeks ago and assumed I caught a bug, only for it not to go away after several days. But it's time I face the facts...During the deepest and darkest days of my grieving, I didn't think about birth control. It was irresponsible and stupid, but I just didn't have it in me to think logically. My only focus was getting through each day and praying for there to eventually be a light at the end of the tunnel.

Gage was obviously too high to think about it, and he probably assumed I was on something. He never asked, and it never crossed my mind...until now.

Once I'm almost positive I'm done throwing up, I wash out my mouth and brush my teeth, then head back into the kitchen to make a bacon-less egg and cheese sandwich. I'm mixing the eggs when something on the television catches my attention.

"In our dirt of the day, our sources have confirmed that Raging Chaos's drummer, Gage Sharpe, has been discharged from New York Medical after a recent overdose that our sources say was an attempt at ending his life..."

I rush over to the television to hear what she's saying, but she's already moved on to her next bit of gossip. Could it be? No, there's no way. There are a million Gages out there, right? What are the chances that...?

Grabbing my phone, I click on the internet and search Gage Sharpe, then click on the images, and sure enough, the gorgeous face of the man I spent almost three months with pops up. It's been over three months since I've seen him, but the moment my eyes land on his curly brown hair, broody blue eyes, that strong jawline, and the single brow—that's sporting a simple bar through it—quirked up, silently telling the world to fuck off, my belly does a quick flip-flop.

I drop onto the couch—my food forgotten—and spend hours learning everything I can about the mysterious man who carried me out of the cemetery and, in his own way, took care of me for months. Once I'm done, everything suddenly makes sense: the nice apartment, him not working, his roommates...Gage Sharpe is the drummer for Raging Chaos, one of the world's hottest rock bands...and he's also a drug addict.

My hand instinctually goes to my belly, knowing what I have to do. If what the news is saying is true, then Gage not only overdosed on drugs but he also did it with the intent of ending his life. I pray to God that he's okay and gets the help he needs, but I will do everything in my power to keep the little miracle growing inside me safe, including making sure Gage never finds out. I already lost two babies and a husband to drugs, and there's no way I'm going to let that happen again. I didn't protect my babies the way I should have last time, but I won't ever make that mistake again.

Nine

GAGE

Free time...

My life has become a routine of wash, rinse, repeat, but it's not a bad thing. I know what to expect, thrive on the structure and stability, and even revel in it. I haven't done a single drug in months, and my body recognizes that it's better because of it. But my brain...fuck, it still craves the high every goddamn day.

"I'm not ready," I tell Pamela, the woman who's been by my side every step of the way. From the first few weeks of hell during detox to the months I've spent trying to analyze every part of my life so I can go back into the real world and function like a normal adult. Only I feel like one of those animals who've been injured and saved, spent months getting rehabilitated, but because they've spent so much time there, they've become domesticated and wouldn't be able to survive in the wild.

"Why don't you believe you're ready?"

"Because I did drugs for six years, and I've only been drug-free for three months." The thought of going back into the wild scares the shit out of me and makes my heart race in my chest. We've been talking several times a day every day this week to help prepare me, but it's not fucking helping. I've had three anxiety attacks and had to be hospitalized because I thought I was having a heart attack.

"Gage, do you think it's possible you're scared because you've refused to speak to anyone outside of these walls? You're afraid of stepping back into a life you've only known while high?"

"Yeah," I agree, the lump in my throat forming. "That, and failing my friends, and then turning to drugs and then ending up right back here. I'm not ready."

I clutch my chest as it rises and falls in quick succession, feeling the stirrings of another anxiety attack. "What if I'm not the same guy they know? What if I can't play the drums and the band fails? What if I can play, and then we go on tour, and I'm back to craving the drugs?" I voice my concerns, the same ones I've expressed all week. "What if I walk out of here and I can't handle it? What if I go to the grave to see Tori, and the pain in my heart hurts so bad that I'm not strong enough to say no?"

Pamela opens her mouth to speak, but I cut her off. "And before you say that's what my sponsor's for, what if he's not there? What if I don't call him because I want to do the drugs?"

With every *what-if*, my heart pumps harder, my palms clutch tighter. Sweat beads across my forehead. "I'm scared," I tell her, not for the first time. "I can't fail them again. They're waiting for me to go back to making music and being their friend, and I'm fucking scared. Please," I beg. "I'm not ready. I need to stay longer."

She releases a soft sigh and nods in understanding, and I instantly calm. "Okay, here's what we're going to do..."

Ten

GAGE

SEVEN MONTHS LATER

AS I RUN DOWN THE SANDY BEACH, THE CHILLY SALT WATER LAPS AGAINST MY ANKLES AS THE WIND WHIPS around my face. It's November in Long Beach, so it's cold as fuck outside, but that doesn't stop me from going on my morning run. The cold air fills my lungs, reminding me that I'm alive.

When I arrived at the beach house after being discharged from Changing Seasons, I spent hours at the beach. Swimming in the ocean, watching the stars at night. Writing lyrics. Finding myself.

With my sponsor, Gabe, by my side, and Pamela doing sessions via video, it felt like I was taking baby steps. Not quite in the wild but not caged either. I hate that aside from a couple of texts, I haven't spoken to anyone, but I needed to focus on my healing. While on drugs, I didn't like the person I was, but without them, I didn't know who the hell I was. And I needed to figure that out on my own. Who I am without the band, without my friends. Without the ghosts of my mom and Tori hanging over my head. I'm still not quite there, but at ten months drug-free, I feel a hell of a lot closer.

A month ago, Gabe moved out, and we now talk daily on the phone. My calls with Pamela are also down to every other day. See...baby steps. Our last conversation was about if I've decided when I'm returning home...*if* I'm returning home. Pamela pointed out that I'm not the same person I was six years ago, and if being in a band is no longer what I'm interested in, the guys will understand.

But I'm not ready to give up the band just yet. And not because they've been waiting for me, but because before the drugs, I loved beating on those fucking drums, and I want a chance to see if I still love them. The only problem is, there's only one way to find out...I have to go home.

And I'm a fucking chickenshit.

I'm slowing to a light jog as I get closer to the house when I spot a woman leaning against the fence. She's wrapped up in a winter coat with a beanie on her head as she rubs her gloved hands together.

"Are you freaking crazy?" Kendall, Declan's wife and mother of his five-week-old twins, yells as I approach. "It's like thirty degrees out here."

She smiles warmly at me, and I pull her into a hug, realizing this is the first human contact I've had in months. "You look so good, Gage," she murmurs, kissing my cheek.

"Thank you. How are the babies?" I ask as we walk up to the house to get out of the cold. I was shocked to learn that Declan—after all the years of crushing on Kendall—finally got the girl. I was also so damn happy for him.

"Perfect. Amazing. Exhausting," she says with a laugh.

"They with you?"

She shakes her head. "I thought it would be best if I came alone."

When she texted me a couple of days ago, telling me that she got my number from Declan and he didn't know she was contacting me, she asked if she could come and see me.

"It's beautiful here," she says, staring out at the ocean. "I can see why you love it."

"I'm hiding," I admit. After she contacted me, I spoke to Pamela, and even without her saying it, I knew it was time to go home. "I needed more time, but I'm ready to go back."

I glance at her, and she smiles softly at me. "I thought you were going to make this hard on me. I even brought in the big guns." She nods behind me, and when I look back, I find Kaylee standing there with glassy eyes.

"Come here, you." I open my arms, and she rushes into my embrace. Over the years, since Tori died, we've remained in touch, despite her and Braxton parting ways for a while. And last year when we went on tour, and they reconnected, we grew close. Tori was her best friend, and she missed her like I did...like I do.

"I heard you got married." Despite not texting or talking to anyone, they continued to send me pictures and messages to keep me updated. They were what kept me going during the hard days, knowing they were living their best life, happy and finding love.

"We did," she gushes, hugging me tighter. "I miss you, Gage. We all do."

"I miss you guys too. I'm sorry it's taken me so long."

"No, no apologizing. We're just so happy to see you healthy. You look so good." Kaylee squeezes my bicep playfully. "And you're all muscular."

I laugh. "Yeah, well, when I'm not spending my days getting high or playing music, I have a lot of time on my hands."

"Speaking of which," Kendall says. "Are you...planning to play music again?" I can hear it in her voice, the concern. Not for me, though. For her husband. He's the reason she's here. Because I've been gone for so long, and the band has refused to play a single chord or sing a single lyric without me.

"I'm going to try," I tell her truthfully. "I can't promise anything, but I'm going to come home and take it one day at a time."

She smiles and nods. "Thank you. The guys have missed you so much."

We hang out for a bit longer and chat, the girls catching me up on everyone, and then they take off after I assure them that I'll be home for Thanksgiving.

I spend the day packing and getting my shit together. Since the apartment's no longer available, I agree to stay with Kaylee and Braxton while I figure out my next move.

Two days later, I arrive at the Blackwoods for Thanksgiving. When I walk through the door, I'm met with hugs and warm greetings. I thank everyone, but notice Declan is nowhere to be found.

"He fell asleep on the couch," Kendall says.

"Give me a few minutes," I tell everyone, needing some time with my friend. I'm close with all the guys, but Declan and I have always had a different connection. Maybe it was because Braxton and Camden found the women they wanted to spend their lives with, leaving Declan and me to bachelor it out together—him with his woman out of reach, and mine...well, she was also out of my reach.

The day I woke up in the hospital and saw the look in his eyes, then learned he's the reason I'm still alive, I'd never felt like more of a failure in my life. Had I not made it, he would've had to live with that guilt, and I promised myself I would never put someone I love in that position again.

"Am I dreaming?" Declan asks, his eyes fluttering open.

"As sweet as it is that you apparently dream about me..." I chuckle. "Nah, it's me, in the flesh."

"Where's everyone?" he asks, glancing around.

"Giving us a minute." I sit on the couch next to him. "I wanted to say I'm sorry. I shouldn't have stayed gone as long as I did, but I needed the time."

"What made you come back?"

"Your wife." I smile at him. "Congrats, by the way. Finally got the girl."

"Kendall?"

"Yeah, she came and saw me. Told me it was time to come home."

He smiles softly. "So where've you been? Why'd you stay away for so long?"

I drop back against the couch and turn my head to face him. "Where do I even begin?"

"How about at the beginning?"

And so, I do...I spend the next hour telling everyone where I've been and the journey I've been on to get here. Admitting that while I'm drug-free, I'm still scared as hell and unsure if I'll be able to play again, let alone tour.

When I'm done, Declan puts his hand on my shoulder and says, "All that matters is that you're here."

"Agreed," Braxton adds. "If the band doesn't ever play another song again, we don't give a fuck as long as you're healthy. You are all that matters."

"We're so damn glad to have you back," Camden says, hugging me. "The holidays wouldn't have been the same without you."

Every doubt I had about coming home evaporates as I glance around, taking in their words. I'm where I belong...with my family.

Eleven

GAGE

THREE MONTHS LATER

"YOU KNOW WHAT YOU NEED?" KAYLEE ASKS AS I STROLL INTO THE CONDO, DRIPPING IN SWEAT FROM MY morning run.

"No, but I'm sure you're going to tell me."

She ignores my sarcasm and hands me a bottle of water. Taking it, I give her a grateful smile and chug half of it down.

"To go out on a date."

I choke on the liquid, and she laughs, making me glare her way. "The last thing I need is to go on a date. A part of my program is—"

"Staying away from relationships," she finishes, rolling her eyes. "Yeah, I know, but that's only for a year, and it's been over a year now. There's nothing wrong with putting yourself out there. When's the last time you were with anyone?"

My thoughts go straight to Sadie. Her bleeding heart and broken soul. She was destroyed and damaged but still so strong. Strong enough to walk away from me after I did the worst thing I could do: push her away.

It was for the best because she deserved more than I could give her back then. Had she stayed, I might've brought her down with me. But that hasn't stopped me from thinking about her over the past year and a half. Once I was drug-free and could think straight, I spoke to Pamela about her, about the guilt I felt for what I did to her.

She asked if I wanted to reach out and apologize, but I didn't want to put her in that position, so instead, I had Easton do it for me. I told him to just make sure wherever she was, she was safe and taken care of. I didn't want to know anything except that she wasn't on the streets somewhere, and if she was, to make sure to get her off them. He got back to me a week later and said she moved to Virginia, was renting a home in a nice subdivision, and she looked good. Not happy, but okay.

"Gage?" Kaylee says, knocking me out of my thoughts. "It's okay to find happiness."

Her words take me back to the past, to Declan saying the same shit about

Sadie. In another lifetime, I would've scooped her up and held her close, keeping her for myself. But I wasn't capable of handling a woman like her with care. I think Kaylee and Declan are right...It's time for me to find some happiness. But right now, the only thing I want to focus on is the band. The guys have had my back, and it's my turn to have theirs.

"I know," I tell her. "And it'll happen when the time is right, but right now, the only happiness I'm after comes in the form of a drum kit." I give her a wink and stalk off to take a shower. Today is the first day the guys and I are back in the studio writing. If all goes well, we'll have our songs finalized in the next couple of weeks and then start recording. Our goal is to release the album this winter and tour next summer.

After taking a shower, I tell Braxton I'll see him at the studio and then go by the cemetery. I haven't been here since the day I OD'd, but with Sadie fresh on my mind, I figure it's time. Since it's been a while, I pick up flowers on my way for Tori, and at the last second, I grab two more small bouquets for Sadie's babies. With her living in Virginia, I imagine she isn't able to visit them the way she did during our time together.

After placing them into each of their holders, I have a seat in front of Tori. I can't believe it's been almost eight years. It's crazy how fast time flies. One minute, I was kissing her at the beach, and the next, I was so low I almost ended my life.

"This is the first time I've visited you sober," I say, hoping wherever she is, she can hear me. "I was lost for a while. The guilt over the way your life ended consumed me. But I know now that what happened wasn't my fault. It was that piece of shit's and your mother's, and I'll never forgive either of them."

I run my fingers through the grass, tugging on a few strands absentmindedly as I gather my thoughts. "While I was in rehab, I thought a lot about you. About children and teenagers in the same situation as you. Scared and feeling like they're alone in the world. For the past several years, instead of honoring your life, trying to right the wrong, I drowned in the injustice of the situation. But that's going to change.

"I'm starting a foundation called Tori's Angels, and it's going to help children and teens in the same situation as you have someone they can go to who will listen. I know now why you didn't tell me. I was too close to you, and you feared for what would happen to me, but had you had someone on the outside you could've gone to..." I choke up, my emotions getting the better of me. "Things could've been different."

Instead of leaving to go to the studio, I spend some time with Tori, catching her up on how everyone's doing—Cam and Layla are in parental bliss with Felix, their six-year-old, and Marianna, their one-and-a-half-year-old. Braxton and Kaylee are still in that honeymoon stage, where they're fucking like jackrabbits every night, which reminds me—I need to start looking for my own place. If I have to hear

Kaylee scream Braxton's name much longer, my ears might permanently bleed. And Declan and Kendall are so much in love that it's sickening to watch. Luckily, they're so busy with their six-month-old twins, Morgan and Nina, they don't have time to fuck like Kaylee and Braxton.

As I tell her about them, I can't help the way my heart swells in my chest, wishing I could have what they have. They've found love and family and aren't alone. I've craved to have all of that my entire life, and now that I'm sober and ready to move forward, I hope to find that one day.

When we're all caught up, I tell her I'll visit again soon and then take off to meet up with the guys. I'm both excited and nervous to be back. It's been years since I've done this sober, and I'd be lying if I didn't admit to being concerned. Luckily, I have my sponsor, Gabe, in case I feel the need to get high, and I'm planning to go to a meeting later today if we get done early enough—if not, I'll go to one tomorrow.

The second I step foot through Blackwood Records' doors, I'm met with Easton and Sophia standing by the front desk.

When she sees me, she comes straight for me, enveloping me in her warm embrace. She's always been the closest thing to a mother figure I've had, and since I've returned, she's been around a lot. She admitted to feeling guilty for not stepping up and forcing me to get help—not realizing just how bad it was—but I told her the same thing I told the guys and their wives. Nobody could've forced me to do shit. I had to hit rock bottom. And once I did, once I came too damn close to ending my life, I was ready to handle my shit and stand on my own two feet. And I'll be damned if I ever fall again.

"You look amazing," Sophia says, kissing my cheek. "Every time I see you, I swear you look even better, healthier. How could we not see it before?" She shakes her head, liquid filling her eyes. "I'll never forgive—"

"Stop," I say gently. "The only thing that matters is that I'm okay. Everyone having my back and being here...means the world to me." I look her in the eyes. "You guys are my family."

Before she can get even sappier, Easton speaks up. "The guys are already in the studio." He gives me a quick hug and pats my back. "Welcome back, son."

My heart races behind my rib cage as I walk into the studio where the guys are. This will be the first time in years that I'm writing, playing, and recording sober. One of my biggest fears is that the music will bring me back to my darkest days and have me craving the high. Then there's the fear that I won't be able to play the same, that being sober will fuck up the vibe, and I'll let the guys down.

Thankfully, the guys don't make a big deal about me being here. Camden tosses a water bottle my way, Braxton throws me a chin jut, and Declan smiles softly. And then we get started on our next album.

The days turn into weeks, and before we know it, we have enough songs to create an album. Everyone has their own way of doing shit, but for us, we'll spend anywhere from a few weeks to a couple of months practicing, recording, tweaking, and then finalizing every song. Then begins the other shit: photo shoots, the artwork, merch designs, deciding which songs will be the single, promoting the upcoming album, planning the tour, and the list goes on.

"I think we should start with 'Deep,'" Camden says, referring to one of the songs I wrote while in rehab. "It's emotional as hell, and my dad thinks we should consider it for the single."

"Sounds good," Braxton says, grabbing his guitar.

"I'm down," Declan agrees.

Slowly, I walk over to the drums, immediately recognizing them as my own and not the studio's.

"We figured you'd want your own," Camden says, sounding unsure.

"Thanks," I mutter.

Pulling my sticks out of my back pocket, I sit behind my kit and take a moment to get a feel for them. It's been a long-ass time since I've played, but the moment my foot presses the pedal and my sticks hit the drums, it feels as though the broken parts of me have been sewn together. I'm not perfect—never will be—but as we come together as a band for the first time in almost two years, I feel whole again.

"Fuck yes," Camden says when the song comes to a close. "This is going to be one helluva comeback album."

His words hit in the pit of my stomach. Had I not fucked up, there wouldn't need to be a damn comeback album.

As if the guys know exactly what I'm thinking, Declan says, "Don't go there. We all needed this break. Camden was busy having kids, and Braxton and I both got married. Kendall and I had twins. I would've wanted time at home with them anyway. We'd been hitting it hard for years, and all of us needed a break. This isn't on you."

Knowing they'll only argue if I point out that an almost two-year break wasn't what anyone intended, I simply nod, once again thankful that my friends have my back. They might not blame me, but I blame myself, and I'll do everything in my power to make sure this next album is the best one yet.

We're about to take it from the top when my phone goes off with a text from Kaylee: **When's the last time you spoke to Sadie?**

Me: Not since shit ended between us...Why?

I never told anyone what went down between us. Declan kind of knows since he was there the morning after—and I'm sure he's smart enough to put the pieces together—but he's never brought it up, and I know he wouldn't talk about it with anyone.

A picture comes through, along with a question: **Is this her?**

I zoom in on it and find myself staring at a smiling Sadie. Her red hair is up in a messy bun, and her eyes are bright, filled with happiness. My heart lurches in my chest at how much I've missed her. Even being as fucked up as I was back then, she still crawled into the crevices of my broken self and embedded herself under my skin. In the short time we spent together, I was reminded of what it was like to have someone to talk to, to share shit with. Most days were bad, so fucking bad, but some days were good.

I close my eyes, recalling how she would look at me and smile every once in a while. It was a sad as fuck smile but still filled with hope and promises of tomorrow. At the time, I wasn't capable of either one, but she was, and seeing how happy she looks now...While I hate the way I hurt her, I know I did the right thing for her.

Another picture comes through, this one of her with her head thrown back in a laugh. *Fuck, she's beautiful.* What I wouldn't give to hear her laughing. She will forever be the woman who got away.

Just as I'm about to confirm that the woman in the pictures is, in fact, Sadie, a third picture comes through that has me freezing in place. A little girl with curly red hair. She's standing next to Sadie, both of them smiling, as Sadie points at something in the distance. The little girl can't be more than a year old, which doesn't make sense since Sadie lost her son, unborn daughter, and husband, leaving her with no one.

"What's going on?" Declan asks.

"How old does she look to you?" I show him the picture.

"Is that Sadie?"

"Yeah. How old is the little girl?"

Camden walks over and glances over my shoulder. "Maybe ten months old, give or take..."

I do the math in my head. The number of months she'd have been pregnant. How long it's been since I've last seen her...That would make the baby roughly eight months. It's possible she met someone after me, but there's also the possibility that—

"Oh, shit," Declan murmurs, speaking my thought out loud. "Is she yours?"

I try to remember if we used protection, but I can't recall ever doing so. I never thought about condoms or if she was on birth control. I was too busy chasing my next high and getting lost in her.

"I don't know," I tell him, "but I'm about to find out."

Twelve

SADIE

TODAY IS VINCENT'S BIRTHDAY—HE WOULD'VE BEEN THIRTY-TWO YEARS OLD. IT'S BEEN EIGHTEEN MONTHS since I've visited my family. When I decided to move to Virginia to start fresh, I never planned to stay away as long as I did. But then I found out I was pregnant and then gave birth, and with every step forward, I couldn't bring myself to go backward...back to the cemetery where my family was buried, back to the heartache I endured. Back to where I left Gage and the jagged pieces of what was left of my heart.

Little by little, with every smile, every laugh, my daughter has helped bring life back to the vital organ in my chest, so I continued to move forward...for her...for us. It's not that I haven't thought about my family. I show her pictures of Collin every day, explain that he's her brother in heaven. She doesn't understand, but one day she will. She'll know that in the midst of all the chaos, she was the calm in my storm. That because of her, I was able to breathe again, *live* again. And so, I stayed away, not wanting to risk falling back down that hole filled with depression.

Until now.

Vincent's mom called and begged me to visit. She hasn't seen me since I left and would like to meet my daughter. When they found out about her, they were confused and upset, but over time, they became supportive. They aren't her grandparents, but they send her gifts and video chat with her as if they are. They love me like their own daughter and, by default, love my little girl as well.

Amidst the dark, my little girl brought light to all of us.

"All right, my little cherry pie." I lift my daughter into my arms and blow a raspberry into her neck, making her giggle. "It's time to get going."

"Ma, Ma, Ma." She shakes her head, trying to wiggle out of my arms. She's only recently started babbling what sounds like Mama, and I swear every time she does it, I want to give her the world. We've spent the morning at A Latte Fun, an indoor playground for kids. I'm hoping to wear her out so when we go to the cemetery, she'll sleep through it. I'm unsure of how being there will hit me, and the last thing I want is for her to see me crying.

"We have to go," I tell her, holding her tighter as I walk us toward the door so I can change her diaper and get our shoes on. "We'll come back again." After changing her diaper, I set her on the cushioned seat and hand her a sippy cup so she can get something to drink while I get her shoes on. Once she's ready to go, I open the stroller and buckle her in, then get my shoes on.

As I'm pushing the stroller out the door, I pull out my phone to let my in-laws know I'm on my way and will meet them at the cemetery when the stroller gets stuck on something. I set the phone into the cup holder and am preparing to get it over whatever hump it's caught on, but when I look up, I realize it's not stuck on anything. It's been stopped...by Gage.

Fuck.

He raises a single brow, the brow with a metal bar going through it from top to bottom, and his eyes pierce into mine. I stumble back slightly, taken aback. I don't remember a lot from our short time together, but I could never forget his eyes, the way they were dimmed and lifeless. Only now, they're bright and filled with life and...hurt...hurt with a mixture of hardness to them, and I know in my gut, somehow, he *knows*.

My thoughts are confirmed when his gaze descends, landing on my daughter. His eyes soften as he takes her in. She's completely unaware of what's happening, babbling away and slamming her pacifier against the tray while she scoops up Cheerios with her other hand.

"Is she—?"

His words are cut off by a woman trying to get by. "Excuse me," she says, annoyance laced in her tone, and it's then I realize we're still standing in the middle of the doorway.

"I'm sorry," I tell her.

Gage backs up, and I push the stroller through, exiting onto the busy sidewalk. People in a rush skate around us as I move to the side before someone trips over the stroller.

I can feel Gage's eyes on me the entire time, watching, assessing. It's been a year and a half since I've seen him, and while he looks like the same man I walked out on, he also looks different. Healthier. But that's always the case with addicts, right? They're up, and then they're down...I saw it over and over again with Vincent. He would be up, on top of the world, making promises, and then he would fall, taking all those promises with him. Until the last time, when he not only took all his promises but also our son with him.

The thought has me needing to get as far away from Gage as possible. Away from his addiction. His ups and downs. But before I can make my escape, he's stepping in front of the stroller, putting his hand on the handlebar and blocking me in.

"Is she mine?" he asks, cutting straight to the chase, his eyes locking with mine.

"She's mine." I jut my chin out in defiance. "Now, if you'd please move, I have somewhere I need to be."

Only he doesn't move. He stands there, in my way, his gaze flitting between my daughter and me. "I know she's yours," he finally says. "She has your beautiful red hair and fair skin. That's not what I asked. Is. She. Mine?"

I know what he asked...what he's asking. But I can't bring myself to say what he needs me to say. It's my job to protect her, to keep her safe, and I can't do that if he has access to her. I already failed my son. I can't fail my daughter too. So despite Gage already knowing the answer, I say the only thing I can say. The only words that will come out of my mouth. The only answer that will protect my little girl, keep her out of harm's way, and ensure that her fate isn't the same as my son's—her lifeless body buried six feet under because I trusted an addict who made promises he couldn't keep.

"She's mine and only mine," I tell him as I pry his fingers from the stroller's handlebar.

"Sadie," he growls, refusing to let me go. "She has my blue eyes and curly hair. Are you going to deny that she's mine?"

"Don't do this. Please, Gage," I choke out, my emotions getting the better of me. "Please don't do this. I...I have to protect her. She's my entire world. Please, let me walk away. Whatever you think you know, just...for her sake, let it go...Let us go."

Gage's eyes widen, and he steps closer to me. "You want me to forget that I have a daughter? A daughter you didn't tell me about? Are you serious right now?"

"Yes...Yes, I'm serious. You're...an addict," I hiss, trying like hell to remain strong. "Do you not remember how she was conceived? What happened *after* she was conceived? I'm trying to protect Rory, and I can't do that with you coming around. So please—"

"Rory?" he asks.

"What?"

"You said Rory. Is that her name?" His face softens as he glances down at her.

"It's what I call her, but her name is Aurora. The name means dawn, like a new day. And that's what she is for me: a new day, a fresh beginning," I choke out, tears filling my lids. "Gage, please." I place my hand on his chest. "She's taken care of and loved and...safe. Please don't do this. Don't ask to be a part of her life and risk hurting her."

Up until now, Rory has been quiet, munching away on her Cheerios and distracted by the passersby, but she must've had enough because she screeches, blubbering out, "Ma, Ma, Ma," grabbing both Gage's and my attention.

With the heat of his stare on me, I reach down and unbuckle her, pulling her into my arms. Her head goes to my shoulder, silently indicating that she's tired and ready for a nap. "I already buried two babies," I tell him. "One because a man couldn't stay away from drugs. I can't do that again. I'm not asking you for anything.

I haven't asked for a penny. I just want to love her and keep her safe." I lay a soft kiss to the back of her head, inhaling her sweet baby scent. "Please. Do the right thing and let me go...let *us* go."

Gage's eyes redden slightly, filled with unshed tears, and I hate myself for asking him to walk away from his daughter, but I have to put my daughter first. I have to protect her at all costs, even if that means keeping her from the man who helped create her.

When he doesn't say anything back, I take that as my answer, and before he can change his mind, I grab the stroller with one hand and push it back onto the sidewalk, needing to get away from him as quick as possible.

I don't look back, don't stop until I get to the train station, and the entire time, I don't think about the guilt trying to catch up with me. I refuse to feel guilty for protecting my daughter. I'm doing what's best for her, keeping her safe. That's what a mother does, and that's what I'll always do until my last breath. I might not have been able to do that for Collin and wasn't given the chance to do that for Rebekah, but I will succeed with Rory. At least Gage didn't argue with me about it. Despite knowing she's half his, he let me go. He heard my pleas and did what was best for her—let us go.

"Oh, Sadie," Janice says when we walk up, pulling me into a hug. "It's so good to see you." She kisses my cheek, then looks down at Rory, who's back in her stroller fast asleep. "I know this is hard for you, but thank you for coming."

We walk over to the three graves, and seeing my babies' names hits me straight in the heart. I'll always grieve for Vincent, but over the years, my sadness for him has turned into anger. He's the reason our little boy died. He put his habit before Collin and took him down with him. Now, he's not here to mourn the loss of our son or feel the pain I feel every day. I would never express my feelings to Janice and Henry since he's their son, and it's not their fault he had a drug problem, but it doesn't stop me from feeling the way I do.

"It seems someone left flowers," Janie says when she goes to put small bouquets into the holders. Vincent's is the only one empty, so she places one bouquet into his. "Did you already come by?" she asks.

"No." I glance over at the nearby grave where Gage visited and notice the same flowers there as in my babies' holders. It's too much of a coincidence...It had to be Gage. He knows I haven't been here, so he left flowers for my babies. The thought has me pressing my hand to my chest and rubbing at the ache forming there.

We spend some time at the graves. Janice reminisces about Vincent, noting only the good memories she has of her son. I join in occasionally, but mostly leave her to it, knowing she really just needs us to be here with her. Vincent was their only child, and the day they lost him, like me, they lost their entire world.

When she's all cried out, she wipes her eyes and asks if I'd like to join them for dinner. I'm about to take her up on it when the sound of the footsteps crunching on the grass catches my attention, and my eyes meet Gage's.

"I'd like to spend a little longer here, if that's okay," I tell her. "Maybe we can meet for breakfast tomorrow? We don't leave until the afternoon."

She eyes Gage curiously but nods. "That would be great. I'd love to spend some time with Aurora when she's awake."

With a kiss and a hug from each of them, they head down the sidewalk, leaving Gage and me alone.

"We have to stop meeting like this," he says.

"Like what?" I ask, confused.

"You know..." He nods toward the graves. "At a cemetery."

"You left flowers." I don't have to explain what I'm referring to—he already knows.

"I did. Yesterday. Those people who were with you mentioned you moved away, so when I returned, after being gone for the past year, and came to visit Tori, I brought your babies flowers too."

"You were gone for over a year?" After it was in the news that he overdosed, trying to take his life, he pretty much dropped off the face of the planet.

"Yeah, I was in rehab," he confirms, "and then spent some time away...after I tried to kill myself."

"I'm glad you're...okay."

He steps toward me. "I'm more than okay. I'm sober and drug-free. Haven't touched anything in fourteen months." He glances down at a still sleeping Rory and smiles softly. "I fucked up so damn badly with you, and I am so sorry. I was at my lowest..." He shakes his head. "I can't take back what I did, and I never intended on contacting you because I know I hurt you, but then Kaylee texted me a picture of you and our little girl and..."

"She's mine," I repeat. "Not yours, *mine*. I don't care about you fucking up. I knew you were an addict when I met you, but I was grieving. I will forever be grateful to you for taking me in when I was grieving and needed a safe place to stay and giving me Aurora. But what we had..." I choke out. "It was nothing more than two fucked-up, broken people getting lost in each other. I don't want or need your apologies or anything from you. I just want you to leave me alone. Let me raise my baby and take care of her."

"I get that," he says. "But I'm not the same guy you met back then. I'm sober and healthy now, and I can't just let you walk away with *our* daughter while I turn a blind eye and pretend she doesn't exist. I get why you didn't tell me. I was beyond fucked up back then, in no place to father a child, and you did what my mother never did...You protected our daughter." He reaches out and slides his knuckles down my cheek. "But I'm here now, and I want a chance to get to know her, to be the father she deserves."

I step back out of his touch. "No."

"No?"

"No," I repeat. "I won't do this again. I won't put her in harm's way. I've been there, done that, got the graves to prove it, and I won't risk her life. I learned the hard way that when I'm up against drugs, I lose every damn time. It's too late for my son, but I can still protect Aurora."

"I'm sober," he says again. "I go to meetings several times a week. I haven't touched a drug in fourteen months, I swear. I just want a chance..."

I bark out a humorless laugh. "You don't think I've heard all this before? I was married to the King of Chances. Gave him chance after freaking chance. No! No, no, no! I'm all out of chances."

I grab the handle of the stroller and am about to walk away when Gage grips my bicep gently but strong enough to prevent me from leaving. "I know this is hard for you, but I can't let you walk away. That little girl is mine too."

"What are you trying to say?" I ask, twirling around and removing myself from his grip.

"I'm saying that I want to be in her life, and I'm asking that you give me a chance to be her dad, please. I don't want to take this to court..."

"Fuck you! I don't care who you are. I don't care that you're some famous drummer for some popular band or that you're worth millions of dollars. My job is to protect her!"

"And I love that you want to do that," he says, keeping his calm. "All I'm asking is to be given the chance to get to know her. Please, Sadie. I don't want to fight, and I'm not trying to take her away from you. I just want to see my daughter."

I stare at Gage as his eyes bore into mine, begging, pleading, and my heart drops into my belly, knowing that I'm going to have to give in. I might be able to keep him away temporarily, but if he goes to court and proves he's sober, they'll give him rights to her because he is her father. And what if he tells them I kept her away, and they try to punish me? The thought of my little girl being taken from me has the blood in my veins turning cold.

"Fine. You can see her."

Gage sags in relief. "Thank you. When?"

"Today, I guess. Since we leave tomorrow."

His brows furrow. "Sadie, I don't just mean once. I want a relationship with her."

"I get that, but we live in Virginia, so unless you're moving there, it will have to be done over the phone. We have an entire life there. A home...I have a boyfriend." More like a guy I'm kind of, barely dating, but I don't mention that.

"I...I can't just move to Virginia," he says, dragging his fingers through his hair. "The band is recording..."

"If making music is more important than seeing your daughter, then that's your problem." I know I sound like a bitch, but I'm not the one with the drug problem who fucked me and then fucked those other women while he was high. He's the one who pushed me away. He's the reason I moved to Virginia. And I'm not about to make this easy on him. I made shit easy on Vincent and look where it got me. Never again.

"No, it's not," he finally says, sounding defeated. "I'll figure something out. Where are you staying?"

"At the W."

"The one near Bryant Park?"

"Yeah."

"That's near me," he says. "If you want, we can go there and order in dinner. Then once Aurora wakes up, we can spend some time with her. There's a park nearby that Kendall and Layla take the kids to."

"Who?" I ask, confused.

"Layla and Kendall...They're the wives of Declan and Camden, my friends and bandmates. I think you met Declan, right?"

"Yeah, and Braxton and Kaylee as well."

"They're good people." He smiles softly. "Anyway, the studio is near Bryant Park, so they take them to the park there a lot."

"Okay. Yeah, we can do that."

We walk through the cemetery in silence, and when we get to the end of the sidewalk, a man rounds the front of the SUV and opens the back door.

"I have a stroller," I say to Gage.

"It can go in the back."

"Her car seat is at the hotel."

"Oh, shit...I mean, shoot. Umm..." He looks around like he's hoping a car seat will suddenly appear out of thin air.

"Just meet us there," I tell him. "I need to change and feed her anyway, and when she wakes up, she's cranky, so she'll need a few minutes."

"That's okay. I can walk with you guys."

The guy standing there clears his throat.

"This is Paul. He's part of our security team."

I nod toward the tall, muscular man, who's the same height as Gage—and with the muscles Gage has added since the last time I saw him, pretty much the same size as well—confused.

"He keeps the paparazzi in line," Gage notes. "We generally don't walk anywhere or take the trains because it can get crazy when a fan recognizes us. It happens here less frequently than in LA, but with me showing my face again and the band announcing that we're back in the studio, it's been a little hectic lately."

"Okay...Well, I'm not going to run with our daughter, so just meet me at the hotel. I'm staying in room 252."

And with that, I walk away, stroller in hand, wishing I never came back here, praying Gage really is sober, and hoping he doesn't destroy my entire world.

Thirteen

GAGE

I HAVE A DAUGHTER. A BLUE-EYED, RED-HAIRED, FAIR-SKINNED, BEAUTIFUL LITTLE GIRL. SHE LOOKS LIKE THE spitting image of her mother, except she has my eyes and curly hair. I don't know anything else about her, though. Her likes, dislikes, when her birthday is... Nothing. But that's going to change. I never imagined having kids, especially not after...

Fuck, I just can't believe it. When Kaylee sent me the image, I knew deep down she was mine. But I was hoping I was wrong. Because if she was right, that would mean while I was getting high, overdosing, and spending months in rehab, Sadie was growing a baby we created in her, giving birth, and raising our daughter alone.

Because I fucked up. I pushed away the first woman I'd connected with in years. I got scared and did the unforgivable. I fucked two women in my living room, knowing Sadie would see. Knowing it would hurt her, and she would walk away from me. I couldn't even tell you what either of them looked like or what their names were. I remember nothing but the look on Sadie's face when she walked out and saw what was taking place. The hurt in her eyes has haunted me for months. It's the reason I didn't look her up or go after her once I was sober. Because she deserves better than what I did to her.

God, it now feels like forever ago, another lifetime, but that's how life works. I might be sober now, but the effects...the consequences of my shitty choices will continue to darken my door. Although is it really a consequence when the result is that beautiful baby girl?

And Sadie...Goddamn, she looks good...*gorgeous*. She was on the skinny side when I found her at the cemetery because she wasn't eating properly. She was beautiful but sad—eyes glassy and features etched with devastation. Now, she looks happy. Her eyes were clear and bright. Every time she'd look at our daughter, she got this twinkle in her eye. She was meant to be a mom.

And a wife. When she told me she was in a relationship, I wanted to punch something. Of course, she's with someone. I barely know her, and even I know she's the whole damn package. The thought of some other guy spending time with my daughter makes me feel sick. Him stepping in and playing daddy...Do they live together? Does my daughter think he's her dad? Are there family photos of them hanging on the walls? After they put Aurora to bed, does he take Sadie to their room and get lost in her?

When we were together sexually, it wasn't about attraction with her. It was about the escape and losing ourselves in one another. I was too high to fully appreciate her body or treat her the way she deserved. But now...she's got curves for days. If I were given another chance, I would take my time and worship every damn inch of her.

I shake those thoughts from my head. She's with someone now. I lost my chance. I chose drugs over her, and that's my punishment: to have to look at her every day, knowing we created a beautiful little girl and we'll never be a family. At least it's not too late for me to be a part of Aurora's life. I don't blame Sadie for keeping her from me. She did what she felt was best, given the situation and her past, but shit has changed. I'm sober and have every intention of being a father to my daughter. I grew up without a dad, and I'll be damned if my daughter does the same.

Kaylee: Is she yours?

I add Kendall, Layla, Braxton, Camden, and Declan to the chat so I don't have to repeat myself.

Me: Sadie's daughter is mine. Her name is Aurora...She calls her Rory, and they've been living in Virginia. She's leaving tomorrow to go back. I'm going over there now to spend some time with them.

Kaylee: I can't believe she kept her from you!

I never told anyone what happened that night, the last night I saw Sadie, but now I have to because I can't have my friends hating the mother of my daughter.

Me: I deserved it. Sadie lost her son and husband when he drove while high and got into a car accident. I found her mourning their deaths (along with the baby girl she miscarried the day before their accident). I brought her to my apartment and spent months with her. When Braxton told us he was moving in with you, Declan asked if Sadie and I were getting serious. I got scared and brought two women home. While I was high on heroin and coke and pills and whatever the fuck else I had taken that night, I fucked them in the living room. Sadie saw and walked away. She had to save herself, and I'll never blame her for that. When she found out she was pregnant, she made the decision not to tell me about Aurora because she was doing what a mother should do...protecting our daughter from me. Do not hate her for that. I don't. Now, I have to prove to her that I'm capable of being a father to our daughter.

A few minutes go by before the texts flood in...

Kaylee: I'm sorry. I didn't know. ((hugs))

Declan: You're not the same person you were back then.

Braxton: We're here for you...

Camden: You're going to be a good dad.

Layla: I respect what she did. I would've done the same thing.

Kendall: If you need anything, please let us know.

Me: Thank you. I'll let you know how it goes. Just got here.

Paul pulls around back so I can take the private entrance up to Sadie's floor. Once we're at the door, I tell him I'll give him a call when I'm ready to go. When Sadie opens the door, the sleeping baby is now awake, attached to her hip, her blue eyes, identical to mine, looking at me curiously.

"Thank you for letting me come over."

Sadie nods. "I'm sorry for being so...mean earlier. I—"

"You don't owe me anything, least of all an apology," I say, cutting her off. "You're hurt and scared, and I deserved everything you said. The fact is, we barely know each other, but we share a daughter, and I'd like to get to know you both. I know I have a lot to prove, but I'm hoping you'll give me the chance."

She sits on the couch with Aurora, who drops her head onto her mom's shoulder and eyes me shyly yet curiously while I sit in the chair across from them.

"I can't believe we have a daughter," I muse, unable to take my eyes off her. "Can you tell me about her? What's her middle name? When's her birthday?" There's so much I want to know, and I feel like I don't have enough time. It's already almost dinnertime, and they leave in the morning.

"Her middle name is Rebekah...Aurora Rebekah Sharpe, but as I mentioned before, I usually call her Rory for short."

When she says her name, Aurora pops her head up, giving her mom an adorable toothy little smile. "Mama." She presses her tiny hands to either side of Sadie's face and places a loud, wet kiss on her nose, making Sadie laugh and my heart jump straight the fuck out of my chest.

"Aw, you give me kisses?" Sadie asks, her voice soft and filled with love. It makes me wonder if my mom ever spoke to me like that. The only memories I have are of her crying. She was always sad and down, never could get ahead. When I was old enough to understand how rough shit was, I can remember thinking that one day I would make enough money that she would finally be able to smile. Never got the chance, though.

Aurora answers Sadie's question by giving her another kiss before she scrambles down and plops onto the ground, crawling over to a bin of toys.

"She'll be one on May fourth," Sadie says, her eyes following Aurora as she dumps a bunch of toys out and grabs one, bringing it straight to her mouth. When she seems entertained, Sadie turns her attention back to me. "Rebekah was—"

"Your baby girl," I finish, recalling the name of the baby she lost. It's on the gravestone, and even though I was high all the damn time back then, I remember her telling me about her.

"Yeah," she says softly. "I wanted to honor her since she never had the chance to be part of this world."

"It's beautiful and perfect. And you gave her my last name?"

Pink tints her cheeks. "I did...I wanted so badly to tell you about her, but I was just so scared. When I saw on the news that you overdosed and almost died." She swallows audibly. "I just couldn't do it," she breathes, tears filling her eyes. "I kept imagining what happened to Collin, happening to her, and..."

"Stop," I tell her, crossing over to the couch and pulling her into my arms. "I hate that I missed out on the first ten months of her life and that you went through your pregnancy and giving birth without me, but you did the right thing. I'm clean now, but it was a long-ass road to get here. I'd like to think had I known about her, I would've gotten clean quicker, but there's no way of knowing."

Sadie looks up at me, and I thumb away the straggling tears resting on her cheeks. "I was so lonely and tired," she admits, breaking my heart. "So many times, like when Rory was in the NICU, and I was scared, or when I brought her home, and she was up all night crying, and I wasn't sure what was wrong, I wanted to reach out and tell you just so I wouldn't be so alone, but the fear of what could happen if you showed up high was too strong."

"I'm so fucking sorry," I rasp, hating myself for putting her in that position, for not being the guy she needed and could count on back then. I've failed so many damn people in my life but letting Sadie and our daughter down hits the deepest because she's already been hurt and let down, and when she needed someone the most, I not only pushed her away but inadvertently pushed my daughter away as well.

"She came eight weeks early and spent two weeks in the NICU while her lungs finished developing," she says, once she's gotten ahold of herself. Backing up slightly, she pulls her phone out of her back pocket and scrolls for a few seconds before turning it around so I can see what's on the screen.

"That's her?" I ask, taking in the tiny little human with wires all over her, lying in a rectangular glass container.

"Yep. Four pounds, one ounce." She flips to the next picture of her holding Aurora. The woman in the photo is filled with exhaustion, black circles under her eyes, but there's also a soft smile of happiness there. The next several photos are of Aurora getting older: smiling, laughing, crying. Sitting up, crawling...It's insane how in only ten months, she's transformed from an itty-bitty little thing to a crawling, babbling, laughing baby.

"She's put on some weight," I say with a laugh when she flips to a picture of Aurora in the bathtub, bubbles covering her lower half and the top half filled with adorable baby rolls. Kendall and Declan's babies have them too. Declan always jokes, saying they eat too much even though they're both breastfeeding.

"Did you breastfeed?" I ask. It doesn't matter either way, but I want to know everything. I hate that I won't know unless I ask, but I did this to myself.

"I did. She actually recently weaned off, and her pediatrician said since she's so close to a year old and healthy, she can go straight to milk and regular food. She loves sweet potatoes and carrots and hates anything green." She laughs, putting her phone away as Aurora crawls over with a cup of some sort in her mouth.

She pulls herself up and hands it to Sadie. "Mamamama."

"She also loves stacking things and knocking them over," Sadie says, taking the cup from her daughter and then picking her up. She walks over to where Aurora just was and plops down, setting her in her lap.

I watch as Aurora helps Sadie stack the cups, one on top of each other. When they place the last one, Sadie cheers and claps, and Aurora joins in, just before swinging her fist and knocking them all to the ground. For a second, she stares at them, then she looks up at me and giggles. Fucking giggles. And my heart—my bleeding, battered, blackened heart—comes back to life.

As I'm frozen in place, Aurora grabs a cup, bites down on it, and crawls over to me, stopping just before me and dropping it into my lap.

"She's sharing with you," Sadie says softly, snapping me out of it.

"Thank you," I say awkwardly. Aside from chilling with Felix, Layla and Camden's six-year-old, I don't have much experience with kids, especially not with babies. I'm around Declan and Kendall's twins, but I haven't interacted with them much. They're around six months old and just now trying to crawl. They do this weird rocking back and forth thing that makes them look like little turtles trying to take off. It's kind of hilarious.

"Baba!" Aurora yells when I don't move.

"She wants you to build the tower," Sadie explains, a hint of a smile on her face.

"Oh, all right. Sure." I take the cups from Sadie and start to build the cup tower while Aurora watches with a glint in her eye, silently conveying she's about to cause destruction. The second I set the last cup on the top, she claps, not stopping until I join in.

I watch as she makes sure I'm clapping and excited before she swipes her hand out and sends the tower to the ground, cups flying every which way. Her eyes meet mine, and she giggles that fucking giggle, and once again, my heart feels as though it's been resuscitated.

"Baba!" she squeals, grabbing a cup.

"She could do it a million times," Sadie says, playfully rolling her eyes when I take the cups and start stacking them again. "You don't have—"

"I've missed out on ten months," I say, not allowing her to finish her thought.

"If she wants me to build this tower a hundred times, I'm okay with that." Our eyes connect, and Sadie nods in understanding.

And that's how we spend the evening: building towers and knocking them over until Aurora is hungry and starts to whine. Sadie feeds her some baby food while I order us dinner. And once it arrives, Aurora eats some more. She reminds me of an adorable little bird as she opens her mouth, and Sadie feeds her little bits of her food. As I watch the two of them sitting across from me, for the first time in years, my heart feels so damn full. Wanting to take a few photos of my daughter, I pull my phone out and snap a few pictures of them eating and laughing.

When Sadie sees what I'm doing, she turns Aurora around and says, "Say cheese." Aurora obviously doesn't say that, but she does giggle, which is even better. I take another picture, then switch it to video so I can capture the sound, knowing when I'm back home and alone, and they're over seven hundred miles away, it'll be the only thing I'll have of my daughter to get me through until the next time I can see her.

Fourteen

GAGE

WHEN IT'S TIME FOR HER BATH, SINCE SADIE DOESN'T KICK ME OUT, I STAY AND WATCH, MEMORIZING EVERY babble, every giggle, dreading the moment when they leave to go back to Virginia.

Sadie lets me participate in Aurora's bedtime routine by reading her favorite book to her and explains that she usually goes to sleep earlier at home, but being here has thrown her off a little bit. Not being at home in her room has messed up their structured routine.

"Can I come visit?" I ask once Aurora is fast asleep in her portable crib.

"Gage..." Sadie sighs, shaking her head. "I...I don't..."

"I know," I say, not needing her to finish. "This is all a lot to take in. I get that, and I know you have a boyfriend, but fuck..." I glance at the sleeping beauty who's half mine. "I want a chance to get to know her."

Sadie's eyes fill with liquid as she nods. "Can we please just take this slow? She doesn't know you, and it's just all so unexpected."

"Yeah, of course," I say, willing to agree to anything that will get me time with my daughter. And then a thought hits me. "Does your boyfriend...?" I clear the emotion from my throat. "Does Aurora think he's her dad?" I choke out.

Sadie's eyes go wide. "No." She shakes her head to emphasize her answer. "No, he's never even met her."

I sigh in relief.

"We only recently started dating, and I didn't want to bring her around him unless we were serious. My best friend from college, Sarah, lives in Virginia, which is why I moved there. She's married with two kids, busy running her own spa. When I first moved there, I didn't know I was pregnant, but it worked out. Rory is close to the same age as her youngest, so sometimes, she'll watch her so I can have some alone time." She shrugs. "Between working full time and Rory, it's easy to forget to make time for myself."

Speaking of which..."How are you on money?"

She narrows her eyes, and I quickly raise my hands, waving the metaphorical white flag. "Sadie...It's obvious you take care of our daughter just fine, but the last time I saw you, you were homeless."

She sighs and nods in understanding. "I wasn't homeless. I just didn't want to go home. It was the last place I saw my family alive, and it was too hard. After you..." She clears her throat, ready to skip over what I did, but one of the most important parts of recovery is facing what I've done, so before she can continue, I finish the sentence for her.

"After I brought two women home and had sex with them in the living room."

Her eyes fill with hurt. "Yeah," she whispers.

"Sadie..."

"Gage, I don't really want to go there. We weren't together, and you didn't owe me anything."

"Maybe not, but what I did was still wrong. There were a million other ways I could've pushed you away, but I chose the one that would hurt you the most."

"Why would you want to hurt me?" she asks, her voice small.

This isn't exactly the way I want to end my time with her, but it's a conversation that needs to be had...One she deserves.

"The reason I had a drug problem was because my high school girlfriend committed suicide...and I'm the one who found her."

Her eyes go soft, and she moves closer to me. "I'm so sorry."

"She had been lashing out for a while, but she wouldn't talk to me. After she died, I found a note from her that said her stepdad had been raping her for months. He was threatening to send her away and hurt me. She had tried to tell her mom, but she wouldn't listen. It all became too much, and she felt the only way out was to end her life."

"That's horrible."

"It was. My mom was murdered when I was twelve in a motel room where she was prostituting. They claimed it was an accidental overdose, but I'd seen her pimp shoot her up too many times. When Tori died, I felt like I failed her and my mom, so to cope, I started using.

"The band took off for LA, and we quickly hit it big. The next several years were a whirlwind of recording and touring. The guys tried to get me help several times, but I wasn't ready. I was a functioning addict."

She nods in understanding but doesn't say anything, letting me explain.

"When I met you, I was teetering on the edge. While we were together, I toned it down a bit, getting lost in you. It had been so long since I connected with another person that I craved you more than the drugs...just barely.

"The night you found me with those women, Braxton announced he was officially moving out and in with Kaylee, and Declan asked if you and I were getting serious and if I planned to move you in or get our own place.

"Realizing how close we'd gotten scared the shit out of me. I had already failed my mom and Tori, and you had lost so much. I knew I wasn't in a place to take care of you like you deserved, so I went out and got fucked up, then brought those women back, knowing once you saw them, it would push you away."

Her pouty lips curve into a small frown, and I hate myself all over again for what I did. "I was using heavy shit, Sadie. Heroin and coke...I don't even remember that night, to be honest. But when I woke up and found your letter, enough surfaced for me to put the pieces together. The day you walked away began my downward spiral, ending with me hitting rock bottom."

"The overdose," she whispers.

"Yeah. It all just became too much. I was missing you and hating myself for what I did to you. I went to the cemetery and visited Tori...and I just..." I shake my head, the words failing me.

"Did you mean to overdose?"

"Yeah, I did," I admit. "It was a moment of weakness, but that's all it takes. Declan found me, and they saved my life. I checked into rehab and spent the next ten months getting sober."

Her brows shoot up. "Ten months?"

"Ninety days in rehab, then seven months in isolation with my sponsor and therapist. I needed time to figure my shit out. I'd spent so long being high, I wasn't sure how the hell to function sober and clean."

I pull my keys out and show her my most recent chip. "It's glow in the dark." I shrug. "One year clean." I flip to the other one I keep on my keys. "One day at a time."

"I'm so proud of you, Gage," she says, placing her hand on mine that's holding the tags.

"Thank you." I sniff and place the keys back in my pocket. "A part of recovery is going to meetings and seeing a therapist, but another part of it is facing the shit I did while I was high, which includes facing what I did to you. I know it's going to take time for you to trust me, but I'm going to work every day to earn it. To show you I'm not that guy."

"I hope so," she says, her voice wobbly. "Vincent swore so many times he was clean, and I know you aren't him, but you have to understand that drugs are a hard limit for me, so trusting you is going to be extra hard."

"And I'll just have to work extra hard to earn your trust," I tell her. "Now, you were saying...After I hurt you and you left, you went home?"

"Yeah. I went home and finally mourned. I cried and cried until all the tears dried up. Then I cleaned out the house and put it up for sale, only keeping some of Collin's things, like pictures he drew and photos I took...I gave Vincent's parents his stuff since I didn't want any of it.

"The day I learned who you were from the news running the story of you overdosing, I also learned I was pregnant. I was already living in Virginia and renting a two-bedroom home, living off the little bit I made from the sale of the house. Between that and the savings we had put away, I could afford to be home with Rory. But I love working, so recently, I started working again. I'm an editor, so I can work from home. I do it when Rory is napping and after she goes to bed. It keeps me busy and stops my brain from turning to mush."

"You're amazing," I tell her, meaning that wholeheartedly. She was at her lowest, lost her entire world, and managed to turn her life around all on her own.

"I don't know about that," she says shakily.

"You are." I take her hands in mine. "Thank you...for being the mother and father Rory needed. I promise you, from today forward, I'll be there in any way I can be. I know you don't need the money, but I'm going to pay you for back child support." She opens her mouth to argue, but I don't let her speak. "Please. She's my daughter too, and I want to take care of her. It's bad enough I won't be able to see her every day. Please let me at least do this."

She swallows thickly and nods. "Okay. And to answer your earlier question, yes, you can come visit. Just...please don't make me regret it."

Fourteen

BONUS SCENE

GAGE

to sleep."

"Everything okay?" I ask, drinking my own coffee.

"Yeah, I think her nap ran too late, so she wasn't tired...at all." She mock glares at Rory, who's eating her Cheerios and drinking her milk without a care in the world.

"Why don't you go take a shower, baby-free, and I'll keep an eye on Rory while you get ready? I was thinking we could take her to the park."

At the word park, Rory's ears perk up. "Pa pa!"

"Umm," Sadie says, looking nervous. "I can just bring her in the bathroom with me..."

"Sadie," I tell her, placing my hand on her arm. "I'm not going to leave this house with her." I pull my keys out of my pocket and hand them to her. "I'll watch her eat and then play with her in the living room so you can have a little while to yourself."

She sighs and smiles carefully. "Okay, yeah. If you need anything..."

"You'll be ten feet away," I assure her.

After Sadie's done with her coffee and breakfast, she gives Rory a kiss and tells her she'll be right back. Rory waves bye-bye, then goes back to chomping on her cereal.

When she's done, she raises her hands, so I take her out and set her on the floor. She crawls to the bins of toys Sadie keeps in the living room and goes through each one, flinging them out and making a huge mess. I can't help laughing at how adorable she is.

When she finds the toy she wants, we play with it until she gives me an odd look and the room starts to stink.

"Did you take a shi—go poop?"

Rory looks at me with an unreadable expression.

"C'mon, princess. Let's get you cleaned up."

I lift her into my arms and carry her into her bedroom, setting her on the changing table. I've never actually done this myself, but I've seen Sadie and my friends do it, and I'm determined to show Sadie I'm capable. The diapers and wipes are in reaching distance, and I go about changing her diaper, only gagging once at the rancid smell.

"How is it possible for your tiny little body to produce that kind of filth?" I ask, making Rory laugh since she has no idea what I'm talking about.

I've just finished changing her and getting some clean clothes on her so she's ready to go to the park once Sadie's ready when Sadie comes out of the bathroom in nothing but a towel.

"Hey," she says, startled. Her hair is up in a messy wet bun, the water from her hair trickling down her slim neck. The towel barely covers her, showing off the swells of her perfect breasts and her thick thighs.

"Hey," I say back, holding Rory, who's wiggling to get down. "I changed Rory's diaper and got her dressed."

Sadie smiles. "I'll be done soon. The shower in the master bath has low pressure, so I take my showers in the other bathroom."

While she finishes and Rory plays, I look up plumbers in the area and save them so I can call them on Monday for Sadie.

Once she's dressed and ready to go, I put Rory in her stroller while Sadie packs her diaper bag, and then we're off.

When we arrive at the park, I carry her over to the swings and set her in since Rory isn't walking yet. As I push her, she squeals in delight, kicking her feet and jabbering away. I snap a couple of pictures of her, my heart feeling so full I wonder if it's going to implode in my chest.

"Hey, are you okay?" Sadie asks, and it's then I realize I have tears in my eyes.

"Yeah, for the first time, it feels like everything is perfect." I pull her to my side and kiss her temple. "Thank you for giving me the most precious gift."

Sadie looks up at me and smiles a watery smile. "She's the rainbow after a horrible storm. A piece of hope."

After the swings, Rory goes down the slide several times, and then we play in the sand with the toys Sadie brought. Once Rory's exhausted, we put her in her stroller, and she falls asleep as we walk to a restaurant nearby to have lunch.

Every moment I spend with them is amazing but also bittersweet because I know I'm going to have to leave them soon enough.

Fifteen

GAGE

"OH, MY GOD, SHE'S SO FREAKING ADORABLE," KAYLEE SAYS, WATCHING THE VIDEO OF AURORA GIGGLING. "And her eyes are totally yours. And her nose...well, aside from the nose ring."

"When can we meet her?" Layla asks, watching the video over Kaylee's shoulder.

"I'm not sure," I admit. "They're back in Virginia, and Sadie asked that we take things slow." It's been three days since I've seen them in person, but every night before bed, Sadie has called me so I could say good night to Aurora.

"Makes sense after everything she's been through," Declan says.

"I'm having back child support sent over to her, and she agreed to send pictures every day. I was thinking maybe this weekend I'll fly there and see where they're living and spend some time with them." I haven't spoken to Sadie about it yet, but when she calls tonight—if she calls—I'm going to bring it up.

"I'm very proud of you," Sophia says, squeezing my shoulder. "You're handling this all very well. If you need anything, you know we're here for you."

"I know, and I appreciate it."

The truth is, I'm not handling this well at all. I've been to two NA meetings and had an emergency session with my therapist. Finding out that I have a daughter who I missed ten months with because of my addiction has been rough. I have a lot of regrets, and I can't help feeling like I've already failed her and Sadie.

I started seeing Viola—my therapist here in New York—once I moved back when Pamela recommended I have someone to talk to in person. She understood where I was coming from but also pointed out that I can't change the past, which is something I have issues with.

With my mom, I wanted to go back and save her. Same with Tori. Now, I regret not getting my shit together sooner, so Sadie wouldn't have had to go at it alone, and Rory would know I was her dad from the beginning. But I can't change any of that. All I can do is make shit right moving forward, which seems damn near impossible when they live over seven hundred miles away.

"All right, ladies, lunch has been fun, but we need to get back to work," Camden says, standing and giving Layla and Marianna a kiss.

We spend the next few hours hammering out another song and nailing down the instrumentals with our producer. The songs are coming along smoothly, and if we continue like this, we should be able to start officially recording in the next few weeks.

As we're finishing up for the day, my phone vibrates in my pocket, indicating an incoming call. Sadie's name flashes across the screen, so I click accept, and her face, along with Rory's, displays.

"Hey Gage, are you busy?" Sadie asks.

"Nah, we're just finishing up in the studio." I stand and wave to the guys, giving Sadie my full attention. Braxton follows me since we rode together because I'm still staying with him and Kaylee.

"If you want to call back—"

"I'm good." There's no way in hell I'm going to turn her away when she calls me. I don't care where I am or what I'm doing.

"Okay, well, it's Rory's bedtime." Every night she's called me around this time, so I can "be there" to say good night to Rory.

"Did you guys have a good day?" I ask, walking through the hall and out to the awaiting SUV. Braxton doesn't say a word, but I can tell he's listening as he sits beside me.

"We did. I finished editing a book, and we went to the park. Rory's new favorite thing is the slide, and I swear she went down it a hundred times. Oh! And another tooth came through. She now has four teeth." She smiles, looking so proud, and I feel so damn lucky that my daughter has such an amazing mom.

I connect my AirPods and stay on the phone while Sadie reads Rory a bedtime story and then goes through kissing her good night. And then she points the phone in my direction and says, "Rory, wave bye-bye to Daddy," and holy shit, my heart implodes in my chest at the word Daddy. It's the first time she's referred to me as Daddy, and it's officially my favorite word.

Rory smiles lazily at the screen and lifts her hand, her fingers squeezing open and closed, and I do the same to her. "Good night, Rory," I say. "I...I love you and miss you," I choke out, needing her to know. She's too young to know the words or understand what I'm saying, but that won't stop me from saying them.

Sadie swallows thickly. "Night, Gage."

"Night. Thank you for calling."

We hang up, and I sit in silence, staring at my phone, wishing I could be there with them. Seeing my daughter for five minutes a night isn't enough, but I don't know what else to do. I pull my keys out of my pocket and glance at the tag I got when I started NA: *One day at a time.* I need to remember this.

"Hey, man, I'm going to go to a meeting," I tell Braxton when we pull up to his place and get out.

"All right." He pats me on the shoulder. "I know we've all said it, but we're here for you. You've been thrown a major curveball, and it's got to be a lot to handle."

"I did this to myself. If I wouldn't have been high..." I take a deep breath, remembering what Viola said about the past. "Rory's not a curveball. She's my daughter. I just need to figure out how all the pieces fit. I hate them being so far away."

"I didn't mean it like that. I just meant that you were heading in one direction, and suddenly, you're being spun in circles. It's okay if you don't figure it all out right away. You only just found out about her a few days ago."

"Because I was an addict and fucked up big time. Rory and Sadie deserve better than this shit."

"Speaking of which..." Braxton smirks. "From what Declan said, you and Sadie were pretty hot and heavy before. Any chance you two have picked up where you left off?" He waggles his brows, and I groan.

"Are you two seriously gossiping like a couple of chicks?" I punch him playfully in the arm. "Quit it."

"Still didn't answer the question."

"Her husband was an addict. He's the reason her son is dead. I met her crying on their graves, unable to go home after she lost her entire fucking world." I glance at the bustling pedestrians and cars on the road. "She didn't tell me that I have a daughter out of fear of history repeating itself. The only thing I can hope for is a chance to be a father to Rory.

"Besides, she's already seeing someone. She said it's not serious, but..." I shrug.

"What if she was willing to give you a chance?"

I think back to the way she felt in my arms, in my bed. The way we could talk for hours or just simply walk in silence. Even as fucked up as I was back then, I knew Sadie was a fucking keeper. It's why I pushed her away. And that was when she was at her lowest, grieving and devastated. Spending time with her now...Fuck, I already know she's the whole damn package. She's got a good head on her shoulders, is a damn good mom to our daughter, is sweet and forgiving—I mean, even hurt and pissed, she still let me in—and gorgeous...beyond gorgeous.

"I'd scoop her up so quick and never let her go," I admit. "I'd spend every day of our lives making sure she never hurt again. Making sure she felt loved and cared for. She spent so many years caring for others, putting up with her husband's shit, my shit. When she walked away, she wrote me a note..." I swallow thickly, remembering the words. I've looked at them every day since she walked away. "Even after I hurt her, she still told me she believed in me. Told me to fight and find happiness."

I choke up, wishing I could go back and make better choices. "She could've been my chance at happiness, but I fucked it all up," I admit to Braxton. "Now, my punishment is that I'll have to watch someone else be her happiness."

"I think you should talk to your therapist," he says, shocking the hell out of me since we rarely discuss my recovery. "You *both* deserve happiness, and there's no reason you can't be each other's. Yeah, you messed up, but you don't deserve to be punished for it."

After going to an NA meeting and chatting with Gabe for a while, I text Viola, asking for an emergency session. She's available an hour later, and we spend our time talking about the possibility of Sadie and me.

"What would you think about me meeting her?" Viola asks at the end of our conversation.

"Rory?"

"Well, her too. But I meant Sadie. As the mother of your daughter and the woman you clearly have feelings for, I would love to speak to her to see where she stands. Even if you two don't end up together, you'll be co-parenting for the rest of your lives. Maybe the next time you talk, you can bring it up and see what she thinks. It's up to you."

The next few days fly by, filled with music and Sadie and Rory from afar. I'm missing them like crazy, so when the guys mention taking the weekend off to spend time with their families, I ask Sadie if I can come visit, telling her I'll stay in a hotel so it's not awkward. Thankfully, she agrees, and Saturday morning, I'm on an early flight out. Since the town she lives in is quiet, I leave Paul behind and rent an SUV at the airport.

On the way to Sadie's place, I stop and pick up breakfast and coffee, remembering what she liked from our time together.

She opens the door with Rory on her hip, and as I stare at the two of them, dressed in their pajamas with their messy hair, Rory's head resting on Sadie's shoulder, my heart feels as though it's whole again, and I know whatever it takes, I need to make both of these girls mine.

"WHAT THE HELL IS THIS?" SADIE HISSES, WAVING HER PHONE IN THE AIR, WITH HER FACE RED IN ANGER. We've spent the day together. After Sadie let me spend some time with Rory while she showered and took a little bit of time for herself—I offered after she mentioned Rory was up all night and she was exhausted—we took Rory to the park, stopped for lunch at Sadie's favorite deli, and then ordered in dinner. We did the whole bedtime routine together, and I read Rory her story before she fell asleep. The day has been perfect, and I can't wait to do it all over again tomorrow.

Not wanting to overstay my welcome, I helped Sadie clean up, then went to kiss Rory good night one last time before heading out, but when I walked out to say goodbye to Sadie, I found her at the table fuming.

"I'm not sure," I tell her, walking over.

"This," she says, punctuating the word as she shoves the phone into my face.

It takes me a second to see what I'm looking at, but once I do, I frown in confusion. "That's your child support paperwork. I told you I was going to pay back child support. My attorney insisted you sign the paperwork as proof that you understand you're receiving it." I shrug. When I told him about Rory and Sadie, he told me he would take care of it. He wanted to file for joint custody, but I didn't want to jump ahead and put Sadie on the defense. My hope is we'll figure it all out together, but I figured while we're doing that, I could show her I'm serious by paying her what I owe her. It's at least a start...

"Yeah, I can see that. There are way too many zeros. Are you trying to pay me off or something?" She glares my way. "If you think you're going to pay me off and take my daughter from me—"

"Whoa," I say, shaking my head. "Have you heard of Raging Chaos? I make a damn good living. Even taking the last year and a half off, I still have income coming in, and my financial advisor knows his shit, knows how to properly invest, so while I wasn't doing shit, my money was still multiplying. I would never try to take our daughter from you...ever."

"Shit, I'm sorry. I was just in shock. But Gage, that's a lot of money. Like the kind of money people ask for when they kidnap a kid and want ransom."

I chuckle at how adorable she is. "It's seventeen percent of what I earned during the ten months Aurora has been alive. That's what child support is based on in New York."

I can tell when she does the math in her head because her eyes go wide. "Holy shit."

"Aurora is my daughter too," I tell her, sitting at the table across from her. "Which means it's my job...my *right* to take care of her as well."

"You're right," she finally says. "Thank you."

We're both quiet for a few moments, and my thoughts go back to my conversation with Braxton the other day. I glance over at the television and take a chance. I know she has a boyfriend, but it's not like I'm propositioning her for sex. "It's still early. Want to watch a movie or something?"

Her eyes widen before she averts her gaze. "I should probably get some work done," she says, standing. "Rain check?"

"Yeah, sure." I nod and stand as well, taking the hint. "See you tomorrow?"

"Yep. See you—" She flinches. "Shit, tomorrow..."

"Yeah...Sunday."

"I know." She rolls her eyes. "Sarah was actually supposed to take Rory for the afternoon. Mark had asked me to go to a show with him."

"Who?" I ask, even though I have a feeling I already know.

"Mark. He's the guy I'm...dating. I can cancel..."

"I can stay with Rory," I blurt out.

"While I go on my date?" she asks incredulously.

"You aren't going far, right? I watched her while you showered. I played with her and changed her diaper and got her dressed. It will give me a chance to spend some more time with her, just the two of us, and she seems comfortable with me. I know her routine…"

"I don't know," she says, looking a mixture of confused and sick.

"I won't go anywhere with her," I promise, knowing that's a hard limit for her after what happened with her late husband and son. "If there's an emergency, I'll call for help."

Her eyes bug out. "Gage, this is a lot. A big responsibility. I'm sorry. It's just too much, too soon. I can't…not yet."

My heart drops, but I don't argue because I get it. It's one thing to be with Rory while Sadie is in the other room. It's a whole other thing for her to leave Rory with me alone. It's going to take time for her to trust me, and I need to be patient.

"I don't want to fuck with your plans," I say instead. "I can come over in the morning and play with Rory while you get ready, and then take off once you're ready to go."

"You sure?" she asks slowly.

"Yeah, I'm sure."

She walks me to the door, and even though I probably shouldn't, I lean in and kiss her cheek, my lips lingering for a fraction too long on purpose. "Thank you for today. I had a really good time."

"Of course," she squeaks out, telling me she's not entirely unaffected by me. "I'll see you tomorrow."

I spend the rest of the night writing music, the words flowing. I don't know if it's being sober or spending time with Sadie and Rory, but lately, I can't stop putting my thoughts and feelings onto paper. When I send them to the guys, asking what they think, Camden says he wants to add it to the album, and the other guys agree.

Braxton: Does this mean you crashed and burned?

I roll my eyes at his question. The truth is, I was expecting it. I can't write a song about a guy wanting a woman who wants someone else without it raising questions.

Declan: With Sadie? Wait, is this song about her? She has a boyfriend??

Me: Yes, she has a boyfriend, and no, I didn't crash and burn.

I wouldn't call asking her to watch a movie and getting turned down crashing and burning. That was me just trying to put feelers out to see if she would even be willing to spend some time with me alone—which she wasn't.

Me: Sadie's the mother of my daughter and nothing more. Leave it alone.

Thankfully, the guys listen, and the texts stop for the night, but that doesn't stop me from thinking about her and how much I wish she could be more.

Sixteen

SADIE

"OH, SWEETIE." I PUSH THE SWEAT-COVERED HAIR STRANDS OFF RORY'S FACE, HATING THAT SHE'S NOT feeling well. There's nothing worse for a parent than having to watch your child go through being sick and feeling helpless.

The day after Sarah watched her, while I went on my date with Mark, she called and said her kids were both running fevers and had all the symptoms of a cold. She apologized, not knowing they were coming down with something, and I told her she was being ridiculous. We can't possibly know every time our child is going to be sick. She could pick up anything from anyone: at the park, at a restaurant...germs are part of life.

That night, Rory woke up from a coughing fit in the middle of the night. The next morning, the sniffles came, and along with them came the fever. Now she's tugging on her ear in pain, and I'm sure it's due to an ear infection.

"I'm going to call the doctor right now," I tell her, pressing a kiss to her warm forehead. While I'm making the appointment, she falls into a coughing fit, getting so worked up that it ends with her throwing up.

"Mamama," she cries, fresh tears filling her lids.

"It's okay, sweet girl," I tell her, my heart cracking in two. "We're going to give you a bath and then take you to the doctor."

The pediatrician confirms she has an ear infection, then mentions it sounds like there's wheezing in her chest, and that she's concerned about her being dehydrated, which leads to hours at the hospital while she's given chest X-rays and hooked up to an IV with fluids.

Thankfully, her lungs are clear, but after her labwork comes back, the doctors diagnose her with RSV, and since she was born premature and RSV can be severe, they insist on keeping her overnight to monitor her. Since the safest place she can be is at the hospital, I don't protest it, but have you ever had to force an eleven-month-old to sleep at a hospital?

By the time she's discharged with a nebulizer and prescriptions for her ear infection and cough, I'm so beyond exhausted. When we get home, I prop the mattress of her crib up with a pillow underneath in the hopes of her getting some sleep, and I crash in my own bed.

My eyes are barely closed when there's a knock on the door. I jump up, praying to the sleeping gods that it doesn't wake Rory, and run to answer it. When I open the door, I find Gage looking a mixture of scared and pissed off.

"Are you guys okay?"

"What?"

"I've been calling you for the past two days, and you haven't answered!" he barks. "When you didn't call me two nights in a row for bedtime, I got scared and got on a plane."

Oh, shit! "I'm so sorry," I whisper, opening the door so he can come inside. "Rory got sick, and I gave her my phone to watch a show in bed, and it must've died. I took her to the doctor, and we ended up staying in the hospital overnight, and I was just so worried and exhausted, I forgot about my phone."

Gage's features morph from pissed to worried. "Rory's sick? Is she okay? Why the hell didn't you call me?"

"I..." I begin, ready to make an excuse but cut myself off because no matter which way I slice it, I'm in the wrong. "I forgot," I admit, shaking my head. "I'm so used to doing this all myself that I literally forgot about you. I'm so sorry."

Gage's face falls, and I feel like the biggest piece of shit. He's been trying so hard to be in our daughter's life, even though he's long distance. I would be so mad if I found out she was sick and in the hospital, and Gage forgot to tell me.

"Can I see her?" he asks, his voice resigned and distant.

"She's sleeping, but you can go peek in."

He nods and walks to her room. A few minutes later, he comes back out. "Can I come back tomorrow and see her?"

"Of course," I say, stepping toward him. "Gage, I really am sorry. I was just scared, and it was all a lot. She has a respiratory virus, which can be serious for babies born prematurely, and an ear infection. I went into mom mode and blanked out. It doesn't by any means make it okay, but I just want you to know I didn't not tell you to exclude you. You're her dad, and in the future, I'll make sure to keep you informed."

"It's okay," he says softly. "I appreciate it. Is she okay now?" Somehow, him not yelling or getting mad makes me feel worse. If the situation were reversed, I would've freaked the hell out on him.

"She's on medication for her ear infection and cough and has to do the nebulizer twice a day. I also have a vaporizer going in her room."

He nods. "That's good. Do you need anything?"

"No. I'm just tired. It's been a long couple of days."

Another nod. "All right, well, I'll get out of your hair and let you get some sleep. I need to go see if the hotel has availability. I'll be back in the morning."

"Or you can stay," I blurt out.

He quirks a brow.

"I have a guest room. Well, it's my office, but there's a bed in there. That way, you don't have to spend money on a room." Another pop of his brow. "You'll be here in the morning when Rory wakes up." This gets his attention.

"You sure you're okay with that?"

"Yeah, of course. You're her father. I really am sorry for not calling you."

"All right," he says. "I'll stay. It'll be nice getting to see her in the morning when she wakes up." He smiles softly. "Thanks."

After showing him the bedroom and then saying good night, I head to bed, knowing all too well Rory will be up bright and early, and if I don't get some sleep, it's going to be another long-ass day.

MY THROAT ACHES WHEN I SWALLOW.

My eyes burn.

An itch in the back of my throat bubbles up and forces me to cough.

Dammit, I'm sick.

I knew this was a possibility, but I was hoping the vitamin C I've been popping would help my immune system. Guess not.

I groan, reaching over to take a sip of my bottled water, and then wince when it hurts going down. Just great. Nothing more fun than trying to care for my sick baby while being sick myself.

And then it hits me: sick baby. Why isn't my sick baby crying?

What time is it?

The sun peeking through the blinds tells me it's daylight.

I jump out of bed and run down the hall, finding Rory's room empty. And then I remember Gage spent the night. My heart picks up speed. He wouldn't have taken her anywhere, right?

He was upset that I forgot to tell him that she was sick, but he wouldn't have just up and left with her to punish me.

Oh, God! What if he left to get breakfast with her?

Memories from the past surface.

Me miscarrying.

Sleeping in.

Vincent taking Collin to get breakfast.

Neither of them ever coming home.

"Oh, God, please no."

"Hey, you okay?"

I twirl around and find Gage standing in the doorway with Rory attached to his hip.

"Oh, thank God. I thought..." I shake my head, unable to finish my thought.

"You thought I left with Rory," he finishes, his lips curving into a frown.

"Yeah," I breathe.

"I told you I wouldn't," he says. "She woke up a little bit ago, and you were coughing like crazy, so I didn't want to wake you up. I changed her diaper and fed her breakfast, and we've been watching some good ole *Sesame Street* on the couch."

"They still make that show?"

"I don't know, but I found it on YouTube, and she seems into it."

"Thank you," I tell him. "I'm sorry for—"

"Stop apologizing. This is all new to both of us. It's going to take some time, but we'll get there...one day at a time." He smiles softly. "Why don't you help me give Little Miss Sick her meds and then take some yourself and go lie back down? I can chill with her while you get some rest."

I sigh in relief, thankful to have Gage here with us, especially now that I'm sick as well. Going through her meds, I give her the cough and ear medicine before popping some meds myself and then going back to bed.

I pass out instantly, not waking up until it's dark outside. Confused and disoriented, I check the time and see it's eight o'clock. Holy shit, I literally slept all day. I go pee and brush my teeth, then walk out to check on Gage and Rory, finding them in her bathroom. I stand in the doorway, watching as he gives her a bath. She must be feeling better because she's splashing away and laughing as he pretends one of her toys is a shark coming after her to tickle her.

As I watch them together, a feeling of warmth spreads through my chest. I don't regret my decision to walk away and later protect her, but I'm glad that, unlike Vincent, Gage has committed to getting and staying clean. I wonder if I would've pushed harder and forced Vincent to go to rehab if things would've been different, but then I remember what Gage had said one night when we were talking about his recovery—that nobody can force an addict to get help. He has to want to do it himself. And Gage wants to be clean.

"Hey, how're you feeling?" Gage asks, shaking me from my thoughts.

"My throat hurts, and I have a cough, but not too bad."

"Good. I got you some chicken noodle soup." I stiffen at his words, and he must notice because he adds, "I had food delivered."

Dammit, I did it again. I assumed the worst without giving him the benefit of the doubt. It's not fair to continue to project my insecurities and past on him when he's trying so hard to move forward. He's been clean for over a year and deserves to be given the benefit of the doubt.

"Thank you. Soup sounds really good."

"Mamama!" Rory yells, her hands coming down and splashing her and Gage.

"Hey, sweet girl." I walk into the bathroom and lean down to kiss her forehead. Did you have a good day with Daddy?" She answers by splashing again, this time giggling.

"Go eat, and once she's done, I'll put her pajamas on and bring her out to say good night before I put her to bed."

"Thank you," I choke out. "You being here...means a lot to me." Too many times, Vincent would choose the pills over being a husband and a father. I spent years wishing and hoping for a partner, only to be alone. Gage doesn't understand what him being here really means to me.

Gage deserves a fresh start, to be given the chance to be the father he's trying to be, and it's time to give him that chance.

Seventeen

GAGE

"AND THEN THE PINK PRINCESS WITH HER PINK TUTU DANCED ACROSS THE STAGE. THE END."

"Dada," Rory squeals, slapping the book closed and climbing off the couch. I swear every time she yells *Dada,* I want to give her the damn world. Setting the book down, I follow her as she crawls across the floor to her favorite cups. She's dressed in a pink onesie and tutu that matches the book I just read to her, and she looks so damn cute. I snap a picture of her and send it in a group text to my friends, and seconds later, the women are texting back that they can't wait to meet her.

Sadie is still under the weather, so she's been sleeping a lot the past few days, leaving me to spend time with Rory. As she hands me the cup, silently demanding I stack them with her, I have no clue how the hell I'm going to walk out the door tomorrow and get on that flight to go home. Every day I spend here makes it harder to leave. A month ago, I didn't even know I had a daughter, and now I can't imagine living without her...except I don't actually live with her. I visit...occasionally. Since I've known about her, I've spent more days on the phone with her than in person... until this week. And spending time with her, watching as she grows and changes, makes me realize everything I'm missing when I'm gone. And it fucking sucks. But what choice do I have?

As I stack the cups, Rory falls into a coughing fit, and I check the time to see if I can give her some more medicine. She hates taking it, throwing a tantrum every time, but eventually, she gives in, and it helps.

"Time for medicine," I announce, lifting her into my arms and carrying her to the kitchen. The second she sees the medicine, her eyes fill with tears, and I wish I could snap my fingers and make her and Sadie better. Unfortunately, life doesn't work that way, so I set her on the counter, holding her so she doesn't fall, and fill the syringe with her cough medicine. She whimpers, her bottom lip jutting out, and my heart breaks.

"I know, princess, but it's going to make you all better," I tell her.

"Hey, is she okay?" Sadie asks, stepping into the kitchen. Her eyes are a bit puffy, and her hair's a damn mess, but fuck, if she isn't as beautiful as always. Every time I look at her, I'm reminded of what I had and lost.

"Yeah, I just gave her some cough medicine." I carry Rory back into the living room and set her down in front of the cups. She immediately remembers that she never knocked them down and swipes her hand out, sending them crashing to the floor with a laugh.

"It's the little things," I joke, making Sadie chuckle.

Rory grabs a cup and stands, glancing at her mom, sitting in the loveseat several feet away.

"Mama!" Rory babbles, trying to hand her the cup.

"Come here," Sadie says, extending her arms. Up until now, Rory's refused to walk unless she's moving across the furniture, so when she takes a step toward Sadie, Sadie's eyes go wide in shock as I whip out my phone.

"Mama!" Rory yells as she puts one foot in front of the other. I get every step on camera, not stopping the recording until Rory's in Sadie's arms and she's giving her daughter kisses, telling her how proud she is of her.

"Let's see if she does it again," Sadie says. "Ror, give Daddy the cup." Rory's eyes go straight to me, and the fact that she knows who I am has me choking up with emotion.

Sadie sets Rory on her feet, and instead of her dropping to her knees, she starts walking toward me, waving the cup in the air while she smiles wide. "Dada!"

I watch her, frozen in place, as she wobbles over to me. Once she arrives, I lift her into my arms and kiss the tip of her nose. "Look at you walking."

"I can't believe she's walking," Sadie says, smiling at Rory.

"I got it on video. I'll text it to you."

"Thank you. She seriously needs to stop growing. It's like every day she wakes up, she's speaking more words, doing something new...growing out of her clothes." She sniffles. "Sometimes, I feel like I took being a mom for granted with Collin. I was so busy dealing with Vincent that I didn't get to enjoy Collin like I do Rory. It's probably not healthy, but I want to spend every minute with her, not wanting to miss a single moment."

"It's not unhealthy," I choke out, feeling the same damn way. "You know what it's like to lose people you love, so it makes you appreciate those in your life that much more."

"HEY, WHAT'S GOING ON WITH YOU?" CAMDEN ASKS, WITH ONLY CONCERN LACED IN HIS WORDS. IT'S BEEN FIVE days since I left Sadie and Rory to come home. I didn't want to leave, especially not with both of them still somewhat sick, but I couldn't leave the guys hanging, and we had the studio scheduled to nail down more songs. We're almost halfway done with the songs, and then the recording will begin. When I told Sadie I needed to go, she didn't argue. Just simply thanked me for being there and said she'd see me soon. She might not need me, but fuck, if I'm not starting to need them.

They call me every night, but it's not enough. Not after spending five days with them. Waking up with them, having breakfast with them. Getting to see my daughter every day. Watch her walk for the first time...By the time I was reluctantly saying goodbye, she was crying for me and not wanting me to leave, and fuck if that didn't make it that much harder to walk away.

The problem is, I can't be in two places at once.

"Gage? What the hell, man? You've missed the cue three times now. You need a break?"

"I'm sorry," I say, snapping out of it. "I'm good."

Camden stares at me for a long beat, then nods. "All right. Let's take it from the top."

He starts to count down when my pocket vibrates with an incoming text. I yank it out in case it's Sadie, and sure enough, it is.

Sadie: Rory's cough has taken a turn for the worse. She's having trouble catching her breath, and they're admitting her to the pediatric unit at the hospital to monitor her. I'm here now, but there's no service, so I won't be able to talk. I'll call you when I can.

I've barely finished reading her text when I'm jumping out of my seat and heading for the door.

"Gage!" Camden barks. "Where are you going?"

Shit! I forgot where I am. "Rory's having trouble breathing. She's been admitted to the hospital. I gotta go," I choke out, hating that in order to be there for my daughter, I'm letting the guys down, but my daughter will always come first. "I'm sorry..."

"What? Don't apologize," Declan says. "Go be with your daughter. Let us know if you need anything."

I nod and haul ass out the door. On the way to the airport, while I'm looking for a flight, Easton texts that the Blackwood jet is available, and he's already let them know to get it fueled and ready. I thank him and then text Sadie to let her know I'm on my way on the chance it will go through.

A couple of hours later, I arrive at the hospital. A nurse shows me to Rory's room, and when I walk in, the sight in front of me damn near sends me to my knees. Rory is in the crib with Sadie sitting in a chair next to her. Both girls are asleep—Rory wheezing softly while Sadie's head is pressed up to the bars of the crib, her hand outstretched through a bar and her fingers laced with our daughter's. I imagine Rory scared and crying and Sadie trying to comfort her, and my heart cracks open, blood dripping all over the damn floor.

I should've been here. Sadie shouldn't have to go through this on her own. She's not the only parent, and she deserves to have a partner by her side. My mom never had anyone, and I won't let that happen to Sadie. I can't have my daughter growing up and thinking it's the norm to see her dad more over the phone than in person. And it's not fair to the guys for me to keep taking off and leaving them hanging. It's also not good for me to keep stretching myself thin. I want...*no, I *need* to stay healthy and clean, and I can't do that if I'm constantly being tugged in every direction. If I feel like I'm failing everyone, including myself.

As I watch Sadie and Rory sleep, I consider every option, every road in front of me to take, and even though it's going to hurt like a bitch, I know what I have to do.

I step outside and consider if I should call or text the guys. It's late, and they're probably with their wives and kids, so I choose to text them—I'm also a fucking pussy and, even though it needs to be done, I hate that I have to do it.

> **Me: You guys will never know what it means to me that you had my back all these years, that you waited for me and refused to move forward until I was ready, but I can't be part of the band anymore. My entire world is in Virginia, and I can't be in two places at once. Any songs I wrote or contributed to, I'll sign over to you guys. I'm sorry, but you need to look for a new drummer.**

I hover over the send button, and once I hit it, bile rises up my throat, and I run to the bathroom, throwing up everything in my stomach. Then I turn my phone off so I can focus on my daughter and walk back inside her room, refusing to regret my decision.

A little while later, Sadie wakes up. When she sees I'm here, she looks a bit shocked to see me, like she wasn't expecting me to fly out to be with her and our daughter, and I promise myself she'll never have a reason to doubt me again.

"How's she doing?" I whisper, handing her a bottled water I grabbed from the shop.

After she downs half the bottle, she says, "Okay, I guess. They have her on a mechanical ventilator to help get good oxygen in and the bad out. They explained it all to me, but it's a lot to process. She was so mad and fought them, so they sedated her to calm her down." Tears fill her eyes, and I cut across the room to pull her into my arms. "I was so scared, Gage. One minute, she was fine, and the next, she was having trouble catching her breath. I thought..." She sniffles. "I thought she was going to die."

"Nothing's going to happen to her," I vow even though I have no right to say that. "You did the right thing bringing her here." I situate us on the couch with her in my lap, and surprisingly, she lets me. "You're an amazing mom, and our daughter is so fucking blessed to have you."

She snuggles into my chest and sighs. "Thank you for coming."

"You don't ever have to thank me for being here for our daughter. This is where I belong...and I won't be leaving anymore."

Her head pops up in confusion. "What?"

"I told the guys I'm leaving the band. I can't keep being in two places at once, and where I belong is with Rory...and you."

"Gage..."

"I know you have a boyfriend, but you're the mother of my daughter, and we're going to be spending the rest of our lives raising her together. Just please let me in as her father. That's all I'm asking."

She nods in understanding. "For the record," she murmurs, putting her head back down to my chest. "I no longer have a boyfriend." I still at her words. "He wasn't happy about being kept on the outside, and I couldn't let him in. So I ended things."

"Can you let me in, Sadie?" I ask, tipping her chin up to look at me. "I know it's scary as hell, especially with how shit started with us, but can you give me a chance, please?"

"I'm going to try," she says. "You're right. It is scary, but I'm really going to try."

The next several days are filled with doctors and nurses and a very upset Rory, but thankfully, the ventilator does what it needs to do, and with her medication, she's released with a clean bill of health. Since I came without any clothes, and I refused to leave my daughter, the nurses were nice enough to bring me scrubs I could wear and offer us a shower to use.

Rory is still groggy from all the medications, so when we get back to Sadie's place—which I paid to be completely cleaned and sanitized—she plops onto the couch next to me and rests her tiny head against my arm.

"I'm going to go shower," Sadie says, smiling over at us as I turn on the television and click on one of Rory's favorite shows.

"Take your time. We're good."

I pull my phone out that I've been neglecting and scroll through the messages from the guys, asking me to think about this before I make any rash decisions. It's easy for them to say that when their entire world is under one roof, but in order for me to be with my daughter, I have to drive eight hours or get on a plane.

Since I came with nothing, I'll have to go back and pack, and then I need to find a place to live here near the girls. It's going to take a little bit, but at least once it's done, I'll be near them.

Me: I'll be back soon to get my stuff, and I can sign whatever paperwork you need me to sign.

Declan: I really wish you would reconsider. We can figure shit out.

Me: It's not fair to you guys or to Sadie and Rory for me to always have one foot out the door.

Camden: We get it.

Braxton: Yeah, but we sure as hell don't like it.

Eighteen

SADIE

"ALL RIGHT, SWEET GIRL. WHAT DO YOU SAY WE GO TO THE PARK AND GET SOME FRESH AIR?" RORY SHRIEKS and wobbles toward the door at the mention of the word park. "First, we have to get dressed." I laugh, lifting her into my arms and carrying her to her room.

We're both finally free of illness, so it will be nice to get out. It feels like we've been cooped up in the house—or hospital—for weeks. I've just finished changing her diaper and getting her dressed when there's a knock on the door. Gage didn't mention returning today. Actually, aside from saying he's moving here once he gets everything sorted, he didn't specify when that would actually be taking place.

"Let's go see who it is," I tell Rory as I walk to the door. I check the peephole and recognize the woman. At first, I can't remember from where, but then it hits me.

"Hello," I say when I open the door. "How can I help you?"

Kaylee, Braxton's wife and Gage's good friend, smiles softly at me. "I'm Kaylee Lutz," she says, extending her hand.

"I know, Braxton's wife. We met when I was staying with Gage a while back."

She nods. "May I come in? I was hoping we could talk."

"Sure." Rory's shyness toward strangers has her clinging to me when I try to set her down. "Would you like something to drink?" I ask, remembering my manners. "I have coffee, water, juice..." I cringe, and Kaylee laughs.

"I'm good, but thank you." She smiles at Rory, who peeks at her through her lashes, curiously. "She's beautiful. With your red hair and Gage's blue eyes, Gage will be scaring the boys off left and right when she's older."

"Oh, God," I groan jokingly. "She just started walking. Don't turn her into a teenager yet. I don't think I can mentally handle that."

Kaylee laughs. "I met Gage when we were in high school. He was best friends with Declan, Camden, and Braxton, and I was best friends with Tori and Layla." At the mention of Tori's name, I go still.

"The guys' dream was to make music. Every day, we hung out in the studio while they wrote and played. Everyone knew they were going to blow up. They were that damn good. The music seeped from their pores. They lived and breathed it like it was an extension of them. I can't remember a day when Gage didn't have those damn drumsticks sticking out of his back pocket." She laughs, but it sounds far away as if she's reliving that time in their life. I stay quiet, letting her say what she obviously came here to say.

"Gage never had a real family growing up. He had his mom, but she wasn't all there, and he spent more time as a kid trying to take care of her than she took care of him. The day he met Camden, though, he found his family. The moment Camden welcomed him into the fold, the guys became inseparable. Where one went, they all followed. I didn't become close with them until our sophomore year, but everyone knew those boys were more like brothers than friends.

"When his foster parents all but kicked him out when he turned eighteen, Cam's parents even insisted he live with them. And when Tori died, they helped him move forward the best they could."

She sniffles back emotion. "The guys knew he was struggling with drugs, but he wouldn't talk about it. When I went on tour with them, I saw it for myself and told them they needed to do something, but they were too close to Gage. They loved him and accepted him the way he was. They knew he was still grieving, and instead of pushing him to get help, they enabled him."

I nod in understanding, knowing all too well how that works. One of my biggest regrets is not forcing Vincent to get help or, at the very least, walking away from him when I knew he wasn't going to get the help he needed. It's easy to point fingers at the family and friends, but I know firsthand that it's not that easy to force someone to get help.

"For a minute, he started to calm down a little. He didn't seem to be using as much..."

"When we were hanging out," I say.

She nods. "We all hoped you'd be the one to save him, but we had no idea that you weren't in any place to save yourself, let alone him." She smiles sadly, and I know Gage told them about my past.

"After you left, things got bad, and he tried to end his life." She swipes at a tear, then glances down at Rory, who's now sitting on the couch flipping through the book that she can't read.

"I'm not in any way blaming you, especially now knowing what he did to make you leave. I just wanted to give you the whole story..."

I nod and sigh, thankful Gage didn't make me out to be the bad guy. "It really hurt," I choke out. "I know that we weren't together, and promises weren't made, but it still really hurt."

"What he did was wrong on so many levels, and I'm sure it makes it really hard to trust him again."

"I can tell he's changed," I admit, needing to give him some credit. A few times while he was here, I heard him talking to his therapist, and more than once, he said he needed to go to a meeting. "But yeah, it's still hard to let him in, but I'm trying."

Kaylee smiles softly for a few seconds before her features morph into a frown. "When he left for rehab, we thought it would be ninety days, and he'd come home clean. But ninety days turned into ten months. The guys refused to play without him. They wouldn't record a single song until he came home because they're more than a band…They're family.

"It took Kendall and me going to him to bring him home because he was scared of how things would be now that he's sober. He didn't want to fail anyone or let anyone down. He views Tori's and his mom's deaths as his failures. And now, ever since he found out that he's a dad and you've been doing it on your own, he thinks he's failed you and Rory." I don't miss that she calls her Rory instead of Aurora—a nickname only I, and now Gage, call her. Which means he's been telling them about her enough that she knows her nickname.

My stomach drops, and now I understand where she's going with this. Gage is moving here, giving up the band to be with his daughter, to make sure he doesn't fail us, which means he's leaving the only family he's ever known and ultimately failing them.

"I didn't ask him to move here," I blurt out, suddenly feeling like I need to be on the defense.

"Oh, I know," she says gently. "It was his decision. He's torn between being in New York with the band and being here with you and Rory. But he doesn't want to be away from you guys anymore." She leans forward and locks eyes with mine. "Gage doesn't know I'm here, and he probably would be pissed if he knew I was, but I had to come and plead with you. Beg you not to make him choose."

I swallow thickly with where this is going. "This is my home. You can't expect me to move back to New York for Gage. He might be doing good right now, but he's still an addict. What happens when he starts using again?" I say, shaking my head. Moving to Virginia was my fresh start. I hate that I'm not near my son's and daughter's graves, but in a way, it's for the best. It forced me to move forward, to focus on myself, on healing. If I go back…

"His entire family is there," Kaylee says. "His therapist and sponsor and his meetings. He needs us," she chokes out, "and we need him. The guys need him. I know it's selfish of me to ask, but please, don't let him walk away from us, from the band. It took him so long to get here, to be sober and finally start living again. If you would just be willing to move there, he could have everyone and everything he loves in one place. He needs this, Sadie. He needs to record this album sober and know that he did it, that he didn't let his brothers down. Please, give him that.

"I know you don't owe him that, and he might not even deserve it, but please. He needs it."

Tears prick my eyes, hearing the emotion in every word she speaks, but I don't think I can do it. I don't think I can move there and leave my home and the little bit of support I have behind.

"I'm sorry," I whisper. "I just...I don't think I can do it."

Her face falls, but she nods in understanding. "It's okay. I had to try." She stands and smiles sadly. "If it's okay, could we come and visit one day? Like an actual official visit? Gage has sent us so many pictures and videos, and he doesn't stop talking about you two. Everyone is dying to meet you both."

"Of course," I say, standing to walk her out.

Once she's gone, I spend the day with Rory, but I can't stop thinking about everything Kaylee said. When bedtime rolls around, like every night, we FaceTime Gage. He's usually at the studio or in his room, but tonight when he answers, it looks like he's around a bunch of people.

"I'm sorry, you're busy..."

"What? No," he says. "I'm at the Blackwoods." He moves his phone so I can see everyone. "This is Easton and Sophia, Camden's parents."

I don't know how I didn't put it together until now, but I immediately recognize Easton as the pop star that I spent many years listening to...still do. "Hey," I say, suddenly shy.

"This is Sadie and my princess Rory."

Rory hears her dad's voice and instantly perks up. "Dadadada!"

Gage beams. "Hey, princess," he says softly.

"Hey, Sadie," Sophia says, her smile filled with kindness. "We've heard so much about you. Hopefully, we can meet you one day."

"That would be great," I say.

"Oh, Gage," a woman says, forcing her way into the picture. "She's so beautiful. Look at that red hair. They're both beautiful."

"This is Layla," Gage says, rolling his eyes playfully. "Camden's wife."

"Hi!" She waves.

"I wanna see da baby," a little girl says, crawling onto Gage's lap.

"This is Cam and Layla's daughter, Marianna. See the baby?" he says to her. She nods. "That's my daughter."

"Baby!" Marianna says at the same time Rory says, "Dadadada!" grabbing the phone and pulling it to her face as if she can touch him through it if she gets close enough. Her lips press against the screen, and she makes a kissing sound.

"She's giving you kisses," I say with a laugh, pulling the phone back.

Gage smiles sadly. "I'll be there soon," he says to Rory. "Then you can give me real kisses."

My heart drops as everyone around him goes quiet, obviously knowing what him coming here means—leaving them.

"We can call back in a little bit," I say through the lump of emotion that's filled my throat, making it hard to breathe.

"Nah, just give me a second to go somewhere quiet. Sophia makes the best food, so when she demands I come over for dinner, I can't say no."

I nod, unable to say anything. I know he's not doing this on purpose. He doesn't know Kaylee was here earlier, but I'm questioning everything now after hearing her and seeing all of the family and support Gage has in New York.

Once he's alone, I read Rory her book, and then we both say good night to Gage. After I give her two kisses—one from me and another from Gage—I leave the room, closing the door behind me.

"I've been looking at places," Gage says once I'm back in the living room. "I'd like to see them in person before I sign a lease, so I'm going to stay at the hotel for a little bit until I decide which place is my best option. I was, umm..." He clears his throat. "I was wondering if maybe, after a while, I could take Rory to my place. Maybe once you can trust me enough, she can spend the night. You could spend the night too..." My eyes go wide, and he backpedals. "I mean, like, so you know she's safe with me. Not like that. Although, if you wanted..." He scrubs his hands over his face. "Fuck, this is all coming out wrong."

I snort out a laugh. "It's okay, I get it. We'll figure it out. One day at a time, right?"

"Yeah," he says softly. "One day at a time."

"OH, GOD, THIS IS SO CRAZY," I SAY FOR THE MILLIONTH TIME AS I PUSH A SLEEPING RORY DOWN THE STREET in her stroller. "What was I thinking? What if this is a mistake? A huge mistake?" I mutter to myself as I walk into the Blackwood studio where Gage texted me a little while ago, saying he was. Apparently, he's there to sign a bunch of papers to terminate his contract. So instead of meeting him at the hotel, I came straight here to stop him.

After I got off the phone with Gage, I sat in the living room thinking about everything and weighing my options. I came to the decision to move back to New York so he wouldn't have to leave his band, and he would get to see Rory every day. Before I could second-guess my decision, I packed us a bag and booked us a flight. And now, here we are, walking up to the front desk at Blackwood.

"Hello, how may I help you?" the woman asks.

"I need to see Gage Sharpe."

She snorts a laugh. "I'm sorry, ma'am, but this is a closed studio. If you—"

"Sadie?" a masculine voice says. I glance over and find Easton, dressed in a suit, walking over. "What are you doing here? Is everything okay?"

"Yes...No." I sigh. "Gage said he was here."

"He is. Is he expecting you? We're about to go into a meeting."

"That's why I'm here," I say, then take a deep breath, knowing if I say the rest, I can't take it back. It wouldn't be fair to Gage to say I'm moving here and then change my mind. "I've decided to move here...so Gage doesn't have to leave the band."

Easton's eyes widen, and then a smile splits across his face. "Oh, Sadie." He pulls me into a hug. "Thank you, but are you sure?"

"I am. I need to talk to him first, but yeah, I am." I've spent the entire night and morning thinking this through.

"All right, then how about we go see him, yeah?"

I follow Easton down the hall and into the large room where Gage and the rest of the band are all already sitting.

"Sadie," Gage says, noticing me immediately. "What's going on? Is everything okay?"

"I need to talk to you...alone."

His brow furrows, but he nods. "Okay..." He glances around. "Can we use your office?" he asks Easton.

"Yeah."

Gage walks us down the hall and into a gigantic, over-the-top office filled with records and expensive wood and plush furniture. I'm so distracted by it all that I forget what we're doing until Gage says, "Talk to me."

"I want a contract," I blurt out. "I want it in writing. If you do any drugs, whether it's powder or pills or even smoke weed, you forfeit your rights to Rory." Gage's eyes bug out, and I groan, hating the way that came out. "I'm moving here... Rory and I are moving here, so you can stay and play," I explain. "I'm an editor and can do that anywhere, but you need to be here with the band. And you have family here. I don't...I don't have anyone. Not really."

"You have me," he says, stepping toward me. "If you let me in, you have me."

"I'm scared," I admit, trying like hell to push back the tears. "That's why I want it in writing. I want you to be tested every few months, and if you come back positive for any kind of drugs, you have to let Rory and me walk away. I know that seems harsh, but—"

"No, that's not harsh," he says. "Your late husband lied to you, and you need the reassurance. I understand, and I agree."

"You do?"

"Yeah, I'll sign whatever you want because I *know* I'm never using another drug again." He glances down at Rory and then back up at me. "I have too much to live for."

I sigh in relief. "Thank you for understanding."

"No." He shakes his head. "Thank you. You have no idea what this means to me...you being here." He envelops me in a hug. "I'm going to earn your trust, Sadie, one day at a time. And then..." He pulls back and looks into my eyes. "I'm going to earn your heart."

Nineteen

GAGE

"GAGE...WHAT DO YOU MEAN, MY HEART?" SADIE ASKS, LOOKING A MIXTURE OF SHOCKED AND NERVOUS. I didn't mean for it to come out the way it did, but now that it's out there, I might as well own my intentions.

"I want you," I tell her straight up. "I messed up back then and wasn't in a place to start something with you, but I knew, even blitzed out of my mind, that you were a keeper. And that's what I want...to keep you."

She swallows thickly, and I cup the back of her neck and look into her beautiful emerald eyes that remind me of a fresh start. "I know it's going to take time for you to let me in, but I need you to know my endgame. It's you and me and Rory under one roof. And not because we share a daughter.

"I felt it back then, the connection we shared, in *and* out of bed, but I was too damn scared and high not to fuck it all up. I pushed you away, thinking it was for the best, wanting you to move forward and find love and happiness, but there were so many days I considered reaching out, especially once I was clean, wanting to beg you to give me another chance. And then I find out you had my baby.

"Fuck, it's like fate stepping in on my behalf. And I would be a damn fool not to take advantage of this second chance I've been given."

She sighs into my touch. "I get it. Even back then, I felt the connection between us while I was grieving, but I don't know if I can put myself out there again. I'd like to think I've healed from my past, but the pain goes beneath the scars, where nobody but me can see."

"I get it," I tell her, feeling her words in the deepest part of my soul. "I think that's what drew me to you. Our shared pain. Knowing no matter what we do, we'll never be the same again."

She nods in understanding. "I want to try, to see where things go. I can't make any promises, but I want to try."

"That's all I'm asking. For a chance." I frame her face and press my lips softly against hers, breathing in her scent for several seconds before I back up and give her some space.

"I should probably get going," she says softly.

"Where are you staying?" I ask, still in shock that they're really here. One minute, I was sitting down to sign the paperwork to terminate my contract with Blackwood, and then the next, I'm kissing her in Easton's office after she tells me she's moving here...for me.

She shrugs sheepishly. "I didn't exactly think this through."

"Sadie." I cup the side of her face. "Are you sure about this? If you need to think—"

"No, I'm sure. I just didn't think through how it would all unfold." She laughs nervously. "I rented a room at the W temporarily. One day at a time, right?"

"We'll get it all sorted," I promise. There's no way I'm going to let her and our daughter sleep at a hotel long term, but this came so out of the blue, I'm going to need a minute to gather my bearings and get everything figured out.

"Dada," Rory says, her voice gruff from sleep.

"Yeah, princess, I'm here." I kneel in front of her stroller, watching as she rubs the sleep from her eyes.

"Dada." She sits up and lifts her arms, wanting me to take her out. "Dada!"

"We really should get out of here." Sadie laughs. "I imagine you have band stuff to do, and the last thing anyone wants is this crazy child being let loose."

I chuckle at how adorable she is. One thing about Blackwood Records is that it's family-oriented. Someone's kid is always hanging around. "Or you could stay," I tell her. "The guys will be stoked to find out that I'm still in because of you. I'd love to introduce you to them in person."

"You sure they won't mind me crashing?"

I pick Rory up, and she hooks her little legs around my hip, her arms wrapping around my neck. "Nah, they're going to be excited to meet you."

Sadie pushes the stroller behind me as I guide her back to the office where I left the guys waiting. When we enter, they stand, all looking a mixture of nervous and curious.

"Sadie's moving here," I announce. "I'm not going anywhere."

The guys whoop and cheer while Declan picks up Sadie and swings her around. "You are the damn MVP," he says, setting her down. "Thank you."

"Hell yeah," Braxton says, picking her up next. "Thank you."

"This means so much to us," Camden says once she's back on her feet. "Seriously, we can't thank you enough. We were just plotting how to somehow convince you to move here."

"His wife already did," Sadie says with a light laugh, glancing over at Braxton.

"What?" I ask. "Kaylee spoke to you?"

Braxton groans. "I should've known. Let me guess, yesterday?" Sadie nods. "When she disappeared for several hours, I knew she was up to something. She didn't threaten you, did she?" Braxton grimaces, making Sadie laugh.

"No, she was very sweet. We spoke, and she gave me a lot to think about. I'm an editor and can do that from anywhere, and the truth is, New York is my home. Not particularly the city, but I love it. I ran from it, but it's time I came home."

I make a mental note that Sadie doesn't like the city. My goal is to find her—well, hopefully us—the perfect house, and knowing that she prefers the suburbs helps.

"This calls for a celebration," Camden says. "I say we take the day off and head over to my place for a barbecue, get to know the newest members of Raging Chaos." Camden tickles Rory's side, and she giggles, snuggling closer to me.

"That sounds perfect. What do you say?" I ask Sadie. "Up for it?"

"Sounds good."

"OKAY, SO HEAR ME OUT," KENDALL SAYS, WIPING HER MOUTH.

We've just finished eating delicious burgers Declan grilled, along with a bunch of sides the women whipped up when the guys told them we were coming over to celebrate the band moving forward. Ever since we arrived, the women have been all over Sadie and Rory, wanting to get to know them. I've never been so thankful to have the friends that I have. When Sadie mentioned she needed to get going soon to check in to her hotel so she could get situated, everyone looked at her like she was crazy.

"I have a condo near the studio." Kendall looks from me to Sadie. "It has two bedrooms, two baths with an upstairs loft that can double as a playroom, and a gorgeous view overlooking Bryant Park. I was renting it out since it's not really a seller's market right now, but the tenant had to break his lease to move for work. With a good cleaning, it will be move-in ready."

"Wow," Sadie breathes. "That sounds amazing. I'd like to eventually find a place outside of the city, but for now, that sounds perfect. How much would it be a month?"

Kendall's eyes flit over to me, and I shake my head, silently telling her it's not happening. There's no way in hell Sadie is paying shit, especially when she came here for me. "I'm sure we can figure something out," she says. "If you want, I can show it to you tomorrow."

"That would be great. Thank you."

We hang out for a little longer, the kids all playing while the adults bullshit, and when Rory gets cranky, making it clear it's time for her afternoon nap, we say bye to everyone, so I can take them to the hotel. The guys and I will be back in the studio first thing tomorrow, but I want the rest of the day with my girls to get them situated. I hate that I don't have my own place to bring them back to, but I'll be doing that while I work on winning over Sadie.

"She went out like a light," Sadie says with a laugh, plopping onto the seat next to me.

"She played hard."

"Yeah, she did." She smiles softly. "I loved watching her play with everyone. Aside from Sarah and her two kids, it's usually just Rory and me. I've been thinking about joining some kind of mom's group, but they're a bit intimidating," she says with a laugh. "Your friends, on the other hand, are so warm and welcoming."

"They like you," I tell her, turning to face her. "And they're not just my friends. They're my family, and they can be yours too, if you want them to be."

She smiles. "I think I'm going to take Kendall up on her offer. I have no clue about the city in terms of where to live, and if she lived there, I'm sure it's nice."

That's an understatement...Kendall's place probably costs a month what most pay a year for their mortgage, but I don't mention that, not wanting her to change her mind. Kendall is a huge pop star and wouldn't live anywhere that isn't top-notch. I've never been there, but I have no doubt it will have the best security and top-of-the-line everything. It will be the perfect place for Sadie and Rory to live while I figure everything out.

Speaking of which..."There's something we should talk about."

She quirks a brow. "Okay."

"As you know, I'm part of Raging Chaos, and while New York is a hell of a lot tamer than LA, with us recording again and announcing our next album and single soon, plus doing some promo shit that goes along with releasing, people, especially fans and the paparazzi, will come out of the woodwork. With me being gone, they want answers, to figure out where I've been and what I've been up to. I'd like to post about you and Rory to beat them at their own game, confirming I have a daughter before they can fly in like vultures and attack.

"That also means, though, that you're going to need a guard with you and Rory when you leave." Her eyes go wide, so I explain before she jumps to the wrong conclusions. "Nobody's going to hurt either of you but having someone with you means if they get too close, take shit too far, you'll have someone to protect you. They're nosy fuckers and will want to get your pictures and ask questions. Rory's and your safety are my top priority. If we were living in LA, it'd be insane, but luckily, New Yorkers are chill for the most part. I just don't want you to be blindsided by it all."

I edge closer and cup the side of her neck. "I know it feels like a lot, but shit will calm down, I promise. Aside from the months when we're releasing and touring, our lives are pretty normal."

She snorts out a laugh. "Yeah, okay. That's cute that you're trying to keep me calm, but I've seen the videos and posts and know nothing about your life is normal...but it's okay, I get it. I'm not going to run...unless you push me away again, that is."

"That's never happening," I vow. I take a deep breath, then ask her something

I've been wanting to ask but have been afraid to. "How would you feel about meeting Viola, my therapist? She mentioned you attending a session with me, not only because of us possibly dating but also because we're co-parenting Rory. I just..." I swallow thickly, trying to word shit correctly. "I want to make sure you know how serious I am about staying clean, that you feel like you can talk to me about anything."

I hold my breath in fear that it's too much too soon, and I'm going to scare her off. My fear deepens when tears prick her eyes until she speaks. "I don't want to compare you to Vincent because it's not fair to you, and I'm working on not doing that, but so many times I asked him to speak to someone, and he would tell me he was, but when I would ask if I could join him, he'd tell me he wasn't ready. I learned that he wasn't really seeing anyone, that he would lie and work late instead, so you inviting me to meet with your therapist means the world to me, and I would love to meet Viola and speak with her. I want to support you in any way I can. And not just as the woman who you're *possibly* dating..." She smiles a watery smile. "But as the mother of your daughter, who you're co-parenting with, and...as your friend."

After we hang out and talk for a bit, I make my exit, not wanting to overstay my welcome. But not before I ask if she'll come by the studio tomorrow. She's never seen me work, and I know Rory is too young to really understand it, but I'd love for her to see me in my element, to have them there as part of my world. She says she'd love to come by, so we plan to go see the condo afterward.

When I walk in the door, I find Kaylee and Braxton sitting on the couch. He's holding her while she cries in his arms.

"What's wrong?" I ask. I was with them at the barbeque earlier and they seemed fine.

"Oh, nothing," Kaylee says, waving me off.

"It's not nothing," Braxton adds. "We've been trying to get pregnant, and we thought she was. The test showed positive."

"But I'm not," she says through her tears. "Apparently, you can have a missed miscarriage. It happens to a lot of women, and they don't even know it."

"I'm sorry," I say, hating that two of the best people I know are struggling to get pregnant, when they'll make amazing parents. Sometimes, life is just plain fucked up.

"Thanks." Kaylee releases a deep sigh. "So, Sadie seems really sweet..."

"Yeah, she is. Thanks for what you did...going to see her."

Kaylee's cheeks stain pink. "I didn't want to overstep, but I was afraid she didn't know how important music is to you."

"It's not as important as her and Rory, but I'm glad I get to have both." My gaze flits from Kaylee to Braxton. "But more than that, I'm glad I get to stay here with you guys."

Kaylee grins. "Ditto."

"They're coming by the studio tomorrow to watch us practice."

"Good." Kaylee smiles softly. "You deserve this second chance, Gage. You've worked hard to get to this point."

Wanting to give them their space, I head to my room, where I spend the rest of the night looking for homes in the 'burbs. I might deserve a second chance at finding love and happiness, but I don't deserve Sadie possibly giving us a chance, not after the shit I pulled back when I was high and hell-bent on destroying everything good in my life. On the other hand, she deserves the entire world, and I'm going to make sure I give it to her.

Nineteen

BONUS SCENE

SADIE

"Umm..." I stand, holding Rory on my hip, wondering what I've gotten myself into while she tries to get down to play with Layla's daughter and Kendall's two kids.

A woman is sitting with them, and when I eye her, Kendall says, "That's Jessica, my nanny. Yes, I'm a rich be-otch and have a nanny." She shrugs. "Actually, I have a couple of them, and I wouldn't survive without them. She's awesome, so put Rory down so she can play, and we can have our Mommy date."

"Way to make a first impression," Layla says with a laugh. "The nannies are only for when we do Mommy dates and when we're working. Kendall's merging from workaholic to stay-at-home mom, and it's taking some time, and I work part-time at Blackwood as their videographer." She snatches one of the bottles from Kendall. "I'll take white, thanks."

I'm still frozen in place, trying to take it all in, when Kendall snorts out a laugh. "Oh, don't give us that look. It's Mommy juice." She winks, and I bark out a laugh, walking over to Jessica and handing her Rory. There's a safety fence so the kids can play without leaving the room.

When I was invited over for a playdate, I wasn't sure what to expect, but the women drinking wine at eleven in the morning while the kids play with the nanny wasn't it. But I'm not about to judge because after spending the past year and a half practically alone—with a couple of playdates with Sarah when she isn't working—I'm craving adult interaction, and I love how down-to-earth these women are.

"Morning!" Bailey says, sauntering in with her son, Mathew, in tow. "Oh, wine! White, please."

She sets her son on the carpet next to Rory, who's now playing next to Kendall's twins, and Marianna, who's laid out on the rug, watching a TV show.

"Sadie?" Kendall prompts. "Did I scare you off?"

Bailey snorts out a laugh. "That was quick. What did she say?"

"That she's a rich be-otch with a nanny." Layla laughs.

"Well, she is." Bailey shrugs. "But she's also a damn good mom and an awesome sister and friend." She kisses her sister's cheek and follows Layla over to the wineglasses.

"I'll take white," I tell them.

Kendall grins. "Perfect."

With a bunch of platters of food laid out across the counter, we make ourselves each a plate and then sit at the table that's in seeing distance from the kids.

"So spill," Kendall says. "Is it true? Does Gage have his dick pierced?"

"What?" I splutter, spitting my drink out and making Layla laugh and Bailey groan.

"No one cares about Gage's dick or whether it's pierced," Bailey says with a glare.

"*You* don't care," Kendall argues, "because you don't like dicks."

Bailey sticks her tongue out and takes a sip of wine.

"I asked Declan if he'd get his done, and he blew me off. So is he?" Kendall rests her chin on her hand and gives me her full attention.

"He is," I admit, and Kendall squeals.

"I knew it," she says. "Brax's is pierced too, and Kaylee said it's ah-maz-ing. Do you concur?"

"Let's just say, that piercing appeared in every one of my fantasies for the past two years when I was alone, getting myself off," I say, making the three women giggle.

"That's it! I'm going to convince Declan to get one." Kendall pulls her phone out and starts typing.

"And that's her sober," Layla says with a laugh. "Imagine once she's had some wine."

"So I was thinking we should go to The Hamptons this summer," Bailey says. "Cynthia's convinced me to buy a place there." She rolls her eyes playfully.

"Oh, yes!" Layla agrees. "Since the guys won't be touring until after the first of the year, I'd like to spend a few weeks, maybe even a month there, over the summer. How about for the Fourth of July?"

At the mention of the holiday, my thoughts go back to Collin and the last conversation we had. He wanted to buy fireworks.

"Sadie," Layla says softly, "are you okay?"

It's then I notice my chest is rising and falling in quick movements, and tears have gathered in my lids. "I...I should go..." I go to stand, ready to bolt, but before I can, Kendall drops her hand over mine.

"Whoa, wait," Kendall says, turning serious. "Talk to us. We might have started as Gage's family, but we're yours too."

I glance around at the women all looking at me with warmth and concern etched in their features. Aside from Gage, I haven't spoken to anyone about my past.

Not even Vincent's parents because it's too hard, and they feel too guilty.

"My son...Collin...he loved the Fourth of July. The last time we were together when he was alive, he wanted to get fireworks. That night, I miscarried, and the following day, he was killed in a car accident. He never got to celebrate...*We* never got to celebrate."

"Oh, Sadie." Layla jumps out of her seat and throws her arms around me, enveloping me in her warmth and comfort.

"I'm sorry," I groan. "I'm such a drag...I'm like the worst Mommy date member ever."

"Stop it," Kendall says. "That's what family is for. To listen...to simply be here. And we're here. Just like my family was here when I was supposed to get married and jumped out of a church window instead, and then later found out that two different men could be the father of my babies." Her eyes go comically wide, and I have no choice but to laugh through my tears.

"Oh! Are we sharing stories?" Kaylee asks, sauntering into the house. "Looks like I'm here just in time." She gives Layla a kiss on the cheek and joins us.

"We're sharing how effed up we all are," Kendall informs her.

"Oh, I'll go next." Kaylee playfully raises her hand. "I wanted to push Brax away, so I pretended to cheat on him and let him believe for years I actually did." She snags Layla's wineglass and downs it. "And now that Brax and I are together, we're trying to get pregnant, but my body hates me, and I keep miscarrying." Layla pours her another glass, and she downs it. "Layla, your turn."

"My family was here when I was going through a horrible divorce, and afterward, my ex tried to kill both my son and me," Layla says, pouring herself some wine and taking a sip.

"Bailey, your turn," Kendall says.

"Umm...well, I'm a lesbian."

The women snort out a laugh.

"Okay, so all of us *besides* Bailey have issues." Kendall rolls her eyes, and Bailey shoves her playfully. "Our point is, we're not perfect." She takes my hand in hers. "But we're family, and we have each other's backs. And even though we've just met, we got yours, too."

I smile at the group of women, who I imagined would be stuck-up like the women I met in the past in the mom's group, and take a breath of fresh air, feeling like maybe I've found my tribe.

GAGE

"WHAT THE HELL?" DECLAN GROANS, GLARING MY WAY. "SADIE'S HANGING OUT WITH THE WOMEN DURING their Mommy meeting."

"Yeah, so...Is there a problem?" I had to practically convince Sadie to go to Kendall's, ensuring her the women were all nice and would be welcoming. If one of them did something to make her feel uncomfortable...

"Great, that's Layla," Camden whines when his phone goes off, and he looks at it.

"What the hell are you guys going on about?" Since it's clear we're taking a break from practicing, I stand and shove my sticks into my back pocket. Pulling my phone out, I check on Sadie and make sure everything's okay. Once I've texted her asking how it's going, I turn my attention back to Declan. "What the fuck is going on?"

"Ever since the women got drunk and Kaylee bragged that Braxton's pierced and it makes sex even better, Kendall's been begging me to get pierced."

I chuckle. "Well, it does," I agree. "But what's that got to do with Sadie?"

"Mommy meeting is code for drinking wine and gossiping," Declan explains. "The women do it once a week. Apparently, Sadie confirmed that you're pierced and said it's so good, she's been fantasizing about it."

"She said that?" When we were together, I was high most of the time and didn't think I made it good for her, so if she's bragging about me, that's a damn good sign.

"Yeah." Declan glares. "Think maybe you can ask her to keep her opinions of your metal dick to herself in the future? You and Brax might be okay with holes in your cocks, but I'm not."

My phone goes off, and I pull it out to find a text from Sadie: **Hey! I'm good. Everyone is really sweet...making me feel welcome. We're going to meet up again tomorrow. Is that okay?**

Me: You don't have to ask me to do anything. I'm just glad you're getting along with my family.

Sadie: I am! Although...I'm probably going to need Paul to drive me home. I might've had some wine, and I'm not sure I'll be sober enough to drive home when our playdate is over. Do I just text him when I'm ready?

I chuckle at how adorable she is. Because of my posting on social media, the paparazzi have come out of the woodwork, wanting to get the first picture of my daughter and girlfriend. I asked Paul to take her to Kendall's this morning, but she insisted she could snag an Uber home. Not wanting to argue, I let it go, then told Paul to be on standby.

Me: He's at your service, baby. Have a good time. Just don't gossip too much. ;)

Sadie: Oh, my God! You know...

Me: Know what?

Sadie: Goodbye

I crack up laughing, and the guys all glance at me like I've grown another head. "What?"

"Nothing," Declan says. "It's just...happy looks good on you, man."

I roll my eyes, secretly agreeing. "Let's get back to work. This isn't a damn Mommy meeting."

Twenty

SADIE

Gage: Are you still coming by?

I GLANCE AT THE TIME AND SIGH IN EXHAUSTION. RORY WAS UP HALF THE NIGHT IN TEARS OVER A TOOTH coming in, and since I didn't bring any of her medicine with me, I had nothing to help with the pain. I could've called Gage and asked him to pick something up, but I kept telling myself she would calm down soon. She finally passed out from exhaustion a couple of hours ago, and I'm not too keen on waking her up.

Me: Rory had trouble sleeping last night and is still sleeping. I don't think it's going to happen. Rain check?

I feel horrible that I had to cancel on him the first time he invited us to the studio, but everyone with kids knows parenting rule number one: never wake a sleeping baby.

Gage: Is she okay? Do you need anything? I can come over.

My heart warms at how devoted he is to being a good dad. I would be lying if I said a part of me wasn't scared to let him in, especially after our past, but so far, he hasn't once made me regret it, and while the self-preservation part of me wants to run and hide, the adult in me, who's been through hell and back, knows that even though life can be scary as hell, it can also be taken from you at any minute. Which means I'm pretty much stuck somewhere between wanting to live life to the fullest with no regrets and not making the same mistakes that have already cost me everything once before. Yeah, it's as exhausting and complicated and confusing as it sounds.

Me: Thank you, but we're okay. I'm going to attempt to get a nap in while she's sleeping, and then I'm supposed to meet Kendall later regarding the condo. Have a good practice.

I've just set my phone on the table and have swung my legs onto the couch when a cry comes from the bedroom, followed by "Mama!"

"Good morning," I say, walking into her temporary room and finding her standing in her crib, bouncing up and down.

"Ow, ow!" she squeals. Since she's not crying, I assume she's trying to say *out*. It amazes me every day how fast she's growing and learning. After losing Collin, it makes me appreciate Rory and every milestone that much more. Sometimes, I see little similarities in how they smile and laugh, and it makes me both happy and sad to see pieces of Collin living through her.

"Well, since you're awake, want to go see Daddy?" I ask, lifting her out of her crib and setting her on the bed to change her diaper since there's no changing table here.

"Dada!" She giggles, clearly happier than she was last night.

"Okay, we'll go see Daddy."

On the way to the studio, Kendall texts me that she has an appointment, but can meet tomorrow, if that's okay. As much as I hate being stuck in a hotel, she's doing me a huge favor, and it'll be quicker than me finding a place, so I agree without complaint. Even once I see the condo, I'm still going to have to deal with hiring a moving company to have all our stuff moved here. Since I was renting month to month, I'll at least be able to give notice and cancel the lease next month.

When we arrive, Easton stands by the front desk and greets us, offering to walk us back to the studio where the guys are practicing. We slip into what Easton refers to as the control room, and he ensures me that if Rory makes any noise, the guys won't be affected or disturbed.

The second we walk inside, the music hits our ears. From listening to their earlier albums, I know that while they're a rock band, they're on the calmer side— less screaming, more passion—giving off a Fallout Boy meets Matchbox Twenty vibe. My dad was a huge music buff, and I grew up listening to all types of old-school music.

The thought of my dad causes a dull ache in my chest. My parents tried for years to have a baby, but it wasn't until my mom was forty-seven and my dad was fifty-three that she mistakenly got pregnant with me. They were so excited but also scared because of her age. Everything turned out okay, but them having me later in life meant I didn't have any siblings. I also lost them in my early twenties, shortly after I got married and gave birth to Collin.

I glance out at the band, zeroing in on Gage, remembering what Kaylee said about him being an orphan and the only family he has is his band. A deep sense of understanding tugs at my heartstrings. In a lot of ways, we're both alone in this world, seeking love and acceptance, a safe place to land when we fall, and if I let Gage in, we can be each other's soft landing.

"All right, that was good," Camden says. His gaze meets mine, and he nods subtly. I expect him to tell Gage I'm here, but instead, he says, "Let's do 'Bleeding Heart' next." The guys nod, and then Gage, who's sitting behind his drum kit, counts them in and then starts. I don't know anything about music, but holy shit, the way he hits the drums wakes up something in me that's been dormant for a long time. I don't know if it's the passion in his eyes or the way his muscular forearms and biceps flex every time he hits the drums, but damn, it's suddenly hot in here.

Declan and Braxton both join in with their guitars, and a second later, Camden starts singing. His eyes meet mine once again, and as he sings the first line, he winks at me. At first, I wonder what the hell is going on until Easton murmurs, "Gage wrote this song," and then it all clicks.

Emerald eyes, soft smile, big heart
She's everything a man could ever want
Makes it bittersweet to know there's a chance
She'll never be mine
Someone like me doesn't deserve her time
But that doesn't stop me from wanting to take what's mine
From wanting her heart to be mine
Her body, her soul, all mine

So I'm holding on, biding my time
Waiting for the chance
To prove I'm worth her time
She captured my heart
Broken, bleeding
It was useless, barely beating
But with one look, one touch, she brought me back to life
Now I'm living, breathing
Every day I'm healing
And I want the same for her
I want to be the one for her

It won't be easy, but I'm determined to heal her bleeding heart
She's got no reason to let me in
To give me the chance to make shit right
But I'm not going to stop
Until I've reached into her chest and taken hold of her broken heart
It's bleeding crimson all over the floor
But I'm going to heal it, fix the broken, and bring her back to life
So she's living, breathing, feeling what she does to me

So I'm holding on, biding my time
Waiting for the chance
To prove I'm worth her time
She captured my heart

Broken, bleeding
It was useless, barely beating
But with one look, one touch, she brought me back to life
Now I'm living, breathing
Every day I'm healing
And I want the same for her
I want to be the one for her

By the time the song ends, tears trail down my cheeks like twin waterfalls, knowing that song was about me.

And if I didn't already know, when Gage's eyes connect with mine, raw emotion etched in his features, it's confirmed.

Camden tells the guys they're done practicing for the day, but Gage is already heading our way. I don't know where Easton and the guy working the sound booth went, but when Gage walks in, it's only him, Rory, and me.

"I thought you weren't coming..."

"Rory woke up." I shrug, trying to play off the fact that my body buzzes with electricity, and my heart feels like it's been resuscitated. "You wrote that song for me."

Gage grins. "I did."

He steps closer, his hand about to touch somewhere on me when Rory shrieks, "Dada, ow!"

His attention turns on her. "What's wrong?" He bends so he's at her level.

"Ow! Ow!"

"Sadie, is she okay?" he asks, worry in his tone as he unsnaps her straps and lifts her into his arms. The second she's out of her stroller, she claps, a huge smile spreading across her face.

"I think she's learned a new word," I say with a laugh. "Ow seems to be *out*, only she can't say the t yet."

Gage sighs in relief, smiling at his daughter. "Is that what you wanted, princess? To get out of your stroller?" She presses her hands to the sides of his face and smushes his cheeks together. "Dada!"

"I'm so glad you guys are here," he says, kissing the tip of her nose and making her giggle. "Have you heard from Kendall?"

"She had to reschedule. I think we're going to meet up tomorrow." I shrug. "But on the positive, it means we're free for the rest of the day."

Gage grins. "What do you say we go get something to eat and take it to the park?"

"That sounds perfect."

After saying bye to the guys, we take off. Since the park Gage wants to go to is a bit of a ways away, we throw the stroller in the trunk and have Paul—Gage's main bodyguard—drive us to grab the food.

We stop at a deli that Gage swears is the best in New York. Since they're old-school with no online menu or ordering, we get out so I can check out what they have.

We're walking across the sidewalk, with Paul behind us, when a woman says Gage's name, making both of us look her way. She's too old to be a fan—at least not one who would fangirl over him—so it must be someone he knows.

"Sandra," Gage clips.

Her gaze bounces between Gage, Rory, and me, landing and staying on me. "I'm sorry. You just...you look so much like my Tori..."

"Don't you fucking mention her name," Gage snaps, stepping in her face. "And when you see me on the streets, you don't approach me, ever."

"I'm sorry...I..."

"I don't give a shit," he says, his words coming out so cold that a chill races up my spine. Without waiting for her to respond, he takes my hand and pulls me into the deli. We order our food, the tension thick, and then head to the park, stopping once along the way for Paul to run in and grab us a blanket.

When we arrive at the park, one I've never been to before, it's quiet with only a few people meandering about. We walk for a while, looking for a good spot.

"How about here?" Gage asks, pointing at a shaded area under a big tree that's not too far from the playground. While he lays the blanket out, I cover Rory with her blanket since it's cool outside and she's fallen asleep in her stroller.

We eat in silence, and the entire time I can't stop thinking about what that woman said—that I look like her daughter. If that's true, is that why Gage is attracted to me? Am I a weird replacement for the woman he lost all those years ago? I can't imagine that's a healthy coping mechanism.

When the silence—and tension—gets to be too much, I open my mouth to ask about what happened, but before I can get a word out, Gage speaks.

"You both have red hair and green eyes, but that's where the similarities end. Tori's mom was always good at playing games, and I have no doubt that she was playing games when she said that bullshit. She might've looked like a grief-stricken mom, but she knew her husband was sexually molesting and raping her daughter, and she chose to ignore it."

"She knew?" I breathe, my eyes going to a still sleeping Rory, unable to fathom how a mother could ever know that her child was being raped and do nothing about it. A monster like that deserves to burn in hell...they both do. "Are you sure?"

Gage nods. "Yeah, Tori wrote me a note before she ended her life. After she died and I read it, I went after her mom and stepdad. She knew and chose not to believe her."

"Did he pay?"

"Kind of." Gage swallows thickly. "I went after them, specifically him, saying I would expose him to the world. He was a cocky bastard and didn't take me seriously, saying he would destroy my credibility and reputation, ending my music career before it even started.

"Easton overheard and forced me to get on a plane to LA. He said to let him handle it, that he would make sure he pays, but I would regret it if the last thing everyone remembered about Tori was that she was a rape victim." Gage's eyes glisten, and I find myself gravitating toward him, taking his hand in mine and threading our fingers together.

He glances down and smiles sadly, then brings our joined hands to his mouth, pressing a soft kiss to my hand. "As much as I wanted to expose him to the world, I agreed. Tori deserved more than to have her memory tainted. It was his word versus hers, and she wasn't alive to fight back. So I got on the plane and trusted Easton to handle it. A few days later, Glen...that's her stepdad's name...killed himself."

"Well, if that doesn't prove his guilt..."

"Yeah," he agrees. "It sucks that nobody will ever know what he did to her but knowing that he's been permanently removed from the earth and will never hurt anyone else again and that Tori's mom is now alone and has to live with the guilt of knowing she didn't do shit when her daughter went to her and begged her to listen is a decent consolation."

"Rory will always know she can talk to us," I tell him, feeling like he needs to hear that.

He nods, half with me and half lost in his thoughts. "Yeah, we'll make sure of that."

After a few minutes, he circles back to the initial topic. "Tori was beautiful, with red hair and green eyes. She was wild and carefree." A small half-smile forms on his lips. "But she was young. We both were...She loved to smoke and drink and had a reckless streak to her. I loved her the only way a teenage boy could, and after she died, that love morphed into guilt."

His eyes meet mine. "When I saw you crying at the cemetery, my mind went to Tori, not because of your looks, but because when our eyes collided, I saw in you what I often saw in her: devastation. You were so damn sad and lost, and that's what drew you to me. I couldn't save Tori, so I wanted to save you."

Gage laughs humorlessly. "Fuck, I couldn't even save myself."

"Stop," I say, moving closer to him. "When I had no one, you were there. When I landed myself in jail, you were there. And when I couldn't go home, you gave me a safe place to stay until I could function again."

"And then I pushed you out the door by fucking two women," he growls, shaking his head and moving back slightly, so we're no longer connected.

"I need you to know, no matter how slow you want to go, I'm okay with that. Just the fact you're giving us a chance means the world to me. I'll do whatever it takes to make you trust me again, to show you that you're all I want and that you mean the world to me." His gaze sears into mine, pleading with me to know he means every word he's saying.

"It is hard," I admit. "Sometimes, when I would think about you, the memory of you with them appears, and it hurts. But I won't be that woman who throws your past in your face. You're clean and working hard to have a fresh start, and it's not fair for me to bring up what you did while you were high. But you're right, I do need for us to take things slow, so I can protect my heart."

Gage nods in understanding, framing my face with his hand. "One day, you're going to trust me with your heart." He leans in and brushes his lips against mine. The act is soft and sweet as if he's showing me that he can go slow and take things at the pace I need.

"I promise you, Sadie," he murmurs against my mouth, "when you're ready to give me your heart, I'm going to protect it and keep it safe." He gently sucks my bottom lip into his mouth, and butterflies erupt in my belly.

And as I kiss Gage back, I feel the truth in the lyrics he wrote for me—slowly, with every word, every promise, every action, he's bringing me back to life.

Twenty-One

GAGE

"THIS IS TOO MUCH." SADIE SCANS THE ROOM WITH WIDE EYES, TAKING IN THE SPACIOUS LIVING ROOM AND kitchen. She follows Kendall down the hallway and gasps when she sees the master bedroom completely furnished. "I can't accept this." Kendall ignores her, showing her the second bedroom that's also furnished, complete with a crib, changing table, and dresser. "Nope, I can't do it." She cuts in front of Kendall before she can continue with the tour. "Did you hear me? This is too much. I can't move in here...accept all of this, and I can't even imagine how much it all cost."

"You can and you will," Kendall says. "You being here means Gage gets to remain in the band, the band my husband is part of. Heck, it means there's still a band because everyone knows those guys were not going to record without Gage. This"—she waves her hand in the air—"is the least I can do, and I'm only supplying the condo. Gage bought all the furniture."

Sadie's eyes land on me. "Gage." She sighs. "You didn't have to do this."

I shrug, not wanting to point out that her furniture was all cheaply made and that she and Rory deserve the best of everything. She provided a beautiful, loving home for our daughter, and that's all that matters, but since I'm able to give them the best, I'm going to damn well do so. Money doesn't mean shit to me, but her happiness does.

"Wait a second," she says, walking over to the dresser where there's a picture frame with a photo of Collin and Sadie. She put it on the dresser so Rory would grow up, knowing about the brother she never got to meet. "How did this get here?"

"All your stuff is here," I tell her. "I left your stuff in boxes in your closet, figuring you would want to go through them yourself, but I set up everything else. I didn't want you to have to deal with all of that with a toddler in tow. The place is move-in ready."

Sadie's eyes soften. She's been in the hotel for almost a week now, assuming Kendall was too busy to meet her to show her the place while we were getting everything ready. Not once did Sadie complain, though, when I know it was rough living in a shared space with an almost one-year-old. Speaking of which, with Rory's birthday coming up, I should ask Sadie how she wants to go about celebrating.

"Thank you," she says, hugging me tightly and nestling her face into my neck.

Kendall waggles her brows and mouths, "*You did good,*" before quietly exiting so we can have some privacy. Rory is with Layla since Sadie assumed the place would need to be cleaned before attempting to move in. Over the past week, while the guys and I have been practicing, Layla, Kendall, and Kendall's sister, Bailey, welcomed Sadie into their little mom circle

At first, Sadie was nervous and a bit overwhelmed, but after their first playdate—where the women had what they call a Mommy Meeting, which includes drinking wine and gossiping—she was excited to have made new friends while Rory played with the other kids. I learned from Declan that Sadie's been fantasizing about my pierced cock—and Kendall and Layla tried to convince their husbands to get pierced as well—she met me back at the hotel all smiles. The next day she joined them at the park, and the day after, they all met at that indoor playground. It means a lot to me that she gave my friends a chance and gels so seamlessly with them.

"Where's Kendall?" Sadie asks when she pulls back and realizes that we're alone.

"She left."

Sadie pouts. "I wanted to say thank you."

"You can tomorrow. We're going over to their house for a barbecue."

Her eyes meet mine, and a soft smile curves at the corners of her lips. "Does that mean we're alone?"

"It does," I say, unsure where she's going with this until a tiny twinkle fills her gaze, and she steps on her tiptoes to press her mouth to mine.

"That means I can thank you properly," she murmurs against my lips. Every night, after I'm done at practice, I've been going over to the hotel to hang out with Sadie and Rory. While Rory's awake, our focus is on her, playing and eating dinner, running through her bedtime routine, but once she's asleep, Sadie and I get alone time.

We spend the majority of the time talking and getting to know one another, but for the past couple of days, we've split our time between talking and kissing. I can't remember the last time I simply kissed a woman—for so long, I resorted to fucking, keeping any and all emotion out of the act—but I have to admit, kissing Sadie has become one of my favorite pastimes. Her lips are soft and pouty and when she sighs into the kiss, my cock twitches, loving the sound as much as I do.

"You don't need to thank me," I mutter. "But I sure as hell won't stop you from kissing me."

Our mouths connect, our tongues gliding along each other, and I revel in her sweet taste as I lift her into my arms, carrying her out of Rory's room and back into the living room. I go to set her on the couch next to me, but her legs lock around my waist, and she remains on my lap when I sit down. Every time we kiss, I let her control the situation, not wanting to go faster than she's ready for. She deserves my patience and for us to take each step at her pace.

With her straddling my lap, she deepens the kiss, running her fingers through my hair and fisting the strands, silently demanding more. I break the kiss, trailing fiery kisses along her neck, suckling on her soft flesh, reacquainting myself with every inch of her, memorizing every freckle and beauty mark. When we were together before, I was too high to appreciate what I had, but now that I'm sober, I refuse to take any part of her for granted.

"Oh, God," she breathes when I suck on the sensitive spot just under her ear, no doubt leaving a mark. Her center grinds down on my crotch, and I slide my hands down her hips and cup her pert ass, loving the way her soft body feels against my own.

She releases my hair and lifts her shirt over her head, exposing a black lace bra that shows off the swells of her breasts and hardened nipples.

Not wanting to assume anything, I meet her eyes. "May I?" I ask, praying to God she doesn't say no.

"So polite." She smirks. Leaning forward, she sucks my bottom lip into her mouth, nipping at it playfully. "Yes, Gage, you may touch me."

Not needing to be told twice, I take her lace-covered breast in my palm and suck on her nipple through the material. She groans, her fingers spearing through my hair again as I take her other breast and suck on that one too.

After giving them each attention, I pull back and flip the cup down to get a good look at her. Her breasts are creamy like the rest of her body, with tiny freckles dotting her skin. She mentioned her mom was Irish, and she took after her. With her tits nestled in my hands, I lick her pink nipples, my tongue swirling around the tip before I bite down on them.

Sadie groans, jutting her chest toward me. "More," she breathes.

I lick her nipples again, but she shakes her head. "No, not that...umm..."

"What, baby? What do you want?"

Her pale skin flushes pink, telling me she's embarrassed by whatever she's trying to say, so I drop her tits and take her face in my hands. "You never have to be embarrassed by what you want. Whatever it is, I'll give it to you."

She sucks her bottom lip into her mouth and nods slowly. "I want you to bite me again. When we were together before, you would do that. And sometimes, you would be kind of rough. I never thought I would like sex like that, but I do."

Fuck, this woman.

Capturing her mouth with mine, I kiss her hard and deep, stroking my tongue against hers. Needing her to know, to *feel* how badly I fucking want her. I pull back slightly and lick across her bottom lip before I bite down on it...*hard*, making her groan into my mouth.

Releasing her, I grab her tits again, this time less gentle, and take a nipple into my mouth, sucking roughly on the tip.

"Oh, yes, just like that," she murmurs, throwing her head back and grinding herself against my hard cock. If she keeps doing that, she's going to get us both off.

The harder I suck and bite, the harder she grinds against me, stroking my dick through the material while taking us closer to the edge.

"Oh, oh, God," she breathes, telling me that she's close. Her thighs tighten, and I have no doubt she's about to come when my phone rings in my pocket, making us both stop. I want nothing more than to ignore it, but with Rory at Camden and Layla's, I can't chance it's her, and something's wrong.

When I voice my thoughts, lifting Sadie off my lap—leaving us both unsatisfied—so I can grab my phone, she nods in agreement.

Sure enough, it's Layla.

"Hey, is everything okay?" I ask, wincing when my words come out sounding all breathy like I was just in the middle of a hot as hell sex session.

"Hey," she says slowly, clearly picking up on my vibe. "Sorry to bother you. Everything's okay, but I think Marianna has an ear infection, so I need to take her to the pediatrician. Camden can watch her, but I just wanted to check with you guys first."

"Nah, it's all good," I say, standing. "I'll come get her right now."

"You sure?"

I glance down at Sadie, who's still without a shirt, looking up at me with a mixture of heat and concern. "Yeah."

"What happened?" Sadie asks, her voice as out of breath as mine.

"Marianna has an ear infection, so Layla needs to take her to the doctor. Why don't you stay here and start unpacking your boxes, and I'll go pick up Rory and grab us some dinner?"

We talked about me announcing that I have a daughter, but I haven't posted anything yet in my attempt to take shit slow. I've been keeping our relationship a secret from the world, which means, aside from the picnic at the park, we've been spending our time behind closed doors in her hotel room.

Sadie's entire body visibly stiffens, and I wonder what I said wrong until I replay my words in my head. She's afraid of me picking up Rory...of driving with her. Of me being high and getting both of us killed. I want to be offended that after a year of me being clean and weeks of showing her that I wouldn't risk Rory's life, she would still think like that, but I can't be because she told me she needs to take things slow, and I have to give it to her. After what she's been through, I'm not sure she'll ever fully trust me, but I'm going to work every day to earn it.

"Paul will drive us," I add, texting Paul to pick me up.

"Oh, okay." She leans over and kisses me softly. "Thank you...for understanding."

"One day at a time," I tell her, kissing her back, knowing that even me going with Paul without her is a big deal and a show of trust.

I'm waiting for Paul to arrive when I reach into my pocket to get my phone and realize I've forgotten it. I must've left it on the table, and there's no way I'm going to get Rory without Sadie being able to get ahold of me. I run back upstairs to grab it and let myself in, so I can run in and out without bothering Sadie, but when I get inside, I hear a noise coming from somewhere in the condo.

Concerned something might be wrong, I head down the hall, following the noise. The door to the bedroom is shut, so I knock. "Sadie!"

I hear, "Oh, shit," which has me opening the door, thinking something is wrong before she can finish telling me to wait. "You okay?" I ask, finding her lying on the bed.

"Yep," she squeaks out, sounding all kinds of weird.

I glance around, wondering what's going on, when I hear a buzzing sound. "Do you hear that?" I step closer.

"Nope, don't you need to go get Rory? You should go get her...Don't want to make Layla wait."

The way she's talking a million miles a second has me walking into the room, confused and curious. "You don't hear that noise?" I ask, ignoring her comment.

"I said, I don't."

I'm now next to the bed, and the noise is loud as fuck. There's no way she doesn't hear it...I drop onto my hands and knees since it sounds like it's coming from under the bed, and she screeches, "Stop!" as she leaps toward me, damn near jumping on my back.

Realizing the noise is coming from the drawer and not under the bed, I pull it open and find a dark pink-looking rose thing...vibrating.

"What the hell is this?" I ask, lifting it.

"Oh, my God, Gage! Give it to me," Sadie shrieks, trying to snatch it from me. "It's mine!"

And that's when it clicks—Sadie on the bed, acting weird, begging me to leave, sounding guilty and now embarrassed. The vibration is a goddamn vibrator, and I just walked in on her about to get herself off.

"It won't turn off," she mutters. "I think I've overused it." She covers her face with her hands, making me chuckle.

"Hey," I say, removing her hands. "You don't need to hide anything from me. Besides, the thought of you lying in this bed, fingering yourself, is sexy as hell."

"I wasn't fingering myself. It's a clit stimulator."

"Oh, yeah?" I glance down at it and notice it's the shape of a rose, and the center is what's vibrating. "Show me how it works."

Her eyes go wide. "What? No!" She shakes her head at the same time as I nod mine.

"Yes." I grab her legs and pull her down the bed to lie on her back with her head propped up by the pillows. Since her clothes are still on, I'm assuming she must've pulled her shorts and panties to the side to use it, but I'm not having it, so I yank them down her legs, exposing her neatly trimmed pussy and creamy thighs.

My phone is going off somewhere in the house, but I ignore it. Paul can fucking wait, and Camden can keep an eye on Rory for a few minutes while I get my woman off.

"Spread your thighs, baby."

Despite her initial protest, she does as I say, giving me the perfect view of her glistening pussy. Between our dry humping and her using the toy, she must be so damn wet. I lift the still vibrating rose thing to my nose and inhale. "Fuck, Sadie, I can smell your juices on this thing."

She groans, her eyes turning hooded.

"Show me how it works," I repeat, handing it to her.

She takes the vibrating rose from me and slowly puts it between her legs, nestling it against her pretty pink pussy. The moment it touches her clit, she shivers in anticipation, and I want nothing more than to replace that plastic shit with my tongue. I've never been jealous of an inanimate object until now.

"Were you thinking about me when you had this between your legs?" I ask, lying on my stomach and giving the inside of her thigh a kiss.

She nods, her chest rising and falling in quick succession.

"What were you thinking about? Tell me."

"I was thinking..." She swallows thickly. "I was thinking about how much I want you. I was imagining the rose was your mouth, licking me." She moans softly, the toy bringing her closer to her climax.

"Oh, shit," she breathes, her lust-filled eyes meeting mine. "I'm so close."

Having had enough of that toy bringing her the pleasure I want for myself, I pull the toy away and chuck it to the side, the damn thing still vibrating like crazy.

"Gage! What the—?"

Pushing her thighs apart, I dip down and lick my way slowly up her slit, causing her words to turn into a needy groan.

"Mine," I growl, taking her clit between my lips and sucking on the swollen nub. "Tell me this pussy is mine."

"Oh, God. Yes, it's yours," she breathes as I lay my tongue flat on the sensitive area and begin massaging circles, working her up the same way that toy was. The only difference is that, like this, I get to taste her juices and feel her body shaking in pleasure. I work her up higher and higher until she explodes around my tongue, coating me with her orgasm. I don't stop, wanting every bit of her desire until she's pushing my head away.

"That was way better than my rose," she admits, her tone relaxed and sated.

I crawl up her body and kiss her. I expect her to pull back since my mouth is coated with her pleasure, but instead, she licks the seam of my lips and moans. My dick swells in my pants at the sound, wanting to join the fun, but I push the thought aside because we're taking shit slow.

My phone rings in the background, and with one more quick kiss, I get off her, grabbing the toy and pressing the power button several times until it finally stops vibrating.

"Oh, thank God," she mutters. "That thing is getting thrown in the garbage."

I laugh, tossing it at her.

"Ewww, Gage!"

"What? It's your juices." I lick my lips, and she rolls her eyes. "Paul's waiting for me. I forgot my phone. I'll be back soon."

"Or...we could go together," she suggests. "Go out to dinner."

"We'd be seen together," I point out, "and nobody knows about you guys yet."

"So you can tell them. Post it while we're on our way." She crawls over to me and wraps her arms around me, still naked from the waist down. "Rory's your daughter, and I'm your girlfriend. I don't want us to be a secret. If you want people to know, I'm okay with that."

"You're sure?" I ask, loving that she used the word girlfriend to describe what she is to me. "Once we do this, there's no going back. No matter what happens, it will all be in the public eye."

"I'm sure." She presses her lips to mine. "I trust you to make sure we're protected."

And just like that, with that one sentence, I fall even harder for the woman in my arms. She has every reason not to trust me, yet here she is, slowly giving me her trust. As I look into her vulnerable green eyes, I vow to never break that trust.

"All right, let's do this."

Twenty-Two

SADIE

As Paul drives us to pick up Rory, Gage goes over what he's going to post on social media with Bailey—who's in charge of Blackwood's social media—and my thoughts drift to the past hour. How we explored my new home. Things getting heated with Gage until the moment was cut short because Rory needed to be picked up. Gage walking in and taking over when I was attempting to finish what we started.

After he made me come, I thought he would try to take the next step and have sex. I wasn't sure how I would react, afraid the flashbacks and memories of him being with those other women would hit. Until the moment came when I orgasmed, and then he pulled back, not even trying for more. I didn't have a single thought about our past, not a flash of what happened the night he pushed me away, and it made me realize that I'm ready to move forward with Gage. I was just as shocked as he was when I referred to myself as his girlfriend, but I must admit that it felt right when the word came out. Being with Gage *feels* right.

He's spent the past month and a half showing me every day how much he's changed and how important Rory and I are to him. Two of the days after practice, he texted to let me know he was going to a meeting before coming over, extending an invitation to join him when I'm ready. He said he doesn't want to keep the two worlds separate, that his recovery is a part of his life and will always be, and he wants us to be a part of that. I never got that from Vincent, and I know now it's because he wasn't really trying to get clean. He was lying, putting on a front, and hiding shit, but Gage...he's up front about everything. And that makes me want to take the next step with him.

"Is this okay?" Gage asks, handing me his phone. As I read the statement he typed up—stating that after the past sixteen months of working on himself, getting clean, and fighting every day to stay that way, he's back, and with him is his daughter and girlfriend—tears fill my eyes. While meant to be positive and uplifting, his words are a harsh reminder that if Gage had been successful at taking his life, we wouldn't be here. Rory never would've gotten to meet her dad, and Gage and I wouldn't be getting this second chance. The statement is accompanied by a selfie we took while at the park with Rory. We're smiling at the camera with her in the middle.

"Promise me something," I tell him, turning to look him in the eyes. "Promise me that no matter what happens between us, no matter where life takes us, you will always fight for your life. Rory needs her daddy. She needs him to be clean and *alive*. And..." I choke up, my emotions getting the best of me. "I need you too. Even if we don't work out, I need you as Rory's dad."

Gage reaches out and swipes my falling tears. "I promise, Sadie, I'm never going back to being that shell of a man again. I love my life. I love my daughter, and I'm falling in love with you. And no drug is worth the risk of losing you guys."

I sigh in relief as he pulls me into a hug. "I know you're scared," he murmurs into my ear. "And you have every right to be, but I promise, I'm here, I'm clean, and I'm going to fight every day to stay that way. Not just for you guys but for me too."

He holds me tight for several long beats before he backs up and looks at me, his eyes glassy with emotion. "We got this...one day at a time."

He posts it, and within seconds, comments and likes start flooding his notifications. "I haven't posted in over two years," he says with a nervous laugh, scrolling through the feed. I can't read them all, but the ones I catch are sweet, welcoming him back and congratulating him on becoming a dad. A few are from women asking to have his baby and wanting to screw him, but I refuse to let those bother me. I'm not oblivious to the fact that Gage is more than hot and has been Raging Chaos's *bad boy* for years, doing drugs, partying, and having sex with women he didn't bother to get to know. But that Gage isn't the man sitting next to me, and maybe it makes me foolish or naïve, but until Gage proves otherwise, I'm trusting him to be the man he is now.

"All right, well, I've had enough of that," he says, swiping out of the app and pocketing his phone. "Let's go get our princess and have our first family dinner in public."

OUR FIRST PUBLIC FAMILY DINNER IS AT A LATTE FUN, WHERE WE SPEND HOURS PLAYING WITH RORY. GAGE jumps on the trampoline with her, goes down the slide with her in his lap a couple dozen times, swims through the ball pit, and shows her how to draw with chalk all over the chalkboard wall. And when our little angel turns into the devil at dinnertime, he never once loses his patience as he gently calms her until her cries turn into giggles.

Once we've eaten and Rory is back in her stroller, we stroll downtown with Paul lingering behind. Gage said he doesn't bring Paul everywhere he goes in New York, but he doesn't want to take a chance with us—better safe than sorry.

"What the hell is that?" Gage asks when we stop in front of the Easter Bunny.

"The Easter Bunny," I say with a laugh. "Tomorrow is Easter, hence the reason for the barbecue at Kendall and Declan's place."

"Do you celebrate Easter?"

"Yeah, I mean, I did when Collin was alive. I'm not super religious. We didn't go to church or anything, but we'd celebrate all the major holidays like Easter and Christmas." I shrug, a lump of emotion clogging my throat. "Rory's not old enough to understand, but once she's a little older, the Easter Bunny will bring her a basket, and Santa will bring her presents."

Gage nods toward where the bunny is sitting. "It looks like people are getting their pictures taken with it. Want to get Rory's taken?"

"Sure. She's not really dressed for it, but I guess it doesn't matter."

The line isn't long, so we only have to wait a few minutes before it's our turn. Gage pulls Rory out of her stroller and walks over to the bunny, who extends his arms to place her in his lap. Rory isn't having it, though, and latches onto Gage like he's an extension of her.

"I think I'll just sit next to you," Gage says, keeping hold of his daughter, who doesn't appear impressed by the bunny in the slightest.

I step back to take a couple of pictures of them when an overwhelming sense of déjà vu hits me. I try to shake it off, snapping photo after photo, but it's too strong and threatens to take me under.

"Join us, Sadie," Gage says, calling me over.

"I can take your picture," the photographer adds.

I have a seat on the other side of the bunny, and the photographer tells us to smile, snapping a picture, but something feels off, and that's when it hits me.

I was here before...with Collin.

Once we're done, the photographer gives us a ticket so we can go to the counter and purchase the photo. The woman takes the ticket and scans it, and our photo pops up on the screen. Only instead of seeing Gage, Rory, and me, my brain changes it to Collin and the bunny. The image knocks me back a couple of steps, and I bump into Gage. Thankfully, Rory is in her stroller, and Gage catches me before we hit the ground.

"Are you okay?" he asks, his voice filled with concern.

"I..." Images of Collin running to the Easter Bunny, smiling for the camera, and then hugging him take over my brain, making it hard to think, speak, *breathe*. My little boy...He's gone. He'll never experience another holiday again. No more bunnies or Santas...He'll never open another present or look for hidden eggs.

"Oh, my God, are you Gage Sharpe?" a woman says. "I am a huge fan. Oh! And you must be his girlfriend. I saw the post on Instagram."

She continues to fangirl, but all I can focus on is trying to keep my shit together. But the thoughts and images hit me like a freight train, and the next thing I know, everything goes black.

"SADIE," GAGE SAYS SOFTLY. "WAKE UP, BABY."

I wrench my lids open and find I'm lying on a couch in a room I've never seen before. "What happened?" I croak, trying to sit up. The room spins, so I close my eyes for a few moments before opening them again.

"I think you had a panic attack and passed out," Gage says.

"I took Collin to see that Easter Bunny."

"Oh, baby." He wraps his arms around me. "I'm so sorry."

"It's not your fault. I forgot until you guys sat down, and then it hit me. It's been almost two years, and it still hurts so much," I choke out.

"Mama," Rory says softly, using a tone she rarely uses.

"Paul grabbed her and the stroller so I could carry you into the office," Gage says.

"Mama," Rory repeats, reaching out for me. She's too young to understand, but babies can sense when something is off.

"Hey, sweet girl." I lift her out of her stroller and hug her tightly, needing to smell her baby scent and feel her heartbeat.

"Did that fan see me pass out?" I ask, flinching at the thought of someone getting it on camera.

"Nah, I signed something for her, and she took off before you blacked out. The manager saw it all go down and opened the office for us to get you out of the public eye. But even if she did, the only thing that matters is that you're okay."

"God, I can't believe I did that," I mutter. "What if you weren't with us, and it was just Rory and me?"

Gage cups the back of my neck and turns my face to look at him. "You're the strongest woman I know, but sometimes it's okay to be weak. You've been through more shit than most people, and thinking about what-ifs won't do you any good. I was here...I *am* here."

"I miss him so much," I admit softly. "Every second of every day. Sometimes, without realizing it, my guilt hits. Like with the Easter Bunny...Collin will never have that experience again. And here I am, living my life, taking Rory to see the Easter Bunny, laughing and making new memories while he's buried in a cemetery. I know my thoughts are irrational—"

"Hell no, they're not," he says. "Your thoughts are what drove me to drugs. The guilt I felt over losing her, over not being able to save her. I know we talked about you meeting with Viola for me, but have you considered talking to someone on your own?"

"What is that supposed to mean?" I ask, pulling back and out of his reach. "I'm not going to turn to drugs." Sure, I had my moments, but I got through the roughest part and made it to the other side.

"I didn't say you were." He sighs, and I instantly feel bad for snapping at him. "I was just trying to say that I understand and can relate, and maybe talking to someone will help. You've been through a lot and haven't spoken to anyone about it."

He makes a valid point, and while I'm doing okay, for the most part, having a panic attack and blacking out from a memory is probably something worth speaking to someone about. Especially since it's happened before—thankfully before Rory was born and only once afterward, while she was sleeping.

"You're right," I concede. "I'm going to talk to someone. It can't hurt, right?" I drop my head to his shoulder. "Aren't we quite the pair?"

Gage chuckles. "Hell yeah, we are."

Since the manager had the photo printed for us, we're able to leave through the back door so we don't risk being seen. It's getting late, so we drive straight to the condo after Gage lets me know that he had someone pack up all our stuff in the hotel room and check us out. I should probably be a bit annoyed that he's packed up and moved my stuff twice now without my consent, but I'm too appreciative to question it.

When we get inside, Gage insists I take a bath to relax while he gives Rory one. My nerves are still a bit rattled, so I take him up on his offer and use the time to unwind, meeting him back in Rory's room as he's finishing her bedtime story. She's already fast asleep, so I give her a soft kiss, not wanting to wake her up.

"How are you feeling?" Gage asks, sitting on the couch and pulling me onto his lap.

"Better." I snuggle into his chest. "Today was really nice...aside from me blacking out."

"Yeah, it was." He kisses the top of my head. "But that bunny was creepy as fuck, Sadie. You sure you didn't black out from that?"

Appreciating his attempt to lighten the mood with a joke, I laugh into his chest. "He's not creepy. He's a cute little bunny."

"Babe, he's the shit nightmares are made of. Did you see how Rory reacted? Even she recognized the creepy vibes. And who in the hell decided to make it a normal thing where animals sit on benches and kids sit on their laps?" He mock shivers. "Are there other scary animals I should be aware of?"

"No," I say, sitting up with a laugh and playfully slapping his arm. "But there is Santa."

"Oh fuck, I forgot about him," Gage groans. "I think we need to start a new tradition. One that doesn't involve our daughter sitting on creepy-ass men's laps and taking photos with them."

I wrap my arms around Gage's neck. "What about me? Can I sit on creepy-ass men's laps and take photos with them?"

"Fuck no," Gage growls, gripping the curves of my hips and pulling me closer to him. "The only lap you're sitting on is mine."

His mouth crashes against mine, and all thoughts of the Easter Bunny and Santa and blacking out go straight out the window as I get lost in everything that is Gage.

"Stay the night," I murmur against his lips.

"You sure?" he asks, breaking the kiss and resting his forehead against mine.

"I want you to spend the night...in my bed." My eyes lock with his as I grind down on his hard crotch. "I want to finish what we started earlier today."

Twenty-Three

SADIE

GAGE DROPS ME ONTO THE CENTER OF THE BED AND THEN BACKS UP, REACHING BEHIND HIM AND LIFTING HIS T-shirt over his head, exposing his tattooed chest and six-pack abs. When we were together before, I never took the time to appreciate his body, too lost in my grief, and because of the drugs, his body wasn't as defined. But now, as he pulls his hair back, tying it up into a knot, I can't help but take in the way his biceps and shoulders ripple as he lifts and lowers his arms. The way his abs somehow get even tighter when he reaches for his jeans and unbuttons and unzips them. My eyes stay trained on him as he pushes his jeans and boxers down his muscular thighs, and my jaw damn near drops when his thick, veiny cock springs up, and the glint of metal catches my attention.

Oh, God...that piercing, the one that goes through the head of his dick from top to bottom—I looked it up once out of curiosity, and it's called an apadravya. And even though I was hurt by what he did when he pushed me away, that piercing has appeared in my thoughts and fantasies on several occasions when I was alone and needing a visual to get myself off.

Gage steps out of his clothes and reaches for his cock, stroking it up and down slowly, teasingly, as he smirks knowingly at me. I *might've* mentioned to the other women during our playdate how hot Gage's pierced cock was. And Kendall and Layla *might've* said something to their husbands about wanting them to get theirs pierced. And Gage *might've* found out...But in my defense, Kendall gave me wine and practically dragged it out of me.

Wanting Gage's pierced cock in me ASAP, I reach up to remove my own shirt, but he shakes his head, then stalks forward, crawling onto the bed and toward me like he's a lion, and I'm his prey. I get up on my knees and meet him halfway, and he lifts my sweater dress up, tossing it to the side.

"You're so damn perfect," he murmurs, dipping his head and trailing hot kisses across the swells of my breasts before he reaches behind me and unclasps my bra, removing each of the straps and setting my breasts free of their confines.

Taking them in his hands, he licks and sucks my nipples while I reach down and stroke his cock, using the bit of precum that's seeped out as lubricant.

"I want you in me," I groan when he sucks hard on my nipples, sending a jolt of electricity straight to my core.

"Soon, baby," he murmurs, leaning in and taking my bottom lip between his teeth. He tugs on it, then bites down before licking the bit of pain away.

Gently, Gage pushes me onto my back and peppers kisses along my flesh, stopping to lick my pebbled nipples, then works his way down my torso, pressing open-mouthed kisses to each of my hip bones. He stops at the top of my mound and kisses me through the material before removing my panties and dropping them onto the floor.

With my legs spread for him, he disappears from my line of sight and devours my pussy, licking my clit and working me toward an orgasm. Just as I'm about to come, he thrusts a finger and then two into me, curving them up and pushing me straight off the ledge.

Only once my legs have stopped shaking and my body has come down slightly does he stop and look up at me with a satisfied smirk on his face. "I could eat you every damn day," he says, making a show of licking my juices off his lips.

"I wouldn't protest." I shrug, lifting onto one elbow and wrapping my hand around his neck to draw him closer. "But right now, I really need you inside me."

Our mouths connect at the same time as Gage enters me, his tongue sliding past my parted lips as I release a moan, my body stretching in the best way to accommodate his thick erection.

Once he's all the way in, he stops and focuses on kissing me, tasting, coaxing, consuming me. And then he moves, his piercing rubbing my walls and eliciting pleasure. The last time we were together, it was about grieving and getting lost, escaping our heartbreak. But as Gage kisses me tenderly, his body moving in and out of me in a lazy rhythm, this is nothing like before. Gage isn't fucking me to forget. He's making love to me, showing me in every kiss and every slow thrust how much I mean to him.

Flashbacks of the night he pushed me away hit me hard, and I try to shake them out, but like my panic attack earlier, they have a mind of their own. Images of those women touching him, caressing him, pleasuring him. I take a deep breath, reminding myself that the Gage from back then isn't the same Gage who's in me, kissing me. This Gage...*my* Gage is clean and sober.

As if he can hear my thoughts and sense my insecurities, he breaks our kiss, his eyes meeting mine. "Stay with me, Sadie," he murmurs, brushing his soft yet strong lips across my own. "You're the only one for me. Stay right here with me, where we belong, in this moment, together."

"Gage," I whisper back against his lips. "Please don't hurt me."

His heated gaze sears into me. "The only thing I want to do is love you, baby."

As our mouths connect once again in a fiery-hot passionate kiss and our bodies come together in the most intimate way, I know that letting Gage in is worth the risk of getting hurt. Because for the first time since my world came crashing down on me almost two years ago, I feel like I'm finally living again...because of Gage. Because through the darkness of our despair and grief, we created our own light: Rory. And through her, as if it were fate, we've found our way back to each other. And while whatever we're doing might end in heartbreak, I'm going to do as Gage asked and live in the moment with him. Let him love me and spend every day loving him. Because really, isn't that all we have—right now, at this moment?

"I CAME IN YOU," GAGE MURMURS AS HE SPOONS ME FROM BEHIND, PEPPERING KISSES ALONG MY NECK AND shoulder. After we both found our release, instead of cleaning up, he rolled us over and demanded to hold me for a little while. And since I wasn't ready for the moment to end, I didn't argue.

"I'm on birth control, so we're good." Although the point of protection is also to protect us from STDs, and we haven't had that talk yet.

Once again, it's as if he can read my mind because he turns me over to face him and says, "I'm clean. I haven't been with anyone since you."

I flinch at his words since they're not entirely true. "You were with those women after me," I say, hating to ruin the mood but feeling the need to say it.

"Maybe." He sighs. "But I don't remember that night at all. I passed out and couldn't tell you what happened. I know I must've been with them in some way for you to walk out the door, and I saw them when Declan woke me up, but you're the last person I remember being with. I was tested for everything because of the drugs and the possibility of what I'd done, and I'm clean." He pulls me into his arms and nestles his face in the curtain of my hair. "I would do anything to take the hurt away that I caused you, but the truth is, without you walking out the door, I never would've gotten the help I needed. It was you..." He pulls back and looks into my eyes. "It was you coming into my life and making me feel, and then walking away and making me miss you, that led to me hitting rock bottom and getting help."

I nod in understanding. "I didn't see you have sex with those women. One was going down on you, and the other was all over you, but you weren't really participating. Maybe you didn't have sex with them. Maybe you did. We'll never know. All that matters is that we're both here now. You're clean and sober, and we're living for the moment. I won't punish you for your past because it's not fair to you, but I will tell you right now, like the papers we signed for Rory, that if you use, we're gone. The same goes for if you cheat on me. I won't tolerate it."

"That'll never happen," Gage says, his voice strong and determined. "I meant what I said, Sadie. You're the only one for me. I want your present, but I also want your future." He kisses me softly, tenderly, making me sigh into his touch. "And I'm going to spend every day showing you that until you fully understand and believe it.”

"BABY, WAKE UP," GAGE MURMURS INTO MY EAR.

I crack a lid open and see it's still dark outside, then listen for Rory. When I don't hear her, telling me she's still asleep, I shake my head and roll away from him, wanting to sleep a little longer. When you're a mom, you never take sleep for granted, and when you spend all night getting fucked by a man like Gage, well, you need every minute of rest you can get.

"Rory's awake, baby, and the Easter Bunny came."

"What?" I ask, rolling back over and looking up at him. "What are you talking—?"

As if on cue, Rory shrieks from her room, "Ow, ow!" demanding to be let out of her crib.

She goes quiet, and then a loud bang rings out, making Gage and me go running. When we arrive at her room, we find her toddling toward the door, a huge grin lighting up her face.

"Holy shit," Gage breathes, lifting her into his arms. "She just pulled a damn Spider-Man and climbed her ass out."

"Ow, ow!" She giggles as Gage blows raspberries into her neck and settles her on the changing table to change her diaper.

"The crib is at the lowest point. Looks like it's time for a big girl bed." I give Rory a kiss on her forehead.

"Big girl bed?"

"Yep, a toddler bed. It's low to the ground so she won't fall out like in the crib. Collin moved into one just after his first birthday," I say, remembering the day we surprised him with his race car bed. It was just before Vincent got promoted at work, before he started working too many hours, despite his dad telling him he didn't have anything to prove. Before the pills came into play and turned my husband into a stranger. Picking out the bed was one of the last memories I have of him being sober and of us as a happy family.

"Well, it looks like Princess Rory will be getting a big girl bed for her birthday," Gage says, bringing me back to the present. "Everything's closed today for Easter, but we can go shopping tomorrow." He leans over and gives Rory a kiss on her cheek, then sets her on the floor.

"Where'd you get that dress?" I ask, watching as Rory toddles out of the room in a cute multicolored pastel dress with tiny Easter eggs all over the tutu.

"The Easter Bunny brought it." Gage shrugs.

"Oh, yeah?" I say with a laugh, remembering he said the Easter Bunny came when he was trying to wake me up. "What else did he bring?"

"Mama!" Rory shrieks.

"Better go find out." Gage winks, taking off after Rory.

The living room is filled with pastel-colored balloons, and on the coffee table, right at Rory's level, is a massive Easter basket, filled to the brim with toys and stuffed animals.

After taking a picture of Rory with the basket, Gage sets it on the floor, and Rory attacks it, finding a large stuffed bunny and bringing it to her chest to hug and kiss it.

As I watch Gage and Rory tear through the basket, memories of Collin's excitement hit me hard, but instead of letting myself wallow, I allow myself to embrace the memory before I bring myself back to the moment and sit with Gage and Rory, choosing to live in the now.

"Thank you," I tell him, kissing his cheek after we lay Rory down for her morning nap. After she wakes up, we'll head to Declan and Kendall's for an Easter barbecue.

"For what?" Gage pulls me into his arms and sits on the couch with me on his lap.

"For playing Easter Bunny when I couldn't."

He quirks a brow, so I explain, wanting him to know what's going through my head. A part of letting him in means talking to him, even when it's hard. "When we were visiting the Easter Bunny, I wasn't completely honest. I said that when Rory got older, she would get a basket, but the truth is, when Collin was Rory's age, we celebrated the holidays. I would dress him up and take pictures for Christmas, Easter, and even Valentine's Day. We would go see Santa and the Easter Bunny, and even though he wasn't even a year old yet, there were presents under the tree from Santa and a basket from the bunny.

"But after he died, I stopped celebrating, and when Rory was born, I was so afraid to move on without Collin, to create new memories without my baby boy, that I kept telling myself Rory was too young, and I'd do it once she was older. But it wasn't her age. It was my guilt that was stopping me." Tears fill my eyes, and Gage immediately wipes them away.

"She deserves to have these moments, even if she won't remember them, and I should've given them to her."

Gage frames my face in his hands. "Everyone grieves in their own way, and that little girl is so damn loved by you. Maybe you weren't ready to have her sit on some creepy people's laps yet, and you didn't buy her a basket, but she's loved every day."

"They're not creepy!" I laugh through my tears. "They're magical."

Twenty-Four

GAGE

"I SAW THE PICTURES OF COLLIN SITTING ON SANTA'S LAP, NEXT TO HIS EASTER BASKET, WHEN HE WAS clearly younger than Rory. Dressed for the Fourth of July, his first birthday pictures. When Sadie was unpacking, she had a box of his stuff, and she left it open, and I looked. I saw. So when she told me Rory was too young and then had the panic attack, I called you, wanting your take on it," I tell Viola with Sadie sitting next to me.

We're at my therapist appointment together. Viola wanted to start small, get to know Sadie a bit, so she's talked about moving to New York, being an editor, and how we picked out a toddler bed for Rory yesterday—pink with a girly canopy that Rory loved.

When she asked how our Easter was, it led to Sadie telling her how hard it was for her. Yet she felt like she wasn't alone anymore because she had me, and that when she dropped the ball, I picked it up. So I felt it was only fair that I was completely honest with her.

"I knew there was a chance I was wrong," I continue, "and that it was just a coincidence, but something in me had me follow my gut, so I went out to the twenty-four-hour Walmart while Sadie and Rory were asleep."

Taking Sadie's hand in mine, I bring it up to my lips for a kiss. "When I saw the look on your face," I say, directing my words at Sadie instead of Viola. "As you watched Rory excitedly tear through the basket, snapping picture after picture, I had a feeling I was right. I wasn't going to ask, though. I didn't want to upset you. So when you brought it up and thanked me...letting me in...it meant the world to me."

Sadie sniffles. "Sometimes I want to talk to you, but I can't. Not that you won't listen, but it just doesn't come out. Like the words are stuck in my throat. Memories surface, and I feel like I'm being choked by the emotion."

Viola smiles softly at Sadie. "That's completely normal. This week, I'd like for you guys to try something."

I groan playfully, already knowing what's coming. "This is when she gives us homework," I tell Sadie. "Viola loves to give homework. It's not like the homework we had in school, though. It's worse. Because it makes you actually think and feel, and unlike in school, you can't fucking cheat."

Viola laughs. "Your homework is to buy a notebook and keep it on the counter until one of you needs it. When you feel like you can't speak," she says to Sadie. "Or you want to express how you feel." She looks at me. "I want you to write in it and give it to the other person. Communicating doesn't always have to be speaking. Gage writes songs, and you edit novels. Writing can be communicating too."

After thanking Viola—and Sadie agreeing to join me again next time—we head out. Since Kaylee and Braxton are spending the afternoon and evening with Rory, we use the alone time to pick up gifts for her upcoming birthday and order a cake. We've decided to do her birthday at A Latte Fun, renting the place out for the afternoon since Rory loves it there.

"Where are we going?" Sadie asks when Paul drives toward her condo instead of Kaylee and Braxton's place.

"I'm taking you out on a date."

Her eyes widen, and then a bright smile spreads across her face. "Really? Where? What about Rory?"

"We'll pick her up after dinner."

"I can't even remember the last time I ate at an adult restaurant without Rory." Sadie laughs.

We go by the condo, where a dress and heels wait for Sadie, thanks to Kendall, who had them sent over in her size from some trendy boutique she loves. While Sadie gets changed, doing her hair and makeup, I change into a suit since the place we're going to has a dress code.

When she steps out, donning a tight-fitted, off-the-shoulder emerald dress that matches her eyes and shows off every perfect curve she has, I reconsider going out, so I can eat her for dinner instead.

"The only reason I'm not canceling dinner and laying you out on this table is because you're too beautiful not to show off." I kiss her hard, my tongue delving past her parted lips so I can have a taste of her before I reluctantly pull back.

"You look sexy in a suit," she says, running her hands along the sleeves of my jacket. "I want to go to dinner, but maybe if we eat quickly, you can lay me out on the table for dessert."

With a chaste kiss on the corner of my mouth, she saunters away from me in her fuck me heels, leaving me determined to make dinner a quick affair.

Paul picks us up and drives us to Plush, a restaurant owned by Brody Fields, a friend of Braxton's. When I asked him where I should take Sadie since I've been out of the game for...well, ever, he said he'd take care of it for me. As we're led back to our private room, I make a mental note to buy Braxton that guitar he was talking about at practice the other day to thank him for hooking me up.

The hostess seats us, and I sit on the same side as Sadie, wanting to be close to her during dinner because there's no way I'm going an entire meal with her looking like she does and not touching her. After ordering our drinks and food, the server returns with Sadie's white wine and my water and lets us know our dinner will be ready soon.

Since the room has a private balcony, when the server leaves, I take Sadie's hand in mine and walk us over to it.

"Dance with me?" I ask, pressing the button on the wall that adjusts the volume. Sadie nods and steps into my arms, encircling her hands around my neck while mine wrap around her waist. Her head rests against my chest, and as we sway to the music, I can't help but feel like I'm right where I was meant to be. I have a healthy, amazing daughter, a beautiful girlfriend, and I'm living my life instead of barely surviving. After I lost Tori, I never imagined this for my life and didn't think I deserved it. Maybe in a lot of ways I don't, but fuck if I'm not going to hold on to it with everything in my being.

"Do you think anyone would know if I dropped to my knees right now and sucked your dick?" Sadie asks, shocking the hell out of me and making me laugh. I'm over here lost in my emotions, and she's thinking about my damn cock.

Jesus, can she get any more perfect?

Without waiting for an answer, she backs up and closes the French doors that lead to the private room where we're supposed to be eating dinner, then smirks like a goddamn little minx before she drops to her knees. At the same time, I stand frozen in place, wondering if she's really about to suck me off right here on the private balcony in Plush.

She answers my thoughts when she unbuttons and unzips my pants, then pulls my cock out. Wrapping my semi-hard shaft in her hand, she presses a soft kiss to the head, looking up at me through her lashes. With her eyes never leaving mine, she darts her tongue out, licking the metal piercing, then sucks gently on it. She parts her lips and takes me all the way down her damn throat, not stopping until I'm bottoming out in the back.

"Holy shit," I breathe, grabbing the railing with one hand for support and her head with my other to...fuck, I don't even know what I'm grabbing her head for. All I know is that her hot, wet mouth wrapped around my cock is the sexiest thing I've ever seen and felt, and if I don't slow her down, I'm going to explode in less than thirty seconds like a pubescent fucking boy.

But before I can say or do anything, she takes me all the way into her throat again, hollowing her cheeks and sucking me down like she doesn't have a damn gag reflex, and I'm done for. I come down her throat, watching as she takes it all, swallowing every drop until I'm completely drained. And when there's nothing left, she slowly pulls her mouth off my shaft, stopping at the head to kiss it.

I pull her into my arms and crash my mouth down on hers, not giving a shit that the taste of her is tinged with the salt from my cum. Spinning her around, I back her against the stone wall and shove my hand between her legs, groaning into her mouth when my fingers land on her soaked-through panties.

Pushing them aside, I thrust two fingers into her, my thumb finding her swollen clit. I finger-fuck her like I'm kissing her, slow and deep. She detonates around my fingers a few short seconds later, soaking my hand. And when her legs nearly give out on her, I grip the curve of her hip to hold her up as she comes completely undone.

We stay like this for several moments, both of us catching our breaths. Once we're somewhat composed, we head back inside the private room, finding our food waiting for us.

"When I was growing up, my mom said I wasn't allowed to have any snacks before dinner because it would ruin my appetite." Sadie smirks. "She was totally wrong because I'm still hungry...for dinner and more of you."

Fuck, have I mentioned how damn perfect my woman is?

"DADA, DADA!" RORY GIGGLES, DROPPING HER LITTLE BUTT ONTO THE IN-GROUND TRAMPOLINE SO I CAN JUMP and make her fly. When I do what she wants, and she flies into the air, I catch her in my arms, making her laugh harder.

It's the day of her birthday party, which is also her actual birthday. It's crazy to think my princess is already one. I've only known her—known about her—for two months, but it feels like she's a part of me. I can't imagine her or Sadie not being a part of my life. I'm not technically living with them, but I'm there every night, and I haven't once not slept next to Sadie since the night she asked me to stay. I'm working on finding us a home, and once I find the perfect place, my plan is to propose and ask her to move in together. I never had a home growing up, and while the condo is great, I want to give Rory what I always dreamed of: the big house and even bigger backyard with a jungle gym and a dog running around.

"You must be Gage," a woman says, making me glance up from my daughter. I instantly recognize her as the woman from the cemetery.

"Ga ga!" Rory exclaims, reaching for her.

"Hello, sweetheart," the woman says to Rory before turning her attention back to me. "I'm Janice, and my husband, Henry, is saying hello to Sadie. We're... Vincent's parents." Her eyes dim at the mention of his name.

"It's nice to meet you." Sadie's mentioned them a few times since we've been together, telling me they've stayed in touch and consider Rory like a granddaughter. I didn't put the two together until now, though. That the couple from the cemetery are Sadie's in-laws.

"I just wanted to say thank you," she says softly. "Sadie has told us so much about you, and it's clear you make her happy. Vincent might've been my son, but I wasn't oblivious to the way he treated her and chose drugs over her."

Her admission has me swallowing thickly because I also chose drugs over Sadie once upon a time. As if she can sense my thoughts, she adds, "He refused to get help, and instead of doing what we should've done and cut him off, we enabled him. Sadie said you've been clean for over a year now. That's all I wanted for my son..." She runs her fingers through Rory's hair. "Seeing Sadie so happy makes me happy, and I know I have you to thank for that."

"She and Rory are my world," I tell her honestly. "Their happiness is everything to me, and I'll always do everything in my power to make sure they're happy." I hand Rory over to Janice, making it clear that includes having no issue with her and her husband being part of our lives.

"Hey, you," Sadie says shyly, stepping over and kissing my cheek. "I see you've met Janice."

"I have," I say, tucking her under my arm. "Things are about to get crazy since we finished our album and will start promoting it, but we should get together for dinner when it calms down." I don't miss the way Sadie sighs in relief against my side.

"That would be great," Janice says, kissing Rory and setting her down so she can run and play with the other kids she's made friends with.

She walks over to her husband, who's chatting with Easton, and Sadie wraps her arms around me tightly, looking up at me. "Thank you."

"You don't have to thank me for accepting your family. Vincent and I both fucked up. The only difference between us is that I was able to get help before I killed myself. I know how fortunate I am to have this second chance with you and be able to have Rory in my life." I lean down and kiss her soft lips. "I could've easily been in the same position as him, and I'll never, for a second, forget that."

"Mama! Dada!" Rory yells, wanting our attention.

"Let's go sing 'Happy Birthday' to our princess," I murmur to Sadie. "Then figure out a way to make her stop growing."

Twenty-Five

GAGE

"I'M SENDING YOU GUYS A SCHEDULE FOR THE UPCOMING PROMO AND ENGAGEMENTS YOU'LL BE REQUIRED TO attend," Mario, our publicist, says, glancing up from his phone. We've finalized the album, titled *Calm After the Storm*, and are going over all the shit that comes next. "But I wanted to let you know that tonight you'll be performing at Ruckus. I know it's last minute, but the artist who was supposed to perform got sick." The name of the club sends a shiver down my spine. It's been over a year since I've been in a club, and Ruckus is one of the crazier ones. I spent too much time in VIP, getting high after our performances.

"Tonight?" Camden groans. "Tomorrow's Mother's Day."

"Layla will be working as well," Mario says. "Since you guys are making a comeback, we'll document everything into a vlog series. It's all in the informational packet I emailed."

"She approved that?" Camden asks, pulling out his phone to call his wife, who's one of Blackwood's videographers and has been mostly on leave since she gave birth to Marianna—aside from doing a few small gigs like Kendall and Declan's music video.

"I did," she says, walking in, all business. "I actually just got out of a meeting a few minutes ago, or I would've told you. You know I've been thinking about going back to work, and your dad agreed to me coming back part-time, working with you guys on the promo for your upcoming album."

Camden grins, no doubt loving that he'll have his wife around. One of the things that sucks about putting out an album is how busy we get with promo. I'm already dreading all the time I'll be away from Sadie and Rory, but it's all part of the game, and once it's done, we'll take some time off before we go on tour. I'm hoping to convince her to join us, at least some of the time, so I don't have to go too long without seeing my girls.

"Anything else?" Braxton asks, standing and ready for this meeting to be over.

Mario looks over his notes. "Nope. Be at Ruckus tonight at eight o'clock for the sound check."

We all take off, and I head home, only stopping at the deli to pick us up dinner.

Since Paul is driving, I allow myself to get lost in my thoughts. I'd be lying if I said I wasn't nervous about tonight. It's the first time I'll be back in the environment that enabled me to drown myself in my sorrows and grief. Somehow, it feels like I'm being given a test that I still don't feel prepared for even though I've studied. I pull out my phone, texting Kaylee to see if she's going. She immediately responds that she was planning to, but if I want Sadie to go and need a sitter, she'd be more than happy to watch Rory. I thank her and tell her that I'll let her know, and then I text my therapist, asking if she's available. When she hasn't responded by the time I get home, I put my phone away to focus on my girls.

When I walk in the door, Rory is crying, and Sadie is cradling her in her arms. It's not often Rory cries. I don't have any babies to compare her to, but she seems extremely chill. Unless she's teething, she sleeps all night and rarely throws tantrums.

"What happened?" I ask, dropping the food onto the table and walking over to them.

"I was trying to get some editing done, and she got into the cabinets...slammed her finger in the door."

"Is she okay? Do we need to take her to the hospital?"

"She's okay." Sadie sighs. "It just hurt and scared her. She refused to take a nap today, and I'm running behind on a manuscript that's due. I usually work while she naps or sleeps, but I've been a little preoccupied lately." She glances at me, her cheeks staining pink, and I smirk, remembering the way I took her last night in the shower after we put Rory to bed and then again in bed while we were watching TV. I can't get enough of her, and the moment Rory is asleep, I spend our time together all over her. I hadn't thought about the fact that means she isn't getting her work done, but she hasn't once complained or said anything.

"Do you want me to take her so you can get some work done?" I ask, reaching out for Rory, who's calmed slightly, and taking her into my arms.

"No, it's okay. But I need to get this done tonight, so maybe..." She twists her lips, and my stomach drops at the thought of her not wanting me to spend the night.

"I actually have a thing tonight," I say, knowing her going is out of the question. There's no way I can ask her to attend a show when she needs to get her own work done.

"Oh, okay," she says, her lips turning down into a slight frown.

"It's a work thing," I explain as Rory lays her head on my shoulder and cuddles into my front. "I was going to ask you to come. It's at Ruckus."

"The club?" She sounds as worried as I feel. I don't want to weigh her down with my shit since she's stressed enough as it is, so I force a smile and shrug like it's not a big deal.

"Yeah, we're performing our new single there. It'll be videoed and put on

YouTube to help generate a buzz around the upcoming album. It gets fans hyped. We don't do it often anymore, but since we've been gone for a while, it'll help put our name back on the board."

"Makes sense," she says. "Looks like Rory finally fell asleep." She nods toward our sleeping little girl. "Hopefully that doesn't mean she'll wake up in the middle of the night." She rolls her eyes.

"Should I wake her up?" I ask, unsure what to do. Every day I learn something new about parenting.

"No, just lay her down, so we can eat in peace." She waves me off. "How long until you have to leave?"

I glance at the clock. "I need to get ready and head out in about an hour."

"What songs are you guys playing?" Sadie asks as we eat, making small talk while she also messages back and forth with one of her clients, who's asking her questions about a manuscript she sent her.

"A mixture of our new songs and some old," I say, trying not to freak out over having to enter that club. Every time my brain goes to the music, the people, the drugs, I feel like I want to throw up. I knew this day would eventually come, and I thought I was ready, but now I'm second-guessing myself.

"Hopefully, it's just three songs, and then we're out," I mutter, pushing my food away. The last thing I need is to throw up on stage.

"Yeah," she says, her attention on her texts. I watch her for a few minutes, hating how stressed she looks. I mentioned she doesn't need to work, that I can provide for us, but she just gave me a crazy look and said she appreciated it, but this is the twenty-first century, and she's an independent woman. I think it was meant mostly as a joke, but deep down, I'm sure a part of her doesn't want to depend on another addict—even if I am a recovering one.

Sadie glances up from her phone, catching me staring, and quirks a brow. "You okay?"

I want to tell her I'm nowhere near close to okay, that I'm freaking out on the inside, wondering what the hell I'm thinking going into a club so soon, but when her phone goes off again and she groans in frustration at whoever she's conversing with, I simply nod.

After dinner, Sadie says she's going back to work while I jump in the shower and get ready for tonight. With my nerves making me anxious, I take an extra-long time in the shower, trying to rid myself of the anxiety weighing on me.

After kissing Rory—who's still asleep—and Sadie goodbye, I head out to meet the guys at the club. Since it's one of those events where we need to be seen, we drive together, and our security follows us in. Even with the late notice, the area is filled with screaming fans as we walk up the black carpet that leads to the club. With a lump in my throat the size of a golf ball, I try to act as chill as possible. My phone goes off in my pocket, and when I look to see if it's Sadie, I find a text from Viola:

Hey Gage, I was tied up. I can talk now if you want to call me.

I want to tell her I can hide in the fucking bathroom to talk to my therapist, but the band needs me, so instead, I shoot her a text that it's all good and I'll see her at our next appointment. Then I pocket my phone, willing myself to summon up the strength I need to get through tonight.

Twenty-Six

SADIE

where I am.

Me: At home...

Kaylee: Oh! I thought you were at Ruckus. I told Gage I could watch Rory for you if you needed a sitter. I just got here. The guys sound so good. Braxton was worried about Gage since he hasn't played for an audience since he's been back, but he seems to be doing good. Did he seem nervous before he left?

Her text is accompanied by a short video of the guys on stage, playing a single I've heard them rehearsing in the studio, "Hurricane." Kaylee zooms in on each of the guys, all of them clearly in their element until she gets to Gage. He's playing, nodding his head in the way he does when he's focused, but something about his eyes has me pressing pause. He looks distant, disconnected, like he's just trying to get through the motions. Her question has me thinking about earlier tonight. I was so caught up in the chaos of my job that I was only half there while we were eating dinner.

Did he seem nervous? I can't remember...But regardless, even if he didn't appear to be, tonight is a big deal, and I'm not there to support him.

And then I remember what he said when he first got home. *I was going to ask you to go...* I was so distracted that my only focus was getting time alone to finish my edits.

Dammit, I should be there, supporting him.

Pulling up my contacts, I call Janice. It's late, but she and Henry have always been night owls. "Hey, sweetie, is everything okay?"

"Yes...no. Gage is at his first show since..." I swallow thickly, realizing by the second how badly I've messed up. One of the main reasons he was scared to record again was because of everything that comes with being in a rock band. He mentioned on several occasions that he was afraid the music would always be associated with his addiction, and he worried he wouldn't be able to separate the two. "Is there any way you could come over and watch Rory? I know it's late and at the last minute, but—"

"Henry and I will be right over," Janice says.

"Thank you."

While I wait for them to arrive, I get dressed in my most "club-appropriate" attire, thankful it actually fits since it's from pre-kids. When Henry and Janice get here, I call for an Uber and arrive at the club a little over an hour after Kaylee texted me. There's a chance the band isn't even playing anymore, but since I haven't heard from Gage, I figure it can't hurt to go in and see if I can catch him still playing. Since my name isn't on the list, I text Kaylee, who meets me at the door. The second our eyes lock, I know something's wrong.

"The guys can't find him," she says. "Security is looking for him right now. They finished playing, and part of the contract is that they hang out and have a drink. One minute, Gage was there, and the next, he wasn't."

I rush past her, my heart pounding, needing to find Gage. I can feel it deep inside me as if a string connects us that something is wrong. The club is packed, and there's no way I'm going to find him in this chaos, so I pull my phone out and dial his number. It rings several times before he answers. "Sadie," he whispers, his voice sounding broken.

"Gage, where are you?"

"I...I'm having..."

"Baby, just tell me where you are. I'm here, at Ruckus."

"Bathroom."

I hang up and search for the bathroom. After asking someone, I find it and push past the guys standing outside, waiting for their turn. The door is locked, so I get a manager to let me in. At first, he's unsure, but when I explain who I am and who's in there, he reluctantly does as I ask.

Shutting and locking the door behind me, I find Gage sitting in the corner, his face in his hands, and his body visibly shaking.

"Gage."

His head shoots up, his glassy eyes meeting mine, and I cut across the room and into his lap. "Oh, Gage." I frame his face with my hands. "Did you...did you take anything?" I hate to ask, but I need to know where to go from here.

"No." He shakes his head. "It just...it was too much." He drops his head against my chest and releases a guttural sob. "I was okay playing, but then we were supposed to stay, and I should've left. The guys said I could leave, but I didn't want to let them down and have people talking shit that I dipped out early, so I stayed."

I hold him tight while he cries, peppering kisses all over his face, needing him to know I'm here. When he finally calms, he takes a deep breath and looks into my eyes. "You came."

"I'll always be here. We're a team. You just have to tell me you need me, and I'll be here. Always. Just like when I had a panic attack, and you carried me to safety, or when I was drowning in my grief and couldn't give Rory the Easter she deserved. You were there for me, and I'll always be here for you." I kiss him softly on his lips, then stand, so he can get up as well.

Gage threads his fingers through mine, and we walk out of the bathroom together, ignoring the looks he's getting. Hopefully tomorrow people will just assume we were having sex in the bathroom.

Wanting to get out of there as quickly as possible, Gage texts the guys to let them know that he left, and he'll talk to them tomorrow, and then we head out. Paul drives us home, and after thanking Janice and Henry for keeping an eye on Rory, we shower and change into comfortable clothes.

"I need to call my sponsor," Gage says once we're cuddled on the couch. "I'd like for you to meet him."

"I'd be honored."

"Gage, how are you?" Gabe says, wiping his eyes and clicking a light on.

"I'm...all right...now." He turns the phone so I'm in view. "This is Sadie, my girlfriend and Rory's mom."

Gabe smiles. "Nice to meet you."

"You, too."

"I had a show tonight," Gage admits softly, so unlike the rock star persona other people see. "I wasn't going to use, but it brought back a shit ton of memories and scared the hell out of me. I didn't like feeling like that."

Gabe nods. "What did you do?"

"Went to the bathroom and hid like a little bitch."

"Hey!" I say, glaring at him. "Don't you ever say that again. You didn't hide anywhere. You got out of the situation the best way you could. This was your first time being at a club. Of course, it's going to trigger you. You're human. You could've easily allowed yourself to drown in the feeling and used, but instead, you handled it. And that's more than what many recovering addicts would do," I say, trying not to compare Gage to my late husband, but I can't help it. Looking at Gage, seeing how hard this is for him, but also seeing how strong he is without even realizing it, makes me so proud of him. "You did the right thing, Gage. You got yourself out of the situation."

"She's right," Gabe says, making me jump. I completely forgot he was on the phone. "It could've ended much differently."

"I froze," Gage says. "I should've called you. I didn't call anyone. I just sat in the bathroom and freaked out."

"But did you use?" Gabe asks.

"No," Gage breathes. "Never again." The conviction in his voice sends shivers down my spine.

The guys talk for a few more minutes, and Gage mentions he's going to attend a meeting tomorrow and call Viola for an emergency appointment, and then they hang up.

"I'm so proud of you," I tell Gage, climbing into his lap.

"What if this is a sign that I can't have the career I used to have? What does this mean for the band?"

"Of course, you can have it. You just have to take it one day at a time and adjust accordingly. You said it yourself, you should've left, but you stayed when we both know your friends, your *family*, would never have wanted you to stay if they knew how you felt. You can have the music without the lifestyle, and the guys will understand. Hell, they're all married. They're just trying to make music and entertain the fans themselves."

I wrap my arms around his neck and look into his blue eyes. "Let people in, Gage. Let me in. We love you and support you."

Gage stills under me, and I realize what I've just said. I could play it off, but there's no point since I meant it. "I love you, Gage. And I want to be here, by your side, and the person you call when you're feeling alone. Tonight, you should've told me how you felt. In the future, talk to me."

"Fuck," Gage mutters, crashing his mouth down on mine. He kisses me hard and rough as if he's trying to convey every emotion he feels in that one kiss. When we break apart, he rests his forehead against mine. "I love you so much, Sadie."

Twenty-Seven

GAGE

"DADA!" RORY SQUEALS, WAKING ME UP. I ROLL OVER AND FIND SADIE STILL ASLEEP. AFTER GETTING HOME and talking to my sponsor, I spent the next couple of hours getting lost in her. I showed her how much she means to me and how much I love and need her. We didn't fall asleep until the sun was damn near coming up, so she had to be exhausted.

Carefully, so she doesn't wake up, I grab Rory and change her diaper and get her dressed. It's Mother's Day, and even though I already bought Sadie a gift, I want to do more to show her how much she means to Rory and me. I consider calling Paul to pick us up, but since it's a nice day out, I write Sadie a note, letting her know I took Rory with me in her stroller—so she doesn't freak out—and then we take off on our mission to spoil Sadie.

On the way to the store, I pick up some flowers and make a pit stop at Eternal Cross Cemetery. After placing the flowers on Tori's tombstone, I push Rory over to where her brother is.

"This is Collin," I tell her, taking her out and setting her on my lap. "He's your big brother." I know she doesn't understand, but Sadie wants her to know about him, and I completely support that. "Collin, this is your little sister, Aurora. We call her Rory." Rory squeals at the mention of her name, and I kiss her cheek.

Glancing between Collin's and Vincent's graves, I speak to them, hoping if there's a God, and they're in heaven, they can hear me. "I just wanted to let you know that I'm going to take care of Sadie. I love her, and like you, I want her to be happy." I turn my attention to Vincent's grave. "The only difference between you and me is that I survived. But I promise I'm going to live every day loving and taking care of Sadie, showing her how special she is."

I look at Collin's. "I'd give your mom up in a heartbeat if it meant you were here with her, but since it's not possible, I promise to make sure your spirit lives on. Your mom thinks about you every day, and even though you're not physically with us, you'll always be the best part of her."

I set flowers out for both of them and then lay the last bushel on the grave where Sadie's daughter was laid to rest. So much heartbreak in one place...Sadie deserves for her heart to be filled with love and happiness.

"All right, princess. We're going to pick up breakfast and then head home to Mommy."

"Pa pa!" she shrieks, pointing at the small park.

"Fine, but only for a few minutes."

When the stroller turns in the direction of the park, she yells in excitement. We spend the next half hour playing in the park, and luckily, when I say it's time to go, she doesn't freak out on me.

On the way home, we stop at the bakery and pick Sadie up breakfast and pastries, then stop at the store to get balloons. Her gift is already at the house.

"Boon!" Rory squeals, pointing at the balloons when they fly through the air as we walk back to the house. When we arrive, Sadie is lying across the couch, still in her pajamas, and reading on her tablet.

"Happy Mother's Day," I say, leaning over and giving her an upside-down kiss.

"Boon, Mama, boon!" Rory yells, making Sadie laugh.

"Thank you," she says, sitting up. "Did you have fun?" she asks Rory.

"We made a pit stop at the park." I set the food out and hand her a coffee. "We also stopped by Eternal Cross." Sadie nods in understanding, even if she doesn't completely understand.

I set Rory in her highchair and put some eggs and pieces of a biscuit on the plate for her, along with her sippy cup filled with milk, while Sadie sips her coffee and watches.

"What?" I ask, wondering if I'm doing something wrong.

"I trust you, Gage," she says, shocking the hell out of me. "I trust you with our daughter, and in the future, if you want to drive with her, I trust you to keep her safe."

Knowing that she wouldn't say that lightly, I pull her into my arms and kiss her. "Thank you. That means the world to me."

After we eat breakfast, Sadie opens her gifts. I got her a necklace with a Mom charm on it—hanging from it are her three babies' birthstones. She has me put it on her and tears up, thanking me. The next gift is from Rory. The other day Sadie had to run out to the store, so I stayed with Rory, and we created a picture for Sadie, using her hands to make a heart. I wrote a poem underneath it, and Rory scribbled on it, adding her own touch.

"Gage," Sadie gasps. "This is perfect." It's already framed, so we can hang it up in the living room. "This has been the best Mother's Day ever. Thank you."

"I have one more gift for you," I tell her, handing her the envelope. She opens it and in it is a certificate to a day spa. Unsure what she would want, I purchased everything they offer, just in case.

"I've never been to a spa," she admits sheepishly. "Thank you."

"When I was growing up, my mom used to say all she wanted was a day at the spa to relax. She never got that day at the spa, but I'm so happy I can give one to you. I want to make you happy," I tell her, taking her hands in mine. "Rory and I are beyond lucky to have you, and I want you to know every day how much you mean to us."

Sadie nods, her eyes turning watery. "We're lucky to have each other."

We spend the rest of the day together, and then go to dinner with everyone for Mother's Day, heading back to Easton and Sophia's place afterward for dessert.

"Can we talk about last night?" Camden asks when everyone is hanging out and bullshitting. Normally, I'd be pissed he's throwing my shit out there, but since everyone in the room is family, I get it. They blame themselves for not speaking up when I was spiraling.

"I want to be part of the band," I tell everyone, as Sadie takes my hand in hers to remind me that she's here and by my side. "But I don't want..." I shake my head. "I *can't* be part of that lifestyle. The clubs and after-parties. I know I've been clean for over a year, but I was addicted for over six years. I didn't want to do drugs last night, but I couldn't handle the situation. It was too much for me, and I had a panic attack. Sadie found me in the bathroom."

Easton clasps me on the shoulder. "That's the first damn time you've ever told us your feelings, son," he says. "Thank you." He steps around and sits in front of me. "The only requirement in your contract is to make music. If something is put on your schedule that isn't good for you, you tell me. Get it?" I nod. "I'll make sure it's taken care of, *always*. You come first. All of you do." He glances at Cam, Brax, and Dec. "We're a family, and the only thing that matters is that you're healthy and happy."

Sadie sniffles, cuddling into my side, and I tuck her under my arm, glancing down at her. "See," she whispers. "You're not alone."

"No," I say, looking around at the people who, despite not being blood, are my family in every way that matters. "I'm not."

"HOLY SHIT. YES, RIGHT THERE," SADIE MOANS AS I DEVOUR HER PUSSY WITH MY FINGERS AND TONGUE. AFTER putting Rory to bed, Sadie and I showered the day off. She said she needed a few minutes, so I got dressed and picked up, knowing she likes it when the house is clean before she goes to bed. I was just finishing the dishes when she called me into the room, where I found her spread eagle on the bed dressed in a tiny as fuck black lace bra and panty set.

Her body coils tightly, and then, with a flick of my tongue, she soars, coming hard. Needing to be in her, I flip her onto her belly—the way I know she likes—and pull her up onto all fours before I line myself up and thrust into her from behind.

"This...You and me...is perfect," I groan, pulling back and then pushing into her. My hand comes down on her ass, making a cracking sound as it connects with her flesh.

"Again," she moans, wiggling her ass like the damn minx she is.

I pull out, smack it again, then plow into her, hitting deep.

"Oh, God, yes, again."

I do as she asks, fucking her with deep, lazy thrusts, alternating between smacking her sexy ass and massaging it. When her pussy tightens around me, telling me she's close, I pull her up so that her back is flush with my front and massage her clit until she's screaming my name in pure ecstasy, taking me straight over the edge with her.

Once we've both gotten a handle on our breathing, I pull her into my arms, our bodies naturally tangling up in one another. We should probably clean up since I'm sure my cum is dripping out of her, but the thought of her being full of me, even if she is on birth control, is such a damn turn-on. One day, I'm going to put another baby in her, and this time, I'll be there to watch her belly grow and swell. There was a time when the thought would've sent me to drugs, but now, it reminds me why I need to stay clean.

"I want this," Sadie says, shaking me from my thoughts. "Every day." There's no way she could know what I'm thinking, but the fact that we're on the same page tells me just how perfect we are together.

"I do too." I kiss her on her lips.

"What I mean is..." She bites her bottom lip nervously. "I want you and me... here...every day."

"Baby, you've got me." I glide my hand down her side and squeeze her peach of an ass. I don't know why she's suddenly acting like this, but I'll gladly remind her every day that I'm not going anywhere, that she and Rory are it for me.

"No...Ugh," she groans in frustration. "I want you to move in with me," she blurts out, her eyes going wide. "If you want to," she adds softly.

Rolling her onto her back, I cage her in my arms as my heart pounds against my rib cage. She spreads her legs and wraps them around me, pushing my hard shaft back inside her. With my cum still inside her, I slip right in.

"One day, I'm going to put a ring on your finger," I murmur, pressing a kiss to the corner of her mouth. "Then I'm going to put another baby in your belly." I kiss the other corner. "But until then..." I place a kiss on her neck. "There's nothing I want more than to go to bed and wake up with you in my arms every day for the rest of our lives."

Twenty-Eight

GAGE

"WHAT'S UP, LA?" CAMDEN YELLS OVER THE ROARING CROWD. "YOU MISS US?" THE DEAFENING SCREAMS OF the fans are enough to make even the cockiest musician's heart sing. We're playing at the Summer Music Festival: an annual festival that houses all types of bands on the beach in LA. It's been over two years since we've played here, and I have to admit it's nice to be back. It also helps that as I gear up to play, Sadie is standing on the side of the stage, smiling and waving at me.

When the band got the news that we'd be playing a short set—which lines up with our single that released yesterday—I talked to Sadie, and we decided to make it a little getaway. Three of the nannies who work for Kendall and Layla have come along, so Rory's safely tucked into bed at our house in Calabasas with the other kids.

"Damn, it feels good to be back," Camden adds, making everyone scream all over again. He talks to the crowd for a few minutes, then announces that we'll be playing some new songs and to let us know what they think.

My gaze goes to my woman, who's dressed in a tiny black dress and tall as hell boots that go almost to her knees, cheering us on, and my heart swells in my chest. For the first time in a long time, I feel good about playing. It's not realistic to think she can be at every show but having her here while I work through my shit helps. Knowing that when I'm done and walk off the stage, she'll be there waiting for me makes me feel like the luckiest fucking guy in the world.

The first song starts, and that one rolls into the next. Before I know it, Camden is announcing the final song for the night, "Bleeding Heart."

The second my sticks hit the drums and Camden starts belting out the lyrics, I'm instantly overcome by the words, succumbing to the feeling that I get every time I hear the song I wrote for Sadie...

Emerald eyes, soft smile, big heart
She's everything a man could ever want
Makes it bittersweet to know there's a chance
She'll never be mine
Someone like me doesn't deserve her time

But that doesn't stop me from wanting to take what's mine
From wanting her heart to be mine
Her body, her soul, all mine

It's crazy to think about where we were when I wrote the song and how much our relationship has developed. I know without a doubt she's the one for me, and I'm going to propose soon. Life is too damn short, and I want to make her my wife.

Throughout the entire song, our eyes stay locked on each other, the sexual tension building with each word Camden sings. Words don't need to be spoken, the lyrics speaking for themselves. And by the time the song ends, and Camden is saying good night to the crowd, thanking them for being amazing, I'm pushing off my seat, throwing my sticks toward the crowd, and taking off after my woman.

As I stalk toward her, the heat in her gaze tells me she wants me as much as I want her. And when I close the last bit of distance between us, lifting her by her ass into my arms, she squeals, encircling her legs around my waist.

"I need you," she breathes, her mouth connecting with mine. I find the closest empty room and slam the door behind us. Pushing her against the door, I reach between us and grab her thin panties, ripping them straight off her body. She shrieks in shock, then kisses me harder, devouring my mouth with hers. I thrust a couple of fingers into her to make sure she's good to go and find she's soaking fucking wet.

"This is going to be hard and quick," I warn, knowing full well that as turned on as I am, there's zero chance of me drawing it out.

"Yes," she hisses as I pull my cock out and thrust it into her. With her weight above me, I go deep, and she groans, no doubt in a mixture of pain and pleasure as she takes every inch of me.

"Oh, God," she moans, her head falling back and her eyes rolling toward the ceiling. "That damn piercing is going to be the death of me."

I chuckle, loving that it brings her pleasure. After Tori and before Sadie, I never gave a shit about a woman's pleasure. I only got it for the pain it brought me. But seeing the way she loves it makes me glad I got it.

"Sadie," I groan. "I need you to touch yourself, baby." I hate that she'll have to help get herself off, but there's no way I'll be able to do it for her in this position.

"I'm already there," she breathes, bouncing herself up and down on my dick like it was made specifically for her pleasure. A moment later, she explodes around me, her pussy choking my dick like a vise, siphoning every drop of cum from me.

As I stay where I am, keeping her pinned against the door, her juices drip down and coat my balls. Walking us over to the table, I pull out and set her down, spreading her legs so I can see her glistening pussy dripping with my cum. She stays quiet, but I can feel her eyes on me as I push my fingers into her.

"What are you doing?" she asks, her voice coming out breathy.

"I want to have another baby," I admit, making her body tighten around my fingers. "I want my cum to fill this tight pussy over and over again until we make a baby." I press my thumb against her clit as I finger her, the only sound coming from her slick pussy.

If I was worried my admission would turn her off, I would be dead wrong because Sadie's moans get louder with every word I speak. "I want you swollen with my baby. And I want every man who sees you to know that I was inside you and we created that together.

"Do you want that, baby? Do you want me to fuck a baby into you?"

My question sends her over the edge, and she comes, yelling, "Yes," as I finger-fuck her right through her orgasm.

When she opens her eyes, she looks a mixture of sated and exhausted, and I chuckle at how fucking adorable she is.

"Did you mean that?" she asks, nibbling on the corner of her lip.

"That I want you pregnant? Yeah, one hundred percent." I pull my fingers out of her and stick them into my mouth, sucking her juices off them. When she sees what I've done, her eyes hood over, her tongue darting out across the seam of her lips.

I push my fingers back into her, then withdraw them, lifting them to her lips to paint her pouty mouth with our essence. "Any time you want to stop taking your birth control, I'm good with that."

"Are you sure?" she breathes.

I lean in and press my mouth to hers, kissing her tenderly, and she kisses me back. "I want everything with you," I murmur against her lips. "Anything you'll give me, I'll take and cherish."

"You have me," she says, framing my face. "All of me."

"WHY IS IT WHENEVER I'M ON A DEADLINE, RORY DECIDES SHE'S TOO GOOD FOR NAPTIME?" SADIE GROANS, dropping her head onto the desk and dramatically banging it on the wood, making Rory giggle.

"Mama bang bang." Rory toddles over to the desk and smacks her hand on the desk, mimicking her movement. "Rory bang bang."

I snort out a laugh and lift Rory into my arms. "I don't have anything else to do today. Why don't I get Rory out of your hair so you can work, and we'll bring home dinner?"

Sadie's head pops up. "Have I told you how much I love you?"

I chuckle. "Every day." I lean over and kiss her, and Rory does the same, copying me. "What do you say, princess? Want to go play at the park?"

"Yay!" Rory shrieks, smacking the sides of my face with her tiny hands. "Pa Pa!"

After changing her diaper and getting her dressed, I grab the stroller and buckle her in, shoving the diaper bag in the undercarriage.

"Say bye to Mommy," I tell Rory, who waves to Sadie.

"Bye, baby. Love you." Sadie glances at me. "Both of you."

"Love you."

The walk to the park doesn't take long, and once we arrive, Rory takes off like a bat out of hell, ready to make the jungle gym her bitch. She stops at the swings first, and I spend the next twenty minutes pushing her while playing duck and tickle. She giggles the entire time, thinking it's hilarious every time I duck and then pop up and tickle her.

When she grows tired of the swing, she runs to the jungle gym, climbing up the four levels that lead to the slide. I follow to make sure she's safe, and then run to the other end so I can catch her when she slides down, lifting her into my arms and blowing raspberries on her belly when she hits the bottom.

The third time she climbs up the levels, I run to the end to meet her, only when I get there, she isn't sitting on the slide ready to slide down.

"Rory?" I yell, just as a loud shriek pierces my ears. The cry that comes after can only be described as gut-wrenching. I run back, unsure what the hell happened when I see my daughter lying on the ground, crying in agony.

I jump into action, ready to pick her up when I notice her arm is dangling at the elbow. Her eyes, filled with pain, meet mine, and I swallow down my emotion, needing to help her.

"I've called an ambulance," a woman says as I carefully pick my baby up and rock her gently in my arms. As we wait for the paramedics to arrive, a flashback hits me hard...

"Excuse me...Are you Gage Sharpe?"

I glance up and find a nurse standing above me. Unable to move, I simply nod, and she sits next to me.

"I'm not supposed to say anything. Tori's parents didn't want it to be mentioned, but I've seen you here for hours, and I heard your friend mention you were her boyfriend."

Were...past tense...because Tori is dead. She hung herself, ending her life and leaving me to mourn her.

"There's something you should know. Tori was pregnant."

I snap my head toward her. "What?"

"She wasn't far along, only about twelve weeks, but when they did the autopsy, they confirmed it was a girl. I'm sorry," she says, gently placing her hand on my arm. "I just thought you might want to know."

The nurse sits next to me for several minutes while I sob into my hands, wondering why Tori would take her own life, knowing she was pregnant with my baby. She had to know I would take care of her. It doesn't make any sense. And then I remember the note...

"Can you...is there somewhere I can go to be in private?" I ask.

"Yeah. Follow me."

She leads me to a small room with a couple of cots and a table. "This is where the doctors and nurses sleep when we work long shifts," she explains. "Lock it behind you, and make sure you close it when you leave."

"Thank you."

I lock the door behind her and then sit on the cot, pulling the note out with my name scrawled across the front.

Dear Gage,

Let me first start by saying how much I love you. If you're reading this, it's because I'm gone, and for that, I'm sorry. They say suicide is a selfish act, and I never understood that, until now, because even as I write this letter to you, the only guilt I feel about ending my life is that I'm hurting you. You're not only my boyfriend, but my best friend, which is why it's so hard to write this letter. There are some things you need to know. But before I tell you, I need you to promise that you won't tell anyone. I'm only telling you, so you understand that my taking my life isn't because of you. If anything, the only reason I didn't do it sooner was because of you. Because of how much I love you. Every time I imagined my future, it was with you. All I ever wanted was to create a life with you. I thought I could be strong, but I'm not. I'm weak.

What I'm about to tell you, needs to stay between you and me. Once you're done reading this letter, I want you to burn it. Then get on a plane and go to LA and become the best damn drummer the music industry has ever seen. Promise me, please. Do this for me. Nothing will bring me back, and I don't want you to ruin your life because of him.

Glen. For the past several months, he's been coming into the pool house when you're not here and raping me. I know what you're thinking. Why didn't I tell you?, For a couple of reasons. One, I was scared of what you'd do. I know how much you love me and would do anything to protect me, and I couldn't put you in that position. So instead, I went to my mom. I thought she would believe me and protect me like a mom is supposed to, but instead, she said that I'm sick and need help.

And then I heard them talking. You went to them and begged them to help me. God, I, love you for that, but there's no helping me because they don't want to help me. They want me gone. Glen is planning to run for mayor, and he sees me as a loose string. He's planning to send me away and if you stand in his way, he's going to ruin you. He's rich and has connections, and I can't let him ruin you like he's ruined me.

There's something else you need to know, I'm pregnant. I don't know how far along I am, but there's a chance it's Glen's. He caught me taking a test and told me he's going to take the baby away from me. I can't let him do that, Gage. I'd rather die than let him take anything else away from me. I don't expect you to understand, but please know that I'm sorry and I love you. You're the best person I know, and you deserve to be happy, to have the family you never had, and I'm so sorry I couldn't be the one to give it to you.

Be amazing.

Xo Tori

I shake myself from the past, refusing to let it take me under, and continue to soothe my daughter the best I can.

When the paramedics arrive, they take Rory from me, needing to assess her.

"Dada!" she yells, trying to reach for me. "Dada!" As her tear-filled eyes beg me to fix this, I pull out my phone, dialing the only person in the world who will make this better. The person I need by my side.

Sadie...I need Sadie.

Twenty-Nine

SADIE

I'M LOST IN THE WORDS OF A COZY MURDER MYSTERY WHEN MY PHONE RINGS, GAGE'S NAME COMING UP ON the screen.

"Hey, you. How—"

"Sadie, I need you." The way he says my name, the pleading in his tone causes my body to go cold. Something's wrong. Very wrong. "It's Rory," he adds, and it's then I hear my baby girl screaming in the background. My heart clenches in my chest, feeling as though a barbed wire is wrapping around it, causing the organ to bleed out. "We're on the way to the hospital."

The hospital. They're on their way to the hospital. The recollection of Janice telling me that my husband and son were brought to the hospital but didn't make it flashed before my eyes. Collin's lifeless body, surrounded by his favorite toys he'd never play with again, being lowered into the ground.

"Gage," I gasp, the rest of my words getting caught in my throat.

"I'm so sorry, Sadie," he says, his words laced with raw emotion. "I need you to come to the hospital, please."

"Tell me she's going to be okay," I beg, sliding on my flip-flops and running out the door.

"She's hurt, but she's okay," he says. "I'm so sorry. I fucked up."

"Which hospital?"

He asks someone and then says, "New York Medical." My stomach drops. That's the same hospital Collin and Vincent were taken to. Surely, God wouldn't do this to me twice, right?

"I'm on my way."

Twenty minutes later, I'm running through the front doors of the hospital and straight to the desk. "I'm the mother of Aurora Sharpe. She's been brought in by ambulance."

The nurse clicks away on the computer. "She's in the pediatric unit, room 157. Follow the animal prints on the floor, and it will take you straight there."

I do as she says, and a few minutes later, I barge into the room, where I find Gage holding a sobbing Rory.

Her eyes meet mine, and she cries harder. "Mama, ow, ow."

"Oh, thank God," I breathe, seeing that she's alive. "I'm here, sweet girl," I tell her, cutting across the room, over to her and Gage.

"I'm so sorry," Gage whispers, carefully handing me my baby. "Try not to move her arm. They think it's broken." His glassy eyes meet mine, and tears slide down his face. "I'm so damn sorry. I should've been there. I should've caught her." He shakes his head, his words making no sense.

"What happened?" I ask, cradling Rory in my arms and checking her out. Her left arm is swollen and in a tiny sling.

"She was going down the slide. Every time, I would wait until she sat down, and then I'd go to the bottom to catch her. She must've stood back up and gone to the edge. I was at the bottom when I heard her scream." Gage flinches, and fresh tears spill down his cheeks. "She fell off the side." He hangs his head, shaking it back and forth. "They think her arm is broken. They gave her medicine for pain, said it should be enough so she's not hurting, and they're preparing to have an X-ray done."

"Gage, it's okay," I tell him, reaching out and squeezing his forearm. "These things happen."

"She could've hit her head," he rasps. "Could've broken her neck. You trusted me to take care of her, and I failed you. I failed her." He steps away from us, giving us his back. "I failed my mom and Tori and our baby...And now this. Rory could've fucking died." He turns around, his features etched in pain, and my heart aches for him.

"What do you mean, Tori and your baby?" I ask. I know about Tori and his mom, but he's never mentioned a baby.

"When she killed herself, she was pregnant. I had no idea until the nurse came and told me."

"Oh, Gage." I walk over to him with Rory still sobbing in my arms. "Why didn't you tell me?"

"I was afraid," he admits softly. "I was afraid if I told you that I couldn't keep Tori's baby safe, you'd think I couldn't keep Rory safe. You've already lost two babies." He swallows thickly, his sad blue eyes locking with mine. "Looks like it ended up happening anyway. Maybe if I'd told you, this could've been prevented."

"Don't you dare go there," I say, refusing to let him do this to himself. "That is not the same thing. You were not responsible for your mom's death or for keeping Tori and her baby safe. There's nothing you could've done to protect or save them." I reach out and lay my palm on the side of his tearstained cheek. "You can't let that guilt weigh on your shoulders. It wasn't your fault, just like Rory getting hurt wasn't your fault. It's part of being a parent. Every day, all we can do is love our babies and pray they're safe. But at any moment, they can be taken from us."

I lean over and kiss Rory's forehead, and she sighs softly, her eyes fluttering closed, the pain meds and exhaustion making her sleepy. "Yes, she got hurt. But it could've happened with me or anyone watching her. Life is unpredictable. You can't keep shouldering the responsibility and blame."

I sit on the chair and pat the one next to me, and Gage joins me. "Were you clean and sober?"

"Of course," he chokes out.

"Were you watching her?"

"Yeah, but—"

"It was an accident. She broke her arm, and that sucks, but it was just that... an accident."

"She was in so much pain."

"Did you take care of her?" I ask, already knowing the answer but needing him to hear it. "Did you hold her in the ambulance and make sure she knew she was safe?"

He nods, tears pricking his eyes. "I was so scared, Sadie. I had a flashback from when Tori died, and I was scared it was going to take me under."

"So what did you do?"

"I called you," he chokes out. "I'm so sorry," he sobs. "If you don't want me to take her—"

"Nope," I say, pressing my fingers to his lips, refusing to let him finish that thought. "I don't trust you any less with her than I did before the accident. You did everything you could." I lean over and kiss his wet lips. "I love you, Gage."

We sit in silence for several minutes, and then the technician comes in, bringing an X-ray machine with her. She takes pictures of Rory's arm and then the doctor confirms that it's broken. After realigning the bone, a bright pink cast is put on her arm—her choice—and then we're discharged with a prescription for meds and a referral to see the pediatric orthopedic doctor in four weeks.

Gage remains quiet when we get home, holding Rory and lying with her while she falls asleep. I give him his space, reading a book since I can't focus enough to work.

Once she's asleep, he comes out and sits next to me, lifting my legs into his lap. "Thank you for being there," he says, massaging my feet.

"We're partners," I tell him. "When you need me, I'll be here, just like when I need you, I know you'll be here too." He squeezes my foot and smiles softly at me.

We sit in comfortable silence, both of us lost in our thoughts. I don't know why, but the song he wrote for me plays in my head, and I sigh, thinking about how true the lyrics are.

"For what it's worth..." I sit up and climb onto his lap. "You healed me. My heart was broken and bleeding, and you fixed it by giving me the greatest gift...our daughter." His eyes light up in understanding. "It's because of her, because of *you*, I'm finally living again."

He wraps his arms around me, and I kiss him tenderly on his lips, then nestle my head into the crook of his neck, enjoying the comfort of being held by Gage.

"There's something I need to do, and it'd mean a lot if you'd join me," he says after a few minutes. "Do you think you could ask Janice to come over and watch Rory? We won't be long."

"TORI, I'D LIKE YOU TO MEET SADIE. I WANTED YOU TO MEET HER BECAUSE SHE AND RORY, OUR BEAUTIFUL daughter, wouldn't be here if it weren't for you." Gage sniffles, and I wrap my arms around him, holding him tight. "I hate that you're gone," he says, "but something good, something bright came from the darkness of your death. I met Sadie."

He pulls a crumpled paper out of his pocket and opens it up. "It took me a while to do as you asked, but I've finally done it." He glances at me, a small smile playing on his lips. "I've found happiness." He pulls a lighter out of his pocket and sets the corner of the paper on fire, dropping it onto the stone of her grave.

"She asked me to burn the letter after I read it," he explains. "I held on to it, reading it over and over again, wanting to remind myself of how badly I failed." He places his hand in mine. "I think it's time to move on. To let go of the past and focus on our present...on our future."

Epilogue

SADIE

SIX MONTHS LATER

"THANK YOU, NEW YORK, AND HAPPY NEW YEAR!" CAMDEN YELLS AS THE CROWD SCREAMS IN EXCITEMENT. It's New Year's Eve, and Raging Chaos just finished their performance in Times Square. It's freezing cold outside, but there was no way I was missing their performance. Rory is at home with Janice and Henry, warm and toasty and fast asleep. Gage made plans for us to stay at a hotel overnight to ring in the new year once their show is over.

"One more thing," Gage says, shocking the hell out of me and everyone else. He plays the drums. He doesn't sing...or talk. "Sadie, can you come out here, please?"

It takes me a second to wrap my head around what he's asking, but when he smiles my way and nods, I put one foot in front of the other to join him on stage.

"What are you doing?" I whisper-yell.

"This is my girlfriend," he says to the crowd, making them cheer.

"Hi." I wave my hand quickly.

"I've thought about how to do this a million times, but every time it feels like it's not romantic enough, or the timing isn't right," he says. "So I figured tonight would be perfect. What better way to start the new year than with you as my fiancée?" He quirks a brow. "Shoot, I probably should've proposed first. And now that I'm thinking about it, if you say no, it's going to be a crappy way to start the year."

The crowd bursts out in laughter at Gage's botched proposal, and I join in, shaking my head. "Well, there's only one way to know if it will be a good or bad year," I say, only realizing too late that because of the mic on him, everyone can hear me.

"Oh, yeah." He fumbles with his pocket and then pulls out a black box, popping it open. "Since the day I met you, I knew you were a game changer. You're the lightness in my dark, the healer to my broken. You remind me every day that life is worth living, so I would love nothing more than to spend my life with you as my wife."

Gage drops to his knee and holds out the ring. "Sadie Ruiz, will you do me the honor of becoming my wife?"

"Umm..." I lift my finger to my chin and tap it playfully, and Gage chuckles. "Yes, I would love to be your wife."

A massive grin stretches across his face as he pushes the ring onto my finger and then stands, lifting me in his arms and twirling me around.

"It's probably for the best anyway," I whisper, so only he can hear. "We already have one child out of wedlock. Maybe this baby will be born with his or her parents married."

Gage stiffens at my half-joke and releases me, his blue eyes locking with my green. "Are you...?" He looks down at my still flat belly. I only just found out this morning. I planned to tell him once we were alone tonight after the show.

"I am...We are." I smile a watery smile, and he pulls me into his arms, hugging me tightly.

"Fuck, baby," he murmurs into my ear. "Thank you."

"Do we have time to stop at Eternal Cross on the way to the hotel?" I ask as we make our way off the stage. "I'd like to tell Collin he's going to be a big brother again."

Gage nods and tugs me into his side, kissing my temple. "We have all the time in the world."

Bonus Scenes

BRAXTON

"IF WE DON'T GET MOVING, WE'RE GOING TO BE LATE FOR…" MY VOICE TRAILS OFF WHEN I ENTER THE bedroom and find Kaylee sitting on the bed, holding something in her hand.

"Kaylee…"

She glances up and smiles at me, tears filling her lids. "I'm pregnant."

My heart swells in my chest at her words. "You're sure?" We've been waiting. Since she's miscarried twice early on, we decided not to take a test until she's missed her period a couple of times. She's missed it two months in a row now.

"It says I'm pregnant." She holds up the test and shrugs. She should be excited, jumping with joy, but she's scared. We've been trying for over two years.

"That's awesome," I tell her, sitting next to her and pulling her into my arms. "Call the doctor so we can go in and have it confirmed."

Because of a cancelation, we're in the doctor's office four hours later. After Kaylee gets blood drawn, she's given a gown to put on, and a few minutes later, the doctor returns to do the ultrasound herself.

Unsure exactly how far along she is, the doctor does one internally, and after a few clicks of the button, a *whoosh, whoosh, whoosh* fills the silence.

"That's your baby's heartbeat," the doctor says with a smile. "You're roughly ten weeks, and everything looks good." She goes through and explains everything in detail, and once she's done, she gives us a printout of our little bean.

"I can't believe we're having a baby," Kaylee says, staring at the picture. "It's really happening."

"Hell yeah, it is. Let's go celebrate."

GAGE

SADIE, I WAS THINKING FOR LUNCH WE COULD…" I STEP INTO THE BATHROOM AND FIND MY WIFE STANDING in a puddle of water. "Umm, babe, I think—"

"My water broke." She glances up at me with a huge smile on her face. "It's time."

"What?" I rasp.

"It's time to have the baby."

After calling Janice and Henry to come over and watch Rory, we head to the hospital. Since we've preregistered, we're checked in quickly, and the doctor comes in to check Sadie.

"I…need…drugs," she breathes, clearly in a crazy amount of pain. From the time her water broke till now, her contractions have increased in strength.

"Unfortunately, that won't be possible," Dr. Bromfield says. "You're ready to push."

"What?" Sadie shrieks.

The nurses get her ready, and less than an hour into pushing, our baby boy enters the world, screaming his head off.

"I don't think he wanted to come out," Sadie says jokingly as the nurse hands him to her so she can bond with him.

"I don't blame him," I say with a wink. "If it were up to me, I'd live my entire life inside you."

She snorts out a laugh. "You're so dirty." She glances down at our baby. "Welcome to the world, Asher Sharpe." She kisses his forehead, and I snap a picture, getting choked up. I wasn't here for the birth of Rory, so I've been soaking up every moment of Sadie's pregnancy, and if I have it my way, I'm going to knock her up several more times.

"All right, Daddy," she says, looking up at me. "You ready to hold your son?"

I set my phone down and carefully take Asher into my arms. He's so tiny, only twenty-two inches and seven pounds. His eyes aren't open yet, and he's calm now, sucking his lips like he's hungry. I lean in and kiss his head that hasn't been properly cleaned yet and know that my heart, which was once broken and bleeding, is now healed. Because there's no way it could hold the amount of love I feel if it weren't completely intact.

DECLAN

"DO YOU HEAR THAT?"

"Hear what?" I ask my gorgeous wife.

"The silence."

I laugh. "That's what happens when your husband takes you away on vacation without the kids." I pull her into my arms. It's our anniversary, and I surprised her with a weekend getaway to The Hamptons. Nothing fancy, just some alone time with my wife.

"I don't even know what to do with myself," she jokes, lying back on the couch. We just got back from dinner, and it's almost nine o'clock—which is pretty much our bedtime these days.

"How about a game of rummy?" I suggest.

"Sure." She grins and sits up, grabbing the cards out of her purse.

Anytime she's alone, she likes to play solitaire, and when she's with her family, they play rummy. Shortly after we moved in together, she asked me to play. Since then, it's become our nightly tradition. After the kids are asleep, we'll play while we talk about our day. Afterward, we go to bed and watch *The Vampire Diaries* and *The Originals*. Sadly, we're nearing the end, and I'm not sure what I'll do with my life once it's over—but I'll never admit that to her.

"We might be the most boring couple in the world." She laughs, sitting at the table. "We're kid-less for the night, and here we are, about to play rummy."

"Do you want to go out?" I ask. "Hit one of the clubs?"

"Hell no," she scoffs, shuffling the cards. "I'm good right here. I'm completely content being boring."

"How about we make it a little less boring?"

"How so?" She quirks a brow.

"Whoever loses each round has to shed an article of clothing." I waggle my brows, and she laughs.

"Okay, and first one to five hundred wins."

"And what does the winner get?" I ask.

"What do you want?"

I think for a moment. "If I win, we have another baby."

She snorts out a laugh. "Okay, if I win, you have to get your cock pierced."

"Seriously?" I groan, realizing too late that I walked right into that one. My crazy-ass wife has been begging me to get my dick pierced ever since she found out Braxton and Gage are both pierced.

"Hey, you want your prize to be a human life," she points out.

I chuckle. "Fair. All right, deal."

In the first round, Kendall wins 170 to 150.

I take off my shirt.

In the second round, I win: total is 290 to 310, my lead.

Kendall takes off her shirt, and the entire next round, I'm distracted by her pert nipples poking through her lacy bra.

She wins that round, and the total is 420 to 410, her lead.

I take my pants off.

"Next round, someone could be a winner," she says, dealing.

"Yeah, me, and when I win, we're getting started on that baby making tonight."

"When I win, we're making your appointment to get pierced as soon as Forbidden Ink opens," she says, referring to our go-to tattoo and piercing studio.

We play in silence, both of us focused on winning. Based on what we've laid down so far, our points are pretty close. We both have a couple of cards left in our hands. At my turn, I pick up and set my three cards down, but I'm left floating.

Kendall picks up and grins, setting three cards down. We're floating. I pick up again, and since I can't put the card anywhere, I go out, ending the game.

We count up our points, and when she says she has a hundred and forty points, I know I've lost because I have twenty points less. Kendall knows it too when she glances up at me and sees the look on my face.

"Gah! Yes! Yes! I won…" She jumps up and dances around the room. "I won! I won!" Then she plops down into my lap and straddles my thighs. "But so did you."

I lean back, confused. "And how is that?" And then it hits me. "Are you…?"

"Yep," she says with a smile stretched across her face. "I'm pregnant. Well, at least I think I am. I haven't tested yet since I did it without you the last time. I brought one with me so we could—"

Before she can finish her sentence, I'm picking her up and carrying her to her luggage. "Where's the test?"

"In my makeup bag."

I grab it, still holding on to her, and then carry her into the bathroom, setting her down so she can take the test.

She pees in a disposable cup and then dips the stick in…and then we wait. Not even two minutes later, the word appears across the screen: PREGNANT

"Hell yes!" I pick her up and spin her around. "You're pregnant." Our lips fuse, and our tongues tangle. "Thank you," I murmur against her mouth.

"You don't have to thank me." She laughs, kissing the corner of my mouth.

I drop to my knees, so my face is even with her still flat belly. "Hey, little one…Or maybe it's little ones." I glance up at her. "Wouldn't it be cool if we had twins again?"

CAMDEN

"TO FAMILY!" MY DAD SAYS, RAISING HIS GLASS AND TOASTING FROM THE HEAD OF THE TABLE.

Everyone raises their glasses as well, and repeats, "To family."

It's Thanksgiving, and we're having it at my house this year since Layla, the kids, and I moved into a new home. Since she's pregnant with baby number three, we wanted more room, so we found a place not too far from Gage and Sadie on a small piece of land just outside the city.

But even with the bigger house, with the number of adults and kids we have, we had to bring in another table and several extra chairs so everyone could sit together.

As we eat, the conversation flows about the next album, how the kids are doing in school, and the different milestones they're reaching. It's crazy how far we've come from the four heartbroken single guys heading to LA to follow our dream of becoming rock stars, to becoming husbands and fathers. The road hasn't always been smooth, but as I look around at my friends and family, I wouldn't change a thing because every moment, every trial and tribulation, led us to right here.

"Daddy, I'm done!" Marianna says. "Can I go play karaoke?"

"Me too!" Nina agrees.

"I wanna go play too," Rory adds.

"Go ahead," I tell them. "Make sure you wash your hands first."

The three girls scurry off.

"Do you think this one is a boy or a girl?" Layla asks, laying her head on my shoulder. Since everyone is together today, we've decided to do one of those gender reveals everyone apparently does these days. We purchased a black balloon, and when you pop it, it will reveal a pink or blue balloon.

"I'm not sure," I say, kissing her temple. "Both kids are pretty easygoing, so I could go for either."

Just as I finish my sentence, the music from the karaoke machine starts up, and the three girls' voices ring out through the house.

"I remember when Kendall would sing karaoke," Dad says, grinning at Kendall.

"Thank God for auto-tune," I joke.

"Hey!" She glares. "I could probably sing your songs better than you."

"Is that a challenge?" I ask.

"Damn right, it is."

"Fine. We each pick one song for the other person, and whoever sings it better wins."

"Who's going to be the judge?"

"The kids, of course." After all, they're the most honest out of everyone.

"You're on."

Everyone laughs as we both get up and head into the living room.

"Hey, Mari…" My words are caught in my throat when I catch a glimpse of the three girls singing their hearts out into what they think are microphones.

"Oh, my God!" Layla shrieks, running toward the girls and snatching them up.

"Mommy!" Marianna cries. "That's not nice. I was singing in my microphone."

"Mine doesn't work." Rory pouts. "It just keeps vibrating."

"Mine too!" Nina agrees.

"Mine lights up," Marianna says, glaring at her mom as she takes the three vibrating dildos from the girls and hauls ass to the bedroom while everyone cracks up laughing.

"Let's go wash your hands," Kendall says. "We don't know where those… microphones have been."

"Yeah huh," Marianna argues. "They were in Mommy's drawer."

"FIVE…FOUR…THREE…TWO…ONE…" LAYLA POPS THE BALLOON, AND SEVERAL PINK BALLOONS FLY INTO the air.

"Yay! We're having a girl," Marianna cheers.

"Another one?" Felix pouts. "Mom, you need to handle this. One of her is enough."

Layla barks out a laugh. "Talk to your dad, honey. He's in charge of that area."

"Sorry, kiddo," I say, ruffling his hair. "Next time, I'll try for a boy."

About the Author

Reading is like breathing in, writing is like breathing out.
— Pam Allyn

Nikki Ash resides in South Florida where she is an English teacher by day and a writer by night. When she's not writing, you can find her with a book in her hand. From the Boxcar Children, to Wuthering Heights, to the latest single parent romance, she has lived and breathed every type of book. While reading and writing are her passions, her two children are her entire world. You can probably find them at a Disney park before you would find them at home on the weekends!